IF YOU COULD
SEE THE FUTURE...

HOW FAR WOULD YOU GO
TO CHANGE IT?

BOOKS IN THE
PROJECT W. A. R. TRILOGY

ULTRAXENOPIA

TYPE X

SUBJECT ZERO

COMPANION NARRATIVE
THE RICHTER FILES

PROJECT
W.A.R.

THE
COMPLETE
TRILOGY

M. A. PHIPPS

PROJECT W.A.R.
THE COMPLETE TRILOGY

Cover design by Mirella Santana

Interior design by We Got You Covered Book Design

WWW.WEGOTYOUCOVEREDBOOKDESIGN.COM

SHIRE-HILL PUBLICATIONS
UNITED KINGDOM

ISBN: 978-1-914483-07-3

TRIGGER WARNING

Contains dark themes and scenes of violence

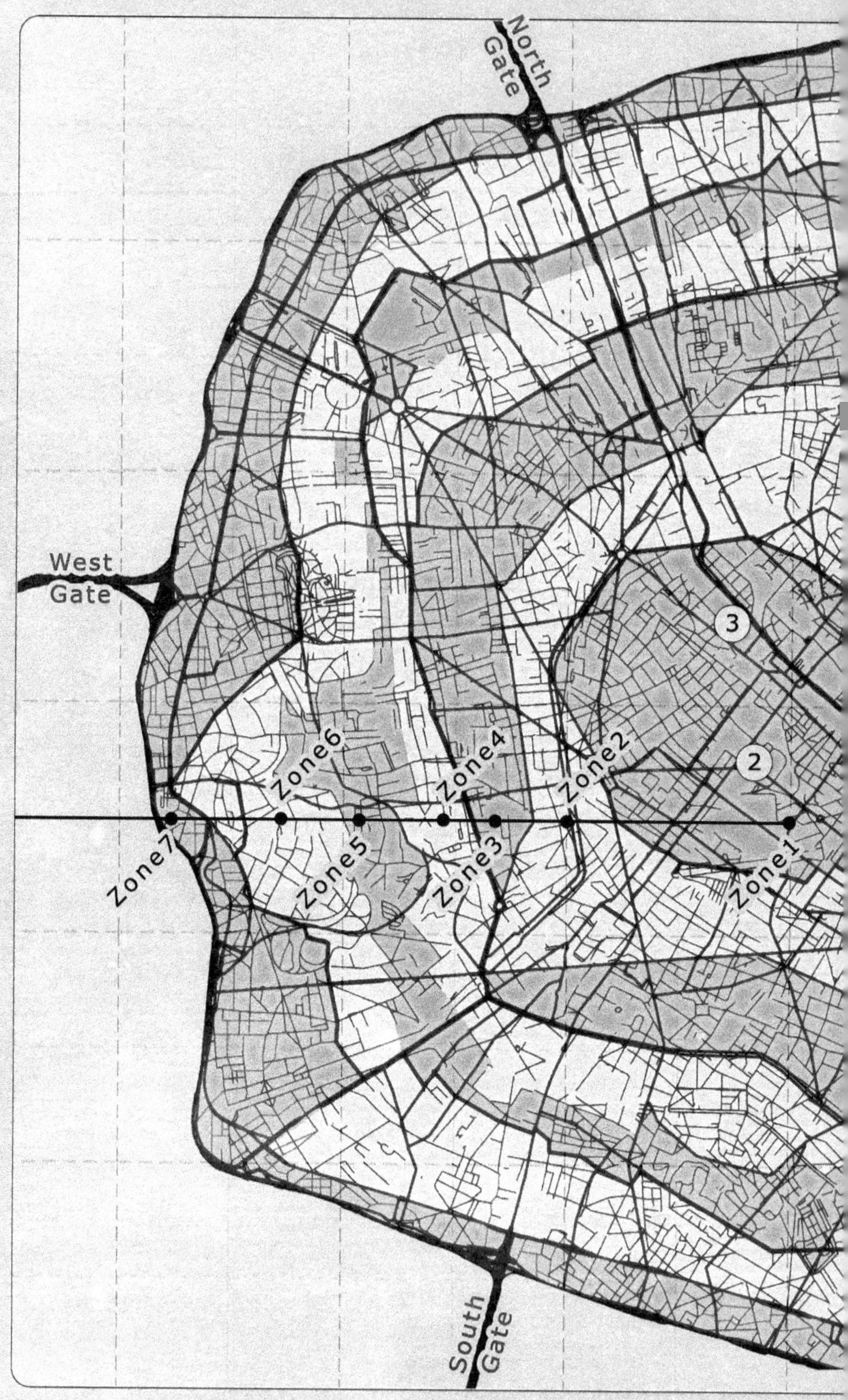

North Gate
South Gate
West Gate
Zone7
Zone6
Zone5
Zone4
Zone3
Zone2
Zone1
3
2
Department of Infrastructure - Document #00425

THE HEART
Population - 8.788.000

1. W.P. Headquarters
2. Magistrates Building
3. The DSD
4. Wynter's House
5. The Vega

4

1

East
Gate

5

STATE PROPERTY

ULTRAXENOPIA

WHEN THE WILLFULLY BLIND FINALLY OPEN
THEIR EYES, THEY SEE SOCIETY FOR WHAT IT IS:

BROKEN.

ONE

"THE TRAIN IS NOW APPROACHING *Central Station. Disembark here for W. P.*
Headquarters and for access to the Department of Interzonal Affairs."

I glance out the window. The darkness of the tunnel disappears in an instant, and before I can blink, the train is back above ground. The towering buildings of the capital rush past in a blur, blending into one confused mass of gray. Nothing stands out.

Everything is the same.

Grabbing my bag, I rise from my seat. The movement of the train is smooth and steady, but my fingers grip the nearest pole out of habit. Usually, I do this just to have something to keep my hands busy, so I don't accidentally fidget. This time, I do it to support my legs, which are in danger of giving out beneath me at any moment.

Taking slow steps, I make my way toward the door. A small group of passengers has already gathered in front of it, their faces blank and postures stiff, ready to start another monotonous day.

Sweat beads along my hairline and under my armpits as warm bodies close in on all sides, keeping their distance so as not to touch me but close enough I can feel the heat of someone's breath against the back of my neck, each pant keeping in time with my heartbeat. I should be used to this after thirteen years of education and countless weeks of preparation exams. By now, I'm no stranger to the crowds of Zone 1.

But today is different, and relief courses through me when the train decelerates and the doors spring open, flooding the car with a welcome swell of fresh air. An automated voice bellows over the loudspeaker, telling passengers to watch their step while disembarking. Other than that warning, the train and platform are silent. No one says anything. No one forces their way forward to get out of the car any quicker. Everyone is patient. Everyone waits their turn, just like always.

Including me.

Claustrophobia claws at my chest as I murmur the same words I repeat to myself every day. The same words I've been rehearsing on a loop since I was five years old. "Don't stand out. Blend in. Remain invisible."

Those are the rules I live by—that everyone lives by.

Those are the rules that ensure we all survive.

When I descend from the train, I'm immediately swallowed whole by an overpowering rush of noise. Footsteps intermingle with the jumbled beeps of turnstiles, combining in a cloud of sound, which echoes like thunder through the station lobby. Keeping my head down, I follow the silent herd shifting toward the station exit, each step nothing more than a sluggish crawl forward.

As I join the procession forming by the glass barriers up ahead, my fingers grope my coat, fumbling in the deep pockets for my government-issued rail card. Once I reach the front of the line, I scan my card across the machine just like I have every other day for as long as I can remember. Just like everyone else before me.

Another beep.

My feet carry me forward when the turnstile opens.

The warm glow of daylight reaches down to meet me as I trudge up the concrete staircase leading out into my birthplace, a massive walled-in city known as the Heart. Despite the cloudless day and hot sun overhead, the biting cold of autumn stings my cheeks.

A shiver races through me as I stand to one side of the exit to get my bearings and gather my nerves, my eyes flicking upwards to observe the detachment in each of the empty faces around me.

No one who passes says anything to me. No one asks how I am. No one looks at each other. Everyone minds their own business, just as they're supposed to. Just as *I'm* supposed to.

Bile rises in my throat, but I urge it back down.

"Don't stand out. Blend in. Remain invisible," I whisper under my breath.

Inhaling, I peer down at the silver watch on my wrist, and a mumbled curse escapes my lips when the numbers ignite across the mirrored face, telling me I'm running short on time. I can't afford to be late.

Not today.

Crossing my arms, I glance to the east in the general direction of my destination, careful to avoid eye contact with anyone passing. My skin tingles as if it's on fire, and my stomach twists into an uncomfortable, tight ball at the thought of what this day represents.

Ignoring the itch of anxiety crawling over my skin, I fall into formation with the crowd on the sidewalk.

The building I'm looking for isn't far—a few minutes' walk from the station at most. But with every step, the pounding of my heart grows more violent and my lungs tighten until I'm practically wheezing. I swallow, desperate to cast off the dread gripping me, but the sensation only continues to worsen.

Mere moments feel like hours before my feet skid to a stop. The carved stone of the familiar sign seems to sprout up from the ground like a petrified tree, looming over the spot where I stand with the same threat as the sky-scraping building behind it.

W. P. Headquarters. The workforce placement educational facilities where the rest of my future will be decided after the events of today. I suppose you could say this building is the foundation and epicenter of our society. Every person in this city—regardless of who they are—will intimately know this place. From our early days of education up until our eighteenth birthday, at which time a single exam at this very establishment determines the rest of our lives. Pass and move on to your designated career. Fail and receive a one-year sentence in Detention as punishment for lacking discipline, followed by a lifetime of the worst jobs imaginable—and not only in terms of pay.

I inhale around the rising lump in my throat.

You can do this. You've studied. You know what you're doing. With those reassuring words bouncing around in my skull, I breathe out and step forward through the revolving glass doors.

The interior of W. P. Headquarters is dreary and lifeless, just like everything else in the Heart. The furnishings are all gray, made of metal and glass, and security cameras mark every corner and wall. At least a dozen people stand in front of me, waiting in a line in the vestibule to gain entry to the building.

More beeps. More turnstiles.

As the minutes pass, a prickle of nerves forms an ache in my legs, coaxing me up onto the balls of my feet then back down onto my heels again. I know I shouldn't move around. Fidgeting is dangerous. Fidgeting makes me noticeable. And yet, every attempt to stay still is met with opposition from the very atoms making up the composition of my body, as if I can no longer control what it's doing.

To distract myself from my building unease, I bite the inside of my cheek and focus my narrowed gaze on a television embedded in a wall to my left. On the screen is footage showing the aftermath of a recent fire or bombing. I'm not sure which. I hadn't heard about an attack, which means it must've only just happened today. Some people are screaming. Others are covered in blood. Several corpses litter the ground.

I strain my ears to hear what the broadcaster is saying but try not to seem too interested. Curiosity is also dangerous and a sure-fire way to draw unwanted attention.

"Thirty-two are reported dead in the devastating attack that occurred an hour ago on a hydroponic factory in Zone 4. Although investigators currently have no leads as to the motive behind the attack, it is believed to be the work of the insurgent group, PHOENIX. Anyone with information regarding the organization's whereabouts is urged to come forward and report to their local Enforcer unit. Any citizen found to be withholding information or aiding the terrorists will henceforth be branded an enemy of the State"—the newscaster pauses for dramatic effect—*"and executed."*

A shiver ripples through me at the words "enemy of the State." That's what the government brands anyone who doesn't follow their rules. All it takes is a single mistake and boom, one-way trip to Termination.

A heavy weight returns to the pit of my stomach as I force myself to look away from the screen. From this point on, I keep my gaze fixed ahead of me.

After another ten minutes of waiting, the turnstile offering access to the building is finally within my reach. The only thing standing between us is a squat middle-aged woman sitting behind a sleek black counter, who signals with a crooked finger for me to step forward.

"Name?" she asks.

I balk under the intensity of her steely gaze, my voice choking out the words, "Wynter Reeves."

"Identification chip," she grumbles, holding up a handheld device.

I extend my left arm without hesitation, keeping as still as humanly possible as the gatekeeper moves the scanner over my wrist. A light at the top of the machine turns green. She then grabs my pointer finger and presses it against an upraised metal square on the counter where a needle juts out and pricks me for blood. I don't even have time to wince before a numbing agent steals away the pain.

"You're all clear," the woman grunts, looking around me and signaling to the next person in line.

The gate in front of me opens with a swish, the glass barriers sliding apart in welcome. My stomach turns as I press into the main lobby. The room is empty aside from the balding receptionist, who sits behind a marble counter stretching the full length of the two-story high wall. His head is down, his unblinking gaze glued to the computer in front of him.

"Name and purpose of visit?" he asks before I've even reached the counter.

"Wynter Reeves," I answer in a timid voice. "I'm here to take my placement exam."

His eyes dart to mine, and he holds out his hand.

"Identification chip."

Walking forward, I once again stretch out my arm, biting my tongue as the man repeats the process I just went through. My lungs hold in my breath the whole time as I wait for that little light to turn green. I only exhale when the machine beeps its approval.

I'm not new to any of this, and yet, my nerves are shredding my insides as if I'm five years old all over again and this is my very first time in this building. It probably only feels that way because so much is hanging on my exam.

If I screw this up, my life is over.

Silence is my companion as the man confirms my information on his computer—another check to ensure that I am who I say I am. Once he's satisfied with what he sees in the database, he hands me a laminated badge with my name and the word 'Examinee' typed in bold underneath it.

"The examination is on Floor 5. Reception up there will check you in."

I cast a nervous glance over my shoulder, following the man's outstretched wrinkled hand to the elevators at the far right side of the lobby as if I haven't used them a thousand times before. With a mumble of thanks, I turn from the counter, grateful no one else is around to notice how badly my legs and hands are shaking.

You have to calm down, I tell myself, running through the mental pep talk I've been practicing in front of the mirror at home every day the last week.

Dragging in a faltering breath through my nose, I head for the nearest elevator and swipe a finger across the silver call button. A glowing blue number appears above the steel doors, counting down to my location on the ground floor. The seconds tick by slowly, and while I wait, I use the time to fix the Examinee badge to the front of my shirt. My frazzled nerves make my fingers clumsy, and the badge nearly slips from my grasp several times. After four failed attempts, I manage to clip the pin shut.

I'm only on my own for about thirty seconds before several other students gather around the elevators. I recognize a few from my classes, and based on the Examinee badges clipped to their shirts, we're all convening for the same reason. Still, despite our mutual purpose for being here, no one says anything to each other. No words of greeting. No whispers of encouragement. Despite sharing this monumental milestone in our lives, every one of us is alone.

The elevator arrives with a ding, shaking me free from my morose thoughts. Since I was the first to arrive, I enter in front of the others, shrinking into the corner beside the control panel where I timidly press the call button for the fifth floor. The last person to step onto the elevator is an older man with deep brown skin and close-cropped black hair, who swipes a finger across the button for the fourth floor. As he positions himself in front of the closing doors, it occurs to me that I recognize him, although I can't work out where from.

After a moment, the elevator ascends, and my eyes drift to each separate floor number as they take turns lighting up above the stainless steel doors, the bright cobalt glow illuminating our metal surroundings. The only other movement comes from the red light blinking like an eye above the dark lens on the security camera in the corner to my right. Although I try to ignore it, I can't escape the feeling that the camera is watching me.

That the people behind it are watching me.

My heart jumps into my throat when the elevator pings and the doors slide open for the fourth floor. The older man who entered behind everyone else steps off without a backward glance, clearly in a hurry to get somewhere. I watch him storm away, once again wondering where it is I've seen him before.

When the doors close behind him, I risk another glance at the camera, the scrutiny of its gaze stronger than ever. Swallowing, I wipe a bead of sweat from my forehead.

A moment later, the doors open to the fifth floor. As I was the first one in, I'm the last one out, but I don't mind the wait. Those extra few seconds give me time to compose myself.

I take a much-needed moment alone then step out of the elevator into a busy reception area. I've never been on this floor—all my classes were always on the tenth level or higher—although, it looks just like any other part of the building: clinical and cold. Pressing my arms to my sides to keep them from trembling, I join the line forming in front of the counter at the opposite end of the room. Upon reaching the front, I find myself standing before a pretty short-haired woman who looks to be only a few years older than me.

"Name?" she asks.

"Wynter Reeves," I answer for what seems like the hundredth time today.

She holds out a delicate hand. "Identification chip."

Once again, I offer my arm and stand still as my wrist is scanned for the chip underneath my skin. The woman smiles when the light on the machine switches from red to green.

"The examination will be in Room Three," she says. "Follow this hall and you'll find it on your left."

With a nod, I turn away from the counter and continue down the corridor to my right. Room Three is situated at the end of the hallway. Five other students are lined up outside the door, waiting to pass through the final checkpoint and gain admittance into the exam room. Just like everyone before me, I wave my wrist across the screen affixed to the wall beside the door. Another beep. Another green light. Unlike the others, at this checkpoint, when the machine scans my chip, the screen lights up with a diagram of the exam room and indicates which desk I've been allocated. I study it for a moment then step through the doorway.

My heart hammers against my ribcage as I plop down into my designated seat and hang my coat and bag on the back of the hard metal chair. One by one, the seats around me fill up as the other Examinees file into the space, but, despite the number of students present, the room is eerily quiet. The silence only makes me more unsettled.

My lips twitch.

It's going to be okay.

Chewing on the inside of my lower lip, I glance down to assess my desktop. The computerized screen is deactivated, and in the top left corner, a red light burns under the glass, flickering in and out like a flame. Swallowing, I hold my wrist out over the sensor, spurring the computer to life. White floods my field of vision apart from where my name is emblazoned in large black letters across the top of the screen.

WYNTER A. REEVES

Today's date appears underneath it: October 14th, 2061. A longer number is printed just below that, which reads 73956241. I'd know that number anywhere. Hell, I know it as well as I know my own name. It's my identification number. The number I was assigned at birth to designate my place in the State. In many ways, that number is all I am.

Other than that, the screen is blank.

A low buzzing draws my attention to the front of the room where a projector flashes a blue-tinted image across the full length of the bare wall. A stern-looking man manifests before us like an apparition, announcing himself to be the CEO of W. P. Headquarters.

As my eyes trail over his features, I see the older man in the elevator whose face I recognized but struggled to place.

Until now.

I knew he looked familiar.

The way he stares out across the room is unnerving, his expression cold and unwelcome, as if taking the time to speak to us is cutting into a thousand other things he'd rather be doing right now. His gruff, authoritative voice booms around me, sending a chill of fear down my spine.

"The examination will begin momentarily. You will be given three hours to complete it. Anyone who finishes before this time may press the call button to submit their exam. Once you have submitted your exam, no revisions will be allowed. Good luck." With those concluding words, the projector shuts off.

A breath catches in my lungs when the door to the room snaps closed, locking with a deafening click.

There's no turning back now. You can do this, I remind myself, although I don't quite believe it.

An automated female voice screeches overhead, echoing through the space and setting every hair on my body on end. *"The exam will now commence. You may begin."*

As silence returns, the screen below me flashes black and then white again, revealing the first part of the exam. My fingers wrap around the electronic stylus attached to the side of the desk, gently raising the pen from its holder, and with a quivering breath, I dive into the series of questions which will singlehandedly determine my future.

The automated voice returns every fifteen minutes to tell us the clock is ticking.

"Two hours, forty-five minutes remaining."

"Two hours, thirty minutes remaining."

"Two hours, fifteen minutes remaining."

The squawking reminders are grating, but I force myself to shut them out and concentrate only on the exam. For the most part, the answers come easily to me, although, there's the occasional question that seems out of place, as if it doesn't belong. Are these continuity errors, or are the test makers trying to throw me off—to confirm whether I belong in my projected sector or if I should be sacrificed to the lowest depths of society?

"Two hours remaining," that annoying voice nags.

Sweat trickles down the sides of my face, and my stomach churns, threatening to bring up my breakfast. I try to swallow—to push down the sudden bout of nausea—but my throat is dry and my tongue is brittle, like old sandpaper, making it impossible. When I blink, my eyes lose focus until my surroundings are an indistinct spinning blur.

I shake my head to clear it, squinting hard at the screen, but the jerking movement only makes my vertigo worse.

"One hour, forty-five minutes remaining."

My lungs tighten as if to suffocate me, but I push through my discomfort, nudging my face a few inches closer to the screen, desperate to complete my exam.

Terrified of what will happen if I don't.

My gaze skims over the next hazy question, but only one part of the sentence is clear.

"...end..."

As I repeat that single word in my head, spasms erupt across my body and a strange pressure pushes at me from the inside, as if my organs are about to burst out of my skin. Control eludes me as I writhe in my seat, and I know without having to look that the other Examinees in the room are all staring at me.

I wish they wouldn't.

I wish this would stop.

I want to continue the test.

I don't want to fail.

I don't want them to see me.

I don't want to stand out.

A cry escapes my lips and echoes in my ears, ringing in my skull like a bell. Pain floods my head, and a tremor rolls over my hand, weakening my already limp hold on the stylus.

The world and all sound seem to move in slow motion as the pen slips from my fingers and clatters onto the tiled floor at my feet, the impact acting like a trigger as everything around me abruptly goes black.

TWO

WHEN I OPEN MY EYES, the exam room is gone.

I turn around in my seat. The pain that consumed me before has diminished, but it's replaced by fear, confusion, and disbelief, which all attack me at once, overpowering the part of my brain that might actually be able to comprehend what's happening.

Is this a dream? A hallucination?

My legs quake as I push to my feet, my fingers clutching at the chair to hold me to the one real thing in this delusion. The air is thick with dust, but through the impairing fog, I recognize my surroundings. I glimpse the familiar sight of the Heart in the details crumbling around me. But there are no people crowding the streets. No lights. No sign of life at all. There's only me, standing here all alone, as the world I once knew succumbs to destruction.

Panic boils beneath my skin, squeezing my lungs in a vise grip. My eyes close on instinct, but some unseen power wrenches them open again, forcing me to watch every second of this nightmare. To see what I can only assume must be the end of the world.

In the blink of an eye, the destruction explodes in a torrent of flame, devouring everything. A blinding flash burns across my vision, but when it clears, the desolate landscape is nowhere to be seen.

Did I just imagine that?

Sweat suctions the thin fabric of my clothes to my body, and I wince away from the horrible screaming that it takes me a moment to realize is coming from me. I clamp my mouth shut to silence my building distress and tighten my grasp on the chair. Wisps of darkness dance in front of my eyes, and as they fade, I'm both relieved and terrified to find myself back in the exam room.

My chest constricts as I glance around at the other Examinees, every last one wearing the same wide-eyed expression. Despite the silence, I know what they're thinking. Those words from the news broadcast earlier vibrate through my head like the pitchy whine of a bad frequency.

Enemy of the State, their faces all say to me.

A sharp metallic stench fills my nose, and I stumble backward, suddenly light-headed and nauseous. I touch a shaking hand to my nostrils and pull it away, a strained whimper escaping my lips when I register the blood coating my fingers. Only one coherent thought rises from the depths of my panic.

Something's wrong with me.

My head snaps up at the click clack of footsteps, my attention narrowing on the moderator entering from the door in the back corner intended for staff. The harsh look she gives me slices through my terror.

I can't stay here. This realization slams into me, knocking the air from my lungs, and without another thought, I lunge forward and smack my hand against the button on my desk, submitting my unfinished exam. I don't have a plan, and I definitely haven't considered the consequences of what I'm doing. All I know is I need to get out of this building.

Grabbing my bag and coat off the back of my chair, I sprint for the exit, waving my wrist in front of the sensor controlling the lock for the door, which scans to check if I've turned in my exam. The response is immediate as the light turns green and the door springs open, granting me my much-needed freedom.

The lock bolts back into place behind me, separating me from the other students still in the exam room. Good. Fewer people to follow me, not that any of them would ever dare to get involved.

As I race down the hallway, I feel the ghostly weight of the other Examinees' stares on my skin, burnt into my back like an unwanted tattoo. I try to shake off the memory of the look they all gave me, but I find it again in every passing expression along my route to escape. Confused glances follow me in my panic.

I rush into the reception area for the fifth floor and come to a grinding halt in front of the elevator, keeping my eyes tilted downward. A stinging pain radiates across my palm as I slap it repeatedly against the call button. Why are elevators never on the floor where you need them?

"Excuse me, miss!" the woman with short hair calls after me.

The elevator arrives in the nick of time, and I bound inside to escape her just as she steps out from behind the counter. Letting out a breath, I slump against the back wall, taking in the mirrored surface of the steel doors, where my distorted reflection stares at me as if to ask me what the hell I'm doing. I shake my head, mortified by my appearance. My skin is ashen and glistens with sweat. My hair is plastered to my forehead and cheeks. My eyes are so bloodshot, the whites of them are barely even visible. Red smears stain the bottom half of my face.

I pull on my coat and press the cream-colored sleeve against my nose to staunch the bleeding. My gaze darts back up to my disfigured reflection and hangs there as my descent continues.

The seconds seem to drag as I consider what grim fate awaits me the moment these doors open again. I don't know what to expect. I wasn't even thinking when I ran out of the exam room. I should've composed myself and finished what I came here to do. Second chances aren't given in our society, and it's very likely, if not guaranteed, that my behavior before will come back to haunt me. Second chances don't exist.

This won't be forgiven.

The number signaling for the ground floor glows blue as the elevator slows to a stop and the doors slide open, offering me up to my fate like a sacrificial lamb to the slaughter. To my surprise, no one is waiting to apprehend me. The lobby is empty except for the balding receptionist, who doesn't spare me a glance. The exam moderator and short-haired woman upstairs must not have reported me. Yet.

The vestibule beyond the lobby beckons me onward, but I falter, unsure if I should go any farther. Maybe, if I turn myself in now, the State will be lenient and let me off with a warning. Maybe it will show me mercy.

A choked laugh rises up in my throat.

No, I tell myself. *It won't.*

Because the State doesn't know what mercy is.

Gritting my teeth, I focus on the one thing standing between me and the way out, and with one more backward glance at the man, I race toward the turnstiles up ahead. All I have to do is prick my finger so the computer can verify my identity.

A little blood, that's it, and then I can leave.

I press my finger to the small silver pad, offering the turnstile payment in blood and silently thanking whoever it was who thought to leave the exit turnstiles in this building unmanned. I don't even wait for the numbing agent, pressing onward the instant the partition slides open. A burning sensation radiates across my skin, my finger throbbing in protest, but I'm too set on getting out of here to care about pain.

I press on through the revolving glass doors into the welcoming chill of autumn. The breeze cools my flushing skin, but I'm too preoccupied with my fear to be able to enjoy the relief.

The people walking past me on the sidewalk all keep a wide berth, eyeing me uncertainly. I might as well have a sign over my head with the word 'danger' written across it in large red letters. Their reactions don't surprise me. Every last person in the Heart lives in fear, and I've given them cause to be afraid and wary of my erratic behavior.

As far as they're concerned, I'm a lost cause.

I pull up my coat collar and press my face deeper into my sleeve, shrinking into myself. My nose doesn't seem to be bleeding anymore, but I'm too scared to pull away the fabric in case someone recognizes me.

Better to keep my identity obscured.

I retrace my steps to Central Station, keeping my eyes on the ground as I try to walk at a normal pace and not run. My pulse quickens when I fumble, nearly dropping my rail card, and crash into a woman standing to my left. Muttering a half-hearted apology, I thrust myself through the nearest available turnstile.

I make it to the platform just as the next train arrives. Rushing on board, I head for a seat in the back, sinking against the wall of the car. I don't dare move a muscle the whole ride home.

In the twenty minutes the journey takes, my thoughts spiral out of control, bringing me to the brink of hysteria.

Stop running, my head tells me. *Turn around. Turn yourself in now before it's too late.*

My fear is strong, but my will to survive in this moment is stronger. When the train reaches my stop, I jump out of my seat, and for the first time in my life, I don't politely wait my turn to disembark. My hands wedge between the bodies in front of me, pushing forward through the crowd like small battering rams. Disgruntled complaints reverberate in my ears, but I ignore them, leaping onto the platform, and race through the station without looking back.

Once free of the confines of underground travel, I encounter fewer people. *Witnesses,* my brain has the nerve to remind me. At this time of day, the roads are mostly empty as everyone is at work or on the train, heading for one appointment or another. Regardless, I keep my head down as I walk and slow my pace to avoid further unwanted attention.

When I reach my street a few minutes later, I choke out a laugh at the welcome sight of my family's designated living quarters two blocks down. I'm almost there.

Sanctuary is almost in reach.

Our home is one in a row of terraced houses. Out of the seven zones in the Heart, we're fortunate enough to live in Zone 2. Zone 1 is reserved for high-ranking officials and other citizens of importance, and Zones 2 through 7 house everyone else. Residences are all allocated based on job placement, status, and wealth—the closer you live to the center of the city, the better off you are. When I was younger, we lived on the border to Zone 1, but our quarters were downsized a number of years ago due to the shrinking size of my family. I don't have any siblings and my father…well, he's not around anymore. For the last eleven years, it's just been Mother and me.

I run up the steps, skipping two at a time, and sweep my wrist across the security panel positioned above the handle on the door. The lock clicks open as soon as the scanner registers my chip, acknowledging me as a resident of this household.

Throwing a nervous glance over my shoulder, I race inside and slam the door shut behind me. My heart jackhammers in my chest, and I close my eyes, leaning back against the wall. Strangled breaths weave in and out of my lips.

It's strange. I know I'm in trouble—or if I'm not already, I will be soon. *Really* soon. Yet, now that I'm home, the events of today seem more like a bad dream than reality. Right now, in the refuge of my house, I can almost forget them and pretend that I'm safe.

Once my heart rate and breathing have returned to normal, I push away from the wall and head for the stairs. Mother won't be home for several hours yet, so I have some time to think of a lie to explain what happened with my exam. Assuming I'm not dragged away to Detention before then—

My feet pause beneath me at the muffled sound of voices coming from the other end of the hallway.

No one is supposed to be home.

"Mother?" I squeak, the word catching in my throat.

My footsteps echo off the white tiled floor as I shift away from the stairs and continue toward the reception room. Despite the sudden silence, I get the sense I'm not the only one here. The faint glimmer of light at the end of the corridor only confirms my suspicions. At this time of day, all the lights should be off.

"Mother?" I call again, my tone strained.

"I'm in the reception room," she answers.

Terror rushes through me as a thousand thoughts fly through my head. *Why is she home? She shouldn't be home. Does she know? What is she going to do?*

I scramble toward the sliding interior door, which is slightly ajar, first having the sense to take a look at myself in the mirror hanging on the wall at the end of the hallway. My coat absorbed most of the blood from my nose, but I still look ghostly pale.

Sick even.

Something's wrong with me, I think for the second time today. The realization twists my gut.

I scrub my sleeve across my face to erase the dried remnants of blood flaking on my pasty skin, hoping Mother won't notice how bedraggled I am. I then shrug off the coat and stroll into the room where she waits for me to break the news of my exam, keeping my expression neutral, as if today has been just another ordinary day.

The moment I cross the threshold, it becomes clear at once that my facade won't fool my mother. She glares at me from her seat on the sofa, flanked by two soldiers holding guns.

Enforcers. The thought is like a knife to my chest.

I would like to say I'm shocked by how quickly they've acted, but the State's policing units are always efficient, handling anyone who might pose a threat. But am I a threat? I had a panic attack, that's all. Sure, I didn't finish my exam, but is that such a big deal? Does what I did really warrant this kind of reaction?

The Enforcers rise to their feet, moving toward me in suits of black armor, their faces masked by opaque helmets, shielding their eyes. My mother stands alongside them, and when she meets my gaze, it's as if she's a different person than the woman I've known these past eighteen years. The distance in her face sets me on edge. The way she looks at me...

I've only ever seen that expression once before.

"There's nowhere to go, Wynter," she murmurs. "Submit."

My eyes spring wide, and the fear hits me all over again, shattering my brief illusion of safety. Submit? To what? My mind races with the possibilities, each one more dreadful than the last. Chances are I'll be sent to Detention for immediate Re-education. That's what the State always does to anyone who fails their exam. Not that I've ever seen or met anyone who's been re-integrated into society after that. Not that I would. The dregs stick to Zone 7.

I open my mouth to say something to plead my case, but my voice catches on a grunt when I take a defensive step away from the soldiers, my back slamming into something solid behind me.

Whipping around, I stare up into the expressionless face of a third man blocking my only escape. The white laboratory coat he's wearing confuses me. He isn't clothed in the Enforcers' regulation uniform, so who is he? And why is he here?

I barely have time to consider these questions before he plunges a needle into the side of my neck. My surroundings blur as the room goes hazy, and suddenly, my body is unbearably heavy, as if gravity is trying to crush me down to the ground. With what strength I can manage, I reach out to my mother.

Help me, I beg, but the words don't pass my lips.

My knees buckle beneath me, and as my eyes flutter closed, her voice floods my ears, unfeeling and cold.

"Do what you must," is the last thing I hear.

THREE

A GROAN BREAKS THROUGH MY lips as my eyes struggle to open. The light beyond my lids is like a sun searing into my vision, and I wince, my body lurching back as if I've been burned by a flame. I try, time and again, to see past the glare, but my vision is bleary. All I can make out is white.

The plodding of shoes against tile pounds through my head like beats on a drum, dull and distant, as if I'm hearing every step from under water. Mumbling voices join the low tread of footsteps, making me aware of several people around me. But I don't know who they are. I don't know why I'm here.

I don't know where I am.

I try to make sense of the last thing I remember. In my mind, I see my mother again, accompanied by the two Enforcers as well as that third unknown man. I can also recall the pinch of a needle in my neck, but anything that occurred after that moment is lost to the black hole of unconsciousness. And now, I'm here.

Wherever here is.

Only one lucid train of thought takes hold in my brain. *Am I in Detention? Is this my Re-education?*

Over the next few moments, the grogginess in my head eases, bringing the room into focus. Grunting, I try to push up into a sitting position, but when I move, something solid constricts my body, pinning me flat to the surface beneath me.

I raise my head just enough to peer down at my chest, and it's only when I glimpse the steel band restraints across my legs and torso that I'm able to feel them. Panic washes over me as I fight to get free, thrashing and screaming until my voice is hoarse and I lack the energy to keep struggling. Ragged breaths scorch my lungs as my body goes limp.

I press my eyes shut for a minute then open them, risking a glance back down at my legs. I've been stripped of everything I was wearing before, right down to my watch. A skimpy white hospital gown has replaced my exam-approved clothes, and I'm strapped to a metal table in the middle of a bright room I don't recognize. A heart monitor beeps beside my head, mimicking every racing beat of my heart, while an IV stand is positioned on my other side, leading down into tubes protruding from the crook of my right elbow and hand. The second I glimpse them, that surge of panic returns. Suddenly, I no longer care why I'm here. I don't need to know what these people—whoever they are—intend to do to me. I just need to get out of this place.

"The subject is awake."

My gaze snaps in the direction of a woman's voice, locking on at least a dozen people standing a few feet to my right, all clothed in the same white coat the man who drugged me at my house was wearing.

Fear creeps across my skin like an itch as I glance between the curious faces observing me. One man scribbles down notes on a computerized tablet while another scratches his chin and looks me over like I'm bacteria in a Petri dish that he's viewing under a microscope. An older woman approaches me with a syringe clasped in her slender hand, her eyes dull and lacking even the slightest hint of concern. The others share her blank expression.

As I take in their faces, reality hits me. Laid out on this table, I'm helpless and weak. I can't move. I can't run away. I can't even find the strength to fight back when the woman pushes a needle into the vein at the crook of my elbow.

A hiss escapes me as she takes three vials worth of my blood, the deep red filling the glass tubes to the brim. Once finished, she removes the needle and sticks a small round bandage over the puncture mark in my skin. She then turns and walks away without saying a word.

As she crosses the room, I narrow my eyes, trying to sharpen her indistinct figure, but my head is still reeling from whatever I was injected with earlier. Through the smog clouding my head, I can make out her fingers tapping against a touchscreen keyboard embedded into the surface of a long countertop lining the white wall to my left. A hologram image projects above her head, displaying several rows of jumbled text, but my vision is too fuzzy to make out the words, my eyes swathed by dancing black cotton balls.

The woman swipes her fingers across the keyboard again then pivots to face a steel bowl set out on the gleaming countertop beside her. Part of me believes that bowl wasn't there before, but the drugs racing through my body are making it difficult to be sure of anything. Except the fear.

That much I'm certain of.

A sizzling sound floods the room as the woman pours the contents of the three vials into the bowl. Sparks of electricity jolt across the exterior, reacting to my blood, and wisps of smoke rise up from the metal, casting a slight haze over the counter.

Satisfied, the woman peers back at the hologram image, appraising it for a moment before tapping her nails against the keyboard again. At the press of a button, a lid snaps over the bowl and the metal container spins in place.

Each rotation is faster than the last, and as the bowl moves, a code manifests overhead—line after line of incomprehensible symbols scrawled across the glowing hologram image. I try to make sense of them, but there's nothing there to make sense of. I might as well be looking at a foreign language.

"Doctor," the woman gasps. "You need to see this."

Terror consumes me at her incredulous tone.

What is she seeing?

What's wrong with me?

Hysteria once again overpowers my senses, and I'm consumed by the need to escape this place. But I have no energy. My mouth is too dry to swallow, my head is spinning, and the fluorescent lights overhead are making me unbearably nauseous. Bile inches up my throat. I pull against my restraints one more time, my teeth clenching together to counter the strain.

The soft thud of footsteps draws my attention away from my struggle, and my body goes still as my eyes flick to the side, locking on the man now standing next to the woman, his hands tucked behind his waist as he examines the hologram image, his mouth set in a serious line. He's young—no older than his mid-twenties, if that—and he's tall, with auburn-brown hair parted neatly to one side and a clean-shaven jaw. Rectangular, thin-rimmed glasses frame perceptive gray eyes.

The woman leans toward him as he studies the hologram, her voice just loud enough for me to hear over the hum of the spinning bowl. "Her blood type," she whispers, her husky tone dripping with awe. "It's...*changing.*"

I may not know much about science, or anything medical having to do with the human body, but I know enough to be certain that what she's saying isn't possible. Not without unnatural intervention, at least.

The man straightens, adjusting his spotless white coat.

"Fascinating," he murmurs.

His eyes shift to mine, and the traitorous monitor beside me betrays me with a string of rapid beeps, the high-pitched computerized echo of my racing heart revealing my fear.

As the man approaches, his pale lips curl into a smile. "Hello, Wynter. My name is Dr. Richter. I'll be taking care of you."

Taking care of me?

"Why am I here?" I breathe, my voice raspy. "What are you going to do to me?"

"Shh, hush now," he croons, patting my shoulder. "I assure you, all your questions will be answered in time." He lowers his eyes, and I follow his gaze to his hand where a syringe is laid out on his palm. It takes me a moment to realize the glass vial is empty. "But for now"—a wave of vertigo hits me as the sharp features of his face melt into a blur—"you must sleep."

"How…" I trail off, my tongue too heavy to speak.

I lift my head as much as I'm able to, spotting the last of a blue liquid disappearing into my body through a thin tube in my arm. The drug acts quickly, stealing my words.

As the drowsiness returns to pull me under again, the doctor's smile is all I see.

FOUR

WHEN I COME TO, I'M in another room I don't recognize. Unlike the room I woke up in before, this one is smaller and only has space for a table positioned at the base of a single bed and a toilet, shower, and sink, which are all crammed together against the wall opposite me, off to the left-hand side of the door. Everything is gray and metallic.

Cold.

Disoriented, and with a fair bit of effort, I push myself into a sitting position. My head is bleary and drug-addled, and my back is stiff, my muscles aching, no doubt from sleeping on the hard mattress beneath me. The springs creak when I shift my weight.

I swing my legs over the side of the bed and plant my feet on the floor, abruptly going still. A wave of nausea grips my stomach, making me wary of moving any more for the moment in case my body decides to throw up. Lifting my eyes, I study the confined space while I wait for the queasiness to pass, noting how there aren't any windows—just plain concrete walls boxing me in on all sides. A camera sits in the far corner to my left, hanging just below the ceiling, an ominous red light blinking on the side of the lens. Just like in the elevator at W. P. Headquarters, it's as if I can sense the people here watching me. I can feel their penetrating gazes without even seeing their faces, especially that of the doctor I met.

Richter, he called himself.

A second wave of vertigo slams into me, and I fly forward, stumbling to the sink, gripping the edges to catch myself. An eternity seems to pass before the nausea subsides.

Exhaling a shaking breath, I glance up into the mirror above the steel basin and let out a gasp. A deranged-looking girl stares back at me from the glass. Purple smudges stain the skin under her eyes, giving the appearance of bruises against the unhealthy pallor of her yellowish skin. She looks sick.

Really sick.

I look away, mortified by my appearance, haunted by the realization burning my thoughts like a hot iron brand searing into my flesh. The thought first occurred to me during my placement exam, and it's been chasing me since, begging me to face the truth.

And the truth is…something is wrong with me.

I choke back a sob as the walls around me seem to inch closer, pressing in on all sides. As my pulse thunders in my ears, my eyes snag on the corner of the mirror, catching on the reflection of a bundle of clothes folded in a pile on the mattress behind me.

Thankful for the distraction, I return to the bed and run my fingertips across the rough fabric. Also gray. Also cold. As my pulse evens out and my anxiety eases, I look down at the sweat-soaked gown chafing my skin and then back at the fresh clothes on the bed. Noting the difference makes me feel even filthier.

My gaze flits to the shower with longing. *Get clean. That's all I can do at the moment. Get clean now. Worry later.* But as my fingers graze the edges of the gown to remove it, I freeze, remembering the camera in the corner behind me. Just how much are the people here watching me? Are they observing everything I do?

I peer over my shoulder at the blinking red light and push a faltering breath out through my lips. A full minute passes before I come to the disheartening conclusion that privacy likely isn't something I'll be granted here. Goosebumps rise across my skin at that notion.

Pushing the thought away, I shrug out of the thin gown and immerse myself under the cascade of lukewarm water that rains down from the shower head when my shaking fingers turn the handle. My muscles tense as my fingernails move over my face, scraping away the dried blood and sweat—a reminder of what happened at W. P. Headquarters.

Behind the hum of the running water, my fear is stronger than ever, a constant deafening scream in my head. How long has it been since I was taken? It can't have been that long ago, can it? It scares me that I have no way of knowing for sure considering how many times I've been drugged by my captors. I settle on assuming it's only been a day or two since the fiasco with my placement exam. Maybe, if I'm lucky, my stay here won't be extended much longer.

I bite back a laugh and shake my head at my pitiful attempt to console myself.

Deep down, I know the truth. However long these people plan to hold me, it will be for a while. I won't see the outside of these walls any time soon. Hell, if I'm in Detention, like I fear, I'm looking at a minimum sentence of a year. The thought makes my insides quiver. A year? For running out on my exam?

It could be worse, I remind myself. *They could've sent you to Termination.*

My fingers tremble as they grasp the handle and turn until the rush of water fades to a trickle. A white towel hangs within reach, and I grab it, wrapping the starchy fabric around my body. As I step out of the shower, I keep the towel draped around me while I change into the clean clothes provided on the bed in an effort to protect whatever modesty I have left. The pants are dark gray—almost black—and comfortably loose, although itchy against my skin. The top is a lighter gray and a few sizes too big for my body, hanging to the middle of my thighs. My feet slip easily into a pair of flat shoes I find tucked just under the foot of the bed.

As my hands work to towel-dry my hair, I risk another glance at my reflection. My complexion is brighter now, although those bruise-like bags remain under my eyes, making me look like I haven't slept in weeks. A knot forms in my chest as I comb my fingers through the damp strands of hair. The short brown ends drip onto my shoulders while my bangs lie slick against my forehead. I look awful, but this is the best I can do under the circumstances.

Once I'm dressed and dry, I plop down on the mattress, unsure what to do with myself. My hands clench and unclench, my fingers wringing the end of my shirt, as my eyes skirt over the room, taking in every detail no matter how small and unimportant it seems at first glance. On every pass, my focus catches on the white table at the end of the bed.

On a hunch, I tap the glossy surface with the tip of my finger, and as expected, a screen flashes to life under the glass, revealing a menu offering a multitude of options to the user. They range from food and drink to other basic necessities, like toiletries and assistance—not that unlike the food delivery computers provided in every home in Zone 2. In this instance, the hospitality of the device is bewildering considering my prison-like surroundings.

I press the icon for food, opting for something bland in case my nausea decides to make a comeback. Almost as soon as I select my choice, a robotic arm descends from a sliding panel in the ceiling above me, holding a tray and presenting a meal that looks like a feast to my growling stomach. The arm sets the tray down on the table then retracts into the ceiling, leaving me alone with my food.

I'm reinvigorated after gorging on broth and bread, and for the first time since waking up in this place, my mind is clear and not bogged down with drugs. I stretch my legs and return to my feet, assessing my surroundings with renewed focus. There's only one route into this room, and I'd be willing to bet it's locked from the outside. I approach the door, scanning my eyes across the surface. No latch. No handle. No defining feature of any kind. Just a slab of steel blocking my only hope of getting out of this place.

As I flatten my palm against the cool metal, a shrill beeping seeps into the room from the other side of the threshold, as if in response to my touch. I rip my hand away and take a hurried step back at the same moment the door springs open.

A middle-aged man with sparse facial hair stands in the hallway beyond, his face devoid of emotion. He's wearing white clothes that are similar in style to mine, and he holds a large computerized tablet in the crook of his arm, the screen flat to his chest.

"Dr. Richter would like a word with you," he says, his pale eyes locking on mine. When I don't respond, he moves to one side of the doorway and extends his hand, gesturing for me to step into the corridor. "Follow me, please."

My racing heart climbs up into my throat and suffocates me as I inch out of the room. The hallway I step into seems to go on for miles in both directions, dotted with identical doors and at least ten other passages branching off on both sides.

Through the glare of the fluorescent lights overhead, I examine the labyrinth and consider my options. I could run, but it's unlikely I would find my way out before I get apprehended again. This place is a maze, and every turn looks the same. Any chance of escape is non-existent.

With a sigh of resignation, I give in to my lifelong habit of self-preservation, falling behind the man and matching the timing of his every step like a shadow. I don't like it, but I have to do as I'm told. Doing as I'm told is how I survive.

As we walk, I notice the man keeps his distance from me, and he only acknowledges my presence again when we reach our destination, stopping in front of a door that looks the same as every other one we've passed in this place. I wait to the side as he enters a sequence of numbers into the keypad above the handle. Each pressed number results in a beep, and with the last digit, a light on the console turns green and the door sweeps open, granting us entry.

The man steps back and signals with a rigid nod for me to enter the room. I have a bad feeling about this, but what other choice do I have except to obey? When I cross the threshold, the first thing I notice is a metal table, accompanied by two chairs facing each other. The room itself is plain and gray, apart from the wall on my left, which holds a large tinted mirror. A surveillance camera hangs in the far corner, watching me from its place by the ceiling.

"Take a seat," the man instructs. "Dr. Richter will be in momentarily."

As I look back over my shoulder, he sweeps his hand to the side of the table with the chair facing the mirror. The door then closes between us, locking me in.

My stomach clenches when I take a seat, my nerves writhing as the seconds tick by. Several minutes pass before the door slides open again. Dr. Richter strolls into the room, grinning as he sits down in the chair at the opposite side of the table.

"Hello, Wynter. How are you feeling?"

I gape at him, unsure what to say. Words suddenly spew from my lips like vomit. "I want to see my mother," I blurt out without thinking.

The smile slips from his face, and he looks down at his hands where they rest locked together on top of the table. "I'm…afraid that's not possible."

"Why?"

He smiles again, although more gently this time. "Since you had yet to be reassigned to a new sector at the time you were apprehended, you were still technically and lawfully under the guardianship of your mother. She has since relinquished her custodial rights, and you are now under the care and ownership of the State. Well…" He pauses. "The DSD, if we're being precise."

My eyes widen, and my blood runs cold. The DSD. The Department of Scientific Discoveries—a harmless enough name that ironically coincides with the last place in the world I would ever want to be. The DSD makes Detention look like a playground and is where the State conducts human experimentation, poorly hidden behind the guise of research. It's also the home of Termination. The home of everyone's worst nightmare. Only criminals and those determined to be unredeemable are sent here, so what could they possibly want with me? Am I a criminal?

Am I unredeemable?

"This is your home for the foreseeable future."

Terror courses through me, rendering my tongue completely useless. I can't speak. I can't think.

I can't breathe.

"I understand what I'm telling you must come as a shock. But I assure you that you are perfectly safe and will be treated with civility during your stay here."

"And how long will that be?" I croak out in a whisper.

I glare at him as the truth strikes without mercy, the pain of it like sharpened claws slicing into my skin over and over again, stripping me down to the bone. My mother gave me up to these people. My own mother! Anger rockets through me, scorching everything in its path in a blistering wave of fire. All that's left in its wake is the betrayal tearing my heart into pieces.

My eyes clamp shut, but the darkness behind my lids only makes the spinning in my head worse.

"I'd like to discuss what you were doing prior to the incident."

My eyes snap open and lock on Dr. Richter, his right brow slightly cocked in a quizzical expression. As I process his words, it occurs to me that he never answered my question.

"What incident?" I ask.

He leans forward, fixing me with his metallic gray gaze. "At W. P. Headquarters, during your exam."

I shrink back as a chill creeps up my spine. The memory of my hallucination is fresh, the destruction I witnessed still vivid in my mind.

"Is that why I'm here?" I gasp, breathless.

The smile returns to his lips, and he rests back in his seat, drumming a finger against the table. The seconds seem to drag as he considers my question.

"Yes," he says after a torturous moment.

My cheeks flush with heat as I scramble to find some excuse that will get me out of this mess. "W-What happened was a misunderstanding," I stammer. "I panicked, but I'm ready now. I'll retake my exam. It won't happen again—"

Amusement hooks into his features as he holds up a hand. "That won't be necessary."

Dr. Richter reaches under the table and produces a tablet, which he places between us. His fingers flit across the screen, and although there's a certain finesse to his movements, his mannerisms seem almost…forced. Insincere. As far as I can tell, the only natural thing about this conversation is my fear.

The fear I'm feeling is definitely real.

"Could you confirm the following, please?" he asks. "What is your full name?"

"Wynter Arabelle Reeves," I mutter, curious why he's asking when he already has this information.

"Identification number and date of birth?"

"73956241. October 14th, 2043."

He wavers for a moment to look down at the tablet. "Blood type?"

"O negative," I answer automatically. But as I grumble these words, a woman's voice fills my head.

"Her blood type. It's…changing."

Suddenly, I'm not so sure.

Dr. Richter nods, keeping his gaze on his tablet, then proceeds with his methodical line of questioning. "Mother's name?"

My teeth grit together as I think of my mother. Of what she did. Of how she didn't even defend me, her daughter. Her only child.

Her sole living family.

"Evandra Reeves," I hiss, blinking tears from my stinging eyes.

Dr. Richter ignores the sharp edge in my voice.

"Father's name and date of death?"

I startle, unsure why he's asking me this. Why does it matter what my father was named or when he died? He's not here anymore. To the State, you don't matter unless you contribute, and the dead can't do anything except haunt the living.

Swallowing, I try my best not to make it obvious the question has upset me. "Freston Reeves," I whisper. "September 9th… 2050."

"Address?" Dr. Richter continues without pause.

"A19, Unit 34, Zone 2."

"And what business did you have the other day at W. P. Headquarters?"

It takes every ounce of willpower I possess not to raise an eyebrow at him. He knows what I'm going to say, so what's the deal with this interrogation?

What exactly does he want with me?

"I was taking my placement exam," I say, drawing out each word in a slow careful breath.

He looks up. "What sector were you projected to enter?" There's a genuine curiosity in his tone.

"Financial." I knot my hands together under the table. "The banking branch."

An unsettling smirk upturns his lips. "You must be quite intelligent to have been designated to that particular career. Financial often leads to a stable and fulfilling life."

I blink, taken aback by his comment. He sounds just like the advertisements displayed in the classrooms throughout all my years of education, pitching one job or another to students. They were meant to target our interests, paving the way for the assessments that would determine what career would be ideal for each of us and play to our strengths.

At least, that's how the State wants the process portrayed, when in truth, our paths are already dictated from the day we're born based on our genetics. It's a widely known fact that our supposed strengths lie in our blood, which is why so many people end up with the same career selection their parents had. My mother works in the financial sector—hence why we live in Zone 2, Financial, among everyone else who works in banking, insurance, and in the departments that manage our State-allocated pensions. Generally, unless you screw up really badly—like, say, by running out on your exam—you'll just end up exactly where you started, following in your parents' footsteps.

Looks like I take after my father.

It's like that everywhere. Zone 1, Authority, is where our lawmakers and officials work and reside, superior in status to everyone else in the Heart. Zone 3, Commerce, is where the shopping departments and health centers, along with their employees, are located—with the exception of smaller emergency facilities, which are sprinkled throughout the other zones—while all the Heart's hydroponic farms and food production workers are based in Zone 4, Agriculture. Zone 5, Defense, is home to the city's Enforcers and their training grounds. Zone 6, Labor, is the base of all construction and engineering facilities and laborers. And then there's Zone 7, Detention…the zone home to those in the least desirable jobs and the location of the Heart's Detention facilities.

When it comes to work and residential status, everyone is kept separate, isolated to their delegated zones. There are exceptions, like when someone has an impressive IQ and qualifies for a job above their initial projection or when someone breaks the law and is sent to a Detention facility. That's why I've never seen anyone who's been sent for Re-education integrated back into society. The State makes it a point to keep us with others just like us, like pigs trapped in separate pens. No one residing in Zone 2 at this moment has ever been on the other side of the law.

Unlike me.

I shiver at the thought, clenching my jaw. I already know what my life would've been like. I don't need Dr. Richter to remind me, especially now that I have no idea what's going to happen moving forward. After all, I'm fairly certain that imprisonment at the DSD will leave a big black mark on my permanent record. My career and residential prospects will be tarnished by this. Assuming I make it out of here alive and get the chance to have a career. Or a life.

Dr. Richter knits his hands together again and stares at me over the rim of his glasses. Although I expect his question, it still catches me off guard.

"Could you please describe what happened during your exam?"

I pinch my lower lip between my teeth. Should I tell him the truth? What will happen if I do? Better yet, what will happen if I don't? I want to know what happened to me just as much, if not more so, than he does. If I tell him, maybe I'll get that answer.

"I…honestly don't know," I admit. "One minute, I was fine. The next, I had this splitting headache, my vision was blurring, and…" I trail off.

"And?" he presses, his gray eyes piercing.

"And…then, it was like I was someplace else. I was seeing things around me that weren't actually there, even though it really felt like they were. I was…

hallucinating, I guess. Before I could make sense of what was happening, I was back in the exam room."

My pulse accelerates as I wait for Dr. Richter to speak. His stern expression tells me little.

"What *exactly* did you see?" he asks after a moment.

I hesitate, swallowing past the sudden lump in my throat. Why does he care what I saw? It was just a delusion.

It wasn't real.

Was it?

A one-word answer breaches my lips without thought.

"Destruction."

His eyes enlarge just enough for me to notice the change, but before I can properly assess his stunned expression, he clears his throat and looks down at the table, typing something into the tablet.

"I'd like you to examine the following documents." He turns the glowing screen around to face me before adjusting his glasses, pushing them farther up his nose. "Let me know if anything from this information seems familiar to you."

My fingers shake as they hover an inch above the glass surface of the tablet. At Dr. Richter's encouraging nod, I scroll through what appear to be identification records, but I've never met or even heard of the people they belong to. I have no idea what I'm supposed to be looking for. The only similarity I notice between them is the cause of death listed at the bottom of each. They all suffered from one form or other of mental deterioration, and in the end, it killed them.

My stomach turns as my eyes trail over a sentence written in the record for a thirty-year-old woman named Leela.

Suffered from vivid hallucinations.

Just like me, I realize.

I flip through the other records, noting the same line inscribed at the bottom of every one. Panic induced or not, hallucinations aren't normal, which means I could be crazy, too. I could be like the people in these files, and I could just as easily end up the same way.

Dead.

"I'm sorry," I whimper, ignoring the sharp pain in my gut. "I don't recognize any of them—"

"Don't focus on the records, focus on their traits. Their physical appearance is key." Dr. Richter waves a dismissive hand, urging me to look again.

At his behest, I flick through the documents two more times, examining each picture with scrutiny. I'm not sure what he wants me to see. When I open my mouth to speak, he cuts me off, placing a mirror on the table in front of me.

"Look into it," he prompts.

Furrowing my brow, I peer into the mirror, fixing my gaze on my own mismatched eyes. One green. One blue. The same as they've always been since the day I was born.

"Have you ever heard of Ultraxenopia?"

I look up from my reflection and shake my head, my heart pounding as Dr. Richter reaches across the table, retrieving both the tablet and mirror.

"Like the people in these documents, you have a rare genetic defect known as Heterochromia. To put it in simple terms, your eyes are two different colors. Although the disorder itself is harmless, we are beginning to link it to a more serious condition. A phrenoextratic disease called Ultraxenopia."

He pauses, allowing a few seconds for this new information to sink in. Dread overtakes me, but I have no idea what any of it means.

A serious condition, he said.

But how serious?

"Ultraxenopia targets the occipital lobe of the brain, which affects our visual processing, along with the superior temporal gyrus, which helps us process sounds. As the condition takes root, it manifests by showing its victims things that aren't really there."

"Hallucinations," I breathe.

"Correct. But these aren't typical hallucinations by any measure. What you experienced during your exam…it wasn't a delusion, Wynter. What you saw might've been in your head, but it was *real*. It was a vision, and in that moment, I believe what you saw was a glimpse of the future."

I resist the urge to laugh, wondering if this is all some sick, twisted joke intended to torment me before sending me on my merry way to my death. A glimpse of the future? Now, who sounds crazy.

And yet, there's a part of me that wants to believe him. That needs something or someone to blame for the unexpected dissolution of my life. Besides, if what I saw wasn't a vision…

What was it?

"That's impossible," is all I can manage to say.

Dr. Richter doesn't seem surprised by my skepticism and responds by pulling out a handheld black device, which he sets on the table in front of me. With a swipe of his finger, a flickering hologram appears between us, revealing surveillance footage.

I instantly recognize the exam room at W. P. Headquarters. In the blue-tinted footage, I can hear the automated female voice droning on in the background, and I can see myself sitting at my allocated desk, my hand scribbling furiously across its surface.

My eyes follow my recorded movements, watching for the first signs of my breakdown. I glimpse them in the odd jerk of my head and in the way my back hunches over my desk. Finally, the hallucination takes hold, and I rise to my feet, staring blankly around me as if I'm seeing something beyond the walls of the room. The events that follow happen just as I remember them, from that bloodcurdling scream right up to the moment I chose to run away. The footage cuts out when I race out of the room.

Dr. Richter clicks off the device but says nothing. Shaking my head, I meet his gaze.

"That's impossible," I say again, louder this time.

"Perhaps," he says. "But, I must tell you, the tests we've already run show remarkable things. Things that, quite frankly, wouldn't be possible if you were normal. Nonetheless, we won't know for certain until we run more intensive tests. I'd like your permission to do that."

I scoff at his words. My permission? Like the DSD needs permission to do anything. "Won't you just do them anyway, regardless of what I say?"

"Yes." His lips peel back into a grin that I'm sure is meant to be reassuring but looks malicious, revealing predatory white teeth. "But I prefer my subjects to be cooperative. Besides," he adds, "you'd be providing a great service, not only to the advancement of science but to the State. What other reason could you need?"

Apprehension spreads through me like a poison, infecting every inch of my body. I can't trust this man, I know that. But what choice do I have except to cooperate? And if I *do* cooperate…what then?

Dr. Richter repeatedly taps one finger on the table, pressing me to speak. With a nervous twitch, I lick my cracked lips.

"If I cooperate…will you let me go?"

He averts his gaze and stands without saying a word, pushing the metal chair away from the table. The legs scratch against the floor, making me wince.

He then heads for the door, which swings open at his approach, and, pausing in the threshold, he turns and offers me a clipped smile. I know without having to ask that our conversation is over.

Inclining his head, he steps out into the corridor, leaving me alone again in the room.

As the door shuts behind him, I come to terms with the only answer I'm left with. He didn't say it out loud, but he didn't have to. His silence said it for him.

They will never let me go.

FIVE

I DRAW IN A STRANGLED breath as two female attendants strap me down to the table. My eyes burn as I try to breathe past the assault of my heart as it attempts to punch a hole in my rib cage, driving my terror that much closer to the surface where I can no longer ignore it. I have to keep reminding myself that I agreed to this.

I agreed to let Dr. Richter run his tests.

Any sane person would ask me why—not that I had much say in the matter. Even if I hadn't relented, he would've proceeded and I would've wound up on this table. But, behind my fear, I'm curious to see what happens next. Regardless of what it takes, I want to know what's happening to me. I have nothing else. No home. No career prospects. No family.

I only have the need to understand what I saw.

Dr. Richter approaches the foot of the table and waves a hand, dismissing the two women beside me. With an obedient nod, they both slip away, stepping out of my line of vision.

"Are you ready?" he asks.

My lips press into a thin line. "That depends. What are you going to do to me?"

He smiles as if it'll reassure me. It doesn't.

"I want to recreate the experience you had the day of your placement exam. Hopefully, that will be enough to prove that I'm right about what you are. About your condition."

And if it isn't? I want to press, but I can't find the words. Instead, I mutter, "How do you plan to do that?"

"Well,"—he skirts around the table until he's standing next to my head—

"we're going to inject you with an inhibitor that will slow down the normal functions of your brain. Once the inhibitor has set in, we'll send magnetic signals to a localized part of the occipital lobe, which is where the visions stem from. These signals should then follow a path to the superior temporal gyrus through a string of vibrations. If all goes according to plan, this will stimulate a response that should replicate what you experienced before."

And if it doesn't go according to plan? What then? But my fear of the answer prevents me from speaking.

My gaze drops away. I don't really understand what he said, but I grasp enough to come up with one final question. The only question that really matters.

"Will it hurt?" I whisper.

I peek up, and his smile deepens as he places a firm hand on my shoulder. "You'll feel a minor discomfort at most. Nothing to be concerned about. Rest easy. No harm will come to you here."

His fingers curl around my shoulder and squeeze, but his grip is too tight to be consoling. The straps securing me down keep me still and prevent me from wriggling away from his touch. I hold my breath until he lets go of my arm.

The seconds tick by in silence as he directs his attention to the equipment around me. To steady my nerves, I concentrate on the ceiling, counting the fluorescent lights and white tiles. None of my attempts to distract myself work, and my gaze snaps to the side at the clicking of footsteps. Another female attendant approaches the table, her face and eyes blank of any emotion—not that unlike everyone else in this city. Reaching for my arm, she wipes something wet across the skin at the crook of my elbow.

"You'll feel a slight pinch," she warns.

I grimace at the piercing sting of the needle, biting my tongue to keep from crying out as the attendant trails a line of tubing from the IV bag hanging from the stand beside the table down to my throbbing vein. Once everything is connected, she grabs a syringe of silver liquid off a nearby pushcart.

"Everything is ready."

At these words, Dr. Richter returns to my side, and a shudder of panic jolts through me when his fingers tug down the front of my gown, exposing the top of my chest. I struggle against the restraints as the same two thoughts strike me again and again.

I've changed my mind. I don't want to do this.

Tears curve down my cheeks as I bite back the protests pressing at the brink of my lips. I don't speak because I understand that what I want doesn't matter. I don't speak because fighting back will only draw this out and probably make it worse. Much worse. After all, the DSD owns me. I am their property to do whatever they want with.

At that thought, I go still and give in to what's coming. Thankfully, Dr. Richter's fingers move quickly, attaching three circular pads in a straight line just under my collarbone. Once he's finished, the sound of my heartbeat projects through the room.

I can hear my fear in the unsteady palpitations of my racing heart. The beeps grow more erratic when a metal halo drops down from the ceiling and encircles my head, at least a dozen bars extending from the inside of the ring and moving inward, pressing into my skull. Trapping me like an animal in a cage.

A buzzing sound fills my ears as a dew of sweat beads across my skin, a growl of frustration swelling in my throat as fear and anger go to war in my chest. Clenching my jaw, I peer sideways, watching Dr. Richter out of my peripheral vision. His back is turned toward me, his attention fixed on a glowing blue hologram screen above the white counter.

Beside him, a panel in the countertop opens, revealing a wide glass tube that looks to be at least a foot in diameter. It rises up, containing a handful of small silver objects, which float as if suspended in water. A purple aura pulsates around them as they orbit each other like tiny planets.

Dr. Richter nods. "Introduce the inhibitor."

I cast a terrified glance first at the woman then at the syringe in her hand. She pushes the needle into the tube hanging from the IV bag, injecting the silver liquid, which works its way through the plastic down into my vein. As it enters my arm, the drug feels strange—cold like ice, sending a chill through my body, followed by a wave of fire.

A convulsion tears through me, and I thrash against the table, a cry lodged in my throat.

"Thirty seconds until the inhibitor will enter the subject's brain," a deep male voice reports from across the room.

I try to look at whoever spoke, but I can't turn my head. The halo holds me still.

An automated female voice projects from the loudspeaker, counting down to what I'm certain will be my demise. *"Twenty-five seconds remaining."*

As terror consumes me, I have to remind myself this would've happened either way. Even if I hadn't agreed to it, Dr. Richter would've run these experiments.

In the end, I never had a choice.

"Twenty seconds remaining."

My heart is pounding. I can feel it. I can hear it.

"Ten seconds remaining."

I don't want this. I'm scared.

"Five seconds remaining."

My eyes find Dr. Richter's as my mouth shapes the words needed to beg him to stop. But all that springs free from my dried lips is silence.

"Four…"

The floating objects cease mid-orbit, almost as if time has frozen around them.

"Three…"

The purple glow brightens as the silver balls move outward, shifting away from each other.

"Two…"

They draw together again with a flash and a bang, like an elastic band that's been pulled taut and then snapped. The entirety of the room goes white, blinding me.

"One…"

When the countdown hits zero, a scream explodes from my lungs. It's as if a thousand lightning bolts have all struck at once, hitting me in the same place in my head. I gasp for air, trying to breathe through the pain. But it's everywhere.

It's *everywhere.*

My vision clears just enough to make out the sharp planes of Dr. Richter's angular face. I follow his unblinking gaze to the silver objects, which have commenced their rotations. After a few orbits, they slow again, pulsing, and then—

"Again," Dr. Richter hisses.

This time, when the lightning strikes, my body goes limp.

"Her heart rate is dropping," a distant voice warns.

Dr. Richter doesn't even spare me a pitying look when he bites back, "Continue until there's a response."

No more… I try to plead, but I can't find my voice.

Over and over again, the lightning cuts into me, sawing my brain in half. I scream until I can't scream any longer and I lack the energy to do more than simply lie still, waiting for this torment to pass. The pain is too much.

I just want it to end.

When the lightning finally stops, the bursts of white surrounding me fade until my mind is lost to unending blackness. All that exists around me is pain, and I am floundering in a sea of it, drowning.

Surrendering to the waves determined to crush me, my eyelids droop closed, and my body gives in to the welcome embrace of unconsciousness.

SIX

THE TORTURE CONTINUES FOR SEVERAL months. Every day, I'm dragged back into the blinding white laboratory and strapped to the metal table against my will. The events that come after always follow the same routine. The testing continues until I pass out, and when I come to, I'm back in this claustrophobic prison. There's nothing to do in this room except wait.

Wait for my torment to start all over again.

In the few moments of clarity I have where I can focus on something other than my constant agony, I think of Dr. Richter, obsessing over what he said in that strange mirrored room. How he promised no harm would come to me here.

I was stupid to believe that lie. What was even more foolish was allowing myself to believe my time here would ever actually end.

I'm not leaving this hellhole, I know that now. I'm just another dispensable tool to these people. My life means nothing to them, and when I eventually exhaust my usefulness, I'll be disposed of just like all the other victims before me. People don't leave the DSD. Not unless they're in a body bag.

My eyes trail over the puddles of liquefied mush scattered across the floor around me. Dr. Richter won't kill me, and he won't let me die. I've tried enough times to be sure of that. At first, I gave in to this madness, thinking there must be an end to it—that I could survive if I just held on and didn't allow myself to give up.

I know better now.

When I stopped eating altogether, they just forced that upon me in the same way they force everything else, even resorting to more invasive methods to provide sustenance when all other attempts to feed me had failed. They always find a way, no matter what.

There's nothing I can do to stop this.

I cringe at the memory of what these people have done to me, recalling one episode in particular, the brutal recollection still vivid even through the fog of near starvation. It was a typical day. Another failed experiment. Weak and worn down to my breaking point, I knew I wouldn't last much longer and I'd had enough.

I then dragged my withering body into the corner beside the toilet, hiding in the camera's one blind spot. I was cowering at death's door already and knew it wouldn't take much to push me the rest of the way.

At peace with the idea of ending my life, I jammed my fingers down my throat and regurgitated what little nourishment my body was still clinging to. But, somehow, Dr. Richter knew what I was doing, and as I retched, orderlies stormed into the room to stop me. One of them pinned me to the floor as another forced a tube down into my stomach. I gagged as they pumped me full of whatever it would take to keep me alive. To keep me in a physical state where they could continue to run their experiments.

I attempted to scream, but I couldn't. I tried to reject the feeding tube, but I couldn't. Their hands held me down as my body convulsed, and in the end, I couldn't fight them.

This method has now become a daily occurrence.

My eyes flicker open and closed, fighting sleep. The floor is cool against my clammy cheek, bringing a fleeting relief to my burning skin. There's an obscene smell perfuming the air that I'm well aware is coming from me, but I lack the energy to shower. I haven't washed in a long time now, apart from occasionally cleaning my teeth to spare myself from the constant rancid taste of bile and vomit. As for the rest of me, I guess I don't see the point.

I'm going to die anyway.

My eyes drift closed as fatigue overwhelms me. Through the haze of my wavering consciousness, a familiar beeping scratches at my eardrums, the sound so faint that, for a brief second, I think it's only in my head. But then the door springs open and footsteps beat against the floor and I realize it's real.

The torment is about to happen again.

No! I want to scream. Certainly, it hasn't been a whole day already?

The hands wrapping around me are rough as they peel my body off the sticky cement floor. Since I'm no longer able to support my own weight, they haul me to my feet and hold me upright, keeping a strong arm snaked around my back to brace me. In the beginning, they had to restrain me when they did this, but they don't bother anymore. They don't have to. Any fight I had has long since diminished.

I narrow my eyes at the man looming over me, who pushes my head to one side and plunges a needle into the skin of my neck, his face devoid of any emotion. I know with that single vacant look that he doesn't care what happens to me here. No one does. Once claimed by the DSD, you're on your own.

The injection works its way through my system, but whatever the drug is, it doesn't quite knock me out. I'm still conscious, albeit just barely. My body, on the other hand, is paralyzed from the neck down. I can't fight, run, or do anything other than feel the lingering caress of pain.

The orderlies drag me out of the room and through the halls, leading me back to my place of torture. My feet burn from the chafing of my bare skin against the smooth tiled floor, making me wonder where my shoes went. I can't recall when I last saw them. The man supporting the bulk of my weight doesn't bother to lift me and spare me this one discomfort, even though he could do so with ease. Just goes to show what they think of me here.

Once again, I'm reminded of Dr. Richter's promise. No harm will come to me?

If I had the strength, I'd laugh.

At first, I don't notice when we enter the testing room, my head groggy from lack of sleep and mind delirious from the endless pain engulfing my body. My senses only sharpen when the cold metal surface of the table grazes my aching skin, snapping my brain to attention.

The fear buried inside me crawls back to the surface as what follows happens just as it did the first time. The IVs. The monitors. The group of doctors in white coats. The metal halo around my head.

A whimper rolls over my lips, but I can't find the will or the energy to cry, even though that's all I want to do. Maybe because, despite how desperately I crave death, I don't want the people here to have the satisfaction of knowing they've broken me.

I don't want *him* to have that satisfaction.

"Proceed," Dr. Richter says with a smile.

A scream rips from my lungs as the lightning bolt cuts through my head, strike after strike exploding inside my brain and setting my vision on fire. I grind my teeth, searching for the strength to fight through the pain, but the ceaseless assault is unbearable. There's no escaping the agony, just like there's no escaping the fact that this will eventually kill me. But when?

When will this torment finally stop?

Please, I beg my body. *I don't care what you do. Just make it stop.*

For a moment, the strikes come to an end. I sag as much as the halo around my head and the steel bands retraining my torso and legs allow, gasping and gagging up the minimal contents of my stomach. Sweat drenches my skin, plastering the paper-thin gown against my emaciated limbs. I blink several times to clear my blurred vision, but the room and everything in it is obscured. All I can make out are indistinct figures.

A male voice enters my ears from somewhere on my right. "There's been a neural oscillation of her central nervous system."

I don't know what that means. I don't even care.

Until—

"Again," Dr. Richter commands.

No! I try to scream, but the word is cut off in my throat by the electric current passing through the halo straight into my head. It shoots through me in repetitive jolts, disabling every part of my body and rendering my thoughts incoherent. Tears stream down my face, and I cry out with each stab.

End this! I plead with myself. *End this!*

Another stab.

End this!

I release a strangled scream, but the sound is swallowed by the inky darkness stretching across the laboratory, drowning the sterile white of the room until all I can see is black. When my surroundings come back into focus, I'm standing in what I think is the middle of Zone 1, looking out upon a vast scene of destruction. It's just like it was the first time I saw it this way. Every last detail is exactly the same, from the murky air right down to the debris by my feet.

I turn in place—equal parts astounded and horrified by the crumbling city around me—and realize, although begrudgingly, that Dr. Richter's experiments seem to have worked. He's encouraged my brain to recreate what I saw during my exam, but what comes now that he's succeeded? What can he possibly garner from having me relive this frightening hallucination?

Vision, I correct myself. It's strange to admit, but I can feel in my bones that it's true. What I'm seeing…

It's the future that awaits us.

A shiver passes over my skin at the crunching of footsteps in dirt, and the hairs on the back of my neck all raise, like the hackles on a growling dog. Stance rigid, I crane my head, peeking over my shoulder.

A breath catches somewhere between my lungs and my throat as I meet the piercing gaze of the man standing behind me. He looks to be a few years older than me—his early twenties if I had to venture a guess. Disheveled blond hair lay matted against his forehead, slick with dirt and sweat, and his hazel eyes are bursting with warmth but also tinged with the unmistakable coldness of grief.

Gray smudges from the ash in the air stain both his cheeks.

I glance between his face and the gun in his hand, then back again, rooted to the spot by fear. Tears flood his eyes, and one breaks loose, cutting a clean line through the filth on his skin. As another tear follows, his lips move, shaping words, but the silence swallows each one. Even when I strain my ears, his voice still doesn't reach me.

Although my eyes and mind are entrenched in this vision, it's as if my body and hearing are stuck back in the laboratory at the DSD. They anchor me to my horrific reality.

"We can't get a clear picture, Doctor," a female voice announces from somewhere on my right.

"You have my authorization to proceed with the intravenous method we discussed earlier. Do whatever you feel is necessary. I *want* that picture."

A hand runs over my face, but I can't see it. I can only feel the fingers prying my eyelids apart and the burning sensation sinking into my pupils. Screams rip from my chest, but the restraints hold me still.

Bursts of static distort the stranger's face as a searing heat radiates over my eyeballs. It's as if two knife-points are piercing my pupils, and no amount of begging will make my suffering end. I am at Dr. Richter's mercy, and he doesn't seem to know what that word means.

More screams escape as the burning continues. A jostling movement knocks my head, and then everything jumps into sharp focus.

"There! Stop! We have a clear picture now!"

The pain ceases at once, and everything around me goes still. At a glance, my surroundings seem unchanged apart from the sudden deafening hiss of wind, which whips back and forth around me, kicking up a fog of dust.

I peer at the man through the haze, wondering if I'll be able to hear him now, but his face is a blur. Tears obscure my vision, hiding his face.

"I'm sorry, Wynter," he breathes, giving his head a slight shake. I blink the moisture from my eyes as his fingers slacken, and the gun in his hand drops to the dirt with a resounding thud.

"End the session," Dr. Richter commands.

The pain in my eyes returns as the vision dissolves and I fall back into welcoming darkness. Unconsciousness envelops me, but I'm shaken awake by a hand forcefully slapping my cheek.

"How do you know him?"

A weary breath passes through my cracked lips. "What?"

My eyes inch open. Dr. Richter stands over me, his leering gaze pressing me for answers I don't have.

In my peripheral vision, I take note of the silver cart positioned next to the table. Two bloody needles lay on the tray, attached to thin tubes.

"No harm will come to you," he had said.

I blink, and tears stream down the sides of my face.

"The facial recognition server has brought up a match," a woman says from the other side of the room. "The man in question is Ezra Laramie, age twenty-two. Suspected member of PHOENIX."

PHOENIX?

Dr. Richter lunges forward and grabs me roughly by the neck. "How do you know him?" he asks again, yelling this time.

"I don't!" I cry, my voice feeble and raspy.

He glares at me, searching my eyes for a lie, then straightens and releases his deadly grip on my throat. Exhaling through his nose, he takes a step back.

"You will," he promises, his tone lethal.

When he snaps his fingers, orderlies appear at my side as if popping out of thin air.

"Take the subject back to her quarters," Dr. Richter instructs them.

The orderlies unclip the restraints and raise the halo, then lower my trembling body from the sweat-drenched table. As they drag me toward the door—showing no compassion or mercy in how they handle me—my unfocused gaze creeps back toward Dr. Richter.

"Contact the authorities," he barks at a pink-faced older man, who jumps and runs from the room. "I want a red alert sent out on the fugitive."

I don't understand why he's so angry. What's caused this reaction in him? Why does he want the man I saw arrested? Is it because they think he's in PHOENIX?

Or is there another reason?

I raise my head, releasing a single strained word. "Why?" But he doesn't hear me, and within seconds, I'm once again surrounded by darkness.

SEVEN

I GRUNT WHEN MY body hits the hard concrete floor, the impact jerking me awake. Black spots dance in front of my eyes as the orderlies retreat for the hallway, the echo of their footsteps rattling around in my brain like loose screws shaken free of their bearings. My fingers dig into my aching skull as the locking mechanism of the door clicks into place, trapping me once again in my prison.

My arms shudder beneath me when I push myself up, my elbows giving out under my weight when a stabbing in my temples drags me down to the floor. With each stab, I'm assaulted by what I saw in the laboratory, the images burnt into the backs of my eyelids, ensuring I can never escape them.

My eyes squeeze shut as my body convulses, and in my head, I see the man from my vision again. The silence between us is filled with those same three bewildering words he muttered before.

"I'm sorry, Wynter."

I press my cheek against the cold concrete and draw in one deep breath, then another. Gradually, the stabbing in my temples recedes. As the pain fades away, the stranger's face dissolves into darkness.

My eyes flutter open, my blurred vision slowly adjusting to the familiar surroundings of my room. My cell. As it all shifts back into focus, I glance at the table at the end of the bed. My mouth and throat are so dry the muscles are spasming, tightening like a hand around my neck. I can barely breathe past the sensation.

Desperate for water, I claw my way toward the table, dragging my limp legs behind me. The drugs Dr. Richter's underlings sedated me with have worn off a little, leaving my body paralyzed only from the waist down—a slight improvement but still crippling enough that relief eludes me. Between my unbearable thirst and the worrying, periodic pain eating away at my brain, Dr. Richter seems surprisingly determined to let me suffer for someone who claims to want me alive.

Fresh beads of sweat rise across my flaming skin, and my head is spinning by the time I cross the room to the glossy white table. With the last of my strength, I fling my hand onto the computerized surface, blindly pressing the touchscreen. As my fingers slip away, a robotic arm descends from the ceiling with what I hope will be my salvation.

To my relief, the arm places a transparent cup on the table, which I can see is filled almost to the brim with water. I reach for it hungrily and slump against the side of the bed, downing the cure for my thirst within seconds and without once stopping to take a breath. The instant I'm finished, my fingers slacken, and I drop the plastic cup to the floor.

Exhausted, I lean my head against the stiff mattress and close my eyes, eager to sleep off the events of today before the orderlies return tomorrow and I have to go through it all over again. Despite my fatigue, the memory of what I saw replays in my head on a loop, nagging at me. I can't shut it out anymore than I could shut out a screeching alarm drilling into my ears.

Who was that man I saw? Why was he sorry? How does he know me? Or, if what I saw was the future like Dr. Richter claims…

How *will* he know me?

The part I struggle to wrap my head around most is the idea of the man being a member of PHOENIX. If that's true, that means he's a terrorist. An insurgent. An enemy of the State. And if what I saw in my vision is real, then I have to assume this means I will eventually have ties to PHOENIX as well.

But how? I'll never leave this place alive, and no one is coming to save me. There's no way our paths would ever cross. Besides, I've always played by the rules. I'm not a rebel. I don't want to stand out. I don't want to fight back against the State or join a renegade organization, despite what I've been through here.

All I want is to survive.

In the midst of my frantic thoughts, it occurs to me that this is the first time I've actually been able to put a face to someone in PHOENIX. Their arrests and executions are never broadcast on the news—"So we don't give them the infamy they yearn for," my mother explained when I once asked her why. All we, the law-abiding citizens of the State, know is that the organization is comprised of criminals who would do anything and go to any lengths to ensure the collapse of society. I guess I've always figured its members would look the part they've been typecast to play.

The role of the monster.

But that man, Ezra Laramie, he seemed…normal, for lack of a better word. Grief-stricken, panicked, even, but normal. The way he stared at me with that pleading expression, tears sliding down his cheeks…

Is that what a monster would look like?

Doubt spreads over my skin. Throughout my eighteen years in this world, I've been guided and shaped by the information supplied by the State and by the adults who know better than me. But now, I can't help wondering how much of what I've been force-fed my whole life is true. Even worse, how much of it was a lie? I've never questioned the State's teachings before. I never had cause to.

Until now.

Suddenly, I'm overwhelmed by the desire to find out the truth of this world for myself. To discover what's happening to me. To unbury the facts concerning the society we live in. To learn the truth about PHOENIX. I need to separate fact from fiction…

And I think I know where to look for those answers.

The only path forward is to track down Ezra Laramie, if not to get the answers I seek then to find out why he appeared in my vision. There has to be a reason. Besides, searching for PHOENIX—fearsome terrorist group or not—seems like a better alternative than staying here and suffering through another one of Dr. Richter's experiments.

I can't go back in that laboratory. Not after what I've just seen or what Dr. Richter and his lackeys put me through today. Regardless of whether they plan to kill me or simply run more tests, I can't take any more.

So, I need to escape. But how? No one leaves the DSD alive, and I can't exactly fight my way out. Plus, there's the other glaring issue. Even if I do manage to escape, how will I find Ezra Laramie?

The answer strikes me with the same intensity as before, and on reflex, my body doubles over as a sensation unlike anything I've ever felt before explodes inside my brain.

I'm too tired to scream, so I bite down on my tongue to distract myself from what feels like my skull splitting open. Blood pools in my mouth, and the metallic taste is almost pleasant compared to the pain.

As the stabbing in my head eases, the square gray room fades into the inky blackness of what looks to be a narrow street. The shine of halogen lights reflects off the broken asphalt from a dingy bar in the distance, pushing back the gloom. Even from the opposite end of the street, I can read the sign over the door with ease.

THE VEGA

Each glowing letter flickers in turn as the bulbs buzz with a sinister hum.

I glance at a signpost behind my left shoulder, printed with the location name B42. The rusting metal also bears the circular symbol representing Zone 7.

A cry swells in my throat as the pressure inside my brain re-emerges and expands outward, beating against the walls of my skull as if searching for an escape. Or maybe it's just determined to cause me as much pain as possible. In my ears, I hear the unmistakable sound of glass shattering, and as a scream rips from my lungs, I lurch backward, a ringing vibration filling my head when it slams into something hard behind me. My chest heaves as my gaze moves across my fuzzy surroundings, noting the cold gray walls of my cell.

Bed. My head hit the bed.

My eyes flick up to what remains of the mirror above the sink then down to the floor where the rest of the glass lies scattered around my feet in large fragments. How did it break? Confusion barrels through me as I reach out a shaking hand and carefully pick up a shard. A shallow network of cracks spreads over the glass like a spiderweb, distorting what I can see of my face. The whites of my eyes are blood red again, and my pupils are blown wide, reducing the green and blue irises to a thin, barely visible rim.

I gape at my reflection in horror. How long have I looked like this? Days? Weeks? Or is my appearance a result of today's "successful" experiment? Either way, what's happening to me?

What has Dr. Richter done?

Clutching the jagged shard in my hand, I allow my head to flop back against the mattress and snap my eyes shut, lacking the energy to face all these questions right now. Time passes in a fitful daze as I drift in and out of consciousness. I'm not sure how long I stay this way, but eventually, the feeling returns to my numb legs, rousing me a little.

It's the shrill staccato of beeps outside the door that shakes me fully awake. My body tenses as my gaze moves from the closed door to the security camera in the corner to my left. The red light is still blinking, watching me, but if I'm going to escape, it's now or never. I might not survive the next experiment.

I turn, squaring my back to the camera, and wedge the glass shard in my hand beneath the mattress while resting my cheek on the blanket. To the unsuspecting eye, it will look like I've just moved into a more comfortable position to sleep. Hopefully.

The door springs open at the same moment my hand drops to my side. Forcing a yawn, I make a show of opening my eyes, blinking sleepily at the tall female attendant in the doorway. To my complete lack of surprise, her blank expression matches the emotionless demeanor displayed by everyone else I've encountered here. Hell, it's the same look I've noticed on almost everyone throughout my life.

Everyone except my father.

The woman spares a quick glance at the shards on the floor, a hint of curiosity raising one thin brow before she looks back up at me. "Dr. Richter would like to speak with you. Once you're dressed, I will escort you to meet him."

She watches my every move with predatory focus as I push up from the floor, trying to find my balance on shaking legs that seem hell-bent on not supporting my weight. Trembling, I reach for the pants folded on the bedspread behind me, taking my time to slide them on underneath the sweat-soaked gown as I try to figure out my next plan of action. When I raise my arms to change into the starchy gray shirt, my body spasms, and I have to bite my lip to keep from crying out. A fresh pair of shoes sit beside my bed—the first I've noticed in weeks—which I slip my feet into, suppressing a whimper.

"Follow me," the woman says, her tone clipped.

As she turns into the hallway, my gaze falls to the mattress. *Now or never*, I remind myself.

I let out a breath and drop to one knee, yanking the shard out from its hiding place and tucking it inside the left sleeve of my shirt. The woman reappears in the doorway, annoyance creasing her brow, just as I press the glass flat to my wrist. I quickly look down at the floor and pretend to adjust the heel of my shoes.

After a convincing delay, I rise and follow her out into the otherwise empty corridor. The path we tread is familiar, even though I've only walked it once before. Eventually, we stop beside the closed door of our destination—one of many in an identical sea of doors but only one out of a few that I fear.

The woman enters the unlocking code into the keypad, each piercing beep like the smash of a hammer driving into my skull. When the door slides open, my eyes fall on Dr. Richter, who is already inside the room waiting for me.

"Take a seat," he orders.

I look back over my shoulder at the woman, but I only catch a glimpse of her face before the door slides shut between us.

Curling my fingers over the shard in my sleeve, I shuffle over to the chair opposite Dr. Richter.

He gives me a quick once-over. "You look like hell."

I clench my jaw. "What have you done to me?"

He removes his glasses and wipes the lenses clean on the lapel of his white coat. "I haven't done anything that your body wouldn't have naturally embraced on its own. I merely sped up the process."

My mouth goes dry. "What do you mean?"

Dr. Richter meets my gaze with a smirk, returning his glasses to their perch on his nose. "You are evolving. Developing abilities those unlike you can only dream of possessing. Although I was uncertain of it before, this last trial has confirmed my suspicions. You are precisely what I thought you would be."

What. Not who, I note.

"You said I wouldn't be harmed. You said I would be treated with civility—"

"Yes," he admits, interrupting me with a shrug. "But sacrifices must always be made for the advancement of science."

Sacrifices? I nearly scream.

How can he act so apathetic about what they've done to me? What *he's* done to me? What I went through was torture, plain and simple. Not that I shouldn't have seen it coming considering that's what the DSD is known for.

I chew on my lower lip for a moment, mulling over the questions piling up in my head. Is what he said true? Would the changes happening in my body have occurred anyway, even without his experiments? Was this pain, this agony, always inevitable?

Dr. Richter's voice is like a slap to the face, pulling me from the abyss of my thoughts. "I brought you here today to discuss what you saw." When I don't speak, he lets out a sharp exhalation, pinching the bridge of his nose between his thumb and forefinger. "Your vision." He sneers, clearly losing his patience. "Was it a continuation of what you saw during your placement exam?"

I shake my head. "More like…a missing piece out of the middle."

His eyes flash behind his glasses as he leans toward me, folding his hands on the table. "How does it end?"

His tone unnerves me, sending a jarring chill over my skin. I hesitate, and in this moment, I'm more certain than ever that my life is in danger. That certainty reaffirms my need to escape.

Dr. Richter pushes back his chair and jumps to his feet. Slamming his fists down on the table in front of me, he raises his voice, shouting, "How does it end?"

I notice the subtle twitch of his cheeks and the way sweat beads along his neatly combed hairline. His fingers curl inward until his hands are in fists, the knuckles straining white against the metal surface of the table.

As his composure crumbles, I feel something that could almost be mistaken for happiness. For the first time since waking up in this horrible place, it's almost as if the roles are reversed. Now, he's the one showing weakness.

Now, I'm the one with the power.

"We all die," I say with a smile.

EIGHT

AVERTING HIS GAZE, DR. RICHTER looks down at his tablet and swipes a finger across the top of the screen. In a calm voice, he says, "Could you please come back in?"

The woman from before re-enters the room, her expression hollow as she stands in the doorway like an obedient soldier, awaiting her orders.

"Take the subject back to the laboratory and prep the team for another session," Dr. Richter instructs.

"What?" My fingers grasp the edge of the table as panic weighs me down in my seat.

"So soon?" the woman asks, looking genuinely taken aback as she furrows her dark manicured brow.

Dr. Richter ignores the woman's question and approaches the door, brushing past her and stepping one foot out into the corridor. He then pauses to look back at me, his body straddling the threshold.

"We will retrieve the vision in its entirety, no matter what it takes."

I blink, my jaw dropping at the lack of remorse present in both his gaze and tone. Doesn't he realize that his last test could've killed me? Does he even care?

I shake my head. "You know I can't control it—"

"You will learn to!" he growls. The anger behind his words spreads into his skin, flushing his cheeks until his whole face is ruddy. "You *will* lead me to him!"

To him? I muse, thinking of the blond stranger's face. *Or to PHOENIX?*

What is Dr. Richter actually after?

As this question takes shape in my head, a scream rips from my lungs, ravaging the inside of my throat. A sharp pain slices into every inch of my skull, and as the pain spreads, a violent spasm tears through my body, rattling me down to my bones. In what little awareness I manage to cling to, I wonder if I'm going to die. *Finally,* part of me thinks with relief while the rest of me screams, *No! I'm not ready!* Wrenching to the side, I fall out of my seat.

As my body seizes against the cold floor, a crystal clear image ignites in my brain. I see that bar again. *The Vega,* I recall from the glowing halogen sign. Except, this time, I'm inside the establishment rather than seeing it from the outside. An older man with a bushy beard and a shining bald head stands behind the wrap-around bar, drying a wet glass with a questionable looking gray and brown rag that's definitely seen better days. Before him, three people sit at the high counter, one of whom I recognize.

It's him, my brain registers as the image quickly fades before thrusting me into a fresh hell of pain. My hand shoots out and clutches the nearest table leg as I ride out the stabs in my head. Sweat and tears drip from my face to the floor.

"What have you just seen?" The rich timbre of Dr. Richter's lilting voice is a faint thrum on the edge of consciousness. The deafening ringing in my ears is almost enough to drown him out.

The soles of his shiny black shoes squeak against the floor as he closes the distance between us. Crouching beside me, he grabs hold of my shirt, his knuckles roughly grazing my collarbone.

"Answer me!"

His outburst ejects spittle onto my cheeks, but I don't raise a hand to wipe it away. I don't move at all. I don't even speak. I just glare into those soulless gray eyes in silence, determined not to cave.

Sneering, Dr. Richter loosens his claw-like grip on my shirt and shoves me away as he rises. My body careens to the side, and as I collide with the ground, my head slams into the tiles. Black spots stain my vision, and a moan rumbles low in my throat.

Biting back a sob, I reach up a trembling hand and grab the edge of the table. Slowly, I pull myself up to my feet, keeping one hand on the metal surface for support until my legs are steady.

Once I'm certain I won't tip over, I risk a wary glance at Dr. Richter. His focus has turned from me and is now fixed in the direction of the open doorway, his eyes locked with the female attendant's, who stands with a hand in her pocket, as if waiting for him to give her an order. My pulse skyrockets when he nods and she pulls a syringe free from her sterile white coat.

Tensing, I stumble back into the corner. I won't let them do this to me. Not anymore.

Never again, I silently vow.

Remembering the shard of mirror pressed close to my wrist, I shake the glass piece loose from my sleeve. The jagged edges dig into my palm. "Stay away from me," I whisper.

The woman inches toward me, disregarding my warnings, her hand clutching the syringe. My fingers tighten around the glass.

"I said stay away from me!" My arm shoots upward as I brandish the broken piece of mirror like a knife.

The woman hesitates, pausing mid-step, assessing the threat with a curious tilt of her head. I blink a few times to bring her face into focus, but her features are a blur, the sweat dripping into my eyes blinding me as I scramble for a way to escape this. But there is no escape, is there? The only way this ends is with me back on that table.

The only way this ends is with me dead.

Pressure pushes against the walls of my head, coaxing a strangled hiss from my lips. As the room spins, I wrap my free hand around the top of my skull, as if that will somehow keep my brain from exploding. My nails dig into my scalp as the pressure worsens, sinking into the skin, drawing blood. The warm sticky wetness seeps into my hair and runs in a single thin line down my cheek.

A shriek surges up from my lungs, and as the cry breaks loose, all the pain flows out of my body. The pressure shoots out of my head like a cannonball, targeting the mirror behind Dr. Richter, which shatters into hundreds of pieces, the shards falling away from the frame to reveal a hidden observation room on the other side of the wall. At least ten doctors stare back at me with shell-shocked expressions, every last one of them unmoving and exposed.

Chest heaving, I shift my sights back toward the woman. She hasn't moved from her previous spot, her body frozen and face contorted in terror. A tingle of energy buzzes over my skin, a wave of power rising up from within, pulsating like a beating heart as if it's a separate entity living inside me. As if it has a mind of its own. It reaches out for her, fed by my fear.

When my eyes narrow, her fingers slacken, dropping the syringe to the floor. My lips twitch. She reaches for her head, her fingers sliding over her scalp as she gasps. Blue streaks materialize, starting about an inch from her hairline, and creep across her face, displaying a swelling network of veins, which disappears down her neck and under her shirt.

Her eyes roll back, and she falls to her knees. Foam bubbles at the corners of her mouth as she writhes, the saliva mixing with the red tinge of blood. A panicked voice in the back of my head tells me she must've bitten her tongue, but I lack the ability to care. If anything, I only want to cause her more pain.

Dr. Richter drops to his knees and flips the woman onto her side, holding her firm against him throughout the convulsions. His eyes find mine as his lips shape hurried words, shouting at me, but I can't hear him.

My eyes squeeze shut as the pressure returns to my head, crushing my brain like a grape in a fist. My legs buckle, threatening to drag me back down to the floor, and every intake of air is a struggle as the chaos around me seems to slow to a standstill.

But then, the universe springs back into motion, forcing time into a forward lurch and popping the soundproof bubble around me. My eyelids pry apart at the inhuman wail that suddenly pierces my ears, and I glance down to find the attendant thrashing in Dr. Richter's arms, her skin so white it's almost translucent. Blood trickles in a steady, constant stream from her nose and ears as if her insides are melting.

With one last heaving cry, the woman goes limp. Dr. Richter stares at her unmoving body for a long moment before daring to meet my gaze. "What have you done to her?" he asks, his voice breathless.

A wave of dizziness knocks me off balance, and a surge of bile rushes into my mouth as whatever power possessed me releases its unwanted hold on my mind. It's as if a fog has been lifted off my senses, returning me to myself. I shake my head a few times to clear it.

The woman's still body catches my eye, and I know without having to ask that she's dead. Did I really do that to her? I couldn't have…could I?

I peer down at my hands. Although I didn't physically touch her, they might as well be covered with her blood. A tear streaks down my cheek.

I did this. I killed her.

Swallowing the urge to vomit, I stagger forward one unsteady step then force myself to take another. This place is destroying me, and if I don't jump at the chance to leave now, it'll consume not only what remains of my sanity but my humanity. I can't let that happen.

My entire arm trembles as I inch toward Dr. Richter and lift the shard of glass to his throat. "Take off your coat." When he doesn't move, I push the sharp tip of the mirror into his jugular until it draws blood. Only a pinprick but enough to show him I'm serious.

"All right," he says quickly. "Let's just remain calm. You're in shock, I can see that. Let me help you."

"Help?" A barking laugh rocks my body. "I don't want any more of your *help*." I spit the word like it's acid on my tongue. "I just want to leave. Now, I won't say it again. Take off your coat."

His lips press together as he shrugs out of the pristine white garment, and when he hands it to me, I pull it on, even though he's several inches taller than me and the fabric swamps my body. I look like a child dressed up in her father's clothing, but I only need it to disguise me enough that no one here will spare me a second glance. That's all it is. A disguise.

Well, the closest thing I'll find to one, anyway.

Peering at the empty doorway, I back away slowly from Dr. Richter, keeping my weapon raised in warning. My steps are calculated and cautious, spurred on by the tenuous belief that I might get out of here and actually achieve what no one before me has managed.

I might leave the DSD alive.

That thought gives me the courage to step out of the room, and yet…once I'm in the hallway, a burning question I can't find the strength to ignore any longer holds me back against my will. Pausing, I clench my hands into fists and peek over my shoulder at Dr. Richter. He hasn't moved from where he still sits on the floor, his gray eyes cast down at the small puddle of blood under the attendant's head stretching out across the white tile.

"That man I saw… Why do you want me to find him?" I ask.

His mouth hitches up into a tiny smile. "He's a criminal. And all enemies of the State must be brought to justice."

Enemy of the State…

"Is that really the reason?"

"Why?" He looks up at me through his glasses, cocking an eyebrow. "Is that who you're planning on running off to for help?"

I strain my jaw, afraid to say anything that might give even the slightest indication where I'm going after I leave this prison.

Dr. Richter seems to see right through my silence.

"If you think you can trust him, you're wrong. If you think he'll protect you, he won't."

Keeping my face blank, I glance down at the body beside him. "I don't think I need protection. Do you?"

As these words leave my lips, I turn away and press on down the corridor, desperate to put as much distance between myself and Dr. Richter as possible. I don't want him to see the tears in my eyes or the mask of false strength as it slips from my face. I just need to get away from him. Far, far away. Even if that means I have to join PHOENIX.

Trust doesn't come into the equation for me.

Still, his warning follows my every step as I move through the building, keeping my pace slow and controlled to avoid the attention of the watching cameras. At any moment, an influx of Enforcers will probably arrive to detain me. But no one comes.

No one tries to stop me.

My heart pounds in my ears, muting my footsteps, as I progress through the labyrinthine facility, taking blind turn after blind turn with no idea which direction I should head in. After countless corridors and what feels like several hours of searching, the main lobby slides into view.

Dread tickles my skin as I assess my surroundings. The space is large—spanning at least two stories—and open with minimal furnishings, which are all in varying shades of white and gray. Everything is clinical and clean. There's also nowhere to hide. The path to the doors is wide open, but to get there, I'd be in plain sight of the enemy.

A grimace warps my lips as I consider my options. Getting here was easy enough, but escaping from W. P. Headquarters was easy, too, and look how that fiasco turned out. Getting out of the DSD is a whole other story. I also can't figure out why Dr. Richter hasn't raised the alarm. He's had plenty of time to do so, and—tracking chip aside—it's not like I have a home to run to this time that he can track me down to and corner me at. I could go anywhere in the city, so why hasn't anyone come after me?

What is he waiting for?

I press my back to the wall beside me and glance around the corner, eyeing the row of revolving glass doors standing like sentries at the opposite side of the lobby. My way out. The *only* way out. Four guards keep watch by the long line of turnstiles separating me from liberation.

I draw in a wheezing breath, shrinking back out of sight, as panic claws at my throat. This won't be possible. It won't. There's no such thing as escape from this place.

My teeth grit together as I force myself to think of the man I saw in my vision. Possible or not, I've come this far. I can't give up now. I at least have to try.

I have to find out who he is.

Exhaling through my nose, I thrust the shard of glass into the right pocket of Dr. Richter's white coat. Then, before I can talk myself out of this half-baked, possibly—*most definitely*, I correct myself—suicidal plan, I turn the corner and trudge toward the doors with confidence, like I belong. Like I'm just another one of the monsters.

My footsteps merge with the others echoing through the lobby, adding to the quiet whir of movement. No one takes any notice of me, igniting a brief flicker of hope, which fades the closer I get to the turnstiles, my eyes landing on the small raised box connected to the closed partitions. Horror and realization both dawn on me at the same moment. If I prick my finger, the alarm will go off. I don't have the security clearance to leave, which means I'll just be handed back over to Dr. Richter and his team of minions. I've been dealing with these security checkpoints for eighteen years and I only just think of this now? What is wrong with me?

Well, aside from the obvious.

My stomach turns when it occurs to me that maybe this is why Dr. Richter hasn't raised the alarm. Why would he if he knows I have no way to escape?

Heart racing, I shift my eyes from side to side, frantically searching for a solution. To my right, eight doctors or maybe attendants—I'm not quite sure which—are walking in a tight-knit group, also on their way out of the building. Out of options, I make the split-second decision to fall into the line they're forming in front of the checkpoint. With my stolen disguise, I easily blend into the mass of white coats.

The weight on my chest eases just a little. "Thanks, Doc," I mutter under my breath.

The shrill beeping of the turnstile computers grows louder as we approach, screaming their approval. Beep, after beep, after beep as each person waiting proceeds forward through the glass barriers. When the man in front of me pricks his finger and the partition before us slides open with a hiss, I take advantage of the opportunity presenting itself.

This is the only chance I'll get.

Holding my breath, I press my chest flat against the man's back and push through the barrier just one step behind him before the gate can close. To my relief, the sensor doesn't pick up my intrusion.

As we come out on the other side, the man throws an odd look at me over his shoulder, no doubt startled by my unexpected proximity. I turn my head to hide my face, grumbling an apology. Before he can say anything in response, I hurry away toward the revolving glass doors.

When I step outside, the frigid winter breeze hits me like a slap in the face—cold but fresh in comparison to the stale, odorous air I've been breathing for months. Relishing the burn of every inhalation, I choke out a laugh and sprint away from this nightmare as fast as my legs can carry me.

As I race into the night, a worrying thought gnaws at me. What if I was only able to leave because the DSD allowed me to leave? Because Dr. Richter let me leave? What if, the entire time, he was watching me but chose not to intervene?

If that's the case, there's only one reason I can think of as to why he would do that. Why he would risk losing his precious experiment.

He thinks I'll lead him to the man from my vision.

He thinks I'll lead him to Ezra Laramie.

NINE

MY GAZE LINGERS ON THE metal sign towering over me where the insignia for Zone 7 looms over the road. I have to keep moving. I can't go home, and there's no one else I can turn to for help. There's nowhere left for me to go.

Not if I want to survive.

Clenching my jaw, I peer down at my arm and tug up the white coat's oversized sleeve until my left wrist is exposed. Even though it isn't visible, I know the chip is there, buried under my skin—a homing beacon to Dr. Richter, telling him exactly where I am.

A stuttering breath trickles out from between my trembling lips. I can't put this off any longer. I escaped from the DSD hours ago, and at every point I stopped to remove the chip, one excuse or another held me back from doing what has to be done to be free of my captors for good. I told myself that if I left it in place, Dr. Richter would be more inclined to keep his distance because it would seem like I was leading him to PHOENIX, just like he wants. That if I removed it before the opportune moment, he would realize what I was planning and send his subordinates to haul me back to his lair. That's what I said to myself as a way of shifting the blame away from my fear.

But the excuses end now.

Tremors run over my fingers as I thrust them inside Dr. Richter's coat pocket, a gasp catching in my throat when the jagged edges of the broken mirror graze my skin. My nerves waver, but I tighten my grip, resolved.

"I can do this," I whisper.

With a hurried glance at my seemingly deserted surroundings, I slink into a nearby alley, stepping out of sight of any hidden prying eyes into a shroud of darkness. The cover of shadow obscures my vision, but that might be for the best. I don't want to see what I'm about to do anyway.

My hand twitches as I drag the sharp edge of the glass in a horizontal line a few inches above the hem of the coat, cutting back and forth through the fabric with rough jabs until a mangled strip comes loose from the stitching. I then roll the torn fabric into a ball and jam it inside my mouth, biting down.

Exhaling through my nose, I angle the pointed tip of the mirror against my naked wrist. Fear pulses through my body, and for a moment, I don't move any more than that, daunted by the potential consequences of what I'm about to do. One single slip is all it would take. One mistake and I'll die here in this alley.

At least then I would be free of Dr. Richter.

I shake my head to rid myself of that thought, pushing away the horrific mental image of my possible death. The chips are located in this spot for a reason—so people won't attempt what I'm so foolishly about to do. But it has to be done.

There's no other way.

Clamping my teeth down, I push the shard into my wrist, piercing the flesh before I can talk myself out of it. A grunt swells in my chest, but my cries are muffled, muted by the ball of cloth in my mouth. Blood pools from the wound and drips from my arm onto the pavement below.

My fingers work the glass, turning the tip around inside my arm, as my nerve endings scream, making me light-headed and nauseous and a million other things in-between. Still, I jiggle the mirror, searching, even as drowsiness overwhelms me.

I squeeze my eyes shut so I don't have to look at the blood, the red somehow startlingly clear in the gloom. I bite down harder, straining my jaw.

I have to stay awake. I have to find it. I repeat these words to myself like a chant, clinging to consciousness, until, finally, after what seems like hours of agony, the glass tip scrapes something hard.

The chip.

Gasping, I fall back against the brick wall behind me and peek one eye open, trying not to jostle my arm. Through my blurring vision, I can just make out the glint of gold protruding from my wrist like a splinter.

I tilt the glass shard flat against my palm to free my pointer finger and thumb, which I use to pinch the small piece of metal, tugging it all the way free from my wrist. Wincing, I let out a shaking breath and carefully hold it up to eye level.

Fortunately, the chips, which are implanted right after we're born, are only good for identification and tracking purposes—and for making payments, since they're directly linked to our personal bank and pension accounts. They don't keep any record of vital signs, though, which means, if I leave the chip here in one piece, it'll look like I've just stopped to rest for the night. Dr. Richter and his team won't have any way of knowing I cut the damn thing out until tomorrow morning when they realize I haven't moved for a while and consider the option that I might be dead. By the time they come to investigate, I'll be long gone from here. Hopefully.

The vertigo swarming my head makes me think otherwise, threatening to topple me over. If I allow this exhaustion to consume me, I know I won't get up again. If I let it take hold, I'm as good as dead.

Fight. Stay awake. You have to keep moving.

At this thought, a burst of adrenaline rushes through my veins, and I find my balance, managing to stay on my feet. Before this energy can fade, I flick the chip into the densest patch of darkness at the other end of the alley where a large brick wall forms a clear dead end. The shadows swallow that small discarded piece of my identity whole.

I hiss as a burning pain expands over my wrist—the freezing night air grazing across my torn skin only making my discomfort worse—and with a low growl, I glance at the open wound and the blood, which is showing no signs of stopping or even slowing down any time soon. My jaw slackens, and the balled up fabric falls from my mouth, unraveling across my outstretched arm as a cloud of steam billows in the air in front of my face from where my hot breath reacts to the icy cold. Aware I need to get the bleeding under control if I'm going to last beyond the next ten minutes, I bite at the cloth, my teeth working in an awkward partnership with my fingers, wrapping it around my wrist and pulling the fabric as tight as I can bear. This makeshift bandage won't be enough to staunch the bleeding, but it'll have to do until I can close up the wound. Or before I bleed to death.

Whichever comes first.

I blink a few times to clear the fuzzy haze from my eyes and pull Dr. Richter's coat sleeve back into position, the cuff hiding the bulk of the bandage. My fingers loosen to drop the shard but tighten at the last possible moment when I consider that I might need it again. Any weapon is better than no weapon at all, especially considering where I'm going.

Resolved, I drop the bloodied glass back inside the deep pocket.

When I push away from the wall, my legs buckle without the support, and the world spins on its axis as a sudden dizziness turns my stomach. Lurching forward, I retch several times, spewing stomach acid and bile onto the pavement.

Once the nausea stops triggering my gag reflex, I stumble out of the alley toward freedom. My feet drag, and I trip every few steps as I walk, searching for the sign from my vision, shivering against the cold. The night is thick, and the fog clouding my eyes only makes my task that much harder.

The streets are empty. I've never been this far from home before, and I can barely even believe I'm in the same city considering the significant differences between this zone and the one I grew up in. The buildings are derelict, the roads cracked and filthy, and the narrow homes are stacked so closely together they resemble shacks more than actual houses. The State must not bother with upkeep this far out from the central zones. There aren't even any security cameras hidden among the eaves of the buildings or attached to the street lamps that I can see—although, that's a good thing for me given the fact that I'm trying to stay off the DSD's radar.

Still, despite my need for invisibility, a shudder of fear ricochets up my spine. Crime in this zone must run rampant without the constant watchful eye of the State. For all I know, I could be walking through these streets with a target on my back.

As I trudge forward, frantically searching the shadows for danger where it might not even exist, I find myself feeling sorry for those unfortunate enough to live out here, regardless of whether they're lawbreakers. Those born here are innocents, subjected to the horrors of residing in an outer zone. In Zone 2, I never had these concerns.

Unlike where I'm from, Zone 7 marks the edge of the city—the final zone before reaching the wall separating us from the unknown dangers outside. Other cities lie beyond the Heart's borders, but travel to them is prohibited without special clearance from the Board of Travel, which is typically only granted to those individuals working in the highest sectors of society. Or to Enforcers, for the rare occasion when their particular skill set is required somewhere else.

This zone is also the home of Detention, the group of facilities I initially thought I was imprisoned at when I first woke up in the DSD. Looking back at everything I've been through, I think Re-education would've been preferable to Dr. Richter's experiments, even if that meant undergoing brainwashing or whatever it is they do to keep people in line once they're released after their sentence. Even if it meant I would've spent the rest of my life in a terrible, low-income job and living in a slum just like this one.

Anything would've been better than torture.

The toe of my shoe catches on a dip in the pavement, and a gasp rips from my lungs when I trip. My arms thrust out to break my fall, my fingers clasping around the nearest object they can find to save my face from the tarmac.

When the ground is no longer rushing upward to meet me, I drag in a few shaking breaths to steady myself. Cold metal digs into my hips, pulling my gaze to the street sign supporting my weight. The emblem for Zone 7 fills my limited field of vision, along with the name of the road.

B42

I blink, struggling to believe what I'm seeing. Up until now, part of me was still convinced the visions were nothing more than hallucinations concocted by my unhinged brain as a way of processing the stress from, first, my placement exam, and then from my time at the DSD. But seeing this sign in front of me, *really* seeing it, surrounded by a dreary street I've never been to and yet recognize… It's enough to tell me this is actually happening.

It's enough to tell me the visions are real.

My eyes skirt along the empty road, following the path as I see it again in my head. There's no one around, but it's late, and, if I had to guess, past curfew. I can't imagine anyone takes that risk, not even in the outer zones since Enforcers could be on patrol and are probably less lenient with the citizens here, considering their inferior status. Despite not having any cameras to watch them, it seems even the people living in the slums of Zone 7 abide by this one law of the State.

Everyone except for me.

At the far end of the road, I glimpse the bar from my vision. The exterior of the run-down building is just as I remember it, right down to the halogen sign hanging above the wide metal door. The lights seem to flicker at my approach, the bulbs buzzing with a hum of warning.

My feet maneuver around the rain-filled potholes, my steps slow and breathing labored. By the time I reach the door, my heart is beating so hard and fast I can barely think straight.

Swallowing, I raise my hand only to hesitate with my fingers an inch from the rusty handle. Whatever—*whoever*—I find on the other side of this door will change my life, I know it. The actions I take here will set me on a path I won't be able to turn from. If I step through this door, all hope of my old life is gone. Am I ready for that?

Nodding, I brace myself and pull.

As the door swings open, I'm greeted by low amber lighting and the musty, stale smell of old smoke. The stench leaves a strange taste on my tongue, and I grimace, snapping my mouth shut when the odor hits me. Breathing through my nose, I straighten my face into a neutral expression and step into The Vega.

As soon as I pass over the threshold, every eye in the room turns to look at me as if my presence has set off an alarm, stopping me short. I loiter by the doorway, unsure what to do.

Driven by my natural inclination to blend in, I inch forward and plop down on a stool at the bar. The bald bartender watches me with one eyebrow cocked as he dries the glass in his hand with the same dirty rag I saw in my vision. A toothpick sticks out of the left corner of his mouth.

"What can I get ya?" he asks in a gruff voice.

I lick my dried lips, suddenly parched and desperate for a drink. How did I not realize how thirsty I am until now?

"Water," I croak.

With a laugh, he shakes his head and picks up another glass to dry it. "Yer in a bar, sweet cheeks. Water ain't exactly on the menu. You'll have to order somethin' a bit more toxic."

I bite my lip. Alcoholic beverages aren't common in Zone 2. In the higher echelons of society, drinking is seen as a degrading habit, and because of that, it's no longer legal in many places across the Heart. The only reason it hasn't been banned in the outer zones is because consumption still provides a steady income stream—and escape from reality—for the poor. With little else to rely on, they need the support. Either that or the State is hoping it will eventually kill them.

Although I've never consumed alcohol before, I know from my schooling that it won't ease my thirst. Besides, I have no way to pay for a drink now that I don't have my chip. But, from the way the bartender glares at me, I know that if I don't order something soon, there's a good chance I'll be asked to leave. Or be forcibly removed. Then everything I did to get here, like murdering that attendant and nearly killing myself by cutting the tracking chip from my wrist…

All of it will have been for nothing.

As I consider what to do, my eyes trail over the dark, stuffy room, taking in the familiar but unfamiliar surroundings. They almost complete one full rotation of the space before catching on the occupied stool two seats down from mine.

As I take in the shadowed profile of the man sitting there, I forget all about the bartender, who still stands in front of me, waiting for my answer. The sole focus of my attention is the man perched on that seat.

"Well?"

The bartender's deep voice shakes me free of my thoughts, and I force my gaze back to him, clearing my throat. "I'll have what he's having."

I look left, risking another glance at the stranger from my vision. The reason why I'm here.

The bartender follows my gaze. "Sure thing."

He buzzes around behind the counter, returning a moment later with a large glass of amber liquid, which he places in front of me with a disgruntled frown, observing me with narrowed eyes. I wait for him to ask for payment, but he says nothing, instead moving on to serve another customer. I let out a breath, confused but relieved. I've dodged a bullet. For now.

I stare at the tall, chipped glass with uncertainty. I have no idea what to say or do from this point—I didn't plan anything beyond getting here. Maybe because I didn't think I would actually make it this far.

Or maybe because I know how crazy this all is.

I let my gaze drift back to Ezra Laramie, watching him out of my peripheral vision. Pushing aside my shock that he even exists, I ask myself what I should do. Should I tell him I was kidnapped by the DSD after seeing the end of the world during my placement exam? After having a vision that, following months of torture, he just so happened to appear in? I wouldn't blame him if he didn't believe me. Hell, I wouldn't blame him if he were to try to kill me at the mere mention of the DSD.

My fingers wrap around the glass, gripping tightly, and I lift the brim to my lips, hoping the drink will help clear my head. The taste washing over my tongue is unpleasant, and I sputter and choke as the bitter liquid slips down my throat. Coughing, I shove the glass away from me.

"It's an acquired taste."

My body tenses at the enchanting cadence of his voice. Although I've only heard him speak once, I know I would recognize that sound anywhere.

My heart slams into my ribs as I pivot on my stool. When our eyes meet, he jerks his chin toward my glass, his gaze flashing briefly down and then back up again, locking on mine. I glance at the barely touched liquid, embarrassed.

He swings around on his own stool to face me. "You're not from around here." It's not a question.

"I'm here on business," I answer quickly.

"Business?" Skepticism creases his brow, a slight smile tugging up one corner of his mouth as he throws back the rest of his drink. "There isn't much business going down in Zone 7."

My throat tightens. "Not even with PHOENIX?"

The stool legs creak as he shifts over onto the seat between us, bringing himself closer to me. Leaning in so his lips are practically touching my ear, he growls, "I don't know who you are, but you won't find anything involved with PHOENIX here. I'd stop looking if I were you."

He pulls away, his hazel eyes returning to mine, as Dr. Richter's warning purrs in my head.

If you think you can trust him, you're wrong. If you think he'll protect you, he won't.

A shiver coaxes goosebumps to rise on my arms. I push away my unease, focusing on why I came here. It doesn't matter who I do or don't trust, and like I told Dr. Richter, I don't need anyone's protection nor do I expect it. The people of the Heart have always only cared about themselves and their own individual survival. Why would PHOENIX be any different?

No, all I want are answers.

And, like everyone else, I just want to survive.

"Then why else would you be here?" I ask before muttering the one thing I know will definitely get his attention. "Ezra Laramie."

His eyes spring wide as his name breaches my lips in a hiss, and in response, he jumps to his feet, stumbling back a few steps. The stool he was sitting on tips and clatters to the floor with a bang.

As he backs away from me, his gaze drops to the coat tucked around my frail body, his attention fixing on the insignia embroidered over my breast.

His eyes dart back up to mine. "Who are you?"

Before I can answer, he pulls something free from his belt and throws his arm up, pointing a gun at me.

My heart pounds in my ears as I slide off the stool, my balance unsteady as I stare down the polished black barrel.

"Who are you?" he asks again, shouting this time.

The other dozen or so people in the bar are all standing as well now, watching our altercation with interest. Every last one is also holding a weapon, including the bartender, who fixes me with a glare that could melt steel as he pulls a shotgun out from under the counter.

As panic twists my insides, it occurs to me this bar must be a safe house for PHOENIX members. The people in this room are all likely part of the group or support it in one way or another, explaining why my vision led me here.

Gulping, I turn my attention back to Ezra.

"This isn't how it looks."

"Is that so?" He sneers. "Because, from where I'm standing, it looks like you're one of *them*."

"I'm not." My protest is weak and unconvincing, even to my own ears.

He pushes the cold muzzle of the gun against my right temple, sending a shudder through my body, which rocks me right down to my marrow. He takes a step closer, lowering his voice to a venomous snarl. "And why should I believe you?"

I tense my jaw, spitting my response through clenched teeth. "If I was one of them, reinforcements would already be here."

The State doesn't play games. As a member of PHOENIX, he must know that better than anyone. The State wouldn't waste time sending in a single person to clear out this bar when it could more efficiently get the job done by sending a whole team to exterminate the lot. If I was one of them, the Enforcers would already be here.

If I was one of them, he would already be dead.

A flicker of doubt crosses his face, and he wavers. The point of his gun moves away from my skin, coaxing an unbidden whimper from my throat. His eyes cling to mine, making my heart beat even faster.

"We can't take any chances," an older man grumbles behind him. "We should kill her to be sure."

Terror shreds my composure to pieces as Ezra pushes the gun against my forehead. "How do you know my name?" he presses.

I stare at him, unsure how to answer that question. He won't believe the truth—not yet, anyway. And if I lie, that'll only give him cause to shoot me.

I swallow again, trying to push down the rising lump in my throat intent on choking me. My tongue feels too big for my mouth, and I can't seem to remember how to breathe properly let alone speak.

A shadow spreads across Ezra's face, seeping into the details of the bar and casting the world around me in a muted gray darkness. My fingers reach for the counter to steady myself, but my hand doesn't find the edge.

As I sway, Ezra takes a reflexive step back, his expression switching from anger to horror. My vision doubles as I follow his line of sight to the growing puddle of red on the floor by my feet.

My eyes drift down to my wrist, noting the red staining the sleeve of Dr. Richter's white coat. *I've bled through the bandage,* I realize, my thoughts hazy. *Looks like blood loss will be what kills me.*

I should've known what I did would catch up with me. I was stupid to think this would end any other way but with me dead.

My knees buckle, and I stagger forward a step. As I search for something to focus on, I see Ezra…just like he was in my vision. Everything about him is exactly the same. His face. His hair. Those hazel eyes. But unlike the vision, there are no tears. And why would there be? We don't know each other.

He won't cry for me when I die.

I stumble again and collapse to the floor, the bar vanishing into the dark void of blood loss. Arms snake around me, breaking my fall, warm against my shivering body. A sob escapes my throat at their touch.

Unconsciousness creeps in at the edges of my vision, but flickers of Ezra's face—present and future—help to keep me awake. He must've been the one who caught me. He shouts over his shoulder at someone behind him, but I can't make out what he says. His hands are covered with blood. My blood. A pressure pushing down on my wrist makes me moan.

All at once, the pain and fear are both gone, and when Ezra looks down at me, doubt flooding those haunted eyes, I can't help it. I smile. Maybe I do it because I'm delirious, or maybe I'm just relieved I won't have to face death alone. I don't really know. And it doesn't really matter.

Not anymore.

"I saw you," I breathe, pressing a bloodied hand to his cheek as the world goes black.

DSD
I SAW YOU.

TEN

AFTER A WHILE, THE DARKNESS recedes, but the light doesn't seem ready to welcome me yet. The few sounds around me are faint, as if there's a glass box separating me from my surroundings, and everything is blurred, like my senses are dulled. Like I've been drugged. I fight to open and close my eyes, determined to climb my way out of unconsciousness.

A white hot pain overwhelms my left wrist, and my body shudders against what feels like a rickety bed, my skin ice-cold and slimy with sweat. My face and head burn as if they're on fire.

Through my muddled vision, I can just make out the silhouette of a person beside me. Their face isn't clear against the bright light behind them, but something about their posture reminds me of my mother. I try to reach out to them, but my arm is too heavy to lift it. I can't even find the strength to raise a finger.

"Where am I?" I rasp. My voice is distant, as if it's coming from someone else and not me.

A gentle hand brushes a strand of damp hair from my forehead. "Shh…you're safe." A woman's voice.

Mother's voice?

"Mother," I breathe. "Mother, is that you?"

A stray tear escapes from one eye and slides down my cheek, tracking over my skin. Although my mother betrayed me, although she gave me up, right now, I want nothing more than to be in her arms. To wrap myself in her reassuring embrace. To feel protected.

To feel safe.

Safe… This woman, whoever she is, claims that I'm safe. But how can I be?

The State is after me, their hunt spearheaded by the DSD, and now, there's the added problem of PHOENIX thinking I'm their enemy.

How can I ever possibly be safe?

My eyes squeeze shut, but more tears break through.

"Mother," I gasp again. "Mother…"

The stranger's hand once again touches my cheek, and I take comfort in the feel of their soft skin against mine. I don't need to know why she's doing this, who she is, or even where I am. I just need to not feel so alone anymore.

"What are you doing in here?" a familiar voice asks.

I recognize it at once.

Ezra.

The woman retracts her hand. "She needed medical attention, you know that. I figured it was best to keep an eye on her until she's out of the woods."

Quick footsteps fall against a hard surface.

Concrete. It sounds like shoes on concrete.

"What she *needs* is to wake up and answer our questions."

"She's not the enemy, Ezra," the woman mutters under her breath.

Silence for a moment.

"How can you be so sure?"

She scoffs. "She cut the tracking chip out of her wrist. Why would she do that? Why would she risk her life if she was one of them?"

I'm not one of them, I try to say. My voice fails me.

"Maybe that's what they want us to think. Some elaborate ploy to gain our trust. To infiltrate our ranks." He lets out a humorless laugh.

"Believe what you want. But I think she came to us because she needs our help. Only desperation would make her do something so stupid."

Help. That single word claws through the space in my head, probing until Dr. Richter's voice resurfaces from the depths of my memory. *"Is that who you're planning on running off to for help?"*

I picture Ezra's face. The grim way he looked at me in my vision. The tears on his cheeks as he said he was sorry. Those images are slowly overlapped by reality until all I see is the anger in his eyes. The distrust in his expression. The way he held a gun to my face.

No. No one will help me.

"Always the optimist." Ezra snorts. "What makes you think she *wants* our help?" It's impossible to miss the doubt edging his voice.

"Look at her," the woman pleads. "I know I'm not a doctor, but I know enough to tell you something's not right. Someone's done something to her. Something bad. I just… I can't put my finger on what."

Ezra grunts. I imagine him sulking, crossing his arms and glaring down at the floor. He seems the type.

"When will she wake up?"

"I honestly don't know. She's running a high fever and severely dehydrated, not to mention extremely malnourished. Plus, there's the risk of infection, the chance of sepsis being the biggest concern." She pauses, and then there's a rustle of movement as her hand returns to its previous place on my cheek. "I'm doing everything I can, but I'll make sure you're the first to know when she does."

There's an unease in her tone I didn't notice before. Well, I notice it now, and I know what it means.

She doesn't think I'll wake up.

She doesn't think I'll survive.

Maybe it would be better for everyone if I don't.

A door slams shut, and my eyelids flutter open for a second, but they're too heavy to hold up. When they slide closed again, the darkness returns, drawing me into unconsciousness like an ocean wave determined to drown me. I succumb to its pull, too tired and weak to fight against my fatigue any longer.

I fall back into the black depths of sleep, knowing full well the woman's hand is the only thing holding me to this world.

ELEVEN

"HELLO?"

A voice calls out from somewhere in the distance, seducing me away from the clutches of death. My eyelids twitch open, but everything in my range of vision is fuzzy, and the light hanging over my face is too bright, making it impossible to see anything.

"Can you hear me?"

My eyes squeeze shut as a surge of panic courses through my body, weighing down my limbs. This is all too similar, too reminiscent, of my first conscious moments at the DSD. Even the fear gripping me is exactly the same.

A cry sticks in the back of my throat. I don't want this. I just want to go home. *Do I, though?*

My mother's face drifts to the forefront of my thoughts, her gaze cold and unfeeling, reminding me of her betrayal and of how easily she gave me up, as if I meant nothing to her.

No. Home is no longer an option.

"She's awake."

I peek open my eyes again, drawn to the voice filtering into my ears. A woman's voice.

It's familiar, I realize.

I anticipate the searing blindness of the light, recoiling a little, but the harsh glare doesn't burn as badly this time. My eyelids flick open and closed several times until the bleary fog hindering my vision clears enough for me to glimpse the young woman leaning over me. She looks to be in her early twenties and is tall and lean with light brown skin and shining brunette hair that hangs down her back in a perfectly straight glossy curtain. Large dark eyes gaze back into mine, beaming with a kindness that's alien to me.

Relief smooths out her worried expression, her lips curving into a smile as she exhales a strained breath. My stomach turns when the sound of her sigh is overshadowed by the low tramp of footsteps. I blink again against the blinding light as another figure steps into view, but all I can make out is a black silhouette.

As the room around me fully comes into focus, I'm able to see the face of the person staring down at me with disdain and distrust.

I'm able to see Ezra Laramie.

"It's time to talk," he says, his tone curt.

I wedge my elbows behind me to push myself up into a less vulnerable position, but everything hurts, and my attempts to sit up end in failure. Grimacing, I collapse back against the mattress beneath me, which smells strongly of mildew and sweat.

The woman lurches forward and takes hold of my shoulders, earning a sidelong glare from Ezra. "Careful. You're still weak," she murmurs.

The room spins as she helps me upright and props me into a sitting position against the cool concrete wall. The cot I'm sitting on is wedged into one corner of what looks to be a small storage space.

A sharp pain stabs behind my right eye and spreads across the side of my face, traveling up into my hairline where it fades to an irritating prickle. I press the heel of my hand against my temple, but this does little to ease my dizziness or the lingering ache in my head.

I wince. "What happened? Where am I?"

Ezra lets out a laugh that sounds more like a growl. "Someplace where no one will find you."

My trembling fingers comb through my hair as I try to recount the events from before I woke up here.

"What zone am I in?" I press, glancing around the small space. "How…how did I get here?"

The woman takes hold of my hand and brushes over my skin in soothing strokes with her thumb. "You blacked out from blood loss in a bar in Zone 7. If it wasn't for Ezra, you would be dead." She speaks slowly, keeping her tone calm and every word level. "That was seven days ago. You got pretty sick and were in and out of consciousness for a while. Do you remember any of that?"

My wrist throbs as if in response to her words, and I peer down at my arm, trying to piece together memories that seem reluctant to surface. I remember finding Ezra at The Vega, but our conversation after is a bit of a blur. All I can recall with clarity is his face in the middle of so much darkness.

I swallow. Could what she said be true?

Did Ezra really save my life?

My lips part to speak when a bang makes me jump, sending my racing heart up into my throat. Ezra and the woman both turn toward the door, which swings open, creaking on rusty hinges.

A tall man with messy black hair and shining blue eyes, who looks to be more or less my age, stands in the doorway, watching me with interest. His lips twist with the slightest trace of a grin. "Is that her?" he asks, cocking a mischievous eyebrow.

Scowling, Ezra crosses his arms. "Hey, I thought I told you to stay out of this."

"And miss all the excitement?" Rolling his eyes, the newcomer steps into the cramped room and kicks the metal door shut behind him with his boot.

Shoving his hands into his pockets, he ambles closer, stopping a foot away from the cot. Up close, I can see just how blue his eyes are.

"Hmm…she's pretty cute for a spy." He tilts his head, giving me a once-over.

"I'm not a spy," I grumble, frowning.

A slight movement draws my gaze over to Ezra, who holds up Dr. Richter's white coat. "Then why did you have this?" he asks. "They don't just hand these coats out to anyone."

My mouth is a desert as I force out the words, "It's complicated." They escape in a whisper.

Ezra drops the coat onto the mattress beside me. "Okay, then how do you know my name? When I asked you this question before, all you said was 'I saw you.' What did you mean by that?"

I said that?

I can practically feel the color drain from my face, and I hesitate, unsure what to say. I can't tell him the truth. The skeptical look in his eyes is the only indicator I need to know he'll never believe me. None of them will. Not without seeing what I can do for themselves.

"That's…also complicated."

His upper lip curls back into a sneer as he takes a step toward me, reaching for the gun on his belt. The woman steps between us to defuse the situation, throwing up her hands.

"Look," she says to me over her shoulder, keeping the bulk of her attention on Ezra, "we want to believe you, but you need to help us out a little. Just tell us something. *Please.*"

Her eyes dart to mine again, their chocolate depths pleading. She wants to help—I can tell as much by the subtle nod she gives me—but I'm so used to not trusting anyone that I'm reluctant to try doing so now. Trust is a luxury no one in the State can afford. Plus, the last person I placed my trust in handed me over to a sadistic monster to be tortured.

She's not Mother, I remind myself. Besides, it's not like I have much choice in the matter. If I don't tell them what they want to know, they might kill me. And if I do…well, they may still kill me. Both options are equally risky. I suppose I could try to escape, but all that's waiting for me is the DSD, and no way in hell am I ever going back there.

I risk another glance at Ezra before looking down at my hands. What was the point of escaping Dr. Richter, of cutting the chip from my arm, of any of this, if I don't get the answers I came for? I've found Ezra, like I set out to do, but I should've known that wouldn't be enough. He doesn't trust me. To him, I'm the enemy. That won't change, and he won't give me anything unless I give him something first.

"My name is Wynter Reeves. A couple of—" I falter when the realization strikes me. "I…I don't know how long it's been…"

How much time has passed since the day of my placement exam? It feels like years since I walked into W. P. Headquarters for the final time.

"Since what?" the woman asks, her warm hand still wrapped around mine.

I meet her expectant gaze and let out a breath. "Since I was taken by the DSD."

"Come again?"

The black-haired man gapes at me, and Ezra shoots him a death glare, snapping his name like a curse word. "Jenner."

The other man, Jenner, pulls a face behind Ezra's back, mocking his stern expression. If Ezra notices, he doesn't bother to comment.

I glance between them then look up at the ceiling, fixating my attention on the fluorescent strip lighting, even as it burns into my retinas. "I was taken following my placement exam. By the time I got home, the Enforcers were already there waiting for me."

"What did they want with you?" Ezra presses.

My cheeks flush. "I…I didn't complete the exam," I admit, hanging my head in shame. "I panicked and submitted it only half-finished."

"That doesn't make sense," the woman says. "The DSD doesn't deal with minor crimes. That would be a Detention sentence at worst."

"Is blowing off your exam even considered a punishable offense?" Jenner questions. "I thought you only get sent for Re-education if you fail."

"That's not why I was apprehended," I interrupt, my patience with this topic wearing thin. How many times have I been forced to think about that day? To relive exactly why I was taken?

All three sets of eyes looking at me narrow in confusion, but no one says a word. The shadow of curiosity crossing Ezra's face urges me to continue.

Sweat breaks out across the back of my neck.

"Something happened during my exam having to do with this rare condition I have. I didn't even know about it until someone at the DSD told me I have it. This guy named Richter. He's a…a doctor, of sorts."

Ezra and the woman exchange stunned glances.

"Richter?" she gasps. "Are you sure?"

When I nod, Ezra asks, "Did you happen to catch his first name?"

"No." My hand reaches for the white coat beside me, my thumb grazing over the blood-stained left sleeve. "But this belonged to him. I took it to disguise myself just before I escaped."

"You escaped?" Jenner scoffs, giving me a dubious look. "That's impossible. No one escapes the DSD."

An unsettled feeling weighs like lead in my bones. Because he's right. It *is* impossible.

No one escapes.

"Dr. Richter thinks I can find something the DSD is looking for. They could've stopped me at any time, but they didn't. All that security and they just let me walk out the front door? Trust me, this isn't the first time I've questioned what happened, which makes me think they had an ulterior motive. They probably figured, if they let me go, I'd eventually lead them to what they want."

"You mean us," the woman guesses.

Ezra reaches for the gun at his hip again, but then, at the last second, seems to change his mind. Crossing his arms, he examines my face with a level of scrutiny that tells me he's searching for any holes in my story.

He's looking for a lie.

If only I was lying…then that would mean the horrors I went through at the DSD weren't real. It would mean this is all just a terrible nightmare.

"Is that why you cut out your tracking chip?" Ezra asks after a moment.

My eyes burn, and I can't find the strength to hold back the tears that now begin to stream down my cheeks.

"I can't go back there. I can't let them find me again. I did what I had to do to escape him."

A strange expression twists Ezra's face at these words. It could almost be pity. Or even regret. But, just as quickly as it appears, it dissolves, and all I find in its place is a mask of stone.

"Is that why you came to us? What about your family?" the woman asks, her tone soothing.

If only I had family to go to. Someone who would protect me from everything that's happened, or, at the very least, attempt to. Assuming protection from the State is possible.

Too bad I don't have anyone like that. I thought I did, but…

"My mother was the one who gave me up to the DSD. As far as I'm concerned, I don't have a family anymore."

"Wait a minute," Jenner says. "Am I the only one who feels like I'm missing something? I get why you would come to us for help, what with us being awesome outcasts of society and all, but—and I mean this with the utmost respect—how the *hell* did you even find us?"

Another question rings loud in the silence that follows. One none of them are daring to ask, probably out of fear of what it would mean.

How did the DSD know I could find them?

Images of The Vega manifest in my head, memories from the first time I saw it—in a vision in my cell at the DSD. How do I explain that to them? I had never heard of my condition until Dr. Richter made me aware of it, and even then, I didn't believe him at first. Chances are, no one in PHOENIX would have heard of it either. To them, the truth will just seem like a lie—a crazy story to get around telling them exactly how I found The Vega. How I found Ezra.

The seconds tick by, the silence pressuring me for an answer I have no way to give.

"That's difficult to explain," I mutter weakly when nothing else comes to me.

"Try," Ezra warns, his voice a threatening rumble.

My eyes cut to his. "You wouldn't believe me if I did."

"Oh, yeah? Why's that?"

I curl my fingers into tight fists as a ringing sound vibrates through my skull, making me dizzy. My fingernails dig half moons into my palms. "I didn't find you using…conventional methods."

Jenner's eyes flick between me and Ezra, his dark brows dragging down into a vee. "What does that mean? Like, you used a sniffer dog to find us or something? Wait…maybe you *are* the sniffer dog?"

The woman shakes her head, frowning at Jenner, before shifting her focus to me. "Most people don't know about PHOENIX's affiliation with The Vega. We're just trying to figure out how you did so we can make sure our people are safe. You said yourself that the DSD is somehow using you to find out our location. I'm sure you can understand how this might look from our point of view."

"I do," I breathe, my voice hitching. "And I promise, I didn't come here to cause problems for any of you. It's just…how I found you… Well, it's the sort of thing you'd have to see to believe."

"Then show us." The demand escaping Ezra's lips is ice-cold, yet I can sense a tremble of fear in his tone. On the surface, it reminds me of my mother's final words the last time I saw her before I woke up at the DSD. Before she handed me over to Dr. Richter. Before my life turned into a nightmare. But, beyond that, the fear in his voice reminds me of how I've felt every single day the last eleven years.

The fear in his voice reminds me of loss.

"I can't—" I begin to say, but I barely get the words out before Ezra unholsters his gun.

"Show us!"

He steps forward and jabs the metal barrel into my temple, but I don't recoil, unfazed by his threat. Something about what I've said has upset him, that much is clear, although I struggle to understand what. Regardless, I suspect he won't pull the trigger. Despite the crazed look in his eyes, I've witnessed another side of him that surpasses his distrust and anger—the side portrayed by the man in my vision. The memory of that man, of his words and his tears, is the one reason I have to believe he won't hurt me. If that side of him didn't already exist, he wouldn't have bothered saving my life at The Vega. I would be dead, the future I saw would be changed, and Dr. Richter would've been right to warn me about him.

But he wasn't. I know in my gut that he wasn't.

I stare up at Ezra, unwavering, as the room around us explodes into chaos.

"Ezra!" the woman shrieks, grabbing his arm.

"Hey, man, put the gun down!" Jenner pleads.

Ezra's upper lip peels back into a snarl, but he relents after a moment, clipping his gun back onto his belt. Scowling, he turns and storms from the room, the door slamming into the wall as he throws it open with way more force than necessary.

Just before stepping into the corridor, he pauses long enough to say, "She doesn't leave this room." He then trudges off without looking back.

The woman exchanges a long look with Jenner as the echo of Ezra's tromping footsteps gradually fades, leaving the three of us in an uneasy silence. He glances between us then lets out a loud groan.

"I'll go talk him down," he grumbles.

The woman nods, and we both watch as Jenner slumps his shoulders and heads for the open door, muttering something under his breath that involves a few choice curse words and something about being on babysitter duty. Once we're alone, she sits down beside me, unsettling the springy mattress.

"I'm sorry about Ezra. He…" She trails off, biting down on her lip. "He has a lot on his mind," she finishes lamely, following the words with a sigh. She clamps her hands together, her posture rigid, as if there's something on her mind and she's reluctant to say it. Finally, she asks, "That doctor you mentioned…what did you think of him? Was he a good man?"

I blink up at her, bemused by her question.

A good man? I suppress a laugh at the thought. Good is the last word I would use to describe him.

"No," I answer, my tone as sharp and cutting as the glass shard that sliced through my wrist. "But I don't think anyone in that place is good."

Her face drops, and a wave of guilt washes over me. I don't understand her reaction. Why does she seem so sad? What does she have to do with Dr. Richter?

She smiles at me, but, behind her kind facade, I sense her disappointment. It burns in her eyes like twin flickering flames.

Seeing it only makes my guilt worse.

As she clears her throat, tears pricking at the corners of her eyes, a realization stirs in my chest. The words to voice it spill from my lips in a rush. "You're so different from what I imagined. PHOENIX, I mean. You're nothing like how the State portrays you."

You don't seem like monsters.

She smiles again, although, this time, her expression is coy, as if she's in on a secret the rest of the world doesn't know. Arching an eyebrow, she lets out a soft tinkling laugh.

"That's because we're the good guys."

TWELVE

BLOOD SPATTERS ACROSS THE FLOOR, staining large patches of the white carpet red. Grunts followed by whimpering sobs flood the house, but no one seems to care except me.

No one else steps forward to help.

My father drops to his knees in the middle of the reception room of my first home—the house I grew up in near the border to Zone 1 before Mother and I were relocated. Dribbles of blood seep from between his cracked lips, and I hardly recognize him past his facial injuries, his left eye swollen shut, the other tinged red where burst blood vessels have all but overtaken the white. His cheeks are marred with black and purple bruises, disfiguring his alabaster complexion.

My feet stumble backward as a cry lodges deep in my throat. Why is this happening?

And why is no one else trying to stop it?

My mother snatches my arm and jerks me away from him, dragging me back toward the hallway.

Mother's here now, I tell myself with relief. *Surely, she'll try to help.*

"Take her out of here. She doesn't need to see this," my mother hisses over her shoulder as a strong pair of hands lift me clean off the ground and haul me out of the reception room. Through my panic, I notice the man's black helmet, a standard element of the Enforcers' regulation uniform. The tears streaming down my splotchy red cheeks are reflected in the opaque shield hiding his face.

I stretch my hand out in desperation, screaming at the top of my lungs. My father looks up, his remaining good eye glassy, when I cry for them to leave him alone.

When I beg them not to take him away.

My cries cease as he mutters the last words he would ever say to me. "I'm sorry, Wynter."

Time seems to slow as I fight against the hands restraining me, but I'm not strong enough to escape them. As I struggle, my father's voice replays in my thoughts like an echo.

"I'm sorry, Wynter."

Static skews his face, and then he's just gone, taken from me as quickly as he was when I was a child.

I blink, heavy sobs wracking my lungs, as the memory of the worst day of my life falls away, piece by piece disintegrating into ash until all that's left before me is an endless wasteland of destruction.

I turn in place, taking in what remains of the Heart, my gaze catching on a familiar face—the only one among the apocalyptic nothingness. Ezra's here, just like the last time I saw this. Tears leave lines on his cinder-smeared cheeks as his lips shape the same words my father once said to me. Words that are now like a bullet ripping straight through my heart.

"I'm sorry, Wynter," he whispers.

Static again as their voices surround me, blending together and ringing in a torturous loop with the sole intent of driving me mad.

"I'm sorry—"

I clutch my head, dragging my fingernails over my scalp, as if that will somehow pull the voices out of my skull.

"I'm sorry..."

My eyes burn as the black hole of my shattered heart consumes me, and I drop to my knees, praying for the vision to end. I can't take it anymore.

"Wynter..."

I can't take it.

"Wynter?"

My eyes spring open, thrusting me back into consciousness. My chest heaves as I take in the details of the small storage room, the cramped space empty aside from a few shelving units and the uncomfortable folding cot underneath me. Warm tears wet my cheeks and leave a salty residue on my lips. I brush them away when the door creaks open.

"Wynter? I'm coming in."

I sit up just as the woman I met before walks into the room holding a thin metal tray. The sight of solid food makes me realize just how hungry I am, and my stomach growls at the delicious scent wafting into the space alongside her, coaxing a knowing grin onto her lips. I can only imagine how they fed me when I was unconscious, but I'm sure this method is preferable for both of us.

Her smile deepens when our eyes meet, as if she's genuinely happy to see me again, although I can't understand why she would be. If my nightmare just now has reminded me of anything, it's that standing against the State gets you killed. Harboring a fugitive is worse, *much* worse, and if you're caught, you'll wish for death before the DSD is even finished with you.

Her smile falters when fresh tears slip down my cheeks, and she sets the tray on the floor before taking a seat on the squeaky cot beside me.

"Are you all right?" Her fingers are warm as she places a gentle hand on my arm.

I flinch away from her touch, giving a quick jerky nod, but my unsteady breaths reveal the truth I'm too much of a coward to voice. My lips quiver with the threat of a sob as I wipe the moisture from my face.

"I had a dream about my father. About the last time I saw him alive."

"I'm sorry," she whispers, her voice consoling.

I don't know how to react to her sentiment. In the Heart, we're encouraged not to show our grief, and above all, never to express it to others, especially if the person our grief is aimed at was found guilty of breaking the law. *"Enemies of the State don't deserve to be mourned."* That's what the State has always taught us. And yet, even now, years later, I still can't help mourning my father.

I look down at the floor, unaccustomed to showing such weakness—to showing any emotion at all. *"To suppress is to survive,"* my mother's voice says in my head, surfacing from the depths of my memory, like a hand reaching out to catch me from falling. *"Don't let anyone see what you feel."*

So, that's how I lived until my time at the DSD. I followed three rules to ensure what I felt would always stay hidden from watchful eyes, just like everyone else in the Heart. Together, we feel nothing, and in feeling nothing, we are kept apart.

But the people here—this woman, Jenner, even Ezra—they all wear their emotions plainly, putting what they feel on full display for anyone around to witness. They don't bother to hide what's in their hearts. They don't try to mask who they are.

As I stare at the floor, my unblinking eyes boring imaginary holes into the concrete, I realize that I envy them. How they live here is in direct opposition to the forced emotional seclusion the State has manufactured in our society. I can only imagine how freeing it must be to allow yourself to be who you are, to let yourself feel what you truly feel, without fear of punishment.

"Do you mind if I ask what happened to him?" she says after a moment of silence has passed.

I glance at her out of the corner of my eye as the lump lodged in my throat seems to double in size.

"He was executed for treason," I breathe, every word a burden I can't seem to shake. "My last memory of him is of when he was taken. I never saw him again after that."

I don't know what I expect from her. Shock, maybe? Horror? Disgust? After all, it's not uncommon for people to distance themselves from someone who's been touched by death the way I have. Distance is safer. Distance ensures we remain unnoticed, that we're invisible to the State.

And to be invisible is to stay alive.

But she doesn't look at me that way. Instead, I see something in her gaze no one would ever dare publicly reveal. Pity. It shines in her eyes, along with an understanding of sorts, as if she can empathize with my pain.

As if she's felt that sort of grief, too.

"You know, everyone here has lost someone or something to the State. But that's why we fight. So our losses don't have to be for nothing." She folds her fingers around mine and shifts closer, bumping my shoulder with her upper arm. The warmth I sensed from her before is only intensified by her touch. "We aren't that different, you know. I don't know why you were looking for Ezra, but maybe...you belong with us. Maybe you're here for a reason."

A frown tugs down the corners of my lips, and I resist the urge to snort. "I'm not so sure about that."

You don't know what I am.

You don't know what I've done.

The memory of that female attendant at the DSD comes rushing back, triggering a surge of bile to climb up my throat. Even now, I can see her seizing body so clearly.

Swallowing, I shake the recollection away.

I wish I could find the words to explain that I didn't search for PHOENIX because I desired acceptance. I only wanted to find Ezra to help me grasp what's happening to me. So I can get answers about this world I don't fully understand. So I can figure out what role he will eventually come to play in my life and in that terrible future I saw.

The woman chuckles under her breath. "I am. You and me... We're more alike than you know."

I lean away from her, gaping a little, unsure what to make of her bold but blind sense of trust. She grew up in the State, didn't she? She must know how dangerous trust can be.

"How can you say that when you don't even know me?" I ask, my voice failing to hide my amazement.

She squints at the ceiling as if considering her answer. "Call it a gut feeling. I just... I see the same fear in you I once saw in myself. That I *still* see in myself."

"What are you afraid of?" The words leave my lips before the thought has even fully registered.

I should know better than to pry—in the State, such an act is forbidden—but I can't help myself. Ever since the day of my placement exam, it's as if the rules of my old world are slipping away a little bit more every day. At what point will those rules no longer matter to me? At what point will I be free of their tether?

A kind smile unfurls across the woman's face when she meets my gaze again. "Everything."

I know what that feels like. To always be scared. To worry I'm only one breath away from doing something that would see me following in my father's footsteps far sooner than I would like. Hell, I know that feeling better than most.

Her unabashed honesty resonates with me in a way I wouldn't have ever expected. Maybe because this isn't how our world works. We don't make eye contact. We don't develop close relationships or talk to each other on a personal level. We don't show warmth or compassion to others, like she's displaying to me now.

In my world, fear is used to keep us apart, whereas she's using it to bring us together.

"I meant what I said before. I'm not here to cause any problems for you."

"I know," she says. "I can tell just by looking at you. You're one of the good guys, too."

I scoff. "Well, I'm definitely not a spy for the State."

Her eyes light up at my words, and she taps a finger against her lips, as if deep in thought. "So, maybe it's time we prove that to everyone."

Everyone?

My brow furrows when she jumps to her feet and tugs me off the bed, still clutching my hand. "Come on. I bet you're dying to stretch your legs and get out of this stuffy room for a while."

I hesitate, digging my heels into the floor as she tries to pull me toward the door. When she looks back at me, I stammer, "I-I don't know. Ezra said I wasn't allowed to leave this room." I don't want to make him any angrier or distrusting of me than he already is.

She rolls her eyes, waving a dismissive hand at me. "Despite what he thinks, Ezra is not in charge around here. I have just as much authority as he does, and I say we're going for a walk. If he has a problem with it, well, that's on him."

My heart hammers against my ribcage as she drags me along behind her, ignoring my protests.

"Oh, by the way," she adds as she throws open the door. "My name is Rai. Rai Dorne."

When she smiles once more, I'm disarmed by what I glimpse in her gaze—not just kindness but an offer of friendship. Such a concept is foreign to me. After all, friendship doesn't exist in the State. Maybe it's because of that deprivation I find myself wanting to know what it's like. Is someone like me even capable of it?

I trail Rai through a series of hallways, the footpath just wide enough for us to walk side by side. Fluorescent lights hang at even intervals overhead, placed between a maze-like network of pipes, which follow along the full length of the low ceiling. The damp, musty air has a mossy taste to it, and as we walk, I notice there aren't any windows. If the lights were to fail, we'd be swallowed by darkness.

The realization that follows this observation doesn't bring me any comfort. After so long trapped in the stifling confines of the DSD, breathing recycled air, the thought that I might be underground makes me anxious. It triggers memories I'd rather forget.

"Are you okay?" Rai asks.

I force a smile onto my face but say nothing.

For the first ten minutes or so since leaving the cramped storage room, Rai and I are alone. I follow her steps through the compound, wondering how such a place could exist without the State knowing about it, which in turn only reminds me of all the secrets I'm hiding. Why I'm here. What's wrong with me.

The fact that I've murdered someone.

"We're more alike than you know," Rai had said.

Are we, though? I wonder.

The longer we walk, the more often we cross paths with the other residents here. They all stare at me with the same expression: confusion at first, followed by distrust. I don't blame them for viewing me as a threat—I'm sure they all know what happened at The Vega by now—but after the first dozen or so glances, I lower my eyes to escape the judgmental scrutiny of their gazes.

I only look up again when we enter a large cavernous space, the warehouse-like room empty apart from a border of benches and some crates, a handful upturned to double as seats. At the opposite end of the room, Jenner waves at us.

"Hey!" he shouts, his voice carrying in an echo.

Ezra stands beside him, staring me down with a look that says he does not share his companion's enthusiasm to see me. Even from a distance, I can sense his suspicion and something else all too reminiscent of loathing. Those emotions emanate from him like heat from a fire.

If I get too close, I might get burned.

Jenner runs toward us, skipping every third step. He stops next to me, flashing a broad grin as he bites into an apple. "How's it going?" he asks, spitting a little.

Before either of us can answer, Ezra skulks across the room, his furious gaze fixated on Rai. "Why did you let her out?" he barks.

Huffing, she plants her hands on her hips and tosses her long hair over her shoulder with a graceful sway of her head. "I already told you, she isn't our enemy. We should stop treating her like one," she snaps back.

I glance between them, taken aback by their annoyance with each other and afraid of being caught in the line of fire. I can feel their impending argument like the first drops of rain in the air.

Beside me, Jenner lets out a sigh. When I look over at him, he winks and then slings an arm around my shoulders, pulling me close to his side. "Hey, why don't we go sit down and have a chat? Sound good?"

I look back at Ezra and Rai. The fight I predicted is now erupting between them, an explosion of anger volleyed back and forth, like they're playing a verbal sport. It's amazing they can understand anything they're saying with the way they're screaming over each other. I can hardly make out a single word. It makes me wonder what they are to each other that gives them the right to speak so openly. Confrontation is frowned upon in our society. Confrontation means disobedience, and disobedience makes you an enemy of the State. Like most things, disobedience is dangerous.

Then again, I suppose they're free of those rules here.

I allow Jenner to steer me away to an unoccupied seating area in one corner of the large room—far away from Rai and Ezra but not so far we can't still hear the distant drone of their bickering. Once we settle on one of the benches, he reaches into a nearby crate and offers me a bottle of water.

"Thanks," I mutter.

He leans back, looking at me for a moment, then stretches his right arm out in front of me.

I peer down at his empty hand.

"I don't think I've properly introduced myself yet. The name's Jenner Rhodes."

Unsure what else to do, I extend my fingers, shivering a little when his skin grazes mine. As we shake hands, a memory hits the front of my thoughts.

My father once told me this is how people used to greet one other, but, like most things, the gesture died away along with everything else that existed before the State came into power. I can't help wondering why. Did the State outlaw this simple greeting, or did people just stop wanting to know one another because of their fear of betrayal? When did we stop caring about anything but our own survival?

We sit in silence for a while, staring out across the vast, empty space. Ezra and Rai have given up on their fight and subsequently stormed off in different directions. Part of me worries I should've followed Rai when she left, but I find Jenner's company too comforting to move. If I wasn't in good hands, she wouldn't have left me here.

"I agree with Rai, you know," he says. "I don't think you're one of *them*." It doesn't escape my notice how he spits that last word.

"You seem to be the only ones," I point out.

A crooked smile hooks up the left side of his mouth. "Nah, you're an innocent, I can tell. I've seen those bastards up close enough times to know the difference." He leans in, his breath warm against my ear. "Don't worry. Everyone else will see that soon enough."

Even Ezra? I'm tempted to ask.

I watch Jenner out of the corner of my eye, intrigued by his carefree manner and easygoing personality. Like Rai, he's choosing to trust me when I haven't given him any logical reason to. Why? Aren't these people supposed to be wanted criminals? Monsters, the State always called them. They don't seem like that to me, but, aside from a surface portrayal of kindness, what do I really know about them?

My thoughts turn back to Ezra. It's hard to believe the man who pointed a gun at my head twice now is the same man from my vision, and yet, even though he's keeping his distance from me, I can sense a connection between us—something that tells me what I saw in my vision was real. And the man I saw in that future wasn't a monster.

None of these people are.

"This place…" My eyes skirt across the dome-shaped ceiling. "None of it is like what I imagined."

Jenner laughs. "I know what you mean. I thought the same thing when I first arrived here. Maybe that's why I find it so easy to accept you considering I *was* you once. Everyone here was, they just don't want to admit it. Change can be hard for some to embrace." He grins at my confused expression. "Ezra's not always such an ass, I promise. He's just trying to keep everyone safe, and responsibility sometimes comes with trust issues."

"If you think you can trust him, you're wrong."

As Dr. Richter's warning once again reverberates in my ears, it occurs to me that Ezra isn't the one who needs to be trusted in this scenario. He isn't the one in question. I am. I'm the one who needs to earn *his* trust, not the other way around.

"It's all lies, you know. Everything they say about us." Jenner hunches forward, resting his forearms on his knees and lacing his fingers together, joining his hands. There's a sadness in his eyes when he stares down at them. "All that violence in the Heart is attributed to PHOENIX, but, in reality, we don't cause any of it. Our goal isn't to hurt anyone. No one here wants blood on their hands."

"You mean the State?" I ask, raising my eyebrows.

He nods but doesn't meet my gaze. "Do you have any idea how it feels to be called a terrorist when you're just trying to survive?"

I sink my teeth into my lower lip, fighting back the burning sensation building along the edges of my vision. I can imagine all too well what Jenner must be feeling. Isn't that how I was treated just because I didn't finish my placement exam? Just because there's something wrong with me that I have no control over? Hell, the people at the DSD acted as if I wasn't even a human being.

But none of that, no matter how much sense it makes to me, explains why the State would lie about PHOENIX. What would it get out of frightening the masses with the constant threat of terrorism?

"If you aren't responsible for the attacks…"

"Fear leads to control, and control guarantees the government's longevity. I suppose that's all the incentive they need. I just wish people knew the truth about us. Mindless violence won't bring about change."

I stare at him for a long moment, haunted by that sentiment. Mindless violence…

Like what Dr. Richter did to me.

"What will?" I whisper.

"Honestly?" He peeks up at me through thick lashes, his expression youthful and uncertain. "I'm still trying to figure that one out."

For as long as I can remember, the State has always portrayed PHOENIX as a force to be reckoned with. To be feared. But, as I listen to Jenner, I can't help questioning who the victims really are in all this.

My exposure to the people here has been limited, but I've seen enough to know they aren't terrorists or murderers. They're no different than the people

I've walked past on the street every single day of my life. They're just a group of scared individuals doing whatever it takes to survive.

The solemn look on Jenner's face makes me eager to change the subject. My thoughts shift back to Ezra and Rai, and a spark of curiosity forms my next question for me. "They're your friends, right? Ezra and Rai? How did they get involved with PHOENIX?"

He scratches his chin. "Well, Ez and Rai have known each other since they were kids. They've gone through all this together, every step of the way."

Together. On a personal level, I don't even know what that word means.

"How about you?" I ask. "How did you end up joining?"

"I...uh..." He runs a hand through his disheveled obsidian hair as his cheeks turn a subtle shade of red. "I had a run-in with the authorities when I was seventeen. It was a misunderstanding more than anything else. A case of wrong place, wrong time. Anyway, Ezra and Rai got me out of that bind. That was three years ago, and they've been stuck with me ever since."

His tone gives off the distinct impression the life of a rebel wasn't something he wanted.

Looks like we have that in common.

"You don't seem too happy about that," I note.

He averts his gaze, wringing his hands in his lap. "It's not that I don't feel grateful toward them for saving my life. It's just that...from the moment they intervened, everything changed. I had to leave my entire life behind, and my family suffered as a result of my idiocy. I couldn't risk going to see them again, not even to say goodbye."

I grimace at the string of thoughts that forms. *Would they have wanted to say goodbye, or would they have been as callous as my mother? Would they have handed you over?*

"When the Enforcers couldn't find me, my parents and sister were brought in for questioning." He pauses, casting a meaningful glance at me. "You know what the DSD is like. My family didn't know anything about where I was or what I did, and yet, they were branded as enemies of the State just because we were related. They were sent to Termination shortly after."

I don't know what to say. What is there to say?

He's right. I do know what the DSD is like. I can imagine all too well the horrors his family would've gone through.

Jenner shakes his head then says, "I know I'm responsible for what happened to them. If I had died or just let the Enforcers apprehend me, the State wouldn't have had any reason to hurt them. It would've left them alone."

You don't know that.

My father's face fills up the space in my mind. Looking back, how close did Mother and I come to receiving the same punishment as Jenner's family?

Were we only spared because he got caught?

"At the same time...their deaths are my reason for fighting, you know?" His eyes lock on me, holding my attention rapt. "I want to prevent these kinds of needless tragedies from happening to anyone else."

A sharp pain clenches my heart, and the sympathy arising within me seems powerful enough to drown an entire city. I can't even comprehend Jenner's pain. Well, I can, but I was young when my father was taken, and with time, those memories will fade. But Jenner...he might not be so lucky.

That pain could live with him forever.

I startle when he pokes me in the cheek with his finger. "That right there," he says through a smile. "That's how I know you aren't one of them."

I reel back as goosebumps rise across my arms, my eyes narrowing in confusion. The way he's staring at me is unnerving. No one's ever looked at me this way before.

"What do you mean?" I ask.

The seconds roll by, but he doesn't answer.

Before I can press him, he looks away, turning his attention to the opposite side of the room. I follow his gaze to see Rai walking toward us.

"How'd it go?" he asks once she's closer.

She pushes a tired breath out through her nose. "He's being difficult, but he just needs some time to mull things over. He'll come around eventually."

I recall the sour expression on Ezra's face when he saw me and the rage in his eyes during his altercation with Rai. Why was he so angry? And what exactly were they fighting about?

Me, probably.

My heart sinks as Rai and Jenner launch into a conversation about one important thing or another, their voices growing faint as I rest back against the wooden slats of the bench and allow my troubled thoughts to devour me. The images in my head replay my nightmare from earlier...except, it isn't my father who I'm seeing this time.

It's Ezra.

My lungs constrict when he speaks.

"I'm sorry, Wynter."

He says those same words again, over and over, always the same words flooding my ears, but they never offer any explanation or give any hint about what will happen between us.

Or why he'll apologize for it.

He says them until I hear nothing else and the other sounds of the world die away.

THIRTEEN

THE NEXT HANDFUL OF DAYS are spent touring the compound in the few hours when I'm allowed out of the storage room—a compromise Rai made with Ezra until we convince him that I'm not a threat. That's what she claims, anyway. But I have a feeling the order to keep me locked up came from someone above them in the PHOENIX hierarchy.

Someone I have yet to meet.

The structure is an underground facility from the pre-State days, but that's as much as anyone is willing to tell me, other than to say that we're safe from the State here. As if there could possibly be such a place.

Rai and Jenner are hospitable, and their friendly manner is almost enough to make me believe I'm not their prisoner…until we pass one of the other residents, and that person's wariness when they look at me triggers the reminder of where I am and why everyone views me as a threat. That single look forces me to remember that I'm not truly welcome here.

It also doesn't escape my notice there are things they make it a point not to show me. Specifically, the exits. Regardless of the kindness they're bestowing upon me, regardless of their words of acceptance, it's evident they don't trust me enough to risk letting me leave. I don't blame them. For all they know, I could be leading Dr. Richter right to them.

"Make yourself at home."

I scowl at Rai, unable to hold back a grimace.

"Really," she insists, pursing her lips and giving me a look that tells me I shouldn't doubt her.

I can't help it. Surely, making myself at home will only cause more problems for me in the long run. She and Jenner might like me enough to want me to stay, but I have a feeling that sentiment isn't shared by the others here. Especially Ezra.

Even now, nearly a week after waking up in this place, I struggle to see how he fits into my life or how we'll get to where we are in my vision. Maybe that's for the best considering the terrible future awaiting us. That destruction should be avoided at all costs, and maybe the way to do that is to avoid him.

Still, at this rate, I'll never understand who he is or the connection he holds to my condition, and the not knowing is what's driving me crazy.

"The first step to acceptance is exposure," Rai says, her musical trill snapping me back to attention. "The people here need to see you if they're expected to trust you, and that'll never happen if you're locked away all the time."

I cock a dubious eyebrow at her. *Last I checked, being locked up wasn't exactly my choice.*

Despite that thought, I say nothing, even though there's an obvious flaw in her logic. In the Heart, people often go their entire lives without trusting anyone, even those closest to them. So, how can she expect a group of strangers to trust me after such a short time together and only the odd interaction in passing? I haven't earned their trust, and frankly, I don't need it. I'm only here to discern the link between Ezra and my vision.

I came here for answers, nothing else.

Rai pauses beside the doorway leading into one of two galley kitchens and turns toward me, taking hold of my hands. "Anyway, this is where I leave you. I have some things I need to see to, and I think Jenner can take it from here. I hope you don't find this too forward, but I've arranged for you to have a shower. I would've taken you sooner, but everything we let you do has to be approved, and unfortunately, there was some…kickback."

"Kickback?" I ask, furrowing my brow.

She rolls her lower lip between perfect white teeth. "The showers are communal, and some of our residents here are…vulnerable. They weren't comfortable with the idea of you, a stranger, being in there with them unsupervised. But, at this time of day, the facility should be empty. Everyone is off doing their chores. Problem solved."

Her eyes flit to Jenner, who looks down at me and winks. "I'll make sure no one bothers you."

Rai says her goodbyes then disappears into the sweltering heat of the kitchen. Once we're alone, Jenner returns to our leisurely stroll, and I follow him through the endless corridors, trailing his every step like a shadow. We walk without speaking for so long I lose track of the time, but I don't mind the silence. His company is soothing and eases my growing distress about being underground surrounded by people who think I'm only here to harm them. It's strange when I put my feelings toward Jenner in perspective to the other relationships in my life. Thinking about it, I wasn't even this comfortable around my own mother.

"How many people live here?" I ask after a while.

"Twenty-six. But with you, we have twenty-seven," he answers.

My feet falter, and I stumble to a standstill.

Twenty-six people?

The fearsome terrorist organization PHOENIX only has twenty-six people?

"Is that it?" The question escapes me in a strangled whisper.

Jenner's lips crack into a lopsided smile. "We're just one branch in a much larger tree. PHOENIX has hundreds of sects in the Heart alone, some of which greatly outnumber ours."

"Oh." A sigh of relief crawls up my throat, but I catch myself mid-breath. I barely know these people, so why should I care if they have the support and numbers needed to stand up to the State? That's their problem. It has nothing to do with me.

Except, with every day that passes, I realize a bit more how untrue that is. I'm no insurgent—I didn't come here to join PHOENIX as some act of rebellion against the society I was raised in. I came here because I was scared and I didn't know what else to do. I'm nothing but a homeless runaway, who found kindness where I didn't expect it. And now, I'm terrified I might lose it. What else do I have without this?

Where else could I go?

"Here we are," Jenner announces, stopping beside an open door leading through to a narrow hallway. There's a bathroom not far from the storage room, which Rai accompanies me to a few times a day, but that facility doesn't have a shower.

As I stare through the doorway, it occurs to me just how long it's been since I last bothered to bathe. Funny how removing the threat of death can put these sorts of things into perspective.

"Rai told me earlier she set aside some clothes for you in the washroom, which is at the end of the hall through this door. I'll wait for you out here while you clean up. I know it's been a while, so take your time."

His nonchalant remark about my lack of cleanliness would be insulting if it wasn't so painfully true. Now that I'm free of the DSD, the awareness of the stench exuding from my skin makes me shudder. All I want in this moment is to wash it away, along with everything bad that's happened to me over these last few months.

My cheeks burn as I dash through the doorway, and I don't dare slow my pace until my feet carry me into the washroom, beyond the reach of Jenner's piercing gaze. Although his presence brings me much-needed comfort, it's also overwhelming at times. The way he looks at me… I don't think I'll ever get used to it.

My breaths are ragged as I step into the empty room, and although I'm thankful for the solitude, I feel like a trespasser, like I shouldn't be here. I whip around at the slightest noise, whether it be the low thunk of pipes or the slow dripping of water, afraid of who might be waiting around every corner or in the shadows.

This isn't like the DSD, I remind myself, letting out a breath. *These are good people. They aren't like Dr. Richter.*

I inhale through my nose, and once my pulse is steady again, I begin to undress. It's like peeling off a second layer of skin, the fabric stiff with sweat and stinking of odors built up over several months that have been collecting on my skin and could turn even the strongest stomach. It's remarkable Rai and Jenner could stand being near me. Come to think of it, the thick, musty stench in The Vega was probably the only thing masking my odor from Ezra.

Wincing at the smell, I kick the clothes off, leaving them in a heap on the white cement floor, before stepping into the nearest shower cubicle and turning the valve until the water is scalding. The heat feels good against my aching skin, and I sense a weight lift off my shoulders the longer I stand under the spray, as if the water is burning away my trauma.

As steam swarms my body, I glance down at my bandaged wrist for the first time since removing the chip. The thought of looking before frightened me, but now, I want to see what lies under the dressing. I *need* to see what I've done to myself. What price I paid to escape Dr. Richter.

My teeth bite along my lip as my fingers carefully unravel the linen covering and remove the gauze. Apart from some swelling and the uneven line of stitches holding my sliced skin together, the wound doesn't look too bad. It doesn't appear to be infected anymore, at least—thanks to Rai. I count myself lucky considering how differently things would've turned out if Ezra hadn't bothered to help me and Rai hadn't worked tirelessly to get me through those first few days when they weren't even sure I'd survive.

From the moment I stepped inside The Vega, Ezra held my life in his hands, even if he didn't know it. As far as he was concerned, I was the enemy. He could've let me die. He could've let me bleed out to ensure his own survival and safety. But he didn't.

He *chose* to save me.

That knowledge, along with several other small discoveries I've made since I woke up in this place, reiterate that PHOENIX isn't at all what I expected based on what I was told growing up. But I'm also still not sure if I should trust them, regardless of what they've done for me so far. As I keep telling myself, trust is dangerous. Trust gets you killed. Plus, I don't exactly feel safe here, and I definitely don't belong with these people, despite what Jenner and Rai keep saying. And yet, I know I *have* to be here—that this place will help me discover the truth, not only about my visions but about my disease.

Ezra is the key, but I'm struggling to reconcile that grief-stricken man in my head with the hardened rebel who wants to keep me locked up. Then again, he was holding a gun in my vision.

Maybe I've been wrong about everything, and my future ends with him using it on me.

An icy prickle trails across my naked flesh as my fingers grip the valve again, the pipes squealing in protest when I shut off the water. As I step out of the shower, my eyes land on the clothes Jenner mentioned. They sit neatly folded in a pile on the side of a wide metal basin—one of many positioned under a long row of mirrors. A toothbrush, a tube of toothpaste, and a towel lie just beside them on the edge of the sink, and boots and fresh socks sit nearby on the floor.

I leave the filthy garments from the DSD where I tossed them before, abandoned in a mound on the floor, happily trading them for the fresh clothes: a pair of tight-fighting brown cargo pants and a faded black long-sleeved shirt. I know I should pick up the physical reminders of my torment and discard them before someone else has to do it, but I can't bring myself to look at them, let alone touch them again. They hold too many bad memories.

Memories I never want to revisit.

My fingers comb through my tangled hair as my eyes lock on my reflection in one of the mirrors. I recoil when I meet the gaze of the gaunt-faced girl in the glass, unprepared for what I see. My skin is pale, almost sallow, and prominent bags hang under my eyes, darkening the skin like bruises. I've deteriorated since I last looked at myself.

Now, I look to be mere moments from death.

I push that thought away and hurry out of the washroom, running from the reality of my disease with the same determination with which I ran from the DSD. In the corridor outside, Jenner leans against the wall opposite the doorway, humming a soft, unfamiliar tune. With his eyes closed, he looks serene, beautiful even. At peace.

More than anything, I wish I could know what that feels like.

His eyes pop open at my approach, and he flashes that charming lopsided grin. "Look at you, all cleaned up. I mean, hey, you were cute before, but now…!"

A blush spreads from my neck to the tips of my ears. I suppose I should take it as a compliment he finds anything physically appealing about me, considering the horrifying effects this disease is having on my appearance. In reality, I suspect his reaction might have more to do with the obvious lack of age-appropriate females residing here. Other than Rai, I don't think I've seen any other females around our age in this place.

Sensing my embarrassment, he changes the subject. "Shall we continue?"

Over the next hour, Jenner leads me through the rest of the compound. There isn't much left to see that I haven't already, but then again, I don't know what more I was expecting. This facility seems to serve as a residence, rather than as a base of operations, and the majority of the rooms are either general living areas or individual sleeping quarters.

When we reach the end of the tour, Jenner guides me back into that warehouse-like room with the domed ceiling where we had our first conversation earlier this week. A crowd has gathered, but we loiter at the outskirts of the space, watching in silence as the two dozen people before us take turns patting a middle-aged man on the back.

They repeat the same phrase to him, over and over, some shouting the words while others sing them. Rai pushes her way into the center of the crowd, carrying a heavy-looking crate of glass bottles. When she sets it on the floor, everyone cheers before reaching for the bottles—which I assume must contain alcohol considering PHOENIX's affiliation with The Vega—like a pack of starving wolves.

"Amazing," I whisper, awe leaching into my tone. "With everything you have going against you, you still find time to celebrate birthdays."

Birthdays are just markers of time with a singular purpose: to denote how many years we have left until we become contributing members of society. In the State, the only birthday that matters is our eighteenth, which is when we go for our placement exam.

At least, that's how it normally is, and how it was in the years after Father died. Before then, he always made that day special and would even give me little gifts when Mother wasn't looking—always disposable, so no one would ever find out about them, like a poem or a piece of music. Nothing tangible. Even though the gift was fleeting, it meant the world to me as a child.

My birthday is when I feel his absence the most.

"Well, it's the little things that make life worth living," Jenner murmurs, his voice so low I barely hear it. "Besides, we have to enjoy this while we can since we could all be dead tomorrow. The birthdays we have now… They could be our last."

Jenner and I don't speak again as we watch the celebration unfold. My gaze moves from one end of the room to the other, observing this brief moment of bliss in the many smiling faces around me. My attention catches on one particular face in the crowd and on the hazel eyes cutting into me, hard and cold.

The second I process Ezra's expression, meeting his gaze, the world around me shifts, and pain explodes inside my head as a spiraling succession of images beats through my brain, each one another stab. Screams rip from my lungs as the vision overtakes me, dragging the room into total darkness.

As I fall to my knees, a new vision takes shape behind my eyelids, bringing me back to the shadowed alley at the border of Zone 7 where I cut out my chip. Before me, an entourage of Enforcers forms a barrier around a group of people all dressed in identical knee-length white coats. I recognize those coats at the same moment Dr. Richter steps into my limited range of vision. He turns toward me with his lips pressed together, glaring down at his hand where a bloodied glint of gold rests in the center of his palm.

The corners of his mouth pull into a sneer as his fingers clench into a fist around the chip.

"Clever girl," he purrs.

My body convulses against the cold concrete floor, my head repeatedly slamming into the hard surface as the vision melts away. I can't regain control of my movements or quell the tremors running over my limbs, and within seconds, the metallic stench of blood fills my nose.

Through the hazy black spots spreading in front of my eyes, I glimpse the vague outlines of figures huddling over me.

"Wynter!" Rai calls out. My name is a panicked cry on her lips.

I try to answer her, but I can't get my mouth to cooperate.

The echo of Jenner's voice reaches my ears. "What the hell's happening to her?" He's shouting, and there's a slight wobble behind every word.

He's scared, I realize. But whether he's scared *of* me or *for* me…I don't know.

The pain spreads, threatening to swallow my body whole. Jenner and Rai lean over me, and through the haze obscuring my vision, I can just make out the concern and fear twisting their faces. But they aren't what I'm focusing on. They aren't what I'm searching for—what I need to see—in this moment before my long overdue death descends, finally ready to claim me.

Ezra stares at me from between the blurred faces, his expression no longer cold and hard, not at all like it was the last time I met his gaze.

Now, as the darkness pulls me under, those sad hazel eyes say only one thing.

He's afraid.

FOURTEEN

MY EYELIDS CRACK OPEN, AND a low moan escapes me when a throbbing pain beats against the walls of my skull, the ache behind my eyes made worse by the blinding light shuddering overhead. I lift my hand to block out the glare, and squinting, I can just make out my surroundings. The storage room is blistering—or maybe I'm feverish and it's my skin that's on fire—and the scent of dust and mold clouding the air is more potent than usual.

That smell isn't coming from me, is it?

My tongue darts out to lick my dried lips. I don't remember ever being so thirsty.

Once my vision adjusts, my arm drops back beside me and a frown tugs down the edges of my mouth. Ezra, Jenner, and Rai all stand by the door, keeping their distance from me. For good reason, too. They've witnessed what I can do—what I told them they'd have to see to believe—and shocker, here I am again...

Back in my little prison.

This can't mean anything good. I tell myself their fearful expressions suggest they're merely taking measures to be cautious—although, for my sake or theirs, I'm not sure—but that line of thought does little to comfort me. Can't say that I blame them.

I would be frightened of me, too.

Every part of my body hurts as I move to sit up, the forward motion triggering a jolting stabbing pain in my temple. I press the heel of my hand against my forehead, hoping the pressure will counterbalance the ache. When that doesn't work, I drag in a deep breath and try to ignore the dread twisting my stomach.

My visions are getting worse, my reactions more severe. This level of pain...

It's not normal. Losing consciousness isn't normal. What will happen when the side effects of this disease become too much for me to bear?

What if, next time, I don't wake up?

The idea of death hovers at the front of my mind. Not that long ago, the escape of it would've been welcome, but now, I find myself clinging to life with every ounce of desperation my frail body can muster. Maybe it's my survival instincts kicking in, or maybe I'm just not ready to follow in my father's footsteps.

Either way, I don't want to die. Not yet.

"It's time you tell us what the hell is going on." Ezra steps toward me, crossing his arms. His leering gaze burns into my face, making me squirm.

My answer slips out between raspy breaths. "I told you it was something you had to see to believe."

His eyes narrow. "What happened to you back there? What was that?"

My tongue sweeps over my dry lower lip once again as I contemplate what to say. It's time to tell them the whole truth before my silence gets me killed, but what possible explanation will make them believe me?

There isn't one, I realize.

I'll just have to throw caution to the wind and hope for the best.

"The condition I have… It allows me to see things," I whisper.

"What kind of things?" Rai asks, staring at me, her almond-shaped eyes wide and pressing. Jenner and Ezra both wear the same expectant expression.

I waver, sucking in another deep breath, and as my lungs push the air out, the words expel along with it. "Things that haven't happened yet."

The hush that follows is agonizing. My attention settles on Ezra first, then on Rai, hoping one of them will say something to quell the strange tension sucking the oxygen out of the room. They make it a point to avoid my probing gaze.

Jenner suddenly unleashes a loud bark of a laugh, making me nearly jump out of my skin. The sound is harsh against the backdrop of silence. "That's impossible," he scoffs.

Rai casts an uncertain glance at Ezra, drawing my focus back to his face, which is pale, his expression pinched and unmoving, as if his features have been carved out of stone. A sinking feeling weighs in my gut as the seconds seem to tick by at a snail's pace. It's as if everyone in the small room is waiting for Ezra to say something.

Especially me.

A strangled breath climbs up my throat when he finally speaks. "What did you see?"

I blink a drop of sweat out of my eyes, my heart racing, as I carefully select my next words. "That doctor I told you about... Richter." I pause. "He was with a group of other researchers along with Enforcers in the alley where I left my chip. They found it. They know I cut it out."

I roll my lower lip between my teeth as a thought occurs to me. It's been nearly two weeks since I escaped from the DSD. Dr. Richter would've found the tracking chip long before now; he wouldn't have waited this long to come find me. Unless...maybe these visions aren't just of the future but of things I haven't seen with my own two eyes—future, past, or present. Which would mean Dr. Richter was wrong and my visions aren't only of what's destined to happen days, weeks, months, or even years from now, but of anything this disease or fate or whatever is triggering them decides it wants me to see.

Just what is all this leading me to?

My father's face surfaces from my memory, gripping my heart and lungs in a vise. Could I see him again if I learned to control this ability?

Would these visions let me see the dead?

"It's not possible!" Jenner repeats, his voice raised.

The mattress squeaks beneath my weight as I recoil, my body shrinking back against the cold wall at the abrupt change in volume. I don't like Jenner shouting. Like water and milk, the two don't go well together. I wish I understood why he's so angry. I wish I knew how to bring back his smile.

He turns on Ezra, his cheeks turning ruddy. "Come on, man, seeing into the future? I think our little captive here must've hit her head. There's no way you can actually believe what she's saying."

Rai reaches out and plants a tentative hand on his shoulder. "Jenner—"

"No!" He sneers, stepping out of her grasp. "It's just not possible!"

Everyone goes silent again, and one by one, they all look down at the floor. Except me. Me, who was taught to never make eye contact or draw attention to myself. My gaze hangs on Jenner. Despite the kindness he's shown me, what I've said has driven a wedge between us for some inexplicable reason. Eighteen years of my mother's lessons ring in my head, telling me to mind my own business, but...this *is* my business, isn't it? I want to know what I did to offend him. I wish I knew how to set it right.

In my peripheral vision, Ezra lifts his head, and his solemn expression coaxes goosebumps up along every single inch of my body. When he speaks, the words that break the silence knock all the air from my lungs.

"Yes, it is."

I stare at him, half in shock and half in confusion. Is he saying what I think he's saying?

Does this mean he believes me?

Jenner poses the questions I can't find the words to ask. "How do you know? How *could* you know?"

Ezra's eyes snap to mine, and for the briefest flicker of a moment, all I see is the stranger from my vision, the tears carving lines down his cheeks. "Because I've seen it before—"

"Ezra," Rai interrupts.

I glance at her, surprised by the warning edge to her tone. My gaze shifts back and forth between her and Ezra as it dawns on me that this revelation isn't news to her like it is to me and Jenner. Whatever information Ezra has that gives him knowledge about my condition, whatever he's been through, whatever he's seen, one thing is certain: Rai knows about it.

Jenner shakes his head. "It's not—"

Anger distorts Ezra's features, and he slams his fist back against the concrete wall behind him. "My mother had the same illness, all right?"

Dropping his gaze, he slumps to the floor and rubs a hand across his eyes. A million thoughts run through my head in this moment, and I can't ignore the monumental realization that there's something else connecting us beyond what I saw at the DSD. Something that proves I'm not his enemy.

Is this link why he was in my vision?

Is this link what drove us together?

"She kept muttering these strange things that didn't make any sense." Ezra's voice is low, as if he's speaking to himself, and I find myself leaning in, eager to take in every word. I focus on his moving lips with rapt attention. "Everyone thought she was crazy, even my father. That's why he had her institutionalized. I guess he figured she wouldn't get better. At least, not without professional help. I can't really remember how long she was in the asylum since we were never allowed to visit. All I know is she died alone in that place."

A gasp rises in my throat, but I swallow it. Like the Detention facilities, asylums are located in Zone 7, far away from respected society. Unlike Detention, where we're told rehabilitation is possible, those unlucky enough to be institutionalized will never see the light of day again. Institutionalization is a death sentence— they might as well be sent to Termination. After all, the State only cares about contributing citizens, and those institutionalized cannot contribute. Even old age is frowned upon, although the State rewards a lifetime of servitude with cushy pensions once we reach seventy to entice compliance. But those at asylums... The only reason I can think of as to why they aren't disposed of like criminals is because no laws were broken resulting in their sentence. The State probably fears the outrage that would ensue if it started executing people just because they're unwell.

I think back to my first real conversation with Dr. Richter. As we sat on opposite sides of that long metal table, he had asked so many questions and explained things I still have difficulty wrapping my head around. He also showed me the files of the other known individuals who suffered from this disease. From Ultraxenopia. Individuals who probably died in an asylum—or, in more recent years, as the result of Dr. Richter's experiments once he realized what they were and the DSD got hold of them. Looking back, I wish I had thought to memorize their names. Maybe then I would know if Ezra's mother had been in that pile.

"It was the unusual circumstances of what happened to my mother that contributed to the selection of my brother's career," Ezra continues. "I guess now I know he's finally gained some insight into her condition after all these years."

"What do you mean?" But as the words breach my lips, it dawns on me that I know the answer. It can't be a coincidence. Not after the way Ezra and Rai— who I now know were childhood friends, thanks to Jenner—both reacted when I mentioned him.

"That doctor from the DSD… His name is Austin."

A door seems to open in front of me, revealing an obvious physical resemblance between Ezra and Dr. Richter. I can't believe I didn't notice it sooner. Although their eyes are different colors, they share the same angular jaw and the same furrowed brow. Even their noses and hair color are similar, the latter only differing by a few shades. Whereas Ezra's is dirty blond, Richter's hair is tinged auburn, warmer in hue, which I find ironic, considering his cold personality. Not that Ezra is exactly a fuzzy ball of sunshine.

I don't want to be right about this, terrified of what it could mean if I am. Because, if Dr. Richter is a monster…what exactly does that make his brother?

"Are you sure?" The question barely makes it past my lips, my voice hitching.

As Ezra nods, Rai, who has been silent up to this point, extinguishes any remaining doubt I have. "We knew which sector he was projected to enter."

"Wait a minute. One of those DSD scumbags is your *brother*?"

I look over at Jenner, watching as tremors of rage pin his arms to his sides and his hands clench into tight fists, the knuckles draining of color until the skin is bleached bone white. Before Ezra can answer, Jenner lunges across the small room, closing the distance between them. He only manages to grab hold of Ezra's shirt before Rai steps between them, shoving him back.

"Jenner! That's enough!" she shouts.

His upper lip curls back, revealing his top row of teeth, but he releases his grip. Seething, he turns away from us, cursing.

I risk a glance at Ezra, and it only takes a few seconds for me to recognize the emotion warping his expression, having felt the very same conflicted feelings toward my own mother that he must be feeling right now. But is his resentment directed at Jenner or at the brother who's causing this rift between them?

Scowling, he runs a hand through his hair. "Listen, I haven't seen or spoken to my brother in years. We became estranged shortly after my mother's death, at which point, he got permission to go by her maiden name, probably as a middle finger to our father. When I left home to join PHOENIX, he cut off all contact. He wanted nothing to do with me, and I never bothered to find out what he was up to. Case closed."

As Ezra speaks, I'm distracted by the look on Rai's face and by the tears glistening in her eyes at his words. Once again, I'm left wondering about her connection to the man who tortured me. Since she and Ezra have known each other since they were children, that must mean she knew Richter, too.

"You should've said something," Jenner grumbles, clicking his tongue with a disapproving tut. "That's a messed up thing to keep from us. Do you even realize what kind of danger that connection can put us all in?" He lets out a humorless laugh. "Lies and omissions like that make you no better than the State."

I wrap my arms around my legs, pulling them close to my chest, keeping my back to the wall and trying to make myself as small as possible. This conversation might have started with me, but it sure as hell hasn't ended with me.

Now, I'm nothing but an unwanted intruder.

"Jenner, let's go for a walk," Rai pleads.

He casts a begrudging look at her before stomping into the corridor, slamming the door shut behind him. She moves to follow but hesitates long enough to brush a hand against Ezra's shoulder. They exchange a silent glance, but neither one of them utters a word.

My eyes dart between them as Rai pulls open the door. Ezra doesn't move from his spot on the floor, his posture stiff and gaze downcast, and as Rai steps out of the room, the door clicks shut behind her, leaving the two of us alone.

FIFTEEN

"I THINK I KNEW THIS whole time," Ezra murmurs. It's the first time he's spoken since Rai and Jenner left the room several minutes ago. "From that moment in The Vega when you said that you saw me, the way you said it…" He laughs under his breath. "Even then, I think I knew you and her were the same. I could see it—the fear and pain behind your eyes that I always saw in my mother's."

I hesitate, unsure what to say. We've both been affected by Ultraxenopia and made victims of it but in far different ways. I don't know if I can understand what he's been through any more than he could possibly comprehend what I've suffered.

As I stare at him—his eyes, both familiar and yet those of a stranger's, swimming with a glimpse of tears born of grief—I ask myself who this condition is worse for. The person who has to bear the brunt of the disease? Or the ones left behind who have to watch them deteriorate?

This line of thought never occurred to me before now since my own mother gave me up without question. She was all I had in the world. There was no one else for me to leave behind. No one to watch me succumb to this illness.

No one who loved me to watch me die.

I bite back tears and look down at my hands where they fidget in my lap, pinching the hem of the shirt Rai lent me—now soaked through with sweat and blood—between my trembling fingertips. When Ezra appeared in my vision, I didn't give much thought to who he was as a person. On the surface, he was simply my ticket out of the DSD, a cardboard cutout representing my freedom. After months of torture, finding an escape from Dr. Richter was all I cared about. Sure, his presence piqued my interest, but who he was—his life, his pain—were of little consequence to me.

But now, instead of a potentially imaginary stranger in my head, he's a living, breathing person in front of me, and I can no longer ignore the who behind the hazel eyes boring holes in my skin or what horrors or trauma made him that way.

For the first time, I realize how selfish it was of me to seek him out. With what little I know about his family and past, I can't help wondering if my being here is a problem for him. I can imagine all too easily what he's been through between the death of his mother and the broken bond with his brother—my own life an eerie mirror image of his pain. But what if those similarities between us are stirring up memories he'd rather forget?

What if the very thing drawing us together is also the thing that pushes us farther apart?

"Austin…" The forlorn timbre of Ezra's voice drags my gaze upward, and when our eyes meet, he clears his throat, hesitating for a moment before finally asking, "What did he do to you in there?"

I cock an eyebrow. Can he not guess what I went through? Maybe he just doesn't want to envision the suffering his own brother is capable of inflicting.

The memory of those unfeeling gray eyes washes over me. "I'll spare you the gruesome details, but I *will* tell you Richter won't stop until he gets what he's after. He didn't have any issue with risking my life in pursuit of it, and I doubt he cares about anyone else's."

Ezra frowns, turning his eyes to the floor. "It's my fault."

I blink, taken aback by this confession. "What? How do you figure?"

Silence stretches between us for so long I begin to think he won't answer. Then, in a quiet voice, he says, "My brother and I have always had different stances when it comes to our political viewpoints. Between the two of us, I've always been the more liberal one, dedicated to justice and helping others, whereas he's always been all about the future and his personal contribution to society. The perfect citizen of the State. Despite that, we got on well enough, but our relationship took a turn after our mother passed and it only worsened when I told him I was leaving home to join PHOENIX. He spouted off the typical nonsense about it being a terrorist organization and that I was setting myself up for a hard life at best and a painful death at Termination at worst. But, I knew in my gut, it was the one place where I could really make a difference and do something more with my life. Where I could escape the confines of a tyrannical government that was dictating my every decision and that had snatched my free will away the second I was born." Passion blossoms behind every word as he rants, his eyes alight with fire and fury. He pauses to lick his lips and draw in a breath. "So, I ignored him and did what I wanted to do. It didn't help the situation that Rai chose to come with me."

There it is again—that connection between Dr. Richter and Rai. But what *is* the connection? What were they to each other back then?

What are they to each other now?

As if reading my mind, Ezra adds, "My brother and Rai have a complicated history. Let's just say, her joining the rebellion wasn't the future he had envisioned for them."

It takes me a moment to grasp what he means. Ezra's relationship with Dr. Richter is estranged—he admitted that much earlier when Jenner freaked out about them being related. But what about Rai's relationship with him? What happened between them before she left home to join PHOENIX?

I recall the way she asked me if I thought Dr. Richter was a good man and the devastation that had filled her gaze when I said no. As I remember that moment, I find myself wondering if her affection for him was mutual. If it was, how did she feel when she left him?

If it was…does that mean he wasn't always a monster?

"How old were you when this happened?" I ask.

Ezra scratches the back of his neck while his other hand picks at a thread on his pants. "Well, I left home right before Austin took his placement exam, so fifteen. Rai was seventeen. It's been almost eight years, and neither one of us have seen or heard from him since."

Eight years… Is nearly a decade long enough for someone to forget that kind of abandonment?

I think back to my time at the DSD, reliving the sequence of events that occurred the day Dr. Richter's tests were finally successful. The day he saw my vision. The day he saw Ezra, his younger brother, again. The hairs on the back of my neck stand on end at the memory of the crazed look that flared in his eyes when he realized who it was I had seen.

No, I realize. Eight years isn't enough.

Ezra peeks up at me, his expression almost gentle, not that unlike how it was in my vision. Silence once again swells between us, and as the seconds tick by, I try to work out why someone like him would ever shed tears over someone like me. Brusque demeanor aside, he's a far better person than I am…or have ever been. He left behind the comfort of society to help other people, while I'm just trying my best to survive.

I don't deserve his remorse.

"I'm sorry, Wynter."

Why? I wonder again. *What are you going to do?*

"Why did you really come looking for me?"

I suck in a breath, unprepared for this question. I don't know why—he's already pressed me about that day and why I came to The Vega. I suppose I'm flustered by it this time because I know I won't keep getting away with some half-assed answer about the truth being complicated. If we're ever going to move forward, if I'm ever going to understand what's happening to me and what part he plays in my vision, then I need to tell him what happened.

He needs to know what I saw.

"During one of your brother's daily experiments on me, I saw you in a vision. By that point, he had already run more tests than I had bothered to count, and that was without the added motivation of knowing he could use me to locate PHOENIX or anyone else the State might want him to find. If I had stayed, he would've used my visions to hunt every last one of you down. Or kill me in the process of trying."

"So, you left," he finishes, slightly breathless.

I nod, ignoring the sharp pain that shoots through my left wrist when my hands squeeze into fists. "My reasons for leaving were purely selfish. I was being tortured. It was escape or die. I wish I could pretend otherwise, but the truth is, I didn't fully understand Dr. Richter's motivations or who else would be in danger because of me. Because of what I'm capable of."

I avert my gaze, not wanting to see even a hint of the disappointment I'm certain I'll find if I look Ezra in the eye. With this admission hanging in the air between us, I must look so small and unworthy of his help.

Swallowing, I force myself to continue. "That last day, once I'd made up my mind, I saw a glimpse of The Vega just before I escaped. I didn't have anywhere else to go, and it felt like the vision was pointing me in a single direction, a beacon of light guiding my way through the darkness that had cast such a huge shadow over my life in such a short space of time. The opportunity fell into my lap, so I took it, and that path led me to you. I'm only here because I want to understand why. And because I didn't know where else I could go where *he* wouldn't be able to find me."

Ezra sits up straight and narrows his eyes. "What was your vision about? The one where you saw me."

I shift, uncomfortable beneath the touch of his gaze, as reluctance overwhelms me. Maybe because there was an intimacy to what I saw that I'm embarrassed to voice. Or maybe because I don't want to burden him with what that future means.

Ezra cocks his head to one side, and there's something subtle about his expression that reminds me of how he looked at me in my vision.

Of how he *will* look at me.

"I-It was just you and me," I stammer. "You were saying you're sorry."

"Oh?" A trace of amusement crosses his face. "What was I apologizing for?"

My throat constricts. "I don't know."

And I'm not sure I want to.

His eyes flutter closed, and he exhales, his sigh strained. For whatever reason, he doesn't press me on the matter. "I suppose I do have a lot to apologize for. Rai would happily tell you as much."

My pulse quickens. "Like what?"

"The way I've treated you, for one," he answers with a lazy shrug.

He opens one eye to look at me, and an unfamiliar heat rises on my face, which I quickly hide behind my uninjured hand. My words escape through the cracks between my fingers. "You weren't sure if I could be trusted, I get it. The precautions you took were necessary."

"But the way I treated you wasn't. I should've at least listened to you first, been open to offering you the same help I've extended to everyone else here. The truth is, I was blinded by hate. I was blinded…" He trails off.

I arch a brow. "Let me guess. By the white coat?"

A laugh more like a huff parts his lips. "Yeah. Once I saw that DSD insignia, my fear took over. I allowed it to cloud my judgment."

Except, that's not entirely true. If it was, he wouldn't have bothered to save my life when I was bleeding out at The Vega. Despite what happened between him and his brother, despite his fear of the DSD, he pushed all those feelings aside to help me, a stranger who would've died if he hadn't.

Ezra pushes up from the floor and crosses the room in a handful of steps, holding out his right arm in front of me. As he stands beside the cot, waiting for me to take his hand, there's a split second where I see the man from my vision. He looks at me with those bewildering tears in his eyes, whispering those same three words that now haunt my every waking thought. But why is he begging me for forgiveness?

What is he going to do?

I blink, and suddenly, the Ezra of the present is back and the future that seems so far but so impossibly close is gone. A ghost of a smile plays at the edges of his mouth, and as my eyes drop down to his hand, I will myself to jump across this chasm between us. To do the opposite of what Dr. Richter warned me about in the moments right before I fled the DSD. To do the one thing I've been too scared to attempt since the day my father was taken from me.

To trust someone.

To trust Ezra.

The instant my hand slides into his awaiting grasp, he steps back and yanks me off the mattress. The nerves in my stomach flip when he turns and tugs me along behind him toward the door.

Panic seeps into my voice when I ask, "Where are we going?"

Ezra flashes a sly grin at me over his shoulder, the warmth lighting up his face unexpected and bright, like a ray of sunshine breaking through storm clouds.

"Out of this room," he says, his tone buoyant. "You're not our prisoner anymore."

SIXTEEN

EZRA LEADS ME ON AN unfamiliar path through the corridors, the air between us charged with a strange sensation that makes my skin prickle and itch. I'm not sure what it is I'm sensing. The silence permeating the air isn't exactly unpleasant, but there's a noticeable shift between how he was acting before my latest vision and how he's acting with me now. A slight smile teases at the corners of his lips, only adding to my confusion. Maybe I'm just picking up on the fact that the distrust he's been clinging to seems to have vanished.

I watch him out of my peripheral vision, wary of the unknown motivation behind his sudden change in attitude. As much as I want to trust him, the difference is far too great and came on too quickly to be convincing. For that reason, I don't buy it. There's something he's not telling me.

Something he doesn't want me to know.

"Here we are."

He pushes open an oval-shaped bulkhead door to my right, stepping over the metal lip into the small but cozy space beyond. Curious, I peek past him into the empty quarters, immediately taking note of the bed. I don't need to look at the plump mattress for more than a few seconds to know it's way more comfortable than anything else I've slept on for months.

"I think you'll find this much more to your liking. We aren't in the business of holding prisoners here, and that other room is actually more of a storage closet, so it wasn't really a long-term solution."

A breath sticks in my throat. Long-term? Does this mean he wants me to stay here with PHOENIX? Rai said something along those lines, but is staying here really even an option for me?

Hope swells in my chest, but its presence is fleeting, like a fire doused by a downpour of water. Too many bad things have happened to me in my life, and now, my brain is programmed to think nothing good ever can. Or will. Even the thought of a new life here with people who might actually care about me is marred by doubt and suspicion.

My movements are cautious as I step into the tiny square room, my gaze skirting along the gray walls. Although the aesthetic is reminiscent of my cell at the DSD, this space still feels like home in a way the terraced house I shared with my mother in Zone 2 never did. Maybe because I always sensed a distance between us—a deep river she wasn't willing to cross, further proven when she handed me over to Richter. But here, the people didn't turn me away the second my life was in danger and I needed their help. Here, every river they face has a bridge.

Upon coming full circle, I meet Ezra's gaze, a frown forming between my brows.

"I know what you're thinking, and don't worry," he says. "You aren't taking this bed away from anyone. This place is big enough that we actually have rooms to spare."

"That wasn't exactly what I was thinking."

"Oh." Uncertainty flashes across his face. "Okay, then what were you thinking?"

I hesitate, watching my foot as the bottom of my shoe scuffs against the concrete floor. "I was wondering if it's okay that you're offering me this. If you actually have the authority to decide who is and who isn't a prisoner here."

His expression hardens. "You let me worry about that. I'm on your side now. That's all that matters."

But why are you? I want to ask. Is he only doing this because of his mother? Because we're victims of the same disease? Or is it because of something else I'm not seeing?

What's changed?

I'm tempted to press the matter, but I hold back the words of protest building up in my throat. I don't want to test the limits of Ezra's graciousness when we finally seem to be making progress.

My teeth bite down on my lower lip as I sneak a longing glance back at the bed. There's no reason why I shouldn't accept this small comfort. If I reject it, I'd only be doing so to punish myself. Between months of torture at the DSD and my recent brush with death from blood loss and sepsis—according to Rai when I pressed her one day about the time I spent unconscious—I think I've been punished enough. Clearly, Ezra seems to think so, too.

The silence between us drags on for a few seconds too long to be natural.

Clearing his throat, Ezra looks over at the door. "I'll get Rai to find some extra clothes for you. There are bound to be some lying around here somewhere. If not, we'll figure something out."

"Thank you," I whisper.

When I speak, that ghost of a smile returns and it's like I'm looking at a different person than the man I met in that dingy bar in Zone 7. In the brief time I've spent with Rai and Jenner, I've discovered how compassion can be a driving force, especially when distanced from the draining nature of the State, which discourages such sentiments. Sympathy—or in Ezra's case, empathy, considering he's seen what I'm going through before with his mother—can alter a person's mindset toward anything, regardless of the circumstances.

Or, in our case, because of the circumstances.

Since learning I suffer from the same disease his late mother had, Ezra's visibly softened toward me—his eyes now warm and curious rather than hard and glistening with distrust and suspicion. By now, he must know I'm not a spy for the State but a victim of it, just like everyone here. Just like his mother, who was abandoned in an asylum to die alone. Otherwise, why would he be doing all this? I have to believe he wouldn't show me such kindness unless he knew I wasn't a threat.

An awkward hush fills the room as I shuffle forward and plop down on the bed, the mattress welcoming my weight with a creaking sigh of the springs. A smile spreads across my face as I fall back against the blankets, forgetting Ezra's presence and pushing aside the unending stream of questions plaguing my mind.

I've only been here for a brief time, but I can sense something changing within me, as if all the emotions the State has encouraged me to repress my whole life are inching closer to the surface. Perhaps, like me, they're reaching for freedom. Freedom from a life of conformity. Freedom from fear.

Freedom to live life how I choose.

"I'll, uh…leave you to get settled, then," Ezra says.

Rubbing a hand across the back of his neck, he turns for the door, stepping over the raised threshold without uttering another word. I follow his rigid movements with narrowed eyes, wondering why he suddenly seems so out of sorts. But the answer never comes to me and I'm too exhausted to care.

Shrugging, I relax against the soft mattress, and as my body unwinds, a fog of sleep washes over me. My eyes drift closed, embracing the darkness, but I'm pulled back into full awareness by the sound of my name.

"Wynter."

My eyes peek open and lock on Ezra where he wavers in the doorway. As he stares at me, I realize this is the first time I've heard him say my name—well, the first time in person and not in my head—and hearing it reminds me of what I saw in my vision. Of that future where we stand together, just the two of us alone at the end of the world.

"I have to ask." He hesitates, averting his gaze. "Did my brother say what he wanted with you?"

I bristle at the mention of Dr. Richter. I understand why Ezra would want to know more about my time at the DSD and my connection to his villainous brother, but the memory of what I went through is distressing, and I'd really rather not talk about it if I don't have to. Still, knowing what I do about his mother and accepting that the story of my disease doesn't only belong to me, I decide he deserves to know.

Frowning, I shake my head and sit upright. "No. Just that I'd be doing a service to the State if I cooperated. I know he planned on using my visions to lead him to PHOENIX, but he never told me anything else. I assumed I was just some guinea pig for him to study and then dispose of once I'd exhausted my usefulness."

I consider this line of thought for a moment. Now that I know Dr. Richter and Ezra are brothers, I wonder what the former really wanted with me. Did he just want to locate PHOENIX so he could track down Ezra and get his revenge? Or was he hoping to find Rai and bring her home? Or was it a combination of both and also doing his duty to the State? Perhaps, it was something else altogether.

Ezra stares at the wall behind me, his eyes glazing over. Then, as if coming to some internal revelation, he crosses the room and crouches in front of me. "I think it might be best if we keep this to ourselves for now. Don't tell anyone else what the State wants with you, and whatever you do, don't mention your condition or my brother, okay?"

I gape at him, bewildered by his unexpected request. I get why he wouldn't want me to say anything about Dr. Richter—the news of their familial connection might not reflect well on him considering how long he's kept it a secret—but I don't understand why he wants me to hide the rest. What does he think will happen if I don't? Aren't all the people here also running from the State?

Don't they protect their own?

But you're not really one of them, are you? an annoying voice in the back of my head reminds me.

"I can't control what's happening to me," I snap. My tone is sharper than I intend, but I don't apologize for it. I lost much of my ingrained politeness thanks to the hell I went through at the DSD. "And a friendly reminder, I *just* had a seizure in front of everyone living here. Sure, maybe they won't think much of that now, but they will the second it happens again. And when that time comes, they'll start asking questions."

He knows I'm right—I can tell as much by the disgruntled expression spreading over his face. The effects of this disease will be impossible to hide. Sooner or later, the others will demand to know what's wrong with me and why I'm really here.

Sooner or later, the truth will come out.

"No one else has to know the details," he says. "Let them think what they want. The important thing is that we keep you safe."

Why? I want to ask. Why is what happens to me so damn important to him? Hopefully not because of anything having to do with his brother or the DSD. Then again, refugees or not, these people are part of a rebellion. It would be foolish of me not to acknowledge that a tool of the enemy is also a weapon against it.

A shiver runs across my skin at the thought.

As I silently question Ezra's reasoning and motives, something occurs to me. "Are you just saying this because of what happened with Jenner?"

Ezra lowers his gaze. "You know, I can count on one hand how many times I've seen Jenner mad. Like, *actually* mad. I must've really pissed him off."

"Will he forgive you?" My voice catches a little, and I take a deep breath to hide the unease racing through me. Forgiveness is as much a part of my world as empathy or understanding. The State doesn't care about your point of view or why you did anything. It only cares if you follow the rules and what punishment you deserve should you break them. Forgiveness is never even on the table.

"Of course." Ezra waves his right hand dismissively. "We've been friends for years, and it'll take much more than one fight to jeopardize what we have. He'll calm down once he realizes I've done nothing wrong."

I can't even fathom that notion—one built around the concept of forgiveness. Forgiveness doesn't exist in the State. One mistake, and you're guilty. End of discussion. And guilt always leads to punishment of some kind, some worse than others. Some deadly. People don't even risk arguments with family or friends out of fear of what outcome it might lead to.

Ezra, Jenner, and Rai were all raised in the Heart, just like me. They would've experienced the line we all have to toe for the sake of avoiding the vengeful wrath of the State. And yet, it hasn't escaped my notice that, ever since my arrival, all they've done is argue, as if the submissive traits they had growing up have all worn away the longer they've lived outside normal society. It's fascinating to watch, except for the fact that the disagreements are almost always because of me. I might not know them well, but that doesn't mean I want to be the wedge that drives them apart. I came here to find Ezra, to find answers about my condition and the future we're all unknowingly barreling toward. Not to make his life or anyone else's harder than it already is.

"You know, I wasn't too receptive to the idea when Rai first ran it by me, but I've been thinking a lot and I agree with her now." Ezra laughs at the confused look on my face, the sound flooding my body with warmth while simultaneously spreading through me like a chill. A gentle smile curls up his lips. "You should stay," he clarifies. "You belong here as much as any of us. Maybe more so considering the bastards you've run from."

That feeling of hope returns to my chest, but it's fleeting, a weak flicker, like a faltering heartbeat.

"I'm not a rebel, so I don't know how much help I'd be," I admit. "I didn't come here to try to change the world."

Only my own.

He shrugs. "No one in PHOENIX is claiming to be a hero. We're all just trying to get by and do whatever we have to do to survive. Sound familiar?"

My eyes widen. That does sound familiar. My entire life has been built around the need to survive. Ever since my father was arrested and executed, I've been on constant alert, always in sight of the State's watchful eye. But here, the State can't reach me or see me. Here, I can do more than just survive and spend my days living in a bubble of fear.

Maybe, here in this place, I can live.

The memory of my vision floods my head as Ezra rises from the floor and shifts onto the bed beside me. The unspoken connection I sensed between us intensifies the closer he gets, like heat against my skin. I flush, wondering if he feels it, too.

We sit, side by side, neither one of us daring to penetrate the hush with empty words. As the silence thickens, what Ezra said about hiding my condition drifts back to the forefront of my mind. What will these people do when they find out why I'm here? What will they do when they find out what I am?

"I know we didn't exactly get off on the right foot, and it might seem odd given my recent behavior, but you can always talk to me if you need to get something off your chest. I'm not a bad listener."

I peek over at Ezra, and he smiles again, raising one tawny brow in encouragement. The words stick to the roof of my mouth, held back by eighteen years of forced emotional suppression. I gave in with Rai, but even then, I knew opening up on that level to someone could reveal a weakness they could then exploit. And that's exactly what it would be if I spilled my guts to someone who I would've sworn hated me only an hour ago. It would be weakness. It would expose the desperate desire for human connection I didn't even realize was present within me.

At least, that's what the State has trained me to think. But now, as my eyes fix on Ezra's, the alternative hangs before me. Perhaps divulging my concerns is the first step in bringing us closer together and will help me uncover the extent of our connection and how it leads to that desolate future.

Maybe this is the key to understanding my visions.

"You haven't seen how everyone here looks at me," I blurt out, unable to keep the agitated edge out of my voice. "I've lived in fear long enough to recognize the signs. They're terrified of me."

I almost miss the avoidance I encountered every single day in the Heart. I'm not used to so many eyes staring at me. I'm not used to being viewed as the enemy. In some ways, I almost feel like the evil creatures from the fairy tales my father told me when I was young—dark, haunting stories forbidden in our society. Stories he never told me around my mother. To the people here, my motives are unknown. To them, I could be dangerous.

To them, I might very well be a monster.

You killed someone, that infuriating voice chimes in. *They'd be right to think that.*

Luckily for me, they don't know what I did. I don't even allow myself to wonder how much would be different if they knew the truth.

Ezra places a hand on my shoulder, and to my surprise, I don't shy away from his touch.

"I'll talk to them," he promises.

"Is there really any point?" I press. "They're going to find out about me eventually. You can't hide the truth from them forever. Then, they'll realize they were right to be afraid."

Ezra holds my gaze for a moment, searching for answers I have no incentive to give, then says, almost to himself, "You're right. Maybe we shouldn't, then."

My stomach clenches. "What do you mean?"

"We tell them the State's after you without saying why. If they ask, we make something up. Something that won't give anyone reason to—" He clamps his mouth shut, cutting off the rest of whatever he was about to say. When his eyes shift to mine, I furrow my brow at him.

Reason to what? I nearly scream.

Ignoring my silent question, he says, "It's been a long time since we had anyone new join our sect, so they probably just want some assurances that you aren't going to get us all arrested. Or killed. Once that suspicion is gone, they'll accept you into the fold. They just need to believe you're one of us first." He jumps off the bed and extends his arm in front of me, his hand palm up in offering. "It's a bit of a long shot, but I have an idea. You in?"

I stare at Ezra's hand, leery of his scheming expression. As if to reassure me—or possibly warn me—a slideshow of images from my vision manifest in my mind, once again showing me those hazel eyes and the tears over whatever it is he's going to do that makes me wonder if I should trust him.

Warnings flash like neon lights behind my eyes, but I ignore them and slide my hand into his. I'm not sure what's running through his head, and that frightens me. But, at this moment, at least for right now, I want to believe he has my best interests at heart. I want to believe he's on my side, as he claimed. I want to believe I can trust him.

Now, it's time to find out if he's lying.

SEVENTEEN

I WATCH EZRA, TRAILING A few feet behind him, my eyes trained on his back every step of the way. His stride is confident, which is almost reassuring, considering what he's planning on doing. Almost.

"Are you sure about this?" I ask, a slight tremble to my voice.

"As sure as I'll ever be." Despite these words, he doesn't meet my gaze.

I shadow him through the labyrinth of corridors as we retrace the path Jenner and Rai took me on just this morning, before I passed out from my vision. The fluorescent strip lighting seems to get brighter the longer we walk, sprouting black spots in front of my eyes and giving me flashbacks to Dr. Richter's experiments.

I swipe the back of my hand across my forehead, brushing away a sheen of sweat. I don't know why I'm so nervous. Regardless of what happens next, the path I'm on can only lead one way, meaning any worries I have about the situation are pointless. From what I've seen, the future—*that* future—is set in stone.

A shudder races over my skin at the thought. I'm not sure if it's comforting or terrifying knowing that nothing Ezra is about to do really matters.

He leads me back to that large central room, the space empty compared to how crowded it was the last time I was in here, before I collapsed. As we pause at the threshold, I spot Rai and Jenner huddled together on a bench in the distant left corner.

Jenner notices us almost at once, his eyes flickering from me to Ezra, where they hang for a moment, narrowing in lingering indignation. I'm tempted to smile or wave or whatever it is normal people do in greeting, but all I can think about is the way he reacted when I told him, Ezra, and Rai the truth about what's wrong with me. About what I can do. Of the three of them, I figured he would be the one to believe me.

Of the three of them, he was the one who didn't.

A hollow ache wraps around my heart and spreads outward, infecting the rest of my body, until I'm nothing more than agitated nerves in a shell that merely resembles a person. To distract myself from the gnawing sensation, I focus my attention on Rai. Her mouth shapes words, but I can't make them out.

Jenner says something back, waving his hands in an animated gesture as he casts a sidelong glance in our direction, but Rai just rolls her eyes and grabs at his arm, jumping to her feet and dragging him up along with her. He doesn't put up a fight; he just scowls, shoving his hands into his pockets like a sulking child. When Rai crosses the room, he follows behind her, keeping his gaze pinned down on the floor.

Once they're both within earshot, Ezra jerks his chin toward the exits. "Gather everyone for an emergency meeting. It's time we introduce Wynter properly."

Rai hesitates, examining Ezra's face for a moment, as if hoping to glean more information from his silence. Or maybe she's wondering if he has permission to go through with this. From where I'm standing, his stony expression gives nothing away, but she must see something in his gaze that assures her because she nods and veers out of the room to complete the task given to her, no questions asked. Jenner, on the other hand, stops dead in his tracks, his eyes no longer on the floor but locked on my face. Unlike before when I was tempted to smile or wave, I only want to look away. He doesn't even spare a second glance at Ezra.

A gasp parts my lips when Ezra's hand grazes mine, my heart jumping into my throat as his fingers move up my arm and come to rest on my shoulder. Heat flushes my skin when he meets my gaze, but I'm not sure if it's the intense look on his face causing this reaction in me or the fact that Jenner is watching us.

"Wait here," he instructs in a quiet murmur, his breath tickling my ear.

Fire ignites in my blood at his touch, but the unexpected thrill rushing through me is nothing compared to the sinking sensation taking hold of my stomach. I can't explain it, just as I can't explain why, as he walks away, I feel exposed and alone. After all, I'm used to a life of isolation. That's all I've ever known. But life in this compound is nothing like life in the State, and without him beside me, I have nothing to shield me from the wary stares of the handful of people present in the room. The distrust blazing in their eyes as they stare at me is like an inferno burning over my skin.

I immediately lower my gaze, unable to face the suspicion assaulting me from all sides. Ezra's plan won't work. No one here will ever believe I'm not a threat.

They won't trust me. They can't. They—

Know what you are, a crooning voice finishes in my head. It reminds me of Dr. Richter. Hell, maybe it is. Maybe all that torture has rooted his cruelty into my very subconscious and it's only now rearing its head to torment me. *They can sense the danger emanating from you,* the voice continues. *They suspect what you did…murderer.*

I shiver as goosebumps rise along every inch of my body. No, I refuse to believe that. They can't know. How would they? Not even Ezra knows. Then, a more disturbing thought strikes me, hard and fast, like a knife to the chest. If he did, would he still say he's on my side? Or would he turn against me?

I swallow as the dull thud of footsteps resounds in my ears, and the hairs on the back of my neck stand on end when black boots enter my line of vision. Dread sends my heart racing as my eyes leap upward, fixing onto the face of the person they belong to.

"Hey."

The left side of Jenner's mouth pinches into that kind, lopsided smile I've grown so fond of, but behind it, he seems nervous. Uncertain. The slight dimple in his cheek fades when he frowns and rocks back onto the heels of his feet.

"Listen, I'm sorry about earlier. I didn't mean to imply that you're a liar or anything. It's just…what you said… It put this nagging thought in my head. If *I* had this power you supposedly have, if I had known what was going to happen to my family, would things be different now? Would they be alive? Would I have still found myself in the position that forced me to choose between death at the hands of the DSD or joining PHOENIX? I guess, on some nonsensical level, it didn't seem fair you had this advantage and I didn't."

Advantage?

I've never looked at it that way. To me, it's always been more like a curse. I suppose, from an outside perspective—from the viewpoint of someone not suffering through this disease—I can understand why he might see it like that.

Dr. Richter certainly did.

I open my mouth to attempt to say something consoling, but the words fail to form on my tongue. Jenner's experienced a devastating loss and bears the burden of that pain even now, so I can appreciate why he would think what I can do is unfair, even though he isn't alone in his grief. Even though others have also had their fair share of it in their lives. Including me.

"Then, hearing about Ezra's brother… Well, I guess that just kind of tipped me over the edge. Ez and Rai know everything there is to know about me, and today, I realized, I can't say the same about them. Which, of course, made me wonder what else they aren't telling me."

"I get it. They've become your family. If you can't trust them, who can you trust?" I ask. If only he knew how much that concern haunts me, too.

"Yeah." He grimaces. "Exactly."

An awkward hush spreads between us, wrapping the room in an almost tangible silence that presses down on my lungs, strangling my breaths. As I search for something to say, desperate to return to how things were before he knew the truth about me, I realize how much I miss the Jenner I've come to know over the course of the last week. The Jenner who made sure I felt comfortable and welcome when nearly everyone else avoided me out of fear. The Jenner who, despite being a stranger, disclosed things to me that were personal— things we're taught not to dwell on or share in our world because nothing and no one should matter more than our purpose within the societal structure of the State. The Jenner who showed me it's okay to feel. The Jenner who I could call my friend when I never knew what friendship was before coming here.

I search for him in the features of the man standing before me. To my relief, he stares back at me through those piercing blue eyes.

"So, this *gift* of yours…" He casts a quick look over his shoulder, dropping his voice to a conspiratorial whisper. "Is it always like that?"

I wish I could lie. I wish I could say what I know he wants to hear, but what good would that do either of us? It wouldn't make this disease any easier to bear. It wouldn't cure me or take away what I've been through or what still awaits. If I were to lie, I'd only be doing so to spare myself from his inevitable horror.

No, being dishonest at this point is useless. I can't lie to him about it any more than I can lie to myself.

"For the most part, yeah." I shrug, as if it's no big deal the disease ravaging my body keeps treating my brain like an over-boiled egg about to explode from the pressure constantly building up inside it.

"Wow." He balks, and it takes him a few seconds to recover as he comes to terms with my confession. Nostrils flaring, he drags in a breath and lets it out slowly, muttering, "That must *really* suck."

His bluntness pulls a laugh out of me, but the sound is strained as it springs from my throat. Jenner doesn't seem to notice. He laughs as well, and after, we just grin at each other, comfortable in our silence again.

The smile only slips from his face when his eyes drift from mine, glancing over my right shoulder and narrowing at something in the distance behind me. Swallowing, I follow his gaze to where Rai stands in the closest of the two doorways to the large central room, ushering a small group into the space. Ezra arrives through the other entryway a few minutes later, bringing what I assume must be the rest of their community.

Jenner and I say nothing as we watch Rai and Ezra herd everyone into the room. When he doesn't move from my side, I glance up at him, but the confusion and worry I expect to glimpse on his face are nowhere to be found. He doesn't know what Ezra's going to say or how much he's about to reveal about me—for all he knows, it could be everything—and yet, he doesn't seem concerned. If anything, he's unnervingly calm.

That's because he trusts Ezra, I realize. Jenner might be furious with him right now, but he knows Ezra wouldn't go out of his way to hurt me, even though I'm a stranger to them. Even though my being here puts them all in danger. Because, to Jenner, I don't deserve the hand I've been dealt and he views me as an innocent, even though I'm the furthest thing from it.

I can't help wondering if he would still think that if he knew I killed someone.

The residents of the compound shuffle into the middle of the room, sharing curious glances and voicing their suspicions about why they've all been called together. As a murmur of confusion carries through the space, buzzing through the air in an incoherent wave of jumbled words, Ezra weaves through the crowd, gripping the edge of an empty wooden crate in his hand. Pushing out a breath, he drops the crate to the floor, steps up onto it, and locks eyes with the perplexed sea of faces.

In one cohesive movement, the crowd shifts its attention from Ezra to me, and my body buckles beneath the weight of the speculative whispers, even with Jenner's comforting presence beside me. His fingers wrap around my shoulder and squeeze.

When Ezra lifts his arms, the drone of conversation dies away, replaced by an eager, expectant silence. I peek up at him out of the corner of my eye, noting the way his chest rises and falls with each breath, as if he, too, is anticipating what will come next.

As his arms drop back to his sides, he speaks, his voice an authoritative boom of thunder cracking through the room. "I know you're all wondering about our latest addition. About who she is and why she's here. Well, let me put the rumors to rest. The answer is simple. She's here because she needs our protection, the same as any of you."

"From what?" A man who appears to be a few years older than Ezra steps forward from the crowd, grasping the hand of a young girl, who stumbles after him, her face as white as a sheet. Her wide eyes dart to mine, shining with fear.

I glance over at Ezra as he clasps his hands behind his back and lifts his chin, standing just a little bit taller. Although his stance is strong and his expression commanding, I see this facade for what it is: a lie.

Just like the lies he's about to spew about me.

As the overhead lights reflect off the sweat beading just beneath his hairline, a realization hits me. I glimpsed it before when I collapsed in this room, and I see it again now, glowing in the amber-tinted depths of his gaze. The look I find there gives away his true feelings at this moment, just as it gave away his grief in my vision.

He's afraid.

"Re-education," he answers, not missing a beat. "Her nerves got the best of her during her placement exam, and she ran out before finishing it. You all know what the State is like. Punish first, ask questions later."

Ezra doesn't elaborate any more than that or clarify when my exam actually was. The way he says it would make anyone think my exam occurred the day we met at The Vega, as if I'd sought out PHOENIX right after. Considering what we're trying to hide, it's best if that's what everyone thinks.

A rumble passes through the crowd as some bob their heads in agreement while others look even more perplexed than before. I peek at Jenner, then over at Rai, but they're both masters of deception, their faces still and blank, as if this information isn't news to them, reaffirming the lie. I suppose it isn't, but they also know Re-education was never what Dr. Richter had planned for me.

They trust Ezra, I repeat to myself as my eyes crawl over the group. *They trust that he knows what he's doing.*

"Typical. The exam is a joke," one woman scoffs, offering me a pitying smile.

But the man beside her doesn't look as convinced.

"Is it true she confronted you in The Vega while wearing a DSD-issue coat?" he asks, his dark eyes fixing Ezra with a challenging stare that sends a chill over my skin.

When Ezra doesn't answer straightaway, my anxiety heightens, constricting my lungs. Jenner, sensing the tension coursing through me, once again squeezes my shoulder, his warm fingers an immediate comfort to my nerves. I melt into his touch, wishing this could be over.

Before I can look back over at Ezra to see what he's doing and try to work out how he'll skirt around the truth this time, he recovers, expelling his next lie with ease. "Yes, we met at The Vega. She had been running since morning, was tired, thirsty, and had stumbled into the bar looking for water. As for the coat, her mother works at the DSD as a lab technician in Engineering. She stole it from their house to disguise herself before making her way to Zone 7. Bumping into each other was nothing more than dumb luck."

It takes all the self-restraint I can muster not to raise an eyebrow at him in disbelief. My mother…an employee for the DSD? If it wouldn't reveal that we're lying, I'd laugh. My mother works for an insurance company—the closest she comes to torturing people is denying them cover when they make a claim.

Pushing the sheer absurdity of the notion aside, why would Ezra say my mother works for the DSD after he was so insistent no one find out about his brother? Won't the people here view me as an even bigger threat if they think my mother works for the most feared institution in the State? Then again, we needed a believable explanation to account for the coat—too many people at The Vega saw me that day—and without a plausible cover story, it would be easy enough to discover the truth if someone here wanted to dig deeply enough or poke at the holes in Ezra's lie. As for the rest of what he's said, about our meeting being nothing more than coincidence, no one else was part of our brief conversation that day. No one knew why I was really there or that I knew exactly who Ezra was the moment I saw him. But the coat…

Everyone at The Vega saw it.

An outcry of panic drowns out Ezra's voice, and as his gaze passes over the crowd, I realize why else he opted for this lie. He's feeling everyone out, seeing how they react upon learning that someone they know is related to an employee of the DSD. It's risky, but he wants to see if they'll turn on him if they find out about Dr. Richter.

"They'll come after her!" one woman screams, hysteria creeping into her tone.

"They'll kill us all!" cries another.

Countless outbursts flood the room with everyone trying to talk over each other, and the distrust I sensed from these people before is intensified now that they've swallowed Ezra's falsified version of the truth. But unlike before, when that suspicion was kept at a safe distance, the general feeling in the room is hostile.

Now, these people are out for my blood.

Ezra meets my gaze as the crowd inches forward, closing in on me, but he doesn't look worried or even surprised by this chain of events. Was this his plan all along? What is he hoping to achieve by stoking the flames of their fear?

Jenner pulls me back a few steps as Rai puts herself between me and those standing at the front of the group, her arms spread wide, forming a barrier. "They can't track her," she shouts over the uproar. "She cut out her ID chip—"

The crack of a gunshot brings an end to the chaos, silencing everyone in the room. All eyes turn to Ezra, whose hand is raised high above his head, tightly clutching his pistol.

"Let me finish," he says, his voice stern, like a parent disciplining their children. "Even if the State was interested in locating Wynter, it would struggle to find her since her tracking chip is gone. She cut it out before we met at The Vega. As it stands, the only person at risk here is her mother, who will now be viewed as a traitor on the basis of helping her child escape. That's how the State will swing it to cover the scandal, and the missing coat will be all the proof it needs to convict."

His words fade to a soft murmur in the back of my mind as dread pools in the pit of my stomach, a poison slowly flooding my system. He's right. I remember thinking as much when Jenner told me the story about his family and how they were all executed at Termination when he disappeared from their lives. Mother and I got lucky when Father was arrested, but what about when I was taken into custody after my placement exam? She had seemed so calm that day with the Enforcers stood on either side of her, but what happened after that? Is my mother still alive, or did she succumb to the same fate as my father?

"So, she sacrificed her mother to save herself? Is that really the kind of person we want here?" a woman at the front of the group asks, her tone biting.

Her words are a slap to the face, and it takes all the self-restraint I can muster not to flinch. If it wouldn't jeopardize our cover, I'd set the record straight about exactly the kind of person my mother is.

Luckily, I don't have to.

"We've already spoken to Wynter about that, and she has assured us her mother is every bit the heartless savage the DSD is known for recruiting. If anything, she did us a favor by framing her. One less monster for us to deal with."

My heart seizes at that word. *Monster.* Doubt shivers through me. Despite everything she's done to earn the title, my mother still isn't as bad as me. Between the two of us, *I'm* the murderer.

Between us, I'm the real monster.

When no one speaks up again, Ezra continues. "I know you're afraid, but just try to remember how *you* felt when you first left life in the State to join PHOENIX. We didn't know you, and yet, we never treated you the way we're all treating Wynter now. She isn't the first of us to have ties to the DSD. If you'll recall, we even saved some of you from a one-way trip to Termination. This isn't anything new, so why are we treating her as if she's different?" He pauses a moment, letting what he's said sink in before adding, "I'm asking you to trust me the same way you did when you came here. I didn't lie to you then, and I'm not lying to you now. I promise, she isn't a threat."

Sure, I agree. *So long as I don't leave.*

Ezra's eyes meet mine, and, in that moment, I know we're thinking the same thing. If I were to wind up back in the hands of the DSD, it's almost guaranteed Dr. Richter would use me to hunt down PHOENIX. He would tear open my mind and rip out my thoughts until every last rebel was accounted for.

The only way that won't happen is if he never finds me again. The only way that won't happen is if I never leave this place.

"And if the DSD *is* looking for her? What then?"

A middle-aged man with pale blue eyes and ashy blond hair moves to the front of the crowd. I recognize him immediately. It was his birthday that everyone was celebrating earlier.

The birthday I interrupted with my seizure.

He looks up at Ezra, crossing his arms. Unlike the others, his expression is calm but pressing, as if demanding an answer. As if he's entitled to one.

A spark of curiosity festers within me, and as I study his face, I remember how Ezra dodged my question when I asked about his authority here and how Rai had insisted he isn't in charge. But what about this man? He's at least twenty years older than either of them, making him a more suitable age for leadership.

Could he be the one who's been making every decision about my presence here?

Ezra offers a nonchalant shrug. "Well, if the DSD *is* looking for her, it's probably in our best interest to ensure they don't find her. We're in a position of power if we have what they want."

Although his words hold no malice, my heart still beats against my ribcage as the doubts I told myself to ignore flare up again, overtaking my thoughts.

I knew before I went looking for Ezra that he and the others in PHOENIX might not accept me, just like I knew I was walking into the middle of a decades—if not centuries—long war. But after everything I've been told, after everything Rai and Jenner have done to make me feel welcome, is this what it's come to? Is this why Ezra's taking my side now and trying so hard to get me to trust him? After everything he said to me…am I only a pawn?

Or is this just another lie to protect me?

Once again, I'm reminded of the last thing Dr. Richter said, just before I escaped the DSD.

"If you think you can trust him, you're wrong."

I didn't want to believe him then. I still don't. But I can't deny that part of me wonders if he's right.

Can I really trust Ezra Laramie?

"So, she's a tool against the enemy?" someone asks, calling out from the back of the room.

This idea spreads through the space like a ravenous wildfire, moving over every face staring at me. Several members nod their approval while others look at me, confused—probably trying to figure out how I can possibly be used to their benefit.

The whole time, Jenner's hand stays on my shoulder. His grip tightens to console me, but I find little comfort in his touch as the discontented mob moves forward. If anything, his hand is a cage. It holds me in place, refusing to let go.

Maybe I made a mistake coming here.

This isn't the first time this thought has crossed my mind, but I brushed it off and told myself I was just being paranoid. But, now, as I stare out at the crowd, I realize my suspicions were right. I don't belong here.

And I never will.

Another gunshot cuts through the air, returning the room to a tense state of silence. Lowering his arm, Ezra jumps down from the crate.

He steps toward the group, which parts down the middle, making way for his approach. Once he's standing in the center of the room, he spins in a slow circle, looking at each face in turn.

"Why are any of you here? Perhaps you joined PHOENIX following the death of a loved one, or maybe you were fed up with the unjust nature of our society. Either way, you wanted an out and we gave you one. It's no different for her."

Every set of eyes in the crowd follows the direction of his outstretched finger, landing on me. The scrutiny of their combined gazes sends a rolling shudder over my skin.

"If we abandon her now just because we're afraid, then what the hell do we stand for?" he growls.

Another unsettled murmur casts a cloud over the room. Some people voice their uncertainty, while others hang back, too afraid to speak. Really, who can blame any of them for reacting this way? They're worried their sole means of survival is threatened, and thanks to me, everything they've worked so hard for could change or collapse at any moment.

I never wanted to negatively affect anyone's life—I just wanted to save my own, and now, my selfishness has put these people in danger, more so than they even realize. Everyone here has sacrificed so much already. It isn't right that we're asking them to risk what little they have left to protect me, someone they don't even know. I haven't earned that loyalty.

I don't deserve it.

Ezra keeps talking—his voice building in volume and urgency, ringing in my ears—and I gape at him, hardly able to believe what I'm hearing. My heart picks up speed, beating in time with each syllable. "By accepting those who run, we make ourselves stronger. And that strength will, in turn, make the State weak! Wynter is one of us now. So, let's start acting like it."

Why is he doing this?

Why is he fighting for me?

An ominous hush blankets the crowd, but with the silence comes something that wasn't there before. I glimpse whatever it is in their faces, their expressions now shed of that familiar suspicion.

I risk a glance at Ezra, and although he meets my questioning gaze, he says nothing.

One by one, the people gathered in the room shuffle toward me, but their advance lacks the anger and hostility it held before. Regardless, fear bubbles under my skin, and I hold myself still, ready to face their judgment. Instead, they each take a turn welcoming me, with some even going so far as to also offer a kind word or smile. I struggle to think of anything to say in response, unnerved by this strange procession.

As the crowd thins—everyone departing the room now that the meeting is over—my eyes keep straying to Ezra's. Once everyone has gone, he crosses the empty space, closing the distance between us. Rai repositions herself in front of me and pats my hand, although her expression is cautious.

Beside me, Jenner crosses his arms. "Well, *that* was interesting. Quite the yarn you spun there, Ez. You don't really believe they're all okay with this or that anyone actually bought that lie, do you?"

"I'm not an idiot," Ezra scoffs. "Although, it would've been fine if Nolan hadn't opened his mouth. I just needed to buy some time so I can figure out what to do and how to guarantee Wynter's safety."

"*We,*" Rai corrects him. "And you know, maybe we won't need to do anything. We don't even know if the DSD is still looking for her."

Ezra and I both stare at her, giving her the same dubious look. Rai glances between us, raising her eyebrows.

"Of course, they are." I shake my head. "Richter won't stop until he's found me. You don't—"

My mouth snaps shut, cutting off the rest of that sentence. I was about to say they don't know what he's like, but then I remembered that's not true at all. Ezra and Rai probably know Dr. Richter better than anyone. Even me.

Unless he really has changed since they knew him, in which case, my pointing that out will only serve to make them both feel worse. The situation is volatile enough already without me adding any fuel to the fire.

Ezra lets out a long, withering sigh. "I have a really bad feeling about all this. I just wish we could know what he's planning."

As he says this, Jenner and Rai both look at me, and the same unspoken question is written across each of their hopeful faces. I know what they're thinking without having to ask.

If we knew what Dr. Richter was planning, we could assess the risk and make our own plans accordingly. Plans to keep everyone here safe, even me. Plans that might actually give me a future.

And they want me to be the one to find that information. They want me to use my visions to help them. Trouble is, I can't control this power. Like I tried to tell Dr. Richter, I'm of no use to anyone.

Ezra flashes them both a steely glare, clenching his jaw. "No. That's not an option."

"Why?" Rai asks. "I mean, I know it's not ideal, but, if we want to be sure, what other choice do we have? It's not like we have anyone on the inside to help us, and it wouldn't take much for someone like Nolan to pick apart those lies you just told. Besides, don't you think it should be Wynter's choice? Let's ask her—"

"No," Ezra says again, his voice a threatening snarl. "We aren't using her like that. Case closed."

"Hey, earlier you were just as eager to toss her out of here as everyone else," Jenner says. "What's with the sudden change of heart? Why are you so against the idea of her helping us?"

Variations of this question have been nagging at me, clawing at my insides where they sit, heavy, in my chest. They've lived there since Ezra told me I was no longer their prisoner, and they reside there still now, questioning my wavering determination to trust him.

I want to believe his intentions are good. I want to believe his desire to keep me safe is out of remorse for what happened to his mother and not because of some diabolical scheme to use me. But I'm not so sure I do believe that. I'm not convinced he doesn't have other motives. After all, my time with Dr. Richter has made me aware of the deceits people are capable of.

The seconds tick by without anyone speaking, and in that silence, I suddenly hear it—what it is Ezra's refusing to say. The unspoken truth hits me with the force of a lightning strike.

Of course, I know. If I'm really honest with myself, I think I've known for a while. How could I not, given what happens every time I have one of my visions? The effects this condition have had on my body are proof enough of the fate waiting for me.

How else could this all possibly end?

"Because he thinks it'll kill me," I breathe.

Ezra recoils, and the look on his face cracks my heart into a thousand irreparable pieces, leaving behind a black hole in my chest. I glance away, unable to bear the pain I find in his gaze that seems to mimic my own so acutely. To my horror, the expressions on Jenner's and Rai's faces are worse.

Rai looks at Ezra, her gaze pitying. "Your mother died in an asylum, Ezra, and with her, died any answers about what she went through in there. We don't know it was her illness." Her somber tone implies the many other unspoken things that could have ended his mother's life.

"We don't *not* know it was her illness either," he retorts. "Austin was pretty damn convinced of it."

"Austin was in denial and was looking for anything to blame that would give him some sense of purpose." She sighs, and it's a heavy, weary sound that tells me they've had this conversation before.

"He's right," I mutter, the words escaping of their own volition, triggered by my acceptance of the facts.

And the fact is, this disease will kill me.

Rai's eyes dart to mine. "Wynter…" Her tone is gentle, as if she's talking me off a ledge.

As she takes a step toward me, I stumble backward, shying away from her hand, which reaches out to touch my shoulder. She freezes in place, and the wounded way she stares at me makes me want to bury myself under a rock and never resurface.

So, I do the next best thing.

Their voices chase after me as I turn and run from the room as fast as my legs can move. I ignore their calls, sprinting blindly through the corridors, racking my brain for the best place to go. Where the hell can I go?

As I run, I realize how frightened I am. At my weakest point, I would've welcomed death into my arms, but now, the idea of it is like a slow-moving drug trying to paralyze me. It creeps through my veins, crippling my every breath.

At first, I feared death at the hands of the DSD. Then I escaped and the new threat became PHOENIX. As the days passed and I grew closer to Jenner and Rai, that fear began to fade and I dared to imagine a new life for myself. But there is no life to be found in death, and death from this disease is unavoidable. I can't run from it. I can't fight it.

My only option is to succumb.

Tears obscure my vision, but when I wipe them away, new ones rise to take their place, blurring the path ahead. A growing heat attacks my body, the corridor increasingly hazy and warm until the growing inferno seems to burn through my flesh, consuming me.

A fever presses down on my head, hot and heavy and relentless in its fury, matched only by the brutal stabbing pain in my temples. I continue to run, but my legs weaken with every step.

I fling myself through the next open doorway and stagger forward until the details of the room take on some form of clarity, sliding into view. *The washroom. I'm back in the washroom.* Dizzy, I throw myself into the nearest shower cubicle, my fingers convulsing against the cold metal handle. A scream breaches my lips when the water emerges from the pipes and strikes against my fiery skin.

The vision explodes in my head at the very same moment the water devours me, the images sharp and eerily clear, as if what I'm seeing is actually happening. As if it's in front of me.

As if it's real.

The emptiness. The debris. The destruction. Every detail is the same, aside from one addition.

This time, I also see myself.

A steady trickle of blood streams from my ears and nose, mixing on my trembling lips with the tears spilling from my eyes, which are entirely black. A choked sob escapes me, warped by the harsh wind.

"I'm afraid!" I cry. "I don't want to kill anyone else. I don't want to do this. I don't want to die!"

A sharp breath catches in my chest, and as the image around me shifts into that terrible ending with the world swallowed by a blinding light, it occurs to me how wrong I've been about everything.

What I witnessed at the DSD might've led me to PHOENIX, but nothing I saw was ever about them at all. Or about Ezra…despite the central role he's seemed to play in those visions. From the beginning, this has always been about me. About this disease.

About what I am.

Rai. Jenner. Ezra. Everyone here… They're nothing but unwilling victims I'll drag down with me when this all finally comes to an end.

The walls crack beneath my touch. My fingers slip away, rushing upward to claw at my skull, as the pressure building inside me teeters on the brink of exploding. With a scream, it rushes out of me in a wave of release.

The pipes in the walls burst through the concrete, showering me with a surge of water and pounding into my aching bones, forcing my already weak body down to the floor. As the ongoing rush of water pummels my skin, I surrender to the pain and to impending unconsciousness, lacking the will to fight any longer.

Darkness casts a thick veil across my eyes, and I give in to its call. As I do, one tormenting thought rolls through my head.

The vision has always been about me.

I am the one who will end the world.

EIGHTEEN

"WYNTER."

Someone calls my name, but I can't see who they are.

Everything is hazy.

All I'm aware of is pain.

I'm trapped somewhere between unconsciousness and waking with the fog in my head muffling the voices around me. I can't tell them apart. I can't even remember who they belong to.

"Is she breathing?"

"I don't know—"

I try to wrap my head around the words in my ears, but the pictures overtaking my thoughts make it difficult to concentrate. They come together, forming a vision, and the world ends in front of me just as it did that first time. There's nothing I can do to stop the destruction. Nothing I can do to protect anyone from the person I now know will cause that future.

From me.

"Why is there so much blood?"

Static distorts my surroundings, warping the image. When it settles, forming a clear picture again, Ezra steps into my line of vision—his eyes locked on mine and a gun in his hand. Tears leave streak marks on his cheeks, cutting through the ash and dirt on his skin.

"I'm sorry, Wynter."

Why? I want to ask, but my lips refuse to move. *Why do you keep saying you're sorry?*

Static again. This time, when it passes, I only see myself—or rather, the monster this disease is turning me into. Black soulless eyes. Blood covering my skin, symbolizing the evil power rotting within me. It's like a parasite weaving itself through my body. There can be no running from it. No escaping it. This frightened but deadly creature...

"Help her. Do whatever you have to."

This is what I will become.

Warm arms swaddle my legs and torso, lifting me up as if I weigh nothing. As the ground falls away, a soft voice speaks into my ear. "Wynter..."

Tears burn my eyes as recognition tugs at my brain, guiding me toward a place I have no hope of reaching in my current state. A place I'm not sure I'll ever reach again. Darkness washes over everything, pulling me into the long-awaited embrace of what I'm sure can only be death.

I don't want to die.

"Please, wake up..."

A strangled breath expands in my throat as my eyes flutter open, the lids heavy, weighted with exhaustion, but the fatigue quickly ebbs. As I force them wide, the room around me comes into sharp focus, and I glimpse the plain walls of my new living quarters—the one part of this compound that's mine.

I blink. No one else is here. Despite the echo of voices still speaking to me, I'm alone.

This must be a dream. I turn in place. *Of course, it's a dream,* I chide myself. Why else would I be standing when only seconds ago I was sleeping? No other explanation makes sense.

Unless, of course, this is something else altogether.

"Wynter."

A shiver shoots up my spine as the familiar timbre of Ezra's voice seeps into my ears. I know it so well now. It's always in my head, always speaking to me. Haunting me. Interlaced in my every waking thought.

A dizzy spell leaves me unsteady on my feet as I glance at where he stands in the doorway, glaring at me with an incensed expression that rips the air right out of my lungs.

"Ezra—"

"You can't do this," he growls, interrupting me. Anger pushes out every word and burns behind his eyes, unnerving me. I've never seen him so irate before, and that's saying something considering how many times he's held a gun to my head.

I gape at him, swallowing, and hesitation creeps into my tone as I dare to ask, "Do what?"

A wary breath spills from my lungs when he doesn't respond. Bracing myself,

I repeat the question, my racing pulse throbbing across every inch of my body until I can feel my beating heart everywhere.

Again, he doesn't answer me, and when I repeat myself for a second time, someone else talks over me, overpowering my voice with their own.

"I have to."

Confusion throws me even further off balance as it suddenly registers what I'm seeing and I transition from being at the center of this vision to a spectator on the outside of it all. My mouth goes dry as I pivot until my gaze settles on the other me—the future me—where she sits on the edge of the mattress. She busies herself unwrapping and then rewrapping her wrist on repeat, avoiding Ezra's seething gaze. She doesn't see me. To her and to the Ezra at this point in time, I'm nothing more than a ghost.

"Look at me," he pleads, glaring at her.

When she doesn't, he storms toward the bed, tears the bandage from her hands, and tosses it aside. Neither one of them spares a second glance at the bundled dressing as it falls to the floor.

"You have no idea what you're getting yourself into," he says. His tone, though abrasive, is edged with panic.

"And you do?" Her eyes jump up to meet his.

I don't recognize the indignation stretched across her pale face. *My* face. I didn't even know I was capable of it. Even during my time at the DSD, I don't recall experiencing anything quite that potent, not even when I killed that attendant. Except fear, of course.

Fear is the one emotion I've always been permitted to feel.

A scream of frustration builds in my throat as I watch the two of them stare each other down, waiting for the other to concede. Why is he so furious with me? What did I do to upset him this time?

I'd wager the other me has these answers, but she doesn't share them with me, unaware of my presence. I wish she would, even just a hint.

Anything to help me avoid this.

What good is having the power to see the future if I can't understand what I'm seeing? What good is this power if it can't be used to sidestep the events I'd rather not happen?

Another shiver rocks my body as the friction in the small room reaches its breaking point. Shaking her head, the future me pushes up from the bed, and for a moment, she hesitates where she stands next to Ezra, her fingers stretching outward, almost as if she's reaching for his. She freezes with her fingertips less than an inch from his hand, then drops her arm and steps toward the door.

It's at this moment I witness something I could've never anticipated. Something I might not believe if I hadn't already experienced the accuracy of these visions first-hand.

Before the other me has even taken two steps, Ezra snakes his arms around her waist from behind and pulls her body flush to his chest, preventing her escape. She goes still in his embrace as he holds her close, her eyes—one blue, one green—impossibly wide.

Their breaths weave together, ragged and wanting, and slowly, he spins her around to face him before leaning down, closing the distance between them. Warmth flushes her cheeks, turning the skin a deep red, as she rises up onto the tips of her toes—meeting him halfway—her body acting on reflex in the heat of the moment. To any other onlooker, it would seem as if she's done this a thousand times before. But to me, the shock of this moment runs deep.

I let out a breath and run a fingertip over my lips, and I swear I can almost feel him, even though I'm not the one Ezra's kissing. My pulse spikes when the two pull apart, and, for the first time since this vision began, the expression the other me wears on her face matches the stunned look plastered on mine. Bewilderment sinks into the depths of her eyes as she takes a shaking step away, forcing some space between them again.

I try to speak, even though they won't hear me, because I don't understand what the hell's going on and I can tell the other me doesn't either. How could she? Ezra and I are from different worlds. Maybe it didn't start that way, but he escaped our warped society far sooner than I did. He's had time to adjust to our inbuilt emotions whereas I still struggle to know what I'm feeling. The desperate look in his gaze…

I don't know what to do with it.

"I don't want you to go," he whispers.

I sense his warm breath against my cheeks when he speaks, as if the two of us are connected across time. I suppose, from that very first vision, we have been. Despite the suspicion, despite the distrust, I always sensed something between us, anchoring our fates together in a way I couldn't understand or explain. And from that very first moment I saw him, something in me began to change.

From that moment, I knew I would never be the same.

And I haven't been. Since I met Ezra, Jenner, and Rai, everything I've always been told to suppress has been steadily surfacing, exposing emotions I've never been permitted to feel without me even realizing what was happening. Ever since I found Ezra, the rules I followed to survive my day-to-day life in the State have ceased to exist, not because I've forgotten them but because they don't need to. Here, I can allow myself to be who I really am, whoever that person is.

Here, I think I finally understand freedom.

"Stay here," he murmurs. "Stay with me."

Stay? I blink, unsure what he means. Where else would I go? Where else *could* I go?

A veil of darkness whisks me away, and as it fades, my eyes open, thrusting me back into reality. As my hazy vision adjusts to waking, I consider the possibility that what I saw just now was only a dream. That seems far more plausible than the notion of Ezra and I ever being together that way. But, if what I just witnessed *was* a dream and not a vision, why would I see that?

What could've triggered those thoughts about Ezra?

A sudden vertigo swirls through my throbbing head, my scalp burning as the pain in my temples urges bile up into my mouth. I swallow it, pushing down the nausea until I'm confident I won't vomit or choke.

Exhaling, I take stock of my surroundings. I'm in my new quarters, just as I was in my dream, but this time, I'm actually lying in bed, my head sinking deep into the pillow.

See? I say to myself. *It was a dream. Just a dream.*

My body aches in protest as I push myself up, my muscles and bones screaming in pain as if every inch of me has been broken and reset, healed, then broken again in a cycle of torture. Unlike in the storage room, when I battled infection and I—according to Rai—was lucid enough at times for her to feed me small doses of soup, this time, an IV stand is positioned next to the bed on my right, the thin feeding tube trailing from the bag connected to my upper arm.

What's happened to me? Based on the way my head is pounding, I think I can assume the worst. Gradually, the memories resurface, confirming my fears, and I remember the cracking tiles in the shower, the burst of water knocking me down, the blood...

The vision where I end the world.

I bite back a sob as the memory of my terror spreads under my skin like a rash with no cure. A whimper parts my lips, and as a deep breath responds in the darkness beside me, I freeze, nearly collapsing back into my pillow in fear. Holding my breath, I squint at the shadowed person sitting in the solitary chair pushed up against the left side of the bed, my tired gaze locking on the dozing figure's face.

"Ezra...?"

How long has he been here? Has he stayed by my side the whole time I've been unconscious?

He starts when I mumble his name, bolting upright, his eyes blown wide, searching the shadows for danger where there is none. Unless, of course, you count me, which he should, especially after this most recent vision. When his gaze locks on mine, he visibly settles, letting out a breath of relief.

"You're awake," he says, the words weighted. Then, rubbing the sleep from his eyes, he asks, "How are you feeling?"

I cough to clear the dryness from my throat and force a one-shouldered shrug. "Honestly, I've felt better."

He lowers his gaze, his expression distraught. "I'm so sorry," he breathes, his voice barely audible.

Why? I want to ask, just like I've wanted to ask him a thousand times before. But the question is eclipsed by the recollection of those three fateful words that led me here. To him.

"I'm sorry, Wynter."

"Still not it." When he blinks at me, confusion creasing his brow, I manage a smile. "You're not off the hook yet."

Comprehension spreads across Ezra's face, and I can tell he's remembering the same moment I am, when he first gave me this room and I finally told him about my vision and the words he'll eventually say to me.

Despite the fleeting grin he offers back, his eyes swim with guilt. He stares at me with such remorse in his gaze, as if what's happening to me is somehow his fault, even though we both know it isn't. I can't even blame Dr. Richter for my condition, despite all the horrible things he did to encourage its progression.

No, if anyone is to blame, it's my mother for abandoning me to die as a result of these visions. Because that's what this disease will do.

It will kill me and take everyone I care about with it.

This realization crushes my chest, affecting me far more than I expect it to. I barely know these people. How have they buried themselves underneath my skin and in the depths of my heart so quickly? How, after being subjected to the harsh world I was raised in, did I not even notice I was letting them in?

Driven by a need for comfort, which I was always denied growing up in the State—even by my own mother—I reach out, squeezing Ezra's hand where it rests on his knee, touching him for the first and possibly only time, with what little strength I have left.

To my relief, he squeezes back.

"Where is everyone?" I ask, turning my face away slightly to hide the tears welling in my eyes.

"Sleeping." Ezra tugs his hand from mine and lifts his arms above his head, stretching, then sinks back into his seat with a sigh. "It's nearly dawn."

"How…" I hesitate, taking a moment to build up the courage to ask the only question that truly matters right now. "How long have I been out?"

Ezra seems reluctant to meet my gaze, his own rife with unease and something else… Something almost like fear. He only answers when I arch a questioning eyebrow at him. "Six days," he whispers.

A rush of panic ripples through me.

Nearly a week? It's been that long?

My teeth bite down hard on my lower lip until the metallic taste of blood fills my mouth. The longest my unconsciousness has lasted as a result of these visions has only been a half-day at most. To jump from that to an entire week…

Trepidation rips through me. I already knew my condition was worsening, but if things continue to progress the way they are now, then I don't have much time left.

My hands tremble in my lap as I consider what this drastic change could mean, not only for me but for everyone here. For Ezra, Jenner, and Rai. Is the abrupt escalation of my symptoms a sign that my apocalyptic vision is creeping closer?

How long before we're all out of time?

"There's something else." Ezra stares down at his fingers as if purposely avoiding my gaze, fidgeting with the hem of his shirt. "The other day, we received a transmission from someone who claims they want to work undercover for PHOENIX. He's a high-ranking member of the State. You've probably heard of him."

I blink, my brow furrowing, as I try to wrap my brain around such an impossible concept. Why would anyone installed in a position of power within the State's hierarchy want to switch sides?

"Who is it?" I ask in a breathless voice.

A long moment passes before Ezra looks up at me. "His name is Wren Bilken. He's a senior advisor for the State, who works in direct correspondence with the city magistrates. He's also the CEO of W. P. Headquarters."

My hands clench into fists, sending spasm-like jolts of pain up both of my arms, especially through my left wrist, which still aches from the incision where I cut out my chip. Right now, though, I barely notice the pain.

Wren Bilken. I met him once briefly when I was sixteen, and that one time was more than enough. He conducted my work placement interview and ultimately decided which sector I was projected to enter. He personally oversees all education leading up to the exam from the moment we're first old enough to enter school.

I only saw him two other times in my life—in the elevator at W. P. Headquarters and again on the screen, wishing us luck at the beginning of my exam.

Unease settles deep in my bones. Something isn't adding up. Why would Wren Bilken, of all people, have any desire to help PHOENIX? How could someone in his position benefit from the State losing power?

Plus, doesn't anyone find it suspicious that he sent this transmission only *after* I came here? The timing can't be coincidental, and if it is, why didn't Bilken reach out sooner? PHOENIX has been around for years, so why now? And how did he even figure out how to contact them?

What isn't Ezra telling me?

"It's a trap." The words breach my lips in a rush.

Ezra gives a stilted nod. "Probably. But even so, we'll take the bait. We don't really have any other choice in the matter."

I gape at him, startled by his cavalier attitude. What could the transmission have possibly said that warrants putting himself in harm's way? What did it say that could justify his death? Because that's what will happen if he goes. He'll die, and the answers I came here for will die along with him.

"Listen to me," I hiss, reaching for his hand again. Maybe if I touch him, he'll actually listen. "Wren Bilken isn't someone who will turn against the State. Whatever he's asking you to do, *don't*. This has the DSD written all over it."

The frustration running through me is like an itch I can't scratch. If my body wasn't still weak, I would jump out of this bed and shake some sense into him.

Scowling, Ezra rips his hand out of my grasp and jumps up from the chair with a huff. "By all means, give me another option," he begs. "You're new here, so you don't know what it's like. Living in isolation. Relying on generous benefactors for food and other necessary supplies. Rarely ever seeing the sun. We're basically a glorified homeless shelter, and honestly, I don't know how much longer we can survive this way." Groaning, he runs a hand through his hair. He looks exhausted, as if he hasn't slept in days. A pang of guilt strikes my chest. Considering how long I've been asleep, maybe he hasn't. "We've been waiting for an opportunity like this for a really, *really* long time. What Wren Bilken is offering could change everything for us."

"How?" I ask, the volume of my weak voice building strength. "What information is he willing to give you? What is he asking for in return?"

"Nothing." He answers a little too quickly, and I narrow my eyes, certain he's omitting something important. "He just wants us to meet him in person first to hammer out any details before we agree to anything permanent."

I glare at Ezra, amazed by how foolish he's being, especially since I know he isn't stupid. Something weird is going on. This is obviously a trap. He must know that as well as I do.

So, why is he going along with this plan?

"You could die." These words are like sawdust in my mouth.

His eyes latch back on mine, and he smiles. A small, sad expression that's all too reminiscent of how he looked at me in my vision.

"I know," he says, his tone resigned. "But I don't have a choice. It isn't my decision to make."

Whose is it, then? I'm tempted to press, but I've lost the will to argue about this. Nothing I say will change his mind. He's going, with or without my blessing.

Instead, in a half-hearted breath, I ask, "When are you leaving?"

He holds my gaze, his voice filling the space between us, which seems to span the width of an ocean in this somber moment. The air is heavy with something that feels strangely like mourning. "Tomorrow night."

So soon?

I think of all the days I've been asleep in this bed—how many hours I've wasted unconscious, which I could've spent getting to know Ezra better. Hours I could've spent learning who he really is and getting answers to the questions that have been piling up ever since that first vision of him. Hours I could've used to finally decide if I trust him, although, in my gut, I know that I can...and that I already do. Someone doesn't sit by your bed for six days while you're sick if they plan to stab you in the back.

So much wasted time...

What if these are our last moments together?

What if he doesn't come back from this mission?

I clamp down hard on the inside of my cheek. Although I'm silent on the outside, on the inside, I'm screaming.

"How will you get to wherever it is you're going?"

I don't really know why I ask. It doesn't matter, and the answer won't make any difference. Maybe I'm just trying to stall the inevitable. The more questions I ask, the longer he has to stay here with me where it's safe.

Safe...

A fluttering sensation stirs in my chest, like the wings of a butterfly beating against the bone cage surrounding my heart.

I wonder, when did his safety start mattering to me? Before this latest vision, before I slipped into a coma, I was still trying to figure out if I could trust him and dealing with the realization that this disease will eventually kill me. So, why does that seem so unimportant right now?

Why does my heart ache at the thought of him leaving?

It's the dream's fault, I tell myself. That dream of us kissing that's making me imagine something between us that isn't really there. Or maybe that's just an excuse I keep telling myself to avoid how much this whole situation reminds me of how I lost my father.

And I really don't want to lose anyone else.

"The compound is linked to a web of underground tunnels that have exit points throughout the city," Ezra explains, his tone steady. Distant. As if he's trying to push me away. "It's the safest method for us to travel without being seen since the State's scanners can't detect our heat signatures through all the metal underlay in the ground."

As he speaks, an idea strikes me as suddenly as those lightning-like bolts Dr. Richter drilled into my head so many times during each of his experiments. It's insane, but it's also the only way to keep us together.

Despite the unexpected friendships I've found in Jenner and Rai that have made me want to stay, I'm only here because of Ezra. He's not going anywhere without me until I figure out what part he plays in the future awaiting us, however small it may be. Every day, that vision is inching closer, and the time I have left to understand it and how it comes to happen is running out. We can't waste any of it apart.

"I want to go with you."

It's a futile request. I'd be putting myself in danger, which is the opposite of what Ezra has said he wants, and by leaving this place, I'd only be making it easier for the State to find me. For Dr. Richter to find me. Not to mention, I doubt anyone here would actually *let* me leave considering the threat to their safety if I were to tell anyone the location of the compound.

Regardless, I can't bear the idea of Ezra leaving me behind, of going where I can't follow. Not if there's a chance he might not come back, despite what my vision keeps showing me. As I already told him, I'm not a rebel. I'm not here for PHOENIX.

I'm here for him.

Besides, he saved my life at The Vega when he had no logical reason to, and I guess a part of me feels like I owe him. Maybe, by going on this mission, I'll find a way to repay him...even if all the future holds for me is pain. Pain he might be responsible for.

Pain that'll spur him to say those three words.

Ezra sits back down in the chair, fixing his bloodshot eyes on the floor, staring at nothing in particular.

"What?" I goad. "Aren't you going to say no or try to tell me that's a bad idea—"

"No," he murmurs, cutting me off. "If there's one thing I've learned in the short time we've known each other, it's that you're nearly as stubborn as I am. Besides, Rai and Jenner will be glad for the company."

I let out a stunned breath. "Seriously?"

I was so prepared to fight him on the matter that him relenting so easily takes me aback. I don't know what to think of it. What happened to keeping me safe? What happened to someone else making the calls about what I'm allowed to do here and where I'm allowed to go, even with supervision? I had expected at least some kickback from him, not this weird capitulation that doesn't make any sense.

Another thought occurs to me. Is he breaking some rule by saying yes to my request? Or is this just a ruse to get me to do exactly what the person in charge here wants me to do? Maybe he always knew I'd ask.

The sadness in his gaze makes me fear the latter.

"Sure." He shrugs. "You can be our lookout. You'll see the enemy coming long before any of us do."

A smile splits his face, and he lets out a forced laugh that makes me wince. I fail to find anything funny about this. Ezra is a walking contradiction—one minute, I'm a prisoner, the next, he's determined to keep me safe, and now this…whatever the hell this is. I can barely keep up with how often he changes his mind.

Then there was his vehement opposition when Rai and Jenner asked about using my power. How is what they wanted me to do any different than what he's suggesting now?

If anything, his reaction back then exposes the truth behind his choice at this moment. After what happened to his mother, he wouldn't want me to use my power this way—not unless someone else is forcing his hand. Not unless there's something he doesn't want me to know. Something he's determined to hide.

And I'd be willing to bet that something is why he's agreed to let me tag along.

Dread claws at my skin, but I bury it down deep and urge myself to think only of the task ahead. Regardless of what's coming, we'll face it together.

I will follow him, wherever this transmission leads.

NINETEEN

I PRESS MY BACK AGAINST the cold wall, trying my best to stay out of everyone's way. I want to help, but I don't know where to begin or even how to prepare myself for the task ahead. This mission will go against everything the State has instilled in me over the last eighteen years. Every rule I followed, every ideal it taught me to aim for…

What we do tonight will unravel them all.

I can't help wondering who I'll become without the State always whispering in my ear, telling me who I'm meant to be. Once we make contact with Bilken, I'll be just the same as everyone else in PHOENIX—an outcast who's turned her back on society. There will be no returning to the life I once knew.

Not that I ever planned on going back anyway or that it's even an option given what I am, not to mention my impending death and the potential destruction of the world if I can't figure out how to change that future. Even if I hadn't met Jenner and Rai and learned the truth about PHOENIX and the attacks on the State, the DSD ensured going back to a normal life would never be an option for me. I'm stuck on this path.

Now, I need to embrace it.

My chest rises and falls with a sigh as my eyes scan over the shelves laden with supplies. So far, I've only filled my pack with water and food, although I should really be looking at the weapons. I've been avoiding those particular shelves out of cowardice and sheer inexperience. I don't know anything about guns. Even if I held one, I wouldn't know how to use it.

Ezra loads ammunition into his pistol, and I wince at the sharp click of metal on metal as the slide locks back into place. My eyes follow the deft movements of his long fingers until his hand suddenly freezes around the black grip. He looks up at me, his hazel gaze hard and unreadable. The hairs on the back of my neck stand on end, and I shift my weight from foot to foot, uncomfortable beneath the heat of his stare.

What could he be thinking right now? Perhaps, he's second-guessing his earlier decision and has changed his mind about letting me come. I wouldn't be surprised. If anything, I'm stunned he hasn't backtracked on it sooner. I still can't figure out why he so readily agreed to let me join them after making such a fuss about keeping me safe and especially after insisting he wouldn't use my power because of the risk to my life.

As he crosses the room toward me, I can already imagine it—his stern voice stating I'm staying behind and my own pitiful attempts to protest that decision. What would I even say? What *could* I say that wouldn't end up sounding like the ramblings of a mad woman?

My lips part to speak, but my lungs release only air.

Ezra's eyes are probing as he comes to a standstill in front of me. I gulp down a breath, anticipating his order. But it never comes.

Instead, he extends his hand, his fingers spread out in offering. The gun he was prepping before lies flat against his palm.

"You'll need it."

I blink, stammering, "A-Are you sure?"

Because I'm sure as hell not.

A grin pulls at his lips as he nods. "I trust you. Besides, we should all go armed, just in case."

"I trust you." A weird sensation floods my chest at these words, and yet, they still don't make me feel any better about the situation. Regardless, I wrap my fingers around the metal—the surface warm from Ezra's touch—taking a firm hold of the handle to appease him. It's heavier than I thought it would be, which only serves to heighten my unease.

Although I've killed before, it wasn't intentional—I didn't realize what was happening, couldn't control what I was doing. But this… Using this gun would be my choice. If I'm going to carry this weapon, I need to be prepared for the very real likelihood it may be used to take someone's life. If I pull that trigger, I won't be able to blame my condition for my actions or pretend the resulting death was a terrible accident. It would be entirely my fault, and I would have to carry that guilt.

Could I do it?

Could I use this weapon to kill if I had to?

As the others prepare their supplies, I consider whether it's necessary for me to have a gun of my own. I don't have a clue what I'm doing with it, and everyone else is already armed. What if I shoot the wrong person by mistake? What if I accidentally hurt Jenner or Rai?

Or Ezra. Nausea grips my stomach at the thought, although I struggle to understand why. We barely know each other—he's a stranger to me, even more so than the others—and yet…the notion of his death hurts the most.

But am I really afraid of losing *him*, or am I afraid of what will happen if I never get the answers I came for? Without those answers, without understanding his part in my vision and the why behind those three words, will I be helpless to change that future?

Will I be helpless to stop myself from becoming a monster?

Jenner brushes up next to me, making me jump, and slings an arm across my shoulders. "Don't worry," he says, his breath hot on my ear. "I'll take care of you. But, if it would make you feel better, I can give you some one-on-one shooting lessons."

My brow hitches upward as he takes a step back, pulling his arm away from my neck. Turning, he lifts his gun and smiles.

"All you have to do is find your target, and once you have him in your sights, release the safety and just squeeze the trigger."

Time seems to slow as I follow his gaze, and my heart almost stops when I see where he's aiming.

"Bang!"

My hand flies to my mouth as I gasp, but Ezra only seems annoyed by the outburst. Reaching forward, he closes his fist around the end of Jenner's gun and pushes the barrel away from his chest.

"Stop messing around," he snaps.

Jenner snorts and hits Ezra in the left bicep, who then punches him back, suppressing a grin. I glance between them, unnerved by this faux display of violence considering the situation we're about to find ourselves in. At least Ezra and Jenner seem to be getting along again.

As I watch them laugh and joke with each other, it really hits me what we might be walking into. How many of us will make it out of this, if any? Perhaps that's why Jenner feels the need to hide behind a shield of light-hearted behavior. If that's the case, I don't blame him.

I don't want to think about what awaits us either.

"Is everyone nearly ready?" Rai asks. Her fingers adjust the thick strap across her chest, which is attached to a flat bag on her back.

"As ready as we can be," Ezra says. His eyes fix on mine. "Are you ready?"

Panic constricts my lungs, suffocating my breaths, but I nod, although my terror is slowly eating away at me from the inside. I'm frightened, not only for myself or for the others who have agreed to go on this mission, but for all those who we're leaving behind.

What will become of them if we don't come back? How will they know what's happening or if any of us have been captured?

How will they know if it's safe to stay here?

These worries beat around in my skull as I shadow the determined steps of our party through the compound, hanging at the back of the group. The corridors we traverse seem to go on for miles until we enter an area I wasn't shown during my tour.

The passages here are dark and narrow—a maze most likely built with the intention of disorienting any intruders. I find myself noting the directions we turn. Left. Right. Right. Left again. We carry on for at least twenty minutes, but the pattern changes every time I think I'm getting the hang of the route, putting a dent in the mental path I've been drawing.

I can understand the precaution. If an enemy were to overrun this place, the maze would have them turning in circles, giving those living here time to escape. Assuming they have another way out.

Eventually, we wind up in a cramped, tapered room that appears, at first glance, to be a dead end. Squinting through the shadows, I note the outline of a hatch door embedded in the opposite wall.

This is it, I realize when Ezra steps forward.

The first leg of our journey starts here.

I stand back while everyone else congregates around the circular door, once again doing my best to stay out of their way. Accompanying us are three older men who haven't said a single combined word since we set off from the compound's supply room. The man with the bulky frame, whose bulging muscles threaten to explode through his shirt, is named Duke, but I never caught what the other two are called. Frankly, I don't care enough to ask.

A deafening metallic squeal cuts through the silence as Duke grips the large wheel attached to the hatch and turns it three times, his large arms straining. At the end of the third turn, he yanks the door open, letting in a rush of stale air and heat.

One by one, we step into the blackness of the tunnel beyond the opening. A thin layer of water covers the ground, soaking the outside of our shoes, but my feet stay dry thanks to the thick socks and rubber inserts Rai gave me just this morning. Now, I get why she was so insistent I wear them.

Beams of light illuminate the rounded walls as the others all click on their flashlights. I reach into my pack in a hurry to do the same, always keeping one eye on Ezra, watching him at all times out of my peripheral vision. He huddles with Rai, shining his light over the black disk-like device in her hands, which looks vaguely familiar. As a hologram materializes in the air just above the gadget, it hits me where I recognize it from. It's identical to the one Dr. Richter used to show me the surveillance footage of my exam.

Ezra moves the beam of his light in a circle, signaling for us to gather around the glowing map of what I now realize is the tunnel system. The layout is so intricate and complex it would take me weeks to work out the tangled web of passages or understand where each one leads. Rai, on the other hand, seems to read the map with ease.

After examining the hovering image for barely more than ten seconds, she stores the device back inside her pack and retrieves her flashlight. Turning, she directs the blinding beam down the left side of the tunnel where the route branches off in a fork and leads in two separate directions.

"It's this way," she says.

The others each make a note of the route, and then we all follow Rai through the waterlogged passage, walking for ages without speaking a word. The only sound is the repetitive splash of our footsteps, the echo of which trails our group like a stranger stalking our every move in the shadows.

I cast a wary glance behind me—not because I'm afraid someone's following us but because every step brings us farther away from the compound and from relative safety. Despite the community's cold reception toward me, the compound still felt a thousand times safer than where we are now and especially more so than where we're heading.

So, why did I leave? Did I really opt to come just to stay close to Ezra—a guy I don't even know all that well, who may or may not play a vital part in the future where I destroy the world? Sometimes, I question my judgment, especially since I'm risking a one-way trip back to the DSD if we get caught. Is my need for answers about my condition—about Ezra—the only reason I'm going on this mission? Or is something else guiding me down this path?

Something like friendship.

I sense a camaraderie with Jenner and Rai that I never knew growing up in the State. Before them, I didn't have friends—such a concept was incompatible with how I was raised. But what about Ezra? Is he my friend?

What exactly are my feelings toward him?

My pulse quickens, my hitched breaths deafening in the dank hush of the encompassing tunnels as images from my dream fill my head once again. A shiver rolls over my skin, but I force my thoughts elsewhere.

To distract myself from the mental picture of Ezra's lips against mine, I reflect on what I've been told about the transmission from Bilken and, for the first time, urge my brain to show me what's going to happen once we get through this tunnel. I've never tried to call to my power before, mainly out of repulsion toward the pain that comes with it, but the fear lurking under my skin is worse than any possible side effects.

Although I insisted on joining this mission, I can't shake the suspicion that my greatest nightmare awaits us at the end of this path. If I'm right and the DSD is behind this…

We're all as good as dead.

Slowing my steps, I focus my thoughts…but nothing happens. No vision, no static, or flickers of people or places. Nothing. Not a single glimpse of the future, past, or anything remotely helpful at all.

I push out a disgruntled breath and press on, picking up the pace to catch up to the others. I'm so consumed by my apprehension of the unknown, I fail to notice Ezra walking beside me.

"Are you nervous?" he asks in a quiet breath.

I flinch at the sound of his voice, and he frowns, his eyes hooded and dark with what seems like concern.

When I don't say anything, he lowers his voice even more. "Whatever happens, I'll look out for you. I promise I won't let anyone hurt you."

"Why?" I counter, rounding on him. "Not that long ago, you were ready to kill me yourself. Now, what? You're suddenly my protector?"

A swell of guilt bubbles up in my chest. I don't know why I'm so angry, but I do know my frustration is misplaced. Even if Ezra is hiding something from me, I also know he's trying to make amends for how I've been treated, and, I imagine, attempting to fix some of the damage his demented brother inflicted on me. Why should I begrudge him that? If anything, I should encourage that forgiveness since it'll only bring us closer and perhaps clarify this mystifying connection between us.

There's also the possibility he feels responsible for me because of my condition. He couldn't save his mother from this disease, but maybe, somewhere in the back of his mind, he believes he can still save me. Or, at the very least, just be there when everyone else has abandoned me to suffer through it alone.

As my thoughts come full circle, a scream of vexation builds in my throat, poking at the brink of my lips. If he really does want to keep me safe, then why did he say I could come on this mission? What does he think he's protecting me from?

Or, maybe, the better question is, who?

An apology hangs on the tip of my tongue, but I swallow the words, torn over what to say and whether or not I'd actually mean it. I glance at Ezra, but he doesn't say anything either.

We continue our trek through the long, winding tunnels, the minutes passing with a silent monotony that would make even the strongest person question their sanity. The unchanging rhythm of our forward progression only falters when we reach yet another crossroads.

Rai digs through her pack for the handheld device and clicks it on with a tap of her finger. The hologram flares to life, throwing a soft blue light across the walls around us.

"Where do we go next?" Ezra stops beside her and peers down at the map.

"Well, based on the information in the transmission, we're roughly three miles away from our target." Rai pauses to trace a finger along the glowing blue lines, then raises her flashlight and shines it down the path to our right. "That's the way we need to go."

As she stores the device back inside her bag, Ezra turns to face the rest of us. "We'll stop now for a quick ten-minute rest. Check that all your guns are loaded, and make sure you stay hydrated."

From the murmurings around me, I gather we'll reach our destination an hour or so before midnight. Taking advantage of our last chance at peace before facing the very real possibility of death—or, in my case, a return to torture at the DSD—I drop my pack to the ground and lean back against the damp wall with a sigh, making sure to sit on the sloped edges of the floor to avoid the thin layer of water.

I choose to rest on the opposite side of the tunnel as everyone else in the group, needing some time and space to think. Aside from the lingering concern that there's something Ezra isn't telling me, and realizing that I know absolutely nothing about our mission, it's dawning on me that I'll only get in everyone's way once we get there…wherever there is. In my weakened state, and with no control over my visions, I struggle to see how I can make myself useful.

Why did I think it would be smart for me to join them? And why the hell did Ezra agree?

The shuffle of approaching footsteps draws my gaze upward, dragging me out of my spiraling thoughts. Jenner hesitates a few feet away from me, holding out a canteen of water.

"May I?" He jerks his chin toward the ground.

Accepting the offered water, I take a tentative sip as Jenner plops down beside me, filling the empty space with his comforting warmth and calm demeanor, both of which I need to assuage me right now.

Several moments pass without either of us speaking, and as the seconds stretch on, the quiet turns threatening, like a hand reaching out in the darkness to choke us. I'm overcome by the urge to say something—*anything* to break the silence—when mutterings reach me from the other side of the tunnel.

My eyes drift to the man sitting across from me on the opposite slope, the toes of his boots touching the gully of water separating us. Beads of sweat glisten along his upper lip, his mouth twitching as he chants the same handful of sentences over and over again.

"We will not die. We will be reborn among the ashes and overcome any adversary who stands against us. We will endure. We will survive. We will not die…"

My heart rate quickens with every word he recites until I find myself repeating them back in my head.

We will not die…

Jenner nudges my arm to get my attention. "Are you okay?" he asks.

Glancing up, I look from him to the man and then back again. "What does it mean?"

Frowning, he fixes his gaze on the mumbling man, his expression pensive. Forlorn. "I guess you could say it's our motto. A sort of promise we all make to keep the rebellion going, even after one of us dies. We'll never give up. We'll keep on fighting until there's nothing left to fight for. We'll rise past the deaths of those who paved our way, like a phoenix rising from the ashes."

While I admire the notion behind such a sentiment, it fills me with the worst kind of dread. I don't want to think about anyone dying, least of all Ezra, Jenner, or Rai. If I could have it my way, we'd all turn around right now and race back to the compound. To safety.

"You know," Jenner says, his voice dropping to a rumbling whisper, "Despite everything, I'm surprised Ezra let you come with us." His eyes turn back to mine, holding me to him, and my stomach clenches as the weight of my returning uncertainty bears down on my shoulders.

From the moment Ezra relented to my request, I've wondered about his unspoken motives. Why am I here? What help can I be to these people? Why did he let me come? Surely, he didn't only agree just because he knew I'd fight him on the matter.

"Why?" I ask past the sudden tightness in my throat.

Jenner shrugs. "Well, if the transmission really is a trap set by the DSD, we stand to lose the one thing that could give us the advantage against them."

"So, she's a tool against the enemy?" That's what someone had asked when Ezra rallied everyone before my illness put me into a coma. Clearly, he wasn't the only one thinking it.

I don't like the implication behind Jenner's words—the idea that I'm a pawn to be used, thrown back and forth between two opposing sides. Of course, no one in PHOENIX aside from him, Ezra, and Rai know what I can do.

Do they?

When I don't say anything, Jenner hastily adds, "I asked him about it, but he just said you'd be safer with us than alone at the compound without anyone who knows what's really going on. I couldn't exactly argue with that, not after seeing how riled up everyone was. Suspicion brings out the worst in people, not to mention, I'm not sure anyone else would know what to do if, you know... *you had one of your visions.*" He silently mouths the end of that sentence, his eyes flicking left and right, as if he's worried someone might be listening in on our conversation.

I merely blink at him, confused. *Riled up?* Does he mean before Ezra's speech... or after? Everyone at the compound accepted me because of what Ezra said, didn't they?

Jenner's expression goes slack at the look on my face. "Shit. You don't know, do you?"

"Know what?" The words barely penetrate my lips.

An eternity seems to pass in the time it takes for him to answer. "You have to understand, in small communities, rumors spread. It's inevitable."

"What sort of rumors?"

His eyes drop to his hands, which fidget nervously with his canteen. "Like ones connecting you to the transmission from Bilken."

I open my mouth to ask why anyone would link me to Bilken, even though I already know why they would. I knew I couldn't be the only one who thought the timing of the message was coincidental.

Jenner clears his throat. "Only Ezra and Nolan know what was on that transmission, but that doesn't stop the rest of us from having our own theories."

"Nolan?" I recognize the name, but I can't place the face. Too many details from the day Ezra made his inspiring speech about me are fuzzy thanks to the crippling side effects of my vision.

"He's the Head of our sect. The transmission from Bilken was addressed directly to him."

This revelation only further compounds the nagging feeling that's been eating away at me. "Where does Ezra fit into that? And how did Bilken even manage to contact PHOENIX?"

Jenner waves a flippant hand. "Ezra's sort of his second-in-command in our merry band of misfits, so anything requiring us to go out on missions or considered need-to-know, he knows. Nolan's more of a behind-the-scenes kind of guy." His expression darkens. "As for the transmission, I heard it was encrypted in this week's Enforcer rotation schedule. We monitor that stuff to time our movements topside, and Rai picked up on the abnormality in the code."

"How did he know you'd be checking the schedule?"

Jenner shrugs again. "Smart guy, I guess? I mean, it's common sense that we would."

I nod, but foreboding claws at the back of my brain. Exhaling, I murmur, "If I ask you a question, will you answer me honestly?"

He pulls back just enough to give me a curious look, his eyebrows dragging down into a vee. "Sure," he says, although he seems anything but.

"Do you think…" I trail off, my resolve paper-thin. Steeling myself, I force out the words. "Do you think PHOENIX would hand me over if someone in the State gave you an offer that was too good to refuse?"

Someone like Wren Bilken.

He freezes with the canteen an inch from his mouth, the water dribbling down over his chin. Lowering his arm, he asks, "Like what?"

"I-I don't know. Something that would ensure your safety, maybe? Something that would allow you to lead normal lives…"

Jenner snorts. "The last thing anyone in PHOENIX would want is to go back to the State's twisted version of *normal.*" He spits that last word like it's left a foul taste in his mouth.

"What about Ezra?"

He arches an eyebrow. "What *about* Ezra?"

I roll the words around on my tongue for a few seconds before finally pushing them out.

"Would he hand me over?" I breathe.

Jenner's eyes nearly bulge out of their sockets. "No way!" he retorts, his tone accusatory, his expression livid. "Why the hell would you even think that?"

My cheeks flush, burning red-hot with shame.

Because I want to trust him but I'm afraid, and everyone else I ever trusted has either betrayed me or died.

Instead, I say, "Because there's something he's not telling me, and I don't understand why else I would be here." It's not a lie, but it's not the whole truth.

Gradually, the shocked look on Jenner's face softens.

"Listen to me." His voice is both soft and hard, like a warning wrapped in a consolation. "Every person in our sect has Ezra to thank for saving their lives. Every single one, even me. *Especially* me," he adds with a humorless laugh. "He found us all and guided us to a new life, to safety, and yet, I've never seen him fight or stand up for anyone the way he has for you. I don't know what's changed, but he's risked his good standing with everyone we know just to keep you safe, which has to say something, right? Plus, he's too stubborn to back down on anything, so trust me, he's not about to give you up or send you packing to the DSD. You don't deserve what they did to you, and you sure as hell don't deserve to go back to those assholes."

"But you don't know what they did to me…"

And really, Ezra doesn't either.

"You're right," Jenner admits, his gaze slipping away. "I can't even begin to imagine what you went through. That's how I know it was bad."

Before I can comment, Ezra waves a beckoning arm from farther on down the tunnel. "On your feet. We're moving out."

Jenner stands, offering me his hand, and I take it, dodging his eyes as he pulls me up, helping me back onto my feet.

"Thanks," I mumble. Bending forward, I grab my pack and hoist the thick strap over my shoulder.

Jenner opens his mouth to say something, but the splashing of footsteps nearby cuts him off. We both turn toward the sound to find Ezra beside us, face pinched, lips pulled tight, and eyes narrowed.

"Head up the group with Rai," he barks at Jenner, who seems to be the source of his annoyance.

So much for them playing nice again.

Jenner either takes no notice of Ezra's hostility or just doesn't care. He runs a hand through the messy charcoal strands of his hair. "Sure thing." He then winks at me and walks off, leaving the two of us alone.

Every beat of my heart is erratic as Ezra inches closer, demolishing the distance between us with only two steps. I glance away before I can see his expression and focus on adjusting the straps of my pack, unsure what to say. Unsure what to think. To my dismay, the belt attachment doesn't want to cooperate.

"Here, let me help you."

Ezra takes the bag from my fumbling fingers, and, as he reaches around my torso, his hands graze my back, sending an involuntary shiver racing through me. I hold my breath. Even through my shirt, the skin he brushed against tingles as if his touch remains, branded into my flesh. In a strange way, the sensation reminds me of those lightning-like bolts used to spur on my visions at the DSD. Except, now, the electricity is far from painful.

Now, it almost brings me pleasure.

I swallow and lift my gaze to the ceiling, searching for something to distract myself from Ezra's unexpected proximity as he adjusts the tightness of the straps. The wet stone offers little in the way of diversions.

Ezra shifts, and the heat of his body against mine tempts the memory of my dream to the surface again. Despite how hard I fight to shove it back down, the mental picture of that imagined kiss floods my head. I've barely thought of anything else.

I tell myself it's because such affection isn't commonplace in my world. Most people are too afraid to let anyone that close because they fear betrayal or because they don't want to risk losing them and living with that pain once they're gone. Affection barely even exists within families—I certainly never saw it between my parents, assuming it ever existed at all. And, as such, I never expected it for myself. After all, as my mother always drilled into me, affection is weakness. Love is weakness.

And weakness can be used against you.

I figured, when the time came, I'd be partnered through one of the State's partnership agencies and I'd fulfill my required contribution to population growth, just like everyone else. I never allowed myself to think I could ever have anything more.

And that's exactly what that dream of Ezra has stirred in me—this idea that I could find something real and meet someone who actually cares for me. It's given me hope that I could, one day, have love.

Assuming I don't destroy the world first.

"There." Ezra's voice shakes me free of my thoughts. "Now, the pack won't come loose if we need to make a quick getaway."

Our faces are unbearably close when he says this, and I can't stop myself from looking at him, my eyes drawn to his lips, as if pulled there by a magnetic force. The memory of their touch overwhelms me.

I glance away, hoping the darkness of the tunnel will hide the heat flaring up in my cheeks. If Ezra notices my embarrassment, he doesn't say anything, but I'm not sure if I'm relieved by his silence or disappointed. I suppose a combination of both.

Clearing his throat, Ezra takes a step back and falls into line behind the others. As he walks away, a shaking breath expels from my lungs, and my pulse throbs across every inch of my skin, leaving me flustered and disoriented. I'm completely incapable of understanding what I'm feeling, and right now isn't the time to get lost in thoughts of anything but our impending mission.

Priorities, Wynter, I chide myself.

Drawing in a steadying breath, I push whatever this is taking hold of me to the back of my mind to revisit later and follow Ezra's lead down the tunnel, trailing a few steps behind him.

Our trek continues in the same eerie quiet as before but with an added level of tension. As we trudge along, my eyelids grow heavy, the humdrum sound of our repetitive footsteps making me drowsy, lulling me until I'm practically sleepwalking.

I snap out of my daze when a hand grabs my arm.

"Wait," Ezra hisses, holding me back.

He's stopped walking, and my eyes, now wide and alert, dart between the drawn features of his face and the retreating figures of our friends. My heart pounds like a hammer against my ribcage as Rai, Jenner, and the rest of our party disappear into the shadows.

Once the others are out of earshot, Ezra releases his hold on me. I glare at him, bewildered by his behavior, but he doesn't meet my gaze.

"I get it, you know," he says after a moment. "After everything you've been through, why the hell should you trust me? But I'm not like my brother. I'm on *your* side. I don't know how else I can make you believe me."

The frustration in his tone ties my stomach in knots, but the pleading in his eyes is what breaks me. Sweat drenches the palms of my hands as I whisper, "Trust has nothing to do with this."

"Then what?" he presses. "Help me understand."

His eyes jump to mine, and I wince as their scrutiny cuts through the protective wall I've built up around myself over the last eighteen years. Every day was just another brick in the barrier separating me from anything outside myself that could hurt me.

The pained edge to his voice sends that wall toppling over. "Please, Wynter."

I cross my arms over my chest, shrinking into myself. "I'm just struggling to understand why you're so determined to help me, to *lie* for me, when you were all too quick to hold a gun to my head, not once but twice since we met. Is it because Richter's your brother? Because of your mother?"

I don't voice the last option—the fear bubbling up in my chest that he might be planning to use me to PHOENIX's advantage. Or his own. Not only because

I don't want to believe it, but because I can't bear to hear if it's true.

It isn't, I tell myself. *It can't be.* Because, despite my constant wavering on the matter, I trust him. I do. What I don't trust is the effect desperation can have on people when they run out of options. And Ezra… His entire life is a series of difficult choices and limited recourse. The reality is, he's not in a position to put me first. To choose me, a girl he just met—someone who has only brought the reminder of pain and chaos back into his life.

Ezra scratches the tip of his finger against his chin, considering me. "Would it be ironic if I said it's complicated?" An unexpected smile tweaks the edges of his lips as I bite back a laugh at his words. Not that long ago, I enraged him with this very same explanation, and now, here we are, the roles reversed.

However, our humor is short-lived, and his smile fades as he rubs a hand across the back of his neck.

"What I told you about my mother…" He hesitates, as if choosing his next words carefully. "A lot of my anger about the situation stems from the fact that there was a time when I thought she was crazy, too. She would say the same thing to me every day, over and over. Always the same thing. *'One green, one blue. Look for winter.'* I had no idea what she was talking about. Her words seemed like a warning, but after a while, I tried to ignore them because nothing happened and my father constantly insisted it was just random gibberish. After she was locked away, I forgot all about it…until you came along."

I suck in a sharp breath as he takes another step toward me.

"At first, I didn't trust you for obvious reasons, like your link to the DSD and how easily you found us. I thought for sure you were lying. But then you told us your name, and something clicked in my head. One green." He points at my left eye. "One blue." He then points at my right. "That's when I realized what she had actually been saying."

He stands so close to me now, I can feel his every word on my lips when he speaks.

"Wynter, she had said. Look for *Wynter.*"

"She saw me?" A million questions fly through my head, but I don't know which one to give voice to first. My indecision chokes me, making me mute.

"From the moment I heard your name, I recalled that gut feeling I had when I was younger, the one that once made me so sure what my mother said was a warning. And, for a while, that's what I thought it was. I thought you had been sent by some higher power to tear our world apart," Ezra says.

Apprehension ripples through my body as I wonder where this conversation is heading. He isn't entirely wrong. I am going to tear their world apart. Just probably not in the way he's thinking.

Still, I can't tell him that. Not yet.

"And now, you don't think that?" I hedge.

"I can't really explain it. Another gut feeling, I guess. But when you collapsed… and then when you told us about that vision, I knew."

Staring at me, he brushes a hand across my cheek, tucking an errant strand of hair behind my left ear. The bewildering thrill of his skin against mine rips a gasp from my lungs and makes my knees tremble.

His next words are a weighted whisper in the silence of the tunnel.

"She wanted me to protect you."

TWENTY

"ARE YOU SURE THIS IS it?" Ezra squints at the ceiling.

Rai nods. "It's as close as we're going to get."

We all stare at the rusted hatch door overhead. Danger lurks on the other side of the metal, its call a hypnotizing temptress, urging us to climb up into its mouth where it can then devour us whole. Shadowy fingers slink out of the darkness and wrap around my ankles, grabbing at me, keeping me from taking another step forward, even though I have to.

My nerves send a hair-raising chill up my spine.

This is the end of the line.

"Give me a boost." Ezra smacks Jenner's arm without looking at him, and the latter turns, knitting his hands together with Duke's, forming a step with their joined fingers and flattened palms. I stand back with Rai, watching, as Ezra places one foot in their grasp and they hoist him to the door, their shoulders providing the needed support for him to keep his balance.

As Ezra straightens, one of the other two men who accompanied us here hands him a long black bar curved at one end, which he wedges between the spokes of the wheel attached to the hatch for leverage. Grunting, he pushes against the thin bar, his weight shifting as he throws his body forward—Jenner and Duke adjusting their stance to keep him steady and upright. The wheel creaks in protest as flakes of decaying iron flutter to the floor.

Inch by inch, the rust loosens and the wheel turns, the squeal of each rotation like an alarm screeching through the stone passage around us. With one final turn, Ezra pushes the door, and it crashes open, slamming against the ground overhead.

A shudder spreads over my skin. What if someone heard that bang? What if we're caught before we even exit this tunnel?

Unease grips my chest as Ezra hauls himself up through the hole, his legs disappearing into the blackness beyond as if he's been swallowed. I wait with bated breath for him to reappear and inform us the coast is clear, trying my best to ignore the niggling thought that something has gone terribly wrong. Maybe the Enforcers are already here. Maybe they've captured him, and any moment now, they'll descend on the rest of us, too.

A moment later, Ezra leans over the opening, the glow of our flashlights reflecting off his face, washing out his features. He holds up a hand to shield his eyes from the glare, and my lips part with a gasp, relief barreling through me, as the beams of light fall away. Clenching his teeth, he bends down to help the next person up through the hole.

Jenner goes first, followed by the two older men whose names I still don't know and then Rai. When it's my turn, I click off my flashlight and, with a boost from Duke, extend my arm to grab Ezra's awaiting hand, which hangs through the opening, ready to pull me out of one darkness and into another. His fingers glide across my skin, sending a shock of electricity racing through my body, which starts at my wrist and travels all the way down to my toes. Holding my gaze, he pulls me up through the hole and, for the briefest moment, into his arms.

Heat swells under my cheeks as I push away and quickly clamber to my feet, scurrying aside to stand with Rai. I don't look back at Ezra to see his reaction.

Duke is the last one out. Once we're all gathered on the surface, he ties a rope around the wheel, then helps Ezra close the hatch, sealing off our escape. For now. We'll come back this way once we're finished.

Assuming we make it out alive.

A biting wind nips at my clothes, and a shiver rips through me as the winter air skims over the hot sweat coating the back of my neck. The damp warmth of the tunnels seems miles away as I peer into the shapeless gloom of the courtyard.

"Where are we?" I whisper to Rai, leaning in to keep my voice as low as possible. I can't recognize our surroundings in the thick darkness.

"Zone 1," she murmurs back under her breath. "Outside the city magistrates building."

My gaze skirts across the expansive plaza, flitting through the shadows and moving up toward the sky to trace the shape of the structure before us. Even without street lights to guide my vision, I can sense the building's familiar enormity.

As my eyes adjust to the night, allowing me to take in the finer details of our surroundings, I'm overwhelmed by the chilling feeling that someone is watching us. All around me, the shadows shift and change as if waiting for us to make our next move.

"Is this really where Bilken wants us to meet him?" Suspicion rings behind my tone.

Rai glances at me, her eyes black in the darkness. "It makes sense. All city officials have offices here, even if they hold their main jobs somewhere else. Perhaps, he figured the more conspicuous the better. Sometimes, plain sight is the best place to hide."

"Unless, it's a trap," I grumble.

Maybe Rai has a point. This building is massive, typically well-guarded—since it's off limits to even normal rule-abiding citizens—and is surrounded by an open plaza, meaning we're sitting ducks out here if anyone does decide to attack. Surely, the State wouldn't expect us to do something so reckless? Then again, desperation makes fools of us all, and it might suspect we'd take the risk if we had a reason to.

A reason like the promise of a potential influential ally.

My thoughts go in a maddening circle as I muse over the likelihood that this mission will turn out the way everyone hopes. Maybe I'm just a pessimist. Or maybe PHOENIX has been exiled for so long they've forgotten what the State is capable of.

Another option occurs to me—one I'm not eager to entertain. Still, I can't ignore the possibility that, maybe, we've been sent here under the guise of meeting Bilken when, in reality, we're here for an entirely different reason altogether. One none of us is even aware of, aside from Ezra, if he's really clued in on the details as much as Jenner seems to think.

I remember what Jenner said about someone named Nolan being the Head of their sect, the one who, presumably, makes the decisions. I don't know who this person is, but—thanks to what I've been through—I see dubious morals and suspect the motivation behind everything now. After dealing with someone like Dr. Richter, I wouldn't be surprised if there was some nefarious reason for this mission. Just as I wouldn't be surprised if all of us were deemed expendable if our deaths meant achieving whatever the aim of it is.

Someone in the group clears their throat, and in the darkness, I find Ezra's face. A sense of urgency hardens his gaze. "In the transmission, Bilken said a door on the northwest side of the building will open at exactly 11:15. The locking mechanism will only allow entry for sixty seconds, so we have to be precise and get there before then. Otherwise, we'll miss our window."

Rai looks down at the device in her hand. The hologram illuminates the courtyard for only a few seconds before she shuts it back off.

"Well, we better get a move on," she says. "We only have eleven minutes."

We move in a tight herd through the densely packed shadows, my legs mimicking the others' hurried pace as much as my fatigued muscles allow. In our haste, we pass at least a dozen entrances to the magistrates building, although none are the one we're looking for. Regardless, I note that not a single door is guarded, which is highly unusual given the classified intel stored inside the building. Where are the Enforcers who would normally be posted here?

Once again, doubt scratches at the back of my brain, but Ezra and the others don't seem to share my concerns, which makes me wonder if I'm overreacting or seeing red flags where they don't actually exist. Is it possible the time I spent at the DSD has infected my mind with paranoia? Because of Dr. Richter—and my mother's abandonment—I find myself questioning everything and everyone, suspecting the worst of their actions. Maybe I shouldn't. Maybe I should just take a step back and believe Ezra when he says he won't let anything bad happen to me.

Rai periodically checks the device, which now serves as our compass, keeping it clutched in her hand as we run. The glow of the hologram diminishes after a moment, shrouding us again under the cover of darkness.

"Five minutes down," she hisses. "Six remaining."

We make it to the correct entrance with only thirty seconds to spare. Panting breaths form steaming clouds in the freezing air as we huddle around the locked door, waiting.

The seconds seem to stretch into hours. I glance first at Ezra, then at Jenner and Rai, tempted to ask them to abandon this mission—to turn back now while we still have our lives. I open and close my mouth several times, but no matter how much I wish to utter those words, I can't find the bravery needed to say them.

At 11:15, the door in question clicks open, just as Bilken promised it would. Gripping his gun in one hand, Ezra uses the other to reach for the door, his fingers twitching as they jiggle the handle. The locking mechanism doesn't fight his advance.

He hesitates, throwing a nervous glance back at Rai, but she just purses her lips and nods, saying nothing. My pulse stutters as it occurs to me what that look between them must mean. They're preparing themselves for what I've been saying from the first moment Ezra told me about the transmission.

This is a trap. That thought beats against the inside of my lips, but I stop it from passing, well aware voicing it won't help anyone or deter us from stepping through this door.

I'm not sure what frightens me more—walking into the unknown or knowing there will be nothing I can do to help the others if we run into trouble. My fingertips brush against the gun at my belt, but touching the metal only makes my restlessness worse.

"Hey." Jenner clamps a hand on my shoulder, his mouth pulling into that crooked smile I always find so reassuring. "Don't worry. Everything will be fine."

For a moment, I almost allow myself to believe him.

Ezra pushes the door open the rest of the way and slinks forward, pressing ahead into the unlit corridor. The rest of us follow behind him with our guns at the ready, our eyes peeled for danger.

I imitate the others, watching them closely. When they press their backs to a wall, I do the same, flattening my body against the nearest object in sight. When they freeze, I go as still as a statue, not daring to move a muscle until Ezra gives the all-clear.

My chest expands and contracts with each breath as my heartbeat throbs inside my ears, a deafening cacophony of terror that spreads, swelling in my throat and then building behind my eyes, making my vision fuzzy and squeezing my windpipe until I can hardly breathe. Everyone else is calm and focused, but their composure only exacerbates my fear.

My gaze cuts through the gloom, searching for Rai. She sits cross-legged by the entrance we came in through—the door propped open by the bar Ezra used on the hatch in the tunnels, its interference keeping the locking mechanism from activating in case it attempts to close and lock us all in. She stares down at a compact computer propped open in her lap, and the illuminated screen radiates a soft green-tinted glow across her face.

As her fingers dance across the keyboard, I slink along the wall, inching back toward the door until I'm squatting beside her in the corner. Curiosity draws my gaze over her shoulder.

Red dots blink across the screen, separated by thin green lines, which form an interior schematic of the building. I only comprehend what I'm looking at this time since the layout closely resembles the diagram from W. P. Headquarters the day of my placement exam—the one I saw prior to entering the exam room that showed me which desk I was allocated.

Rai peeks back at me and winks, then taps a button on the keyboard with a flick of her finger. One by one, the red dots on the screen fade to black.

"Cameras are out," she says with a smirk.

The others all relax at her words and step away from where they stood with their backs pressed flat to the walls, their relief ringing out in a chorus of sighs. Despite easing their rigid stances, everyone keeps their guns firmly at hand.

As Rai stores the computer back inside her pack, I stare at her in awe, wondering how she managed to do that. The answer comes to me quickly.

Hacker.

I remember hearing about the dangers of hackers in news alerts, but I never really understood what they were capable of. Until now. What she just did—shutting off the building's cameras with the same ease as drawing a breath—explains how PHOENIX has remained undetected for so long, how they always manage to elude the State's clutches. If the State can't see them, it would never even know they were there.

The technique is brilliant in its simplicity, and yet, it still doesn't answer one crucial question.

"How have you managed to stay under the radar for so long? Can't the State still track you?" I ask.

When Rai meets my gaze, I glance down at her wrist then at my own where the thick bandage hides the jagged self-inflicted incision. PHOENIX might know how to turn off some cameras, but the State has other methods to track us.

Her hands freeze on her half-packed bag.

"When PHOENIX first started, they used to cut the chips out like you did, but a lot of people died from blood loss or infection. Weapons are one thing, but it isn't that easy to get our hands on medicine because of how tightly regulated it is. Yet another of the State's many methods to keep us all under control. So, there wasn't much anyone could do in the early days except clean them up and just hope for the best. You were lucky we happened to have antibiotics on hand."

As she says this, my thoughts travel back to my school years when we were taught how terrible life was before the State and learned of the previous regime's policy on drug use, medicinal and otherwise. Recreational freedom led to a massive downward spiral of productivity, resulting in a population that had become dependent and lazy. When the State came to power, it chose to keep our health under lock and key for what it claimed was our benefit. Even something as simple as a headache can now only be treated by going to a health center.

No exceptions.

"In those early days, PHOENIX was always on the move. The sects were constantly changing their location to keep the Enforcers from discovering where they were organizing and to protect their suppliers," Rai continues, her voice a low thrum in the silence. "They fluctuated between hiding above ground and below, so the State wouldn't piece together where the real hideouts were.

"During that time, the founding members worked on different ways of disabling the tracking mechanism in the identification chips, going through failure after failure and countless unnecessary deaths in the process. Eventually, they realized that, by using a localized electromagnetic pulse, they could just fry the chips without having to resort to dangerous invasive procedures to remove them.

"The chips are in that place for a reason, to stop us from tampering with them. We just had to find a way around it. The scanner we use now has gone through various updates over the years, but it still does the trick." Grinning, she flaunts her wrist in front of my face. "The chip is just a harmless piece of metal now. The State couldn't track me, or any of us, even if it wanted to."

I gape at her, impressed but also slightly unnerved. The State has always been vocal about the far-reaching extent of its power and knowledge. So much so that, up until this very moment, I didn't think it had any points of vulnerability.

But if what Rai is saying is true, then PHOENIX has discovered a chink in the State's armor, an imperfection—a weakness—that could potentially be used against it. Knowing that, it's terrifying to think what these people might've accomplished if they hadn't abandoned society. Perhaps, if they hadn't been driven away, the world would've been a much better place with their contribution.

Or a worse one, a small voice in my head counters.

Before I can question Rai any further, she jumps to her feet and trots down the hallway, slinging her bag back over her shoulder and securing the strap in front of her chest. I follow in her footsteps, counting every last one as I walk in a futile attempt to distract myself from the deafening beat of my pulse in my ears. By the time I make it to where the others all stand gathered together, I can barely hear what Ezra is saying.

"You three take the first two floors." He gestures to Duke and to the other two men who came with us. "Rai, Jenner, and Wynter will go up with me to the third and forth. Make sure your communicators are active, and call me if you find anything, no matter how insignificant it might seem."

I stand off to one side of the corridor as our group splits in half. Duke leads the other two men down the hallway, while Rai and Jenner hunch over the hologram map of the building, now displayed on the handheld device, mumbling to each other about which nearby staircase would be best to take.

As I push a shaking breath from my lungs, warm fingers brush down the length of my arm. They then grip my hand, forcing me to meet Ezra's gaze.

"Stay close to me," he whispers, "and stay behind me. Remember, no matter what happens, I won't let anyone hurt you, okay?"

With a careful smile, he lets go of my hand and proceeds down the hallway, only looking back once to make sure that I'm following him.

We shadow Rai and Jenner up to the third floor where we find a more extensive corridor stretching before us, long and winding with several different additional hallways branching off from the main path. The construction of the interior is vastly different to the handful of government centers I've been in before. Whereas most other buildings are composed of metal, marble, and glass, the furnishings here consist almost solely of wood. It's a material not often used anymore—I imagine because the others have been proven to last longer. It's all about longevity, just like Jenner said. Or, maybe, that's just the excuse the State uses to get away with eradicating any reminders of the old world.

The world which existed before we did.

After five or so minutes of walking, Jenner waves his hand, signaling for us to stop. I pause behind Ezra while Rai leans against the nearest wall, consulting her blueprint of the building.

"Yo, Ez," Jenner mutters. "Did this Bilken guy say where he wanted to meet?"

"No, but he has an office here, so he probably figured the answer was obvious."

A skeptical look flashes across Jenner's face. "Yeah…maybe. Man, this place gives me the creeps. The sooner we find Bilken and get the hell out of here, the better."

I cast a sidelong glance at him, frowning. If I'm not the only one who has a bad feeling about all this, why are we still here?

Why don't we leave now before it's too late?

This mission doesn't make any sense. Even Ezra couldn't give me a clear, logical answer as to why it was so vital we take such a risk. PHOENIX has been around longer than I've been alive and has managed all this time without someone on the inside to leak them information. So, why change that now? And why Wren Bilken?

Why is he so important to them?

My eyes drift back to Ezra as he lets out a sigh and peers down both lengths of the corridor we're currently searching. "Tell you what, we'll cover more ground if we break off into pairs. Jenner, you and Rai take the east side. Wynter and I will take the west side. Call us if you find anything."

I want to ask if he thinks splitting up is a good idea, considering our group has done so once already, but neither Rai nor Jenner question his judgment, which makes me think I shouldn't either. They each give a curt nod before heading one way as Ezra urges me to follow him in the other.

A prickle of fear raises the hairs on my arms as I hesitate, watching Jenner and Rai walk away. My doubts from before come surging back, and in a quiet breath, I beg the world, or fate, or whatever might have a hand in deciding our futures that this won't be the last time I see them.

"Ready?" Ezra breathes into my ear, his sudden proximity making me jump.

Swallowing, I take a step back and bob my head once in answer.

We continue through the empty corridors, searching the passing rooms, but find nothing. No people. No clues. Just empty offices. I mirror Ezra's steps, keeping pace as we walk, my eyes and ears on high alert for anything out of the ordinary.

As we near the end of yet another long hallway, Ezra stops in his tracks, and I stumble, nearly colliding face-first with his back. Shuffling to stand at his side, I peek up at him.

"What's wrong?"

He silences me with a finger to his lips and jerks his chin toward an upcoming office door just ahead on our right. I follow his unblinking gaze to the name engraved on a gold plate fixed to the wood.

W. BILKEN

My heart sinks as I gape at the plate, and a strange sense of understanding settles in, seeping into the very marrow of my bones. Two possible futures await us from here. Either we'll meet Bilken and he'll turn out to be exactly what he promised…

Or we'll find something else altogether.

Ezra unhooks the communicator from his belt and murmurs into the mouthpiece, "We found something. We're going to check it out."

The nerves writhing in my stomach lash out, making me feel like I'm going to vomit. I draw in a steadying breath and grip my gun tighter.

Despite how frightened I am by the prospect of what lies on the other side of this door, I find solace in knowing I won't face it alone. Ezra and I will confront it together.

And yet, that comfort also fills me with fear. Not that long ago, he was just some unknown man I saw in a vision. I didn't really care who he was beyond the lingering question of why I was seeing him and how he was connected to that future, and I wasn't concerned with his wellbeing or fate.

But now—

Rai's muffled voice diverts my focus away from that thought. Her words are intermingled with static. *"Ezra, don't do anything stupid—"*

Her voice cuts off as he disconnects the call and places the communicator back on his belt, returning both hands to his gun. As he cocks the slide, he catches my eye.

"Remember, stay behind me," he breathes.

I nod again as he pushes open the door.

TWENTY-ONE

THE DOOR CREAKS OPEN ACROSS the wood floor, brushing onto a thick layer of carpet. Ezra steps over the threshold with his gun raised, his eyes intently scanning the darkness, while I follow behind, staying close just like he instructed.

Shadows permeate the office like smog. My pulse pounds just under my skin, and my breaths are ragged as my shaking hand guides my flashlight across our dim surroundings. The beam reflects off a large glass desk positioned in the middle of the room, but in terms of inhabitants, the office is empty.

I creep along behind Ezra, our footsteps muffled by the pristine white carpet spanning the wide stretch of unoccupied floor. The office branches off into two smaller side rooms, separated from the main space by rounded archways decorated with swirling patterns carved into wood the same color as blood.

Swallowing, I take in the details around me, noting how this place seems almost like some sort of parallel universe to the one we reside in. The wood features we saw throughout the rest of the building continue in the foundations here, except, they're accented with the familiar, clean-cut addition of metal, marble, and glass. It's like a strange combination of two worlds. The world I grew up in...

And the old world, which no longer exists.

I inch along the wall closest to me, my gaze drawn to the rounded glass shelves slotted into the built-in wooden casing stretching from floor to ceiling. Along them, hundreds of volumes of browning, tattered books are organized in clean rows, the spines lined up according to size and color. At even intervals, the pattern is interrupted by curious trinkets, some made of metal, others of stone—objects I've never seen before and lack the names for. Objects which serve no practical purpose that I'm aware of, which can only mean one thing.

They're contraband.

Each year, the State makes it a point to perform a thorough search of every residence in the country to ensure no one possesses illegal goods. What were once considered normal everyday items to own are now…

"Forbidden," I whisper.

I stumble back a few steps, knocked off balance by the anger bubbling up within me. There's so much contradiction, so much hypocrisy in this room, it makes me sick to my stomach. Why are State officials allowed these items when ownership by normal citizens isn't permitted? Why are *they* allowed them without consequence when such possession by anyone else is seen as the worst sort of crime?

A crime punishable by death.

Nausea blinds my senses, and my knees buckle beneath me, nearly dragging me down to the floor. Despite everything I've been through between the execution of my father and the horrors of the last few months, I wasn't aware how much I truly despise the State until this very moment. And that hatred festering in me like a cancerous tumor all boils down to the maddening injustice staring me in the face.

What happened when I was a child… At the time, I never even considered the possibility that it was immoral or evil. It was just the way things were. A wrong that needed to be corrected. To a child who didn't know any better, the State was always right. It was everyone else who was wrong.

But now, seeing this—

"I don't think anyone's here."

A gasp more like a squeak breaks through my lips when Ezra lays a hand on my shoulder. Blinking away the tears budding in the corners of my eyes, I nod, averting my gaze, and help him do another sweep of the office. The second search confirms our suspicions.

We're alone.

I don't understand. If the offer contained within the transmission was genuine, then where's our contact? Where's Wren Bilken? On the other hand, if this is a trap, like I suspect, then where are the Enforcers? The State wouldn't leave such an important establishment unguarded, which means it's probably only a matter of time before someone arrives to either kill or detain us. But, if that's the case…what are they waiting for?

What are they hoping to accomplish by waiting?

Ezra crosses the room to the imposing glass desk and presses a hand to the crystalline surface. The hidden screen flickers to life with a shuddering glow, the light slicing clean through the night.

Tap, tap, tap. His fingers skip across the touchscreen, marching in time with my racing heart. Each beat drums in my ears, in my throat, in my stomach, pulsing everywhere at once until my apprehension is all I'm aware of. It grows until it's a physical lump in my chest, blocking the air from reaching my lungs. As I wheeze, my eyes fix on the cause of my panic.

A ball the size of a pregnant belly hangs motionless in the air above the top left corner of the glass desktop, suspended over a brass base by an attached curved bar that runs along one full side of the sphere. Uneven shapes protrude in a bumpy texture across the exterior of the ball with elegant script written in the middle of each. I only recognize one of the names. The rest are unfamiliar to me.

Sweat forms along my brow as I try to recall the name for this miniature model of our planet. The answer rises in the back of my head, digging its way out from the recesses of my memory. It taunts me in my father's voice.

"Globe."

Hysteria crushes me as the memories attack from all sides. My hand shoots out, clutching at the edge of the desk to hold myself upright through their brutal assault. How have I never thought to question this before now, especially considering everything my father once taught me? How am I only just now seeing what the State has been doing to me and to everyone else trapped in its grasp?

We've allowed the government to limit our education, reducing what we're taught down to information those in power deem appropriate for us to know. The State determines what we learn and what we don't, shaping us into mindless followers who are blind to anything other than the controlled system put into place to imprison us. Beyond what I've been told in school and by news reports, I realize now I know nothing.

I know nothing of the world outside this country.

I know nothing of the world outside this city.

I, along with everyone else, only know what the State tells us and wants us to know. Whatever twisted variation of the truth that may be.

Holstering my gun, I trail my fingers across the knobbly surface of the globe and give it a push, my eyes following the rotations, one after another, until my head is spinning. As the sphere turns, Ezra's fingers continue their hypnotic dance across the desktop.

"What's this?"

His voice snaps me out of my trance. A shudder rips through me, but I shake it off and wander to the other side of the desk where I gaze over Ezra's shoulder at the illuminated screen below. I'm not sure what we're looking at but sprawled across the top are two words printed in large red letters.

"Project W. A. R.," Ezra murmurs.

I follow the movement of his hand across the screen, taking in a few disjointed sentences as he scrolls down through the rest of the file. From what I can understand, we seem to be looking at notes recorded by a doctor.

Some lines stand out to me more than others.

DAY 22

Subject refuses to eat.
Have undertaken measures to avoid malnutrition.

My pulse quickens, and my mouth goes dry as the vivid memory of that tube down my throat comes rushing back. Terror settles under my skin, but I force myself to keep reading.

DAY 48

Subject is weak but is withstanding tests.
Appears to be more resilient than past subjects.

A scream claws up my throat, but no sound manages to pass through my lips.

DAY 116

Test has succeeded. Pursuing extracted information.
Will continue testing.

At the end of each entry are the initials AR. If I had any doubt as to who these notes were referring to, seeing Dr. Richter's name would've wiped them away. But I don't have any doubts.

I'm well aware these are all about me.

I want to beg Ezra to stop reading, but I can't seem to remember how to speak. I'm frozen from head to toe, unable to do anything except relive the most traumatic part of my life from the perspective of the very person who dragged me through that hell.

Ezra's eyes dart back and forth, scanning through Dr. Richter's recorded entries. With another tap of his finger, the screen changes.

Then his hand goes still.

Now, instead of documents, we're exposed to the visual evidence of what the DSD did to me. The first image to pop up is a mugshot from just before the experiments started—back when I still looked healthy, before the DSD sunk its claws into me and the torture began. Further images appear, showing the daily disintegration of my health. Video footage is available as well, enticing us with a blinking icon in the bottom right corner of the screen.

Thankfully, Ezra doesn't click it.

A tremor of terror rocks my body, urging my legs to turn and run from this room. I can't bear this. I don't want to see any more. I don't want to relive it.

"My god…" Ezra breathes.

I can feel his eyes on my face, his gaze burning hot, but I can't bring myself to meet it. How can I look at him the same way now that he's witnessed the one thing I wish I could forget more than anything?

My lungs draw in a strangled breath as a realization suddenly strikes without warning. "It's initials," I gasp. "Project W. A. R." I pause, working the monogram out in my head. "W…A…R… Wynter Arabelle Reeves."

I risk a glance at Ezra, and his horrified expression twists my already aching heart to near breaking point. My lips part, but all that escapes is a whimper.

Ezra's eyes soften with understanding, and reaching out, he takes hold of my hand, his fingers settling over mine, slowly easing my distress as I fight back the need to cry and scream and rage over everything that's happened to me. Over and over again, he caresses the back of my hand with his thumb until I'm no longer trembling.

"Why is this here?" he asks once I've calmed down.

My thoughts have been circling around this same question. Why would Bilken have this information on me? He doesn't have any ties to the DSD that I know of, but that doesn't mean Richter hasn't been forced to share information with those above him in the State hierarchy. Even so, I'm failing to see the connection. What interest could the CEO of W. P. Headquarters possibly have in *me*? It doesn't make sense, and considering how easy it was to crack Bilken's computer and access these files, I'm left to conclude that this information was planted here for a specific purpose.

Like for us to find.

But that can't be the case, surely. Bilken had no way of knowing I'd be here. As far as he or the State are concerned, the only people on this mission would've been members of PHOENIX. Assuming they knew that and this file *was* planted here, why would they want PHOENIX to see it?

What does any of this mean?

A sinking feeling burrows in the pit of my stomach, and I can't shake the gnawing thought that we're missing something vital—a piece of the puzzle that would help me see the bigger picture. Doing my best to shrug off the sensation, I lean forward and swipe my free hand across the touchscreen.

My jaw clenches as I scroll through the notes and images, but I don't stop to look at any of them longer than a few seconds each. Ezra stands beside me, still holding my hand, watching my frantic search without saying a word.

A sharp breath catches in my chest when a military order pops up on the computer, positioned at the end of the file. My heart rate increases with every word, and the more I read, the more confused I become. The order requests the use of Project W. A. R. in any future assaults on neighboring countries, but I don't understand why. How would that even work?

When the realization finally hits me, I'm tempted to slap myself for not seeing it sooner. Aside from my ability to witness events at any given point in time, my visions have also revealed what I'm capable of...or will be soon enough. Although I haven't wanted to admit it, what I did to Dr. Richter's attendant was only a small taste of the sort of power I will eventually possess. Even now, I can sense that power humming under my skin, expanding, growing. When it finally matures—assuming I don't kill us all first—Dr. Richter and the State will have the ultimate weapon.

My hands clench into fists as anger swells inside me like a ravenous hunger. They knew all along. *He* knew. Dr. Richter understood what I would become, which not only means he lied to me when I was his prisoner but that he's known this entire time what I was intended for.

Biting back my rage, I comb through the rest of the order, devouring every word. It goes on to request my use for the premeditated protection of the State from any outside attacks. I assume that means it plans to use my visions for more than just tracking down members of PHOENIX, like Dr. Richter claimed.

"Good luck with that," I hiss, seething.

I can't even control this power, so what on earth makes the State think that it can?

Ezra squeezes my hand, and my eyes shift to his, the warm depths of his gaze loaded with so many silent questions. The way he looks at me compels me to speak.

"The State's planning to wage war against..." *Everyone,* I think to myself, but my voice trails off before I can finish the sentence out loud. Shaking my head, I ask, "Why would it do that?"

Ezra scowls at the screen. "Complete control and domination. The State clearly thinks it has the tool to achieve that end, and it seems like it's more than willing to use it."

Letting go of my hand, he leans over the desk and taps the screen once more, flipping through the pages of the file again. I'm not sure what he's looking for, and I don't bother to ask. Instead, I back away, crossing the room, putting some much-needed distance between myself and the documented evidence of what I am.

And of what I might yet still become.

I return to the bookcase I was admiring before and skirt along the wall until I pass one of the two side rooms veering off from the office. Something large and black catches my eye, enticing me through the archway. Ezra calls my name, but I ignore him.

Unlike the main part of the office, this space is comprised almost entirely of glass. Tiny mirrors no bigger than my palm line the sole circular wall right up to the highest point of the domed ceiling where a crystal chandelier dangles from the center of the tiled pattern, exploding downward into a long, pointed sculpture resembling a cluster of icicles. My face fills each of the glass fragments surrounding me.

In the middle of the room stands the imposing object which drew my gaze: a grand piano, its shining ebony surface as smooth and reflective as still water. The sight of such an item here startles me. Whereas the contraband articles in the office were small and could be easily tucked away during a search, something like this isn't owned with the intention of being hidden.

No, this is a display. And a proud one at that.

Goosebumps rise on my arms, and I shiver. Seeing this piano standing here so openly, in plain sight for anyone passing to see, is an affront to all the people who were put to death over the years just for owning instruments like this one. People who just wanted to cling to what little beauty still remained in the world.

People like my father.

This display…

This *exhibition*…

It's a mockery of the individuality and creativity they all suffered for.

Exhaling, I trail my fingers along the ivory keys, just as I did to a similar piano all those years ago when I was first exposed to the greatest secret I would ever know. I was young then, so I didn't understand the consequences.

Not like I do now.

My father wasn't a bad person, and he definitely didn't deserve what happened to him. He was merely a lover of history and appreciated anything that commemorated the old world. He didn't want us to forget where we came from, like the State encouraged us to. Instead, he felt it was his duty to preserve that past. To cherish those little pieces of our history. So, he would restore and collect banned items and stow them in a hidden place no one else knew about, all for the sake of safekeeping that knowledge.

It was for that reason he was executed.

As far as I know, I was the only person he ever shared the full extent of his secret with, and in exchange for my silence, he would teach me about the books and other objects he had collected—some of which were instruments. That secret stood at the center of our relationship and strengthened our bond in a society that discouraged such closeness, familial or otherwise. After all, our loyalty was meant for the State, not for the people around us, regardless of shared blood.

My mother never understood our camaraderie and tried to sway us toward the more commonplace reservation and distance we observed among other families. Over time, her suspicion grew, and eventually, she uncovered what we were up to. When that happened, she didn't hesitate. She did her duty to the State, as was expected, and reported my father.

Looking back, I'm surprised she didn't turn me in as well, regardless of the fact I was only a child, just shy of seven, at the time. If she was willing to hand over her own husband, why not her child?

I suppose she must've felt the blame lay with my father and that I was merely a victim of his influence. Or maybe he begged her to protect me and she honored his dying wish. It was the least she could do.

Still, I can't help wondering…if she hadn't found out my father's secret, if we hadn't been caught, would she have so readily given me up to the DSD like she did? Maybe if our family hadn't already succumbed to such tragedy, she would've protected me the way a mother is supposed to. The way any child deserves.

My eyes brim with tears as my fingers stroke a handful of keys, pressing down just enough to call up each note. As the ping of the strings bounces off the tiled walls, echoing throughout the small space, I recall the melody my father once taught me. I wish I had thought to ask how he knew it.

His face springs to the forefront of my thoughts, and in my memory, I hear the gentle lilt of his voice instructing me to follow his hands. I strike each note at the same moment he does, playing side by side—my father in the past and me in the present—as if we're finally together again. As the music grows, the memory in my head changes.

Behind my closed eyelids, all I see is his face, bloodied and beaten rather than smiling—the way I wish I remembered him. The happy memories were tarnished the moment the State stepped into our lives, and now, instead of his warm voice guiding me, all I hear are the words that have tormented me for years.

"I'm sorry, Wynter."

Tears stream down my cheeks, but I keep hitting the notes, the thrum of the vibrating strings reverberating into my fingertips.

"Wynter."

The coppery stench of blood fills my nose, and the wetness tickles my lips before splashing onto the keys and across my fingers. The sound of each drop *ping, ping, pings* in my ears.

"Wynter—"

A hand reaches out and touches my shoulder, grabbing me just like the Enforcer's hands did that day. I remember the feel of those fingers, strong and firm, as they pulled me away from my father.

Pressure balloons in my head as my lungs fill with air, bursting with a scream that rises up, pushing at the inside of my lips. I won't let them do this to us.

Not again.

A stabbing pain hammers into my temples, and with a shriek, my building power rips out of my body like the lash of several dozen whips. As the pressure pushes outward, the mirrored wall shatters.

Aside from the deafening crack of glass, the only sound that registers in my brain is a strange muffled grunt. Above me, the crystal chandelier swings from side to side as the tiles shower to the carpet like rain.

I spin on my heel, lured by the abrupt surge of energy tearing through my body like a drug, and glare down at the cowering man on the floor, his back pressed against what remains of the mirrored wall. When I take a step toward him to finish what I started, his frightened expression stays my hand.

As he stares up at me, familiar hazel eyes wide with fear, the memory of who he is takes shape in my head, bringing me back to myself and releasing me from my temporary insanity. Horrified, I glance from the bleeding gash on Ezra's right cheek to the glass shards scattered around us.

A single thought breaks through the fog dulling my senses. *What have I done?*

I blink as the pressure regains control, pushing all sense of who I am back down under the surface, like a parasite finally taking over its host. My head snaps to the side, my attention focused, as heavy footfalls plod against the carpeted floor. As I turn, glancing back into the main part of the office, at least a dozen Enforcers file through the doorway.

When they raise their guns, I feel it—this disease, this *power*, taking hold of me. Its sole focus is self-preservation, and it succeeds in its task by ripping the weapons from the Enforcers' hands and turning them back on their owners.

I'm barely aware of what I'm doing as bullet casings launch into the air. The ammunition perforates the beautiful shelves behind the soldiers, breaking the glass and destroying most of the rare objects and books they held. If I wasn't so wholly consumed by this power, I might mourn the loss of such priceless treasures.

Crimson spatters the carpet, and, for the briefest of moments, I have the most bewildering thought that I am like the white fibers under my feet—once pure and untainted but now, thanks to this disease, irreversibly tarnished, slowly rotting as the evil within me spreads. Like this carpet, I am forever stained by the blood I have spilled.

Once the last Enforcer goes still, I release my mental hold on the guns, and when they fall, I welcome the glorious relief of pressure as a weight seems to lift off my skull. Without that pressure to burden me, I drop to my knees, more exhausted than I've ever been in my life.

A familiar warmth catches me before my head hits the floor.

"Wynter," Ezra breathes in my ear. His tone is drenched with worry.

My movements are sluggish as I search for his gaze, my body rigid with shock and fatigue as the last of my energy fades, leaching out of my body like a tide drifting back out to sea. Blood still oozes from the wound on Ezra's cheek, but when I try to lift a hand to wipe it away, he flinches, afraid of my touch.

He's scared of me, I realize.

And he should be.

I glimpse the movement of his throat as he swallows, his eyes flickering away from mine, drifting back toward the open area of the main office space. I follow his line of sight to the mutilated bodies piled in a heap before us, their corpses surrounded by weapons, empty casings, and fragments of the inhumane world I allowed myself to get lost in.

In my head, I'm screaming, *Not again!* But when my lips finally move, they only manage to say, "What have I done?"

Ezra doesn't answer me.

Hot tears stream down my face as I gape at the massacre before us. *I did this. I killed those people.*

Me…

I killed them.

See? that taunting voice says in my head. *You can't change what you are…and what you are is a killer.*

My fingers weave through my sweat-matted hair, gripping my head as a glint of light reflects off the glass on the floor, catching my eye. Hand shaking, I curl my grasp around the nearest shard, but when I raise the broken mirror, I don't recognize the person looking back at me. No, not a person.

WHAT HAVE I DONE?

A monster.

My eyes are black, a far-stretching abyss with only a sliver of white on each side. My usually alabaster skin is gray and sickly, the color contrasted by the streaks of blood seeping from my nose and the corners of my eyes, making me look possessed.

I choke back a sob. Ezra places a hand on my back, and when I try to hide my face, not wanting to see his reaction to this terrible, monstrous thing I've become, his fingers graze my chin, forcing me to look at him.

When our eyes lock, fresh tears burn across my vision and broken cries rack my lungs. Ezra pulls me into his chest, hugging me as tightly as either of us can physically bear. Despite his horror, he holds me close when anyone else would run away.

I slump against his chest and press my eyes shut, desperate for consolation from my guilt, but reality seems intent on dragging me away from even the smallest comfort. My eyes spring open again as slow footsteps pad across the blood-soaked carpet, bringing my worst fear into view.

I glance up, meeting that familiar cold gaze that haunts my every waking thought.

"Hello again, Wynter," Richter says with a smile.

TWENTY-TWO

SEEING HIM AGAIN IS ALL it takes to push me to the edge. The deranged hand of fear rushes out from the darkness in the back of my head where I've been trying to keep it and clutches my throat, crushing my wind pipe until I can't breathe. My screams are silent as I fight for air.

I try to clamp my eyes shut again, begging myself to wake up from this nightmare. But I can't find the strength to look away from the monster in front of me, and even if I could, doing so wouldn't change a damn thing. Because I know this isn't a dream.

This is real, and my torturer has finally found me.

Dr. Richter meets my gaze with his trademark sinister grin, his expression soulless and devoid of feeling—much like the vacant faces worn by the slew of bodies littering the floor. He doesn't seem surprised by the corpses. If anything, he seems pleased by them.

"Austin," Ezra gasps beside me.

I peek up at Ezra, pulling out of his arms just enough to get a good hard look at his face. The shock and pain I find there remind me that I'm not the only one this reunion is hard for.

Steeling myself, I turn my gaze back to Richter. The smile has vanished from his lips, and the gray depths of his eyes have shifted their focus, turning from me and locking instead on his brother. As they glare at each other, it sinks in, more than ever before, that I was right about this mission.

We never should have come to this place.

"Ezra," Richter snarls through clenched teeth.

Dread and anxiety both prickle my flesh as the weight of reality pins me down to the floor. Only one coherent thought manages to form in the swirling vortex filling my head.

I was right. The DSD planned all this.

Ezra unfolds his arms from around me, and I'm cold without his reassuring warmth to keep me sane. As he rises to his feet, the jaws of madness open up from the ground beneath me. Before they can close and trap me in a cage from which I might never escape, Ezra reaches down and snakes a hand around my waist again—a lifeline saving me from my own self-destruction. With a gentle tug, he pulls me upright, away from the darkness and back into the light.

My surroundings are a muddled blur as the room begins to spin, slowly at first, then building…faster…faster…faster… Vertigo distorts my senses, and my knees buckle, sending my body tumbling sideways into Ezra's chest, my fingers gripping his shirt as if it's the only way to keep me here on this plane of existence. He catches me, holding me close to his side.

As my vision clears, bringing the room back into sharp clarity, I focus on Dr. Richter, trying to make sense of this riddle and work out how he's managed all this. Trap or not, there's no way he could've known I would be part of this mission. So, does that mean he's actually here to see his brother and the transmission from Bilken was merely a ploy to reunite them? To finally carry out whatever twisted revenge he's been planning since Ezra and Rai left all those years ago?

I wouldn't put it past him.

Then again, back in the tunnels, Jenner said that the transmission was addressed to Nolan, not Ezra. Does that mean Nolan had a hand in orchestrating this set-up? If so, why? Why would someone in PHOENIX want to work with the State—their enemy? What would he and Bilken get out of this ruse?

Dr. Richter lowers his gaze to the broken bodies sprawled across the floor. As he nods his approval, his fingers graze his chin. "You made short work of those Enforcers. You're progressing much more quickly than I had anticipated."

I bite down on my tongue to keep my anger at bay. After eighteen years living in the State, it should be as easy as breathing to suppress my emotions, and yet, Dr. Richter gets under my skin and affects me in a way no one else ever has. Every word, every breath, out of his vile mouth stirs up a homicidal rage I never knew existed within me.

"What do you mean?" Panic warps Ezra's tone, and a thousand unspoken questions swim in his eyes when he looks at me.

From the moment I read the first words of the military order we found on Bilken's computer, I understood what I am and what the State plans for me to become. Now, Ezra will finally understand, too. He'll see what I've gotten PHOENIX involved with.

He'll grasp how dangerous I really am.

My voice breaches the silence in a venomous hiss as I hurl an accusatory glare at Dr. Richter, my eyes like knives penetrating their target. "You knew this power was more than just visions. You knew what it would turn into, what I would become."

Flashes of vivid memories fill my head, showing me the faces of everyone I've killed—first, the attendant at the DSD and now, the Enforcers sent ahead to confront us. Even with all I've learned about the impossible nature of this disease, I still can't wrap my head around how I did it. I didn't even have to lift a finger. Every movement, every action was done with my mind, and what's more frightening is I had absolutely no power to stop it. It was like I was a slave to my whims. I wanted to kill them, so I did.

It was as simple as that.

Smirking, Dr. Richter gestures toward the glass desktop and the light emitting from the glowing computer screen. "I'm assuming you've seen your file? You should know by now you're not the only one we've tested on. So, yes. Of course, we knew. Did I not tell you that you were evolving and I had my suspicions as to what you were? How else would I have known that, I wonder, if I didn't have extensive insight about your condition?"

His words swarm my thoughts, and a buzzing sound floods my ears as I recall that initial interrogation at the DSD. All those other files he showed me, all those people… I knew the truth ever since Ezra told me about his mother, but still, I didn't want to believe it. I didn't want to believe so many others like me have existed and that they all died at the hands of such evil.

If Dr. Richter is capable of remorse, he doesn't show it.

"Your visions aren't the only reason the State wishes to use you. It's what you are becoming that's of far more interest to us." He steps over an unmoving arm, his shining black shoes squelching against the crimson-stained carpet. "It's fate, really. Even your initials agree. W…A…R…" He purrs each letter. "It's like you were destined to become the weapon that would allow us to conquer the world."

"I don't understand," I breathe, my voice ragged. "Why would you choose to start another war when one is already happening within our own walls?"

Dr. Richter cocks a bemused eyebrow at me. "You mean PHOENIX?" He scoffs—a cruel, mocking bark of a laugh—and pushes his glasses farther up his nose. "They aren't a problem. They never really were."

Ezra tenses beside me, and the confusion on his face mirrors the jumbled tangle of thoughts in my head. Dr. Richter chuckles as he continues to skirt around the mangled bodies between us.

"PHOENIX was more of a menace to begin with, but over the years, you've made yourselves quite useful. What better way to subjugate the public than to frighten them with the constant threat of terrorism? It was the perfect starting point for the State to strengthen its hold. We could've easily disposed of you at any time. Keeping you around just happened to align with our interests."

As much as I wish this was just another deceit, what Richter is claiming lines up with what Jenner said about the attacks blamed on PHOENIX. How they were all devised and carried out by the State. That PHOENIX was merely a scapegoat to mask the real instigator behind those horrors.

Still, if what he's saying is true, that doesn't answer why he constructed this trap. Or what he's hoping to gain in the long run. Why is he here?

Why are *we* here?

"Why go through the trouble to bait them to come here if the plan wasn't to trap PHOENIX?" I ask.

"I'm not after PHOENIX," Dr. Richter says, a slight cryptic laugh in his voice. "Well, not all of them."

"Rai…" Ezra whispers, his skin chalky.

I should've seen this coming. From the moment I suspected the DSD was behind the transmission, I should've known this wasn't only about me. I've learned enough about their past relationship—and of Richter's personality—to know he would never forget Rai's betrayal. Or forgive it.

As I once said to Ezra, Dr. Richter won't stop until he gets what he wants and anyone who gets in his way is an acceptable casualty.

Dr. Richter slides closer to me until the heap of corpses no longer stands between us. Nothing does. He could reach out and touch me if he felt so inclined.

"While I have my personal reasons for being here, I actually came to retrieve you, Wynter."

Ezra shoves me behind him with a sweep of his arm, baring his teeth. An animalistic growl rumbles deep in his throat. "She's not going anywhere with you."

"Are you sure about that?" Dr. Richter flashes his signature smile, and that one look says so many things I don't want to acknowledge. It screams of victory. "Surely, you knew the potential consequences involved with bringing her here. You knew the risk, and you took it anyway. Or perhaps, you couldn't resist the temptation and wanted to see her power for yourself, the same way I always wondered about Mother's. After all, we do come from the same stock, Brother, despite how greatly we might both wish to deny it."

Ezra winces as if Dr. Richter has struck him, then risks a glance over his shoulder at me. I shake my head, hoping to convey what I'm unable to find the words to say. I want to tell him that I know Dr. Richter is lying, and that I know he only brought me here to protect me from something, even if he's too afraid to say what. That he's not the same insatiable monster his brother is. I want to tell him that I don't blame him for whatever comes next, even if it means I end up back at the DSD. Even if all this ends with me dead.

If I was honest with him—and with myself—I would admit that outcome is what's best for everyone.

Tears prick at the corners of my eyes as I swallow, pushing down the lump in my throat. "What now?" My voice is barely audible despite the hush.

"Well, unfortunately, you killed all the Enforcers I enlisted to detain you, not that I'm entirely surprised," Dr. Richter says, without sounding the least bit contrite. "No matter, I've called for more, and they should be here any moment now. Then you'll go back to where you belong."

My fingers grab at the back of Ezra's shirt, my nails like pincers, holding me to him. "You're crazy if you think I'll go with you willingly."

A bored expression crosses Dr. Richter's face, and he shrugs, indifferent to my protests. "If you wish to leave with your new friends, that's your choice. But just know that it's inevitable you will return to my care. Although, if I were you, I'd do so sooner rather than later. That power of yours won't monitor itself."

Ezra whips around, bringing his mouth to my ear. Between us, he holds his communicator clenched in his hand. My eyes flick down to the message flashing across the small screen.

10 E SPOTTED. T2G.

E? T2G?

"We have to get out of here," he whispers in a rush. "The others have sighted more Enforcers, and if we don't leave now, we won't be leaving at all."

Then it clicks. The E must stand for Enforcers and T2G...

Time to go.

I nod. He doesn't need to tell me twice. I don't plan on sticking around here any longer than necessary, not if the end result means I'll wind up back on that cold metal table at the DSD.

Ezra wraps his arm around my waist and helps me toward the door, my body drained from my confrontation with the Enforcers. Dr. Richter stands by, watching us with those unfeeling gray eyes and an amused grin taking form on his lips. He does nothing to stop us or prevent our escape.

Just as I allow myself to believe he's letting us go, his voice plunges into my back, stabbing me.

"There's a cure."

Every inch of my body freezes. Ezra tugs against me with a quiet plea to keep moving, but Dr. Richter's words hold me in place. Against my better instincts, I peer over my shoulder.

"Your condition is progressing far too quickly," he warns. "Without proper treatment, your symptoms will worsen, and we all know where that will leave you, don't we, Brother?"

Where will this condition leave me? I wonder.

Ezra and Richter have only ever seen this disease end with death. But I'm not concerned with *my* death. I'm concerned with the deaths of those I care about. The fatalities I will cause if my condition does continue to worsen. I've already murdered at least a dozen Enforcers, and I'll never forget what I did to Dr. Richter's attendant. I don't want to carry the burden of taking any more lives.

I don't want to hurt anyone else.

Like so many times before, the recollection of that vision of the future manifests in my head. The end of the world takes shape, flaunting the approaching destruction and death I, alone, will cause.

How many people will I kill when that future clashes with the present? How many lives will I take because of this disease? Because of what I am?

A cure...

A cure would take all that away.

"He's lying, Wynter." Ezra's hand tightens around my waist. "We have to go *now*," he urges.

I walk forward a few steps, but my eyes linger on Richter's smug face, searching for the lie I know must be concealed there beneath his conniving guise. I know he'd say anything to get me to go with him, but what if, this time, he's actually telling the truth?

What if there really is a cure?

Can I risk walking away without being sure?

"If you come back to the DSD willingly, I will ensure you get the cure before it's too late."

Too late? When will it be too late? And how long would he allow my condition to progress before administering this so-called cure? How long would he continue to use me before my body would be so ravaged that a cure wouldn't even help me?

I'm hesitant to believe him, given what I've already been through and the fact that he's neglected to mention anything about a cure until now. But I also can't ignore the possibility he's presenting.

That future...

The end of the world...

What if this is how I prevent it? What if the cure is real, and with it, no one else has to die because of me? Because of this horrible *thing* I'm becoming?

The options before me beat against the walls of my skull, but I'm too exhausted to know what to do. If I were to go with Dr. Richter, I'd be giving myself up with no guarantee the cure even exists. Torture and death would mark the rest of my days.

But if I don't go with him, I'd be dooming everyone in the world to die. I wouldn't be the only victim of this disease anymore, and I would be responsible for every life lost because of my cowardice. If I don't go with him, it would only be because I don't want to leave the people who have since entered my life.

Rai.

Jenner.

Ezra...

We've barely had the chance to really get to know each other, but the thought of leaving them now, of never seeing them again, is a physical weight on my chest crushing me. No...if I don't go with Richter, it would only be because I'm selfish.

Because I'm afraid.

Ezra hauls me from the room before I can make a decision, his fingers digging into my side, steering my movements forward when I can barely find the focus to guide my own steps. Side by side, we fumble over the threshold.

Dr. Richter's raised voice echoes down the corridor, chasing us as we limp away from the office. Every word he shouts tempts me back.

"Think about it, Wynter. You know where to find me."

TWENTY-THREE

MY BREATHS ESCAPE IN RAPID succession, ravaging my lungs and leaving my mouth and throat parched. I try to swallow, but every attempt feels like hot gravel grinding against sandpaper, making me shudder with the effort. I'm desperate for water, but there's no time to stop or rest.

Right now, our only focus is getting out of this place.

Ezra's arm tightens around my waist, his breathing strained as he supports my weight while trying to keep a decent pace. I try to ease his burden, but I'm tired and weak, and every step is a tremendous effort. The after-effects of what I did in Bilken's office are wreaking havoc on my body, crippling my muscles and limbs until they stop functioning altogether. At that point, Ezra has no choice but to drag me.

Despite everything I know about his character, I half-expect him to abandon me and save himself, but he doesn't even seem to consider doing that. He simply grits his teeth and carries on as if it's the only thing he can do.

As if it's the only option he has.

The hallways seem to go on forever. Was this building always so big? Darkness creeps in at the corners of my eyes, and I'm not sure if what I'm seeing past the haze impairing my vision is real or imagined. I can't think straight, and the exhaustion consuming me is only making my symptoms worse.

Distant voices enter my ears, jerking me back from the pull of unconsciousness. Ezra quickens his pace, and when we round the next corner, I glimpse the distorted silhouettes of Jenner and Rai at the opposite end of the corridor. Their concerned faces sharpen as we barrel toward them.

"Where the *hell* have you been?" Jenner asks through clenched teeth.

Relief rushes through me as my eyes lock with Rai's. Her golden-tinged brown skin is pink with exertion, and she's breathing hard, her chest heaving, but she appears unharmed as far as I can tell.

Breaking away from Ezra, I throw the full weight of my body at Rai, choking back a sob. Moisture springs into my eyes as my arms wrap around her back, hugging her to me as tightly as I can—as if my brain won't really believe she's here with us otherwise. My useless legs fail to hold me upright, and as I sink to the floor, she kneels alongside me.

"What's going on?" she hisses over my head.

Warmth spreads through my chest as she brushes a careful finger over my cheek, wiping away the blood and tears. I can feel the sticky streaks on my skin, but I lack the strength to care about how frightening I must look to her. All I can think about is her safety and how much I want to get out of here before Dr. Richter finds us again.

Ezra speaks in a hurried voice, filling the others in on what happened while we were separated. "Bilken was a dead end. It was a set-up by Austin. He's here for Wynter."

"He's here?" Rai asks, her tone fraught. A tremor rolls over her hands, and she quickly flattens her palms to my back to still them.

"We have to go right now," Jenner snaps, casting a panicked glance over his shoulder. "The others are already out and waiting back in the tunnels. But they won't wait forever."

Rai unhooks my arms from her body as Ezra steps forward and lifts me up off the ground. My eyes drift from her face to his.

"Right," he grunts, adjusting his hold on me. His fingers brush against my waist. "Let's get out of here."

We continue through the far-stretching corridors in tense silence. Ezra and I trail Jenner's lead, our movements awkward as he holds up the bulk of my weight and we try to keep our steps synchronized. Rai follows behind us, bringing up the rear of the group, to keep an eye out for Enforcers.

We head back the same way we came, since finding an alternate exit would also mean finding a new route back to the tunnels, and we don't have time for that. Taking our original path isn't without its own share of danger, but, luckily, we don't run into any resistance or trouble of any kind along the way.

Like before, the building is eerily empty.

What happened to the Enforcers the others spotted before? I wonder through the residual pain in my head. Has Dr. Richter called them off, or are they lying in wait, preparing to attack us when we least expect it?

Sweat beads along my brow and hairline as we push ahead through the soundless hallways, and a fever flares along my skin, burning hotter with every laborious step. The heat spreads into my nose and travels down into my lungs where it chokes me like a thick layer of smoke.

Despite my suffocation, a scream explodes up my throat as the stabs in my head appear out of nowhere, hitting me in that same familiar pattern. I trip, falling… falling…falling…but through the growing fog darkening my surroundings, I think I hear Ezra call my name. I can just make out the blurred features of his face, his unblinking eyes staring down into mine as he pulls me against his chest.

His voice slips away, swallowed by the sudden onslaught of convulsions that happen every time I go through this. I try to go back to him—to escape the future intent on pulling us apart—but I can't seem to figure out how.

I'm too weak to fight what's coming.

A long moment passes where all I'm aware of is pain. Then, as if waking from a dream, I open my eyes to find myself back in Bilken's office. The broken bodies still litter the floor, their blood soaking into the once pristine white carpet. Nothing is any different than it was when we were here less than twenty minutes ago.

My gaze crawls from one end of the office to the other, starting at the shards of broken mirror on the floor and ending at the window behind Bilken's desk. Dr. Richter stands in front of the panes, his hands knitted behind his back, staring out into the unending darkness of night on the other side of the glass.

"Austin."

A rush of fear sweeps through me at the sound of his name, and sucking in a sharp breath, I whip around to find Rai standing in the doorway. She hesitates before inching into the room, her eyes drawn to the carnage forming a small mountain between them.

"Raina…" Dr. Richter whispers.

As if lured by his voice, she gasps, crying out, "I had to see if it was true for myself. I had to see if it was really you behind all this."

A grimace warps his lips. "And now that you know? How does that make you feel?"

"I just want to know why!" She raises a clenched hand up in front of her chest, as if doing so will hold her aching heart in one piece. "None of this is doing your mother's memory any justice—"

"My mother?" He scoffs, letting out a soft laugh. "My work has nothing to do with honoring my mother."

I glance between them, noting the doubt on Rai's face. The same uncertainty overwhelms me. From the moment I learned about Ezra's and Richter's mother,

I assumed her death was the latter's motivation for pursuing others afflicted with the same condition. Perhaps because of lack of closure, or maybe he really has been working toward a cure this whole time as a way of honoring her memory—not that his personality exactly oozes with sentimentality. Either way, I assumed her demise was the reason for why he is the way he is.

"My mother's illness might've initially been why I showed an interest in this line of science, but after a while, my tragic origin tale no longer held any bearing. All that mattered was progress. And what incredible progress I've made."

His words send a tingle of unease up my spine, even though, in the physical sense, I'm not really here.

Tears well in Rai's eyes. "Then why?"

"Can you think of no other reason?" he asks her. "Can you honestly not figure out why I might desire the power to locate whoever I want?"

"All this...because of me?"

"You gave me no other choice," he growls. "You left me. You *chose* Ezra."

"I didn't choose Ezra!" Denial erupts from her lungs as a single tear spills down her cheek. "I chose freedom over slavery. I chose a new life. A life with meaning and purpose—"

"Slavery?" He sneers. "Is that how you saw it?"

She flinches. "It's how I still see it. Everyone in this corrupt country is a slave, even you."

Nodding, he paces in front of the window. "And what sort of life would you say you have now? Always in hiding. Always running. Where is the meaning and purpose you yearned for in such a sorry existence? What kind of life is that?"

"One I chose." Her voice wavers, breaking a little. "One where my free will wasn't stolen from me."

He stills at these words and glares at Rai with eyes as cold and lifeless as the corpses between them. "It pains me to hear that's how you pictured a life with me. And here I would've given you the world."

Rai shakes her head. "That world you say you wanted to give me is broken. What you were offering me was merely poison wrapped up in a pretty package. It would've killed me if I'd stayed. Would that have made you happy?"

Dr. Richter lowers his gaze but doesn't utter a word, and as the seconds tick by without either of them speaking, I realize any feelings they may have once shared have been pushed aside and overridden by anger. Anger born from the opposing paths they chose to take all those years ago.

Paths that led to very different futures.

What was the defining moment that broke them apart? Was it Ezra's decision to join PHOENIX, or did it go back even further to an event before that? Perhaps back to the moment when Dr. Richter's career path was decided? Or when his mother started showing peculiar symptoms that first drew his interest?

If he had been projected for another sector, would things have turned out differently for them? Would he still have become this obsessive, heartless sadist, or would he have maintained whatever decent qualities once made her care for him?

"I never stopped thinking about you."

Dr. Richter and I both glance at Rai, equally stunned by her confession. My eyes jump back and forth between them, and for a flicker of an instant, I glimpse something in his expression that almost makes him seem human.

That flicker disappears just as soon as it surfaced.

"There's nothing I can do now, Raina. You must know that."

A tight, bitter smile tugs at the edges of her trembling lips. "Once an enemy, always an enemy, right? Isn't that Termination's mantra?" With a trembling breath, she clamps her eyes shut. Tears slip from between her closed lids. "I've known from the moment I left you what would happen if we ever saw each other again. If it's any consolation, I'm sorry. About everything. My choice was selfish, but I never wanted to hurt you."

"I wish an apology was enough, but you've left me no choice now that I see your mind won't be changed. You've brought this upon yourself." Every word is a stone he flings at her, all cast with a single intent.

To maim.

Time seems to slow as he reaches into his pocket, and when he raises his arm, a scream tears from my lungs. Although I race forward, determined to put myself in his path, I know there's nothing I can do. I'm a mere apparition with no substance to intervene or change anything about this moment.

I'm completely helpless.

Still, I reach out a hand, and as my fingertips brush where the barrel of his gun meets the air, a murky cloud descends upon the room, abruptly ending the vision. My surroundings darken, pushing me back into consciousness, as Dr. Richter's voice fills my ears.

"The irony is almost poetic, don't you think? You ran, and yet, the poison still got you."

My eyes snap open.

"Wynter!" Ezra leans into my line of vision, relief washing over his face like a rush of color flooding into pale cheeks.

I inhale through my nose, but my breaths hit a wall. My airway is blocked. I let out a whimper. If I can't breathe, I can't tell Ezra about what I just saw, and I need to tell him right away.

I need to warn him about what's going to happen.

Sensing my distress, he holds a canteen up to my mouth, and the water is a welcome respite, easing the burning pain inside me. The liquid loosens the blood sticking my lips together, helping me to speak.

"Ra—" I wheeze.

Nausea grips my stomach. Gagging, I twist away from Ezra, hurling onto my side, and spew across the wooden floorboards. Icy shivers travel up my spine with each heave.

Ezra's hands are like hot coals on my skin, but I never ask him to move them away as he holds me with one and rubs my back with the other. He keeps me steady until the sickness passes.

Once my stomach is purged, I give a shuddering sigh and allow my body to go fully limp, resting my head in Ezra's lap. For a few moments, I lie still, simply getting my bearings. His voice in my ear brings the world into focus.

"Wynter...what did you see?"

The memory of Rai's face in my head rockets through me. "Rai..." I try to explain what I saw, but my mouth struggles to shape the words.

"What about Rai?" he presses. "She's right—"

He turns, gesturing with his thumb over his shoulder. I follow his gaze, but, like I foresaw, the only person we find standing behind us is Jenner.

Ezra's head snaps side to side, his eyes searching. "Where is she?" he practically shouts. The muscles in his arms strain against my sore body.

Jenner's face goes ashen as he fumbles for his communicator, calling Rai on the encrypted frequency band they're using for this mission. When she doesn't answer, he shakes his head in disbelief. "She was right behind us! Where the hell did she go?"

Ezra grabs my shoulders, his fingers gripping tight enough to leave bruises. "Where is she, Wynter? Where's Rai?"

My head is spinning, and quick, panting breaths part my lips. Pain echoes in my brain like a rumble of thunder after a lightning strike, obscuring everything around me. I can see Ezra. I can hear him.

But it's so hard to reach him.

"Rai..." I breathe, fighting to speak. "Ri...Richter..."

Ezra's mouth flattens into a thin line, the acceptance and fuming rage in his gaze both telling me he's realized what she's done without me needing to say anything more. I suppose he must've known it was always a possibility she would hunt down his brother once she found out he was here. Hell, maybe that's the only reason she came on this mission in the first place. Maybe she suspected Richter had something to do with the transmission and wanted to end things between them once and for all.

"I have to find her," Ezra says.

It occurs to me, past the haze in my head, that he's asking me—*begging* me—for guidance.

My throat is tight, like a hand around my neck, as I manage to push out the words, "Bilken's office."

With a faltering breath, Ezra leans in close to me until our faces are only a few inches apart. The growing distance in his eyes unnerves me.

"I need you to go with Jenner. He's going to get you out of here and help you to safety—"

Dread and panic both smother my chest, and my stomach seems to drop, falling into my feet. I don't know why, but I have a terrible feeling that surges further at his words. It scratches at the back of my brain, saying the same thing over and over again, like a warning. It tells me that, if Ezra leaves me now, I'll never see him again—regardless of the many visions and dreams that have suggested a different future awaits us. After all, how can I be certain those visions are showing me the truth of what will come to pass and not just one possible path?

How can I be sure the future won't change when I least expect it to?

All I do know is that our fates are intertwined, and my gut keeps telling me that if I survive tonight, he will as well. But I can only be sure of that if we stick together. Besides, I only came on this mission because of him. No way in hell is he abandoning me now after everything we've been through. If he leaves, if he *dies*, I'll never get the answers I sought PHOENIX out for. And if I never get those answers, then I exposed them all to my cursed existence for nothing.

No, if he wants to help Rai, he's taking me with him. Otherwise, I fear the worst. Otherwise, I'm certain I'll lose them both. As much as I want to save Rai, I can't let that happen.

As much as I want her to live, I can't watch him die.

"Wait—" My voice cracks as my fingers clutch his coat, holding him to me. Any other words I attempt to utter fail to form. My body isn't cooperating, and it's costing us all valuable time.

"Uh, I hate to spoil a perfectly good plan," Jenner interrupts, "but we have company."

Heavy footfalls trigger tremors in the floorboards, the sound of the enemy reverberating in the distance like the faint beating of drums. My eyes dart to the far end of the hallway as the first Enforcers round the corner, cutting off our intended exit. They raise their guns, preparing to fire.

Ezra jumps to his feet, cursing under his breath, and hoisting me up, he runs back the way we came, dragging my limp body beside him. If he wants to save Rai, he has no choice now except to take me and Jenner with him or risk sacrificing us to the Enforcers, which we both know he won't do. He'll find a way to save us all because that's just who Ezra is.

Clenching his jaw, he tightens his hold on me.

I try my best to keep up with him as he sprints through corridor after corridor back in the direction of Bilken's office. Each step is more draining than the last, sapping me of what little strength I still retain after my vision. Before long, I'm too weak to continue.

Ezra charges ahead, and I can sense his increasing frustration at my slowness. My feet fumble against the floor despite my silent pleas for them to move.

We'll never make it at this rate, I realize.

Ezra must be thinking the same thing because he bends down mid-stride and scoops me up off the floor. He carries me in his arms, building momentum, even with the added burden of my dead weight. As we run, the Enforcers' footsteps fade.

After several minutes, we find ourselves back in the dead end hallway where Bilken's office is located. Ezra's ragged breaths beat against my cheek, matching the frantic tempo of my erratic pulse. Our destination is so close now and moving closer with every second.

Rai's face appears in my head, and I pull at Ezra's shirt, urging him to move faster—ignoring the guilt blossoming in my chest that tells me he would've reached her already if he hadn't been forced to bring me along. Ignoring the realization that says, if she dies, it will be my fault.

No, I tell myself. *We're so close. We're almost there.*

Just a few more steps.

An ember of hope sparks to life in my stomach, igniting my nerves, but it's snuffed out before the flame can form, extinguished by the ringing echo of a gunshot. We don't see Rai. We don't have to. The splash of blood sprayed across the floor mere steps ahead of us is all the indicator we need to tell us what just happened.

At the sight of the blood, Ezra's grip on my body slackens, and he drops me, his arms going limp at his sides. I try to find my footing, but my legs are like twigs supporting a building of bricks. As they give out beneath me, strong arms take my weight.

"I got you," Jenner murmurs in my ear.

I crumple against him, my eyes drifting from Ezra's blank face to the bloodstained wooden floorboards.

This can't be happening. We were here.

We had made it.

"We…we're too late," I breathe.

"No!" The anguish in Ezra's voice breaks my heart. He stalks forward, reaching for his gun, his heated gaze focused on the open office door before us.

I know what he's going to do—or, at least, what he intends to do. He has a new mission, and its focus is one thing and one thing only.

To kill Dr. Richter.

I thrust out a shaking hand, wishing he'd stop and walk away from this vendetta while there's still time for us to escape. One death is enough.

Don't let it become two! I shout in my head, but exhaustion prevents the words from forming.

As if reading my mind, Jenner places me down on the floor, then dives after Ezra, snatching him by the neck of his coat and yanking him back.

"There's nothing we can do! We have to go!"

Ezra turns, his expression livid, and shoves Jenner away from him, who raises his arm. I wince at the sound of Jenner's fist making contact.

Ezra falters, stumbling to the side a few steps. His hand flies up to touch his red cheek.

"Listen to me!" Jenner barks before grabbing Ezra roughly by the shoulders. "Are you ready to die for revenge? Are you ready to let *her* die in the crossfire?" He points at me, his other hand tightening its grip, the skin of his knuckles turning white from the pressure. "I need you," he pleads, lowering his voice. "I can't save her alone."

Ezra balks at these words, the anger in his eyes overshadowed by the most peculiar fear. He stares at me as if he isn't quite sure what he's seeing.

The corridor quakes with the approaching sound of our doom. The Enforcers have almost caught up to us.

If we're going to escape, we have to go now.

Jenner releases Ezra's shoulder and returns to my side, easing me up off the hard floor and cradling me in his arms, holding me firm to his chest. With one last ominous glance in the direction of Bilken's office, he sets off down the hallway back the way we came, then turns right, following the only path left to us even though the route is blind.

My voice is raspy as I bellow for Ezra to follow us, my plea an incoherent rambling as my tongue trips over my words. Ezra hesitates for only a moment, then stalks Jenner's steps, pushing into a sprint to catch up with us. Relief squeezes my heart as I close my eyes, exhausted by this whole ordeal. When I open them again, Ezra's head is bowed, his gaze pinned on the floor, avoiding my gaze. He doesn't look at me again for the rest of our journey. And why should he?

Because of me, Rai is dead.

It takes longer than I'm sure any of us would've liked, but we finally make it back to the courtyard. Thanks to Jenner, we arrive at the tunnels in one piece. He places me on the ground—this time, on my feet—as he braces himself to lift the hatch door. The metal hinges screech, piercing the night air, when he pulls.

A bright light shines up to greet us from the depths of the hole. "What the shittin' hell took so long?" Duke yells, the glow of the beam reflecting off his face.

"I'll explain later!" Jenner positions my body in front of his, supporting my weight. "Catch her, will ya?"

He helps me sit down at the lip of the hole then lowers me into the darkness by my arms. As I drop, my stomach flips, even though the fall isn't far. Duke catches me almost at once, his muscles like rocks as my back smashes into his chest, forcing a groan from my lips.

For a long moment, he doesn't relinquish his hold on me, his eyes taking in the dried blood smeared across my face, his broad mouth slightly ajar in abject horror. His reaction doesn't surprise me, but I still look away.

Ezra follows next, probably forced by Jenner who likely doesn't believe he would follow us otherwise. Once he's back underground, he stands to one side of the group, waiting in silence.

When it's Jenner's turn, he tests the rope attached to the wheel, checking to make sure it's still secure, then jumps, splashing into the thin layer of water.

"Close it up," he orders as he trots back to my side.

Duke cocks a confused eyebrow at the hatch door before lobbing suspicious glances at Ezra, Jenner, and me. "What about Rai?" he asks, his tone wary.

My lips press together. Beside me, Jenner's body goes rigid. We both peer at Ezra, who stares blankly into the darkness around us.

"She's gone," is all he says, his voice lifeless.

Everyone gapes at Ezra's retreating figure as he turns and proceeds down the tunnel. He doesn't spare me a glance as he passes. He doesn't even look at Jenner. He simply walks by, his unfocused gaze set straight ahead as his body sinks into the shadows.

TWENTY-FOUR

THE JOURNEY BACK TO THE compound is long and quiet. No one speaks out of fear of upsetting Ezra, or maybe we just can't find the words to describe our grief. It follows us in the darkness like a stray dog begging for scraps—constantly nipping at our heels no matter how many times we try to shoo it away.

The sadness writhing in my own heart is an unwanted but familiar companion, and with each sodden step through the tunnels, my thoughts naturally drift to my father, recalling the day he was taken from me with unsettling clarity. The pain I felt then… It was exactly like this.

With Rai gone, it's like I've lost him all over again. She had become that person in my life—the parental figure I had begun to rely on since I can no longer rely on my mother and my father is gone, his spirit torn from this world. And, just like my father, her death is my fault. If he had never included me in his illegal activities, if I hadn't been so hell-bent on staying with Ezra, both my father and Rai might still be alive. But, because of me, they aren't, and now, instead of the agony of only a single loss creating a hole in my heart, I'm assaulted with the pain of two.

Now, my grief threatens to break me completely.

It's strange how someone can be there one minute and gone the next, their existence stamped out with the same ease and speed as drawing in or releasing a breath. It shouldn't be that easy.

Her life was worth more.

My eyes flit to Ezra, locking onto his back. He lumbers ahead of us, barely keeping within sight of the reach of our flashlights, the beams like fingers constantly trying and failing to grab hold of him and keep him from drifting farther away. It disturbs me to think how close he came to becoming just a memory, like my father and Rai. If Jenner hadn't intervened, if he hadn't stopped him from going after Richter—

Tears drip down my cheeks at the thought of losing him, this stranger who has somehow grown to mean so much to me despite our initial apprehension and distrust of each other. I scream Ezra's name in my head, but the silence swallows it whole. I scream, and I scream, but he doesn't look back. He just keeps walking, his pace steady and unchanging—the echo of his movements like a metronome counting the steps taking us farther away from what we've lost and will never get back again.

Steps that widen the distance between us.

I struggle to keep up with the others, even with Jenner's help. He holds me close, one arm propped around my waist with the other holding my hand where it lay slung over his shoulder. Every so often, I sense him looking down at me, but I never meet his gaze. Part of me doesn't want him to see the guilt in my eyes while another part doesn't dare turn away from Ezra, too afraid of what might happen if I were to glance away for even a second.

As I stare at the distant shape of Ezra's retreating figure, I imagine his face, expression drawn, the skin of his cheeks slick with tears. Silent, endless tears just like the ones from my vision.

"I'm sorry, Wynter."

I wave the recollection of his doleful voice away because he has nothing to apologize for. If anything, I'm the one who's sorry. No matter which way I look at it, we were in a lose-lose situation. Even if I hadn't stalled him and he had gone after Rai without me, those extra few seconds wouldn't have made any difference. Rai's fate was sealed the moment she went after Richter.

But knowing that doesn't ease my guilt, and I can't help thinking that if I had some control of this power, if I had seen what was going to happen sooner, then maybe I could've done something about it.

Stop it.

Change it…

Can the future even be changed? If it can't, then what's the point of these visions? Why show me such things if they can't be prevented? It's cruel, and I'd rather live in ignorance than be tormented by the inevitable.

Rai's smiling face fills every void in my head. In the short time I knew her, she made me feel loved and accepted, but more than that, she gave me a sense of protection—the only thing I ever really wanted from my mother. She made me feel welcome in a world where I had never experienced that feeling. Or expected to. She was full of hope, gentle, and kind.

And because of me…she's dead.

Time passes in a daze until we arrive back at the compound. Together, Jenner and I hobble toward the round hole in the wall marking the end of the tunnel, and as he lifts me over the threshold, my eyes instinctively search for Ezra. He disappears into the darkness of the maze before I'm even fully through the hatch door.

"Maybe I should go after him," I mutter, gasping, leaning against the nearest wall to catch my breath.

"No." Jenner jerks his head. "What Ezra needs right now is space. We should all just leave him alone."

I open my mouth to protest but immediately snap it shut again at the warning look on Jenner's face. He's right. It's not my place to go after Ezra. Besides, I'm reluctant to chase after him anyway, worried he'll blame me for what happened to Rai. And he should. Why else would he have brought me along if he didn't intend for me to use my power to warn them? To keep a vigilant look out for danger? But if that's what he wanted, why couldn't he have just told me as much? I would've happily gone through the pain of these visions if it meant I could keep them all safe.

Tears prick at the corners of my eyes as a warm hand wraps around my shoulder and squeezes. Sniffing, I peek up, meeting Jenner's gaze. The tenderness I find there alleviates the pain in my heart just a little.

"Hey. You're already starting to look like yourself again," he says, a crooked smile touching his lips.

A flush crawls over my clammy skin, and I swallow, relieved he doesn't elaborate and even more thankful no mirrors are readily available for me to see the damage for myself. Back in Zone 1, Duke had looked at me as if I wasn't a human but a thing to be feared. Not that I blame him. The first time I witnessed the side effects of this disease, I thought I was staring into the eyes of a monster.

You're a murderer, that small voice says in my head, as if I had somehow forgotten. *Of course, you're a monster.*

Jenner returns his arm to my waist and carefully helps me away from the wall before leading me back through the maze without speaking a word. Once again, I find myself memorizing our steps, imprinting the turns we take on my memory. He only breaks the silence about thirty minutes later when we're standing awkwardly outside my quarters.

"You should get some sleep. It's been…" He trails off, looking flummoxed, then shakes his head in dismay. "Well, it's been a long night."

I nod, placing my fingertips on the door handle. "What about you?"

He lets out a sigh, raking a hand through his hair. The sooty strands stick up in several directions. "I don't think Ezra's in the right headspace to report on what happened, so I'll have to do it for him. They're going to want an explanation about what went down out there, not only with Bilken but with Richter and Rai. I don't think we can hide the truth about Ezra's relation to him anymore."

The worry lines creasing his brow set me on edge.

"Who will?" I ask in a breathless whisper. "Nolan?"

Jenner nods. "Among others."

He averts his gaze, and I wonder if he's being intentionally vague—if he isn't allowed to disclose that information or if he just doesn't trust me enough to tell me the details. I hope it's the former. After what happened tonight, I don't want to lose anything else, not even something as intangible as Jenner's trust.

Assuming I ever had it in the first place.

Suddenly, I recall something Ezra said when he first told me about the transmission from Bilken. I had pleaded with him not to go, and he had said it wasn't his decision to make. Like I first suspected then, someone else is calling the shots behind the scenes. Someone else made us go on that mission.

And that someone probably knew it was a trap.

"You mean whoever sent us to meet Bilken," I growl, not bothering to mask my anger.

He nods again but doesn't say anything more. As much as I'm involved in the events that transpired tonight, I'm still very much a stranger to PHOENIX. No matter which way I look at it, regardless of whether or not Jenner trusts me, I'm an outsider.

And outsiders are kept on the outside for a reason.

"I wish there was something I could do."

Rough fingers graze my cheek, applying pressure just under my chin, tilting my head back until I'm forced to look up. Jenner stares down at me, his dark brows furrowed.

"There is," he says, his tone slightly scolding. "You can rest. You've been through a lot tonight."

Maybe he's right. I mean, what else can I do?

Shoulders sagging with exhaustion, I sigh and turn the handle, plodding into my quarters. Jenner catches the door before it clicks shut behind me.

"Wynter." I glance back, meeting his gaze through the crack. "What happened wasn't your fault. It was no one's fault, you understand? I don't want you thinking otherwise."

Although he's wrong, I lack the energy to argue about it. It doesn't matter what he or anyone else might think. What happened to Rai was my fault for the simple reason that I could've prevented it. The pain everyone is feeling right now over her death…

It's all because of me.

I swallow and quickly slam the door shut, needing to escape those piercing blue eyes, which have this way of seeing straight into my soul. Pressing my ear to the metal, I don't move a muscle until his footsteps retreat down the corridor.

Once I'm certain Jenner's gone, I nudge open the door. As tired as I am, my body is filthy and I'm desperate to wash the stain of the past several hours off my skin. With a longing glance back at my bed, I quietly slink into the hallway.

The compound is empty as I head for the washroom. I shouldn't be surprised, considering the late hour, but still, the silence is unnerving. It's as if this place has been abandoned, stripped of all life in the hours we've been gone.

When I finally reach the showers, the fluorescent lights overhead flicker on automatically. I wince, unaccustomed to the glare after so many hours shrouded in darkness.

My fingers tremble as I unstrap my pack and peel off my clothes one piece at a time. The fabric, stained with sweat and copious amounts of blood, drops to the floor with a thud.

Shivering, I reach into an empty shower cubicle and turn the valve until a drizzle of hot mist warms the cool air. The heat is inviting, and I'm about to step under the water when I make the mistake of looking back at the mirrors. A scream catches in my throat when I see the ghoulish girl reflected there.

Blood and sweat are caked on her face and tangled in her wild, unkempt hair, the whites of her eyes streaky and red, as if she hasn't slept in days. Or weeks. Her irises—one green, one blue—have been swallowed by sinister inky black pools.

I stare at my reflection in horror, lifting a shaking hand to my face as if hoping the girl in the mirror won't copy the action. As if this isn't really me that I'm seeing. This girl with her terrifying black eyes…she's nearly identical to how I saw myself in my vision of the end of the world. So, does this mean that moment is creeping closer? Does this mean there's truly nothing I can do to avoid that future?

Hysteria claws at my chest, and in a fit of panic, I hurl myself under the cascading water. My fingers scratch at my aching skin, my nails biting into the flesh, scraping away the dried blood and sweat with fury. The residue rushes in streaks down my naked body, filling the base of the shower with red.

Tears spill down my cheeks, one after another, until my legs give out beneath the weight of my guilt and fear. Collapsing to the floor, I sob into my hands.

I'm not sure how long I sit here, weeping in a pool of crimson water. Seconds turn into minutes, which turn into hours, and yet, the shower is never able to cleanse the horrific images from my mind.

The attendant seizing on the cold tile.

The Enforcers, now a mountain of mangled bodies.

Rai, her blood splashing onto the floorboards.

The world and all life crumbling into ash.

When I finally step out of the shower, my eyes are red and raw from crying. In a sluggish daze, I peer down at my garments where they sit in a heap across the wet tiles. Like the last time I stripped off bloody clothes here, I don't bother to pick them up. They're dirty and I'm clean, so I fail to see the point.

What's the point of anything anymore?

My thoughts are foggy and distant as I trudge back to my quarters, the underground air nipping at my naked skin, although I barely notice the chill. Once back inside the isolation of my room, I collapse onto the bed and cocoon myself in the sheets, burrowing into the mattress as if I don't intend to ever resurface. Why would I?

It would be best for everyone if I don't.

I press my eyes shut. The emotions I've been working to bury are trying to force their way out of the box I've shoved them all into, but I know I won't survive them this time if they do manage to throw back that lid. I plead with my body to let me escape them, but sleep—sweet, blissful sleep—evades me.

When those emotions emerge and the pain strikes all over again, tears well in my eyes, burning like fire and carving scorching lines down my cheeks, leaving a salty residue on my skin. I cry, over and over, until I lack the energy to stay awake any longer and the darkness finally takes me.

I don't even notice my descent into sleep since the world beyond waking is just as grim. Like all the other times, I'm greeted by the familiar scene of destruction as the vision takes me back to the place where all this began and where everything will ultimately end. As I gaze upon the desolate wasteland, it's as if I'm standing at the edge of the world. Everything that ever mattered is gone, and I'm alone, just like I've always been. Just like I should be.

If I'm alone, no one else has to die.

I close my eyes. When they drift open again, nothing around me has changed. Ezra isn't here, although he usually is by this point in the vision.

For some reason, I'm still alone.

Is this the same vision I've grown so used to seeing? Or has something happened to change that future?

A faint moaning draws my gaze over my shoulder, and I whip around, expecting to find Ezra behind me. I blink against the haze of dust and debris, peering through the blinding fog toward several dark shapes rising up from the ground in the distance. As they shuffle closer, their faces sharpen.

My hand lifts to my mouth, stifling a scream, as I scramble backward, my eyes unable to look away from the figures moving toward me. As their feet drag through the dirt and the distance between us shrinks, I realize I recognize their faces. The PHOENIX members living in the compound are all here, looking at me, their hooded gazes vacant.

No, not just vacant. *Lifeless.*

I search the scattered mob in desperation until I spot Jenner's recognizable blue eyes staring at me from the farthest depths of the crowd. His name is barely a breath on my lips as my feet dart forward, cutting a path through their bodies. Heart racing, I push them aside until I'm standing face to face with my friend.

His eyes share the same empty look as the others. Unsure what to do to snap him out of his daze, I press my fingertips to his cheek.

If my touch is the trigger, the screams erupting around me are bullets. They cut through the air in a merciless hail, each shriek another perforation in my sanity, as the people I've only just met...start to die.

One by one, they drop to the ground. Only a few pass quickly. The others aren't as fortunate, writhing and twitching and screaming in the dirt. Their agony echoes around me in each unending shrill note.

My hands slam against my ears to drown out their screams, but, through the chaos, I somehow hear Jenner's voice. When he says my name, it's like a gunshot slicing through the cries engulfing the world.

"Wynter..."A spurt of blood spews from his lips as his eyes slip down to his chest, widening in surprise. I follow his gaze, cupping my hands around my mouth and nose to muffle my sobs.

A red stain spreads from the middle of his torso, expanding outward across the pale fabric of his shirt. I shake my head, but the pressure spreading through my body is building, and as my own scream breaks free of the cage of my lungs, my power lashes out, striking one of the only people I ever wanted to protect.

I can feel it. I can *feel* myself doing this to him, but no matter how hard I try, I can't stop it.

Control is always just out of my reach.

As his blood spatters my face, I collapse to my knees, and clamping my eyes shut, I scream again at full volume. I don't want to see any more. This isn't real. This isn't happening.

Please, let this never happen. Please, make this end.

As if hearing my prayers, the world around me goes silent. Swallowing, I peek open my eyes and pin my arms to my sides to quell the vibrations of fear spreading through me. Jenner is gone. The people from PHOENIX are gone. No one is dying.

I'm alone once again.

I abruptly regret my previous desire to sleep, now wanting nothing more than to wake from this nightmare. I beg my brain to return me to reality, but, instead, my surroundings blur and I realize the nightmare is far from over. The horror…

It's only just beginning.

Ezra steps into my line of vision, materializing in the dusty wind like a mirage. A single tear trails down his cheek when he speaks. "I'm sorry, Wynter."

This is where the vision always ends—just after he says these words. But this time, the vision is different.

This time, the nightmare doesn't end.

As the vision concludes, revealing a harsh truth I've been too afraid to fully acknowledge, I rush forward, yelling out his name. But, no matter how hard my legs push, I can't reach him.

Just like with Jenner, I'm helpless to stop this.

"No, no, no!" I cry.

Ezra doesn't move or scream like the others did. He simply sheds those silent tears as death takes him, starting at his feet and slowly devouring the rest of his body, disintegrating him piece by piece. His smile is the last thing I see, and then he's just gone, mere dust in the wind.

I wake to the deafening sound of my own despair. As my wails reverberate through the room, I bolt upright, my body fighting to breathe through the build-up of thick tears lining my throat. The cool air nips at my exposed chest as the bed sheets crumple around my waist.

Leaning forward, I rub a hand over my face and brush the sweat-matted hair from my eyes. Was what I saw just now only a dream?

Or was it a vision?

If it was the latter like I fear, then that means I will be responsible for far more than just the end of the world.

PHOENIX.

Jenner.

Ezra…

They won't die because of some apocalypse my powers inflict on this planet, alive and then gone in the blink of an eye, their deaths painless and quick.

Nothing about what I just witnessed was quick, and although I always knew their deaths would stain my hands, it's only now I grasp the full extent of what my vision has been saying.

It's always been me…

I will be the one who kills them.

TWENTY-FIVE

I SWING MY LEGS OVER the side of the bed. The air is cool against my naked skin, but I don't move or try to cover myself, my body paralyzed by the haunting images branded into my thoughts, plaguing me.

Pushing out a trembling breath, I wipe a hand over my face and tuck my sweat-matted hair behind my ears.

What I saw could've just been a dream, I tell myself. After all, there were no side effects, no bloody noses or seizures, like there usually are after one of my visions. Like the dream I had of Ezra, it was just that—a dream with no proof of any physical consequence.

Still, I can't help wondering…what if it wasn't?

The end of the world is unavoidable. Try as I might to ignore that fact, the end *will* come and *I* will cause it. And with the end of the world comes the end of all life. The ruin of our planet will go hand in hand with the deaths of everyone, including those I care about. On some level, I always understood that.

But seeing them die like that… Seeing their faces… Hearing their screams… Seeing *his* face… That was the point when this nightmare felt too close to reality. That was the point when I finally came to terms with exactly what my vision has been showing me.

My fingers comb through my still damp hair, the strands messy and tangled with sleep. Sniffing, I draw my legs toward my chest as my thoughts buzz around my skull in a dizzying circle.

Is there no way to circumvent what I saw?

Is there nothing I can do to prevent that future?

Ezra's face fills every available space in my head, and all the times I've seen him—both in person and otherwise—play through my mind on a loop. I see every moment…

Even the ones I don't want to.

I watch him die all over again. Pain stabs my chest like a knife plunging into my heart, the blade pushing deeper until I don't know where this agony ends and I begin. As the grief consumes me, I understand what has to be done. Acceptance sinks into my bones, even as I mourn everything I'll be giving up.

Dream or not, Ezra will die if I do nothing.

Before our mission to Zone 1, I would've been helpless to change that, but I have options now that Dr. Richter has revealed there's a cure. He could be lying, but I can't just assume he is. Not when a cure would solve everything.

Not when I'm already dying and that terrible destruction I saw is racing closer.

A cure would mean we avoid that future. It would stop the world from ending. It would stop me from committing any more massacres like what happened with those Enforcers at the magistrates building. Above all, it would save the few people I care about.

The few people I have left who I want to protect.

A breath puffs out my cheeks as my gaze turns to the spare clothes piled up in the corner. Although my body is still sore from last night, I drag myself out of bed and throw on a pair of pants and a long-sleeved shirt in a hurry. There's no time to waste. Every vision takes me one step closer to that vile future. If I'm going to do this, I have to go now.

I shove my feet into the extra pair of boots Rai gave me and rush through the doorway without looking back. My mind is made up. Nothing and no one will deter me from my decision, but I do need to see to one last thing before I walk away from this place for good.

I make my way through the network of hallways, searching the rooms without any clue where to find Ezra. The compound is immense, and there are countless places where he could be hiding, wallowing in his sorrow. With no other option, I explore every corner. Time might not be on my side, but I refuse to leave until I've seen him and Jenner again, just one more time to say goodbye.

I'll keep looking, no matter how long it takes me.

As I scour the compound, the quiet hum of night gives way to the chaotic din of morning. I'm eager to avoid the watchful leers of my waking neighbors, but I don't have to try very hard to ignore them. They seem just as content to pretend I don't exist.

Maybe they blame me for what happened to Rai.

I shake my head with fervor, discarding that thought. Considering how late it was when we got back, I doubt anyone is even aware of her death yet. Even if they did know about it, that wouldn't give them any logical reason to blame me. No one else here knows about my condition. No one else knows I had the power to save her or that, because of my lack of control, I let her life slip through my fingers. Therefore, if they do end up blaming me, it's only because they never trusted me in the first place.

Tucking my head down, I continue my search. There are more important things to worry about than what the people here might think of me. It's not as if any of them have bothered to get to know me except for Ezra and Jenner. No one else has risked life and limb to look out for me, especially given the short time I've known them.

Maybe the rest of the world can sense what I am and Ezra and Jenner are blind to that danger. After all, look what happened to my father and Rai. They each got close to me, and now, they're both dead.

Tears flood my eyes as it dawns on me that Ezra was right to keep his distance when we first met. I almost wish he had kept it that way.

Leaving would be so much easier if he had.

I swallow. As much as I don't want to tell them, it's only right Ezra and Jenner should know what I'm planning. They have to know. I need them to understand so they won't try to come after me.

It takes over an hour for me to find Ezra. He sits hunched in the corner of the small unlit room where the generators are stored, his head propped on his knees, his body engulfed by shadow. He doesn't look up when I step into the room. Maybe he doesn't hear me, or maybe he lacks the energy to care about anything now that Rai's gone.

I take care not to startle him, sliding to the floor, making sure to leave plenty of space between us to ensure we aren't touching. Despite the distance, I can feel the heat radiating from his body, and as it reaches for me, I fall into the memory of the dream in which he kissed me. How I long to feel his arms around me for real.

I suck in a breath, fighting the desire to shift closer to him. The cramped space isn't helping the temptation—if anything, it's only making me far more aware of his presence. Of his fingers, only inches from mine.

Of his lips, which I can't stop staring at.

I swallow again, biting back my alien urges. He lifts his head just a bit, and my eyes leap to his, taking in his impassive expression. I have no idea what to say. I've never consoled anyone before. In the State, we are raised to accept death without question or remorse. Like with all our other emotions, we're encouraged to suppress our grief. Mine has long since found its way to the surface, but that doesn't mean I know how to alleviate his.

Ezra's eyes flick to the concrete floor, and I follow his absent gaze to a picture lying next to his left foot. He makes no protest when I pick it up, my fingers skirting along the edges of the thick, shiny paper with care. The photograph is crinkled and has faded with age, but the image is clear and I immediately recognize the three smiling faces. They're much younger—only children at the time this was taken—but I'm certain it's them. After everything we've been through together, I would know those faces anywhere.

In the image, Ezra appears to be around seven or eight years old. He's missing his two front teeth and grinning at an older boy beside him. His brother's smile is far more reserved, but there's kindness behind the expression, unlike the way he looks now that he's older and hardened. Richter has one arm slung across Ezra's shoulders and the other draped around a pretty girl's waist, pulling her into his side.

Rai.

She's smiling broadly, her bronze cheeks rosy, her eyes fixed on the tall boy beside her with an admiration that spills from the picture. The affection between them is palpable, even at such a young age.

If only those cheerful faces were aware of the heartache awaiting them.

Choking back tears, I place the picture back down on the floor. I can't stand to look at it any longer knowing I'm responsible for their pain. Even Dr. Richter, who I loathe with every fiber of my being, manages to earn a shred of pity from me.

I cast a sidelong glance at Ezra. On top of the agony of losing Rai, I imagine he's tormented by his reunion with Richter. It must've been awful for him to see his brother again and have to accept that he's no longer the smiling young boy in that photograph. These were two people who once meant the world to him, and now, they're both gone from his life.

"Did you love her?" I whisper.

I've asked myself this question countless times since that heated argument I witnessed between him and Rai when I first arrived here and they were on opposite sides of the can-we-trust-Wynter debate. I'm aware of Rai's history with Dr. Richter, but her past with Ezra has never been as clear to me.

His movements are lethargic as he props his head back against the hard wall. The minimal light flooding in from the hallway reflects off his cheek, highlighting the black and purple bruise forming from when Jenner punched him earlier in the magistrates building. As awful as their brief fight was to watch, that moment likely saved his life. I'll never have the words to thank Jenner for that.

I peek down at my fidgeting hands, clasping them together in my lap to still them. A long while passes before Ezra speaks.

"Rai was like a sister to me. She's been in my life for as long as I can remember." His voice breaks, and out of the corner of my eye, I glimpse the way his body shakes with cries he's trying so hard to hold in. "I took it for granted," he whispers, dejected. "Like an idiot, I assumed she'd always be there."

The tears budding in his eyes finally break through, and as they fall in an effortless and unending stream, I watch him, stunned and lost for words. I've glimpsed his tears in my head so many times, and yet, seeing him cry in person is somehow so much harder and more painful to witness. Each silent droplet breaks my heart a bit more.

"How do you do it?" He turns to observe me, those hazel eyes pleading. His desperation for an answer is written all over his face. "How do you kill someone you love? How could he do that? How—"

He breaks down, weeping, before he can finish that sentence. I gape at him, wishing there was something I could say, but any words I might come up with are trampled by the memory of that all-important vision. I've seen this face so many times. Not quite as it is in this moment, but the sadness…

The sadness is what's familiar.

The recollection of that image strikes again without mercy. I see his face. I see his tears.

"I'm sorry, Wynter."

I blink, and the memory changes. Now, instead of destruction, I see my room here in the compound. Now, instead of tears, I see his lips muttering words I still don't understand.

"Stay here. Stay with me."

The look on his face when he whispered this plea is seared into my brain and into the backs of my eyelids, so it's all I see every time I close my eyes. Even now, those words vibrate through my soul and settle in the crevices in my heart, almost making me feel whole again. They have a bewildering power over me, even though I know they aren't real.

Even though they never will be.

Although Ezra's sobs are like thunder in my ears, that imagined moment between us is all I can think about right now. The kiss, which will never happen because I'm leaving after this.

The kiss I find myself wishing for.

An unfamiliar heat tears across my chilled skin. I know this isn't the time or the place, but something inside me is fighting to get out. Something new. Something different from the monster I'm growing so used to unleashing.

The monster that I'll soon become.

Part of me tries to fight this strange desire while another part wants to set it free—to see what this feeling is and embrace it, especially after so many years of keeping everything bottled up in a cage I never wanted or asked to be in. A cage I never even realized I could have a life outside of.

A life that, thanks to this disease, I'll never get the chance to explore.

With that realization rushing through my head, I abandon all sense of self-control. Wanting just a taste of the life this disease and the State have both stolen from me, I lean in close to Ezra, pressing my hands to his cheeks, and turn his face toward mine, interweaving the tips of my fingers through the disheveled strands of his hair. His cries cease at my touch, and we stare at each other for a moment before I allow whatever this is raging in my chest to take hold of me. Before I allow it to consume me. To *change* me.

The emotions Ezra has been gradually pulling out of me since we met all wash over my senses. The sensation is intoxicating, like a much-needed breath of fresh air, and I can't stop myself from reaching for more, from wanting to explore their depths at least once in my life before it's over for good. Soon, I won't have another chance.

This moment is all I have.

I pull him toward me, finding his mouth, and as our lips meet, every erratic beat of my heart is a ticking time bomb, threatening to explode. My stomach is turning in circles, making me nauseous, and yet, every second of this discomfort is glorious.

This feeling... Is this what love feels like? Am I even capable of such an emotion?

Yes, I realize as I deepen the kiss. What else could this pressure squeezing my heart be?

I think part of me loved Ezra from that very first vision. Maybe these feelings developed as an unintended consequence of fate pushing us toward our set roles in that dire future—of which, his still remains a mystery to me. Or, maybe, the visions were a path of breadcrumbs, guiding me to him because that was what fate intended all along and that future is just the way our tragic story was always meant to come to an end.

Regardless of which came first or caused the other, regardless of the fact we barely know one another, the affection in my heart is real. And knowing that only makes what I have to do worse.

My eyes press shut, and I see us together at the end of the world, facing our future.

"I'm sorry..."

My heart tears open, spilling its contents onto the cold floor, and all too quickly, I remember what will happen if I stay.

With a reluctant breath, I drop my hands to his shoulders and push away, breaking the kiss. His eyes follow mine, but he doesn't say anything. Silence spreads through the room like fog.

Fear creeps through me at his shocked expression, followed by horror, and finally, disgust. What have I done? How could I inflict my complicated array of emotions on him so soon after what we just went through? How could I pursue this knowing what he must be feeling right now over Rai? How could I allow myself to reach for such comfort without taking his own trauma into account?

I scramble to my feet, mortified, and backing away, blurt out, "I'm sorry."

Before he can speak, I'm sprinting through the open doorway, running as fast as my legs can carry me. I don't look back, even though my heart is begging me to stop. How could I be so thoughtless? Ezra was grieving for Rai, for our *friend*, and I was selfish enough to act on my impulses when, instead, I should've been grieving with him. I was only thinking of myself.

I was only thinking of what *I* was feeling.

Once I'm certain Ezra isn't following me, I dart to the nearest wall and plop down to the floor, fighting to breathe through a barrage of tears. As I drag in a breath, my forefinger trails over my lips where the skin still tingles from our kiss.

Regardless of everything that's happened between us, I care for Ezra, possibly more than I've ever cared about anyone. But loving him—if that's what this is—isn't enough to change what's coming for us all, and staying here certainly isn't an option.

Dr. Richter could very well be lying about the cure, but if trusting him is the only way to stop me from killing the people I care about...then I'll do it.

I'll do whatever is necessary to avoid that future.

After a few calming breaths, I scooch my back up the wall until I'm on my feet again. My wobbling legs are unsteady beneath me, but I'm composed enough to move forward. I proceed through the hallways, never once looking back.

This is it.

This is what I have to do for all our sakes.

TWENTY-SIX

I HESITATE OUTSIDE THE OPEN doorway, making sure to keep just out of sight. I had thought this was the right thing to do, but, now, I'm not so sure I can do it. I've been psyching myself up for hours, but after my miserable failure with Ezra this morning, this feels more like a betrayal than the well-intended farewell I was aiming for.

Still, shouldn't at least one person know where I'm going so they don't attempt to come after me later? Or should I just cut my losses and run with no one the wiser about my plan? That's what I'm going to do anyway, so wouldn't it be better for everyone if I just disappear now and save them from further heartache? Besides, goodbyes are unnecessarily painful. I would be sparing them that pain.

I would be sparing myself that pain.

I peek around the corner into the supply room, watching Jenner from my hiding place. He's alone, sitting on top of an upturned crate, his head down, as his fingers nimbly reload the ammunition in various weapons. One after another, he slides a fresh magazine into the grip of each gun.

The frown on his face suggests he isn't doing this monotonous task because he enjoys it. If anything, this is likely his way of getting his mind off troubling thoughts and feelings, such as those stirred up by the loss of a friend. Perhaps he's trying to distract himself from the pain so it won't overwhelm him the way it's already overwhelmed me.

Pins and needles spread over my thigh as the leg I've been leaning on begins to go numb. It seems as good a sign as any. I've stood around long enough.

Now, it's time to do what I came here to do.

Reaching inside and grabbing hold of my courage, I rap my knuckles against the door frame. Jenner raises his head at the sound, and a smile brightens his face the instant he sees me.

"Come in," he urges with a wave of his hand.

My cheeks twitch as my nerves rampage through my stomach, the depths of my belly twisting in such a way I fear its churning contents won't remain there much longer.

Jenner pulls a crate from the corner of the room and flips it over, placing it beside his own makeshift seat. I plop onto the creaking wood, avoiding his gaze.

I must've rehearsed what I plan on saying to him at least a hundred times. Yet, now that we're in the same room, those words are lost to me. As soon as I open my mouth, they disappear into thin air.

"You look a lot better now," he says after a moment, breaking the torturous silence.

I don't have to look at him to know what he's referring to. The blood. The pale skin. The inhuman black eyes. The monster I'm becoming versus the dying girl I am.

A shy smile upturns my lips, but I still can't find the strength to speak. Why is this so difficult? I've known him for, what…the better part of a month? A large chunk of which I've spent unconscious?

It shouldn't be this hard to say goodbye.

I consider turning and leaving at once, releasing us both from the torment of this awkward encounter, but I don't move, my body held in place by the very emotions encouraging me to escape this. Emotions I have to face if I'm going to leave this all behind.

"How are you holding up?" Jenner asks, seemingly oblivious to my internal struggle.

I shrug. "As good as can be expected, I guess. How about you? Did you go see whoever you needed to speak with?"

He lets out a strained breath and rocks back on the crate. I scrutinize his face, noting the dark smudges of exhaustion staining the skin under his eyes.

"Things are…" He hesitates, frowning again. "Well, they're a mess. Truthfully, they have been for a while, we've just been turning a blind eye to it all. After last night, it's only a matter of time until the news of Rai's death begins to spread and everyone learns of Ezra's connection to Richter. Then, everything will be a thousand times worse." With a disheartened huff, he leans his head back against the wall. "Everything around us is falling apart."

His words anchor onto my heart and pull downward, as if determined to tear my body in half. Maybe now isn't the right time to leave, after all. Jenner and Ezra could use me here. I could do some good in getting this place back on track.

But, even as I tell myself this, I know the only way I can truly help is to go. If Ezra is under question after last night, I can't imagine how much worse it will be for me once everyone connects the dots and finds out why I'm really here. Besides, I'm running out of time.

By staying, I would only be making things worse.

"Damn it. Where do we go from here?" Jenner asks, his voice a rumbling growl. "What the hell can we even do? Those assholes are always one step ahead of us. No matter what, we always seem to lose."

He throws his arm backward, slamming the side of his fist into the wall behind us. The room seems to vibrate from the contact, or maybe it's the tremors rocking his body I notice. Either way, I can't put this off any longer.

I have to tell him, and I have to do it now.

"Jenner, there's something you should know."

He blinks, the rage in his eyes dissipating, their depths now alight with worry. "What is it?"

I sink my teeth into my lower lip. "That doctor—Richter. The one who—" But I can't bring myself to finish that sentence. I can't even finish that thought. I swallow, trying to push away the lingering images of Rai and Richter in Bilken's office. "He said there's a cure for my condition," I whisper.

Jenner stares at me, eyes wide and mouth agape. "What? You don't believe him, do you?"

"I'm not sure. I know he probably just said it to lure me back, but…" My voice trails off as I lean forward and brush my fingertips across Jenner's arm. "What if it isn't a lie? What if there really is a cure?"

His eyebrows knit together, and slowly, realization spreads across his face like the first light of day soaking up the horizon. "You're leaving…"

When he recoils from my touch, I pull back my hand and lower my gaze to the floor, flinching. The way he looks at me brings back the memory of the nightmare I had and I can't face it again. I can't allow myself to remember how it felt to watch him die.

"There's something I haven't told any of you—" I falter, uncertain if I should continue. Does he really need to know what I've seen since there might be a way to prevent that future, if Richter's claims about a cure are true? Even if Richter's lying and that future is unavoidable, shouldn't I just let Jenner live the rest of his short life in blissful ignorance? In peace?

No, I decide. *He deserves to know.*

After everything he and Ezra have done for me, *risked* for me, I can't leave without one of them knowing the truth. I need them to know what I'm hoping to change so they can understand why I'm leaving. Otherwise, they might try to come after me.

If that happens, there will be nothing I or anyone else can do to save them from the State.

"The very first vision I had, right before I was taken to the DSD…" I clench my hands into fists and force my eyes upward until they lock on his face. As hard as it is to face him right now, I need to look at him when I say this. I need to welcome this pain because, once I leave this place, that's it.

I'll have no one, and Jenner will be only a memory.

"It was of the end of the world. I saw it all as if I was actually there, as if it was really happening." I speak in a rush, pushing out each word until they fall out of me willingly. But, instead of lifting the weight from my shoulders, they only seem to add to my burden, dragging me down, crushing me. My voice hitches. "As my condition grew worse, I saw more of the vision. And then I saw Ezra. We were the only ones left as everything around us crumbled into ash."

Jenner shakes his head. "I don't understand—"

"It's me. What I am," I interrupt, biting back tears. "It will happen because of me."

His mouth opens, as if he's about to say something, then closes again, snapping shut with a click. In the silence that follows, I glimpse the realization building behind his gaze. He doesn't need me to tell him that he'll die in that future. He doesn't need me to say that I'm the one who will kill him. He knows.

I can see in his eyes that he knows.

Of all the emotions he must be battling with at this moment, I presume fear would land at the top of the list. And he does seem afraid. Yet, there's something in his expression that doesn't suggest fear for himself…but for me. Here I am, telling him we're all going to die because of this rare disease I have, and *I'm* the one he's thinking of. *I'm* the one he's feeling sorry for. It's not right.

I don't deserve it.

"My life ended when I had that first vision, but you…you're all still alive. I can't let anyone else die because of me."

The moment I utter these words, he lunges forward and grabs my shoulders, almost knocking me off the crate in the process.

"I told you what happened with Rai wasn't your fault!" His eyes shine with tears as his hands grip me tighter.

I fight to breathe past the ache in my chest. "You say that, but what if I'd seen it sooner? If I had, then maybe we could've saved her. We both know that, so why don't you blame me?"

Jenner reels back as if I've slapped him, his eyes wide, his hands slipping off my shoulders. I scramble, trying to find the words to explain what I'm feeling.

"That's the dilemma I'm faced with now. Even if what Richter said is a lie, how can I turn my back on the possibility of a cure when I know where that other path will lead?"

"M-Maybe the vision was wrong," he stammers, combing a trembling hand through his mop of black hair. "Maybe—"

"It's not wrong," I snap, my tone forceful. That line of thought will lead us nowhere; it's better to nip it in the bud before it can form roots. False hope won't help anybody right now, me least of all. "The visions never are. Besides, I've seen what my power can do. If you had been in Bilken's office when the Enforcers first arrived, you would've seen it, too."

That moment is hazy to me, even now. But through the fog of confusion, I'm all too aware of what I did to those soldiers. Those *people*. It was the same thing I did to Dr. Richter's attendant. The same thing I almost did to Ezra before I snapped out of my daze.

Murder, that small voice in my head says again.

This power… I can't control it, and I don't think I will ever be able to. I won't live long enough to try. This disease will spread through my failing body until there's nothing of me left in this shell. Until I'm a mindless killing machine intent on destruction.

I jerk my head to escape that image. "I won't be able to live with myself if anyone else dies because of what I am. A cure is the only hope I have to stop this and to keep you all alive."

"But I don't want you to leave." Jenner's gaze is pleading, his voice the barest breath of a whisper.

My lips wobble with the increasing threat of tears, but I push them back and force a smile. "I'm so glad I got to know you…even if it was only for a short time." Rising from the crate, I place my hands on his shoulders, bend down, and plant a kiss on his cheek. "Be safe," I mutter in his ear.

Gulping down the lump in my throat, I turn to face the open doorway, prepared to move on with my goal in sight. Prepared to move on and never look back. But, as I take a step, something stops me.

Something keeps me here in this room.

Jenner's hold on my uninjured wrist is firm, and as he spins me around, I lose my footing, stumbling into the safe embrace of his arms. When he crushes my body to his, I hear everything this moment is trying to tell me. I hear everything *he's* been trying to tell me.

I sense his affection for me in the gentle way his lips brush over mine, but, as he kisses me, I can only think of one person.

And that person isn't Jenner.

After what seems like a lifetime, his hands relax, and he pulls away, releasing his hold on me. His watery eyes peer down into mine with urgency.

"Stay," he begs. "Please."

Stay.

Stay…

"Stay here. Stay with me."

This moment is so reminiscent of my dream, but the details are wrong, like puzzle pieces that don't quite fit together, even though it looks like they should. But Jenner isn't the one I should be embracing right now.

Jenner isn't the one I want to ask me to stay.

The pain cutting through me when I glimpse his expression is worse than anything I endured at the DSD. All at once, I understand why the State is so unfeeling. Why our society is so unfeeling.

This misery… Why would anyone ever *want* to feel this? From what I've seen, even the good things—like love—end in pain, so maybe the State was right to try to spare us from that.

"I'm sorry." The words barely make it past my lips.

Jenner lets out a tiny choked-off laugh, and I can hear the sadness behind it. "If I can't get you to stay, what will?"

I don't answer him. The truth is, nothing will make me stay. Nothing can anymore. Not when there's so much dependent on me leaving.

"Goodbye, Jenner."

The tears finally spill over, running in rivers down my cheeks, as my feet pull me into the hallway. It takes every last ounce of willpower I have to stop myself from looking back.

My movements are listless on my way through the compound. On more than one occasion, I consider running back to the supply room and trying to fix what I've broken. That wasn't how I wanted to leave things between us or how I wanted—or expected—our farewell to go. But I also know if I turn back now, I'll never find the strength to leave.

I plot out my plan of action to distract myself from my sorrow and guilt. The pattern of turns I need to take through the maze to get to the hatch are seared into my memory now. Assuming I make it that far, finding my way through the tunnels beyond should be easy enough. The journey will take a while, but I'll get to my destination in the end.

All that's left is to prepare myself, and then I'll go. I'll do it quick. Just get what I need and make for the door. No more detours.

No more goodbyes.

Ezra's face flashes through my thoughts like a lightning strike. I already tried to say goodbye once, and it didn't go the way I had planned. Still, I can't bear another attempt after everything we've been through, especially considering how I feel about him.

Wiping away the tears obscuring my vision, I fix my gaze on the path ahead, resolved.

No more goodbyes, I promise myself.

TWENTY-SEVEN

I REACH DOWN AND PLUCK my pack off the washroom floor, brushing excess water from the sodden straps. The droplets rejoin the shallow puddle at my feet.

Lips quivering, I glance at my filthy clothes where they lie undisturbed in a heap where I left them. While I know I should clear the mess away instead of leaving it for someone else to clean up, I can't bring myself to disturb it. The bloodstained fabric holds too many bad memories.

Memories I only want to forget.

I tear my gaze away from the clothes and open my pack, checking over the minimal contents inside. Everything looks to be in order, although the flashlight and a canteen of water are really all I'll need to see me through my trip back to Zone 1. My journey there will be one-way. Beyond that, anything I need will be provided for me by the DSD.

I shudder at the thought of being a prisoner again, held captive in that tiny, drab room. A lifetime seems to have passed since I first escaped Dr. Richter's insidious clutches, yet the memory of my time there is still painfully fresh—like a scar from a wound that will never fully heal.

It haunts me, even more so than the guilt that stabs at my heart every time I think about Rai. The trauma I've managed to push back these last few weeks is rearing its ugly head, feeding an anxiety I'm no longer sure I have the strength to suppress. It spreads, creeping through every last inch of me, just like this disease taking over my body.

Bile rushes up into my mouth as a wave of vertigo disorients my senses, making the bright room spin around me. Dizzy, I reach for the nearest wall for support while ragged breaths crush my lungs, scorching my throat.

As I heave, I throw myself over a sink, gripping the edges of the basin so tightly my fingers ache, but nothing comes up. My stomach is empty of everything except the fear of what I'm about to walk into.

For the first time since settling on my decision, it really hits me that I'm going back.

I draw in a few quick breaths through my nose, my inhalations deep and slow, and think about what I want to protect. I picture Ezra and Jenner, and I see all too clearly what will happen to them if I stay. Their deaths are burned into my brain. There's no other way to prevent that future from happening.

This is my only option.

I blink once, then drag my eyes upward and force myself to look in the mirror. It's strange, but the girl reflected there is someone I no longer recognize. Maybe what I'm seeing is the last of my innocence, the ignorant version of me the State created—the version I have to abandon if I have any hope of moving forward. All the pain blackening my heart, all the feelings I wish I had time to explore… They'll remain here at this compound with her.

With the me I need to leave behind.

Turning, I slog out of the washroom and traipse through the corridors as if in a trance. Every step is a struggle, and by the time I make it back to my quarters, I'm worn down by exhaustion.

My legs give out beneath me as I slump down on the bed, and a sigh parts my lips as my hands grip the blanket. I could've had a new life in this place, a life free from the State's control. If things had been different, I would've embraced it. I would've fought to protect this freedom, just like everyone else here.

But things aren't different, and life is far from fair. The fresh start I was offered… It was nothing more than a pipe dream.

I should've known it could never be mine.

Tears prick at the corners of my eyes as I take in every detail of the room one last time. Everything and everyone I've come to care about here…

I silently say goodbye to it all.

An uncomfortable dull pain shoots through my wrist as I draw my legs into my chest and wrap my hands around my knees. Rotating my arm, I peel back the bandage—still damp from my breakdown in the shower—and peer down at the raised incision protruding from the still tender skin.

It's terrifying to think what would've happened if Rai hadn't been around to help me that day. How we all would be walking a different path if she hadn't worked tirelessly to heal me. If Ezra hadn't spared my life and had chosen instead to let me die. Maybe, if they hadn't intervened, Rai would be alive now. If I had bled out in The Vega, we wouldn't be faced with the monumental problem of our impending doom.

Because I'd be dead, and that's the way it should be.

If I had died then, everyone here wouldn't be at risk now. Rai would still be alive, Jenner and Ezra would *stay* alive...

And I wouldn't have to go back to the DSD.

Fat tears roll down my cheeks as I pull my pack onto my lap and lower my legs, letting out a shaky breath. There's a roll of bandaging in the side pocket, which I use to rewrap my wrist, although my efforts are clumsy. Not that it matters. I'm only doing this to delay my departure. Once I'm back at the DSD, the doctors there will tend to my injuries properly, with the added bonus of probably shoving a tracking chip back into my wrist to replace the one I cut out. Dr. Richter might even pretend to care about my health and well-being if it means I give him and the State what they're after.

I smother a humorless laugh and circle the gauze around my arm four times. Once the incision is covered, I have nothing left to do. I'm out of excuses to stay. Besides, I've wasted enough time here already.

Pinching my eyes shut, I suck in a breath. The seconds tick by as I yell at myself to get up—to rise from this bed and march out the door, like I should've done hours ago. I hear my own words shouted back in my head until the voice in my ears sounds nothing like me at all but like someone else.

Like Ezra.

"So, that's it?" he asks.

My eyes spring open and dart toward the doorway where Ezra stands at the threshold, a mere silhouette against the light pouring in from the hallway. His gaze exudes rage as he steps into the room.

"You were just going to leave?"

My tongue trips over itself as I try and fail to find an answer. What can I say? What *is* there to say? I didn't expect to ever see him again, and I still have to leave, regardless of any feelings I think I have for him or any argument he might make to tempt me to stay.

My departure is non-negotiable.

"I take it you spoke with Jenner," I mutter.

My name falls from his lips like a plea as he takes a panicked step forward. "Wynter... You can't do this."

The anger in his tone is like a chisel chipping away at my heart. If only he could see what I've seen.

If only he understood what will happen to everyone here if I stay.

"I have to," I whisper, looking away.

My fingers fidget with the bandage around my wrist, unwinding it, rewrapping it, then unwinding it once more to distract myself from his lingering gaze. His eyes follow my movements, and I can feel them burning into my face, but I don't dare look up.

"Look at me." Crossing the room, he tears the roll of dressing from my hands and tosses it to floor. "You have no idea what you're getting yourself into."

My hands clench into fists. "And you do?"

My eyes snap upward, locking on Ezra, as I'm struck with the sudden urge to slap him. Does he really think I want to leave—that I *want* to go back to the DSD and be tortured for who knows how long before death finally takes me in its eternal embrace?

I'm only doing this so he can survive.

The temperature in the room seems to rise as indignation and frustration swell between us like heat. We glare at each other for what seems like hours until I can't bear the hurt glistening in his eyes a single second longer. It cuts away at my wavering resolve.

Shaking my head, I push to my feet, once more avoiding Ezra's gaze. I hoist my pack off the bed and sling it onto my shoulder, a jittery breath escaping my lungs as I take one step and then another toward the open door. As I brush past Ezra, I stop for a moment and reach for his hand, hesitating. My fingers freeze just short of touching his.

This is why I didn't want to say goodbye. The pain cracking my heart into pieces…

I didn't want to feel it.

Grimacing, I retract my hand and force myself to continue walking. The distance to the hallway seems never-ending, but I fight through the growing heartache in my chest, even as it tears me in two.

Half of my heart stays behind, an anchor holding me to this room, to this compound, determined to keep me here. The logical part of my brain presses onward, but then my legs lurch to a standstill, and I realize something else is also holding me back. It isn't just my heart that wants to stop me from leaving.

Warmth snakes across my waist from behind, and my eyes follow its spread to where Ezra's arms circle around me. They pull me back, hugging me tight to his chest, draining my body of any instinct to fight and instantly erasing my desire to leave.

He turns me around so we're standing face to face, our noses almost touching. I flush at his sudden proximity, my breath hitching at the realization his lips are so close to mine I could kiss him again if I wanted to. Which I do. So badly.

Ezra smiles, as if he knows what I'm thinking, and flattens a hand against the small of my back, pulling me even closer. Then, as if gravity itself is pulling us together, he bends down at the same moment I rise onto my toes, meeting each other halfway.

Just like in my dream, Ezra's lips press to mine, and as the heat from my body melts into his, I stare at his closed eyes, trying to make sense of what's happening. My heart is pounding so furiously I struggle to inhale as it repeatedly slams into my ribs, and my frenzied nerves are pulling my senses in a thousand different directions at once. Pleasure and pain course through my veins, hand in hand.

When we break apart, the raging hurricane of my inexperienced emotions threatens to suffocate me. I gape at Ezra, afraid to blink or speak.

"I don't want you to go," he says, his voice soft. His words are warm against my face as he says them, each one a separate kiss of their own. The touch of them sends a shiver over my skin. "Stay here. Stay with me."

My eyes spring wide. *The dream was real.*

My heart swells with affection and longing until a different thought strikes, cutting through both. It casts a shadow over this bittersweet moment.

I never saw what came after these words. My vision ended with his plea, depriving me of knowing what awaited us next. Because of everything we've been through, I'm not sure if I believe what he's saying…or if I even can. Ezra isn't in his right mind—he's consumed by the pain of losing Rai, and his actions are probably being guided by panic more than logic or sense. How can I be certain he isn't just saying these things because he's afraid of being alone? How do I know he isn't just looking for comfort in the one place he knows he can find it? If I hadn't so brazenly kissed him before, maybe he wouldn't be saying these words now at all.

I recall our conversation back in the tunnels and the confusion I felt when he promised to protect me. I can't help mimicking what I said to him then.

"Why…?"

I anticipate his response with bated breath, even though what he says won't change anything. I'll still leave this place to protect him and Jenner. Leaving is the only way to avoid their deaths. Putting distance between us is the only way I know to save them. The closer they get to me, the more likely they are to die.

His hand trails across my cheek as he frowns. "I don't think I can handle losing anyone else."

My heart sinks, and disappointment settles under my skin. After what happened to Rai, I understand why he would feel this way. He brought these people together, so each death or loss must weigh on him. His own personal burden. But if his grief is why he's asking me to stay, that means I'm nothing more than another number. Another notch in the PHOENIX belt.

Which also means he's using my feelings for him as a weapon to coerce me.

But why? Because he feels responsible for me?

Or because whoever's in charge here doesn't want me to leave?

If Nolan or someone else high up in PHOENIX is working with the DSD like I fear, then ensuring I don't run away is probably their top priority now, especially after Richter failed to retrieve me during our disastrous mission—no thanks to Ezra, which makes me think he isn't involved with whatever shady deal is going on behind the scenes. I still can't figure out what PHOENIX would possibly get out of such an arrangement, but something in my gut tells me I'm right.

Alternatively, if PHOENIX *isn't* involved with the DSD and has no idea what I'm capable of, it's still only a matter of time until they find out the truth. Then, like Ezra even said in his speech last week, these people will grasp how they're in an advantageous position if they possess what the State covets.

It won't matter that I will be the death of us all. The only thing anyone will see is my power and how it can be used as a weapon.

I bite my lip, suppressing a frustrated groan. I wish I could see the full picture and gain a better understanding of all the players on the board. I don't know anyone's motivations, which scares me, although, right now, I only care about Ezra's.

I peek up at him, tormented by doubt.

"Why did you take me with you?" I ask. His eyes narrow as I step out of his grasp. He tries to pull me back, but I push him away as a terrible fear comes alive in my stomach. "Why?" I press through rising tears. They stick in my throat, choking me.

His eyes soften at the look on my face. "Because I was afraid if I left you behind, I would never see you again, even if we did somehow make it out alive. I know it was stupid and risky to take you, but I wasn't ready to say goodbye to you yet. And I'm sure as hell not ready now."

My heart aches with hope, but I shove it away. Because, through the disbelief keeping me silent, I notice the lie behind his words.

What he's saying, no matter how hard he's trying to sell it to me, isn't the truth. Or, at least, it's not the whole truth. There's another reason he brought me that night. A reason he's adamant not to admit.

His touch ignites a shiver over my skin as he tucks a stray lock of hair behind my ear. "When Jenner told me you were leaving, it dawned on me just how badly

I want you to stay. And trust me, it has nothing to do with my brother or mother."

A sly grin appears at the corners of his lips, sending my pulse into overdrive. He's deflecting, using my feelings against me again, but I struggle to care anymore because these words, the ones he says now…they're the truth. I can sense that as plainly as I sense the depth of my own growing affection for him.

Any doubts I have about his motivations for keeping me here drift away and dissolve in this moment. I no longer hear or care about what he isn't telling me.

I only welcome in what he is.

From the day I was born, I've been taught to repress my emotions, brainwashed to integrate into a society it's taken me eighteen years to realize is poisonous. Humans aren't meant to shut out their feelings, and what I never grasped before is you can't. One way or another, they'll climb to the surface. One way or another, they'll find a way to break through.

Stifling my emotions for the better part of two decades leaves me wholly unprepared for this moment. Each emotion tears through me, burning everything that made me who I am until I'm nothing but a pile of ashes. From those ashes, what rises up is the new me.

The me, who, for once, is permitted to feel.

Another shudder rolls over my body as Ezra skims his fingers across my lower lip, wiping away the tears pooling there.

"Please, don't cry," he whispers.

His breath caresses my lips and cheeks as he combs his fingers through my hair, making me light-headed. Bending down again, he slants his mouth over mine, and all the emotions I've been bottling up since that very first vision of him pour out in this kiss.

It's strange to think that I never would've known this kind of connection if my placement exam had gone off without a hitch and everything in my life had continued as normal. From that point of view, looking at what's transpired since then, it's hard not to find the good in my condition. Despite all the bad, it's brought me to Ezra, even if our time together is temporary.

Even if it can never last.

Another tear spills down my cheek, but I ignore the cruel burn of it and focus on my shaking hands as they slide across Ezra's chest and up under his shirt, trembling with uncertainty. Although I don't have the slightest clue what I'm doing, I give in to my confusing urges. I don't want to have any regrets. If this is the only time in my life when I can experience this sort of closeness—a bond of meaning the State has robbed us all of—then I want to do it with someone I care about. With all the pain and grief I've experienced, I just want to feel something good for once.

For a moment, I just want to forget everything else.

Ezra reciprocates my touch, and as we fall onto the bed, I kiss him with fervor, losing myself to my erratic emotions and surrendering myself to this fleeting bliss. Thanks to Dr. Richter and this fatal disease, I don't have much time left in this world, regardless of any possible cure. Even if I don't die after this, I know we'll never see each other again. This world where feelings and love are possible for me will be nothing more than a memory. So, if this moment is all we'll have...then to hell with it.

I plan on making it count.

TWENTY-EIGHT

I LIE STILL, LISTENING TO the gentle hum of Ezra breathing softly beside me. His bare chest rises and falls in slow repetition, his lips parted slightly, releasing hot breaths. A sweaty lock of blond hair lies flat across his forehead, and I'm tempted to reach out and brush the strands away—to touch my hand to his skin one final time. I resist the urge. He looks so peaceful in sleep, and after everything he's suffered through, I don't want to disturb him.

Besides, it's better for both of us this way.

Sitting up, I scoot toward the edge of the bed. The shift of the squeaking mattress doesn't wake him, which disappoints me a little. Although I know this path I'm on can only end one way, part of me wants him to stop me. I want him to pull me back into his arms and take away any desire I have to leave this place.

To leave him.

My feet graze the cold floor as the air nips at my skin, the weight of our handful of precious hours together pressing down on my chest. Every inch of my body aches with the urge to sink back into his embrace and find comfort in his touch as many times as it takes to heal me of this disease and this pain. Instead, I sit still on the bed, hesitating.

How can I leave him so soon after losing Rai? How can I abandon him and Jenner to suffer through the consequences of our mission alone?

Because you have to, I remind myself. *It's the only way to keep them both safe.*

My eyes dance across Ezra's exposed torso, carving the vivid recollection of his body into my brain. Every whispered word we shared, every touch…

At least I'll have the memory of these moments together to see me through what must come next. No matter what happens from here on out, at least I'll always have that brief comfort.

Hours seem to pass in the minutes I spend watching him sleep. It's as if the blood coursing through my veins is hardening into stone, freezing me and holding me in place. It takes all the self-control I can muster to convince myself to go. I've already stayed too long, allowing the night to slip by in his arms. If I don't leave now, he'll wake up, which is the last thing I need. If that happens, he'll just try to stop me—not that doing so will require much effort on his part. If we get to that point, any will I have to leave him will be non-existent.

But, if I go now, while he's asleep, it'll be a clean break for us both.

If I go now, it'll be easier for everyone.

Leaning over his sleeping form, I take in the details of his face—his closed eyes, his long lashes—and plant a barely-there kiss on his lips. I don't apply enough pressure to wake him, just enough to leave my mark. His cheek flinches where my breath tickles his skin.

Biting the inside of my cheek to hold back the tears, I stand and pull on my clothes, careful not to make any noise. My fingers fumble with the strap of my pack, hooking it around my chest, as my feet reluctantly drag me toward the door. My heart sinks a little more with every step. Why does this feel so wrong when I know it's the right decision? The only decision? Why does this hurt so much when I know that my leaving is the only way to keep him alive?

Not for the first time, I wonder if maybe the State has the right idea encouraging distance in its citizens' lives. Affection is dangerous because it's painful, because it leaves you open to get hurt. By pushing us all apart, we're spared that pain and can live our lives ignorant of that heartache. There's sense in that logic, even if it's lonely.

Still, I want to believe it's been worth it—that everything I've been through up to this very moment has been worth the sadness I'll now carry with me. If I can change what's going to happen, if I can save Ezra and Jenner from that terrible future that, even now, haunts my every thought, then it will be.

I would embrace any amount of pain necessary if it meant my sacrifice would save their lives.

I pull open the door but pause at the threshold and cast a worried glance over my shoulder. Will Ezra understand my reasons for leaving, or will he see it as an act of betrayal? Will what we shared be destroyed as a result, just like what happened with Dr. Richter and Rai?

Will Ezra turn against me just as Richter turned against her?

It doesn't matter, I realize. If his hatred is the cost for saving his life, then it's a price I'll happily pay.

The tears spill over now, carving lines down both my cheeks. My teeth bury into my lower lip as I turn and finally step through the doorway.

This time, I don't allow myself to look back.

The compound is silent as I stalk through the unlit corridors, retracing my steps to the maze after a quick stop at the now empty supply room. After a series of memorized turns, the room housing the tunnel entrance slides into view. Since night has fallen once again and everyone in the compound is asleep, there isn't a single soul in sight to intervene or try to stop me. For a moment, I half-expect Jenner to show up until I remember what he said to me yesterday.

"If I can't get you to stay, what will?"

He must've genuinely believed Ezra would be able to change my mind about returning to the DSD. Why else would he have told him what I was planning to do unless he suspected how I felt?

Thinking about Jenner only causes my guilt to resurface, especially after what happened with Ezra. I try my best to push these feelings aside, reminding myself that what I'm about to do is what's best for everyone. Not only for him and Ezra...but me.

Abandoning these thoughts, I flip open my bag and pull out a curved black bar like the one Ezra used when we were last in the tunnels. Positioning myself in front of the hatch door, I wedge the bar between the spokes of the wheel and throw the full weight of my body against it. Sweat beads on my brow as the metal creaks in protest and flaking bits of rust fall to the floor.

Even with the bar, turning the wheel is a struggle, especially with my aching wrist. Still, I keep pushing, determined to see this through, and after a few attempts, the door gives way. It swings open before me as if in support of my mission.

Panting, I stow the bar back inside my pack and clamber through the hole into the blackness of the tunnel beyond. My fingers fumble with my flashlight and quickly click it on. The beam of light breaks through the thick gloom with ease.

I follow the same route Rai led us on to Zone 1, the splashing of my feet in the shallow covering of water providing a much-needed break from the silence. The journey feels longer this time, being on my own. My eyes shift in and out of focus, my body once again lulled by the hum of my steps. To keep myself awake, I rehearse why I'm doing this, chanting the reasons over and over again in my head. If I say them enough times, maybe I'll believe them.

I'm doing the right thing.

This is my only option.

This is the only way to stop the world from ending and to keep me from killing the people I care about.

This is the only way to save Ezra and Jenner.

I continue repeating these thoughts until I arrive in what I think is the general area of Zone 1, based on the timing of my journey. Pausing for a drink to rouse myself from my fatigue, I glance down both lengths of the tunnel, peeling my tired eyes in search of an exit. After another ten minutes of walking, I spot a platform of steps veering off on the left side of the tunnel. Upon further inspection, the platform cuts into the rounded wall and leads up to an obscured rust-covered entrance. I race up the steps with the bar in one hand and throw myself against the wheel.

The door opens after a few attempts, protesting my entry with a piercing shriek. Beyond the exit, another tunnel stretches out before me, but this one is tilted slightly uphill. My breaths are heavy and my feet slip against the grime on the floor as I hurry up the slope.

Flecks of dirt and water spray across my face as I push against the barred gate at the top of the incline. It creaks open into a shallow stream lying under a low-hanging bridge in a park, and as I step into the fresh air, my eyes take in the dim morning light marking the beginning of the sun's ascent over the horizon.

My stomach twists as I shrink back into the cover of darkness. I don't want to be seen in daylight. I don't want to attract unnecessary attention. I don't want outside influences pressuring me to go back to the DSD. I want to do this on my own.

I want it to be my choice.

With a faltering breath, I inch out from under the bridge, scanning the frosty greenery around me for movement. I see nothing except for the slight rustle of leaves and the whipping of branches in the cold morning breeze. Based on the upkeep of my surroundings and the looming buildings positioned along the edge of the park, I know without a doubt I'm back in Zone 1.

Somehow, knowing that makes this all easier. My journey has almost reached its end.

Using the landmarks as my guide, I make my way to the DSD, comparing where I am in retrospect to what I saw when I escaped a few weeks ago. To my surprise, I locate it far quicker than I expected I would. Maybe the fear had imprinted the details of the night I fled onto my brain. Either that, or a part of me always knew I'd eventually have to come back here.

I hesitate on the opposite side of the street, staring up at the domineering building in front of me. I don't think it ever occurred to me before how something so ominous stands in plain view of our society, as if the State is proud of what they do here.

Proud of what they'll soon be doing to me.

My heart jumps up into my throat, blocking my breaths. I try to come up with a reason to run—an excuse to abandon my mission and get the hell out of here before it's too late to turn back. But I can't.

Too much depends on me.

"For Ezra and Jenner," I whisper, steeling myself.

As my feet usher me across the quiet street toward my doom, I think of what my life was like before my birthday. How different I was then. How scared. How the only thing that ever mattered was survival. How nothing else even existed to me.

Don't stand out. Blend in. Remain invisible. Those are the rules I lived by—the rules I thought would keep me alive. I was wrong. But, maybe, with my sacrifice, Ezra and Jenner can survive. I have to believe that. I have to believe doing this can make a difference.

I have to believe I *can* change the future.

Lifting my chin, I storm through the revolving glass doors. As if expecting my arrival—I was probably spotted by one of the many surveillance cameras littered throughout this zone—Dr. Richter is already in the lobby, surrounded by his usual flock of attendants. They all stand in a line facing me.

I stop in front of him, and he meets my gaze, gracing me with that eerie smile of his. If I didn't already know what to expect, I might think he's sincerely happy to see me.

"You made the right choice." He rests a hand on my shoulder—a gesture any normal person might mistake for kindness.

But I, Wynter Arabelle Reeves, am not normal.

Narrowing my eyes, I spit through clenched teeth, "You win. I'll do whatever you want. But you will never go anywhere near Ezra again. Deal?"

Dr. Richter appraises me for a long moment before stepping to the side, his hand sliding from my shoulder as his arm sweeps through the air, gesturing me back into the DSD.

I meet his eyes one final time, the malicious intent in them burning like fire.

His smile deepens. "Welcome home, Wynter."

END OF BOOK ONE

BOOK TWO
TYPE X

WHEN HUMANITY DIES,

THE WORLD DIES WITH IT.

ONE

A HEAVY WIND SLAMS INTO the side of the helicopter, jerking the metal carcass with rough, repetitive jolts, which threaten to send the gargantuan carrier aircraft spiraling to the ground. The two dozen Enforcers around me don't seem to take much notice of the turbulence, their expressions drawn, eyes fixed straight ahead, like robots that have been programmed to concentrate only on the specified task laid out before us.

Propping my head back against the vibrating wall, I focus on the roaring drone of the rotors, listening intently to the constant whir. Steadied by the deafening hum, I drag in a deep breath and let my eyes drift closed, my heart rate evening out as I distance my thoughts from what awaits when we land. More than anything, I wish my consciousness could remain in this state of calm in-between forever. Here, reality is but a dim afterthought.

Unfortunately, such blissful escape isn't an option.

I push out an exasperated breath through my nose and peek open my eyes, scowling at the tingle creeping over my face. Even without looking, I can tell someone's watching me. The burning touch of wandering eyes is a far too familiar sensation by this point—that unavoidable curiosity that seems to go hand in hand with what I am now that my existence is public knowledge.

Hell, after this long, I've grown to expect it.

Looking up, I narrow my eyes into slits, glaring at the Enforcer strapped in the seat directly across from me. He doesn't glance away, which intrigues me considering how skittish others tend to become in my presence. Especially the newer recruits who have only heard stories of my unfathomable power.

Based on this particular soldier's appearance, I'd be willing to venture a guess and wager he's barely older than me. Perhaps we're even the same age, although twenty is unusually young for an Enforcer. Then again, the State is at war. The rules for registration have likely been eased to help expand our ranks for the battles ahead.

If only these soldiers knew how little their presence in this war even matters.

Typically, registration age begins at twenty-five, so the person in question has to work within their designated career for a minimum of six years—since we don't always immediately move into our career roles following our placement exams at eighteen—before they can make the conscious choice to become an Enforcer, a decision not to be made lightly given everything the individual would be sacrificing. For one, service to the State is for life, which means no reneging and going back to your previous career, not to mention that Enforcers all reside in the barracks in Zone 5, which means surrendering any previously assigned living quarters. Secondly, Enforcers aren't allowed to enter partnerships or have families of their own and all existing familial ties must be severed. This rule is in place to prevent deviant forces from ransoming loved ones to gain access to intel or admission to prohibited locations that an Enforcer would be able to access. Not that such an eventuality is even really a threat to the State. Enforcers are nicknamed Loyalists for a reason, and they live and breathe devotion to the governing body. The good of the State must always come first.

To them, nothing and no one else matters.

The young soldier's dark eyes scan over my throat before meeting my gaze again, his pupils blown wide with the same fear written all over his face. The metal ring around my neck chafes against the skin of my collarbone when I shift in my seat. As the Enforcer quickly looks down at the floor, I grasp what it is he's truly afraid of.

The irony of the situation would be amusing if it wasn't so damn maddening. The battle we're about to fly into poses far more danger to the Enforcers aboard this aircraft than I do, and yet, I'm the one he's second-guessing. Or maybe, he's simply doubting the effectiveness of my collar.

I breathe in, holding back a mocking laugh.

Don't worry, I'm tempted to say to him. *You aren't the one who needs to fear me.*

Another bout of turbulence jerks the transport helicopter from side to side, knocking me around in my seat. The straps restraining me hiss as their limits are tested and they tighten against my torso, the tough material digging into my shoulders, rubbing through my bodysuit onto my skin. With the sudden dip in altitude, my stomach flips, making me nauseous, but I'm used to the discomfort.

I'm used to all this.

A crackling pop assaults my ears as the speaker system overhead purrs to life. A few seconds pass before a husky voice speaks, reverberating in a tinny echo through the fuselage.

"We will arrive at our target destination in T-minus two minutes. Make your final preparations and ready yourselves for landing."

I observe the soldiers around me in my peripheral vision, noting their movements with waning interest. A few of them load ammunition into their guns while others reposition their gear—pointless checks that do nothing more than prepare them for a battle they'll never actually see. After all, the Enforcers are only a last resort.

The State has other means to get the job done.

Despite the chaos of motion around me, I remain still, my gaze fixed dully ahead, passing the seconds until landing in silence. As we descend, faint explosions rumble in the distance, the sound muffled by the thick, metal walls. The occasional shock wave rocks the cargo hold, reminding us all what we're about to walk into.

Once again, I peer at the youthful Enforcer strapped into the seat across from me. Beads of sweat dot his forehead and upper lip, his fingers fidgeting as he wrings his gloved hands in his lap. His visible agitation leads me to wonder if this mission will be his first time in the field.

If it is, then he should be glad it's with me.

His lips twitch as our eyes meet once again, and with a choked gasp, he touches the side of his helmet. In response, the opaque bulletproof shield lowers over his face, hiding his frightened expression from view. My mouth presses into a thin, disgruntled line as I wonder how long it will take him to realize that the very person he's afraid of will be the reason he stays alive today.

The reason everyone here stays alive.

The aircraft trembles, shuddering against the angry wind, as we continue our descent. A thunderous thrumming echoes through the large hold as the rotors slow their rotations, creating a vortex where other sounds all cease to exist. The engines stutter to a stop within seconds of the helicopter touching down on the ground.

Around me, the Enforcers unfasten their safety belts as soon as the pilot gives us the all-clear. In one cohesive unit, they rise to their feet, falling into formation and creating a single-file line, like cogs in a well-oiled machine.

A tremor rolls through the cavernous fuselage as the hydraulics scream and the loading ramp drops with a muted thud to the ground. Sunlight beams through the opening in the back of the aircraft, and for a brief moment, it's as if the low-lit interior has been set on fire.

Metal clashes against metal as the soldiers trudge forward, dragging their steel-soled boots across the tread plates lining the floor. I linger behind, watching them move in their herd, refusing to lift a muscle until I'm alone—just like every other mission I've been on. I'm not entirely sure why I do this. Maybe it's my own form of silent protest.

Or maybe it's the only way I feel in control.

When I can't delay any longer, I raise my fingers to the buckles on my harness. Although I know all too well what awaits me the moment I disembark from this aircraft, my hands are steady as they loosen the straps. I've done this so many times now the thought of what I'm about to do doesn't even faze me.

With a resigned breath, I push to my feet, my eyes straying to the loading ramp for the first time since landing. Just beyond it, I can sense the procession eagerly anticipating my impending entrance.

I grimace. It's always the same. No matter where we go or the devastation that follows, the State always makes it a point to parade me around like a trophy.

Swallowing my scorn, I take one step and then another, my stride confident as I inch farther into the thick beam of sunlight, the warmth washing over my face. The metallic clang of my boots rebounds off the aluminum floor despite how lightly I tread, each step like an icepick chiseling away at my eardrums. My sanity suffers the same assault, my senses hyperaware of the alert eyes watching me from below.

As I progress down the ramp, I glance up at the cloudless sky in an attempt to shut out the sea of faces beneath me. It's harder to ignore them than I thought it would be—a lesson I never learn, no matter how many times I'm forced to go through this. Before I can stop myself, I look down at the crowd.

Heads turn and bodies shift at my approach, making room for me to pass as I step off the ramp onto a congested beach. As I make my way through the silent crowd, I sense what the Enforcers around me are thinking. Their every thought radiates like a radio frequency and is visible in their shared wide-eyed expressions.

Astonishment. Fear. I sense them both, although it's difficult to tell which emotion is stronger.

I advance through the parting army, avoiding the hundreds of unblinking stares, instead turning my attention to the gray silhouette in the distance, welcoming the distraction of the growing skyline. As the space between us shrinks, I take note of the militarized units converging at the outskirts of the city. To my annoyance, the nearest patrol stops what it's doing the instant the soldiers there take notice of me.

I press on. The sand merges with an expanse of small rocks, which covers the length of the beach up to the wide road on my right leading straight into the city. The gravel shifts beneath my feet, the crunch of each displaced rock soothing me the same way the rotors did earlier in the aircraft. Just like then, I know this moment of tranquility won't last for long.

A quiet beeping echoes in my ear, abruptly halting my forward march and sending a shiver through my body despite the blazing heat from the sun. I hesitate for a few seconds before pressing the tip of my finger against the receive button on my communicator.

My mouth opens to speak, but words fail to form. Pressing my lips together, I wait for the familiar voice I know is on the other side of this call.

"Can you hear me?" Dr. Richter asks.

His words ring in my skull, triggering my gag reflex and igniting the flame of loathing that always consumes me at the slightest reminder of his existence. I draw in a deep, calming breath before answering. "I can hear you."

"Good," he says after a brief delay. *"The target is two miles to the north of your location. A convoy is ready to accompany you—"*

"That won't be necessary," I interrupt. "I'm already on my way."

At first, Dr. Richter doesn't respond, his only answer a faint chuckle that raises the hairs on my arms. When his voice comes back over the signal, I can hear the smile in his tone. His words are a mocking murmur in my ear.

"It finally seems like we're on the same page. Good luck."

Clenching my teeth, I jab at the button on my earpiece to disconnect the call, growling an expletive or two that I would say to his face in a heartbeat if I didn't know what sort of punishment would follow. If there's one thing Dr. Richter doesn't tolerate, even more so than disobedience, it's disrespect.

When I resume my trek, an eerie stillness engulfs the beach as every eye within a hundred yards homes in on my every movement with interest. The Enforcers in my immediate vicinity all stand at attention, but their posture is almost too rigid, as if they're all worried I'll lash out if any of them dare to move. I shake my head. I couldn't care less about them.

My only focus is getting this over with.

Every crowd I approach separates, allowing me to proceed unhindered toward the perimeter of the city. The blasts grow louder with every step, the tremors serving as a warning that anyone within range of the explosions will die. No one tries to stop me from walking into that danger.

After all, this is what I'm here for.

Tiring of walking on sand and rocks, I redirect my path toward the road, finally moving onto the wide stretch of pavement. The tarmac is worn in places and dented with potholes in others, but the damage doesn't take away from the overwhelming beauty of the city. What little I'm able to appreciate reaches down and touches my corrupted soul.

A sudden déjà vu washes over me as I follow the road into the confines of the city, my eyes trailing over the old stone and brick buildings with their arched windows and crumbling stucco, the architecture such a drastic departure from the cold glass and metal so predominant in the Heart. All at once, I'm no longer sure if what I'm seeing is real or just a tormenting reminder of every other city I've been to in recent months. The details blend together in my broken memory.

After the State launched the first dozen or so invasions, the places I saw became muddled in my brain until I could no longer differentiate between them. Or, maybe, I just didn't care to. Maybe they all look the same to me—much like this city looks to me now—because I'm detached from everything, including my humanity. Maybe, by allowing the recollection of all these different places to bleed into one, I can somehow escape the guilt of what I've done.

I can't even recall why I agreed to all this or why I'm still doing the State's bidding now. It's possible Dr. Richter altered my memory as a way of getting me to comply with his orders, but I don't truly believe he would do that, not when he could instead punish me with the memory of whatever it is I'm forgetting. No, I think something far more ominous is happening inside me. My brain…

I don't think it *wants* me to remember.

For over two years now, I've been the State's puppet and Dr. Richter's prized experiment. A large portion of that time has been devoted to rigorous testing and brutal experiments, all conducted in the name of science. The rest has been spent invading foreign countries with me at the helm of each occupation.

In less than a year, the State has managed to overtake almost everything.

Nothing feels real anymore. Nothing except pain. Even my memories seem distorted these days, and I can't recall the last time I felt normal…if I ever did at all. I remember my mundane life before I became the property of the DSD, when I was merely a student preparing for my placement exam. I can even somewhat remember pieces of my initial time with Dr. Richter when I was first taken into custody, although the events that led to my apprehension are hazy, as is most of what went on after I became the DSD's ward. I've never asked to be reminded of the details.

Beyond that, there's a bewildering gap in my memory I can't make sense of. I know I got away from the DSD for a while and willingly returned on my own, but where I went and why the hell I went back…I don't have a clue. It's as if part of the eighteenth year of my life has been ripped from my brain and tucked out of sight behind a wall built by my repressed trauma. Whatever I'm forgetting hasn't fully vanished; the lost memories, although shrouded in fog, niggle at the back of my brain, living with the small piece of me that still feels human underneath this abomination I've become. But...their presence is growing weaker. Each day, another piece of my humanity is eaten away, taking whoever I was before with it. Gradually, I'm becoming less of who I was and more of what the State has always wanted me to be.

A weapon.

The part of me that still has the strength to fight clings to whatever it is my mind refuses to remember, but it can never break down the blockade constructed around my stubborn memory. Some days, I wonder why I bother, why I don't just give in to Richter and the State and fully abandon my humanity. That's the path I'm heading down anyway, and without humanity, I wouldn't need to feel this nagging, lingering guilt all the time. Whenever I consider this, though, a small voice in my head tells me not to give up, and that small encouragement is all I need to fight another day.

I often wonder if my reason for suffering through this madness lies within those buried memories. I imagine I returned to the DSD to protect something... or someone. That's the only logical explanation. But, if that's the case, what could be so important that I'd allow myself to forget it?

Who could be important enough to drive me to embrace never-ending torture to save them?

My feet slow to a halt as my senses sharpen, detecting the enemy like a bad smell in the air. I'm close. Only a little farther.

Then, this can all be over. For now.

The road curves to the right, steering me through a residential area of terraced houses and apartments. I cast a quick glance at the darkened windows on each side of the quiet street, but there's no visible movement inside that I can see. The small part of me that's still human is thankful for that.

After another few hundred yards, the buildings space out, separated by patches of dead grass and smaller outbuildings. Ahead, the road widens into a fork, like arms opening to welcome me home. My feet never falter as I push forward, my attention focused on my target.

Following the left branch of the forked path, I enter the immense plaza marking the center of the city. Erect barricades and soldiers form a straight line through the vast space, facing me in preparation for a fight, and a handful of tanks sit positioned along the outer confines of the square in a last-ditch attempt to save their home from our invasion.

My eyes scan the area with what little remorse I'm still capable of feeling. This meager battalion must be all that remains of this country's defenses after our recent assaults—a pitiful contingent the State could've eradicated with a single bomb if my wranglers had felt inclined to act.

Of course, I know why they didn't.

A surge of anger rushes through my body, and I can almost hear Dr. Richter's laughter in my ears, taunting me with disdain and malice. This is what I'm here for. Besides, the State is seeking to oppress, not annihilate. Destroy just enough to make our enemies tremble in fear.

Kill just enough to make them surrender.

Distant shouting draws my attention to a man screeching from the opposite end of the plaza, his face distorted by the slight haze of dust hanging in the air like morning fog. The enemy soldiers in formation around him all look in my direction, and my steps slow to a standstill as I stare back at the army, scanning their ranks before squinting my eyes at the officer in command who shouted before. Although I can't see his face clearly, I can sense the exact moment our gazes intersect. Startling, he yells out to me again—his voice wobbling a little this time—but no matter how many times he repeats himself, I fail to understand what he's saying. All meaning is lost behind his foreign tongue.

After a few more wasted breaths, he finally gives up on his futile attempts to converse with me.

The officer rounds on the nearest soldier, his wrinkled skin burning bright red with frustration, the sight of which is visible even from where I stand at the other side of the plaza. The younger man goes ashen when the officer barks his orders, hesitating for a moment before raising his rifle. Thanks to my sharpened senses, I can see his hands shaking as he fires a warning shot. The bullet hits the ground only inches from my right foot.

Letting out a calm breath, I tilt my head and peer at the small graze in the cobblestone below me, assessing the damage. A wisp of smoke hovers just above the charred pockmark.

A soft huff parts my lips as I lift my gaze, zeroing in on the soldier. The moment our eyes connect, an overwhelming pressure cripples my brain. As it takes hold, the part of me that has the power to stop the impending carnage is pushed under the surface until all trace of resistance is gone.

In this moment, Wynter Reeves doesn't exist. The weapon is in control of what happens now.

An outcry of chaos erupts through the plaza, and shouting intermingles with the clicking of metal as the soldiers all aim their weapons at me. When I step forward, the officer belts out another order, this time to the entire battalion. His squawking voice is followed by a torrent of gunfire.

My march forward is effortless as my mind redirects the rain of bullets with practiced ease. The shell casings fall around me in sheets, pinging off the cobblestone like discarded coins. I am a rock, and their attempts are like water, but still, the soldiers keep firing.

As the distance between us diminishes, the enemy's terror becomes palpable—a taste I savor on my tongue because this task demands it of me. Even the projectiles launched by the tanks fail to hit their target. With a flick of my wrist, the barrels bend back on themselves, preventing any further attempts.

Realizing they're fighting a losing battle, many of the soldiers turn tail and run. The one who first shot at me stays behind, his hand furiously reloading as he fires again and again, each attempt more fruitless than the last. Impressed by his determination, I decide to make him my starting point.

They will see what I'm capable of.

They will know who they're dealing with.

As I close in, tears stream down the soldier's face, the moisture on his cheeks glistening in the harsh sunlight. With a gasping breath, he reloads his gun again in one final attempt to strike me down, but before he can fire, I wrap my fingers around the end of the barrel and yank, tugging the weapon free from his grasp. Crying out, he loses his balance and falls to the dirt with a grunt.

The soldier scrambles backward, unable to regain his footing, his complexion rapidly changing from a putrid yellow hue to gray. With a whimper, he cowers against the dry ground, and as his eyes lock on mine, I glimpse the horror shining in the depths of his gaze.

All the while, I feel nothing.

Inhaling, I reach out and grab hold with my power. The soldier arches his back, his head rolling on his shoulders as his screams slice through the air like a knife. Convulsions shake his limbs, and he drags his nails across his face as if to stop the pressure building in his head, creating vertical lacerations that cover each cheek. Specks of blood bubble up and drip from the gashes, coating his skin in a glossy red sheen.

I watch his crazed response with boredom, my mind collected and body still despite the havoc I'm wreaking on his. The half-formed pleas spilling from his cracking lips do nothing to deter my purpose. With a tilt of my head, his spine snaps like a whip.

His cries cease, and the surrounding gunfire follows suit until the plaza is silent and still. Trailing my gaze over the soldier's broken body, I crouch to retrieve his pistol, noting the unit's commanding officer out of the corner of my eye. His mouth opens several times as he trips over the unspoken words refusing to exit his throat. In the ominous hush between us, the terror etched into his face screams just how much he fears me.

I rise and stalk toward him, my every step matched by one of his own as he scurries away. Panic keeps him moving, but it also makes him clumsy. Within seconds, he stumbles over his feet and crashes to the ground with a yelp.

I watch as he writhes like prey caught in a trap it has no hope of escaping, small, weak cries escaping him as he drags himself backward. After a few moments of this pointless struggle, he stops, surrendering himself to his fate. His hands tighten into fists as a stuttering breath parts his lips.

Lifting my chin, I raise the pistol and press the muzzle against his forehead. As my fingers dance along the trigger, I take count of the remaining forces still present, concentrating my senses on every gun directed at me. Closing my eyes, I bend them to my will, manipulating their power.

As I turn the weapons back on their owners, the resulting screams are drowned out by gunfire. Round after round is fired until the last bullet is exhausted and blood splatters the dirt and stone.

My tongue caresses my lower lip as my eyes bolt open, locking on the cowering officer on the ground before me. As my finger finds the trigger, he spouts one final word.

I don't move for a long moment. My eyes simply follow the steady stream of red as it puddles beneath my boots, my mind reeling from what the officer said before I put him out of his misery. What he whispered to me.

What he *called* me.

I hear it again now—the one word he managed to utter in a language I would understand. It rings in my ears, haunting me in the growing silence of the city.

"Monster."

TWO

I GLANCE AT THE ENFORCER beside me as he slides a key card through the thin reader affixed to the wall beside the heavy metallic black door. A small light at the top of the mechanism turns green just before the lock turns with an audible click. The door slides open a second later, granting us entry into the place that's become both my prison and home for the foreseeable future.

The DSD.

I follow the Enforcer, tracking his every move, as two more trail behind me, never more than five feet away at all times. Their clomping steps keep in perfect time with mine, a clear reminder there's no escaping them or this routine existence. Still, I can smell their fear. It radiates off their bodies like heat.

Out of the corner of my eye, I notice the soldier just behind my right shoulder tighten his grip on his gun. I roll my eyes. Their incessant hovering is annoying, but I've grown accustomed to this procession. Dr. Richter claims the constant security around me is necessary, which means I'm never alone outside my cell—with the exception of when I'm on a mission and, even then, I'm never truly on my own. Dr. Richter is always watching from somewhere.

Aside from when I'm in the field, these particular Enforcers are always with me. I don't know their names, and frankly, I don't really care. I don't think I've ever even seen the faces hiding behind their helmets. On several occasions, Dr. Richter has insisted they're my personal bodyguards, but I know better than to believe his lies.

The truth is, I'm nothing more than a glorified hostage.

We follow the familiar path through the brightly lit hallways of the facility's ground level. At one point, the lights overhead made me nauseous, burning into my retinas and leaving fuzzy, dancing spots in my eyes. Now, they're just another unchanging aspect of a life I've learned to embrace.

Our steps slow as we approach the security gate preventing further entry into the building. We always use the back service entrance when going out on a mission and come back in the same way to avoid drawing unwanted attention. Although my existence might be public knowledge now, my whereabouts are not, and the State has every intention of keeping it that way.

Part of ensuring that secrecy is the extra security laid out in this part of the building. A female guard, flanked by two Enforcers and accompanied by a bald man wearing one of the DSD's signature white coats, stands beside a full-body scanner, which all staff members and personnel are required to pass through if they want to progress beyond this point. Even Dr. Richter has to pass through this checkpoint despite being the revered Head of the Research department.

No exceptions, not for him or for me.

The DSD is the one place in the entirety of the State where special clearance doesn't exist—at least, where entry is concerned. The work conducted here is considered too valuable to risk a security breach, so precautions are taken to the utmost extreme. More than anything, these limitations are in place to safeguard me. Their prized weapon.

Their project.

When we get to the gate, the guard steps behind a large podium housing the control panel and gestures for me to enter the scanner with a disinterested wave of her hand. The Enforcers accompanying me all shift to the side, forming a tidy row in front of the wall, as I slip inside the large cylinder.

The tube, which will scan my body for any prohibited and potentially dangerous paraphernalia, is made of bulletproof glass and stands flush with the wall, extending from the floor to the ceiling. Breathing out, I spin in a slow circle as instructed—the guard's voice dulled by the thick glass—ignoring the watchful eyes staring at me. A light flashes at the base of the tube as a metal ring moves up and down along the glass, casting my body in a silver-blue glow as a low humming sound vibrates through my skull and reverberates all the way down to my bones. The scan takes around thirty seconds in total.

Once it's over, I'm escorted to the other side of the gate where my collar is checked by one of Dr. Richter's attendants for any abnormalities that could lead to a potential malfunction.

The metal shackle around my throat is examined multiple times a day, not only for my safety but for the safety of everyone else in this place. My collar is the most cherished possession in the entirety of the DSD. Aside from me, of course, but then again, the collar and I go hand in hand. Without me, it serves no purpose, and without it, I would be useless to the State. Ensuring it remains functional is top priority.

I often find myself wondering about the collar's inner workings and how it functions, but all that matters is it keeps me in check and gives me full control over my powers. Other than that, all I know is what Dr. Richter has said in his vague and incomplete explanations whenever I've dared to ask about it. Something about magnetic signals, probably along the same lines as those excruciating lightning-like bolts he so enjoys shooting into my head. It would make sense if the collar used the same method Dr. Richter discovered could trigger my visions, especially since I'm always in some degree of discomfort, not that unlike what I experience during one of his experiments. Even now, a persistent headache gnaws at my temples and at the base of my skull.

Regardless of how it operates, the collar serves its intended purpose, so I gladly suffer the pain. As Dr. Richter often likes to remind me, control comes at a cost.

The balding attendant examining my collar steps back and nods once to the guard, who barks, "You're all-clear." The instant these words leave her lips, the Enforcers—who completed their own scans during my examination—return to my side, ready to escort me into the depths of my prison.

As we continue onward, their footsteps never fall too far behind mine, each click of their heeled boots a drum being pounded on repeatedly in my head. This reminder of their claustrophobic presence is like an itch lingering under my skin I can't scratch. If I could avoid the repercussions, I'd turn and dispose of them right now just for a moment's peace.

Our route takes us into a large open room located near the center of this level where the personnel from the four different departments of the DSD often meet and converse. Although I'm officially classed as a ward of the DSD, I legally belong to Research, the department Dr. Richter is in charge of. I haven't had any direct involvement with the other three departments: Rehabilitation, Engineering, and Termination. Engineering had a hand in the construction of my collar, using information provided by Research, but I've never crossed paths with any of its employees.

In regards to the inner workings of the DSD, I was stunned to discover that what we're told in school growing up is accurate and not just propaganda to keep us in line. Rehabilitation works closely with Research, concocting medicinal cures for any illnesses that might befall the citizens of the State. They do this through the use of biotechnology and are responsible for overseeing all pharmaceutical manufacturing, which is outsourced to a factory in Zone 6. Engineering creates and maintains the equipment used at the DSD and throughout the State, from the tracking chips to all the other technology used in our everyday lives right down to the communicator Dr. Richter always gives me just before I go out on my missions. And then there's the final department, Termination.

The Grim Reaper of the State.

As we enter the open space, my gaze is immediately drawn to an older woman loitering on the far side of the room. She stares down at the computerized tablet in her hands, her unblinking eyes following every flick of her finger as she leans against a wall in the corner despite the number of empty sofas present. A regulation white coat adorns her tall, slender frame, hiding most of her tight, knee-length black dress.

As if sensing our arrival, she glances up from the tablet, fixing me with deep green eyes. Pushing away from the wall with a broadening grin, she hurries over to greet us. Her heeled shoes click against the polished floor, poking tiny holes in my sanity.

"Hello, Wynter," she says, beaming at me.

I stare at her but say nothing like always, keeping my expression blank. Smile still intact, she peers back down at her tablet, brushing off my lack of response.

Perhaps she's finally grown used to it.

Although she's always been consistently kind to me during these routine interactions, I'm well aware this exchange is nothing more than a formality—the caretaker playing her dutiful role. Now that I've proven my worth to the State, Dr. Richter is determined to keep me in good health, physical and otherwise. No one will say it, but I know my mental state is the department's biggest concern, and as Richter's personal assistant, this woman's job is to keep an eye out for any warning signs that might indicate a problem with his precious weapon. Her false kindness is merely a job requirement, a necessary facade to keep me calm and avoid me snapping and killing her like I apparently did to one of Dr. Richter's other attendants. Or so I overheard some of the staff say once. If that's true and I did murder someone, it's just one of many events I don't remember from my first stay in this hell.

My eyes trail over the woman's smooth complexion, considering her in silence. If her kindness was real, she would've told me her name. She would've tried to console me through the torture of Dr. Richter's experiments. But, after over two years of seeing her every day, she never once has. She hasn't even tried. Every time our paths cross, it's always business as usual.

"Dr. Richter is waiting for you in Exam Room B," she announces, looking up from her tablet again. Glowering at each of the Enforcers congregated around me, she adds tersely, "You may go."

The Enforcers hesitate for a moment, exchanging bewildered glances before dispersing, relieved of their babysitting duties. For now. Their retreating footsteps flood my ears.

Strange. Normally, they escort me all the way to the exam room and then, once that's over, back to my cell.

"Shall we?" the woman asks, her coy expression and the calm timbre of her voice both deceptively warm.

Extending her arm, she ushers me out of the room and down a wide, empty hallway where we walk side by side, retracing a route I've traveled countless times before.

I could walk this path blind if I had to, I realize.

The thought leaves a sour taste in my mouth. Familiarity is something I neither want nor need in this place. And yet, it's something I can't avoid, even when I try to.

As we walk, the woman regurgitates the same statement of praise she spews at me after every mission. It never changes.

Every word is always the same.

"Dr. Richter is pleased with your performance. You should be proud of your progress."

I can sense her eyes watching me, her pointed gaze like fire licking over my skin, as if determined to burn away my exterior. I don't look at her, instead staring blankly ahead until we reach Exam Room B.

The woman's fingers flash across the keypad on the wall, inputting the sequence of numbers needed to unlock the door. As it clicks open, she gestures for me to enter the room.

Exam Room B is like any other room in this building: sterile and cold. A spacious gray space, it contains an examination table, computerized desktop, and various other medical instruments and storage compartments, all lit up by fluorescent white strip lights. I know this room intimately. The only space I'm more familiar with here at the DSD is my cell.

I brush past her and pause at the other side of the threshold as the door slides shut between us. Bracing myself, I draw in a steadying breath and glance up to see Dr. Richter leaning against the metal examination table pushed up against the left-hand wall. Crossing his arms, he observes me with perceptive, gray eyes.

A cool, detached smile appears on his lips. "Welcome back." He stands up straight and pats the surface of the table, indicating for me to take a seat.

A discomforting chill runs over my skin as I cross the room and hoist myself up onto the cold slab of steel, doing as I'm told without question. Once I'm settled, Dr. Richter reaches over my shoulder, and I watch him out of my peripheral vision as he retrieves a small device off the low shelf behind me. Although this has become a sort of ritual between us, it still takes every ounce of willpower I can muster not to recoil from his unwelcome proximity.

My airway tightens as he begins the exam the same way he always does, brushing the scanner against my collar while the fingers of his free hand press into my neck, holding me still. The device beeps once, relaying information to the computer integrated into the desktop positioned just to the left of the table.

"Looks good." He lays down the scanner and thrusts his hand into his right coat pocket, retrieving a slim silver flashlight. Furrowing his brow, he shines it into my eyes. "Now, follow the light."

Once again, I do as I'm told, staring into the blinding beam as he swings it from side to side, assessing my pupils' reaction.

"Excellent." Dr. Richter clicks off the flashlight and stows it back inside his pocket. As he straightens, stepping away to consult his computer, I blink several times to ease the ache in my eyes.

As my vision adjusts, thrusting the room back into sharp focus, I notice Dr. Richter watching me with unnerving interest. No, *assessing* me—his prized pet.

His possession.

A smug smile tugs at the corners of his mouth. "The data collected from your collar during this latest mission has shown extraordinary results. Your vitals are strong, your reactionary responses are beyond superb, and your abilities are evolving at an unprecedented rate. If you maintain this level of progress, it won't be long until your power knows no limits at all."

I press my lips together when he touches my arm, thankful for the fabric separating my skin from his fingers. A shudder rips through me, chilling me to the marrow.

"You've come a long way," he says, his voice a low croon. "When we first began these experiments, we weren't even sure you'd survive. Now, look at you. The perfect specimen I've been dreaming of for over a decade." He leans forward until our faces are only a few inches apart, then lifts his hand and caresses my cheek. His next words reek of demented adoration. "My own little angel of death."

My nostrils flare, and I suck in a sharp breath, my thoughts overwhelmed by the memory of that foreign officer and what he said in his final moments. What he called me just before I killed him.

"Monster."

Dr. Richter drops his hand and turns his back to me, redirecting his attention to the computer. A weight lifts off my shoulders with some distance between us, making it easier to breathe.

"Are we done here?" I ask in a hollow voice. "I'd like to return to my quarters."

His fingertips *tap, tap, tap* against the desktop like tiny nails hammering into my brain. A long moment passes before he answers.

"Not just yet."

When our eyes meet again, I'm struck with the sudden urge to shrink away from his gaze. I suppress the temptation, remaining as tall and still as possible, trying my best to ignore the alarm bells ringing through my skull at the intense look on his face.

His cold eyes narrow. "Who's next?"

A strangled breath parts my lips, and I waver, scrambling to make sense of his question. When I don't answer, he clears his throat and raises a hand to adjust his glasses.

Taking a step closer to me, he clarifies, "I wish to know which governments still pose a genuine threat to our goal."

I gape at him, no longer confused but bewildered. Every other time I've been asked to use my power this way, I was hooked up to a wide array of machines and injected with countless, pain-inducing drugs. This question only came once that part was done. The information I saw was then fed into the DSD's computers, which allowed Dr. Richter and his team to extract and verify the data using real-time visual recordings made of my brain's responses to the experiments, allowing them access to see what I saw and ensure they only obtained the truth. To them, at that stage, I was merely a leech, sucking out and retrieving the desired information for them to then analyze and use.

Reaching forward, Dr. Richter takes hold of my chin and tilts my head back, forcing me to look up at him. "This time, I want you to tell me yourself."

I blink, taken aback by his unexpected request. Why does he want to change our routine? Why ask me when he can just link my brain to his computer and see my visions for himself? He knows what works, so why change the process?

"Why?" I breathe, vocalizing my thoughts.

He runs his free hand through my hair, twirling the dark ashy strands around his fingers. I grunt when his grip tightens, holding me still.

"I think we've come far enough now that I can trust you to be honest with me. Wouldn't you agree?" Smirking, he lowers his eyes to the metal collar pressing into my throat. His unspoken warning is clear in his gaze.

My jaw clenches, holding my anger at bay. For a split second, the thought of lying crosses my mind, but the outcome of that would be worse than just telling the truth. Any suspicion concerning my answer would only lead him to conduct one of his brutal experiments to confirm it. Which, of course, would then be followed by some form of punishment for my dishonesty.

That was one lesson I learned the hard way. The first time I was sent out on a mission—the first time I was asked to kill—I couldn't do it and I lied, which resulted in several Enforcer deaths when they came in to clear out the bodies of the people I was meant to dispose of. The enemy was waiting for them, and the Enforcers never stood a chance. After that incident, Dr. Richter saw to it that I would never lie to him again.

Aside from the risk of punishment, there's the other reason behind my cooperation to consider. Although I'm not entirely sure what it is, it's always there at the back of my mind, haunting me. I might not remember why I'm here or why I'm willing to do Dr. Richter's bidding, but I'm fairly certain risking an attack on the State will put whatever I'm trying to protect in jeopardy.

Peering at Dr. Richter, I nod.

Using my power has become easier with time and practice. What used to cause me agony is now as natural as breathing. All I have to do is focus my thoughts, pushing away all exterior stimuli until I'm aware of nothing outside myself and my mind is pliable to whatever forces of nature are responsible for my visions. Then, whatever it is I had focused on will manifest before me, answering any internalized questions I have, even ones I might not be fully aware of. It's like entering that drowsy in-between state just before falling asleep.

I push out a breath and close my eyes, sinking into that separate level of my mind where I can access my visions at will. I've seen many places this way. Of course, I've also had to visit them after, but I try not to remember that part.

My eyes move rapidly behind my closed eyelids, my brows dragging into a vee as I search for any activity outside the State that could suggest a possible threat or impending attack. Within a matter of moments, what looks to be an impressive military base on the outskirts of an unfamiliar city takes shape in my head. I take stock of the vast collection of artillery and armored vehicles, then move on to the gathering soldiers, noting the insignia stitched onto their uniforms. I focus further and the vision moves inward, concentrating on a group of high-ranking officers surrounding a glowing hologram display of their plan of attack. Although I don't understand what they're saying, the time stamp on the looping footage tells me everything I need to know.

"Well?" Dr. Richter asks. His irritating voice pulls me back to the present.

My right eye twitches as I force my lids open. "An attack by air will occur in four days' time. The intention is to decimate the Heart using isolated missiles, out of fear of sparking a nuclear war, but there are plans for an invasion to ensure the city is completely wiped out if the strikes aren't conclusive."

I'm tormented by these moments—the moments when I hand entire populations over for slaughter. Entire *innocent* populations. After all, this new enemy is only attacking because they're afraid we'll come for them first. Because they just want to protect themselves from the State's increasing hold over the world.

From me.

But what they fail to realize is this pre-emptive move has signed their death warrant. The actions they take now will only lead to their annihilation.

In a bid for world domination, the State has launched an all-out assault on every country standing in its path. It was only a matter of time before we would eventually come for this new target. They know this and hope to catch us off guard by going on the offensive, but what they don't understand is that victory is an illusion.

So long as I exist, the State is unstoppable.

Dr. Richter faces the computer again, his fingertips pecking at the touchscreen keyboard. As he types, a bright blue light shines up from under the glass surface of the desktop, forming a large holographic image, which hovers in the air beside him.

I examine the transparent sphere, glancing at each of the tiny names and symbols denoting the different countries of our world as they appear. Dr. Richter watches my expression as I scan for the insignia matching the location in my vision.

My hand shoots out, pointing to a small speck of light on the globe. "There. The city I saw was there."

Dr. Richter swipes his hand over the keyboard, freezing the rotating image. My heart falters when he approaches again, leaning in close, his gaze locked on the name positioned just above my fingernail. Grinning, he straightens and realigns his glasses out of force of habit.

As he inches away, observing the computer again, it dawns on me how familiar this feels. Staring at the luminescent blue sphere, I'm reminded of something…

But what?

A dull buzzing sound snaps me out of my thoughts, the cerulean light of the hologram fading and returning the space to its usual monochrome palette. Dr. Richter walks back toward the table, positioning himself at my side, his piercing eyes boring into mine as his hand sweeps along the strong curve of his chin. The amusement twisting his lips only fuels my annoyance.

Grabbing his tablet off the low shelf beside me, he slides his long finger across the top of the screen. In a loud, clear voice, he says, "We're ready for you."

The door swishes open, allowing his assistant to re-enter the room. Although she smiles when she sees me, her kindness is a mask. Behind it, she's just as cold and empty as everyone else in this place.

"Take Wynter back to her quarters," Dr. Richter instructs. "We're finished for the day." He then shoos me away with a lazy wave of his hand.

I lower myself off the table and shuffle across the spotless, tiled white floor. The woman retreats into the hallway, and I mimic her steps, more than happy to get as far away from Dr. Richter as possible.

Just as my foot is about to inch over the threshold, he calls out to me.

"Oh, Wynter."

I pause in the doorway and look over my shoulder before glancing back at Dr. Richter's assistant, who waits in the hallway, standing tall with her back to the wall. The obedient servant as submissive as ever.

Internalizing a sigh, I face Dr. Richter.

"One more thing," he says.

Closing the distance between us, he grabs my left wrist and pushes up the sleeve of my bodysuit to expose the crook of my elbow. Before I can react, he plunges a needle into my throbbing vein, adding yet another puncture mark to my already riddled skin.

My blood flows into the attached vial, filling it in seconds. A grimace crosses my lips, and I wince when Dr. Richter yanks out the needle. A cruel smile darkens his features. "Can't forget this." He holds up the syringe and dangles it vertically, waving it from side to side, showing off the container of my blood and once again flaunting his power over me.

Hatred flushes through my entire body like a rush of heat as I roughly tear my arm free of his grasp. As I tug my sleeve back down into its rightful position, I wish for nothing more than to see him dead.

No, I wish to kill him myself.

But overshadowing my loathing is my anger at myself. Thinking he'd forget this part of our little meetings was ignorant of me. Taking my blood has become a daily occurrence—one he derives pleasure from since it causes me distress and pain. Why should today be any different?

What he needs the blood for...I don't know and I'm not sure I really want to. All I do know is it's important to him and that he's collected a vial for every single day I've been his prisoner. Known as Type X, the blood coursing through my veins is a genetic mutation no one has ever seen before.

One of a kind, just like me.

"Get some rest."

The light from the ceiling reflects off the rectangular lenses of Dr. Richter's thin-rimmed glasses, shielding his eyes and making him look every bit the maniacal mad scientist.

Tightening his hand around the vial, he adds, "The attack is in four days. We leave in two." He then turns his back to me, indicating that our meeting is over.

Swallowing, I ball my hands into fists to keep my fingers from trembling. My nails dig into my palms, drawing blood, as I nod and finally exit the room.

THREE

BLUE LIGHT ILLUMINATES THE EXAM room, drenching my body in its radiant glow. My eyes follow the fuzzy edges of the rounded image as it expands, watching as a slew of names manifest across the transparent exterior. They pop up—bright spots absorbing the space where nothing existed just a moment before—as if the places they represent are only just now coming into existence.

Pins and needles prickle every inch of my skin as I pass my hand through the hologram. To my surprise, something hard presses back against my fingertips where I expect to only find air.

The light fades, revealing a wooden globe spinning in front of me on its tilted axis. Seconds ago, what I was looking at was nothing more than a digital projection of a world I have personally had a hand in destroying.

Now, what I'm seeing is something different.

Something important, I realize.

I take a step backward, gaping at the rotating sphere, which stands precariously close to the edge of a large desk I didn't notice before now. A fire of recognition ignites in my brain as my eyes trail along every perfectly cut curve of glass before settling on the screen embedded within the center of the desktop.

I've seen this before, I know it. But where?

My heart jumps into my throat, choking me, as the exam room is swallowed by a whiff of black smoke. Suddenly, all I see around me is darkness.

As the seconds pass, my surroundings sharpen a little, introducing me to a new space comprised of glass, metal, marble, and—oddly enough—wood. The finer details of the spacious room I now find myself in are hazy and out of focus. All except for the globe, which continues to taunt me from its place on the desktop.

A heavy weight seems to sink into my brain, and the odd sensation gripping my chest tightens as that ping of familiarity pulls at my senses. Only one thing manages to break through the fog in my head.

"What's this?" a male voice calls from behind me.

My lungs spasm from the sharp intake of air through my lips, a cold chill sinking deep into my bones as I turn in place, searching for the source of the voice. If someone is hiding in the gloom, they don't make themselves known.

I take a cautious step forward, then go statue-still when a faint buzzing sound reverberates from behind me, setting the hair on the back of my neck on end.

I cast a wary glance over my shoulder at the glass desk, the sole distinct object in the room aside from the spinning globe. The computer screen flashes to life beneath the crystalline surface, flickering in short, sporadic bursts and dousing the room in an onslaught of light.

The glow of the screen is blinding in comparison to the darkness around me, and I have to squint to see through the glare as I slowly inch back toward the desk. After a few moments, my vision adjusts to the harsh sting of the light, unveiling the words written across the top of the screen. They spill from my lips in a strangled breath.

"Project W. A. R."

Static skews the narrow letters, warping them for a second before they disappear altogether. Convulsions of light splash across the walls as a jumbled blur of letters and images race past across the glass screen in their place. I can't keep track of them, nor do I try to.

Behind me, a soft voice mutters in my ear, adding to the chaos of my confusion.

"...*Twenty-two...*"

"...*refuses to eat...*"

"...*measures to avoid malnutrition...*"

I peer behind me, searching for the source of the whispers, but I still see nothing.

"...*Forty-eight...*"

"...*withstanding tests...*"

"...*more resilient than past subjects...*"

Hysteria festers under my skin like rot, spreading with every word and sinking into the cracks in my sanity. My hands flatten over my ears to silence the voice.

A voice I now recognize as my own.

"...*One hundred and sixteen...*"

"...*extracted information...*"

"...*will continue testing...*"

A scream pushes at the inside of my lips, but before I can free it, the whispers cease. I hesitate for a moment then lower my hands, gasping on an inhale, fighting to catch my breath and calm my crazed heart, which I hadn't even realized was racing. Once my pulse steadies, I risk another glance at the screen, looking closer this time.

My attention is so focused, I don't even notice the woman standing on the other side of the desk until she touches my hand, coaxing my startled gaze to her expressionless face. Her complexion is pale and almost colorless next to the exhaustion bruising the skin around her eyes.

One green, I silently say to myself, staring at her left eye. *One blue,* I note, peering at the other. Short, mousy brunette hair grazes the skin just above her collarbone.

Leaning over the desktop, she whispers in a low, hurried voice, "It's initials. W…A…R… Wynter Arabelle Reeves."

Her words fade as the darkness thickens, trapping me in a cage where the bars of my prison are built from an emotion I haven't felt for a long time now. Panic. My frantic breaths are all I can hear in the hush. Although I can't see her, I know the woman—my own distorted reflection—is gone.

The blackness surrounding me is fully opaque now; I can't see anything, not even the desk, although the cool glass surface lingers under my fingers, keeping me afloat in a sea of nothing. Drawing in a breath, I shift forward one step at a time, using the edges of the desk as a guide to find my way, even though my path is blind. But following the sharp curves can only take me so far. Sooner or later, I'll have to step into the shadows and face whatever the darkness has in store for me next.

Thump, thump, thump. Despite my unease, my heart is a steady metronome as I shift away from the safety of the desk. And yet, with every step, I feel myself slipping deeper into oblivion until I begin to wonder if what I'm actually walking into is death.

Death. It's an anchor holding me to the unending nightmare of my existence, so it would be fitting if that's what I'm facing now. I deserve it.

After everything I've done…

I deserve to die.

As that thought finds form, a small speck of light burns in the distance, beckoning me toward whatever it is awaiting me at the other side of this eternal night. The light is faint—a dying ember struggling for life in a bottomless pit of ash—but it keeps fighting, growing larger, brighter, as if it's a living thing leading me toward salvation.

Driven forward by an urgency I can't quite explain, I thrust myself into the welcoming warmth of the light. My fingers tremble as I reach out to touch it.

To my surprise, the light is smooth like glass and cool to the touch like a dry surface of ice. As I flatten my palm, the glow steadily fades and a darker shape rises from its depths until I'm looking at a black piano.

A fresh wave of déjà vu strikes without warning, and I struggle to unravel the recognition cutting a path through my brain as it weaves into my shrouded memories. The thousands of tiny mirrors suddenly cascading around me distract me from my determined attempts.

Instinct takes over, and I throw my hands over my head, forcing the glass fragments away with my power before they can cut into my skin. The shards land at my feet like solidified raindrops, forming a circle around where I stand and leaving me completely unscathed.

I lower my eyes to the fragments where I glimpse the same reflection in every cracked piece below me. *My* reflection, again and again, contorted into an expression of horror.

I can't recall when I last experienced an emotion like the one barreling through me, ripping the air from my lungs. I didn't even think I was capable of such a feeling anymore after everything I've done.

Repulsed by my all too human fear, I try to run away from this nightmare, but my legs are frozen. Even my thoughts are tangled and incoherent as my eyes remain locked on the glass, unable to comprehend what I'm seeing.

That male voice calls out to me once again as the blackness finally devours me whole.

"*Wynter...*"

My eyes shoot open.

"Wynter—"

I blink, drawing in a strangled breath as the bleary figure above me slides into focus. Dr. Richter's assistant leans over the bed, repeating my name and shaking my shoulder.

Recoiling from her touch, I inch back across the mattress and push myself upright, taking in the familiar setting of my prison with a quick glance at my surroundings.

It was only a dream. Relief soothes me for a moment before a darker realization sinks in. Sleep is hard enough for me to come by these days, but dreaming? I can't recall the last time I was blessed with such an escape without it being corrupted by something else. Something riddled with meaning and glimpses of other times and places I don't care to see.

Before Dr. Richter fitted me with my collar, the visions would plague me awake or asleep, but oddly, it was only when I was awake that damage occurred as a result of my illness. It only took a handful of tests to conclude that the reason my body didn't suffer a negative response during unconsciousness—unlike the terrible seizures that crippled me when I was awake—was because my brain would go into stasis, putting me at that deeper state of being the visions spring from, providing a sort of shield from their effects. I could see them in my dreams, but they couldn't harm me. At least, not to the same extent.

According to Dr. Richter, my body views the visions as a foreign intruder and, as such, attacks the part of my system where they originate from. Before the collar, before control, the visions were essentially eating away at my brain. But asleep, my body would simply accept what I saw, mistaking the images for a dream. It wouldn't fight the visions—it would let them in. If anything, the visions I had when asleep delayed my death long enough for Richter to save me.

If you can call this miserable existence being saved.

I brush my fingers across my forehead, pushing back a few rogue strands of hair, the ends sticky with sweat. My chest heaves as a stilted breath parts my dry lips.

My eyes dart to my silent caretaker, who stands next to the bed, watching me with an appraising look that reminds me I need to be careful around her. Although she's always been kind to me, I know better than to trust this woman, who's essentially nothing more than Richter's second set of eyes. Is she taking note of my agitated state? If she is, I can guarantee she'll mention it to him. This change, however slight, in my normal behavior is sure to spark his interest.

Her mouth pulls into a practiced smile. "It's time."

I nod and swing my legs over the side of the bed, mechanical in my movements. As I rise to my feet, the woman turns toward the door.

"I'll be waiting just outside," she says over her shoulder. "Let me know when you're ready."

The lock to my cage clicks back into place when she exits the room, angering the feral side of me the people here and my countless sins have both helped to create. It unleashes its claws and strikes at the underside of my skin, begging for freedom. For vengeance.

For blood.

Pushing my darker tendencies back into submission, I fix my eyes on the wall above the sink where a mirror once hung, if the flickers of memory I have of my first stint at the DSD are to be believed. Now, all that's there is an empty stretch of concrete.

If I could see my reflection, what would I find?

Staring at the cold expanse of gray, I comb my fingers through my dark wavy hair and braid the billowing curtain over my shoulder before tossing it back, leaving it to hang down the length of my spine. A frown forms on my lips when it dawns on me that I don't need to see my reflection to know the answer to my internal question.

Even without a mirror, I barely recognize myself anymore.

Sighing, I cast a sidelong glance at the table positioned at the foot of the bed. My usual gear is folded in a neat pile on top of the computerized glass surface, freshly laundered and waiting for me.

"Just like always," I mutter under my breath.

Crossing to the table, I run a hand over the fabric, closing my fingers around the black nylon jumpsuit. As I stare down at my uniform, I swear I can still see the bloodstains from the last time I wore it—a ghostly reminder that I can never escape what I've done and will continue to do because the State wants me to.

Shaking away that thought, I shift my attention back to the wall above the sink. A faint silhouette marking the concrete is the only evidence I have that a mirror ever hung there at all. I try to envision it there again now, hoping to unlock the memory of what happened to it, but all I see is the rain of tiled glass from my dream.

The recollection of it weighs on my mind, and gradually, the mental image haunting me settles over the room, as if my reality and the nightmare are merging, joining into one. Glass fragments lie scattered across the gray floor of my cell, with a few pieces pooling in the sink and the remainder clinging to the frame on the wall that wasn't there only a moment ago. Each piece reflects the same startled face. Me, but not as I am now.

Me, as I was in my dream.

A gasp tears from my throat as I stumble backward, my legs buckling when they bump into the bed frame, sending me toppling onto the mattress.

As my head hits the bed, I clamp my eyes shut, my lips quivering as I count down from ten, whispering each number in a low, hissing breath—a coping mechanism for these rare moments when sanity eludes me. The instant I reach zero, my eyes reopen.

My pulse throbs across every inch of my skin as I lift my head, my eyes buzzing nervously around the room as confusion threatens to undo me again. The glass fragments that littered the floor only seconds ago have vanished, and the broken mirror hanging on the wall is gone. My prison is once again bare, just as it should be.

Shifting into a sitting position, I shake my head to chase away the madness tickling the edges of my thoughts. It's still there, hiding behind every breath, waiting to take hold when I least expect it. But I can't allow that. If I'm going to survive this place, I have to be strong. No matter what that entails.

As I stand, my fingers grip the material even harder.

Uncertain how much time I've already wasted, I hurriedly dress in the same regulation bodysuit I'm always given for these missions. Black nylon covers me from my neck to my ankles, the fabric only interrupted by mesh paneling on my thighs and forearms and a tactical belt, which is really just for show. My brain is all the weapon I need. Matching combat boots lace up the full length of my shins, ending a few inches below my knees.

Remembering Dr. Richter's new nickname for me, I glare down at the uniform with distaste. An angel of death, he had called me. I can't help wondering if this outfit is supposed to make me look the part.

Once the last zipper is in place, I rap my knuckles against the door to the room. Six beeps flood into the room from the hallway as the woman enters the unlocking code into the keypad on the other side of the wall. A few seconds later, the door slides open.

"Are you ready?" she asks from the threshold, her dark gaze locking on mine as she smiles.

I push past her, refusing to answer.

Like every other time she's accompanied me, we proceed through the long, empty corridors in silence, only communicating when necessary to discuss my next mission. Although we've gone through this routine several times, I can never escape the dread that nags at me. Or the feeling that I'm heading to my own execution.

As we round the last corner before the security checkpoint, Dr. Richter falls into step beside me and the woman slinks away, disappearing from view. Without saying a word, he offers me a minuscule communicator barely the size of my thumbnail. With begrudging acceptance, I swipe it from his hand and insert it into my ear.

"Have you been debriefed?" he asks, his tone bordering on apathetic.

"Yes," I murmur, keeping my eyes trained ahead.

"Good. I'll be here, just like always." I glance at him when he taps his finger twice against his ear.

Silence resumes as we pass through the security checkpoint and persists until we arrive at the back exit of the building where seven Enforcers wait by the door, among which I spot my so-called security detail.

I freeze a few feet short of their position when the blood-curdling chill of Dr. Richter's fingers wraps around my arm. His nails dig straight through the fabric of my bodysuit into the skin of my bicep.

As I turn to face him, he stares down at me with that all too familiar sinister smile. "You know what to do. I'm sure you won't disappoint me."

His eyes bore into mine as he releases his talon-like hold on me and takes a step back. His grin deepens when he raises his right arm in a salute, and it takes all the self control I can muster not to grimace at the gesture.

"For the State." His mocking tone dares me to disobey him. To refuse to answer the sentiment.

I clench my jaw, swallowing my disgust, aware I have no other choice but to play by his rules. To blend in, like I always have, but in a much more dangerous environment nothing could've ever prepared me for.

"For the State," I repeat reluctantly, regurgitating the words like an emotionless marionette.

His lips curl into an even more ominous smile.

Biting my tongue to hold back what I really want to say, I turn and proceed toward the awaiting Enforcers. A few step aside, giving me room to pass, as the one positioned farthest ahead opens the door.

The instant I cross the threshold, stepping out of the recycled purified air of the facility, the soldiers all move into formation—a wall of black circling around me, with each plodding footstep keeping in sync with mine. Our march resounds off the tarmac outside as we make our way toward the armored truck waiting less than a hundred yards away.

During these transitional moments, I always feel more like a convict being transported than a soldier heading to war. I suppose because, despite my vital role in everything the State is doing, that's what I actually am.

A prisoner with no control over my life.

When the doors to the back of the truck bang open, I clamber inside without hesitation, followed by five of the Enforcers as the other two climb into the cab at the front. Once we're all settled, the engine roars to life, preparing to carry us off to yet another battle.

Another slaughter, I correct myself.

Vacant thoughts fill my head over the course of our journey, giving me a temporary reprieve from the grim reality that has become my life. I only snap out of my inattention when the roaring howl of winds surrounding the truck alert me that we've reached our destination.

Within seconds, the vehicle skids to a halt and the metal double doors spring open, granting us permission to disembark. I follow after the Enforcers beside me, and my eyes flick up as my feet touch down on the pavement, settling on the transport helicopter in the middle of the airfield. The rotors begin their rotations, whirring loudly, as the ground crew preps for take-off.

My entourage herds me into the cargo hold, and once we're on-board, I sink into my usual seat and draw in a long, steadying breath. My hands tighten the harness straps around my shoulders and torso, clicking the buckles into position. Then, I sit back and wait.

With little else to do until take-off, I scan the length of the fuselage, watching as the seats around me fill up one by one. The only sensation I tend to experience in these moments is nausea, but right now, I feel something much worse. Something I can't put a name to.

Not knowing what's bothering me sets me on edge, so I do the only thing I can. Focusing my thoughts, I search for anything unusual or out of place in the immediate future. To my dismay, I come up blank. Nothing appears to be wrong as far as I can tell.

Everything is as it should be.

Glowering down at my hands, I blame my sudden uneasiness on the dream I had earlier. I just need to forget it and force it out of my mind, then I can go back to being calm and collected, like I always am.

Like I need to be.

Dragging in another deep breath, I tilt my head back against the vibrating wall and snap my eyes shut. Here, in this helicopter, while on my way to destroy another piece of my dwindling humanity, it occurs to me just how exhausted I am, not just physically but mentally.

Do mass murderers get vacations? I wonder.

That thought amuses me as I fight against my growing fatigue, but the hum of the rotors eventually wins this battle, lulling me to sleep. As darkness descends, wrapping me in its arms, a broken mirror is the last thing I see.

FOUR

*"**WE ARE APPROACHING OUR TARGET** destination. Prepare for landing in T-minus five minutes."*

I jerk awake as the crinkling static of the loudspeaker scratches at my eardrums, sending sharp bursts of pain to my temples. Wincing, I press my fingertips into my forehead and glance around the metal interior of the aircraft. The Enforcers are all preoccupied with last minute preparations, readying themselves for the battle ahead.

Straightening my back, I stretch my arms above my head until my shoulder joints pop. As several eyes dart in my direction, wary of my every movement, I remember the young Enforcer I encountered before my last mission. I recall how nervous he seemed. How scared. Even now, his fear of me is more clear in my thoughts than anything else I've been forced to endure since I returned to the DSD, the pain and horrors of my daily life all blending into one ambiguous, unwanted expanse of time in my memory.

I glance at the seat opposite mine, and for half a second, I expect to see him there, staring at me with those terror-stricken eyes. The face I find instead is much older.

A man rather than a frightened boy.

Normally, I wouldn't spare a second thought or shred of curiosity for any of the soldiers I'm constantly surrounded by—to me, they're just as much cannon fodder as they are to the State. And yet, part of me is interested to know what became of that young Enforcer. I don't see him among the soldiers here, so unless he was relocated to another unit, there's an infinitesimal chance he didn't survive the previous battle, though that outcome seems unlikely since the

Enforcers' involvement in this war has been limited.

Still, that part of me is tempted to search for him and find out if he's alive. Not because I actually care one way or another, but because I'm burdened with the need to know if there's even the smallest trace of humanity left remaining within me. If there isn't... If I'm not capable of feeling something as simple as compassion for another human life...

Then what am I fighting for?

The helicopter touches down on the ground, the roaring winds fading as the rotors shudder to a halt. Out of the corner of my eye, the loading ramp lowers with a metallic whine, welcoming our invasion. The piercing screech of the hydraulics might as well be this land's dying screams.

I wait until the last of the Enforcers have exited the aircraft before finally unstrapping my harness. As the buckles click open, I draw in a breath and concentrate all my awareness on a far-off point in the back of my mind. Almost at once, a wall rises up around my thoughts, separating my consciousness from the surrounding world like an invisible shield.

This routine—this distance—I've learned to create for myself has become a necessary and vital part of every mission. Without it, I can't do what has to be done.

Without it, I can't cope with what I've become.

Exhaling, I rise from my seat, my steps light as I make my way toward the ramp. Each soft, metallic clang of my boots on the aluminum tread plates is like a whispered countdown as I approach the inevitable. Although I despise this part of my missions the most, this time, I choose to face the judgment waiting below head-on instead of attempting to delay it.

That uneasy feeling that had gripped my senses when I first boarded the helicopter creeps back to the surface as I look out upon the sea of faces and register the hundreds of eyes staring up at me. The sensation wriggles through every inch of my body, but I push it away, aware of what will happen should I let that feeling gain control. Exhaling, I force myself to move closer to the confrontation I'd rather avoid.

A shiver ricochets up my spine the instant I step off the ramp, and I pause, my instincts triggered. Something seems off, the air charged with a tension I never noticed on any of my previous missions. Apprehension and my inexplicable need to please Dr. Richter collide, telling me to search for the source of my growing distress. Instead, I swallow those feelings and decide to ignore it.

For once, I'd rather not know what's coming.

A nasal voice distracts me momentarily from my trepidation, drawing my gaze to a tall figure emerging from the crowd to my right. "Your transport is ready—" he begins, but I cut him off.

"I'll walk."

The Enforcer flinches when I speak, as if he thinks I might hurt him. My lips press into a taut, thin line, my face freezing just short of a scowl.

Based on his reaction, it seems the Enforcers have grown accustomed to expecting my silence and submission. I suppose I can see why. Up until this moment, I've been the perfect, obedient pet, catering to the State's barbaric whims. Everything Dr. Richter wants me to be.

Perhaps this is the real reason why the young Enforcer was so frightened of me—because I showed an interest in him that demonstrated an intelligence inside me that proved I was more than the mindless killing machine everyone here believes me to be.

Do the Enforcers think I'm unable to speak? Or think? Or are they just refusing to acknowledge I can, considering the horrors I'm capable of? In many ways, it's like they've forgotten I'm human.

In many ways, maybe I no longer am.

I brush past the man, knocking his shoulder with mine, as my feet stomp toward the popping rattle of explosions in the distance. Perfect timing. The State has begun the preliminary attack.

Once I get there, the baton will pass to me.

My pace is steady as I proceed unhindered toward the city. Like always, countless stares follow my every move, but I never stop or look back at the soldiers.

After a few hundred yards, a soft beeping sound thrums in my ear, the incessant ringing reigniting a faint ache in my temples. With a grunt of exasperation, I jab a finger at the button on my communicator.

"The transport is there for a reason." An undertone of irritation distorts Dr. Richter's voice. The master scolding his insubordinate slave.

I come to a standstill, confused by his words. "You've never minded before," I answer directly.

How many times have I turned down the very same transport he's now reproaching me for rejecting? I prefer to walk into battle. For me, that journey serves as a much-needed calm before the storm, a chance to prepare myself and get my mind ready to perform the job expected of me. Dr. Richter always seemed to understand that, so why is today any different? Maybe he just doesn't want me to get too comfortable with any notion of freedom.

The resulting silence between us carries on for so long I begin to think there's something wrong with my earpiece. I'm about to raise my hand to check my communicator when Richter's voice comes back over the signal. Every word he snarls is a threat.

"Remember why you're there," he growls, his tone snide. *"We're surrounded by enemies, and this battle is key for asserting our dominance in this region. We can't afford to take our time. So, a little more urgency today, yes?"*

Anger settles on my tongue, but I bite back my retort before I say something I'll regret. No good will come of arguing with him—it's a struggle I can never win, and he would punish me a thousand times over to prove as much. Still, despite my incomprehensible determination to keep him placated, I can't take another second of his voice in my head. I'll suffer his wrath for this one indiscretion if it means a return to momentary peace.

Grimacing, I press the button to end the call and rip the small device from my ear with a huff. For a long moment, I don't move, unsure what to do, and as I hold the communicator between my fingertips, I toy with the idea of crushing it in my grasp. Doing so would be easy with my powers. I could even pretend it's Dr. Richter I'm crushing to add an extra layer of satisfaction to the act.

A smile touches my lips at the thought of squashing my captor like the insufferable insect he is, and yet, I can't bring myself to do it. My grin falters as my fingers relax and my hand goes slack, as if my arm has a mind of its own. The earpiece falls to the dirt intact.

"Typical." I let out a humorless laugh. As expected, I'm too weak to go through with even the most trivial and petty acts of rebellion.

I'm always too damn weak.

Lowering my eyes to the scorched desert earth at my feet, I trudge forward one step then another. My destination grows larger in size as I wander farther away from the abandoned earpiece. I'll be punished for discarding the communicator—horrifically, too, I imagine. But, even knowing that, I feel nothing. Not dread. Not fear. Nothing. After everything I've seen and done, I'm not sure I would even recognize such emotions.

My ears prick up at the thundering blast of detonations—five explosions, by the sound of it—my balance unsteady as the ground trembles, rumbling in protest. Without a second thought, I continue in the direction of gunfire and the smoke plumes forming in the sky overhead, finally crossing the threshold into the city where death permeates the air like fog.

In truth, I'm envious of its victims. Death is a constant companion in my life, and yet, I'm never allowed to experience its relief for myself. How I wish I could escape this repetitive war the way my victims have. Death would be a welcome refuge from the nightmare of my every waking moment.

Death would allow me to escape Dr. Richter.

Too bad my handlers would never allow it. Vague recollections of past attempts have made it abundantly clear that there's no point in trying. So, I've resigned myself to this existence and to the understanding that I have no choice but to obey Dr. Richter's every command. No matter what he asks, I'm forced to do as he says. To kill people. To destroy whole cities and watch them crumble to the ground. Because, if I don't do it, he'll make me.

And then, what freedom I still have will be gone.

I touch my fingertips to the rim of the collar, the thick metal band pressing into my neck. They remain there, planted against this tether binding me to control, as I proceed into the ongoing first wave of our invasion.

I barely register the drones or explosions around me, the rubble landing at my feet a mere obstacle I sidestep without even thinking about what I'm doing. Every ringing blast and the occasional scream that follows are muffled, as if I'm hearing it all from behind an impenetrable wall of glass. It's a strange sensation—as if I'm trapped in a separate reality from the battle raging around me.

I walk in a daze with my eyes on the ground, only half-aware of the broken bodies scattered throughout the war-torn streets. I've seen so many corpses by this point, I'm not even fazed by the sight. The blood sinking into the dirt by the roadside glistens in the occasional streak of sunlight that manages to cut through the ash and smoke clouding the air.

A sharp cracking sound snaps me out of my stupor, and my gaze catches on a splintered piece of glass sticking out from under my boot. In the fractured web, I catch tiny glimpses of my distorted likeness.

Face, after face, after face…

As my eyes stare back at me from my reflection, my thoughts are assaulted by a barrage of images. They stretch across my field of vision and drag me into the depths of my mind.

I immediately recognize where the vision takes me first. I'm back in my quarters at the DSD, staring into the rectangular mirror that once hung above the metal sink. But, strangely, I can't see my reflection, and when I press a finger to the glass, it shatters.

Static distorts my surroundings, and when I turn toward the sound, I find myself standing in a cramped shower cubicle. I think I know this place, but I can't remember from where. My hands move of their own accord, clawing at the concrete wall until the surface ruptures beneath my touch, exposing a bursting copper pipe. A grinding moan fills the air as a rush of water spews onto my head and pushes me down to the floor.

Static again.

My eyes squeeze shut, and when they open again, I'm thrust back into the darkness and cascading rain of glass from my dream. The mirrored fragments float around me like large, suspended snowflakes caught in mid-air, allowing me to glimpse my face in each piece.

But is this really *me* I'm seeing? The woman staring out from the shards looks like me, and yet, she's different somehow.

Unfamiliar.

Short brunette hair brushes the top of her collarbone, framing a pale pointed face stained with blood. Her eyes mark the greatest departure from my current appearance. Whereas mine are green and blue, hers are black, devoid of even the slightest glint of light. But that darkness, however different, is how I know we're the same. Because it shows that she's utterly soulless…

Just like the monster I'm always struggling to hold at bay.

As the girl in the glass and I stare at each other, I question which one of us is the real Wynter Reeves. The madness I'm constantly slipping toward—one toe always dipped in its dark, tempting waters—calls out to me in the voice of the unknown man I heard in my nightmare.

"Wynter," he beckons.

The slideshow of images blinding me vanish as my consciousness is abruptly yanked back to reality. I blink away tears as a nearby blast rattles my skull.

Dragging in a shaking breath, I quickly reacquaint myself with my surroundings. My eyes dart side to side, taking in the shuttered houses before falling to the squadron of enemy soldiers gathered at the far end of the street.

I grasp at once from their expressions of fear that they know who I am and why I'm here. I suppose I should have expected as much. With everything the State has done the past year, with everything *I've* done, it was only a matter of time before my reputation would precede me beyond the Heart's walls.

The soldiers close their ranks, raising their weapons to attempt what so many before them have failed to accomplish. I wait for their attack with a heady mix of dread and longing.

A cacophony of gunfire erupts through the city, overwhelming the faint tinkling of bullet shells scattering across the tarmac and dirt. I breathe in as the familiar pressure rises up within me, and I concede, giving in as it takes over my entire sense of self. Focusing, I shove any objection I have to what's expected of me deep down where it won't stand in the way.

As I push forward, my power lashes out at the soldiers like invisible tentacles, crushing them all in my mental grip. The fight is over as quickly as it began—it couldn't have lasted longer than a minute. It's always so easy, as natural to my senses as breathing, and this confrontation was no exception.

I go still, every part of me frozen, as I stare at the shifting fog of dust lining the street, waiting for the murky air to clear.

That's when I hear it.

A whimper cuts through the hush, kicking my defensive reflexes back into full swing. My power purrs along my skin as my narrowing eyes peer through the fading haze. When the dust finally settles, revealing the carnage, I spot the one surviving soldier.

My teeth clack together as my body tenses, my jaw clenching so tightly a stab of pain shoots upward into my cheekbones. I can already imagine what Dr. Richter would say if he knew I left anyone alive.

"It seems you're losing your touch."

I storm forward, determined to put an end to this battle and leave this miserable day behind me. But the closer I get to the soldier, the more I'm able to make out his face. My feet falter when I realize just how much he reminds me of that young Enforcer.

Seizure-like tremors cross his hands, loosening the gun from his shaking fingers until it slips from his grasp, falling to the ground. Flinching, he raises his arms in surrender and drops down hard on his knees.

"Please…"

A single tear carves a path down his cheek, and the faint flicker of my humanity responds, triggering a new vision. In the time it takes for me to blink, the world around me remakes itself and I find myself in a new scene of destruction. I recognize the Heart in my apocalyptic surroundings, but the streets are empty and I'm alone with the cowering enemy. Except, the man I'm staring at isn't the soldier who was kneeling before me only seconds ago, begging for his life. He's someone else.

Someone…familiar.

I gape at the stranger, observing his disheveled blond hair and the streaks of ash on his cheeks. When he meets my gaze, an emotion I can't comprehend in my inhuman state burns in his eyes. A small voice in the back of my head tells me I might not want to understand it.

An unexpected tear spills over, cutting a line through the soot on his skin. He parts his lips to speak, and I'm unprepared for the way my heart trips at the sound of his voice—the same voice I heard calling to me in my dream. He whispers three bewildering words.

"I'm sorry, Wynter."

Although I go rigid when he murmurs my name, my body inches forward, closing the distance between us, as if drawn to him by the insatiable need to understand who he is. The vision fades just before I can reach him.

I fumble as my eyes refocus, and it takes me a moment to realize the person staring at me now is the trembling soldier who surrendered to me mere moments ago. Disoriented, I pause in my advance, and the soldier's expression lights up at my hesitation.

"Please," he begs for the second time, licking the pool of tears from his bottom lip.

When he speaks, I only hear the voice from my vision. That voice, which echoes in my head, haunting me. *Tormenting* me. The face of the blond-haired man consumes my thoughts until I can't see anything else.

Just those hazel eyes.

A rush of doubt spreads through me, hot and fast, and irregular, shallow breaths pour from my lungs as I peer into the eyes of the soldier, his skin ghostly white. His irises flicker from blue to hazel, his face flashing between the two, as a building pressure climbs up my throat like vomit.

I press my palms to my skull, pushing at my scalp until my head hurts, trying to hold in my fracturing sanity. I thought, by building a wall around myself, I could keep the madness at bay. But I can't.

Not anymore.

A strangled gasp springs from my throat as I focus on the soldier's face, but now, I only see the man from my vision. The man I heard in my dream.

The echo of his voice rings again in my ears.

"I'm sorry, Wynter."

A growl breaches my lips as a surge of power explodes from my chest, barreling down the empty road.

"Get the hell out of my head."

The soldier's eyes widen, his mouth popping open to scream, at the same moment I snap his neck.

FIVE

THE DOOR TO MY QUARTERS whisks open, and I dart over the threshold, ignoring the stares of the Enforcers behind me, who all keep their distance just a bit more than usual. The door slides shut again the second I'm inside the room, the locking mechanism clicking back into place with a snap, ensuring my captivity.

The thought would make me laugh if I wasn't so consumed by my suffocating hysteria. After all, I could crush this door and the pitiful lock with a mere thought if I wanted to.

Heavy breaths squeeze my lungs as the tiny room shifts out of focus, the gray walls blurring. My eyes flutter open and closed, but no amount of blinking or straining my vision manages to cast off the fog. If anything, my surroundings only become more obscured.

My panic grows, igniting every nerve in my body, and sweat bubbles from my pores, sucking the black bodysuit to my fevered skin. A heavy weight presses down on my chest as my panic takes the form of a hand tightly clenching my throat. My heart races, hammering against my ribcage.

It took all the strength I possess to remain calm on the journey back to the DSD, although I doubt my performance of feigned composure was in any way convincing. Even Dr. Richter's assistant seemed to sense something was wrong with me; I could tell as much by her unusual silence and the hurried manner in which she left me here in my cell instead of taking me to see Dr. Richter like she always does after my missions. Not to mention the fleet of Enforcers she had accompany us. This change in routine alone is alarming.

Her uncharacteristic avoidance of me was best for everyone in the building. I was and still am like a ticking time bomb, ready to go off at any moment. Who knows what would've happened if she'd pushed me or forced me to talk when I'm already so close to the edge. Hell, I'm dangling from it by one finger. But now that I'm alone, I no longer have to hang onto that edge. I can let go and let the madness swallow me whole.

My hands press over my mouth, smothering my screams and making me light-headed as I struggle to breathe through my fingers. I don't ease my grip, not even when the threat of unconsciousness sets in, my thoughts focused on the paranoia and frustration tearing a path through my head. They unhinge my mental faculties until my mind is splintered into hundreds of fragments. The pieces are all equally broken, and yet, they never quite fit back together, no matter how desperately I try to reconstruct what I'm always so close to losing. Not only my humanity but *me*.

The girl behind the monster.

My teeth sink into my bottom lip, biting down hard, as I peek at the security camera, more aware than ever of its watchful eye. The red light on the side of the lens blinks every few seconds, observing me with unending interest.

A shudder rocks me from my head to my toes, and as I look down at my shaking fingers, I realize I won't be able to hide this. Dr. Richter will find out something's wrong. He'll know.

With my luck, he probably already knows.

Another flush of heat rolls through my body, turning my unsettled stomach. Hurling myself toward the sink, I clutch the side of the basin and turn the tap until a welcome mist spatters my face. But despite the relaxing, cool touch of the water, the heat and nausea remain.

A tremor of dread makes me tremble as a single thought plays in my brain on a loop.

What's happening to me?

Swallowing, I lift my gaze to the shadowed imprint on the wall over the sink. As I stare at the dark mark staining the concrete, I can just make out the ghostlike image of the mounted mirror, projected in front of me like a weak hallucination. The surface shines under the fluorescent lights.

I follow the unbroken edges before meeting the gaze of the woman staring out from the glass. Seconds turn into minutes, but no matter how long we stare at each other, I fail to find any similarities between us—similarities that *should* be there given that she's my reflection. Instead, I only see a stranger.

An impostor who wears the same face that I do.

Her mouth curls at the corners, as if she's about to say something, prompting me a few inches closer. Like a magnet drawn to its polar opposite, I lean in, desperate to know what secret she's hiding. Just when I think she's about to tell me, her lips peel back into a smile. At the same moment, an image explodes inside my brain and the small room falls away.

Suddenly, I'm no longer staring at the mirror but at the man I saw during my vision on the battlefield during my last mission. The man whose voice I heard in my dream.

The man…from what I'm beginning to suspect may actually be a memory.

The vision is the same as it was before—the two of us standing together, alone, as the Heart collapses into chaos and ruin. Tears cut paths through the ash on his cheeks.

"Wynter," he breathes.

Static. The picture wavers, then sharpens again. Except, now, the distance between us has lessened.

Static again.

Closer.

Static.

Closer.

"Wynter…"

Who are you? I try to ask, but my tongue twists, holding my question hostage. *Why do I keep seeing you?*

"Wynter."

Closer.

"Wynter."

Closer.

My eyes snap shut as I press my hands over my ears in a futile attempt to block out his voice. I shake my head when his words echo from the back of my skull, agitation creeping over my skin. It's as if he's speaking from somewhere inside me.

"Get out," I plead. "Get out…"

"Wynter…"

"Get out!"

A shrill beeping penetrates my delirium, and somewhere, in the background of consciousness, I hear the whoosh of the door to my cell fly open. A breath sticks in my throat when I sense the familiar, loathsome presence behind me, like a darkness sinking into the room. The tap of his shoes against the floor sends an involuntary shudder over my skin.

"What the hell happened?"

My eyelids lift as the last of the vision falls away, abandoning me with my tormentor. I don't turn to face him, even though I know he expects me to, instead concentrating on the dark splotch staining the wall where, only moments ago, I looked into a mirror that no longer exists. The hallucination of it and the other me I saw reflected in its transparent surface are both gone.

I swallow, forcing my thoughts to the topic at hand. My tone is flat when I finally answer.

"They're all dead, aren't they? That's what you wanted."

Every click of Dr. Richter's approaching steps carries the weight of my inevitable punishment. His vile presence looms over me from behind, his breath hot on my neck, making me sick to my stomach again. I resist the urge to recoil from him.

"The enemy has, indeed, been eradicated," he croons in my ear. "But, perhaps, you can explain why you also felt the need to slaughter the Enforcers sent in to clean up after you."

Disbelief pulls my gaze over my shoulder where I meet his harsh expression head-on, unsure if I heard him correctly. The colorless eyes staring into mine gleam with truth, but I can't bring myself to accept what he's saying. The Enforcers are only sent into the conquered cities once I've completed my appointed task. They secure what I destroy; I never even cross paths with any of the units except for at our initial landing.

Surely, I couldn't have done what he claims.

"Personally, I couldn't care less," he continues, "but my superiors, on the other hand, *do* care. Our numbers have dwindled thanks to your little outburst."

I break his gaze and peer down at my hands, my thoughts spiraling.

It's not possible. I'm in complete control. I couldn't have—

My inner protests cease when I remember the cowering soldier and the blond man whose face I still see even now, every time I close my eyes.

A lump swells in my throat. Could I have killed those Enforcers without realizing what I was doing?

I bite down on my lower lip and take a careful step away from Dr. Richter, turning so his view of my face is obscured. I don't want him to see it—my lapse in control. I don't want him to suspect that something is wrong.

But, like always, he's one step ahead of me.

He cuts off my advance, putting himself in my path, and grabs me roughly by the chin. His fingers tighten, his nails digging into my skin, preventing my escape. With a hissing breath, he jerks my face upward until I have no choice but to look at him.

"I'll ask you again. What happened back there?"

Once again, I think of that frightened soldier, but my thoughts only hang on him for a moment before the image of that blond stranger fills my head. Just like on the battlefield, their faces seem intertwined, constantly flicking back and forth, showing me one and then the other until their edges blur together. In that strange moment when the madness came so close to taking control, they had both pleaded with me—one for his life, and the other…

I hesitate, more confused than ever. What was that man apologizing for? And why did hearing him say those words feel so familiar?

"I just lost focus," I mutter, clearing my throat. "It won't happen again."

Dr. Richter drops his hand from my chin, and he steps back, giving me a wide berth, as his eyes search my face for the obvious lie. I glance away, hoping he won't see it.

"There's something you're not telling me," he says.

I tighten my hands into fists. "There isn't—"

My back strikes the nearest wall, ripping the air from my lungs, the fingers pressing into my neck cutting off my access to oxygen. As my head slams into the concrete, black spots dance in front of my eyes, blinding me. I try to drag in a breath, but his grip is too tight.

"Don't toy with me!"

I can just make out Richter's face through the haze of my vertigo. His teeth are clenched, his brow is furrowed, and those menacing gray eyes gleam with malice.

I gasp for air, helpless beneath his touch despite the inhuman power raging inside me. His fingers crush my throat, pressing the metal collar into my windpipe. As he leans in, I glimpse the pleasure in his hooded gaze. There's no doubt he's enjoying every second I squirm.

"You are *insignificant*." The fire of his words scorches my lips, his breath unbearably warm on my face. "You are mine to command, and if you can't do the job, I will not hesitate to do it for you. Remember that the next time you lose focus."

His eyes drop to my collar. Another warning. One I've heard before and that I'm willing to bet he's all too happy to act on.

The sole limitation of my power is the inability to see inside his head to find out if he's lying—if this is an empty threat or if what he's implying is actually possible. With the way the collar functions—controlling my otherwise immeasurable and uncontrollable power—Dr. Richter would've been foolish not to program some sort of override feature into the device. If you take on the burden of creating a monster, you also need a way to restrain it. A way to keep it leashed.

Besides, the DSD always has a backup plan, and in this particular case, it's more likely the backup plan is a bullet to the back of my head. Still, as much as

I believe Dr. Richter is lying about his ability to control me, I don't want to find out the hard way that he's not. I don't want him to live up to those threats. I'd prefer to do whatever the State tells me to do than deal with the alternative and lose myself completely.

If I had to guess, I'd say that my willing submission is why Dr. Richter hasn't acted on his threats. He enjoys asserting his dominance over me, bending my will, and I'd rather let him and live with my actions than allow him to violate me any more than he already has. At least, this way, even if I am a murderer, I'm also more than just a puppet being pulled by her strings.

My expression slackens, and whatever Richter sees in my face must be enough to convince him that we've reached an understanding. When his hold on me loosens, my body crumples to the floor.

Wheezing breaths pound against the inside of my throat. I can already feel the bruises forming. Rubbing my hand across my neck, I glance up as Dr. Richter straightens his glasses and smooths out the invisible wrinkles in his coat.

Without looking at me, he states in a calm, unperturbed voice, "See that it doesn't happen again."

My fingers prod at my tender skin as he retreats for the door, turning his back to me. My jaw locks, grinding my teeth together, as I watch him walk away.

A number of thoughts overwhelm me in this moment, but it's the daydream of how pleasurable it would be to kill him that I fantasize about most. I think of him on his knees, begging for mercy, and of how it would feel to deny him that kindness—to torture him slowly the way he's tortured me.

The fatalities I've caused since this war began are nothing in the grand scheme of things, inconsequential even, compared to what his death would mean to me. Whenever I was sent into battle, I was always aware of what I was doing when I took the lives of the armies I was tasked with destroying, and although my actions were horrific, I never felt anything after. Not grief. Not remorse. I simply did what I was told to do because I had no other choice.

But killing Dr. Richter? That would feel *good*. It might even bring me some semblance of happiness, an emotion I haven't felt in as long as I can remember. Plus, it would be so easy.

With a single thought, I could snap his neck.

The door to the room slides open, and time seems to slow as I contemplate whether to act.

Kill him here.

Kill him now.

Be rid of my captor.

Forget everything else.

Bitterness and disappointment flood my body when my eyes follow his looming figure into the hallway, watching the door sweep shut behind him.

In the end, like always, I do nothing.

Frustration ripples through me as I remind myself why I haven't killed him a thousand times before and why I probably never will. The reality is, without Dr. Richter, there's no cure for my condition. Without Dr. Richter, there's no control. As much as I despise both him and the State for what they've done to me, I fear the thought of what this disease can do even more.

So, I obey.

My fingers mindlessly caress the smooth surface of my collar—this shackle around my neck—as I muse over my other reason for sparing his life. There's a reason doing what he wants is important. There's a reason control is important.

If only I could remember what it is.

Sighing, I sink to the floor and prop my head back against the wall, scrubbing a hand over my face. After more than two years, my sanity is finally unraveling. I'm actually surprised it's taken this long given what I've been through. What I've seen.

What I've done.

Once again, I wonder what it is I'm protecting. Whatever, or whoever, I'm doing this for must really be important for me to have held out for as long as I have. Important enough for me to do whatever it takes to hang onto control.

I strain my jaw. I don't enjoy killing. I don't enjoy being this abomination, and I'd rather die than be the State's instrument of death for even one more day. But I came back here for a reason, so if being the DSD's weapon means seeing that through…then so be it. I'll do whatever I have to do until the final breath leaves my body.

Even if that means sacrificing my sanity.

A deranged chuckle escapes me as I glance up at the ceiling, staring into the blinding white lights. I guess it really is like Dr. Richter always says.

Control does come at a cost.

SIX

THE ARMORED TRUCK HURTLES FORWARD at breakneck speed, bouncing over every bump in the road with enough force to send me lurching backward. My head slams into the wall more than once, triggering sharp jolts of pain down my spine and coaxing black spots to rise over my eyes. The Enforcers accompanying me sit perfectly still, but I can feel them all watching me, their stares burning into my flesh, as they look for signs that might indicate I'm close to lashing out. Or having a meltdown, as the rumors are calling it.

My fingers trace small circles across the nylon fabric encasing my thighs as my eyes stare ahead, drifting out of focus. Considering what happened the last time I was sent out on a mission, I should be concentrating on the impending battle and preparing myself mentally. Instead, I allow my thoughts to wander, cycling back through the events of the last two months.

Following my accidental mass slaughtering of nearly two hundred Enforcers, Dr. Richter had no choice but to pull me from combat at the urging of his superiors. For weeks, his team ran test after test on my collar to ensure there weren't any faults that may lead to a more permanent loss of control. Control we've both worked so hard to achieve and maintain.

Control which, as it turns out, relies on me not losing my mind.

That's the thing about the collar. It might stop this disease from killing me and allow me to access my power at will, but it won't prevent me from snapping and killing the people around me if my broken brain tells me to…regardless of if I'm aware of what's happening.

I was out of commission for eight weeks in total—an inconvenient length of time in the eyes of the State, which, for once, has had to fight its own war instead of expecting me to do all the dirty work. Except for when my power of foresight was used to pre-empt any potential attacks, I was sidelined. Not that I minded. Aside from Richter's incessant testing, it was nice to not have to kill anyone for a change.

Of course, when the Research department—my legal guardians—couldn't find any problems with the collar, Dr. Richter had no choice but to reinstate me in my role as his angel of death, although it was obvious he had his reservations. My paroxysm was a mystery he couldn't solve, but since those in charge of the State demanded I return to the battlefield—brushing my outburst off as a one-time fluke—he had no plausible excuse not to comply with their orders.

This mission will be my first engagement since then.

I recall my brief exchange with my tormentor about an hour ago, prior to boarding the transport truck. As I approached the back entrance of the DSD, walking side by side with Dr. Richter, he pressed something small and hard into my hand. Looking down, I saw a communicator identical to the earpiece I discarded during the previous battle.

"Try not to lose this one," he said.

His tone was strained, and faint bruises smudged the skin around his eyes, suggesting he'd had at least one sleepless night. He seemed concerned about the upcoming mission.

Perhaps, even about me.

Of course, I'm well aware that wasn't the case. Dr. Richter isn't capable of concern for another human being, let alone for someone like me. Someone who's almost as monstrous as he is.

No, it was never me he was worried about but, I suspect, his position within the hierarchy of the State. What would his superiors say if what transpired during my last mission were to happen again? What would they do to him if Project W. A. R. turned out to be a failure?

What would they do to me?

The memory of his voice—and the threat that had lingered behind it—fully consumes my thoughts.

"Make sure to take the offered transport this time. That's not a request," he growled.

Nodding, I turned then to join the entourage of Enforcers waiting for me by the exit. Before I could even take a step, Dr. Richter seized my arm and pulled me close to his side.

"Don't disappoint me," he hissed in my ear.

When he released his grip on me a few seconds later, I moved out of his reach before he could grab me again and hurried toward the escape of the doorway.

Although the distance between us was growing, I could feel his eyes burning into my back, following my every movement right up to the moment the doors of the armored truck clanged shut behind me. That, along with the new communicator lodged in my ear, was a stark reminder that I would never escape him.

The truck speeds over another bump in the road, knocking my shoulder into the hard wall. The impact pulls me back to the present, redirecting my train of thought to our mission.

My ears pick up on the hum of the rubber wheels finding traction against the tarmac, and behind it, I note the scream of the roaring wind and what sounds like voices shouting. The truck skids to a sudden stop, and I know without asking that we've arrived at the airfield.

A beam of light streaks across my face, making me wince, when the doors to the back of the truck swing open. Shielding my eyes from the rising sun, I wait for the Enforcers to disembark then follow suit, stepping down onto the pavement.

The instant I'm off the truck, my hand drops to my side and my lips purse, holding back at least ten different words to express my annoyance and contempt for what I find before me.

Roughly fifty Enforcers stand at attention, separated into two even straight lines, forming a path—the only path available to me—to the helicopter. They face each other with their right arms all raised in salute. The same patriotic salute Dr. Richter used at the DSD all those weeks ago to mock me.

Was this his idea? Another way to put me in my place and demonstrate that I can never fight his hold over me, no matter how much I might want to? Or is he trying to tell me that I'm no different from the very State I despise?

A mass murderer capable only of destruction.

My stomach turns as I gape at this demonstration of loyalty, and it takes every ounce of self-control I possess to stop myself from snapping the neck of each Enforcer involved in this spectacle. Acting out would only prove just how much Dr. Richter gets under my skin. That power over me—that ability he has to affect my equilibrium—is what he thrives on.

Gritting my teeth, I urge myself to move. I've stalled too long, and if I don't go now, the Enforcers acting as Dr. Richter's eyes will know something's wrong and suspect the worst. Who knows what my last outburst might have put at risk. I can't afford a repeat of that. Not when I can't even be sure what the hell it is I'm trying to protect.

Not when my hold on control is the price I would pay.

Swallowing my pride, I force myself to take one step and then another, proceeding beneath the canopy of raised arms as if I don't have a care in the world.

I walk calmly, even though my heart is racing and every breath I draw is a struggle. Once I finally emerge from the pathway, I dart up the loading ramp and into the aircraft ahead of everyone else, plopping down in my usual seat at the front of the cargo hold, just behind the pilot's cabin. Keeping my expression neutral, I drag in breath after breath through my nose with as much composure as I can muster. By the time the Enforcers all file on board, filling the empty space around me, my pulse and breathing have returned to normal.

The buzzing hiss of straps tightening and the loud click of belt clasps reverberate through the fuselage, and I can just make out the muffled voice in the cockpit, announcing that we've been cleared for departure. As the helicopter shudders to life, the deafening drone of the rotors drowns out all other sound.

I lean my head back and slowly exhale as the ground beneath us disappears. The sudden weightlessness flips my stomach, which hasn't happened since I first started going out on these missions, making me uneasy. I can't help wondering if there's a deeper cause behind the sensation.

Ever since my unconventional examination—when Dr. Richter had me look ahead without verifying what I saw—my day-to-day life has seemed strangely out of focus, like I'm viewing the world through frosted glass. The dreams, the hallucinations, and the visions of that blond stranger have continued to plague me, although I've done a much better job of hiding their constant torment than I did during the last battle when the confusion of it all made me snap. There have been days I've come close to that precipice—when I've been at the edge of my tolerance—but I always manage to reel myself back by focusing on the nagging feeling that the visions and dreams are trying to tell me something important.

But what?

If I could use my visions to discover that answer, I would, but without any idea what to look for, I'm powerless. I need a clue, a breadcrumb to guide me, but the visions haven't given me a name or anything else helpful to go on. As of now, I have nothing. Even my abilities, which have been used to crush whole armies, have their limitations.

I glare at a non-existent point in the air, trying hard to empty my thoughts, to be still and not focus on anything at all. As fatigue washes over me, I encourage my mind to abandon every thought, every memory—broken or otherwise—and every inclination to see the future. After a few moments, I sense the mental shift into a different level of consciousness somewhere between sleep and awake where nothing and no one can touch me. I push away everything. The unusual distress that's haunted me the last eight weeks. My anger and hatred toward Dr. Richter.

I let go of it all.

I have no idea how much time passes as I sink deeper into my trance-like state. It surrounds me, cocooning me in its hold, until I'm no longer aware of the Enforcers around me or even the thundering rotors as they carry us farther away from who I used to be and closer to who I was always destined to become.

"Project W. A. R.," a voice whispers next to my ear.

My voice, I realize.

A tired breath brushes past my lips as the dreamlike daze lifts from my body, sending me back to reality in a dizzying rush. Blinking, my eyes trail over the inside of the aircraft, then glance down at my fidgeting hands. My fingertips absentmindedly drift back and forth along a jagged scar in the middle of my left wrist.

My brow furrows as my unease returns. How have I never noticed this mark before? I can't even remember how I got it.

Raising my arm to inspect the puckered flesh at eye level, I drag a fingernail along the length of the scar. Fragments of memories lying dormant in the depths of my mind spring to the surface in response to my touch.

First, I glimpse a shard of broken glass. No…not just glass. A piece of mirror, like the one I saw in my cell at the DSD. I watch, transfixed, as the sharp edges slice into the skin of my wrist and dark crimson blood pools from the wound, streaming in rivulets down my arm.

The memories shift then, transporting me to a musty room where I can barely make out the bleary figures surrounding me. I follow their horrified gazes to the floor where a puddle of blood drowns my feet.

A blinding light fills my field of vision, and I blink as a dark shape slides into view, forming the distinct outline of a person. A familiar female voice calls my name, but the blurred edges of her silhouette are all I can see.

My body jerks forward, shaking my paralyzed thoughts free from the memories overwhelming my mind. The straps of the harness tighten around my chest, digging into my shoulders, which ache from the whiplash. Sweat trickles down the sides of my face.

Despite the acute panic flooding my senses, I'm aware of the bewildered expressions hiding underneath the Enforcers' opaque helmets. The soldiers exchange unsettled glances before fixing their unseen gazes back on me.

Sucking in a deep breath, I squeeze my eyes shut, but they spring open again a few seconds later, drawn to the Enforcer on the other side of the cargo hold sitting directly opposite me. My eyes fall to the gun hovering over his lap, the barrel unmistakably aimed at my chest.

My pounding heart jumps up into my throat at the threat, even though the logical part of my brain knows that no human weapon can harm me. That voice of reason screams for me to compose myself, but the lingering images tormenting me are making it so hard to focus.

Calm down, the voice urges. *You have to calm down.*

I drag in another sharp lungful of air, but I'm still breathless, as if I've been punched in the stomach, the burning in my chest verging on painful. My eyes shift to the Enforcers again, anticipating their reactions, but none of them move. Every last one is frozen in suspended time.

Without warning, a vision drops over my eyes, and I observe what it shows me while holding my breath, blind to the present and helpless to intervene. I watch as a gloved hand slackens, dropping an iron-cased ball to our feet. The impact against the tread plate flooring resounds in my ears as the small ball bounces twice.

Clink.

Clink.

With the second bounce, the universe reconfigures itself and time shifts to double speed, returning me to the present.

I blink the sweat from my eyes as my fingers fumble with the straps of my harness, struggling with the clasps. Frustration rips through me as I glance at the upraised loading ramp, but even as I reach out a hand to warn the others, I know there's nothing I can do to stop this. I saw what's about to happen too late.

Now, everyone here will die.

"Grena—!" I scream.

The explosion tears through the back of the fuselage before I can get the full word out. A deafening ringing shrieks in my ears as my half-fastened straps relinquish their hold on my body, throwing me from my seat. A searing pain radiates through me as my body flips and my back collides with the wall opposite where I was just sitting.

A siren wails, and emergency lights spring up through the aircraft interior, dousing every person and every surface in an ominous red glow. As the helicopter loses altitude, the air forms a vacuum, sucking everything it can grasp through the gaping, twisted hole in the metal where the loading ramp used to be—before the blast tore it to shreds.

I gasp, fighting to suck in a breath, as my fingers grip a flailing harness, using all my strength to keep myself from slipping and plunging to my death.

Not even my powers could save me from that fall.

The longer I go without enough oxygen, the more blurred my vision becomes. My head spins, and vomit rises in my throat as the helicopter descends in a

GRENA—!

flaming spiral, heading straight toward the ground.

The siren screams of our impending demise, and tears stream down my face from the violent winds whipping my cheeks and eyes as I pull against the harness and shift my body into the nearest seat. My hands are uncoordinated as I fasten the straps around my chest, pulling them as tight as they'll go. Clutching the armrests, I then clamp my eyes shut and await the inevitable, bracing myself for impact.

For the first time in years, I don't know what to do; I'm powerless in every sense of the word.

I berate myself for once again losing focus. My job is to look out for attacks and prevent them, not sit back as they happen around me. If I hadn't been so distracted—if I had been paying attention, like I'm supposed to—I would've seen this coming.

Suddenly, a thought occurs to me. One that sets the hairs on my arms on end and pimples every inch of my flesh.

There's no way the blast was an accident. State-issued weapons are designed to prevent misfiring, which leaves only one possible outcome.

An Enforcer set the grenade off on purpose.

I don't have time to waste trying to comprehend the motive behind this attack, not when I should be concentrating on how I can stop the aircraft from crashing. I've never had to use my power for something like this before. Could I do it?

Could I save us when my sole purpose up until now has only been to destroy?

Then, another question enters my brain. Should I even attempt to? If I don't and we crash—if I don't and I die—the State will no longer have their precious weapon. Then, I would no longer have to be this monster. I wouldn't be forced to submit to Dr. Richter and help the State in this pointless war. I would finally be free and I wouldn't have to keep suffering for the sake of something or someone I can't even remember.

This could be the escape I've been waiting for.

I waver between these two options for only a moment before submitting to my chosen fate, willing it to happen quickly, ignoring the lives of the remaining Enforcers around me who will be sacrificed for my freedom. The pressure inside the fuselage increases, crushing my lungs as we spin out of control.

I do nothing to stop it.

The alarm continues to blare around me, and the emergency lights burn through my eyelids, reminding me of the blood in the fractured images that assaulted me earlier.

What about answers? asks a quiet voice in the back of my head. *Don't you want your memories back? Don't you want to remember what you gave yourself up to protect?*

I consider this line of thought, vacillating between wanting that missing piece of myself back and the desire for something else I want even more.

Sacrificing answers and memories is a small price to escape Dr. Richter.

A smile curls my lips as I relax in my seat, ready to embrace my long overdue death. As the aircraft spins out of control, what little I can remember of my life flashes before my closed eyes, and past the flickering images, I hear a man calling my name. His voice is familiar, but I can't seem to place it.

My brow furrows when he calls out again. This time, his voice is louder.

Closer.

"Wynter."

My eyes snap open, my surroundings blurred from the ongoing turbulence. As my vision sharpens, I take in the tall figure of an Enforcer standing in front of me. His face is hidden behind his black helmet, but I recognize his stance and the way he stares at me, even though I can't see his eyes.

The soldier who turned his gun on me earlier takes a step forward, closing the distance between us. I stare at him, confused how he's able to stand when the vortex is crushing everything else around us. Unaffected by the pressure, he takes a clunking step toward me, his boots sucking to the floor with a magnetized clang.

Out of the corner of my eye, I glimpse the small metal pin from the grenade responsible for this destruction. It dangles, half-exposed, from his fist.

It was you.

I gape at the unknown Enforcer, but the chaos of the explosion has muddled my head and everything is happening too quickly for me to use my power to find out who he is or what he's hoping to accomplish. Why would an Enforcer attack his own unit?

Was this attack because of me?

He's so close to me now, every footstep a countdown to an end I'm no longer prepared for. My lips part to speak, but the thrashing wind rips the air from my lungs, the howling descent swallowing my voice.

Grunting, I glare into the black shield masking the Enforcer's face, wondering what he's waiting for. As if reading my mind, he raises his gun, and I tense, preparing myself for the shot, eager for the freedom it will grant me. An escape from this life.

He hesitates for only a second before muttering, "I promise, someday, you'll thank me for this."

Then, before I can utter a word, he pulls the trigger and the world goes black.

SEVEN

A SHARP PAIN HAMMERS AGAINST the inside of my skull as my thoughts burst through the tumultuous surface of sleep into consciousness, rousing me one scrambled sense at a time. Even through my closed eyelids, the light shining onto my face is so intense I try to shy away from its touch, but something restrains me, holding me captive under the heat. The more I wriggle, the more it burns and the more I become aware of each stab in my head.

Wincing, I wrench open my eyes, stifling a cry as the blinding light scorches my retinas. Tears form, making my vision fuzzy, but through them, I can just make out my distorted surroundings. Dark gray concrete walls cage me in a square, empty space with only a single door for access. It faces me, standing a few feet away, while a surveillance camera watches me from its perch in the corner.

I huff out a strained laugh.

Someone is always watching.

I breathe in through my mouth, tasting the stale air on my tongue. The damp scent of mildew is oddly familiar, and before I'm even aware of what I'm thinking, my brain supplies the answer to the first coherent question I'm able to form in my groggy state.

I'm underground.

I jerk my head, confused by this realization. How do I know that?

And why do I recognize this place?

Perhaps the stagnant air is laced with toxins and I'm merely imagining things in my last few seconds before death finally claims me.

My lungs constrict at the thought. When the helicopter was plummeting to its fiery doom, I wasn't only prepared to die, I was ready for it. After years of torture at the hands of Dr. Richter, death would've been a welcome relief.

But now, as I try to breathe through the sensation of something heavy pressing down on my chest, I grasp how little I actually want that.

As much as I know I deserve it, I don't want to die.

Fresh tears prick at the edges of my eyes as I glance up at the lights overhead, the glare of the bulbs like a thousand flames burning tiny holes into my skin. My fingers twitch, eager to shield my face from the heat, but when I try to lift my hand, nothing happens.

Cold metal spreads its icy touch over my wrist, and as I lower my gaze, a knot twists my stomach, squeezing tighter when I register the thick, black shackles restraining my hands and feet. It's only now I notice the chair that I'm sitting in. The steel contraption keeps me upright through my disorientation, holding me prisoner.

I test the restraints, first pulling against the ones binding my wrists and then moving on to the ones at my ankles. They don't budge—not that I expect them to—and I lack the energy to try other methods thanks to the drugs coursing through my system, debilitating my body and mind. I'm not sure what my captors injected me with, but whatever it is, it's doing a damn good job of keeping me in this chair.

A stilted breath trickles from between my dry lips. "What d'you know?" I mutter, my words slurring. "It seems the monster is finally helpless."

A loud clang reverberates in my ears, and my eyes drift upward when the door screeches open. A middle-aged man with ashy blond hair and weathered skin meets my gaze from across the threshold but doesn't step into the room. Through my still clouded vision, I note the curious expression spreading over his face, although he's careful to contain it.

As if aware of my observation, he narrows his pale blue eyes, and a faint shudder ripples over my skin at the intense look he gives me. It reminds me of how Dr. Richter looked at me when we first met—that hungry curiosity that made me feel less like a human and more like a prize. As I take in this stranger's face, I can't help wondering if he has the same evil intentions.

A reserved smile pulls at his bearded cheeks, reigniting that vague sense of recognition that keeps assaulting me in this place. Like my surroundings, something about this man is familiar.

Before I can figure out why, another figure appears in the doorway, pushing past the older man and charging into the room. Heavy boots plod in aggressive stomps across the concrete floor, bringing their owner closer to me.

My self-preservation instincts kick in, overwhelming the lingering haze of drugs. As my head finally clears, my focus sharpens on the young man walking toward me.

His gaze is piercing, the depths of his irises pure obsidian, as he glares at me with a malice not that unlike what I'm sure I've displayed toward Dr. Richter on more than one occasion. A lock of brown hair so dark it's nearly black hangs loose across his forehead and dangles in front of one eye.

I glance down at his hands. A folding metal chair is clutched in one and a rifle is grasped tight in the other, the barrel held upright by the strap around his shoulder, his finger hovering just beside the trigger. Dropping the chair, he props it open a few feet away, positioning the seat to face me.

The gun faces me, too.

Ignoring his blatant warning, I redirect my attention to the man in the doorway. It's only now that he steps into the room, approaching the chair with a pleasant but cautious smile, seemingly unaware what I'm capable of. If he does know, he must have a death wish. Either that, or he doesn't realize how easy it would be for me to kill him.

With or without the restraints.

Plopping down in the empty seat, the man dismisses his subordinate with a lazy wave of his hand, keeping his attention on me at all times. Clenching his jaw, the younger man storms from the room, but not before shooting me one last look of loathing.

I glance away, certain meeting his gaze would only further antagonize him. Despite my efforts, I sense his eyes on my face right up until the moment the door slams shut between us.

The latch turns, locking me in with my new mystery captor, and several minutes tick by without either one of us speaking a word. As he watches me with those curious pale eyes, I wonder if he's expecting me to break the silence. If he is, then he better prepare for disappointment. Whatever information he's hoping to glean from me will stay sealed behind my locked lips. I might not feel any loyalty toward the State, but I certainly don't feel any toward this man, whoever he is, either.

Crossing one leg over the other, he leans back and folds his hands around his top knee. His gruff voice slices through the dank hush with ease.

"Hello, Wynter. My name is Rodrick Nolan."

Based on the way he pauses now, I know this is the part of our conversation where I'm meant to introduce myself. Considering he already knows my name, I fail to see the point. I scowl instead.

He clears his throat. "We've met before. Roughly two and a half years ago now. Do you remember?"

I bite down on my tongue to keep my face blank, even though, on the inside, the madness always lingering at the edge of my sanity reaches out yet again. I don't remember this man, but I also don't remember much between my placement exam and when I returned to Dr. Richter's care. That missing chunk of time in my memory… If this man is telling the truth, then he might possess the answers as to what I'm forgetting. He might know why I gave myself up to the State.

He might know what I was so determined to protect.

Or he might be just like Dr. Richter and have his own nefarious plans for me. That would certainly explain why I'm strapped to this chair.

I trace the wrinkles of Rodrick Nolan's face with my eyes, starting at the silver roots of his hairline and traveling down to the gray, almost white, tufts of his beard. The corners of his lips twitch when I tilt my head.

"Where am I?" I ask, ignoring his question.

"A safe place." While his tone isn't threatening, I'm not sure I trust it. And I shouldn't. Not until I know who it is he thinks he's keeping me safe from.

I cock my head to the other side, studying him. "And how I'm still alive? Maybe you can at least tell me that much."

The smile slips from his face as he straightens in his seat. When he leans toward me, I half-expect him to pat my hand, the way my father used to whenever he wanted to comfort me. But he doesn't reach out. He keeps his distance, his words a low buzzing hum in my ear.

"You've been extracted," he murmurs.

My last conscious moments before waking up in this room flood my thoughts. I see the explosion happen all over again. The Enforcers falling to their deaths.

The flashing red lights so reminiscent of blood.

I meet Rodrick Nolan's gaze once more as his voice prattles on, buzzing faintly, as if he's speaking from a great distance instead of sitting only a few feet away. As I consider him, one word he said echoes in my head.

Extracted…

What does that even mean?

"So, you see, we've been working for quite some time to retrieve you, and the opportunity finally presented itself."

This statement catches my attention, pulling me back to our conversation. "And what opportunity was that?"

He blinks a few times, faltering for a moment, surprised by my question. "To rescue you, of course."

A laugh erupts from my throat. "You call murdering at least two dozen

Enforcers and nearly killing me in the process a *rescue*?"

"Our method might seem a bit…extreme," he admits, "but please, understand. Getting to you at all was a challenge. We worked with the only option we had available."

I think of the Enforcers who were there on the aircraft. Their dying screams still ring in my ears, and I can see the way their broken bodies were ripped through the hole in the back of the helicopter formed by the blast, that moment branded into the backs of my eyelids so every time I blink, I'm forced to relive it.

All those deaths…

I suppress another laugh. Doesn't he realize how futile that intervention was?

"If blowing up a transport helicopter was the only way you could get to me, that must mean you're aware of my security level. Which also means you must know the lengths the State will go to, not only to protect me but to get me back. You're a fool if you think rescuing me was a good idea."

He scoffs. "If you're referring to that collar of yours, you can put your mind at ease. I assure you, it's already been taken care of."

A chill crosses my skin at his words. "What do you mean, it's been *taken care of*?" I whisper.

The thought of someone tampering with the device my power has become so reliant on unnerves me. I'd even go so far as to say that it frightens me, and I barely remember what fear even feels like.

"I mean that we've deactivated the tracker," he says. "From what we can tell, your left wrist is inhospitable, no doubt due to the sloppy removal of your ID chip."

I peer down at the long, jagged incision puckering my wrist.

My ID chip…

I sense the flicker of a memory at the edge of my thoughts but it fades before it can fully form.

"It doesn't appear the DSD put it back in," he continues, "and they haven't relocated the chip to your other wrist. So, unless they implanted one elsewhere and we've overlooked it in our search, which is highly unlikely, we can assume the State won't be able to find you." He pauses, giving me a sly smile. "Rest easy, Wynter. You're safe here with us."

I disregard his attempts to assuage my unease as a tremor of anger vibrates through my body. "Do you have any idea what you could've done?" I nearly scream.

Nolan shrugs. "Twenty-four hours have passed without incident. I think we would know by now if control was an issue." He raises an eyebrow, and I gawk at him as the meaning behind his words sinks in.

Just how much do these people know about me?

My lungs seize as if clenched in a tightening fist, and a long moment passes before I manage to speak. I push out the only question I can think of.

"You keep saying *we* and *us*. Who exactly are you referring to?"

Who helped you get me away from the State, and why?

I don't voice the second question. I'm not sure I want to know the answer.

Nolan drags a fingernail through the coarse hairs on his chin. As he considers me, I count all the different ways I could kill him, deliberating whether or not he's a threat.

When I reach the tenth scenario, he clears his throat. "I believe you're already acquainted with the individual who extracted you. He's an old friend of yours, apparently, or so I've been told. Jenner Rhodes. Does that name ring any bells?"

I suck in a breath as my mind replays those final moments on the helicopter. I remember the Enforcer who loomed over me. The one who said my name as chaos devoured everything around us.

"I promise, someday, you'll thank me for this."

"You mean the one who shot me," I correct him.

Nolan chuckles, and as his biting laughter resounds throughout the small room, his face almost seems to warp, changing into someone else altogether.

Now, in his chair, I only see Dr. Richter.

"The gun was adapted, and the bullets were replaced with tranquilizer darts," he explains, as if that justifies his actions. "We never intended you any harm, nor have we caused you any."

Oh, really? I'm tempted to argue. *I'm sure the drugs in my bloodstream would beg to differ.*

I shake my head, confused by this turn of events. If the extraction was intended as a rescue, then Nolan obviously isn't working with the DSD. Does that mean he sees me as a victim in need of protection?

Or am I only here to be used, like I was by the State?

Frustration rips a low growl from my lips. I'm tired of my disjointed memories and of being treated like a pawn in some sadistic game, with no say over my own life or future. How do I know I can believe what he says? This explanation may just be a trick, a ploy intended to gain my trust.

After all, didn't Dr. Richter once use the same tactic?

I drift back to my last conscious moments in the helicopter as it spiraled in a fiery blaze toward the ground. In my head, I see the Enforcer. The one who spoke my name so clearly before shooting me in the chest.

Jenner Rhodes, Nolan said his name was.

An old friend.

If that's true, why can't I remember his face?

Closing my eyes, I dig deep into my subconscious, but the harder I try to find a memory of my so-called savior, the more he seems to float out of reach.

Exhaling, I blink open my eyes and pin my gaze on Nolan again. His face is an ominous guise of composure.

"You're not with the State," I say plainly.

"No," he agrees, that careful smile returning. "I'm not."

Suspicion grips my stomach, giving me pause. It's common knowledge that everyone in our country either supports the State or pledges their allegiance to it out of fear. Those who don't fall into another group—the outlier in our oppressed society.

If he's not with the State, then that can only mean he's with PHOENIX.

Raised voices flow into the room from the hallway, and we both turn our heads at the same moment, distracted by the ruckus outside. When the lock turns and the door bangs open, disbelief punches a hole in my chest at the sight of the man standing at the threshold. The man I've seen so many times in my head. Every detail about him is just as I remember, from that tousled blond hair to those deep hazel eyes.

Eyes, which in my head, brim with tears.

Nolan jumps to his feet. "This isn't the time—"

The man ignores him and steps into the room, his warm honey gaze locked on mine. My heart falters at the stunned look of relief on his face.

"Wynter," he breathes.

His voice pounds through my head, making me wince. I hear it, over and over again, in the back of my brain, behind vague flashes of images.

Memories, no doubt, attempting to surface.

The recollections stampede to the forefront of my mind, assaulting me with recognition but never taking hold long enough for me to remember anything of substance. They dance along the outskirts of my memory, taunting me at every turn.

I only manage to grab broken fragments.

The buried memories overwhelm me, and my body convulses as a wave of pressure builds up in my skull. Even with the collar, I won't be able to contain this. Because it isn't my power about to be unleashed…

It's the madness finally taking control.

I channel my rage to the shackles restraining my wrists and ankles, ripping the metal to pieces. As the clasps drop to the floor, I spring out of the chair and launch myself at the man from my visions. Projecting my power, I throw him backward, pinning him to the wall next to the door. A grunt escapes his lips from the impact.

Before anyone can stop me, I close the distance between us and wrap my fingers around his throat.

"Why do I keep seeing you?" My words are a threatening hiss, but he just stares back at me, his expression soft. Unafraid. I tighten my grasp, determined to choke an answer out of him. "Why?" I ask again through clenched teeth.

The man's face turns a vibrant shade of red as my fingers dig into his throat, cutting off his air supply. To my bewilderment, he doesn't struggle. Instead, a single tear trails down his cheek as he smiles.

My hand loosens ever so slightly, and I gasp as a tidal wave of memories washes over my senses. The recollections rush past, fractured and fragmented, making it impossible to see the full picture, like looking into a cracked mirror.

Still, at the center of it all, I see him.

I see those hazel eyes.

My lips part to press him with another question, but before I can speak, something solid slams into the back of my skull with enough force to knock me off balance. Black spots dot my vision as my knees buckle and a blinding pain drags me down to the floor.

As the darkness of unconsciousness devours me, my fingers slacken, finally releasing their hold on the man's neck.

EIGHT

I COME TO, PULLED INTO waking by the faint sound of dripping water. The rhythmic tempo is like a clicking metronome in my ear, repeating the same words over and over.

Wake up.

Wake up.

My eyes flutter open as my body curls into a trembling ball under the onslaught of light, preparing for the inevitable burn. But it never comes.

I glance up at the bright bulbs overhead, my limbs relaxing when the blinding glow doesn't affect me. The touch of the light is warm, but it never seems to truly penetrate my skin, and as the glare burns into my retinas, I don't even feel the need to look away. It's as if I'm only half-present in this place, dangling in and out of existence.

In many ways, this reminds me of that strange dream I had at the DSD, just before my sanity took a dive off the deep end. I remember the globe. The computer. The distorted version of myself.

And that voice.

I think of the blond-haired man, recalling the feel of my fingers around his throat. I lift my hand, the skin tingling where I touched him, then risk a gentle tap to the back of my head, applying pressure to the spot where I was struck in the skull. To my confusion, the agony from the impact is gone, which means I'm either heavily medicated to dampen the pain…

Or this isn't actually happening.

Comprehension sinks into my skin, and as the pieces fall into place, I recognize what this is.

A dream.

Or a vision, a small voice says in my ear.

A breath parts my lips, and my eyes dart upward when the door to the small room unlocks with a click. A long-winded creak raises the hair on the back of my neck as the steel swings inward on its hinges.

I peer through the growing gap, but nothing waits on the other side to confront me. Still, I hesitate, rubbing my fingers across my wrists where the metal shackles chafed my skin. I can still feel them there, pinning me down, even though I destroyed them beyond all hope of repair.

If only I understood what holds me back now.

Exhaling through my nose, I force myself up from the chair and creep across the floor toward the door. Although I'm aware none of what I'm seeing is real, I'm still astounded by the emptiness of the hallway. The blinking lights and distant dripping unsettle me, urging goosebumps to rise across my skin.

As I glance down both lengths of the corridor, my eyes are drawn to the long stretch of fluorescent lights running along the low ceiling. The dazzling bulbs reflect off the walls where a sheen of moisture coats the concrete, confirming my suspicion that this place must be underground.

A rush of déjà vu overrides my senses, making me slightly dizzy. I shake my head to push the vertigo away, but the sensation digs its claws in deeper, taking hold of my brain, refusing to relinquish its grip.

All the while, that metronomic dripping carries on, taunting what remains of my sanity. The sound is louder now that I'm free of my cell, but I have no way to tell which direction it's coming from.

Straining my ears, I listen and wait. In the silence, I note all manner of things— some real and the rest most likely imagined. The clicking of pipes. A low hum in the wall.

The faint whisper of a voice chanting my name.

Without hesitation, I follow its calls, lulled forward by the strange feeling gripping my chest. The lights overhead flicker with every step, as if encouraging my advance.

Or warning me of it.

I press on until I reach the end of the corridor, pausing at the intersection where multiple passages branch off from my current location. I falter in the crossroads, unsure which path to take. Unsure where I'm meant to be going.

In answer to my silent questions, that voice reappears to guide me through my confusion.

"Wynter…"

My heart stutters, and once again, I don't waver. I follow the echo of my name, continuing through the deserted hallways. At each turn, I'm steered by the call of the voice and by the faint, repetitive dripping behind it.

Now, instead of urging me to wake up, each drop seems to beg me to hurry.

"Wynter," they both seem to shout out.

I pick up the pace, stumbling into a brisk run. The voice whispers my name as I approach an upcoming turn on my right, and as I move into the intersection, I glance down the length of the corridor, curious what I might find. My feet skid to a stop as disbelief halts my steps.

My breath catches the moment I see him—the owner of the voice—standing with his back toward me at the distant end of the passage. He's too far away for me to see him clearly, his body blurred as if a haze of fog separates us, but certainty weighs like lead in my bones as I stare at him. This man—this indistinct figure, which seems so familiar…

He's the one who's been guiding me.

I raise a hand, reaching out to him, although I don't quite understand why. Perhaps out of a desperate need to understand who he is and what it is he's trying to show me. He looks over his shoulder when I take a step forward, and a sad smile is all I can make out on his face as he turns and disappears around a corner.

"Wait," I plead, my voice raspy, like I've been gargling sand. The word barely passes my lips.

Agitation rushes through me, spurring my legs into a full sprint. As I race after him, I never stop to consider what I'm doing or where I'm being led. Danger is a foreign concept to me as I chase the stranger through the maze-like compound.

And yet, no matter how fast I run, I never seem to get any closer to him. Every time I think I'm about to catch up, I glimpse his indistinct face in the distance, waiting patiently to beckon me onward. Then, he disappears yet again, around another corner or bend, always just out of reach.

Throughout this game of cat and mouse, the man's calls grow more frequent until I'm swallowed by endless murmurings of my name. His voice is a lasting thrum in my ears, tapping against my brain at every turn—

Until I reach a dead end.

My heart jumps up into my throat as I stumble. The moment I stop walking, the whispers cease.

The silence is deafening in its vastness as my eyes fix on the door before me— the only possible exit from this path. The door is no different than all the others I've passed in this place, and yet, I can sense something important behind it.

Something I'm not sure I'm ready to see.

I inch forward, extending my hand to grab hold of the handle, but I freeze before my fingers can brush the metal. The gentle plink of dripping draws my attention to a thin pipe above the right side of the doorway. Water seeps from a crack in its rusted surface, as if in a hurry to escape its prison—a struggle I can empathize with.

One by one, the drops fall to the floor, forming a puddle by my feet. For some reason, the sight of it reminds me of blood.

Beside me, the door creaks open slowly, and I tense, preparing for what I might find. Beyond the threshold, I spot a tall figure in the poorly lit room, but I can't make out their face in the darkness. Their features only slide into focus when I make the decision to step through the doorway.

Rodrick Nolan stands propped against a steel desk with his well-muscled arms folded across his broad chest. Deep wrinkles form a vee on his forehead, drawing my gaze to the scowl on his lips.

"This was a mistake," he says. "You saw it for yourself. She's dangerous."

The blond man, whose face keeps haunting me, steps out of the shadows and into the minimal light. As I take in the pinched expression on his face, it dawns on me that he was the mysterious man guiding me through the hallways with his voice. That was why I followed so eagerly; I recognized who was calling for me.

But why?

What am I meant to see here?

Anger brims on the surface of his eyes as he retorts, "She's not dangerous. She's confused."

Confused? I peer hard at his face as a shudder tears up my spine. *Confused about what?*

Nolan shakes his head. "You need to accept the facts. She's not the same person anymore, Ezra."

My heart clenches in response to that name and at the certainty in Nolan's voice that they know me. Or knew me once. But if that's true, why don't I remember them?

What have I forced myself to forget?

"I refuse to believe that," Ezra bites back.

My eyes drift back and forth between the two men, and as I watch their silent stand-off, I realize that the visions, dreams, and hallucinations of the last two months have been leaving tiny breadcrumbs, forming an undeniable path to this moment.

If only I could figure out what my scattered memories are trying to tell me.

"I'm not sure if she's even human anymore, and I don't think you should be so quick to assume she is," Nolan barks in a reprimanding tone. "Surely, I don't need to remind you what she's capable of."

I snort. What does *he* know about what I'm capable of? What does *he* know about my power or about what I've been through?

What does *he* know about what made me this way?

Ezra's knuckles turn white as he curls his hands into fists, his forearms trembling. "I know I can bring her back—"

"No," the older man cuts in. "She's too unpredictable. Our only option is to dispose of her before she gets us all killed."

"That wasn't part of the deal!" Ezra shouts.

Nolan slams a fist on the desk. "The deal was that we'd get her back. That we'd extract her from the State so they could no longer use her in this pointless war. That was what you asked for. I never promised to let her live."

Nolan pushes away from the desk and takes a hulking step toward the door. His stance is clear. This discussion is over.

Ezra blocks his path, grabbing his shirt. "She's one of us. I won't let you hurt her."

Nolan scoffs. "Wynter was with us for less than a month and, need I remind you, she was a burden on our resources for most of that time. First, with her foolish actions with her tracking chip, then because of her illness, which we *weren't* and still *aren't* equipped to deal with—" Ezra begins to say something in protest, but Nolan continues, speaking over him. "She doesn't owe us any loyalty nor do we owe it to her. Besides, you know the other Heads only agreed to her extraction because of who she is. Now, we should do the humane thing and end this, for our sakes…and hers."

This statement takes me aback, and I gape at Nolan, lost for words. What did he mean…because of who I am?

Who am I to them?

Ezra loosens his hold on Nolan's shirt and lowers his gaze to the floor. The expression on his face stirs something within me I don't understand. I've never seen anyone look so helpless.

The older man lets out an exasperated breath and runs a hand through his hair. "Look, I know that's not what you want to hear, and I'm sorry about that. Especially with what you've already been through. Rai vouched for this girl, and you want to honor that. I get it. But you're a smart kid. You know this is much bigger than us."

"She just needs time," Ezra pleads. "She's been through hell, but she'll come around, I know it. Just give her a chance."

Nolan considers him for a long moment before exhaling a long-suffering sigh and sticking up a crooked finger. "You have one week to prove that to me, understand? If I'm not convinced of it by that time, or if she loses control again, I'll shoot her myself. I'll do what has to be done…even if she is Freston Reeves' daughter."

My eyes dart wide at the mention of my father, and as his face fills my mind, the room around me fades—the curtain of this vision dropping away to reveal the final moments of his last day. The memory plays in front of me like a twisted re-enactment.

All I see is blood.

"I'm sorry, Wynter."

Static cuts through the image, and the memory dissolves, returning me to the small room in the compound. Ezra's voice enters my ears, helping me focus and push back my guilt, grounding me.

"Thank you," he mutters to Nolan.

He then turns toward the door and walks toward me—a reversal of the figure I tried to catch in the hallways. Unlike before, when I could never quite reach him, now, he's so close I could touch him.

Once again, I'm overcome by that temptation to reach out to Ezra—to brush my fingers against any part of him I can reach—although the reason for my urges eludes me.

Nor do I understand the sensation that swallows my heart every time I look into his eyes.

"Ezra."

He stops only inches away from where I stand by the doorway and throws a questioning glance over his shoulder. Curiosity shifts my focus to Nolan's stern face, and I'm startled by the menacing darkness thriving in the depths of the older man's hooded gaze.

A darkness I've only seen in one other person.

"Don't make me regret this," he warns.

NINE

THE ROAD TO CONSCIOUSNESS IS a slow one, my thoughts a writhing whirlwind of confusion as what I saw in my dream comes back to me one hazy detail at a time. I recall being led through a maze of long hallways and the figure calling to me, always just out of reach. I remember the room awaiting me at the dead end of the path and the man inside ready to dictate my fate.

Nolan, an angry voice supplies in my thoughts, but his name is eclipsed by another. By the one belonging to the man from my dream.

The man I can't seem to get out of my head.

"Ezra," I breathe. His name is fire in my parched throat, my tongue swollen and dry as if a dozen cotton balls are lining my mouth. As I try to swallow the rising heat, I recall the desperate look on his face, the determination behind his words to Nolan only adding to my bemusement. He wants to protect me. He told Nolan he wants to bring me back.

But bring me back from what?

And then, there was the unexpected mention of my father. How do these people know him?

What did he have to do with PHOENIX?

Shaking away questions I have no way to answer right now, I draw in one shaky breath after another and force my eyes open to get my bearings. I squint against the harsh light overhead, the glare of the bulbs like knives stabbing into my skull.

Now that I'm awake, the spot on my head where I was struck earlier throbs without mercy. I reach up to touch it, curious to see what damage has been done, but my arm doesn't move—my wrists once again shackled to the chair I was able to temporarily escape in my dream.

Sucking in a breath, I glance down at my hands, silently screaming at my fingers to move, to show me some sign that I'm in control of my body, but even they refuse to budge. I try shifting my feet, but it's more of the same. Every part of me from the neck down is still.

My lips spread into a grimace as it dawns on me what Nolan and his people have done. I showed them how easily I could break their restraints, and now, they've taken the necessary steps to ensure my captivity.

In a very Dr. Richter-like move, they must have injected me with a paralytic to guarantee my confinement to this cage. That's the only plausible explanation. Thanks to the drugs I can all too easily imagine coursing through my veins at this very moment, they can keep me chained up like an animal and stop me from, as Nolan phrased it, losing control again.

My eyes flash to the security camera in the corner of the room, lingering on the red light on the side, which blinks every few seconds, just like the one in my cell at the DSD. The people here are watching me, I know it.

I stare up into the camera's lens and picture Nolan, mulling over his words to me and holding them up against what he told Ezra. For someone who claimed to rescue me, he was surprisingly quick to sign my death warrant.

What exactly do you want with me? Why am I really here?

These questions falter at the brink of my lips, sucked back into the void of silence when the door to the room creaks slowly open. A man with jet-black hair pokes his head through the doorway, fixing me with wary blue eyes.

"Wynter?"

The stranger's voice sends a tingle over my skin, raising the hairs on my arms and on the back of my neck. Although I can't pinpoint why, something about his face and voice are familiar.

Licking his lips, he takes a cautious step into the room, raising his hands when I narrow my eyes.

"I just want to talk."

The way he stares at me is unsettling, the depths of his gaze mixed with longing and guilt. I consider him for a long, tense moment before nodding once, determined to figure out who he is.

Maybe if I talk to him, I'll get some answers.

A smile twitches at the corners of his lips, but it vanishes when a second person enters the room. The hostile man with black eyes who accompanied Nolan before storms toward me again and props a folding chair on the floor, the shrill screech of the metal legs scratching against the concrete loud enough to make my eyes water. When I meet his gaze, his upper lip curls in disgust.

I'm used to such disdain. I was its victim every day at the DSD—an abomination who only existed to be feared. Maybe that's the real reason I'm eager to speak with this blue-eyed stranger who seems so inexplicably familiar to me.

Like Ezra, he doesn't look at me like I'm a monster.

As the young guard straightens, he places a hand on the gun slung over his shoulder, drawing my gaze along the curves of his rifle where I glimpse an unmistakable streak of red on the stock. Blood.

My blood, if I had to guess.

"So, I have you to thank for the headache?" I ask, cocking an eyebrow before baring my teeth.

The blue-eyed man inserts himself between us and ushers my assailant away before he has the chance to answer. Scoffing, the guard steps out of the room, slamming the heavy door shut tight behind him.

Sinking into the chair with a sigh, the blue-eyed man runs a shaking hand through his disheveled black hair and offers me the barest trace of a smile. The seconds roll by as I wait for him to speak. He watches me, searching my face, but says nothing.

After what seems like a lifetime of silence, his grin broadens and he whispers, "It's so good to see you."

My mouth presses into a thin line as his voice loops through my thoughts, playing over and over again, like a taunting echo I can never escape.

As it comes full circle, I realize where I recognize him from.

"You're the one who shot me."

He blanches at my words, his eyes springing wide for a second before lowering to the floor. "I'm…sorry about that," he manages after a moment. "But it was the only way to get you out."

A memory tugs at the back of my brain, repeating what Nolan said about my extraction and about an old friend of mine being the one responsible for my rescue.

This man… Although I don't know who he is, he must be who Nolan was referring to.

He must've been that supposed friend.

"How'd you do it?" My tone is curious and, to my own surprise, reverent. This stranger with his kind eyes and sheepish expression single-handedly took down a State transport helicopter carrying two dozen Enforcers and me, the State's most deadly weapon. That took some nerves of steel, which means he's either incredibly brave or really, really stupid. Knowing what I do about the

State, I'd say the latter.

No amount of bravery will save him from what's coming.

"Inside help," he admits, risking a glance at me. "We have someone who knew how to pass me off as an Enforcer and get the security clearance we needed to infiltrate the airfield. They provided the gear to extract you, which was customized to…" He hesitates, grimacing as he forces out the words, "Suit the circumstances."

I flip back through my memories of that moment, recalling the magnetic reverberation of his boots. I remember thinking it odd how they stuck to the metal, holding him upright while everyone else was pulled to their deaths by the vacuum of air.

"And after you shot me?" I press. "The helicopter was out of control. There was no way we were getting out of there alive, and yet…we did. How?"

I note every movement he makes, however small, however seemingly insignificant.

His shame is apparent in every last one.

"The cockpits in the State's transport helicopters double as escape pods. They might not give a damn about their soldiers, but pilots are in short supply—" His voice cuts off abruptly, his hands curling into fists on his lap. Clearing his throat, he shakes his head. "I'm not proud of what I had to do to get us out of there, but it was the only way. I won't apologize for saving your life."

I'm tempted to laugh, but his tone is so sincere it drains the humor from me, leaving an empty feeling behind. Sadness… I think this is what sadness feels like. At least, what I can remember of it.

I see it mirrored in his gaze, burning alongside his obvious guilt. He feels bad about what he did to the Enforcers and, if I had to guess, the pilots. After all, if he was willing to use a grenade in a fully occupied fuselage, chances are he was also prepared to kill anyone standing in the way of our one route of escape. The question is why?

Why was extracting me so important?

"The entire operation was risky, but it was our only option considering how well-guarded you were. We're just lucky it turned out the way it did."

These words spark a train of thought that thoroughly puzzles me. Only a few people were informed about my whereabouts and missions, so how was he able to get close to me when the State made every effort to ensure I wouldn't be seen until the opportune moment? He mentioned someone working from inside the State… Well, whoever they are must've been in close proximity to me. No other explanation makes sense.

My mind races over the mental picture of every face I remember from my days at the DSD. Which one of them is the traitor?

Which one of them helped me escape Dr. Richter?

The man snorts. "To be honest, I'm surprised our plan worked. I thought for sure you would've seen me coming and that the whole thing would turn out to be a suicide mission—"

"It doesn't work like that."

The man's mouth snaps shut as he cocks his head to the side, observing me with quiet deliberation. I waver under the penetrating heat of his stare, a feeling of déjà vu once again washing over me, drowning all my senses. Swallowing, I turn my own gaze to the floor.

"Usually, I don't see anything until the last minute." In the back of my head, I ask myself why I'm telling him this. Surely, I shouldn't be divulging the inner workings of my power to these people.

Regardless, the words keep coming.

"If I want to actively know something in advance, I have to be on guard and at least somewhat aware of what I'm meant to be looking for. Otherwise, I'm as blind to it as anyone else. The price of full control." I scoff. "On the transport, I should've been on the lookout, but I was…distracted. By the time I sensed what you were going to do, it was too late to intervene."

"Would you have…if you'd seen it in time?"

His question catches me off guard, and I glance up, meeting the full force of his gaze. A shadow has spread over his eyes, which now gape at me as if I'm not even human. Finally, something I recognize.

Fear.

"I-I'm sorry," he stammers after a few seconds of staring. "It's just…you seemed so resigned. You—" He cuts himself off and draws in a breath, his chest heaving as he seems to reconsider his words. "You're different from how you were the last time I saw you. Before, you couldn't—"

"Control it?"

His mouth pinches into a line as he nods, his lips then parting with a single whispering breath. "What did they do to you?"

My body twitches in response to his question as the memories of my time at the DSD cripple my brain like a sudden shock of lightning to my nervous system. A shiver crosses my skin as the familiar touch of madness creeps to the surface, calling my name, beckoning to me. Desperate to escape the tightening grip of my inevitable insanity, I say the only thing I can think of.

"If you were certain I knew about your plan—if you thought the State knew—

why did you risk your life to go through with it?"

With a sigh, the man pushes to his feet and grabs the back of the metal chair, folding it and tucking the legs under his arm. As he turns away, he freezes mid-step.

He doesn't look back when he answers, but I can see how every word presses down on his shoulders, like he carries the weight of the world.

"Because you're my friend."

My heart is a chorus of panicked palpitations as the blue-eyed man retreats toward the door. In my head, I imagine the feeling in my hand returning at this moment and my arm raising to reach out to him, my voice pleading with him to stay. That feeling surges up into my throat and explodes in a single breathless word.

"Jenner."

He pauses in the doorway and peers over his shoulder, the fear in his eyes banished by a glimmer of light I've seen so many times on the battlefield.

I swallow before extinguishing it because that's what I do, what I was created for. What I am...

I'm the destroyer of hope.

"That is your name...right?" I ask.

A morose smile pulls at the edges of his lips as he nods. Then, turning once more, he steps over the threshold, pulling the door closed behind him.

TEN

I SQUIRM ON THE SOFA, the chill of the leather seeping through my clothes, twiddling my thumbs as my toes tap impatiently against the white carpet. Straightening my back, I stare at the empty wall on the opposite side of the room, trying to blink only when I absolutely have to—when the burning sensation spreading over my eyes becomes too much to bear. As the minutes pass, my mother's voice rings in my ears, serving as a firm reminder.

"It's not polite to fidget."

Even at a young age, I knew what she meant. After all, she'd said it before. *"Don't do anything to draw attention to yourself. Be still. Be invisible. Do whatever is necessary to blend in."*

Considering everything that's happened to me since I ran out of my placement exam, I suppose I now find the subliminal warnings she ingrained in my childhood to be a bit strange. My mother made the effort of teaching me how to survive day-to-day life in our twisted society, and yet, at the slightest hint of trouble, she abandoned me to its treacherous tides, leaving me alone to drown.

Father, on the other hand, was different. He was a fighter. He never would've given me up.

Not like she did.

His warm fingers brush a strand of hair behind my ear, drawing my focus away from the wall and banishing the chill crossing over my skin. When our eyes meet, his soothing voice melts away the hard exterior I'm forced to wear every day.

Thanks to the cold, unfeeling nature of this harsh world I was born into, such a facade became second nature to me from a young age. I had to be distant at all times, so that's what I was.

But where our world was ice, my father was fire. He always kept me from freezing over completely.

I furrow my brow at him, curious what he must be thinking, when the lines grooving his cheeks deepen, his lips twitching at the corners. The smile fails to reach his eyes.

"You don't realize it," he says, his tone somber, "but your short life has already been robbed of so much, Wynter. Of so many wonderful things that, because of circumstances beyond our control, you'll never have the opportunity to know or discover."

"Like what?" I ask, cocking my head to one side. As I speak, it occurs to me that the voice expelling from my lips isn't that of fully grown adult but a child.

Me, when I was no older than five years old.

As he considers me, I observe his withered face, noting how tired and old he looks even though, in a physical sense—given his age at this point in time—he should be in his prime. Pain grips my heart at the daunting realization of just how much I failed to see—how much I never noticed when he was alive. I was too young to truly understand our world or the immense burden resting on his shoulders.

But now…it's all I seem to see.

"Come," he urges. "I want to show you something."

Driven by the unchangeable events of my memory, I place my tiny hand in my father's. As he pulls me to my feet, I'm overcome with excitement, and I have to remind myself that Mother wouldn't approve of my outward display of exuberance.

"Don't do anything to draw attention to yourself," her voice says once again in my ear.

I bite my lip to keep my emotions at bay.

My father steers me toward the reception room door but stops halfway across the room. Turning, he drops to one knee in front of me, licking his lips as a bead of perspiration dots along his hairline. I glance at his hands at they clasp my shoulders, unnerved by the way his fingers tremble.

"Now, Wynter," he murmurs, his voice dropping to a whisper, "I need you to promise me that you won't mention what I'm about to show you to anyone. Whatever I tell you, whatever you see, today or any day, no one can know. Not even your mother." He hesitates before adding, "Especially not your mother. This needs to be our little secret, okay?"

As I relive this moment, I hear the warning behind his words for the first time.

They should have alarmed me then, when this memory first took place, but they didn't because I trusted him and I was only a child, deaf to such subtle caveats. Mother was always much clearer with her veiled threats, but Father...he was too kind. Too gentle. He didn't want to frighten me.

Maybe if he had, I would've said no that day and he would still be alive.

Instead, the real answer I gave him slips free from my lips. "I promise I won't tell."

"Good." Climbing to his feet, he offers me a smile and pats me on the top of the head. His hand then wraps around mine again, and together, we walk out of the room toward the secret we both were meant to take to our graves.

The secret which ultimately got him killed.

As we step into the hallway, the recollection of that terrible day shifts to the forefront of my memory. The pain of it, the grief, seems to spread from my subconscious until it's practically palpable, extinguishing the lights overhead and casting our surroundings in darkness.

As the suffocating gloom closes in, I squeeze my father's hand for comfort, but all I find in my grasp is empty air. Fear prickles along my skin as I claw at the shadows, but no matter how frantically I search, he's not there. I'm all alone.

"Just like always," I breathe.

The lights come on again without warning, the glare blurred behind the tears springing into my eyes. Blinking them away, I whip around, looking once more for my father...

And finding instead the one memory I can never seem to escape.

I stand in the middle of the brightly lit hallway, staring into the reception room of our first home at the growing puddle of blood soaking into the carpet. My father lies in it, stretching out his arm, but he's not reaching for me—not as I am now. He's reaching for *her*, my younger self. The child just shy of seven years old, who had to stand by and watch as the father she loved so dearly was beaten to within an inch of his life.

As my eyes lock onto his bruised and battered face, the air rushes out of my lungs in a gasp. Cries fill my ears, emitting from the sobbing child beside me, each whimper transforming, growing older and deeper in tone until there's no one else in this nightmare but me, facing this tragedy on my own.

Although several years have passed, at heart, I still am that little girl.

The little girl who was helpless to stop her father from dying.

"I'm sorry, Wynter," he rasps, his voice ragged and strained beneath the weight of his pain. Three simple words, and every single one must've been agony.

My body goes rigid despite the voice in my head screaming for me to run to his side. Behind me, another voice—my mother's voice—reminds me to be still.

Her every breath holds me in place.

A broken laugh rises up from my throat as I realize where this cowardice inside me came from. This weak, submissive shell of a person…

My mother was the one who made me this way.

Fresh tears form a veil over my eyes as I trail my gaze over my father's discolored face. Even with my power, I'm as impotent now as I was as a child—perhaps more so, considering we're separated by time and I have no way to undo what's already passed. There's nothing I can do to protect him from those determined to crush his meager resistance. Nothing I can do to change his fate.

His fingers strain, still reaching for me, as his bleeding mouth shapes the sound of my name. The terrified expression he wears brings me back to the memory I witnessed mere moments before. To that day when I was five.

The day I promised to keep his secret.

"I didn't tell," I try to assure him, but the words stick in my throat. Because, back then, I said nothing. I cried and I screamed, but I never once said what he really needed to hear.

I let him die without saying those words.

My legs buckle, and I collapse to my knees as the grief I've been suppressing for years finally breaks through the wall my mother worked so hard to erect around me. A wall I've only continued to reinforce. As the tears carve burning lines down my cheeks, I lower my eyes to the floor, unable to look at my father any longer. I can't bear to see the question in his gaze.

The question of if I was the one who betrayed him.

Darkness creeps in from both sides, swathing me, at the same moment something warm brushes my shoulder. A ragged breath parts my lips as I snap my eyes upward, unnerved to find myself torn from one nightmare and thrust straight into another.

The blond-haired man stares at me, eyes moist and cheeks smeared with dirt, the gun at his side limply hanging by his fingers. His mouth moves, and I tense, anticipating those familiar three words. The words, which always echo the final ones said by my father.

But, this time, the words are different.

"Please, don't cry," he murmurs.

His breath on my face startles me, given the distance between us, and I reel back, my vision hazy for a moment as my eyelids slide open. Ezra leans over me, one hand on my shoulder, gently shaking me awake.

As my eyes focus on his worried expression, he bows his head and lets out a sigh, his relief apparent in his tremulous exhalation. When he looks up again, he touches a hand to my cheek, his thumb skirting over my lower lip to wipe away the tears pooling there.

My breath hitches as I shy away from his touch, and he immediately retracts his hand before moving back a few inches, giving me space. Without his body to stand in the path of the overhead lights, the full-strength of the bulbs burns into my eyes, branding spots across my vision. I blink several times to cast them away, but the blindness lingers long enough to concern me.

Whatever these people are injecting me with to keep me docile and ensure my captivity is messing with my body's reactionary responses. My senses aren't bouncing back as quickly as they should be.

Wincing away from the light, I glare at the outline of Ezra's silhouette, trying to make out his face against the fluorescent backdrop that seems to set the room on fire. As my eyes adjust and his features sharpen, I note the anger dimming his gaze. His jaw tenses, the muscles twitching.

"Come on," he says in a whisper, as if coming to some internal decision. "I'm getting you out of here."

The hostility festering under my skin dissipates, and I gape at him, too stunned to speak. The last time we saw each other, I had my hand around his throat and was ready to kill him for answers. Why would he come back after that, let alone set me free from my restraints—the only thing keeping him safe from me now?

Isn't he afraid I'll try to hurt him again?

Ignoring my questioning stare, Ezra squats to the floor and pulls a small black device from his pocket. Without saying a word, he brushes it against the arms and legs of the chair, pausing for a few seconds at each until the scanner beeps. When the last shackle has been scanned, the locks pop open, freeing me from my cage.

Like a wild animal bounding at the chance to escape a trap, I shift forward to stand, but my body is stiff and isn't responding to anything I tell it to do. My joints buckle, and, with a grunt, I teeter forward into Ezra's arms. I bristle at the contact, and he goes still in response, sensing my unease.

"I'm not here to hurt you," he breathes in my ear, the fear in his voice evident. "I only want to help you."

Carefully, as if gauging my reaction, he snakes an arm around my waist and rises, helping me up to my feet. To my own surprise, I let him.

Once we're upright, he moves his hands to my shoulders, and a zap of electricity shoots out from his fingertips where they press into my skin, rousing an odd, mildly nauseating sensation in the pit of my stomach. My heart races as a new form of discomfort takes hold of me.

Swallowing, I turn my eyes upward and trail my gaze over his taut expression, taking in the finer features of his face now that I'm close enough to really see him clearly without murderous thoughts distracting me. Before, I wanted to hurt him for haunting me and retrieve answers by any means necessary. But now, the dream I had of him and Nolan has cast a cloud of doubt over my instincts, and I'm not sure how to respond to his presence or to my captivity in this place. Their intentions are unclear to me, and I don't know what to think.

I'm confused, just as he said.

"This way." Ezra coaxes me toward the door, and for some unknown reason, I allow him to lead me, stumbling one step after another to the presumed promise of freedom.

Although feeling has returned to much of my body now that I'm moving and my blood is flowing, I still have to rely on the support of his hands to stay upright. One arm has returned to my waist, taking on the burden of my weight, and as we cross the room, I lean into his side, drawn to the warmth bleeding through his shirt. His fingers fidget against my hipbone, and his arm tightens, bringing that warmth even closer.

With each slow, guided step I take toward the door, the familiarity raging inside me strengthens, taking on a shape in my memory that's almost clear enough for me to see. I recognize this closeness between us…but how?

What am I not remembering?

This question continues to scratch at my brain as we cross the threshold from my cell into the silent hallway beyond. Once free of the claustrophobic confines of the small room, it's easier to take in the details around me. Like the unmoving figure laid prostrate on the floor.

Ezra seems unsurprised by the unconscious body of the guard stationed outside my door and looks instead down both lengths of the corridor, leading me toward the leftward path.

As I inch around the guard's flailed-out arms, I cast a curious glance at his sleeping face only to find the features of the young man I've encountered twice now. Specks of the blood from my head wound are still visible on the butt of the rifle on the concrete floor beside him.

I cock a questioning eyebrow at Ezra. I didn't hear any sounds of a scuffle, although I was barely lucid, let alone conscious, when I woke to find him in my cell. He just shrugs and urges me on down the corridor.

Our pace through the hallways increases in speed as my legs gradually regain their strength. I never ask Ezra where we're going. Maybe I don't want to think about the future for once, or maybe I don't really care. As I learned at the DSD countless times, just about anything is better than being chained up. Even if the alternative is blindly following someone whose very existence is slowly driving me mad.

After several turns, we arrive at a narrow flight of stairs in an unlit part of the compound. Ezra plants one foot on the bottom step and is about to pull me up after him when doubt shrivels my resolve. I lock my knees, refusing to move.

"Wait." I slip out of his grasp and shrink back against the nearest wall, relishing the feel of the cold concrete through the fabric of my bodysuit. Ezra's heat was beginning to grow stifling. "I'm not going any farther until you tell me what's going on."

Even with his face in shadow, I can see the way Ezra stares at me. The hazel eyes, which have tormented my thoughts for weeks, penetrate the deepest parts of my soul.

Assuming I still have one.

My teeth roll over my lower lip, biting back the words on my tongue. The answer to what I'm about to say could change everything I know about myself. About what I am. About who I was...before the State turned me into their weapon. About why I let them control me in the first place.

I hesitate, holding my breath, waiting to see if Ezra will break the silence first. He props himself back against the opposite wall and crosses his arms, staring at me with wide, hopeful eyes, as if he knows what I'm dying to ask.

As if he wants me to ask it, too.

"Why do I keep seeing you?" The words are out before I'm even aware that I'm speaking. Time seems to slow, the world revolving around this one, all-important question.

Goosebumps pimple my skin as the answer tumbles in a rush from his lips. "Because I think you might love me."

The air rips from my lungs. Love?

I'm not capable of such an emotion.

My eyes dart to Ezra's throat, taking in the purple bruises caused by my fingers. A twinge of guilt turns my stomach as a dull pain throbs across my temples. A memory, maybe, attempting to surface.

Ezra pushes off from the wall and steps toward me, closing the distance between us. "I know you're confused, but I'll help you through it if you'll let me. Come back to me, Wynter. Please."

He raises his hand, but I jerk away from his touch just like I did before.

Every time I've tried to unlock my memories, I've failed. What makes him think his attempts will be different? What makes him think he can save me from the monster I've shown the world I am?

What if I'm too far gone to come back?

His hand flinches, and he lowers his arm, understanding etched across his face. "It's okay to be afraid."

"Afraid?" I snort, laughing under my breath. "I don't think I know what fear is anymore."

Everything I've seen…

Everything I've done…

I don't even have the right to feel fear.

"I do," he admits. "That's all I've known since you left. Every day spent wondering if you were okay, if you were alive, if Austin—" He winces as the name expels in a violent hiss from his lips, and I gape him, wondering how he knows Richter, struggling to see the connection, although I can feel it pressing at the edge of my thoughts. He swallows loudly, shaking his head. "I know you thought you were protecting us by leaving, but we needed you. I need you still."

My eyes flash wide at his words. So, I was right—I surrendered myself to Richter's clutches for Ezra's sake…and possibly others.

A strange sensation ripples through me. I had expected to experience some sense of unburdening, of *relief,* once I discovered my reasoning for doing Richter's bidding. I might not be capable of it now, but once, I was able to love— or, at the very least, feel enough of something to put others before my own well-being.

But I don't feel relief; the furthest thing from it. Instead, I'm consumed by an overwhelming dread. Is it because I had something to lose? Something Richter could still use as a weapon against me?

"The Wynter you knew… I'm not her anymore," I whisper as I try to take another step back. The wall behind me prevents my escape.

A small grin tugs at his lips. "You are. I just think you're too scared to remember right now."

"Nothing scares me," I snap. "I'm a weapon. I've killed thousands. I could kill you right now if I wanted to."

He arches a brow, unfazed by my words. "Nothing?" he echoes, his tone incredulous. He steps forward until he's standing so close I can feel his breath on my face. "So, me being this close doesn't scare you?"

I gasp when he cups his warm hand around my cheek and leans in, bringing his face even nearer to mine. A soft laugh fills the space between us.

"I think I frighten you because I remind you of who you once were."

Is he taunting me? I'm not entirely sure. For a split second, I wonder if he's going to kiss me, and I'm even less sure how I feel about that. The last time I saw him, I was ready to kill him. But now?

Now, even I don't know what I'm feeling.

Just as his lips are about to brush mine, he takes a step back and lowers his hand. I gape at him, breathless and slightly dizzy. Even Dr. Richter, who abused me for years, has never sent my body into this sort of panic. No, this is something else. Something I can't explain.

Something I desperately wish I could remember.

He smiles at the stunned look on my face. "I have something I want to show you. Will you come with me?" he asks, glancing at the stairs.

I nod, even though I'm barely able to form a coherent thought in my confusion. Ezra offers me his hand, and I take it, letting him lead me up the small staircase. Maybe I follow because I believe what he said. Or maybe because I want to believe there's some part of me, deep down, buried by the trauma of everything I've been through, that can still love.

That's still the Wynter he remembers.

A secure metal door stands at the top of the stairs, and Ezra only releases my hand for the few seconds it takes to unlock the heavy bolts sealing it shut. The hinges squeal as he pushes the door open, allowing a flood of yellow light to filter in and cut through the murkiness of the stairwell.

My free hand reflexively darts to my face, shading my eyes, but as I peek through my fingers, I realize the light isn't as bright as I thought it would be. I lower my arm, soaking in the warmth on my face as Ezra guides me over the threshold.

The room we step into is like a snapshot taken from the past. Sunlight seeps through moth-eaten curtains, dancing across worn furniture and faded trinkets, which I immediately recognize as remnants of the old world, from before the State rose to power. Dust particles hang in the air like fog, giving the illusion the room is frozen in time.

I wonder how long this space has looked this way, like a half-preserved memory trapped on the edge of our current oppressive existence. It makes me sad, like I'm seeing what could have been had the State not intervened in our lives.

The wooden floorboards creak beneath my weight as I stumble forward, taking everything in. I hesitate a few feet from the grime-slick windows, my thoughts unavoidably finding their way to my father. If he was still alive, what would he think of this place?

What items here would he have tried to preserve?

"They used to call this sort of structure a farmhouse," Ezra says in a distant voice behind me. "It hasn't been used since the Heart's walls were erected, which is why Nolan chose it. This house is built over an old nuclear bunker constructed by whoever once lived here, and for what we had in mind, the location was right. The State will never think to look for us here."

What he's really saying is poorly concealed by his tone. I hear it there, behind every word.

What he means is the State won't look here for *me*.

Feigning indifference, I drag my hand across the top of a floral pink and white fabric sofa. I rub the dust that comes off the grainy surface between my fingertips.

"Where are we?"

The flooring groans as Ezra walks past me toward the front of the house, his gaze locked on a battered wooden door in the corner of the room to my right. As he throws it open, I glimpse the green adjoining hallway on the other side of the threshold, the shaded alcoves preserving the vibrant pigment of color.

He pauses, looking at me over his shoulder, and inclines his head, gesturing for me to follow.

Uncertainty scratches at the back of my brain, but my legs drive me forward, spurred on by a small voice in my memory that keeps telling me I can trust him. Its assurances eclipse every ember of doubt.

My gaze darts from left to right as I sidle into the hallway after Ezra. Without saying a word, he grabs my hand and tugs me toward the large yellow front door. When he yanks it open, letting in a deluge of light, he says the one answer I wasn't expecting.

"Outside."

I step onto the wide, wrap-around porch in shock, my gaze devouring every detail of the dilapidated wooden beams and rafters before turning to the overgrown fields stretching out before us. The neglected landscape continues for miles—a never-ending tangle of browning weeds and plant life fighting to reclaim the earth.

In the distance, I track the movement of the sun as it curves in a steady descent toward the horizon. Just in front of it, outlined by rays of gold, I can make out the silhouette of a city. But not just any city—the city where I grew up.

My home.

My prison.

The Heart of the State.

"This isn't possible," I gasp.

Ezra's fingers tighten around mine. "When you left, we were forced to relocate away from Zone 7 in case the DSD learned of the compound. We weren't sure if the location would be…compromised."

You mean tortured out of me, I think bitterly.

As he speaks, I stare ahead, trying to remember the events from a life that doesn't even feel like my own. How many people were forced to move because they feared I would give them away? How many lives have I disrupted without even being aware of the chaos I was causing?

"Jenner and I didn't think you would tell Richter our whereabouts, but Nolan didn't want to take the risk with so many innocent lives involved. There weren't many options remaining in the city that weren't already in use by the other branches of PHOENIX. We stayed with another group for a while, but the location wasn't compatible with our plan, so those of us who couldn't fight were split up among the other sects while a few select members moved out here to work on the strategy to extract you."

My brow furrows. "You moved out here because of me?" When he nods, I press further. "How? No one ever gets past the walls."

Ezra's mouth pinches at the corners. "Let's just say, our contact in the State has been useful. He provided us with an extensive map of the tunnels that went way beyond what we ever imagined. The system goes on for miles past the walls, we just never knew how far because of the limitations of our own maps. The way out was essentially already set up for us. We just had to follow the right path and claim this place as our own—"

"That doesn't make any sense," I cut in. "If the State knows about the tunnels, they'll eventually figure out where you are."

"I thought so, too, but according to our contact, the State is under the impression the tunnels are unusable. Something about their records saying the system was flooded with toxic gas at one point. I guess no one ever bothered to check to see if they were still abandoned."

Doubt surges back into my brain. Surely, after all these years and so few arrests, the State would've figured out how PHOENIX is getting around.

This loophole seems far too convenient.

Ezra, seeming to read my mind, lets out a humorless laugh and says, "You probably don't remember this, but before you left, my brother told us that PHOENIX was never a real threat to the State's agenda. From what he said, we had actually made ourselves *useful.*" He spits the word. "Although I hate to admit it, I think he was telling the truth. The reason we're all still alive, the reason the State doesn't monitor the tunnels… I think it's because they don't feel the need to."

His brother?

As Ezra's words sink in, Dr. Richter's face cuts through my head like a bullet. Suddenly, the realization hits me.

Dr. Richter is Ezra's brother.

Knowing this should splinter what little wavering inclination I have to trust him, but it doesn't. I think because, somewhere in the fractured remains of my memory, I already knew this.

And I trusted Ezra despite it.

My free hand balls into a fist as I look back in the direction of the setting sun. When I first heard Ezra's voice in my dream all those weeks ago, I thought I was going insane. Part of me still suspects that I'm losing my grip on whatever small piece of sanity I've managed to hang onto, but at least now I know my broken memories do hold the answers I've been looking for.

I just need to find a way to retrieve them.

I suppose I could look back—use the power of my visions to relive those lost moments. But I don't want to see my memories from the point of view of a detached spectator. I want to *remember* them. And remembering them requires an emotional attachment.

The one thing I'm seriously lacking.

"Why did I leave?" I peek over at Ezra. Maybe this is how I do it. By understanding what I sacrificed myself to protect.

He doesn't meet my gaze. "To protect the people you cared about. You were afraid of what your power might do to us if you stayed."

What I would do…

My nostrils flare as I touch my fingertips to the hard surface of my collar. If I loved Ezra like he thinks, then, of course, it would make sense for me to want to leave him. No one is safe around me when I'm in control, let alone when I'm not. I can only imagine the sort of danger I was exposing the people I supposedly cared about to just by being in the same vicinity as them.

I avert my gaze. "You know what I'm capable of." It isn't a question.

In my head, I hear these same words but in Nolan's voice. He told Ezra the very same thing in my vision. *"Surely, I don't need to remind you what she's capable of."*

Out of the corner of my eye, I can see Ezra nod.

"Then why rescue me?" I'm dangerous, and he knows it. So, why? "Why bring me back if you know what I am?"

Ezra unhooks his hand from mine and grabs hold of my shoulders, turning my body to face him. He trails his fingers down my arms, trapping me in a new type of shackle.

My breath catches when our eyes meet and he whispers, "For the same reason you keep seeing me in your head."

He inches toward me once again, but, this time, I don't move, held still by each paralyzing beat of my racing heart. It's strange. Considering what I'm capable of, I've never felt more powerless.

My mouth shapes a number of syllables, but no sound exits my throat. I've lost my voice, and even my brain can't work out what I should say. I don't know whether to push him away or embrace this mystifying connection between us.

Ezra takes another step, the tension in the air between us almost palpable. I can feel it against my skin, in my hair. I can taste the peculiar tang of it on my tongue.

"I don't remember—" I finally manage, breathless.

A smile illuminates his face with a light that is far too bright against my personal darkness. If he comes any closer, I might accidentally smother it.

And I'm now realizing that is the last thing I want.

"It's okay." Unconcerned with the risks, he bends forward until our faces are nearly touching. Shallow breaths beat against the inside of my lungs as the hazel depths staring down at me pin my body in place, using my heart as an anchor to keep me from fleeing.

I couldn't move even if I wanted to.

Leaning closer, he breathes against my lips, "I'll remember for both of us."

I'LL REMEMBER FOR BOTH OF US.

ELEVEN

THE EMOTIONS I'VE LOST MY hold on since surrendering myself to Richter's torment all resurface at Ezra's touch. The sudden influx is overwhelming, and I don't understand any of the feelings rippling through me. I can't even remember what each of them are called. All I know is I thought they were gone and these remnants have only stirred within the empty shell I've become because of him.

Because of whatever we used to be to each other.

Everything I've done the last few years, every step that I've taken—it all keeps pointing me back in one single direction. To him and to whoever I was before I sacrificed my humanity and became a weapon.

For the first time in as long as I can remember, I think I know what it's like to be afraid. Goosebumps pimple my skin and my shoulders tense as Ezra deepens the kiss, flooding my body with a foreign sensation that intoxicates me as much as it sets me on edge. My knees buckle as his hands run over my back, sending a surge of electricity up the full length of my spine and back down through every inch of my body.

I haven't felt this close to losing control since that day on the battlefield when I murdered that young cowering soldier, my mind torn back and forth between that moment and Ezra's presence in my head. While similar to what I felt then, this time, it isn't my power that's sinking its teeth in and ripping my sanity out through my throat. No, something else has me trapped in its hold.

Something I swear I recognize.

Part of me is tempted to give in to this bewildering feeling racing through me, to let it in and surrender myself to the suppressed memories I can sense fighting their way to the surface, while another part can't let go of the detached persona

I've grown so used to adopting. A persona that, time and again, has proved essential to my survival. For so long now, that emotional distance has been my shield—my way of dealing with the horror and death I've inflicted, protecting me from the mental repercussions of what I've become.

If I were to knock down that wall, I'd be inviting in two years of mental anguish, one year of guilt, plus who knows what residual emotions remaining from that gap of time I can't remember. The time Ezra occupied in my life. Since the State launched its war, I've struggled every day to keep that guilt locked away, and I'm not sure I'm ready to welcome it now...or if I ever will be. In many ways, the wall holding it back is as much a part of me now as the lost memories were before.

I wedge a finger between our lips, needing some space to breathe and think. A shiver rips through me when he whispers my name in protest, his breath hot against my skin. "Wynter—"

"Don't. Please," I beg, my voice weak. "You have to understand how confusing this is for me. I look at you and I feel like I know you somehow, but at the end of that thought, you're a stranger. Whatever we were...whatever we shared..." I shrug, tapping the side of my head with my finger. "It isn't there anymore."

Irritation grips my chest, turning my mood sour. Only days ago, I was ready to kill Ezra, and now, we've just shared a kiss miles outside the one place I always thought inescapable.

Oh, and I might be in love with him, although I haven't made up my mind yet on that one.

There's so much to process, so much to work through, but I can't do that if he's stifling me. The memories won't come back just because he wants them to, regardless of how many times he tries to convince me that he knows who I am or what I may or may not have once felt. For all I know, they might not come back at all.

What then? I ask myself. *What will I do if I never remember?*

"People keep talking to me like I'm supposed to remember who they are, but I don't." I step back, tossing my hands in the air with a huff. "It's *incredibly* frustrating, and frankly, I don't know what to believe."

Ezra shifts his weight from one foot to the other and rubs a hand across the back of his neck, as if he's purposefully trying to stop himself from reaching for me again. "You know we're telling you the truth, though," he says. "That *I'm* telling you the truth."

I study him with narrowed eyes, noting the way his words lack a questioning cadence. In a careful tone, I ask, "What makes you say that?"

Exhaling, he migrates his hand from his neck and extends it toward me, grasping a lock of my hair. His movements are careful but confident, his fingertips sliding along the full length of the strands until the ends slip free of his touch.

Clearing his throat, he leans in, and when he speaks again, his voice is husky and warm in my ear. "Would you have let me get this close to you if you thought I was lying?"

His knuckles graze my hip bone, coaxing an involuntary gasp from my lips. I pull back enough to meet his gaze, and the erratic rhythm of my pulse forces me to accept that he's right. I would've never given him the chance to say otherwise if I didn't, on some level, believe he was telling the truth. We've been alone together for at least thirty minutes, and I could've killed him at least as many different ways by now if I had sensed he was trying to trick me.

The trouble is, I'm still not sure what this inexplicable trust in him means to me. Or for my situation.

"No," I finally admit with a sigh. "I don't suppose I would have."

His hand lingers at my waist, sending a wave of heat arcing through me until all my nerve endings come alive at his touch and I can barely breathe from the proximity.

I retreat backward, away from the cage of Ezra's arms, and turn toward the wooden banister separating the massive porch from the tangle of weeds below. Clutching at the railing to keep myself upright, I suck in one steadying breath after another. A warm wind nips at my cheeks as I turn my eyes to the silhouette of the city in the distance, my brain still struggling to believe what I'm looking at is the Heart. It's surreal to see it this way—to know I'm free of the State and the DSD.

Free of Dr. Richter.

I expect to feel relieved…but I don't. Perhaps because I'm still as trapped as I've ever been. First, by an oppressive society and then, by the cruel whims of my captor. Now, not only by PHOENIX but by my amnesia.

Above all, by my collar.

It presses against my skin when I swallow—a constant reminder of what I am and what I would be without it, should it cease to function. My fingertips skim across the smooth metal ridge just as they have countless times before, sometimes in a grateful caress, other times as I debate ripping the damn thing off and letting this disease finally take me. It's a struggle I've been entangled in since the first moment Dr. Richter locked me in this shackle.

As I stare at the far-flung shape of the Heart, this conflict troubles my mind once again, tied up around my current concept of freedom. Dread and acceptance twist my stomach in knots as it dawns on me that distance doesn't matter. No matter how many miles I put between myself and Dr. Richter, so long as I have this collar—this tether—I will never be free of him.

Or from this disease.

As I lower my hand, I recall what Ezra said about why I left him. For a while now, I've suspected that I was only helping the State to safeguard something important to me. Something I could no longer remember, probably out of some misguided attempt to distance myself to protect it. Based on Ezra's claims about our feelings for each other and the way my body reacted to that news, I think I can guess what that something—or someone—was. If I'm right, is that why I'm so anxious right now? Because of some buried fear that I'll hurt him?

Or is it something more I'm sensing?

A faint hum on the wind tickles my eardrums, rousing my battle-hardened senses. My eyes scan the overgrowth as the sound steadily increases in volume, drawing closer. Closer. As it sharpens, recognition sets my senses on fire and I spin on my heel, grabbing Ezra's arm.

"Get inside. *Now*," I hiss.

He gapes at me, confusion dulling the warm honey pools of his gaze. I roll my eyes with an exasperated huff and shove him back inside the house, following his stumbling figure over the threshold. As I kick the aged wooden door shut behind us, I grip my nails into the back of his shirt and tug hard, pulling him down to the dust-coated floorboards. He freezes on all fours, watching me as I crawl into the front room and pull myself into a tight ball underneath the curtained window, the one blind spot should anyone peer through the glass. Once I'm settled, I gesture for him to follow.

We huddle together against the peeling wallpaper, the scent of rotting wood sharp in our noses, keeping as still and silent as possible. Ezra's fast-paced breaths wash over my neck, deafeningly loud in the hush, but they catch when the humming grows so close we can feel the vibration of it through the floor. The wooden boards creak when he moves his left foot.

My eyes cut to his as I press a finger to my lips. The whirring has reached the porch and is so close now it's a low growl on the other side of the window. My body tenses the longer the humming remains in close proximity to me, my instincts taking over my senses as I ready myself for a possible fight. My powers rise, pushing down all sense of self.

But then Ezra grabs my hand, intertwining our fingers, and the bloodthirst writhing in my gut is calmed. Slowly, I breathe out through my nose.

For a moment, I forget all about the threat on the other side of the wall and focus only on Ezra. Nothing has ever steadied me like this before, and I'm not sure what to make of this baffling power he has over me. Only one other person has ever affected me to such an extent, but with Richter, I'm weak. Submissive.

With Ezra, I'm something else altogether, and for the first time, despite having this collar to keep me in check, I can really sense my control. For the first time, I feel *strong*, but in all the ways Dr. Richter never intended.

A shrill beeping interrupts the thunderous hum as a beam of blue light shines through the torn curtains. Beside me, Ezra presses his hands to his ears to drown out the loud scream of the scanner, but I refuse to hinder my senses now that the drugs have finally worked their way out of my body. Pain drills into my back teeth as the high-pitched wail continues, the light touching every inch of the room except for the window's one blind spot—our hiding place. The beam finds even the darkest corners as it searches for any signs of life.

After a few minutes, the scan ends and the blue light dissolves as quickly as it spread. Gradually, the humming dies away and blissful silence returns, although my dread remains. Once the sound is out of earshot, Ezra and I flip onto our knees and risk a glance out the cracked window. Beyond the filthy glass panes, I glimpse two dark shapes shrinking as they fly toward the Heart.

"Surveillance drones," Ezra grunts under his breath.

My eyes never leave the receding black specks. I follow their movements until they merge with the imposing silhouette of the city, wondering what information they'll report to their owner.

"They know I'm here." Dr. Richter's face fills my head until all I can see is his sinister smile.

Ezra takes hold of my hand. "We don't know that."

I shoot him an incredulous look then slump back to the floor, tugging him down alongside me. We sink onto our knees, facing each other. Even if the machine stalking us didn't have an infrared scanner to search for heat signatures in the house, the State has other methods of hunting me down.

"They can track me." I lift my chin, pinching my collar between my thumb and forefinger. It stays in place against my skin, like a hand always around my throat, ready to choke me. "Did you honestly think the State wouldn't keep tabs on their precious weapon?" I spit each word, the venom in my tone clear.

"But we deactivated the tracking chip..." Ezra trails off, seemingly less certain than he was a moment ago.

Pity strikes me like a slap to the face. I wish I could lie to appease him. I wish I could tell him that deactivating the tracker was enough and that the DSD is no longer a problem. But I have never been a very good liar and I know better than anyone the lengths the State is willing to go to. That Dr. Richter is willing to go to.

Tracking chip or no tracking chip, they will find me.

"So Nolan claims," I grumble, peering down at the pale line on my wrist. "But this isn't like the chips they put in when we're born. If the State wants to find me, I'm not sure you can stop them."

We shift position, and for a while, we sit with our backs to the wall, neither one of us speaking, afraid to disrupt the silence with careless words. My gaze trails across the dusty room, taking it in but no longer seeing the details. The wonder that filled me when I first walked into the space is gone, replaced by a building sense of unease.

I can't help wondering if this is how my father felt in the moments right before he died. If the world had lost all meaning to him like it has for me, thanks to what I've become. Who knows, maybe there never has been any meaning and that realization is what I'm keeping myself from remembering.

Maybe I've always been trapped in a battle I can't ever win.

"We'll remove the collar," Ezra whispers. "Nolan said they couldn't, but we'll find a way."

His words are an arrow piercing straight through my heart. I round on him, trying to swallow my anger, but it overpowers my attempts, forcing its way past my lips like a rush of bile.

"Then you may as well kill me now."

Ezra recoils, and a lump forms in my throat at the pained look that spreads across his face. Closing my eyes, I count backward from ten to calm myself down and spare myself from having to see it.

I know I'm not being fair. Up until I met Rodrick Nolan, I didn't think anyone aside from Dr. Richter really knew the ins and outs of what I am. Only the horror stories were public knowledge. Seeing as they're working together, and Ezra seems to have been at least partly responsible for the plan to extract me, I figured Nolan would've shared these details with him. But, from the way he's reacting right now, I think it's safe to assume he doesn't know the truth of my condition. I can't be angry with him for making suggestions when he doesn't understand why they won't work.

A new question forms at the front of my thoughts, pushing all my other quandaries aside for the moment. When we spoke, Nolan made it clear that he understood what my collar is for. So, why hasn't he revealed that information to Ezra? Why would he keep that information hidden from the one person most determined to help me?

Unless…Nolan isn't actually interested in keeping me alive. Why else would he give Ezra a time limit to bring me around without telling him exactly what he's dealing with?

I open my eyes and push a breath out through my nose. "Don't you find it odd that I'm so different now? So in control?"

Ezra's mouth spasms at the corners. He might not want to say it, but I can see in his widening eyes that he's connecting the dots.

"Without the collar, there is no control," I continue.

He needs to know. He needs to understand.

He needs to accept that there is no future where I'm able to be saved.

When he doesn't respond, I press him further. "Do you understand what I'm trying to tell you?"

Tension floods the room like a suffocating smoke as Ezra averts his gaze, his expression solemn. As he turns his face from mine, he nods.

Unable to bear this strange friction between us, I climb to my feet and trudge toward the door in the rear of the room leading back down into the compound. At this point, captivity is preferable to the heavy weight of this strained silence, and it's not like I have anywhere else to go. The State is everywhere now, and if those surveillance drones are any indication, even the land outside the Heart's walls isn't safe. There's nowhere for me to hide anymore.

My days of blending in are long gone.

I've barely made it halfway across the room when Ezra's voice cuts the silence in half, pausing me in my steps. Every word is shrill with desperation. "Richter said there was a cure."

My body goes rigid, and the breath sticks in my throat when I finally peek back over my shoulder. Unfamiliar tears blur my vision. "Don't you get it?"

Guilt bears down on my chest, stronger than anything else I've felt the last few years—stronger even than the emotions that bombarded me alongside Ezra's touch. His kiss.

The hope burning in his eyes fades once he registers the conflicted look on my face.

I swallow, shaking my head, my breath a tremulous whisper. And as I speak, the guilt grips tighter.

"The collar is the cure."

TWELVE

EZRA HASN'T SAID A WORD since I told him the truth about my collar. The truth about the cure—or lack thereof. The memory of Richter's claim had sparked a hope in Ezra's eyes that was agonizing to witness, but the pain that had replaced that hope was worse. Far worse.

My chest still aches just thinking about it.

As we trudge through the maze of hallways in silence, it occurs to me why Ezra is reacting this way—like this revelation has broken something inside him. The lie about there being a cure… That lie is the reason I left him, I know it. Certainty scratches at the back of my brain like a memory begging to be remembered.

If I'm right, then that lie was the trap Dr. Richter used to keep me captive. I suppress a laugh at the thought. I shouldn't be surprised. It's not like it would've been the first time he's used such a tactic to keep me under his thumb. And yet, there's a level of cruelty to this particular deceit that his other lies never quite reached. Because it gave rise to hope, not only for Ezra but possibly for me. I might not remember what led me to return to Dr. Richter's sadistic clutches, but I can imagine having that bait dangled in front of me made my decision a hell of a lot easier.

Knowing that, I can understand why Ezra's so angry. If the cure isn't real, then everything that tore us apart and everything we've both endured since…

If the cure isn't real, then all that was for nothing.

I try to envision myself as I was back then, when I stood at the crossroads of who I was and the monster I've become, faced with the choice of death or life. All I see is the foolish girl who fell for the lie, and her ignorance makes me scoff. How could she have ever believed Dr. Richter? How could she have been stupid enough to think she would ever be free of his hold?

I glance at Ezra, wondering if he believed the lie, too. I suppose it doesn't matter either way. Regardless of what either of us believed in the past, we both know the truth now.

This metal noose around my neck is the only cure I'll ever see.

Ezra avoids my gaze as we walk, making it a point to keep his distance from me. At all times, he stays a few paces ahead, always just out of arm's reach, whereas before it was like he couldn't stop himself from intruding on my personal space. The change pokes at the bubble of suppressed emotion inside me, threatening to pop it and break down the protective shield I'm always building up around myself. I don't like it, this wedge I've driven between us in such a short span of time.

I stare at the floor, musing over what I can do to return things to how they were before this sadness became so prevalent in his gaze. Even without my memories, the tension pushing us apart feels wrong, like I've been separated from a part of myself I didn't even realize was missing. Or like someone has cut off a limb and what I'm feeling is the phantom pain.

Is this how Ezra has felt during the years I've been gone? If so, then that's yet another burden I have to bear—being the one at fault for his heartache. It might've been Dr. Richter's lie that spurred me to leave, but I was still the one who made the decision. I was still the one who left him—and Jenner, too, come to think of it—without any closure.

A vibrating sound emanates from Ezra's pocket, drawing my narrowing gaze to his waist. As he pauses to answer the call on his communicator, I hesitate beside him, turning my eyes to his face, noting the worried wrinkles forming along his brow.

Cursing under his breath, he shoves the device back in his pocket.

"What's wrong?" I ask, even though I know it can't be anything good.

Ignoring me, he scans both lengths of the empty hallway, his gaze suddenly sharp and alert. Annoyed by his ongoing silence, I grab his arm, digging my nails into his bicep.

That earns me a startled glance. Frowning, he shrugs one shoulder and mutters, "I wasn't supposed to let you out of that room."

"Obviously." I huff out a humorless laugh.

Even if I hadn't noticed his skulking demeanor before when he was removing my restraints, it was impossible to miss the unconscious guard in the corridor outside my cell. Not to mention how conveniently quiet it's been since then or the fact that nobody's around. I've grown accustomed enough to imprisonment by now to know a false display of freedom when I see one.

Ezra scuffs the sole of his shoe on the concrete, rubbing at an invisible spot on the floor. A sheepish expression then crosses his face as he presses a hand to the back of his neck. "Jenner's on surveillance duty today, so he's been keeping watch for us. We both knew it was the only way I could really be alone with you."

For as long as I can remember, a camera has always been watching me. Even before my illness surfaced, surveillance was a normal part of my life, and I trained my behavior to not only anticipate that fact but to accept it. My daily life, the DSD, here… It makes no difference. Everywhere I go, someone is always watching.

At the DSD, that someone was Dr. Richter. Here, the person behind the black lens is Nolan, although it's still not entirely clear what he wants with me. As far as I can tell, he thinks I'm a threat.

But if that's the case, why bother to rescue me?

My brow creases as I stare hard at Ezra. If he went to so much trouble to get me alone, away from Nolan's prying eyes, then there must be something about our reunion he didn't want the older man to witness.

I think back over the events of the last thirty minutes, but nothing stands out to me. Nothing except our near miss with the drones and the revelation about my collar, neither of which will be news to Nolan. He already knows all about my struggle with control.

I exhale and press a finger to my throbbing forehead. I can feel my pulse pounding just under my skin. "Let me guess. Your man in charge here has just discovered I'm not in my cage."

Ezra's cheeks redden as he glances away. He might refuse to meet my gaze—a common occurrence between us if this exchange is anything to go by—but I can see what he's thinking written plainly all over his face. He's worried.

No, it's not just that, I realize upon further inspection. He's not just worried. He's scared. But why?

What the hell am I not seeing?

In the back of my mind, a familiar female voice insists that PHOENIX is good, rising to counter the doubt rushing through me. My instincts tell me not to trust it. The look Ezra gives me only strengthens that feeling. But do I lump him in with PHOENIX, this potential new enemy? Or is he separate from it and its unknown intentions?

Is he an outsider, like me?

"More or less," he mutters under his breath.

I lean against the nearest wall, crossing my arms. "I've been meaning to ask, what'd you do to the guard who was stationed outside my door?"

Ezra cuts his eyes to mine. "I did what was necessary to reach you. It's not like he didn't have it coming. He used to be an Enforcer, if you can believe it."

My voice takes on a hollow tone of disbelief. "He had it coming just because he used to be an Enforcer?" I'm far from being a fan of the State's policing and military unit, but even I know that not everyone serves because they want to or feel they have a choice. Some join to raise their status in society, to spare themselves from destitution or life in an outer zone, while some join strictly out of fear. Because they've been brainwashed to believe that loyalty and service to the State will keep them safe from its wrath. And others... Well, look at me. I'm the worst of them all, and it wasn't a path I would've ever chosen.

For all I know, that young man was cornered into being an Enforcer just like I was forced into being a weapon. It doesn't mean either of us believe in the State's creed or wanted to be part of its fight. If he did, if he was a true Loyalist, why would he have abandoned the State's ranks and come here?

"Does that mean I deserve what comes to me, too, because I work for the State?" I press.

Ezra flinches, an audible gasp popping free of his lips. "Of course not. You know that's not what I meant."

"Do I?" I let out a tired sigh. "Because, to me, it seems like I don't know anything at all."

I picture those obsidian eyes in my head and the hostile way the ex-Enforcer looked at me both times our paths crossed. The hatred in his gaze went beyond a simple disdain for my existence, reputation be damned. No, his gaze held the weight of something more.

Whatever grudge he has toward me, it's definitely personal.

"What's his name?"

I don't really know why I ask. Maybe I'm still pissed that he struck me with his gun and I want to know the name of my attacker. Or maybe because I can't stop thinking about how I'm sure I've seen those eyes before...

"Quinn Stohler."

The name draws a blank. Even if I had bothered to acquaint myself with any of the Enforcers I met while on active duty, I've encountered hundreds of them by this point, if not more. I couldn't pick a single one out of the herd any more than I could distinguish between grains of sand on a beach.

It occurs to me that Ezra still hasn't answered my question. "So, are you going to tell me what you did to him or not?"

He scowls, meeting my gaze for the first time in moments. "Why does it matter?

It's not like I did any permanent damage."

I shake my head at his obvious reluctance. "Why won't you tell me? I've seen worse. I've *done* worse. I'm not some frail little girl."

"Because I don't like the way you're looking at me," he counters, his words edging on the brink of explosive. "Because I don't trust Quinn and I don't like the thought of you pitying him. Because I don't like thinking of any scenario where we aren't always on the same side."

I blink stupidly, unsure what to make of his outburst. It's hard to worry about taking sides when I don't even know how many sides there are or what everyone is fighting for. Hell, I can't even remember what or who I was fighting for before the State turned me into its own personal one-woman army.

Ezra turns his back to me and combs a shaking hand through his hair, his shoulders trembling when he whispers, "I put him in a chokehold until he passed out."

My fingers curl into fists, tightening until the nails cut deep across my palms. Why would he risk so much for me when I don't even remember him? When I might *never* remember him?

"You're going to get yourself into trouble, and for what? It's not worth it," I growl.

I'm not worth it.

I push away from the wall and set off down the corridor back in the direction of my prison, ready to put some space between us. I can't think with him so close to me and that hindrance is becoming an inconvenience.

Despite my bravado, my body seems to have other ideas. Even as I try to walk away, my legs gravitate toward Ezra as if we're being pulled together by gravity. The need to be near him, the need to touch him is apparently mutual, guiding my every step. I don't even realize I'm holding my breath until my shoulder brushes his arm and I gasp.

His hand shoots out, grabbing my wrist, and at the barest touch of his skin against mine, I go still. In my head, I'm screaming at myself to go. To keep walking. But I can't bring myself to move.

I peek up at him through my lashes, unprepared for the way my stomach flip-flops when our eyes meet at such close proximity. The warm depths of his gaze glisten with anger.

"*That's* where you're wrong," he says.

A chill ricochets up my spine as his breath skims my cheeks, his words humming across my skin like a caress, twisting my nerve endings in knots. My breath catches as my pulse pounds dangerously close to the surface.

Is this fear I'm feeling?

I'm not afraid of Ezra, despite how conflicted and confused I become in his presence as unfamiliar emotions press in at the edges of what I remember and what I'm forcing myself to forget. But I am afraid of what he's capable of and of what he might be willing to do to protect me. Of what he might end up sacrificing. I might not remember him, but there's still some part of me that doesn't want him to get hurt. I can feel it buried beneath the monster inside me—the monster I wish I could blame for all the unforgivable things I've done on behalf of the State.

But regardless of what I want, Ezra *will* get hurt. That's what always happens to anyone who gets close to me.

Because of what I am, he will never be safe.

His hand slackens, releasing my arm. Turning away from me again, he clears his throat. "We should head back."

Ezra says nothing else as he proceeds down the passage, and because I'm a coward, I say nothing either. Silence once again blankets our journey as I shadow his steps, reliving what he said in my head.

"I don't like thinking of any scenario where we aren't always on the same side."

Why do those words resonate with me so much? Memories spin in the back of my head, but none of them surface, vexing me further.

"Why wasn't it you?"

Ezra wavers, and I stop walking at once, staring at the back at his head as if an answer might burst free of his hair if I just look at him hard enough. When he turns, I step forward before he can speak.

"If what you said about us is true, then why wasn't it you on the helicopter? Why weren't *you* the one who came for me?" My voice breaks, and I hate how pitiful it makes me sound, but I need to know.

I need to understand because nothing makes sense.

"I wanted to, believe me, but Nolan and the other Heads wouldn't allow me to have direct involvement." When I shoot a dubious look at him, he adds, "They said I was too close to the situation, which was really just their way of saying they didn't want my emotions getting in the way of their mission. Who knows, maybe they thought you'd be more likely to figure out what was going on if it was me there and not someone else."

I roll this thought around in my head for a moment. Because of the effect Ezra has over me, would I have seen the attack coming if it had been him and not Jenner who blew up that helicopter to save me?

I picture his face—the man with the messy black hair who risked his life to get me out of the State. Guilt grips my insides, making me nauseous. There's something there, gnawing at me whenever I think of him, but I can't put my finger on what.

"About Jenner... I know you don't remember right now, but he means a lot to you, too."

A choked laugh parts my lips. *Too*. How sure he is of my feelings for him. Maybe he's right. Maybe he's not. Either way, I don't know what to do with his statement. I never asked for PHOENIX to come to my rescue.

I never asked for any of this.

A discomforting hush falls between us again, and with nothing else to say, we're left with no choice but to continue our trek or linger here and wait for the fallout of his decision to let me out of my cell come to us.

As we carry on, this time side by side, I cast the occasional glance at him, watching his expression for changes. The look on his face puts a bad taste in my mouth, but I don't know what to say to ease the tension between us or force any of this to start making sense. I've spent my whole life so detached from emotion, and the last two years only widened the gap between who I am now and who I became during the forgotten time I spent with Ezra.

If only I had my memories, then, maybe, I would know what I'm supposed to do.

The *thud* of heavy footfalls on concrete snaps me out of my thoughts, and my gaze lifts to the distant end of the corridor where six figures all dressed in black storm toward us. The ex-Enforcer, Quinn Stohler, leads their march.

His black eyes focus on me like a missile locking onto its target.

"Well, he looks angry," I mutter.

Part of me is tempted to say, *I told you so*, but I resist that urge. No good will come of antagonizing Ezra when he's only trying to help me.

As the figures draw closer, he thrusts out an arm to stop me from walking and steps between us, positioning himself in the path of the guards.

I open my mouth to speak, but the words catch in my throat when he reaches for my hand. His fingers shake against my palm, causing a spike of adrenaline to rush straight to my heart.

As my eyes jump from the incoming threat to our joined hands, I once again wonder what he's so afraid of.

The click of a round sliding into its chamber draws my gaze to the ex-Enforcer's gun, a black pistol in place of the rifle he usually carries.

The gun is aimed directly at my head.

"What the *hell* were you thinking?" His aggressive tone triggers my defensive reflexes, and I find myself breathing in as my power rises to the surface.

Ezra pushes me farther behind him. "That cell's a bit stuffy, and I thought she could use some fresh air. We just talked for a bit. No harm, no foul."

Quinn expels a biting laugh. "All that just to have a little chat with your girlfriend? She's dangerous. You don't have the authority—"

"She isn't a threat," Ezra interrupts. But, behind his bravado, his body is stiff. His fingers weave through mine, clenching tightly. "Besides, Nolan said I could talk to her."

Quinn sneers. "Yeah, an *authorized* discussion under strict supervision. Do you even grasp what could've happened? You know what she's capable of, right? What she's done?"

Every beat of Ezra's pulse thrums against my fingers, and I can sense the raging current of emotion lingering under his skin about to breach the surface.

When it does, his voice is a crack of thunder.

"She didn't do it by choice!"

"Yes, I did." Ezra wheels around to face me, his eyes terror-stricken. Before he can interject, I add, "I did what I had to do to survive."

Of course, that's not entirely true since it wasn't *my* survival I was concerned with or what led me to obey the State to the extent that I have. I couldn't remember who I was protecting at the time, but now, I know—without a shred of doubt—I did it for Ezra. If past me was willing to go to such lengths to protect him, then I need to honor her wish and continue to do whatever it takes to keep him safe.

Even if he doesn't like it.

"Stop it," he warns under his breath. "I know what you're trying to do, and it won't work. I won't let it."

"I'm trying to point out what you're either too biased or blind to notice." If he cares about me, then he needs to accept what I've done. All of it. Every horrible detail. He needs to understand that I'm not the same person I was before when he knew me.

A frown puckers the skin between his eyebrows. "No, you're trying to push me away." Although soft, his tone is biting.

He's right. I *am* trying to push him away. So long as this collar continues to cradle my neck, the people closest to me will always be at risk, which makes me a danger to them. Without the collar, the control ends, and I can't allow that. But with it, I'm a threat, and I can't allow that either.

I don't want to be backed into a corner where I'm forced to choose between maintaining control or protecting Ezra and anyone else past me was determined to keep safe with her sacrifice. It's better for everyone if he just lets me go now before anybody gets hurt.

Before he gets hurt.

"Enough!" Quinn steps forward, his cold glare fixed on mine, his gun unwavering in its aim. "You're coming with us."

"Lower your weapon." Ezra pushes me farther behind him, acting as a shield, even though I don't need it. Last time I checked, my power makes me practically bulletproof.

I pinch Ezra's shoulder, determined to defuse the situation before it can escalate any further. Incredulity shines in his eyes when I step out from behind him and surrender myself to the ex-Enforcer.

"It's all right. I'll go willingly."

Not that either of us have a choice.

We tail Quinn through the compound, surrounded on all sides by armed guards who remind me of my entourage of Enforcers at the DSD. Everything about them, from their austere expressions to their overly straight postures, gives the impression of trained soldiers rather than outcasts of society. If the State wasn't worried about PHOENIX before, a glimpse at this procession might make them reconsider the threat.

When we arrive back at my cell, I don't struggle against the hands gripping my arms. Although these walls have no power to hold me, I let the soldiers shove me inside the room without even the slightest breath of protest.

As I fumble over the threshold, I look back at Quinn, scrutinizing the ex-Enforcer's face. That distant sense of recognition returns, and more than ever before, I'm certain I know him.

He raises his gun again, signaling for me to take a step back. I lift my hands and do as I'm told, aware he may turn the threat on Ezra if I don't.

Ezra calls my name, a mix of pleading and desperation interlaced in his tone. My fingers twitch, but I don't move more than that. Quinn's heated glare is all the warning I need to tell me what will happen if I do.

"The people here know what I am," I murmur, turning my attention back to Ezra. "I don't blame them for wanting to keep me locked up."

"But you're not a danger to them. We both know that," he argues.

Except, I'm not as convinced of that as he is.

"If you can't do the job, I will not hesitate to do it for you."

Dr. Richter's words pose the real threat, always lingering at the back of my thoughts—even more so now that I'm free of his grasp and he has the motivation to follow through. I may be in control thanks to this collar, but that doesn't mean

I'm not dangerous to every single person around me.

Ezra most of all.

"Nolan will be the one to decide that," Quinn grunts. The ex-Enforcer then grasps the latch and yanks hard on the door, slamming it shut.

Ezra's voice is the last thing I hear before I'm entombed in silence again.

"No matter what happens, I won't lose you again."

Shock freezes my body in place as the glimpse on his face right before the door closed between us sears into my brain, mirroring the image of him I've been carrying around in my head the last two months. I picture that look again now as those three words he always says echo in my memory.

"I'm sorry, Wynter."

A tear trails down his cheek, and when I let out a breath, the image crumbles, joining the growing pile of disjointed memories building at my feet. As I try to gather the pieces, I realize only one thing about my situation is certain.

Nolan, and whoever else is running the show here… They will never let me go. I'd even be willing to bet his promise to Ezra—the promise that he'd have a week to prove I'm not a threat—was just a lie to buy them time for whatever they actually have planned for me.

What Ezra wants—what I felt in that brief moment on the porch, with his lips against mine—is a dream. In reality, this wedge between us will grow. It will expand and warp, hardening, until what we had is nothing more than a memory neither one of us recognizes anymore.

Because this world has a way of destroying anything good, and the twisted intentions of the people against us will always find a way to win.

Besides, how can I accept what Ezra supposedly feels for me after everything I've done? He shouldn't be fighting for me. He should just forget me—that's the safest option. Forget about me and get far, far away.

Otherwise, this will end the way everything else in my life always ends.

With death.

THIRTEEN

THE CONCRETE WALL IS COOL to the touch, like a slab of ice against my back. Keeping my eyes on the far corner of the room at all times, I hug my legs to my chest, determined to make myself as small in the camera's watchful gaze as possible. The red light at the side of the lens blinks in timed repetition, flashing in quick bursts separated by the same two-second pause. It never ends. The red light always returns.

A reminder that the people here are monitoring my every move.

A number of scenarios pound through my head as I consider the best course of action to take. It would be easy enough to break out of this room. The only obstacles beyond these walls are the armed guards working for Nolan, and even with guns, they aren't a threat to me. I could take them all out with ease.

But after? That's the part that concerns me—what I would do once I'm free of the compound. I have nowhere to go, and even if I ran, Dr. Richter would surely find a way to follow.

A vexed breath parts my lips as I lean the back of my head against the hard wall. My eyes unconsciously dart in the direction of the door as I force myself to address the other issue standing in my way of escape.

Ezra.

There's so much I don't understand about him and about our past together, but the few pieces I've managed to connect are enough to make me second-guess leaving without him.

He's the reason I allowed Dr. Richter to turn me into this weapon—this plague on humanity. I might not have a firm grip on my emotions, but sacrificing myself like that has to mean something. I can't run away from him or the ghost of who

I was before all this. If I do…if I abandon Ezra now…then everything I've done would be meaningless.

So, what options does that leave me with?

Exhaling, I push with my legs, my back flat to the wall, sliding upward until I'm standing. Staring at the camera, I pad across the floor like a predator stalking its prey, every step precise and calculated.

I stop beneath the camera, just short of its blind spot, staring up into the black hole of the lens. If I can't leave this place yet, then I'll settle for answers.

I need to know what these people have planned for me.

"I want to speak with Rodrick Nolan." My voice is loud and clear. Steady. Although, on the inside, uncertainty bites at me.

Minutes pass, but I don't move an inch, my gaze never once straying from its target. After what seems like hours of waiting, I pick up the muffled tones of voices on the other side of the door. They argue for a moment until one raises over the other. Then, there is only silence.

The hinges screech, announcing my visitor, and I turn to find Quinn staring daggers at me with that same distrusting look I've come to expect from him.

When he aims his pistol at me, I smile.

"Sit down," he barks, jerking his chin toward the chair in the middle of the room.

When I don't comply, he flips off the safety catch and shifts his finger just over the trigger. The black of his gaze pierces holes in my skin as the click of the metal echoes throughout the small room.

The grin slips from my lips when Nolan crosses the threshold and lays a firm hand on the younger man's shoulder. "That won't be necessary," he says.

His words remind me of my early days at the DSD—of the assurances I was given before Dr. Richter pulled his mask away and revealed the real face underneath. Everything said to me then was a lie, so why should this be any different? If Nolan is anything like Dr. Richter, then this is likely a ruse to gain my trust and lure me into a trap.

Well, I won't fall for it. Not this time.

Determined to show him how much of a threat I can be, I return to the chair, even going so far as to allow Quinn to secure restraints around my wrists and ankles—replacements for the ones I tore through like paper. I'm sure I look much more intimidating this way, like someone they should be afraid of.

Avoiding Nolan's gaze, I observe the ex-Enforcer. As he kneels before me, I notice a slight tremor crossing his hands. When he catches me staring, he pulls them away.

My brows reach for my hairline as a sudden recognition rocks me to my core.

The way he's trying to hide his fear…

I've seen those mannerisms before.

I scrutinize his face, taking in every detail. Now, as I stare into the sable pits of his eyes, it hits me where I know him from.

"You," I whisper. "I *know* you."

As Quinn reels back, all I see is the terrified young Enforcer I encountered two months ago. It seems like years have passed since that moment, and yet, the skepticism that was written all over his face when he glanced at my collar is imprinted into my memory with perfect clarity. I almost can't believe I didn't recognize him sooner.

Quinn stumbles to his feet and takes a step backward, the color draining from his skin as he quickly jerks his head—not enough for Nolan to notice but enough for me to reconsider saying another word on the matter. The warning in his dark eyes clamps my mouth shut.

As Quinn retreats, putting a few more steps of distance between us, Nolan props open a second chair and slowly lowers himself onto the seat. Crossing his legs, he lifts his chin and side-eyes Quinn. "Leave us."

All trace of the fear I glimpsed seconds ago has vanished from the ex-Enforcer's face as he turns for the door, doing as he's been instructed like the perfect, obedient soldier.

As he walks away, I can't help wondering what he was trying to communicate to me. It's almost as if he was pleading with me not to say something that will land him in trouble…but what? What does he think I know? Or—

A thought occurs to me.

What does he think I've seen?

The metallic screech of the door slamming shut behind Quinn jars my senses, making my head hurt.

Nolan lets out a long-suffering sigh. "You'll have to forgive his manners. The methods the State uses aren't to everyone's taste. Many have actually defected to our side quite recently because of such…difference of opinion."

Defected?

I blink, looking from Nolan's face to the door. Does this mean Quinn isn't the only ex-Enforcer working for PHOENIX now? That would explain the other armed guards. Nolan had already admitted to having a contact working from within the State, but it never occurred to me that such betrayal could be so widespread. Growing up in the Heart, I was taught that people are either devoted to the State or against it. It's black and white. One side or the other.

Ally or enemy.

My mother's face pops into my head, and I find myself thinking about her loyalties. She made it very clear which side she was on the two times she betrayed our family. First, when she gave up my father, and again, when she handed me over to the Enforcers the day of my placement exam. For all she knows now, I could be dead.

Would she even care?

I swallow the rising lump in my throat. "And what methods are you referring to exactly?"

Nolan looks at me as if I should already know the answer. "Well, the way they conduct warfare is one example."

My lips pinch together.

I think back to that day on the transport helicopter two months ago, recalling what I can about the first time I crossed paths with Quinn. Although he was afraid of me, he still gave off the distinct impression of someone loyal to the State. Potential recruits have to be to become full-fledged Enforcers. The preliminary checks they go through before they're granted entry into the training program make sure of that, wiping away any doubt new recruits might be holding onto.

So, what could he have seen that was bad enough to strip him of that devotion? Bad enough to make him turn tail and run from an institution he'd pledged himself to?

"You mean me," I realize.

Nolan repositions himself in his chair, and as he uncrosses his legs, he stares at me with narrowed eyes. As I take in his features more closely, I notice the cartilage above his right nostril is slightly bent to one side, as if his nose has been broken at least once.

"So, what is it you wished to talk about?" he asks, his tone cool and unhurried.

Clenching my jaw, I inhale a deep breath, mentally preparing myself for my next words. The musty air burns my nostrils and throat.

"I want you to tell me how you knew my father."

Nolan barks out a laugh, the skin beside his eyes crinkling into tiny crow's feet. "I should've known you'd be eavesdropping." He clears his throat when I cock a questioning eyebrow, then says, "Your father and I go way back. The last time I saw him was just before you were born."

"Care to be more specific?"

He sighs again, running a hand over his beard. "Your mother would kill me for telling you this, but Freston and I were the founding members of PHOENIX. This organization only exists at all because of him. Because of his ideas."

My body deflates, sinking into the chair. "T-That's not possible," I stammer, ignoring the mention of my mother. Numbers spiral through my brain. "That would mean the State's—"

"Barely thirty years old, yes."

The shock of this revelation hits me with the blunt force trauma of a rock to the head. Everything I've always known…about my family…about our society…

All of it was a lie.

It's always been common knowledge that PHOENIX was born around the same time as the State. With one came the other, like twins. The State has never been shy about admitting this fact since it provided the basis for the fear that kept the populace under their oppressive control. But thirty years? That would mean there are people—*lots* of people—still living today who were there when the State rose to power. People who witnessed what society and life were like before the State took over.

How can that be? And how was the State able to suppress this information? How were they able to keep everyone quiet and stop the younger generation from learning the truth? What power could they have possibly used to erase history from the eyes that were present to see it?

As my thoughts continue to chase these questions in circles, something Ezra said pops into my brain and I make a connection I failed to see before.

"Tunnels…" I whisper under my breath.

My father was executed by the State for owning illegal possessions, but he wasn't discovered until I was nearly seven years old because he never kept his contraband at our home. He stored it somewhere else.

Someplace safe, I remember him once telling me.

Where better to hide his secrets than in the tunnels the State thought uninhabitable?

I wrack my brain, but I struggle to visualize the place he used to take me to. It was our special secret, and yet, the where of it never mattered to me. I only cared about the bond of sharing something with him that was ours and ours alone.

Now that I know of his involvement with PHOENIX, I realize how much deeper his crimes really went.

An involuntary laugh escapes me.

He hid an entire rebellion right under our noses.

"Your father was a good man," Nolan says, "and a devoted father, for what it's worth. Although I was deeply disappointed when he chose to cast aside our mission, I understood his reasons and still counted him among my friends. I was sorry to hear about what happened to him."

The memory of my father's bloodied face invades my mind, but I push the image away. I need to focus.

I need to attempt to make sense of all this.

My father created PHOENIX. This rebellion was built on his ideas, and yet, something made him leave it behind. What reason could he have had to renounce what so many others are willing to die to protect?

Perhaps my father and I are more alike than I initially thought. Between him and my mother, I'm starting to think that abandoning people runs in my blood.

"I understand this must be difficult for you to process, and I'm sure you have so many questions, but I'd like to talk about *you* right now, if that's all right."

I frown, searching Nolan's face for any hint of an ulterior motive. We've barely scratched the surface of the lies constructed around my father, and now, he's turning the conversation away in a very deliberate direction. I can't even begin to guess what this man could be after. What is he hoping to learn from me?

Why am I still alive if he believes I'm a threat?

"What about me?"

"You may or may not remember that you lived with us for a brief time. After a mission resulting in the death of one of our members, you fled. Why? What made you return to the DSD?"

At these words, I hear that female voice in my head again—the one that keeps insisting PHOENIX is good. As her familiar sentiment envelops my senses, guilt claws at my stomach, trying to cut through and break free of my skin.

Sweat prickles along my hairline as a disturbing realization dawns on me. This woman I keep hearing—the voice I now realize is the same one always speaking in my head, telling me not to give up... Was she the member Nolan speaks of? The one who died.

Probably because of me.

My teeth sink into the inside of my cheek as Nolan's pale eyes watch me with interest. There's a sharp edge to his gaze that makes me feel like I'm balancing on the point of a knife. One wrong move, and I'll fall, impaling myself.

But what is the wrong move?

I swallow. "I did it to protect everyone."

Nolan arches a wiry eyebrow. "So, you remember?"

"I remember I had a good reason. Good enough to justify what I've done."

All those battles and all the people I've killed... I did what I had to do, and I'd do it again without hesitation, even if that meant giving up what remains of my humanity. Even if that meant never feeling anything ever again. Even if that meant embracing the monster Dr. Richter turned me into.

I might not fully remember my past, but I do know there were people in it worthy of that sacrifice.

People worth protecting.

"You admit to being dangerous, then."

As Nolan's voice slashes through the darkness of my thoughts, I remember what he said to Ezra.

"I'll do what has to be done…even if she is Freston Reeves' daughter."

That threat still lingers behind his eyes.

"I never said that I wasn't," I mutter.

Nolan shakes his head and tsks, as if I've said the worst possible answer. "You must understand, I'm responsible for the lives of many people who are depending on me. I need to be certain you won't pose a risk to them."

I glower at him. This is only the second time we've spoken and I'm already sick of his indirect warnings. I never asked for this. I didn't ask PHOENIX to intervene or for them to keep me here as their hostage.

Some rescue mission, I muse.

My anger boils up, spitting out in a growl through clenched teeth. "If I'm so dangerous, then why are you keeping me here? Why bother to extract me at all?"

For the first time since this conversation began, Nolan looks uncomfortable. A long moment passes before he answers. "When Ezra first brought you to us, we didn't fully understand the situation. Or your importance," he adds after a pause. "When you returned to the DSD, we got word of what they were planning, and… Well, let's just say it became paramount that we get you back."

"Why?" I press. "With the State's attention focused elsewhere, your lives would've gotten easier, surely. For once, PHOENIX wasn't the target. Or were you just that morally opposed to the war? I can't think of any other reason why you'd be stupid enough to intervene this way. Because, I promise you, Richter will find me and when that happens, you're all as good as dead."

A reserved smile tugs at the edges of Nolan's mouth. "You don't know…do you?"

My eyes narrow into slits. "Know what?"

"What the DSD was really planning to do with you."

His words knock the air from my lungs, and I blink once, twice, three times, my eyes watering as I try to remember how to breathe.

"What are you talking about?" I whisper after a moment.

As Nolan stands, the grin creeping across his face widens. "Do you think we would've waited this long to retrieve you if we gave a damn about the State's war? Power can always be taken away."

My pulse quickens as the madness I always feel myself slipping toward reaches out for the first time in days. It drags me to the brink of my own mental precipice, threatening to pitch me over the edge.

What could the DSD have planned for me that was any worse than what they were already doing?

Nolan scoffs. "This is so much bigger than you. Didn't you ever ask yourself why the DSD kept taking your blood?"

The words to answer stick in my throat. Just how much does Nolan know about my time at the DSD? Just how much does he know about me?

Who the hell is his contact?

"Richter wanted to study it," is all I manage to say.

"Ah, yes. Austin Richter. Not exactly known for his honesty, is he?" Nolan cocks a knowing eyebrow.

My heart seizes as if a hand has just punched through my ribcage and is squeezing my only lifeline into pulp. A scream builds in my chest, and I only have enough strength to swallow it down.

Hysteria pushes me closer to the edge. "What do you want with me?"

Nolan steps forward and bends at the waist, bringing his face within inches of mine. Lowering his voice, he murmurs, "It's quite simple, really. I just require your help on one matter."

My eyes bulge as the realization grips me. Now, I know why I'm here and why Nolan went to the trouble of getting me back from the State. Like the last piece of a puzzle slotting into its rightful place, I finally see the bigger picture behind his motivation.

"You want to use me against the State."

A low, throaty chuckle escapes him. "That's the beauty of it. We won't have to."

With that, he turns and retreats for the door, ending our conversation with cryptic words he's sure to know will torment me until I can work out what they mean. I follow his every step with increasing apprehension, but I can't find the concentration needed to look ahead and find out what he's planning. For now, I'm at a loss.

For now, I'm completely blind to what's coming.

His footsteps cease when he reaches the doorway.

"I wonder if you've figured out who our informant is yet. It is, after all, thanks to him that you're here. Who knows," he adds, looking over his shoulder, "perhaps meeting him will help restore your memories."

Nolan curls his hand into a fist and bangs it twice against the door. Beyond the concrete wall, the shuffle of movement reaches my ears, followed by a chorus of voices.

As the hinges creak, I brace myself.

My pulse vibrates under my skin, buzzing like an electric current, as the door shifts inward until I'm looking straight into the eyes of the man who's been working for PHOENIX from within the State.

The man responsible for my extraction.

My mouth falls open as his broad frame fills the doorway, the lights overhead shining across his ebony hair, highlighting the odd peppered-gray strand. His forehead glistens where the glare strikes his deep brown skin just below his receding hairline.

Nolan smiles at my stunned expression, and as I glance between them, I realize nothing, not even my visions, could've ever prepared me for this.

Nolan's voice is like gravel in my ears as he gestures toward the man beside him. "Wynter, this is—"

"Wren Bilken," I breathe.

FOURTEEN

A CHAIN REACTION FOLLOWS THESE words, the whisper of his name on my lips setting the gears in my brain in motion until my thoughts are spinning out of control, bombarding me with flashes of images surfacing from the recesses of my damaged memory. The pictures dart through my head in quick succession, begging me to remember.

I glimpse the corridors of a dingy compound like this one followed by waterlogged tunnels—the tunnel system running underneath the Heart, if I had to venture a guess. Beams of light flash along rounded concrete walls as the splashing of boots through water pulls me back through time to that moment.

Darkness swallows me for the length of two heartbeats, then eases as a large building slides into focus, assaulting my senses with the sudden recollection of that fateful night in Zone 1.

A night I had allowed myself to forget.

A night I wish could remain forgotten.

A pained breath catches in my chest as the memory hits me with the unforgiving force of a blow to the head. Every moment of that horrible night comes back to me in excruciating detail, forcing me to relive it all. I remember why we went on that mission. I remember what I did to those Enforcers and the lies Richter taunted me with that led me back into his sadistic embrace. I remember it all.

Even Rai.

As the memory of her warm words fills the space in my head, I match them to the voice I keep hearing—the voice that keeps telling me PHOENIX is good and that, throughout the last two years, encouraged me to be strong every day.

Is it her ghost that's been haunting me or my own unrelenting guilt? The guilt of being partly responsible for her death.

The guilt of forgetting her.

Tears burn my eyes and carve lines down my cheeks. I can't breathe. I can't think. Madness sinks its teeth into the edges of my spiraling thoughts, and beyond my blurred vision, I make out Bilken's face. His expression is blank. Void of emotion.

For that, I hate him even more.

"She's dead because of you," I growl.

Rage claws at every inch of my trembling body, my control wavering as pressure rises, expanding in my chest, my power eager to escape and lash out at the first available target. I've never enjoyed killing, but, in this moment, I would love nothing more than to feel Bilken's blood on my hands.

"I assume you mean Raina Dorne," he retorts in a bored monotone.

His obvious lack of remorse incites me further, my fingers yearning to clamp around his throat and squeeze until the life drains from his eyes. It takes what little willpower I still possess to keep myself pinned down where I sit.

My hands clench the arms of the chair like pincers, my fingertips leaving indentations in the metal. "Don't you *dare* say her name."

I can feel it so close to the surface now—the wild animal locked within me raring to rip out Bilken's throat with her teeth. As he steps into the room, I'm tempted to let it.

I'm tempted to let the monster loose from its cage.

Bilken keeps his distance from me, hovering just beside the open doorway, making sure to leave a wide berth at all times. As the dark pools of his eyes examine me with the same indifference and disdain I endured every day at the DSD, my anger builds until I can barely keep hold of it.

If I'm not careful, I'll lose control and Nolan will not only have an excuse to kill me, he'd be justified in his actions. While I suspect he plans on disposing of me regardless of what happens here, I can't afford to expedite that particular outcome. Not when so many questions remain unanswered. Not when I have no idea what he's planning or who he'll put at risk with his schemes.

Losing control is a risk I can't take. Not now.

Possibly not ever.

Bilken scoffs. "I believe your ire is misdirected, Miss Reeves."

The fury, guilt, and regret I've been suppressing all stab me in the heart, each one a separate blade. I struggle to breathe as fresh tears slide down my cheeks, the salt leaving my skin sticky and raw, exposing the full depths of my grief.

A grief I had forgotten.

"You were the one who set that trap for us! The trap that got her killed!" I shriek.

Bilken stares at me with cold, unfeeling eyes, his face a stone mask that gives nothing away of his thoughts. Or his intentions. Maybe he doesn't have any. Maybe he's just like Dr. Richter…and me. Maybe we're all the same—puppets who have been taken in and drained by the State, robbed of what makes us human until we're incapable of any emotions that remotely resemble empathy or remorse. We just do what we're told until we've expended our usefulness.

But, if that's the case, why did Bilken switch sides? Why did he turn his back on the State?

What could he gain from such betrayal?

Something tells me this isn't the first time I've asked myself these questions.

"And yet, I wasn't the one who pulled the trigger," he counters, arching a dark brow.

I shake my head vehemently. "It's still your fault she was there. She would be alive if it wasn't for you and your damn transmission."

He shrugs, conceding that point. "Perhaps. But I think the person you're truly angry with here is yourself. After all, you've spent the last two plus years submissive to the man *actually* responsible for your friend's death. My part in Raina Dorne's demise is negligent compared to that disloyalty."

Disloyalty?

I squeeze the arms of the chair until my fingernails ache, the metal whining beneath my grip. Jolts of pain shoot into my knuckles, and as the pressure of my rising power continues to grow, I no longer care about maintaining control—Nolan and his threats be damned. I only care about making Bilken pay for all the pain he's caused.

My eyes slip to his throat, and I think about how it would feel to snap every bone in his spine. I would happily trade my life for just a moment of his suffering.

But as that thought crosses my mind, a familiar voice takes its place in my head, pointing my moral compass in a different direction.

Rai.

"Everyone here has lost someone or something to the State. But that's why we fight. So our losses don't have to be for nothing."

I hesitate.

Rai wouldn't want this. She wouldn't want me to destroy whatever spark of humanity still lingers within me. She wouldn't want me to kill to avenge her death, regardless of how sweet or warranted that vengeance would be.

I wonder what she would think if she could see me at this moment. Would she see a weapon? A murderer? A traitor?

Or would she still see her friend?

Do I even resemble that person anymore?

Indecision stays my hand, and yet, the influx of emotions coursing through me are proving much harder to contain. The pressure keeps building, searching for an escape.

As I struggle to keep my hold on control, Bilken looks down his nose at me and smirks. His condescending expression seems to goad me, as if he actually *wants* me to attack him—to show them all what I'm capable of. Despite what he said, I know Nolan wants that, too.

Why else would he bring Bilken here?

Why else would he dangle this insult in front of me?

This is a test. The realization infuriates me.

Well, I refuse to fall into their trap or be a puppet just like I was for Dr. Richter. I'm done letting other people pull my strings.

I suck in a deep breath, then let it out slowly, but with my unstable mindset, it's becoming alarmingly clear the collar can only do so much when it comes to containing my anger. I haven't experienced emotions like this since Dr. Richter tied me to this shackle, so it hasn't been tested against the limits of my rage, which I'm learning is a trigger capable of shutting down my control. This power wants to be seen, and I'm not sure there's a damn thing I, or anyone else here, can do to stop it.

A small release of energy spills out of my body, relieving the pressure in my chest just a little. Dust sprinkles down from above as fissures form along the walls and ceiling.

"Enough!" Nolan shouts.

I squeeze my eyes shut, and the cracking slows to a reluctant stop. My lips quiver as I count backward from ten.

"How odd." Bilken lets out a derisive snort. "All the reports were quite adamant that she could control it."

My eyes snap open and lock on his face as a feral smile hitches up one corner of my mouth. I lean forward until the restraints creak in protest. "Oh, I *am* controlling it. If I wasn't, you would already be dead."

Nolan steps between us, raising his hands, as if that will somehow ease the friction in the room. He shoots a warning glare at Bilken. "That's enough for now. You'd better step outside before things get out of hand."

Bilken exits the room with a huff, and although a noticeable weight lifts off my shoulders the moment he's gone from my sight, my relief is fleeting.

Nolan returns to the empty chair, ready to pick up where we left off.

"Why is he here?" I snarl once he's seated. "PHOENIX... You're supposed to be the good guys, aren't you? What are you doing joining up with someone like Bilken?"

As I utter these words, a distant voice manifests somewhere in the cracks of my garbled memories. *My* voice asking similar questions and trying to convince someone that Bilken can't be trusted.

Gradually, the recollection takes shape, revealing pieces of a conversation that took place prior to the night Rai died. I knew the mission to Zone 1 was a trap... and yet, we went anyway.

Why?

"I understand how confusing this must be for you. And distressing," Nolan tacks on as an afterthought. "If you must know, it was never Wren's intention for anyone to die. Rai was...an unfortunate casualty."

I sink my teeth into my lower lip to stop myself from laughing. An unfortunate casualty. *Right.* "What were his intentions, then?" I ask.

"To supply us with something valuable that would demonstrate his loyalty to PHOENIX. He couldn't make direct contact without being discovered, and he knew he would only be desirable to us as an informant working from the inside. It was vital his position within the State remain secure, otherwise he would be worthless to us. He's a good ally to have, but even his usefulness has its limits."

I scoff at Nolan's words. I might not like Bilken, but I can still appreciate how much he was risking by extending a helping hand to PHOENIX. I wonder if he's aware that Nolan will toss him aside the second he stops serving a purpose.

"That doesn't explain what happened that night," I mutter.

Nolan waves a dismissive hand. "The State wanted to find you, so Wren volunteered to set up a trap to lure in PHOENIX, since they had deduced you were hiding with us when your trail went cold. He knew Richter would never harm his prized subject, so your safety was guaranteed, and everything else was arranged so the others would have enough time to get out and make it back alive." He hesitates. "Well, most of them," he amends. "Following the mission, we used the intel Bilken left for us to strengthen our foothold and formulate a new plan of attack against the State. Part of that plan was waiting for the ideal time to get you back."

Yeah. So you could use me, too.

I shake my head. After everything that happened that night, he expects me to believe Bilken's offer for aid was actually genuine?

Doubt prickles over my skin like an itch at the same moment a memory cuts through my amnesia. Suddenly, I recall the look in Ezra's eyes when he first mentioned the mission to meet Bilken. Although I had tried to talk him out of it, he insisted we had to go despite agreeing the transmission would likely lead us into a trap.

As the grainy picture of his face sharpens in my mind, I notice the fear in his gaze. It tells me everything I need to know.

"It wasn't Ezra's idea for us to go. It was yours." Nolan was the one who sent us to Zone 1. Nolan risked our lives, and because of that decision, Rai died. "Did you know any of this beforehand?" I continue, "or did you willingly send us to our deaths on a hunch?"

"Don't be so dramatic," he chides. "The DSD wanted you alive, so you were never in any real danger that night. If anything, I was protecting my people by returning you to where you belonged. Really, you should be thanking me. If you hadn't gone back, you would be dead."

And so would you, I seethe silently.

"As for the rest of your accusation, I wouldn't have gotten to where I am today if I did anything on a hunch. I already knew Wren. He and I go way back. We were friends, in the early days before the State became what it is now, so I'm well-acquainted with his character. When the world changed and I made the choice to move underground, your father and I both asked him to join us. He had his own reasons for saying no at the time, but we agreed the invitation was open. All he had to do was reach out.

"As the years wore on, it became harder for him to make contact without getting caught. He couldn't send a direct transmission without leaving a digital trail, which would've implicated us both. I'm sure you know what the result of that would've been."

The memory of my father's face consumes me.

"Execution." I nearly choke on the word.

Nolan's lips press into a line as he nods. "When Wren offered to set that trap for Richter, he put the message to me in the one place he knew PHOENIX would always be watching. We keep a firm eye on Enforcer rotations to make our movements throughout the Heart easier—something the State was clearly aware of, given how long we've eluded its grasp. Knowing this, Wren encrypted the transmission right in the middle of the weekly schedule for a unit stationed in Zone 7. Kind of hard to miss, don't you think? Even a hacker with minimal skill would've been able to spot the irregularity in the program's coding where the communication was attached.

"Within the transmission was a second encrypted message written in a cipher we created years ago, a secret language only the two of us could understand in the event anyone intercepted the message. To the unassuming viewer, it would look like a blip of code in an otherwise normal transmission—an error that could be put down to a glitch in the system or a bad signal that corrupted the communication during upload. Realistically, Wren couldn't have gotten away with the message if he hadn't had a reason to send the transmission, which Richter provided. He wanted to hunt you down, and he didn't care what methods were used to do so. He only cared about getting you back.

"The moment I saw the code, I knew Wren was finally ready to do things my way. I knew it meant he wanted an out. With his position in the State and the information he had access to, I wasn't willing to refuse the opportunity, even if it meant a few unfortunate casualties."

"It never occurred to you that his loyalties may have changed over the years? That he was merely doing his duty to the State by bringing down one of PHOENIX's founding members?"

A spark of contempt burns behind Nolan's eyes. "Pursuing the transmission was the only way to ascertain his allegiance and to make the initial move to set up future communication between us that the State wouldn't be able to track."

"And how did you manage that?" I press. "I was there. We never set up any communication with anyone." *That I remember.*

I don't voice that last part.

Nolan folds his hands in his lap. "Foolish, ignorant girl. That mission was a treasure hunt, and Wren gifted us with not one but *two* priceless gifts that would aid in our fight against the State. While you were off having one of your episodes,"—his lips curl around these words into a sneer—"Ezra located a flash drive containing vital information along with a code for an untraceable contact channel that would operate independent of all other servers, ours included. Setting it up without Rai was a challenge but not impossible."

My body stiffens at the mention of Rai.

"And the other treasure?" I arch a brow. "What was it?"

I think back to that night, trying to discern if we found anything out of the ordinary in Bilken's office. Aside from his offensive collection of contraband, the only notable thing I remember is—

"Your file," he answers, his lips peeling back into a smile. "And the military order detailing the State's plans for you."

For a long moment, I stare blankly at Nolan, trying and failing to put my thoughts into words.

That conversation I witnessed between him and Ezra... Everything he said was a lie. I had already begun to suspect that was the case and this, what he's saying right now, confirms it.

More than ever, I'm certain that I'm here for a specific purpose, and whatever it is has to do with the abomination the State turned me into.

If that's the case, why the charade? From the way they spoke in that small, dark room, it had seemed like Nolan only agreed to extract me as a favor to Ezra and, possibly, because of who my father was. But, clearly, neither of those had any bearing on his involvement or his motivations. No, he only extracted me because he knew exactly how the State planned to use me.

And because he thinks PHOENIX can use me as a weapon, too.

I purse my lips, discontent with his answer. Although some of what he's said makes sense, something still isn't quite adding up.

"Richter knew the order was there," I point out. "Besides, these days, my reputation precedes me. There was nothing in that documentation that would've told you what most of the world doesn't already know by this point."

Nolan nods, sniffing as he brushes a finger against the side of his nose. "Richter overlooked one vital thing when he agreed to set that trap."

"Which was what?" I sigh, exasperated.

Just get to the point already.

A gloating smile spreads across Nolan's weathered face, stretching from ear to ear. "The fact that one simple piece of information in that order showed us how we can defeat the State."

I reel back, unnerved and confused by his statement. I read that order. Everything the report detailed was about Dr. Richter's experiments and how I would be *beneficial* to the State. It didn't mention weaknesses and it certainly didn't say anything about PHOENIX. Even if it had, I doubt Dr. Richter would've allowed such important intel to fall into the enemy's hands.

Unless…he was hoping it would. Unless there's a reason Richter wants PHOENIX involved in the State's senseless war.

My palms press hard against the dented arms of the chair, my fingers flexing and gripping the crumpled edges, which are now warm to the touch from the constant contact with the heat of my skin.

A frustrated growl breaks through my lips as stabbing pains shoot through my temples. What am I not putting together? None of this makes any damn sense, and the more I try to work it out, the worse the pain in my head seems to get. A prickle behind my left eye makes me wince.

"I don't understand," I spit through clenched teeth. "If that's true, Richter must not have known about it. Otherwise, what would he have gained from agreeing to Bilken's plan?"

Rai's face appears before me, a mirage in the cramped warmth of the tiny room, telling me I already know the answer. Dr. Richter even said it himself. He was never after PHOENIX.

At least, not all of them.

"Why do you think?" Nolan barks out a skeptical laugh. "As far as Richter was concerned, your file was placed there intentionally for you to see, so you would realize the inevitable outcome of your illness if you continued to resist him. If it weren't for Wren's plan, he never would've had the opportunity to use the promise of a cure to tempt you back to the DSD. After all, that is why you left, isn't it?"

At these words, one particular memory from the night Rai died comes back to haunt me.

"While I have my personal reasons for being here, I actually came to retrieve you, Wynter."

Although my other memories remain unclear, I remember that night so vividly now. I remember how Richter used my fear against me and presented the possibility of a cure to this disease as an answer to all my problems.

A cure...

"A cure is the only hope I have to stop this and to keep you all alive."

I remember saying those words. I remember believing them because the alternative was too terrifying to face. And I remember leaving because I was afraid my condition would kill the people I cared about if I didn't. Like Jenner.

And Ezra.

How could I have been so gullible? I never should have believed a single word out of Dr. Richter's mouth. Then again, if I hadn't listened, we wouldn't all be here right now because the world would've ended.

And we would be dead.

"You know, you did us a favor by going back to the DSD," Nolan says.

I bristle, pushing farther back on my seat. "What is *that* supposed to mean?"

"Isn't it obvious?" He chuckles, his laughter sharp, like broken glass cutting into my skin. "Without you, the State has no way of anticipating outside attacks. They've spent a lot of time and energy disconnecting themselves from the rest of the world and have made a fair number of enemies who may wish to use that knowledge to their advantage. Enemies they wouldn't have if it wasn't for you.

"If you hadn't gone back, we wouldn't be in the position we're in now, on the verge of changing the world. That was what I realized when I saw that order for myself. Wren had the foresight to include a copy on the drive Ezra retrieved from his office, and the more I tore through its contents, the more I saw the potential of what the State was setting out to do. And with it, I saw all the beautifully ironic ways it could bring about its own downfall."

My eyes widen as the scattered pieces representing everything that's been bothering me all slot together, forming a complete picture.

Bilken's defection. My file. The military order.

My extraction.

"You want the Heart to be attacked," I realize. "That's why you relocated Outside."

Nausea turns my stomach as I struggle with this notion that, despite this astronomical power residing within me, I'm still nothing more than a pawn to these people—a playing piece shuffled back and forth between two opposing, power-hungry sides. No matter what I do, no matter what steps I take, I'm always playing right into somebody's hand.

Playing the role I was destined for.

Every additional word out of Nolan's mouth only makes my nausea worse. "Fear can oppress a population just as easily as it can turn that same populace against the hand that feeds it. For now, the people are loyal to the State because they are unaware they have any other option for leadership. They will never answer to PHOENIX unless they're convinced the State can no longer protect them."

Something tells me this isn't the first time Nolan's given this little speech, and I find myself wondering if this is how he did it. How he got the other leading members of PHOENIX to all agree to my extraction.

I'm not sure what's worse—knowing they want to use me to further their own agenda or that my father's legacy with PHOENIX doesn't actually matter. If it did, they wouldn't be using his daughter this way. If it did, they'd want to protect me from the DSD. If my suspicions about Nolan's ultimate plans are correct, protecting me is the last thing on his mind.

Another memory flickers in the back of my head, and I remember a feeling I had shortly after Ezra and I met. I remember my concern that the change in his attitude was a ruse to keep me close in case PHOENIX ever needed to use me. That was when the thought first crossed my mind…

A tool of the enemy is a weapon against it.

"And you think you can?" I counter. "You think you can protect the people from down here in your sewers and your underground bunkers?"

Nolan sneers. "We can offer them an alternative. A return to a different way of life—"

"What about the war the State has already started? Do you think the enemies we've made will back down just because someone else is suddenly in charge? You said it yourself, the State is open to attack at any time without me there to see it coming."

Nolan rolls his eyes, brushing off my concerns with a wave of his hand. "We will negotiate peace terms with those who wish to see the State eradicated."

I think of all the dead bodies in the countless cities I personally helped to decimate. If I had been on the receiving end of those losses, I wouldn't want peace or settle for it.

Hell, I wouldn't even consider it.

A shudder bounds up my spine, and without meaning to, I imagine our own city at the brink of destruction. How many people will suffer because of PHOENIX's desire to overthrow the State?

How many more people will die because of me?

"Is that PHOENIX's goal, then? To lead?"

Nolan gives a disapproving tut. "I can see the judgment in your gaze, but PHOENIX is not the first to seek power, nor will it be the last. Someone, somewhere, will always think they can do the job better. Besides, if you choose to rise up against those at the top, you have to be prepared to take their place."

I admire this sentiment. Or I would if I wasn't convinced they're empty words intended to conceal a reality I'm not sure is any better than the one we're already stuck with.

I grimace at the thought.

"If you want power, why don't you just take it? PHOENIX has hundreds of sects in the Heart alone. Rebellions have started on less."

Before learning the truth about my father, I never thought to look back on those history lessons he gave me when I was young. Lessons he hid inside stories I thought, at the time, were merely fiction. Now, I realize what he was trying to do. What he was trying to foster inside me.

A desire to break free of the State.

A flush of annoyance reddens Nolan's face. "Believe it or not, I don't wish to lead through fear. If we seized control by force, we would be no better than the State, and, eventually, we, too, would be overthrown when the next rebellion comes along. This is the only way to get the people on our side and keep them there."

For the first time, I feel like I'm beginning to understand the inner workings of what I'm involved with. Only one question remains.

"I understand why you extracted me. With me gone, the State is vulnerable. I get that. But why wait so long to put this plan into motion? Why not come get me when the State's war first began? Why wait when so many lives were at risk?"

Why not stop me before I slaughtered so many innocent people?

I glare at him, watching as he runs a freckled hand through his hair. He sighs, as if my question is too taxing to answer, then says, "Watching the State make enemies was one thing but hearing of how they would destroy them was another. I don't need to tell you how special you are, but I do wonder if Richter ever told you just how special."

The hairs on the back of my neck stand on end.

"What are you talking about?"

Nolan glances once over his shoulder, then peers at me, lowering his voice. "What do you know about your blood?"

My lungs constrict as my consciousness drifts back through my time at the DSD. I relive everything Dr. Richter ever said to me.

I relive every nightmarish moment.

"It evolved," I answer in a slow, stilted breath. "Richter calls it Type X. He said I'm the only person alive with this blood type."

Nolan nods as if he already knows this.

He leans back, steepling his fingers in front of his lips. "What would you say if I told you that your blood was being injected into other individuals who suffer from the same condition as yourself?"

A gasp lodges in my throat. I knew there had been others with Ultraxenopia before me, but I didn't know Richter had continued his search or that he was still experimenting on others like me. Foolishly, I figured his success with my powers would put an end to his errant abductions.

Another realization strikes, adding fuel to the raging inferno of my horror. Is that why Dr. Richter took daily samples of my blood? So he could inject it into other people? The thought makes me sick. Why would he do that? What did he think would happen?

What has my blood done to them?

Nolan continues, ignoring my obvious shock. "When they found a way to keep you alive, you officially became the first of your kind. A new, evolved breed of human. Richter believes infusing your blood into other Ultraxenopia candidates may help speed the evolution process along. He's looking for a way to bypass the incapacitating side effects you experienced before the cure."

My fingers reach up to touch my collar but are held down by the restraints on my wrists. They're sturdier than the last pair, but I could still break them with ease—a notion which does little to comfort me now. As my hand relaxes, I mull over the real reason this noose is wrapped around my neck.

The collar controls my power, but it also stops the pain and deterioration of my brain. It stops this disease from killing me. As I told Ezra, the collar is the cure. Or as close to one as Richter has been able to get.

Not that he's been looking for one. Unless that's why Richter has been injecting my blood into other people with Ultraxenopia—to find a permanent method of control without the debilitating side effects that have killed so many others. But without more collars like mine, Richter would be powerless against them, so what the hell is he up to? Why would he need more test subjects when he already has the most feared person in the world on a leash?

I can't stop myself from blurting out my confusion. "Why would he do that?"

Nolan cocks an incredulous eyebrow. "Why do you think? He's creating an army."

"No." I jerk my head, aghast. "Even he wouldn't go that far."

"Wouldn't he? We're talking about a man who killed the woman he once claimed to love. At least, that's what Ezra said when he finally admitted his connection to Richter in the days after you left. Someone like that… I don't think they're capable of limits. I'm not sure he even knows what they are."

My expression darkens. He's right. Dr. Richter doesn't have any limits. I don't think that word even exists in his vocabulary.

The more I think about what Nolan has said, the more the thought of others having this power unnerves me. Over the past few years, I've both loathed and embraced this disease, but I've found a way to live with it, just as I've found a way to live with everything I've done. I've killed so many people, and yet, knowing I might be the cause of this curse in others is a possibility I never prepared myself for. If Richter achieves his goal, if he creates more weapons like me, then I'll be far more than a monster.

I'll be the mother of all hell on earth.

"Has he managed it?" The words escape in a ragged whisper.

"Not yet," Nolan assures me, "but it's only a matter of time before he succeeds, and then our chance to supplant the State will be lost."

I lick my lips, which are suddenly bone dry. "That's why you waited over two years to come get me, isn't it? You only acted when you did because you had a viable excuse to intervene."

He shrugs. "Enforcers we can handle. A thousand of you? Definitely not. When Wren informed us of Richter's new goals, the other Heads were left with no choice but to approve your extraction, a plan I'd been preparing and pitching for months but which they were all reluctant to act on. Truthfully, if Richter didn't have such a God complex, who knows when, or if, we would've acted. In all our years of hiding, the other Heads have grown complacent. Meek. But now,

I intend to bring us out of the shadows, and it's all thanks to you."

Reaching out, he touches a cold hand to my cheek, and as a grin pulls at his thin, papery lips, I realize that, just like Dr. Richter, Nolan has been wearing a mask this whole time. As it falls away and I come face to face with the real Rodrick Nolan, the voice in my head insisting PHOENIX is good—Rai's voice— disappears, going silent.

Because PHOENIX isn't good.

Not anymore.

"If you keep me here, the Heart *will* be attacked and many innocent people will die."

Snorting, Nolan rises from his chair. "You've killed many innocent people yourself, have you not?"

I swallow, pushing away the resurfacing wave of guilt, which washes over me again at his words. What I've done is in the past.

What matters now is the future.

"You won't have a country to lead if everyone is dead," I remind him. "Mindless violence won't bring about change."

As these words breach my lips, it dawns on me that I've heard them before. Jenner's voice echoes somewhere in my memory.

"I don't wish for it to come to that," Nolan insists, "but such is the reality of war. One of the many downsides, if you will. All we can do is push for peace to be restored before too many have to suffer."

"And what if your plan fails?" I squirm in my seat as that familiar pressure rakes at the underside of my skin, threatening to spill out. "What if the State's enemies don't want peace?"

Nolan hesitates, considering me for a moment, his expression grim. Sighing, he backs away toward the door.

"Then there's no hope for any of us."

FIFTEEN

I SHUFFLE BACK AND FORTH, my feet scraping the floor, as my teeth click against the tip of my thumbnail. The mangled remnants of my new shackles lie in pieces on the floor behind me. After Nolan's stunt with Bilken, the people here will never see me restrained again.

I plan to make sure of that.

Part of me is ready to explode out of this room and tear down anyone who stands in the way of me bringing justice to Bilken and Nolan for the roles they each played in Rai's death—the monstrous and human sides of me for once aligned in their mission. But another part, the emotionally detached part, is too confused to even know what I'm really feeling. It's as if I've been in the darkness for years and, suddenly, someone has turned on a light, lancing my vision and crippling me. I don't know how to see past the glare.

Or if I'll ever find a way past this blindness.

I pace back and forth, unaware of how much time has passed since my reintroduction to solitude and too lost in thought to care. My mind is a cluttered and conflicted mess. No matter how hard I try to make sense of what I now know—what I've learned—there's more I still don't understand.

For all his talk about change and peace, Nolan's plans for PHOENIX would ultimately make him no better than the State. They're simply two sides of the same coin; on the surface, they may appear different but, in the end, they amount to the same damn thing. And he's willing to cause an even greater war if it means turning that coin in his favor.

I know all this, and yet, I have this persistent thought that I'm missing something important.

I run a hand through my long, knotted hair and let out a breath that's somewhere between a grunt and a sigh. Fatigue weighs down my already exhausted body, slowing my steps to a standstill. When was the last time I slept? Or ate? I might seem evolved compared to normal people, but I still have basic human needs. At this point, the only thing stopping me from collapsing is my determination to piece together my memories.

"What can't I remember?" My fingers grip my skull in frustration as I press my eyes shut, concentrating as hard as I can. When the answer fails to come to me, I finally accept the only option I have.

For so long, I've been forced to use this unwanted power. For strategic gain. To kill others. But I've never used it for personal, selfish reasons. Not once. Even when Ezra busted me out of this room and the complexity of what I felt toward him tempted me to look back on that missing chunk of time, I refused that option because I wanted to get my memories back and experience the full extent of what they held—not just see them from an outside perspective like some spectator watching the movie of my life.

Now, though, I understand my decision went much deeper than that, even if I didn't consciously realize it at that moment. I was afraid of what I might find if I looked, what I might have to face. If I'm honest with myself, I still am. As much as I want to remember, I'm not ready to confront the person I used to be.

But what if, instead, I use my ability to see someone else's memories rather than my own? Someone who was there when the State came to power.

Someone who can help me understand what I'm dealing with.

Exhaling a shaking breath, I slide my eyes shut again and steer my thoughts toward the one person I want to see more than anyone else in the world. As his face materializes, I can't help the smile that tugs back my lips or the tears that prick at the corners of my eyes. The image of him becomes clearer as I unwind the clock, sending my mind to a different point in time in the past—before I existed. To a time when he still did.

Back…before all this.

I sense the change as my surroundings transform, only opening my eyes once the world stops spinning. The concrete of my cell is gone, replaced by the dim lighting and furnishings of a study. Ornate paintings decorate the beige walls, the splash of color a stark contrast to the stone mantelpiece framing a crackling fire. A dark, wooden desk sits just beneath a round window embedded in the opposite wall.

"Father…" I breathe.

Terror catapults through my body, but I force myself to take one step then another, my gaze on his back at all times as I slink toward where he sits at the desk, hunched over and sunken into his seat. As I push forward, I note the way his hand whips back and forth in furious repetition, scribbling across the white page of a—

"Book," I realize, the words leaching out in a gasp.

When is this memory from? Father never kept books in our home—although, this room isn't from any home I remember. To the State, books are contraband. They risk spreading ideas, like a sickness. They encourage others to put their thoughts into a permanent form.

And unmonitored thoughts can be dangerous.

Once I'm beside my father, I peer down at his face. He looks so young but serious in a way I struggle to align with the man I once knew. It's strange…like I'm seeing my father but in the body of a stranger. I almost don't even recognize him.

My fingers ache with the urge to smooth the wrinkles creasing his forehead and calm whatever worries are plaguing his thoughts, but when I raise my arm, my hand passes through his head as if he's a ghost. Intangible.

Frowning, I remember where I am and what this is I'm seeing. I couldn't touch him even if I wanted to. Because I'm not really here…

And because he's dead.

Lowering my arm, I glance over his shoulder.

February 28th, 2034

For so long, it was only rumors. First, it was a simple shift in policy, a change in the way the government was run. Then, there were whispers about assassinations and an insurgency that had risen up from within, taking down the established government without having to resort to the more brutal methods of war and rebellion. I'm not sure how they did it. I don't even know where they came from. No one does. All I know is the struggle was over before anyone was aware it had even begun. And now? Now, the State is in power.

The strangest part is there was never a catalyst. Never a single moment that indicated anything was amiss. No grand war or uprising. The rebels simply appeared like a phantom presence and integrated themselves into our society with no one the wiser, taking down those in power from the inside.

Initially, people weren't all that concerned. They just saw the State as a newly elected government and were fooled by the promises made to appease us. But what everyone failed to grasp is that the State was never elected. Hell, it was never even in the running.

It wasn't long before it began to change us. Change the way we live and function. It happened slowly, one minor adjustment at a time to avoid a full-scale panic. But, lately things have been happening more quickly, taking root in a way that makes me fear the path forward will be irreversible if this continues. Our downfall is progressing at an alarming rate, and I'm worried no one else notices it except me.

Sometimes, I feel like I'm going insane.

Horrific acts plague everyday news, but the State hides its crimes behind vague oaths of peace, insisting that everything it's doing is for the greater good. How easily people are deceived. But not me. I feel like I'm the only one who sees these intruders for what they really are and for what they're trying to do to us. Rob us of a shared national identity. Frighten us until we cower and obey. This new government has even introduced birth identification numbers and a compulsory placement exam to help achieve this end. To categorize the population and determine which of us are expendable.

The numbers are to keep track of us, to identify us, and the exam is to transform us into a more efficient society. Or so the State claims. Those masquerading as our overlords say the exam will urge everyone to contribute equally. That it's in our best interest to only focus on our strengths and to be made aware of our weaknesses. In reality, the exam is just another means for the State to assert control over our lives. To make us follow its rules and live the way those in charge want us to. To eliminate those the State views as a burden.

A place for everyone, and everyone in their place.

His hand stills as he tsks under his breath.

No one has a say anymore. We have to do what we're told or suffer the consequences. The majority naturally go for the former out of fear. And that fear is changing us all.

Something needs to be done before the people are too far gone to remember who they are. Before we're all brainwashed by the promises of the State.

Before we lose ourselves completely.

Rodrick agrees with me, and so our mission to find like-minded individuals to join us and to battle this new evil begins. Once we do, all that's left is to turn our thoughts of rebellion into action and take back what is rightfully ours.

We've even chosen a name for ourselves. Our resolve burns like fire, and we will ensure the fight continues even after our deaths, just like a phoenix is reborn from its ashes. Together, we will rise up from the remains of this nation and liberate our people from the tyranny threatening to destroy us.

The fire behind me cracks like a whip, and as I turn toward the sound, the room around me goes black. When the light returns, flooding the space with a cool indigo glow, I realize the stone mantelpiece is gone, the wall skimmed flat and painted gray. Where the fireplace had been only moments ago, there's now a square box embedded flush with the plaster. Small blue flames lick at the glass.

My gaze skirts over the empty walls, and I note the absence of the paintings that adorned the office before. There isn't a single trace of them to be seen, almost as if they never existed.

Now, there's only gray.

My father is positioned now before the round window in the same spot where his desk used to be. He stares out past the spotless panes, his expression distant. Forlorn. A steel desk stands alone in the corner.

A chill crosses over my skin at the familiar presence of metal—a trademark symbol prevalent in our society. Even this desk, from its cold exterior right down to its placement, represents the State. Whereas the wooden desk from the first memory stood in front of the window, this new desk is turned toward the wall as a reminder that there's nowhere to go. Nowhere to hide. Perhaps to tell him he's trapped, just like the rest of us are in the future.

My mouth is dry as I approach my father. His face is older now. Worn by stress. Warped by fear. Although this memory brings him closer to the man I knew as a child, I recognize him even less than I did in the last memory.

With a sigh, he turns and retreats from the window, taking a seat at the desk, his fingers running along the underside of a drawer as he slumps into the accompanying leather chair. After a moment, his hand resurfaces with the journal, and he flips it open, searching for a blank page. A tremor runs over his whole arm when he writes.

Once again, I read the words over his shoulder.

July 17th, 2038

The situation has become increasingly dire. We're struggling to get hold of the needed supplies to keep our operation going, and it's been difficult to find support, especially with the newly instated identification chips monitoring our every movement. The State is tracking us every minute of the day now, hoping to flush out anyone who might pose a threat to their perfect utopia.

He stifles a laugh as he pens the next line.

This place is more like hell.

My father leans back in his chair for a moment, as if considering his next words. I ache for him, I fear for him—for how much he's risking by putting these treasonous thoughts to paper.

My hand hovers over his shoulder, and although neither of us can feel it, I try to touch him again.

"I'm here," I whisper.

But, as expected, he doesn't hear me.

A tear trails down my cheek as I glance back at the page.

A wall at least fifty feet high has been erected around the perimeter of the city, hindering access to the outside world. Travel is prohibited without special clearance, and our home, now known as the Heart, has been separated into seven zones with the outlying area rapidly deteriorating into a slum. It's a place for the State to deposit the waste until they find a way to eradicate it completely.

For the time being, we're allowed to stay in our homes, but it won't be long until they uproot us. Where we live will coincide with the jobs we're assigned, which will only serve to segregate and break down the relationships we have until they cease to exist altogether. Soon, fear will eliminate loyalty, and once that happens, it'll be easy to force us to conform.

To make matters worse, the State has cut off all ties with our trade partners, citing advancements in hydroponics and genetically grown meat as the reason for our increasing isolation. I don't begrudge science. I celebrate it. But, in this case, it's being used as a weapon to keep us all locked in a cage.

A daily cap has been put in place on almost everything. Food. Medicine. Even water. It's all limited, with our daily allowance determined by our personal contribution. Some products, like alcohol, are gradually being phased out from certain zones entirely. The State claims the change is only temporary while we adjust to the new system of distribution and that, with a little time and effort, we'll be able to create everything we need for ourselves, right here inside these walls, without having to rely on trade.

At first, I thought this was just another way to prevent outside interference with the State's plans. But now, I know this move wasn't intended to keep other people out. It's meant to keep us in. At this rate, the next generation won't even know an outside world exists.

He stops for a moment and just stares at the paper as if he's forgotten what he wanted to write. The pen slips from his grasp and lands on the open page with a muted thunk.

I step around my father's chair and force myself to look down at his face. Dark smudges stain the skin under his eyes, which are glassy and red against his pallid complexion.

Why don't I remember him looking this way? Was I blind to it, the way a child would be? Or did something change between this moment and when I was born? Maybe this pain was always hidden behind his smile and I just didn't notice.

My heart aches when he picks up the pen again.

Another big shift concerns the State's supply of Enforcers, which has grown to an extraordinary level in recent months. Nearly tenfold compared to their numbers less than a year ago. The 'join us or die' mentality is spreading like fire, and more are enlisting every day to prove their cooperation and loyalty to the tyrants who have overthrown us.

Loyalists, as they're now called, are rewarded while those who stand against this new rule are weeded out and exterminated like bugs.

Soon, there won't be any of us left.

A few weeks ago, a curfew was also established in an effort to quash any lingering illegal activity, making our goals that much harder to attain. Although this development has drastically affected our mission, it pales compared to the State's latest venture. I really thought these people couldn't sink any lower. They've separated us. They're tracking us. They're controlling everything we do. And now, they're taking away anything that might make us unique or different from each another. Only by making us the same can they oppress us completely.

They claim the raids are meant to cleanse our society and make way for a greater future. A future we will build together.

More lies.

Pyres light up the streets as Enforcers force their way into homes, burning anything that directly contradicts the State's 'improved' idea of society. They'll destroy the slightest reminder of what life was like before the State came to power, even something as simple as a piece of furniture or, God forbid, a book. Anything that suggests another way of life ever existed before the State did.

But I see what they're really doing. They're taking away the old so we have nothing to go back to.

And the public response? People are feeding this ridiculous assault on our freedom by just accepting it, making the situation far worse. I can see the extent of the State's reach in the whispers I hear in passing on the streets. Individuals I've known my whole life are now preaching lies and making claims that are inconsistent with the world we grew up in. I'd like to think they're in denial, but I know the truth.

They've been brainwashed.

I tear my gaze away from the journal, haunted by the image forming in my head. I can imagine the scene my father describes with such clarity. Enforcers storming into homes. Whole identities ripped away as possessions were burned before their owners' eyes.

Memories.

Talents.

It was all taken away.

For the first time, I really understand why my father chose to expose me to his secret. Why he would spend countless hours poring over old books with me and teaching me how to play the piano. It never occurred to me how many people had to suffer for the privileges I took for granted.

How my father had to suffer.

My lower lip wobbles as I reminisce about our "secret missions," as he called them. He'd wait for the days when Mother was scheduled to work—when it was his turn to care for me when I wasn't at school—and after waiting an appropriate amount of time, we'd sneak out through the back door of the house where no one would spot us leaving. We always took different routes to our destination, and although he claimed it was a game, I know now the change was to avoid any regular patterns to our movements that might arouse suspicion thanks to our tracking chips. And, probably, to prevent me from being able to tell anyone else how to get there.

We always ended up at a park—an inconspicuous enough place for a parent to take their child. Once there, he'd blindfold my eyes, and I would stumble along in the dark, gripping his hand, until he finally said it was okay to look. The only thing I remember about that part is the grating sound of metal followed by the smell. The musty odor and dampness to the air that meant we were in the tunnels beneath the city—although I didn't know that at the time. No wonder he always made me change my clothes as soon as we got home. He wanted to avoid Mother finding out what we were up to.

Thinking about it now, I wonder if the place he used to take me to was one of PHOENIX's early hideouts. Where else could he have concealed something as large and conspicuous as a piano? Where else could he have taught me how to play it without us getting caught? The more I dwell on it, the more I marvel at the fact he was able to preserve such an item at all. I can only imagine the risk he took stowing it before it was discovered by Enforcers.

But why did he do it? Were his actions purely sentimental? Or did he gather such relics in the hope that they might be put to good use again someday? So that one small piece of our history wouldn't be totally forgotten.

The scratching of my father's pen grabs my attention, and blinking, I fix my gaze back on the journal.

The world as we knew it no longer exists. They've stolen

everything from us, and in time, they'll take more until we have nothing left to give. If I was smart, I would destroy this journal. I shudder to think what will happen if they find it. Execution, most likely.

Or torture.

It's no wonder so many people are staying quiet and falling into line. The disappearances are just one horror among many, putting everyone on edge. It's impossible to know who to trust anymore, and the State is making it a point to nurture that paranoia.

Whoever is running this show is smart and has positioned their pieces to the utmost advantage. The people are turning on each other at an astonishing rate. Soon, the State won't even have to lift a finger to weed out the dissenters.

The world has gone to hell. If I'm honest, I'm not sure how much more of this I can handle.

He hesitates, the tip of the pen hovering an inch above the paper, his hand shaking, as if he's not sure whether or not he should continue. Sweat beads across his forehead as he clenches his teeth and forces himself to write the next line. His fingers quake so violently, I struggle to read what he wrote.

Eyes narrowing, I lean forward to decipher the barely legible scribbles. My heart plummets into the bottoms of my feet when I finally make out the words.

At least I still have Evandra.

The sight of my mother's name stirs up an anger within me unlike anything I've felt before. My father trusted her to keep him afloat in a world that was constantly trying to drown him. Maybe, at one point, she did. But something changed.

Something led her to betray him.

Shadows flood the room until the only visible light is the glow of the diminishing blue flames in the hearth. The hairs on the back of my neck stand on end as I cast a wary glance down at my father. He sits immobile before the steel desk, his body still and head hung low.

When I look at his face, there's nothing of the man I once knew in his appearance. His skin is sallow and his sunken cheeks are covered with patchy facial hair. His eyes, which were once so full of life and hope, are dark and distant.

Empty.

I reach out to him, desperate to touch his shoulder, but just like the two times I tried before, my fingers once again only find air.

I watch in horror as he pens a new entry.

March 7th, 2043

I always thought love was the greatest force in this world. That nothing and no one could come between us if we had that love. That we would always be on each other's side, first and foremost. Turns out, I was wrong. Our damaged society has achieved the one thing I thought impossible.

It has divided us.

I suspect she doesn't realize this yet. If she did, I would already be dead. She's made it clear where her allegiance lies, but I'm not sure if her loyalties have changed because of fear or if she's simply been brainwashed by propaganda like so many others. Whatever the cause, Eva is no longer the woman I fell in love with. The person wearing her face is a stranger to me.

It breaks my heart to write these words, but I must put my personal feelings aside. From here on out, I must assume a new identity and pretend to be someone I'm not. Even though I had planned to leave her, to go fully underground like Rodrick has, what I want now is inconsequential. My dream of righting the wrongs committed by those who cast their shadow over our lives no longer matters.

I must abandon everything and all that I stand for, and, for the sake of my unborn child, I must stay and wear the mask of a man who conforms. Perhaps, one day, I will escape from this torment, but until then

He stops writing, leaving the sentence unfinished. I wonder if he's too upset to realize he hasn't completed his thought or if he just can't bring himself to put it down into words.

The tip of the pen moves to the next line.

This will be my final entry. With the world the way it is now, even our thoughts are no longer safe. To those who were depending on me

A tear trails down his cheek and drips onto the letters, smearing the ink.

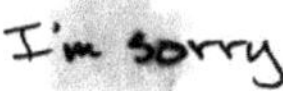

With a shuddering breath, he closes the journal, and as he rises to his feet, his nails dig into the binding, leaving small half-moon marks in the leather.

I watch him, transfixed, as he crosses the room, his eyes unblinking as they stare at the flames. A menacing blue-tinted hue laps across his face, reflecting through the glass barrier.

Crouching, he uses his free hand to lift the glass door, the blaze crackling when exposed to the draft of fresh air. Then, without a second of hesitation, he throws the book into the fire.

The vision ends as the pages burn.

SIXTEEN

MY LUNGS SEIZE AS CRACKS spread along the surface of my heart, the fissures forming an intricate spider web of pain I can barely find the energy to breathe past. The crevices deepen each time I gasp for air, working inward with every strangled inhalation.

Breaking me.

Tears trickle down my cheeks to my lips, blurring the claustrophobic room. Vertigo—probably caused from lack of nourishment—distorts my surroundings and steals the remaining strength from my body, making my head spin. My knees buckle, and I fall…fall…

Fall.

As the floor rushes up to meet me, I'm aware of little other than the pain in my chest. When it swallows me, everything else fades away. The blinding light overhead. The dingy gray walls closing in on all sides. It all vanishes until the only thing visible to me is my father's face. The image of his haunted expression as he watched the flames consume his journal—his thoughts—is burned into my mind like a brand.

I lie still against the cold, damp concrete, unable to move as the grief and guilt each wrap a hand around my throat. I don't try to fight back when they choke me because I deserve this torture, this pain.

I deserve it more than anyone.

"It's…my fault," I whimper in a broken breath.

A bottled-up scream explodes from my lungs, ringing in my ears like the blaring cry of an alarm. I scream until my voice is hoarse and my tears are nothing more than dry, sticky streaks on my skin, uncomfortable and itchy.

I don't know how long my hysteria lasts; the agony in my chest seems never-ending. I cry until there's nothing left in me, and then, I lie still, screaming all over again in my head.

Behind my grief, I hear a man yelling on the other side of the door, his voice muted by the metal but clear. A familiar voice.

Ezra's voice.

"Get out of my way!"

With what little energy I still have, I turn my head in the direction of the doorway, ignoring the way the concrete floor scrapes my cheek. Although I can't see clearly past the muddy haze clouding my vision, I can make out the shape of the door opening. The hinges moan, protesting the weight of the steel, and a shiver crosses my skin when my ears pick up on the thumping of boots retreating down the corridor. Whoever was guarding my cell is off to get reinforcements, if I had to venture a guess.

I blink against the light cascading in from the hallway, and as the dark figure standing at the threshold takes a step into the room, I know in what remains of my soul that it's Ezra.

His body is a blurred silhouette against the harsh lights as he rushes toward me, squatting down to the floor. I tremble beneath the gentle touch of his hand on my back.

"Wynter." He bends forward, bringing his face close to mine until his warm breath grazes my lips. "Wynter…can you hear me?" he whispers.

I want to look up at him, I want to get lost in his gaze, but I can't allow myself that escape. The guilt gripping my heart is too much to bear, and I deserve every single second of this pain.

I clamp my eyes shut. "It's my fault."

Sobs fill my chest as I curl into the fetal position and wrap my arms around my legs, tucking into a ball. I don't know how else to hold myself together, not when I'm so close to falling apart.

Light and shadow dance across my closed lids, indicating movement overhead, but I don't open my eyes to see what Ezra is doing. Part of me hopes he's finally doing what he should've done two years ago—that he'll come to his senses and run from this room before I can break him just like I broke my father.

Another part, the selfish part, wants him to stay.

It's for that reason I don't struggle against him when his arms snake around my back and under my knees, scooping my limp body up off the floor. His strong arms lift me as if I weigh nothing.

"Come on." His voice is low and guttural in my ear. "I'm getting you out of here."

My fingers grip his shirt as he cradles me against the comforting heat of his chest, and for the first time in as long as I can remember, I feel protected. Cared for. Even though we're surrounded by people who only see me as a weapon and wish to use me for their own gain, even though the world could collapse around us at any time…in this moment, I feel truly safe.

As Ezra carries me toward the open door, his stride is steady and calm, but beneath his shirt, I can feel his heart pounding, each thump a feather-light caress against my cheek. I angle my ear, listening to every rapid beat, hearing the cadence of fear in his breaths. They tickle the top of my head, brushing my hair.

What is he so afraid of? I wonder.

When we pass into the corridor, Ezra goes still. I risk a glance up at his face, noting the direction of his gaze and the way his mouth is pressed into a frustrated grimace. His heart, which was racing before, is now a cacophony of vibrating drums in my ear.

I follow his line of sight down the hallway and lock eyes with Quinn, who stares at us both in confusion, his broad chest heaving with the exertion of running. His dark brow furrows as he raises his pistol.

"What do you think you're doing?" he shouts.

Ezra tightens his grip on me, pulling me closer. "Solitary confinement is only making things worse. Can't you see what it's doing to her? She *needs* to get out of this room for a while."

Quinn bites down on his full lower lip and storms toward us, the anger in his eyes like two lumps of smoldering charcoal. As he draws closer, my gaze drops down to his hands. They're shaking just like they were the last time I saw him.

When he's only a few feet away, he growls, "How many times do I have to remind you that she's dangerous, Laramie?"

Ezra's arms tense around me as he barks, "She will be if you continue to keep her locked up! You think I don't know what she's capable of? I've witnessed it first-hand. I've seen what she can do when she's perfectly sane, so trust me, none of us want to find out what happens when she snaps."

I flinch, recoiling from his outburst. His words, although true, are like a slap to the face. All those times he insisted I wasn't a threat… Just as I suspected, he was lying, and now, I have confirmation that he's always known what kind of monster I am.

And yet, despite that, he's here at my side, trying to help me and protect me from harm. Despite what I've done, he still somehow sees me as someone worth fighting for.

Tears prick the edges of my eyes at the thought.

Quinn repositions his hand on his gun, his forefinger dancing just over the trigger. Sweat beads in small droplets along his thick hairline. "Don't think I'll have any qualms about shooting you. *Or* her," he warns.

"I'd really rather you didn't do that."

Jenner emerges from a path to our left, appearing as if from thin air behind Quinn. Grinning, he presses a gun to the back of his head.

Straining his jaw, Quinn lowers his arm. "Nolan *will* hear about this," he promises as Jenner reaches around to disarm him.

"I'm sure he will," Ezra retorts with indifference. He pushes past the ex-Enforcer, and in the charged silence, his whisper is deafening. "Threaten her again and I'll kill you."

He then continues down the corridor without looking back, holding me close at all times as if his arms alone can shield me from anything. I nuzzle my face into his collarbone and glance over his shoulder at Jenner, who raises his hand and then brings it down swiftly, striking Quinn in the back of the skull. Quinn crumples to the floor, and after nudging him once with his boot to make sure he's unconscious, Jenner jogs after us, wiping his pistol on the hem of his shirt. A smear of blood comes off on the fabric.

The three of us progress through the network of hallways, our hurried forward advance reminiscent of that horrible night at the magistrates building. I expect Nolan or his lackeys to show up at every turn, but the compound is silent, the hallways empty. If I didn't know any better, I'd think the place was completely deserted.

As the minutes pass, a heavy drowsiness washes over me, lulling me into the clutches of sleep. Ezra's rocking movements merely push me over the edge I was already teetering at, my body weak with hunger and worn down by the added exhaustion from the vision reel of my father. At the slightest thought of him, his face manifests in my head and the crippling guilt returns.

After what seems like hours of walking, Ezra pauses and kicks open a random door with his foot. He steps into the room with me still in his arms as Jenner follows behind us, bolting the lock.

As we enter the cramped space, I'm alarmed by how much it reminds me of my cell at the DSD. A small cot with gray bedding sits in one corner with a single chair pushed up against the wall just beside it.

Other than that, the room is empty.

Ezra walks over to the bed and carefully places me on top of the mattress, using the pillow to prop my body upright. Once I'm settled, he sinks into the chair with a sigh.

I shutter my eyes and rest my head back against the hard wall. In the silence, my ears catch every noise, from our breaths to the scratching of fabric across concrete as Jenner slides down to the floor.

Fatigue dims my senses, and I'm desperate to sleep, but the itchy clamminess of my unwashed skin and the almost palpable agitation blanketing the tiny room make doing so impossible. Still, I keep my eyes closed, even as sleep eludes me.

"What did you see?" Jenner asks after a while, his voice a tremulous, barely audible breath.

I can sense the expectant way he and Ezra both stare at me, their questioning gazes washing over my skin. My eyes flutter open, but I look down at the blanket beneath me, too much of a coward to face them. I can't. Not yet.

I can barely even face myself.

Dragging in a shaking breath, I pin my arms to my sides and bunch up the thin blanket in my fists. A loose thread sticks out from one of the seams.

"I saw my father." Fresh tears well in my eyes as remorse forms a lump in my throat. It takes several attempts to push out the words. "He died because of me. He wanted to leave, but he stayed because my mother was pregnant. He didn't want to leave me alone."

I think of my mother and of everything I know about her along with what I learned from my father's journal. How she put her loyalty to the State above everything and everyone, including her family. A loyalty which alienated the man who once loved her. A loyalty which got him killed. A loyalty which turned her daughter, her only child, into a deadly weapon.

A monster.

I'm not sure who I hate more—my mother because of everything she's done to us…

Or the State because it made her do it.

I startle when Ezra touches my hand, unused to such casual physical contact. His warm fingers curl around mine and squeeze as a soft breath fills the space between us. "I swear I didn't know about his involvement with PHOENIX until recently. I wanted to tell you, I just didn't know how."

Would it have been easier for me to accept the truth about my father if I had heard it from Ezra? Probably not. I doubt I would've believed anyone until I saw the proof for myself. In that case, looking back was always inevitable.

I needed to get the truth straight from the source.

"I understand why you didn't tell me. We didn't have much time before, and for all you knew, I wouldn't have remembered him anyway."

My focus shifts to the opposite side of the room, settling on the blank wall. During the time I was held captive by the State, I allowed myself to lose sight of so much, but I never forgot my father. Was I trying to punish myself in some way by clinging to the most painful memory I possess? Maybe I just couldn't bring myself to let go of him.

Not when I had already let go of everything else.

"Does that mean you remember now?" Jenner watches me with hooded eyes, but in their depths, I glimpse the faintest glimmer of hope. The way he looks at me…

I've seen it before.

"Some things…" I answer slowly, as if tasting every word to ensure I'm explaining in the most coherent way possible. "I remember everything before I was initially taken to the DSD following my placement exam, and there are some things I remember since, like—"

"Rai," Ezra interrupts.

"And Wren Bilken," Jenner adds.

As I nod, I picture Rai's face in my thoughts. For the last few years, she's been an unseen presence in my life, haunting me like my own personal specter. Now that I remember her, now that I remember that night, the weight of her death is an all too real burden on my conscious. The guilt I've managed to push back for so long strangles me like a thick smoke filling my lungs.

"What about us?"

I glance over at Ezra, not quite sure how to answer that question. His anxious expression ignites a thousand opposing emotions, which all pummel my heart and seem to lodge in my throat, making it all that much harder to breathe. Part of me just wants to kiss him again, while another part wants to run from this room and leave all these conflicting emotions behind me.

Swallowing, I tug my hand free of his and force my gaze back down to the blanket. "Memories are coming back in bits and pieces, but usually only in response to a trigger. The fragments don't even make sense half the time."

Once again, I attempt to piece together the disjointed images in my memory, but no matter how many times I turn them or try to make them all fit together, I just can't seem to grasp the full picture of my past.

Ezra and Jenner don't question me further, and the room descends into uneasy silence, all of us avoiding eye contact as we each fall prey to our own troubled thoughts.

I may not fully remember what we went through together, but I've glimpsed enough, I *feel* enough of who I was, to want to keep them both safe. The trouble is, I don't know how to do that. Up until now, I only ever used this power to destroy. The one and only time I considered protecting anyone with it was when the transport helicopter was seconds from crashing. In the end, I didn't bother. Rather than attempt to save those soldiers, I caved to my impulses and selfish desire for freedom and let them all die so that I could die, too.

A startling realization occurs to me. What if I'm incapable of using my condition for good? What if, by trying to protect one, I inadvertently cause harm to the other? Could I live with that?

Could I live with being responsible for the death of yet another person I love?

Suddenly, I don't find it surprising at all that I chose to leave them when I did. Notwithstanding the risk of what this power might do to them if they maintain their current proximity to me, Ezra and Jenner don't seem to think things through when I'm involved. Our current predicament is proof of that.

And yet, although their recklessness irritates me, I can understand their desperation. They're afraid they'll lose me, just like they lost Rai. Still, that doesn't mean I condone what they're doing. Or that I approve of them putting my well-being before their own.

"Now that you've busted me out, what's the plan?" I ask, my tone just on the edge of acidic.

I glare at Ezra and Jenner, who exchange a wary look but say nothing.

Scowling, I grind out, "If you keep this up, you're going to get yourselves into deep shi—"

"Our first priority was getting you out of that room," Ezra cuts in, meeting my gaze for the first time in at least twenty minutes. "The rest is a work in progress, but I think we all know staying here isn't an option."

"Does this mean you've realized Nolan has been lying to you, then?" When Ezra's eyes widen in puzzled surprise, I add in a tentative whisper, "I saw it. Your conversation with him after I woke up and attacked you."

My fingers twitch at the remembered sensation of my hand around Ezra's throat. I don't think I ever really intended to hurt him, but I still can't shake the regret that gnaws at me, knowing what I could've done. And all for the sake of answers.

Answers no one has freely given me except Nolan.

Thinking about it, he's been far more forthright with me than anyone should be with the person they're holding hostage. His abrupt honesty doesn't make any sense. Even Ezra and Jenner have been reluctant to clue me in on certain things because of my faulty memory, as if afraid of what effect the truth might have on my sanity. But not Nolan. If anything, he's been pushing my limits, testing me as if to gauge what revelation will make me snap. Like Dr. Richter's mind games I endured daily at the DSD, it's almost like the chats I had with Nolan were his way of playing with my grip on control. He wanted to see how far is too far and, in doing so, exert his power over me.

So, was answering my questions all part of his plot to use me, to bend me to his will? What about shoving Bilken in my face or revealing the truth about my father?

Why divulge anything if the plan is to kill me?

My heart races as I spit out each word through clenched teeth. "We both know Nolan never intended to keep me alive."

Ezra bolts upright in the chair as Jenner furiously shakes his head. Their voices overlap one another.

"He won't lay a finger on you."

"We won't let that bastard anywhere near you."

My eyes flick back and forth between them. While I admire their dedication to keeping me safe, they have to know how unrealistic they're being. What power do they have to stand in the way of PHOENIX—or the State for that matter? Hell, I don't even think *I* have enough power for that.

"You say that, but, eventually, he's going to find out where we are, assuming he doesn't already know," I point out. "This place only has so many doors to hide behind. I don't know what you think this will do or how we'll get out of here undetected, but, I assure you, we won't. At the end of this, I'll be back in my cell and you two will be in there along with me."

They don't disagree with me because they know that I'm right. I can see it written plainly across both their faces, just like I can see that we're all thinking the same thing.

We're running out of time to decide what to do.

"When did you figure out Nolan was lying?"

I don't know why I ask. It isn't that important and we have other things to worry about. Still, I find myself needing to know that Ezra didn't allow his feelings for me to blind him to Nolan's obvious treachery.

He lowers his eyes to the floor. "The farmhouse. When you told me about the cure and your collar."

I remember the look on his face when I said it. That expression is printed onto my brain— confusion, grief, and anger all twisted together. It's an image I'll never escape.

"If I thought we had a chance of escaping then, I would've grabbed you and run," Ezra says. "But we didn't, we weren't prepared for it, and we couldn't leave without Jenner. Plus…I wanted to be sure. It's not like we have anywhere else to go, and with the State against us already, I wasn't in any hurry to add another enemy to that list. So, I confronted Nolan about it after we separated and told him what you said. He brushed me off, insisting the collar was a new method to track you, not that it was keeping you in control. He said you were trying to trick me." He glances at the metal ring around my neck as if the sight of it disgusts him. His eyes hang there for an uncomfortable second before turning away from it.

And me.

He shakes his head, his expression morose. "I knew you weren't lying about it. Why would you? Amnesia or no amnesia, that's not who you are. So, I asked myself, what would Nolan gain from withholding that information? What didn't he want me to know? Which then made me wonder why he really extracted you since it clearly wasn't as a favor to us, like he claimed."

Slumping back in the cushioned gray chair, Ezra blows out a loud breath through his nose. As I watch his face contort into a scowl, I remember his conversation with Nolan. One thing he said rings again in my ears.

"That wasn't part of the deal!"

My brow furrows as I peer down at my unmoving hands, the cogs in my head spinning. Then, it hits me. Ezra and Jenner made a deal with Nolan to intervene and steal me away from the State. Only, they didn't know he had his own plans or that he never intended to follow through with whatever empty promises he'd made to them. They were kept entirely in the dark.

But a deal is two-sided, which means they would've had to give Nolan something in return. Payment for my safe extraction. What could they have possibly offered him other than their loyalty, which they've now betrayed?

"The only logical answer was that extracting you would benefit PHOENIX somehow," Ezra continues. "I just didn't realize how until it was too late. Of course, after I confronted him, Nolan wouldn't let us anywhere near you again and, as further punishment, he stripped us both of surveillance access so we couldn't pull any more 'reckless stunts.'" His fingers curl into quotes, his tone a mocking imitation of Nolan's. "What we did…" His voice trails off into a timid whisper as he gestures vaguely around us. "It was the only idea we had. From what we saw and based on what we overheard the guards saying, Nolan was putting you through hell in that room, and it was killing us to be so close and know that, despite all our efforts to get you back, we might never actually see you again. We'd stopped trusting that Nolan had your best interests in mind and thought, maybe, if we got you alone again, you'd remember and we could all find a way to escape. Together."

My heart buckles at that word. *Together.* I'm so used to being alone that I struggle to comprehend what it even means.

As I glance between Ezra and Jenner, I only see good in them. The same sort of goodness I sensed in Rai. Nolan doesn't share that integrity. I knew from our first conversation that something was off about him, a feeling further compounded by the maniacal gleam in his eyes every time he spoke about my power. Based on what Ezra has told me, and what I've gleaned from our few encounters, it seems Nolan's even more like Dr. Richter than I previously gave him credit for.

Lining them up next to each other reminds me of something Nolan said to me about that night in Zone 1. The night Rai died.

That festering undercurrent of doubt returns, itching at the underside of my skin. My fingers grip the blanket, bunching the rough fabric again in my fists.

"Something Nolan said has been bothering me." I look first at Jenner, then at Ezra, building up the courage to speak. My gaze lingers on Ezra's face when I finally force out the words. "Why did you bring me with you that night?"

When neither of them answer, I narrow my eyes.

"I had no weapons training, and let's be realistic, I wasn't exactly in the best condition at the time. I would've been a hindrance more than a help. So, why was I there?" I ask again.

Ezra shakes his head. "Leaving you behind wasn't an option. That's all you need to know."

I frown at him, my fingers once again tightening around the coarse blanket. "That's not good enough. I want to know why—"

He slams his hand down on the arm of the chair. "Because I was afraid I'd never see you again!"

A memory surfaces at his outburst, and in it, I hear him answering the very same question I put before him now. Just like then, I detect the lie behind his words.

"Stop it," I growl. "I want the truth."

"That *is* the truth—"

"Not all of it. I know Nolan is the one who told you to go. I just wonder if you know why he had me go with you."

Ezra's eyes widen a fraction of an inch—enough to confirm he's hiding something.

"What is she talking about?" Jenner asks. His voice seems a million miles away, a dull hum on the edge of this conversation.

The confusion in Jenner's tone brings me relief because it means he doesn't know why I was there either that night. And if he doesn't know, then I can carry on trusting him, just as my hazy memories assure me I always have.

Can I say the same about Ezra? Or are we cursed to live in this repetitive cycle where we constantly omit the truth from each other?

With a deflated sigh, Ezra hunches over, planting his elbows on his knees and rubbing his hands across his face. His fingers press into the skin under his eyes as if trying to rub away the dark smudges there.

I didn't notice it before—how tired he looks. The same bags hang under Jenner's glazed eyes, and I wonder when they last slept or did anything that didn't involve trying to rescue me.

Their unyielding devotion bothers me. Why are they going to so much trouble for someone who barely remembers them? Don't they realize the position they're putting themselves in? Don't they care that helping me could get them both killed?

At that thought, the familiar hand of guilt grips my throat a bit tighter.

Ezra meets my gaze through his fingers. "Taking you with us was better than the alternative."

"Which was what?"

He shrugs as a small, pleading breath parts his lips. "You have to understand how things were. People were frustrated and angry. Fed up. They felt like the life of escape we'd promised them was flimsy and could collapse at any moment, and as a result, many had grown jaded with our way of life. The aid we were receiving from benefactors was becoming less frequent because of the State finding new ways to weed out our supporters. Everything was reaching its breaking point, and we weren't sure how much longer we could sustain the rebellion. Even the Heads of the different sects were growing tired of just sitting around, waiting for something to happen.

"Then, we got the transmission from Bilken, and it seemed like an opportunity had finally fallen into our laps. The offer he was extending… It was our only hope to salvage what was crumbling around us."

His words set yet another recollection free from the cage holding my buried memories. In my head, I glimpse the compound where I met Jenner and Rai, and in the corridors, I see the people who lived there. Their faces all blur into the same terrified mask.

Their hysteria when they found out why I was there echoes deep in my thoughts, and once again, I hear the way some of them called for me to be used against the State just like PHOENIX plans on using me now.

But then, the people of that sect welcomed me into their home just because

Ezra asked them to. Because they trusted him, possibly more than they trusted the real person in charge behind the scenes.

A weathered face pops into my head, showing me a man I saw in the crowd when Ezra made his speech asking everyone to accept me. That middle-aged man, the one who questioned Ezra—

Was Nolan, I realize.

Ezra's voice drags me back to the present.

"When you arrived, there was a general feeling of apprehension because of your ties to the DSD. Then, during that week you spent in a coma, there was speculation linking you to the transmission from Bilken, which made tensions about your presence there worse. Knowing that, how would it have looked if we went on that mission and never came back? Our disappearance... Our presumed deaths... They would've been pinned on you. The people would've wanted someone to blame for the loss, and it would've been *you.*" This last word escapes his lips in a snarl, and he flinches, tearing his gaze from mine. "Fear can do terrifying things to people. It can *make* them do terrible things, even those who don't seem capable of it. Leaving you behind would've been like abandoning a lamb in a hungry lion's den. It wouldn't have ended well."

As I consider Ezra's words, I try to put myself in his shoes. Even without all my memories, I feel like I must've sensed that the PHOENIX members I encountered then didn't trust me. Of course, they would have suspected I was involved if anything happened to Ezra or the others who went on that mission. .

Looking at it that way, I guess he really didn't have any other choice.

As I mull over that angle, I think of Rai—of her death—and wonder if they all blamed me for it. Maybe Ezra and Jenner do, too. I wouldn't hold it against them. After all, what happened that night could've been prevented. If I hadn't been there, Richter wouldn't have either. Despite his past with Rai, he was there for me, for his precious weapon. Revenge was always secondary.

I can't help thinking, if Ezra had just left me behind, maybe Rai wouldn't have dead.

If they had left me behind, I wouldn't have had to go back to the DSD.

"So, you were willing to hand me over to your twisted brother because of some warped idea I'd be safer with him than with PHOENIX?" I press.

Jenner waves a hand to get my attention. "Okay, now I'm really confused—"
Ezra cuts him off. "What are you talking about?"

"That was the plan, Nolan told me himself. He said I did you all a favor by going back to the DSD. If I hadn't, the State wouldn't have gained so much power. If I hadn't, they wouldn't have so much to lose. If I hadn't—"

"You would be dead."

I glance over at Jenner where he sits by the door. It's the first time I've really looked at him since we locked ourselves in this tiny room, and now, it occurs to me why I've been avoiding his gaze. Every emotion, every thought, behind those blue eyes is like a raging fire against my skin. Even the slightest look from him seems to burn me.

He's right. If I hadn't gone that night, I would've never returned to the DSD. Then, Dr. Richter wouldn't have given me the tool needed to control my power. Without control, this disease would've killed me.

Without the collar, I would be dead.

Maybe I should be, I muse.

"Tell me it isn't true," I whisper, my voice thick. "Tell me that isn't why you brought me with you."

Ezra grimaces. "When we received the transmission from Bilken, Nolan spent three days in his office listening to it on repeat. When he finally emerged, he bombarded me with questions about you, then insisted you were putting us all in danger by being there and that we'd only be safe if we sent you away. He kept repeating that we were in over our heads and that we couldn't afford being on the DSD's radar. Then, he told me that if we took you on that mission, we'd meet someone who could protect you far better than we could, someone who was equipped to actually handle your illness. All he said was it was a connection through Bilken. He certainly never mentioned Richter or I wouldn't have taken you anywhere near that place."

My frown deepens. *Speculation, huh?*

If my name was stated in the transmission from Bilken, then it's no wonder everyone there was afraid of me. I wouldn't have trusted me either.

"You heard this message?" I ask.

He shakes his head. "No one heard the full thing except Nolan, and he only told me what I needed to know for the mission. But people overhear things, and rumors spread quickly, especially in confined communities. As Head of our sect, he made the final call about what to do about the transmission, and none of us were in a position of authority to question him. At the end of the day, we were nothing more than disposable foot soldiers for PHOENIX. We had to do what we were told or risk getting kicked out on our asses, which...in a rebellion with so many people and highly sensitive information, like the whereabouts of all PHOENIX's hideouts, *really* means getting locked up until you either remember your loyalties or cave to having a cyanide tab shoved down your throat. Why do you think the State never broadcasts the executions of any PHOENIX members it apprehends? As soon as we're backed into a corner, we end it, so there's nothing left to execute. That's the trade-off with being allowed out on missions."

A shudder rips up my spine at his words. If he notices my discomfort, he doesn't comment.

"But that doesn't mean I took you along with the intention of just handing you over to some random stranger, no questions asked," he says. "That outcome was more of a…worst case scenario. If it looked like we weren't going to make it out of there alive, I took comfort in knowing you might have. I know it seems insane, but I figured, even if the mission did turn out to be a trap, you would survive because the DSD was so hell-bent on getting you back in one piece. And if it wasn't a trap… Well, maybe we would've met someone who had the means to make you better. That was all I cared about. Finding a way to ensure your survival."

"Why?" I breathe. "Why was I so important to you?"

"I—" He hesitates, his glistening eyes threatening tears. Clearing his throat, he chokes out, "I was worried."

"About what?"

"Your…condition. I couldn't be there for my mother when she needed me, but I promised myself I would be there for you. That I would protect you."

His mother?

What does my illness have to do with his mother?

I sense another memory poking at the edges of my thoughts, but it never forms a coherent shape, frustrating me even further. There's something I'm not remembering.

Something important.

"I refused to fail you like I had failed her, no matter the cost to myself or to anyone else. I've spent the last two and a half years attempting to keep that promise. I've said and done what I had to."

If Ezra was linking what was happening to me to his mother, that must mean she had Ultraxenopia. From the rest of his statement, I gather she died, or he wouldn't have gone to such lengths to ensure my survival.

Regardless of his intentions, the rest of what he's said has me on edge. What else has he lied about? What else has he done out of some deluded misconception that his dishonesty would somehow keep me safe?

"You said and did what you had to… What is that supposed to mean?" My heart races in anticipation, dreading his answer.

Jenner snorts. "It means he told Nolan he's in love with you, thinking it would convince the old coot to help get you back."

Ezra's skin flushes a deep shade of scarlet, but despite the vibrancy of color in his complexion, he looks more exhausted and demoralized than I've ever seen him.

I don't know why he'd be embarrassed to hear these words voiced. This isn't the first time it's been made clear that he loves me. He all but told me himself when he last sprung me free of my cell and took me topside.

Unless…those words he whispered to me were just a continuation of some fabricated sob story he fed Nolan. A way to tie up loose ends and ensure the lie played out in my favor.

I think back to our kiss on the farmhouse porch, my lips tingling at the memory. Could a kiss like that not have emotion behind it? I could swear I felt it, but then again, maybe I was only sensing my own repressed feelings. If Ezra was playing a part, the role of my savior out of some sense of duty and debt to his mother, he did it convincingly.

Even I was fooled.

Ezra sighs. "And we were both stupid enough to think it actually worked."

Silence engulfs the room yet again. Ezra avoids my gaze now more than ever, stoking the fires of agitation writhing under my skin. As the sensation spreads, it occurs to me that the crimson tint to his cheeks isn't from embarrassment at all but from shame. And not because of what Jenner said, but because he allowed himself to believe such frivolous feelings, real or not, would've ever made a difference. Nolan doesn't give a damn how Ezra feels, and he certainly didn't extract me because of it. Despite what he might've told them at the time, Nolan only went ahead with my rescue because it suited PHOENIX and played to their plans.

Like I've known from the moment I woke up in this place, I'm only here to turn the odds of this war in someone else's favor.

I chew on my lower lip, sorting back through everything Ezra and Jenner have divulged. If I had known any of this information back when I left them, would things be different now?

Or was the situation always futile?

"Why didn't you just tell me all this at the time? If you had, maybe—"

"You wouldn't have left?" Ezra stares down at his fidgeting hands, his brow puckered and expression pinched. His fingers clutch the hem of his shirt, picking at the fabric. "I did tell you some of it. You just don't remember. The rest of it… Even if I had told you, it wouldn't have mattered. We all know you would've died if you'd stayed."

Except, that wasn't why I left. I didn't care about my life; I cared about Ezra's and Jenner's. I was determined to keep them alive, especially after just losing

Rai. And the only way to do that was to go. Hell, considering what's transpired since, it's clear I should've left even sooner than I did. I should've cut off any attachment between us before it had the chance to form.

I rest my skull back against the wall and turn my eyes upward, looking at the ceiling. A few hairline cracks run through the concrete, spreading out in several directions and intersecting, like the threads of a spider's web. It reminds me of what this power can do.

And also reminds me why I left.

I suck in a breath as a vision strikes without warning, a landscape of destruction unfurling before my eyes, as clear as it was the very first time—when I thought I was having a panic attack during my exam at W. P. Headquarters.

My hand quakes as my fingertips skim the edge of my collar. I never thought I would be relieved to have this tether to Richter, but now that I remember what I sacrificed my humanity for, what I wanted to protect—now that I remember what will happen if I lose control—I realize how important it is that I never take it off.

Even if it turns out Dr. Richter can manipulate me remotely, this collar is the only tool I have to protect Ezra and Jenner and everyone else on this planet from me and the vision I keep seeing. So long as it stays in place, the monster inside me will remain locked in its cage unless I choose to set it free. It might rattle and claw at the bars, but it won't get out.

And that future won't come to pass.

A shudder runs over my skin as I drop my head and fix my eyes on Ezra. "What if I hadn't woken up from that coma? What would you have done?"

"I...really don't know," he admits. "I try not to think about it."

I decide not to press the matter. From his tone, I'm not sure I want to know the answer. Something tells me Nolan probably had a plan in the event of that, too. With my luck, that plan probably involved a pillow smothering my comatose face.

Shivering at that mental image, I quickly change the subject. "So...what do we do now? You guys made the first move, so what's the rest of the plan?"

Jenner leans forward, perching his elbows on his bent knees. "I broke into the surveillance room—gotta love these pre-State bunkers. No ID pads or anything, only old rusty doors." Ezra shoots him a look, and he clears his throat, getting back on track. "Anyway, I looped the corridor footage and locked the system to buy us some time, like Rai taught me to, but we don't have very long. A handful of hours, at most. The thing is, even if we do somehow get past Nolan's security, there's really nowhere for us to go. We can't very well just stroll into the Heart. Not without the tunnels, which means—"

"We need PHOENIX," Ezra finishes.

Jenner lets out a humorless laugh. "Given our current predicament, I highly doubt anyone here would be willing to help us. And even if they did, who the hell in the Heart is going to take us in? We're all alone, man."

I nod in agreement. PHOENIX is as bad as the State in at least one regard. Neither can be trusted, which means we're alone in this war. Three against too many to count.

Enemies here. Enemies there. Enemies on all sides, closing in. And, if the events of my life up to this point are any indication…

The worst is far from over.

SEVENTEEN

WHEN I DREAM OF MY childhood, my father is alive and happy. Except for when I dream of his death. Now, I realize that happiness was just a disguise. In reality, he was as good at fooling me as my mother was at making me believe I was safe. Her betrayal still stings, serving as a bitter reminder of everything I've lost.

And everything I may yet still lose.

Having that vision of my father—watching him chronicle the State's rise to power—has brought the pain of his death that much closer to the surface, as if I'm living through it a second time. Regardless of how much time passes, the weight of my grief never seems to get any lighter.

Or maybe my grief only lingers because of my masochistic need to keep him close. Maybe that's why he's here with me now in this deluded dreamscape— half fairytale and half distant memory—where I can pretend some version of him is alive.

We sit together in the reception room of my first house, the home we shared before his death. Before Mother and I were forced to relocate. When I glance at him, he smiles and wraps an arm around my shoulders, pulling me in for a hug.

I press my face into his chest, even though I can't feel him. Even though this moment never actually happened. Because the me in this dream is the version of me as I am now—a twenty-year-old woman. And my father... He died when I was a child. If he saw me now, I doubt he'd even recognize me.

And yet, as we embrace in the dream, I know that, despite how much he was forced to give up, he never resented me for it. He loved me.

At least, I had that.

At least, that was real.

I close my eyes and breathe in deeply, hoping the action will trigger a memory and I'll catch a trace of what he smelled like. To my disappointment, all I can recall is the musty smell of the place he used to take me on our "secret missions." As it floods my nose, my eyes drift open, but we aren't in the tunnels like I expected we would be. We're still in our home, except, now, I see my father the way I always see him. Bloodied. Beaten. Reaching for me.

Always reaching for me.

When his lips shape my name—the word a faint breath on the tip of his tongue—I realize what it is he's really trying to say. I hear the farewell he's too afraid to whisper as it permeates the silence between us.

The crack of a gunshot makes me jump, and I whip around only to find nothing behind me. When I turn back toward my father, he's gone, and in his place, Rai emerges as if from thin air, manifesting from the depths of my pain. She smiles at me with love in her gaze, and this time, I find that *I'm* the one reaching out.

Tears fill my eyes as I grasp for her ghost.

I choke on a sob when my fingers pass through her hand, then, suddenly, I'm alone in a dark, wide hallway, standing in a puddle of blood. This blood, this symbol of her death…

It's the only thing I see.

"Wynter."

I spin on my heel again, drawn to the distant voice calling my name. Jenner locks eyes with me across the familiar landscape of ruin taking shape around me, but there's something odd about his expression, as if he's neither dead or alive, half-connected to this crumbling world.

My lips wobble, a lump of tears blocking my throat, as I stumble toward him one terrified step at a time. As I draw closer, Jenner's skin seems to lighten in shade, growing increasingly pallid and sickly. When it seems like he can't possibly get paler, he looks down, gaping at his chest. I falter, swallowing loudly, before forcing myself to follow his stricken gaze, my heartbeat hammering in my ears.

Each beat only makes me more aware of my fear.

That's when I see it—the crimson stain spreading over his shirt. It creeps outward, stretching across every untouched inch of skin until his whole chest is consumed.

I recoil as a swell of pressure buzzes under my skin, pushing at the inside of my body. As it claws to the surface, taking control of my senses, it dawns on me that I'm the one doing this.

Me. My power.

I'm the one killing him.

My legs buckle, and I drop to my knees, but I don't feel the dirt or the ground as it rises to meet me. I feel nothing except the pain squeezing my heart.

Clamping my eyes shut, I cover my ears, pressing my hands against the sides of my head.

With a shaking breath, I beg myself to wake up.

"I won't—"

My eyes snap open at the strained timbre, locking onto a familiar face. As I knew he would be, Ezra stands just a few feet away, a single tear drawing a line down his cheek.

When I glance down at the gun clasped in his hand, his fingers go slack and it falls from his grasp, colliding hard with the dirt. A small brown cloud kicks up around his feet as he whispers those three tormenting words that have followed me for years.

"I'm sorry, Wynter."

I wake with a start, bolting upright. Disorientation sweeps over my senses for a moment but clears when I realize where I am. The bare walls of the room Ezra and Jenner whisked me away to seem to close in all around on me.

Sweat pools inside my bodysuit, suctioning the material to my overheated flesh like another layer of skin. The nylon clings to my chest when I tug at the neckline, heightening my growing anxiety. Even counting backward from ten does little to steady my shaken nerves.

Static images from my dream replay through my thoughts, once again assaulting me with the vision that's plagued my life from the moment this disease first reared its ugly head. Aside from my parents, the vision of the destruction I am destined to cause is the only certain thing I remember from before I became this way. Everything else I've seen recently has been distant, as if the memories belong to someone else and I'm just viewing those moments through their eyes. The only exception is Rai.

The pain in my heart when I think of her is as visceral and raw as it was the day she died. What I'm feeling… What I remember… It has to be the full extent of what's in me. If it isn't, if this is the damped down version of that grief, then I don't want those memories back.

Nothing can be worse than this pain.

Even Ezra and Jenner, who I can feel in the deepest depths of my heart that I care for, are like shadows at the edge of my existence. The memories of them never seem to form enough of a shape for me to understand just how much they mean to me.

I peek at Ezra out of the corner of my eye, and a strange sensation twists my stomach at the sight of him curled in the chair beside the bed, his long lashes kissing his cheeks and soft breathes breaching his lips as he sleeps. When I look at him, is it love that consumes me?

Or guilt for allowing myself to forget him?

I run a shaking hand through my hair, but the damp, knotted strands, slick with the grease of several days spent unwashed, tangle around my fingers. Dropping my arm, I press my back to the wall and dig the heels of my hands into my eyes.

In the darkness of my thoughts, I ask myself why I'm suddenly seeing this vision again. Distorted memories of it have bombarded me for months, but nothing as clear and distinct as this dream. Why now? Does this mean we're no longer safe from that path?

Isn't the collar preventing that future?

"What is it?"

I glance at Ezra when he repositions himself in the chair, sitting upright. He stares at me, eyes sleep-soaked but alert.

As he waits for my answer, I can't ignore how reminiscent his expression is of the way he looked at me in my dream.

The way he *will* look at me at the end of all things.

Glancing away, I grumble, "Nothing. I'm fine."

"Wynter."

The mattress creaks as he shifts onto the bed. He's sitting near enough to me now that the heat radiating from his skin is sinking into my bodysuit, tempting me closer. Part of me wants to bridge the space between us and let that heat wash over me. Another part is terrified of what I'll do if that happens.

"I know that look," he murmurs. "Please."

I swallow loudly, hesitating. How do I explain to him what this feels like? The memories I'm trying so hard to regain are like drops of water seeping through cracks in a glass. I'm unable to hold onto anything because it all slips through my fingers before I can touch it.

I shake my head. "It was only a dream."

He can probably tell I'm lying, but what else can I say? I left him once to try to change things—to spare him from the future I'm going to cause. Now, I'm not sure if I'm even capable of anything other than what the State used me for.

Death.

Destruction...

Maybe that's all I'll ever bring to this world.

Can the future even be changed? Or did the actions I took years ago only lead us closer to the outcome I had hoped to avoid? Perhaps that vision is doomed to happen either way. If that's the case, then it was always inevitable that Ezra and I would find our way back to each other.

I take little comfort in that thought. Because, when the time comes, in our final moments together before my power tears into the earth, I'll finally discover why he's sorry.

And the truth is I'm not sure I want to know.

"What time is it?" I ask, determined to direct my thoughts elsewhere.

Ezra peers down at the black watch on his wrist. "We've been asleep for nearly an hour, which means we only have a few hours left until daybreak. We should make a move soon. We don't want to linger here too long."

I skirt my gaze over the barren gray walls. Day and night seem lost in this place, held hostage by the fluorescent lights overhead. We're trapped in a strange cycle of timelessness with each day melting into the next, all time converging into a single unending moment with no interludes to break it apart.

Just like the DSD.

As my eyes sweep past the door, I pause and do a quick double take of the now empty space on the floor where Jenner sat before.

"Where's Jenner?" Trepidation weighs in my gut like a boulder as I snap my panicked gaze back to Ezra.

He crosses his arms defensively, as if anticipating my reaction. "He's trying to make contact with the few friends we still trust to see if any of them will help us once we escape. Our options are limited, but I'm not giving up and neither is he. We'll find a way out of this together."

I grimace. Every word out of Ezra's mouth only makes it that much more apparent that they're putting themselves on the wrong side of history by teaming up with me. Years from now, when people look back on this war—assuming I don't kill us all first—it won't be the power struggle between PHOENIX and the State they remember, it will be the weapon at the center of the chaos. The weapon responsible for so much bloodshed. And when the people ask each other, *Which side were you on?*, they won't care who was in PHOENIX or who was loyal to the State. They'll care who stood on the side of humanity and who took the side of the monster.

By choosing me, Ezra and Jenner will turn the entire world against them, and there's nothing I can do to stop it.

"You're putting yourselves at risk by helping me. You understand that, right?"

To my surprise, Ezra meets my gaze with a smile.

"We'll do whatever it takes to protect you, even if you think you don't need it. Because that's what friends do. We look out for each other. And we're your friends, Wynter."

Friends... Warmth engulfs my chest, but, behind it, his tone threatens to unravel my nerves. Whatever it takes?

Just how far are they willing to go?

"You were right about one thing, though," he says. "We do need to be more careful. A lot of our decisions since your extraction have been made on a whim and were led by emotion more than by logic. Moving forward, we need to be more strategic."

"Why do you think Nolan hasn't come after me yet?" Surely, he must know by now that Ezra and Jenner have broken me out of my cell. Again.

Quinn would've made sure of that.

The more I think about it, the more I suspect that Nolan had to have known this would happen. From what I can see, Ezra and Jenner haven't been that involved with what's going on in this place—or the larger plan PHOENIX is working toward. So, why bother to keep them around if they're only going to get in the way of his plan?

What could they have possibly offered him that would be worth all this trouble?

Ezra runs a hand across the back of his neck, frowning at some unspoken thought. I can't help noticing that he keeps doing this around me, like a tick triggered by my presence.

"I don't know," he mutters after a moment. "A dozen scenarios keep floating around in my head, and I'm trying my best to ignore them all. I'm hoping we won't be here long enough to find out. As it stands, we won't know anything until we hear back from Jenner. Hopefully he was able to make contact with Duke."

The name rings a bell. "Why couldn't he just call this Duke person from here?" Why leave us?

Ezra taps a fingertip on the wall. "No reception. Our communicators won't work down here because of all the conductive material that was used to build this place. Any incoming and outgoing calls have to be received and made from a room called The Pit, which has the equipment needed to boost the signal. But access to it is limited. I guess Nolan was worried one of the defectors might turn on PHOENIX and give our location away to the State."

As the silence returns, building between us again, I consider using my power to find out what the future holds, even though I'm not quite sure what to look for. Fear inevitably holds me back. I don't know if I can handle that vision again. Having to face that destruction, that death, and know I'm the one responsible for it?

I can't bear the guilt any longer.

"Are you hungry?" Ezra asks, nudging me gently with his shoulder. For a few precious seconds, I'm distracted from the very real horrors awaiting us.

I force a careful smile onto my lips. Considering PHOENIX has made it a point not to feed me, I suppose I should feel hungrier than I actually am. With everything going on, I'm finding it hard to have much of an appetite, even if the effects of hunger are wearing me down.

"I guess," I mutter, scratching at my State-issued bodysuit. "More than anything, I could really go for a shower."

He smirks, pinching his nose. "Yeah, you need it."

I elbow him hard in the ribs, and he chuckles, jumping up from the mattress. Turning, he offers me his hand, and as my skin grazes his, an electric current shoots into my fingers and carries through the rest of my body again. I gasp when he tugs, pulling me off the bed.

Once I'm standing, I expect him to let go of me, but he holds on as if we're floating in water and I'm the one thing in the world that can stop him from drowning. I can't help clinging back.

Touching him brings the memories just a little bit closer.

We cross the room side by side, connected at all times by our intertwined fingers. Ezra's grip on me only relaxes when we approach the door and he signals for me to hang back, putting himself in the path of any potential threat waiting outside. Drawing in a breath, he pulls open the door and pokes his head out into the corridor, checking both directions several times. When he's satisfied that no one is coming, he nods and takes my hand again before finally leading me into the hallway.

We progress slowly, not daring to utter a word, always keeping a watchful eye on our surroundings. As we walk, I watch him closely, taking mental notes of every movement. The way his chest rises and falls with each breath. The way his muscles strain at the slightest noise. The way his hand constricts around mine every once in a while as if checking to ensure I'm still there.

The familiarity goading my senses also pulls at my heart, begging me to remember him and whatever it was we once shared. So, why can't I? For someone with my power, regaining my memories should be easy.

I recount my time at the DSD. Even then, I knew something wasn't right with my brain—that I was forgetting something important, maybe even on purpose. I've wondered countless times if I had chosen to forget what it was out of sheer will, as a means to protect it. As much as I hope that's true and that those memories can be restored, I can't help fearing my stint as a weapon wiped away my humanity to the point where those moments disappeared along with it.

No, I insist, reminding myself of the recollections that have surfaced since Ezra and Jenner came back into my life. Like the memory of Rai. Of the night she died. But while certain remnants have returned, the majority remain broken into such tiny pieces I struggle to make sense of the partial picture they show me or how I fit into the muted shades of a past I can't remember. All I can see are splintered shapes and faces I barely recognize.

Resolve burns through me, hot and fierce, and although I'm wary of what pain might come with it, I know it's time to figure out how to unearth the lost pieces and put them back together so I can remember. Not only Ezra and Jenner, but myself. Who I was before I made the decision to leave them.

Ezra tugs at my hand, guiding me through a heavy metal door, which swings shut again behind us. I blink away my daze to find myself standing at the threshold of a washroom.

"Wait here," he whispers.

Unlatching his fingers from mine, he flits around the room, checking each shower cubicle and stall. Less than a minutes passes before he's back by my side.

"It's all-clear. The corridor footage will still be looped for a while, since it's impossible to do anything until the system unlocks, so you should be okay to wash up. I don't think anyone knows we're here, but don't take too long, just in case. I'll be keeping watch outside if you need me."

I nod but say nothing, glancing down at the colorless tiled floor under my feet. My selfish need for cleanliness seems ill-advised considering Nolan could show up at any moment. And yet, I can't ignore the temptation of the showers.

As Ezra retreats back into the hallway, I pad toward the nearest cubicle on autopilot. Reaching for the handle, I grip it and turn, watching with eager delight as a violent burst of water springs forth from the nozzle.

Steam fills the air, forming a foggy layer of condensation on the concrete walls and steel barriers separating one cubicle from the next. The warmth licks over me as I remove my boots and clothes, the dried sweat making the black bodysuit stick to me coaxing a shiver to roll over my skin. Peeling the fabric off, I let it fall to the floor.

Breathing in, I step beneath the piping hot water, and as the drops slide over my skin, each one reminds me of something I've learned or uncovered since arriving at this place. The connection between Nolan and my father. The truth about Bilken. About PHOENIX. My role as an instrument of war, tossed back and forth between two opposing sides.

Rai.

My friendship with Jenner.

Ezra…

Knowing that, one day soon, I could very well end the world and kill everyone in it.

"Why bring me back if you know what I am?"

I had asked Ezra this just before he kissed me when we were on the porch together staring out at the Heart. The recollection of his answer echoes again in my ears.

"For the same reason you keep seeing me in your head."

The bits and pieces I've seen of him re-emerge, and I relive every moment—I *feel* every moment—even the ones I can't remember. How could I love someone but have no memory of them? How could I have no memory of them and still know it's the truth when they say that I love them?

Why else would I have stayed with Dr. Richter if I wasn't protecting something precious to me? What other explanation is there for why I became a willing puppet to the State unless I was harboring feelings for Ezra? I loved him and I want to remember what we had, however small it might have been.

The pipes squeal as my fingers rotate the handle, slowing the spray of water to a steady drip. Leaving my bodysuit and boots abandoned on the wet floor, I veer toward the wall lined with mirrors and sinks on the opposite side of the room. Breathing in, I turn to face my reflection.

The woman staring out from the glass looks like me, but all I see in her mismatched gaze is a stranger. As my eyes trail over her features, I imagine another version of myself. Different, less hardened to our world, but familiar.

And as I picture her in my head, I realize what I have to do.

I concentrate on the next mirror over, biting my lip as it explodes into pieces. The fragments scatter across the sinks and fall to the floor like a downpour of hail.

Stepping back, I look down at a shard by my feet, and bending to pluck it up, I graze my fingers along the knife-like edges.

"Wynter?" an anxious voice calls from behind me.

Straightening, I look over my shoulder, meeting Ezra's startled gaze. The column of his throat shifts nervously as he flicks his eyes along my naked body, their journey ending at the glass piece in my hand.

My grasp is steady when I raise the shard, balancing the tip dangerously close to my throat. His pupils blow wide, and he thrusts a hand out to stop me, his gasp a tinny echo around me.

A smile forms on my lips as I tighten my grip, and exhaling, I whisper the one truth I know with absolute certainty.

"I want to remember."

EIGHTEEN

"WAIT!"

Ezra's panic-filled plea strikes my eardrums as I sweep the shard within an inch of my shoulder. My free hand bundles my long, sodden hair, holding it steady and taut as I move the glass back and forth, using it as a saw. The sharp edge cuts through the strands with ease.

When my fingers slacken after a few moments, dropping the large chunk of hair to the floor, a heavy weight seems to lift off my shoulders. I spin on my heel and glance at my reflection, pinning my gaze on the shortened locks. The ends sit just below my collar.

I study my features. My ashy brunette hair. My eyes—one green, one blue—the defining feature of this disease. Whereas before, the woman in the glass was a stranger, now, she looks familiar. This version of me…

This is what I used to look like.

I blink, drawing in a sharp breath at the abrupt shift to my senses. When I open my eyes again, I find myself standing before a set of silver elevator doors.

The elevator at W. P. Headquarters.

I press my fingertips to the face of my distorted reflection, the steel icy-cold to the touch. Upon contact, ripples spread outward from under my hand as if the doors are made of water.

The vision warps, the walls of the elevator changing, taking the shape of my cell at the DSD. As I turn in place, I realize I recognize this moment from back when I was first taken, following my exam. Broken glass covers the floor by my feet.

I glance down to see my face reflected dozens of times in the fragments, although the eyes looking out from the mirrored surface are black.

"The eyes of a monster," I murmur under my breath.

The air catches in my lungs as my surroundings go black, as if a shadow has cast its veil over the world. I can't see anything. I can't hear a sound past the silence. My senses are all impaired, except for my nose, which locks onto the distinct metallic odor of blood.

Gradually, the darkness eases, revealing thousands of small mirrors looming on all sides, tiled in rows from floor to ceiling along one continuous rounded wall in a space I immediately register as one of the rooms in Bilken's office. My face stares back at me in each tiny mirror.

Face, after face, after face…

A swelling sensation pushes at the inside of my body, and the pressure twists my stomach into knots until I think I might vomit. Although I try to fight it, I can't hold it back and the pressure rushes out of me like a shock wave, bursting the mirrored wall into pieces. Time seems to slow as the shards descend, and I see the monster—I see myself—in the glass fragments falling around me like rain.

Face…after face…after face…

An inhuman cry rips from my lungs, and heaving, I blink again to clear the vision from my eyes, desperate for reality. Desperate to escape the assault of my memories all rushing back to the surface at once. As I breathe in, the washroom slides back into focus.

Goosebumps pimple my naked body, and for a few moments, I don't dare to move a muscle or breathe. My dark tresses lie on the floor by my feet, tickling my toes and ankles. Kicking them away, I peer back up at my reflection.

The stranger is gone; in the mirror, I see only me. The me I used to be. The me I pushed deep beneath the facade of a monster. The me I still am.

I just had to reach out and find her again.

A worried face appears in the mirror just behind my right shoulder. When our eyes meet, a startled gasp tears from my lips.

"Ezra."

Whipping around, I press a hand to my mouth to hold back a sob. Tears spill from my eyes, running down my cheeks, but I don't wipe them away. I bask in the influx of emotions devouring me, rejoicing, because this pain is mine.

And I *remember* it.

My racing heartbeat reverberates behind every breath as I rush forward, closing the distance between us. Ezra seems so far away, and I can't help fearing this is only a dream—that his presence is just another fabrication of my brain intended to torment me. Maybe I'll never reach him at all.

He grunts when my body slams into his, the delicious heat of his skin scorching across my exposed torso, giving me hope this is actually happening. If it's not, if this is just a dream, then I'd rather never wake up again.

I burrow my face into his chest, hugging him as tightly as possible. To my dismay, he doesn't hug me back—maybe because he's afraid. Afraid to believe. Afraid to hope.

Afraid, just like I am, that this isn't real.

With a stilted breath, he presses his hands to the small of my back, pulling me closer. "Do you…remember?"

His words are a delicate, tentative tremor in my ear, ringing of apprehension. The same fear poisons my own head and heart.

I reposition my arms around his neck and snake my fingers through his unkempt hair, taking a moment to breathe the smell of him in and brand our reunion into my memory. His pulse pounds erratically, throbbing against my skin at each point of contact between his body and mine. Every beat coincides with the pace of my breaths.

"Yes." A smile forms at the edges of my lips. "I remember everything."

His arms tighten around my waist, and I cling to him, gripping his shirt with my fingers, as all the emotions I suppressed return at once to consume me.

"I'm sorry," I manage through a wave of fresh tears.

What he must've felt when I left him and, later, when he saw what the State had turned me into… What he must've felt when I came back and didn't remember who he was…

If only I could muster the words to tell him why his suffering was necessary. That I chose to abandon my memories, not because of the longing they stirred in my chest but because I was afraid he and Jenner would be in constant danger if I didn't let them go. With how I was treated at the DSD, sucked of intel on a daily basis, I couldn't hide anything from Dr. Richter. If either of them ever became a target of the State or if Richter ever thought he could've used them against me to ensure my compliance, I would have been helpless to protect them.

Just like I was helpless to save Rai.

Shutting out my past was the only way to guarantee their safety and keep them off the State's radar. And it was my coping mechanism for dealing with the guilt and pain of knowing I'd never see them again.

In the two plus years I was captive at the DSD, Dr. Richter messed with my brain so frequently that blocking out certain things, like emotions and memories, became second nature. A means to an end. With all the experimentation and torture I was subjected to, choosing to forget was how I survived.

And yet, no matter how I try to justify it, no matter how many times I tell myself I did what I had to do to protect him and Jenner, I can't escape the impact of my actions.

I've hurt him, and I'll never be able to forgive myself for it.

"I'm sorry," I whisper again.

Ezra unhooks his arms from my waist and steps back, cupping my face in his hands. With a gentle nudge, he lifts my chin, urging me to look at him. When our eyes meet, he shakes his head and smiles.

Another cry expands in my lungs as he hugs me, and as I shudder against his chest, my hands trail up and down his back, reacquainting themselves with the contours of his body. A blush heats my face as I recall the details of the one night we spent together. The way he kissed me. The way it felt to be that close to another person, especially someone I cared about.

Someone I now realize I loved.

I'm overcome with the urge to experience that closeness again, and I peek up at him through wet lashes, a pleading breath filling the space between us.

"Kiss me."

He answers my demand by slanting his lips over mine, his fingers dancing over my hip bones as he kisses me with a ravenous hunger. My nerve endings spring to life at his touch, igniting a spark that blazes through my veins and settles in the pit of my stomach, setting me on fire from the inside.

After being numb for so long, I can barely handle the sensation. But I need to feel more.

I need to be reminded of who I was before.

Clutching his shirt, I amble backward, dragging him with me toward the showers. A silent question floods his eyes, but I deepen the kiss, refusing to break the connection between us. Luckily, he doesn't seem to want me to.

My feet brush against my discarded bodysuit as we stumble into the shower cubicle I washed in only minutes before. Kicking it aside, I fumble for the handle, grinning against his lips when the water sprays down on us.

Ezra reels back and sucks in a startled breath, his expression uncertain, as if he's concerned we're moving too quickly. I take his face between my hands, urging his hazel eyes to focus on mine.

"I need to feel human," I try to explain.

Water runs across my exposed skin, drawing his gaze down to my naked body. I lean in, bringing my mouth close to his.

"Please," I beg.

When my breath touches his lips, he plants a hand against my lower back and pulls me toward him again. This time, he kisses with slow deliberation, as if he's painting a mental picture and memorizing every detail of my mouth.

My legs weaken when he moves his lips to my neck and shoulders, trailing kisses over my shivering skin, taking care to avoid the metal ring around my throat.

A thought occurs to me, and my hands slide from his back to his chest, gently pushing him away.

Ezra's hands freeze against my waist as he frowns. "What's wrong?"

"True or false. You love me." I bite my lower lip, hating how timid I sound. How starved for some assurance of his affection.

Cupping my face in his hands again, he pulls me in for another kiss. He starts at my forehead, then kisses me once on each cheek, before ending at my lips.

"True," he whispers into my mouth.

Our movements become frantic after that. My fingers work to remove his soaked clothes, while his hands explore my body and tangle in my hair, tugging my head back for better access to my throat. His teeth skim my collarbone as his voice hums against my skin and three beautiful words rise up to my ear in his low, haunting timbre.

"I missed you."

We pause for a moment just to stare at each other. Then, not wanting to waste another second on words, we lose ourselves under the water.

NINETEEN

THE BACK OF EZRA'S HAND brushes along my spine as he zips me back into the damp bodysuit. I clench my jaw when the material suctions to my skin, wishing I had an alternative to this suffocating reminder of my time as Dr. Richter's slave. My nails pinch the fabric to ease the tightness around my chest, but it refuses to give. If anything, the bodysuit only seems to get tighter.

Ezra's breath is warm on my neck as he plants a kiss just behind my right ear. It seems so natural having him this close, and I've never felt more alive or human than I have the two times we've stripped bare and given ourselves to each other. Heat flushes my cheeks at the thought of our entangled bodies. Of his mouth on my mouth. Of his hands touching me everywhere.

Of everything that, for those moments, was mine.

Once the zipper is in place, his fingers move to my shoulders, and they linger there for a moment before grazing down my side and settling at my waist. Squeezing my hips, he turns me around and brushes a wet strand of hair from my lips.

"Promise me, you won't run away this time."

A laugh bubbles up in my chest, but I catch it before it has the chance to escape. It hangs in my lungs as I remember the reason why I left him in the first place.

The vivid memory of my vision whirls through my head, showing me the impending end of the world. I witness the destruction all over again. I watch the people I love die.

I watch Ezra die.

The thought of what awaits us should this collar stop working sends a violent chill through my body that rocks me to the core. I can't bring myself to abandon

Ezra and Jenner again, but I also can't allow that future to happen.

So, what can I do? That vision only started again recently, just before they both came storming back into my life. Does that mean our proximity to each other has something to do with what I keep seeing? I don't suppose I'll ever know for sure.

All I can hope is that the collar will keep me in control, making sure that path is no longer a problem.

"Wynter."

I shake those thoughts away and force myself to meet Ezra's gaze. Behind his probing eyes, I sense his alarm at my silence.

Clearing my throat, I whisper, "I promise."

With a sigh, I cocoon myself in his arms and press my ear to his chest, listening to his heartbeat. It rages against my cheek, beating quickly. Too quickly.

Frowning, I realize he doesn't believe me. Not that I blame him.

I don't believe me either.

To my disappointment, Ezra breaks our embrace. He takes a step back, putting distance between us, then grabs my hand and presses it to his lips, gently kissing each one of my knuckles.

"We'd better go before anyone finds us here," he says with as much disappointment as I feel.

Dread pricks at my nerves. I can't escape the feeling that everything is going to come to a head soon. Whatever Nolan has planned, he's about to make his move.

I can sense it.

Reluctantly, I follow Ezra's lead to the door. As his fingers grasp the handle, my body goes rigid and I freeze, digging my heels into the concrete. The vision flashes in front of my eyes, but my voice is too slow on its rise to my lips. The warning sticks to the back of my tongue as Ezra blindly pulls open the door.

Just as I had already seen, half a dozen men wait in formation around the entryway on the other side of the threshold, blocking our only exit. Ezra drops my hand and shoves me behind him when they raise their weapons.

I know why they're here without having to ask. My gaze scans the hostile group, and I'm not the least bit surprised to see Quinn standing among them.

"Nolan wants to see you," he says.

I knew this would happen. We've lingered too long here without a plan, and now, we're paying the price for our indecision.

Ezra and I exchange nervous glances. Although, I could easily take care of this threat without so much as lifting a finger, Ezra could get caught in the crossfire if I'm not quick enough—a risk I'm not willing to take.

No, my only option is to comply. I already left to protect him and Jenner from the repercussions of my existence once and I'll keep doing what I have to do, I'll obey whoever I have to obey, if it means protecting them again now.

My heart trips at the thought of Jenner, and a rush of guilt tears through me, stealing the breath from my lungs.

Jenner.

Where the hell is he?

When I step forward, Ezra quickly extends arm out to the side, stopping me. I rest my hand on his wrist and nod once, gently pushing him out of the way. Although he relents, his expression is furious.

We're cuffed by separate guards and escorted through the corridors with a gun pressed into each of our backs, urging us forward. As we walk, my eyes flit between the soldiers surrounding us. These men are nothing like the members of PHOENIX I encountered at the other compound. If I wasn't already aware of who was responsible for bringing me here, I might not even believe they're part of PHOENIX at all.

If anything, these soldiers are more like Enforcers.

Hell, given what Nolan said about defections, maybe they used to be.

I suppose this shift was inevitable. If one course leads to a dead end, it's instinct to search for another viable route. To always have a visible path in sight. And that's exactly what PHOENIX has done, all for the sake of what Nolan has led them to believe will be a better future for everyone. They've taken a page out of the enemy's book and are becoming just like them to level the odds, even though they can't seem to see it. They can't see that such methods will cost them their humanity in the process of reaching for power, just like becoming a weapon robbed me of mine.

I cast frequent glances at Ezra, sick to my stomach with worry. His face is pale, and there's a stiffness to his expression that makes me second-guess if he knew how PHOENIX was planning to use me.

If he knew this was going to happen.

It wouldn't be the first time he knew more than he was letting on, the snide voice of doubt says in my head.

I quickly push that thought away.

Quinn stalls before a set of wide doors, bringing our procession to an abrupt standstill. I'm shoved to the front of the group as he pounds the side of his gloved fist against the steel surface, his dark eyes cutting to mine long enough for me to notice the same trepidation I've glimpsed in his gaze two other times now. First, on the helicopter two months ago, and then, when I worked out who he is. Is he trying to warn me about something?

Or is he afraid of what I might do?

He takes a step back as the doors swing open.

The barrel of the gun digging into the lower vertebrae of my spine nudges me forward, forcing me to step into the room. As I stumble over the threshold, my gaze locks on Nolan.

"You look different," he muses, a devious grin curling his lips. He nods in approval. "More like your old self. I can see her there behind those inhuman eyes."

I sneer. "You look different, too. Much more like a psychopath than how I remember. You and Richter seem to have that in common."

The first time I saw Rodrick Nolan—when Ezra made his speech assuring the people of his sect that I wasn't their enemy—Nolan had been that face in the crowd. The silent leader who I now realize was biding his time, playing his twisted, manipulative games from the shadows.

"Good. So, you do remember." His smile deepens, creasing his bearded cheeks. "That will make this so much easier."

Nolan raises one hand, and within a second of snapping his fingers, two men grab Ezra by the biceps and push him down onto his knees, twisting his arms behind his back until he yelps in pain. Quinn presses a gun to his forehead at the same moment a scream of panic tears from my lungs.

Anger sets my veins on fire, and pressure rises in my chest as I lurch forward to intervene.

Nolan's voice stops me dead in my tracks. "Don't even think about it."

Quinn clicks off the safety on his gun as if to echo that threat.

I hesitate, once again doubting myself. Even though I could massacre every last person in this room without receiving so much as a scratch, I'm reluctant to risk Quinn pulling that trigger before I can get that gun out of his hand. Ezra isn't nearly as bulletproof as I am. What if I'm not fast enough?

What if Quinn shoots before I can stop him?

As I watch Ezra struggle, fearing his death, I remind myself why I let Quinn and his entourage drag me to this room and why I'm entertaining this audience with Nolan instead of killing them like they all deserve. For Ezra's sake, for Jenner's sake, I will ultimately do whatever Nolan commands. I will do what it takes to keep them safe, even if that means facilitating this war.

Fury rises in my throat like bile, but I swallow it, shoving it down in an effort to contain the pressure and heat assaulting me from within. My hands clench into fists, tightening my hold on control.

"Now that I have your attention, I have something I wish to discuss with you," Nolan announces in a civil but authoritative tone, leaving no room for argument.

I glower at him. "First, tell me why you're doing this. I'm already your prisoner. Is this little show of excessive force necessary?"

He scoffs, crossing his arms. "You tell me. I can't have you running off before our hand has been played, and with your memories back, you finally understand what's at risk if you don't do as I ask." His eyes cut to Ezra. "Consider this a little incentive to guarantee your cooperation."

The realization that hits me knocks the breath from my lungs. While Ezra has been breaking the rules trying to help me, Nolan's been watching and letting him do it. He's been following our every step, acting as if he's against our reunion, when, ever since my extraction, he's been manipulating the situation to ensure it. He always planned to use me, but, to win my submission, he needed to restore my lost memories so I would have something to lose.

He must've known putting me in close proximity with Ezra stood the greatest chance of achieving that aim. That must be why he waited to come after me each of the times Ezra and Jenner broke me out of my cell. That must be why he let us have that brief time together. He thrust me into a scenario that would potentially trigger those suppressed emotions so that he could turn around and use them against me as soon as they came rushing back.

Which also explains why he was so open with me about PHOENIX's ties to my father and Bilken. He wanted to provoke me on the off chance anger was the key to flipping the switch in my brain that would revert me to who I used to be. The version of me with precious attachments that could be easily threatened.

Well, his plan worked. His goading and being around Ezra and Jenner both pushed me to want to remember my past. Just as he wanted, all the pieces have been fused back together.

And now, as he stated, I know what's at risk.

Nolan closes the distance between us, positioning himself directly in front of me, then grabs my chin between his fingers. His voice is a low, taunting hiss in my ear. "An attack on the State is imminent and unavoidable without you there to warn them. You and I both know this."

He's right. With my absence, the State is vulnerable and open to attack. It's already been two months since I last saw combat. Other nations must be talking by now, suspicious of the intermission. What's to stop them from taking advantage of the lull and attempting to destroy the threat before it has the chance to strike them first? Go on the offensive as a means of defense, just like the last enemy I crushed had planned to. That's what anyone would do.

That's what *I* would do.

Hell, that's how the State justified its whole war.

"With that in mind,"—Nolan drops his hand, releasing my face—"I need you to tell me when we can expect an assault on the Heart so we can prepare."

"I thought you weren't going to use me," I spit.

He shrugs, unconcerned. "Humans are selfish. We're only motivated if we have something to lose, which you do now thanks to your returned memories. So, to protect those you love, I'm *asking* you to grasp the importance of our cause and to help preserve mankind. Use is such an ugly word."

Disbelief expels from my throat in a strangled laugh. "Preserve? Millions of people could die if the Heart is attacked."

"More will die if we do nothing. If the State remains in power, the world will know nothing but war for the foreseeable future. How long before that war escalates? How long before a nuclear holocaust eradicates entire countries? Think of the chaos that could be prevented if we act now. Or, if we're being technical, *don't* act. If we allow an attack on the Heart, we can seize power and rebuild this country into something new. Something better. By helping us, you'd be doing the people, not only of our country but of the world, a great service. You would be a hero."

A great service...

Nausea twists my stomach in knots as I recall something Dr. Richter once said to me. Nolan's words... They mirror the ones Richter used to convince me to let him run his experiments.

"You'd be providing a great service, not only to the advancement of science but to the State."

I clench my jaw. "You know, Dr. Richter said the same thing to me once. Before he *tortured* me. Before he accelerated this disease with his testing. Before he turned me into a weapon and forced me to slaughter thousands of people." Tears are streaming down my cheeks by the time the last word leaves my lips.

Nolan's expression remains unchanged. "I'm not asking you to fight," he insists. "I'm asking you to save lives."

For a fleeting moment, I almost believe him. But then, I remember what he's willing to sacrifice. I remember how disposable other people are to him if they get in the way of his agenda. If Nolan manages to seize power, he'll be ruling over a kingdom of rubble and no one will be any better off than they are right now under the State. If anything, the change might even be worse.

"By threatening one of your own?" I point a shaking finger at Ezra.

Nolan throws his head back and laughs like I'm a silly child who understands nothing. "Every member of this organization is expendable so long as our goal is achieved. Even Rai Dorne, who was an incredible asset, was disposable and could be replaced. No one's life is worth more than the cause."

As he says this, something clicks into place in the back of my mind. Something I didn't quite grasp until now.

"That's why you let Ezra play leader," I realize. "Why he was always the frontman, making the speeches and leading the missions. The people in your sect didn't trust you, did they? They knew the man you were pretending to be wasn't real. You were nothing more than a wolf in sheep's clothing, and I bet they saw right through you."

"Sheep will never trust a wolf," he growls, "but they will always trust another sheep. Ezra was what those people needed because they were terrified and he made them feel safe in a world that had never provided such comfort. He gave them hope. And by inspiring their confidence in our cause, he gained their loyalty, in turn boosting our numbers. In time, that loyalty extended to me, but my hold on them was tenuous. I needed him to help them conform to our ideals and keep them on our side in this war."

Conform? How is that any better than what the State did during its own rise to power—what it *still* does to keep the people in check?

I glance at Ezra. Did he know how Nolan was using him then? How he continues to use him now?

"The reality is, Ezra never had any power. I was the acting Head of that sect, and I made every decision, every move, regardless of what he said or promised. Now, the people who were once so wary of PHOENIX no longer need any convincing to act. They're ready for change, and I will be the strong and ruthless leader they deserve. Together, we will rise up from the ashes of our ruined country and create a new world. "

My left brow hitches upward. "You know, you're beginning to sound an awful lot like the State."

He shrugs again, seemingly unbothered by the comparison. "There's a lot to be said for maintaining control. But, of course, you already know that." Dropping his gaze to my collar, he smirks.

Blood rushes to my cheeks. "What happened to freedom? What happened to not wanting to lead through fear?"

"The ultimate aim is to create a prosperous society built on foundations of peace. But even free people need someone to keep the chaos at bay and to show them, through example, how they should aspire to live. How to better themselves so we don't fall into the trap of generations past, which is ultimately what gave rise to the State. Their laziness and recklessness made them easy prey.

"As for fear, while it isn't ideal, I can't control that any more than you can control your disease without that unsightly collar. Now then," he says, clapping his hands, "will you do as I've asked? Or will our dear Ezra pay the price for your stubbornness?"

Nolan's calculating eyes press me for an answer. I waver, grazing my fingertips along the rim of my collar, the metal hot against my throat.

A string of thoughts jump into my head as I mull over the options before me. Can the DSD still access my collar? Can they remotely obtain the data or see the information it's collected from my recent visions? If it can, then maybe the people there can stop an attack before it has the chance to begin.

Then again, if the DSD could access the collar, wouldn't the State have found me by now?

Wouldn't Dr. Richter have found me?

Not if PHOENIX disabled the tracking chip like Nolan claimed, I remind myself. Without it, there's no way for anyone, not even Dr. Richter, to find me out here. Without it, we're alone against this new enemy.

Without it, there's a very real chance millions more will die because of what I started.

My chest constricts when I look over at Ezra again. If I do this for Nolan, a lot of innocent people will die. I'm not sure I can handle being responsible for any more fatalities when I've already been the cause of so many. But...if I don't help him, Ezra and Jenner will get thrown in the fray and the people of the Heart will still suffer. An attack will happen regardless of what I do.

Because, without me, the State has no way to fight an enemy it can't see coming.

Gritting my teeth, I meet Nolan's gaze and jerk my head once in unwilling agreement. It's all I can do to buy myself some time until I can figure out a course of action that doesn't result in so much death and destruction.

Assuming there is one.

TWENTY

I INHALE THROUGH MY NOSE until my lungs are full, then breathe out, clearing my head of all thoughts. As my eyes slide closed, my inner darkness takes over my senses and the sounds around me fade into a silence so thick and foreboding it raises the hairs on my neck and arms.

As the seconds tick by, my surroundings transform, melting into a mishmash of shapes and colors until my power locks onto the moment I'm searching for.

Despite the fog veiling my consciousness, I'm aware of every person in the room watching me. Their anticipation mirrors my own.

Swallowing my apprehension, I force my eyes open. The city I expect to find—the city I've known my entire life—is gone, devoured by the worst kind of destruction.

A shiver creeps over my skin as I note the stark likeness between my desecrated surroundings and my vision of the end of the world. Mangled bodies lie scattered among the dirt and debris, replicating the deaths in my vision so closely I almost confuse the two. I have to keep reminding myself what I'm seeing.

I have to remind myself that I didn't cause this.

This death…

This genocide…

It isn't my fault.

Are you sure? my conscience asks me, doubtful.

As I examine the full extent of the devastation around me, a realization rips the air from my lungs.

"Project W. A. R.," I breathe.

Of course.

I can deny it to myself all I want, but this attack will only happen because of what I am. Because of what I've done. Because of this disease and what Richter's testing and the State's war turned me into.

This brutal attack and the apocalypse that will inevitably follow…

Both will be my fault.

I take one hesitant step, then another, and as I walk, the scenery around me blurs, twisting and changing until the Heart reverts to how it was when the attack first began. Time turns backward as I will it to move, undoing these horrors.

Explosions suck back into bombs dropped from the sky as life returns to the broken corpses around me, reanimating the people crowding the streets. The rubble littering the ground floats upward, as if gravity has ceased to exist, the concrete and metal reconnecting as the buildings repair themselves. Shattered glass windows piece back together, gleaming with the reflection of a pristine city just as it existed—or will exist—in the moments before the attack.

The cloud of dust polluting the air melts away.

A clock chimes at the edge of the reconstructed plaza, drawing my gaze to the tower behind me, which serves as the focal point of Central Station, overlooking most of Zone 1. I make a mental note of the time before peering at the outer rim of the clock. The date of the attack shines in arching hologram letters.

"Two days."

My eyes snap open, locking on Nolan. An eager smile dances at the corners of his mouth.

"Two days," I repeat, clearing my throat. "The attack will happen in two days, just before sundown."

Nolan traces the shape of his chin with his fingers, contemplating my answer as he scrutinizes my face. I keep still under his leering gaze, determined not to give him any reason to doubt me.

"Very good," he grunts after a moment. "Thank you for your cooperation."

My gaze cuts to Ezra for a fleeting moment—long enough to glimpse the way his chest rises and falls when Quinn retracts the gun from the back of his head. The other soldiers dotted throughout the room follow suit, lowering their weapons in unison.

The tightness around my chest eases a little, but I try not to show my relief on my face. The last thing I need right now is to give Nolan further incentive to put Ezra or Jenner in danger. Seeing how anxious I am for their well-being would surely only provoke him.

Nolan nods at someone behind me, and a moment later, strong hands wrap around my upper arms, pulling me with unnecessary force toward the door. I strain against them, unsure what to do.

I know nothing I say will dissuade Nolan from this path of inaction he's settled on. Corrupted by a need for power that's been cleverly disguised as a desire for change, he'll let millions die to see his plan come to fruition. But this war will only destroy what he's fighting for.

And, in time, it will destroy what I'm fighting for, too.

For that reason, I can't stop myself from screaming, "Their blood will be on your hands! Every death that results from this attack is on you!"

Nolan's pale eyes are vacant as he waves us away. In response, the hands around my arms tighten their grip, yanking me backward so hard I get whiplash.

As I'm dragged toward the door, I'm reminded of the orderlies who tended to me at the DSD. Just like them, these men don't care about my welfare any more than Nolan is acting on behalf of the people in the Heart. If I doubted it before, this moment proves it. PHOENIX. The DSD. They're the same hell but in different packaging.

A hell I'm beginning to think I'll never escape.

"Oh, Wynter," Nolan calls as we pass through the doorway, "one last thing before I forget."

The two guards manhandling me pause at the threshold so I'm hanging half in and half out of the room. Although I'm tempted to break free of their clawlike grasps, I don't bother. No good can come of my resistance at this point.

"I've summoned the Heads of the other sects, who will be arriving tomorrow. Once they're here, I'd like you to meet with them as they'll want to hear what you've seen for themselves." He shoots me a severe look that sends my heart racing before adding, "That is not a request."

As he waves us away for a second time, the guards jerk me around and shove me into the hallway. Their hands dig into my biceps as they drag me forward through the corridors, but I barely notice the pain of their grip.

My only focus is Ezra.

He stumbles ahead of me, sandwiched between two of Nolan's armed goons, head down and hands cuffed in front of his waist. As I watch his every sluggish step, I wonder if he fully understands what he's gotten himself into by trying to protect me. He'll be viewed the same as I am from here on out. A danger to society. A menace to be disposed of.

A threat.

Acid sloshes in my gut at the thought.

Within only a matter of minutes—although it seems more like hours—we once again find ourselves outside the small room that has served as my personal prison in this place. Quinn, who has been leading our procession, unlocks the door and pulls it open, glaring at Ezra.

Ezra lets out a barking laugh, grinning at the ex-Enforcer. "Locking me up so I won't knock you out again?"

A sneer curls Quinn's upper lip, and he launches forward, striking Ezra in the stomach with his knee. As Ezra drops to the floor with a strangled breath, the other guards—excluding the two still tightly gripping my arms—form a circle around him.

Stepping back, Quinn unholsters his gun while the others take turns kicking Ezra in the ribs, face, and legs—whatever part of his body they can reach with their boots. With each impact, spots of red stain his lips and the floor.

Rage burns inside me as I watch the group of men assault Ezra without mercy. With each grunt and moan, I'm consumed by anger toward them for their brutality and anger toward myself for allowing this to happen. As much as I want to intervene, I can't. The gun aimed at Ezra puts a mental leash on my power, forcing me to push all the tempting thoughts of snapping their necks to the back of my mind.

My eyes drift from the gun to Quinn's face, and he smirks at me, clearly enjoying seeing me helpless.

When the beating ends, the men roll Ezra's bloodied body through the open door, into the concrete box of a room. My heart stops at the sight of him, a lump swelling in my throat as memories of a similar moment flash in front of my eyes.

This is just like the day Father was taken.

Quinn lowers his gun and steps into the room, swinging his leg back for a devastating kick that makes me want to rip the limb off his body. As his foot collides with Ezra's stomach for the second time, he spits on the floor.

"Payback's a bitch," he says.

The instant the soldiers release their hold on my arms, I push past them and drop to my knees beside Ezra. My hand brushes across his pale, clammy forehead, sweeping his sweat-matted hair away from his closed eyes. The fingers of my other hand tremble against his neck, searching for any sign of his pulse. It quivers faintly under his skin.

Exhaling, I sit back on my heels as the door slams shut, grimacing when the ear-splitting clang sends an uncomfortable vibration through my teeth. The locking mechanism turns a moment later, sealing Ezra's fate.

And mine.

Guilt rushes through me when I take in his face, the skin colorless in comparison to the ruby blood coating his split lips and nose and the purple bruises blossoming across his right cheek and forehead. Swallowing, I tug at the hem of his shirt, lifting it up to expose his torso. Lacerations and red patches the size of my fist cover his stomach, some of which are already turning black at the edges.

Tears blur my vision, and I bite back a scream. For all I know, Ezra could have internal bleeding or a concussion, neither of which I'm prepared to deal with. I exist to destroy. I don't know how to help him.

I'm powerless to help anyone.

A soft moan behind me has my power surging to the surface, and I whip around, ready for a fight, only to freeze as the guilt writhing within me doubles in weight.

"Jenner!"

My movements are clumsy as I scramble to my feet and hurl myself toward the hunched figure sitting in the corner. Jenner looks up at me with one eye swollen shut and indigo bruises lining his jaw.

"What happened?" I place my hands on his cheeks then quickly pull them away when he winces. His lips peel back, revealing the blood staining his teeth.

His whole body shakes when he lets out a breath. "Same thing that's just happened to Ez from the looks of it."

My nerves ignite with chaotic fury as my eyes drift back and forth between Ezra and Jenner. Even with the collar, I can sense my hold on control slipping. The monster lurks closer to the surface than ever, and if I'm not careful, these feelings of rage—of helplessness—will only continue to fester and grow. If they take over, I won't be able to shove them back down.

And if that happens, no one around me is safe.

A soft yelp jerks my attention back to Ezra who rouses with a start. His eyes blink open, and he coughs a few times, spitting red-tinged saliva on the floor, wheezing as he tries to inhale past the blood. Groaning, he wraps one arm around his stomach and uses the other to push himself up.

When I jump to my feet to help him, he holds up a hand and I immediately go still. Either he's telling me he can do it himself or he's warning me to keep my distance. I'm not sure which, but I respect his wishes, even though it kills me inside that he might not want me near him again after this.

He limps toward us, grunting with every step, and lets out a sigh when he reaches the wall. With a ragged breath, he slides back down to the floor.

"How long have you been here?" he asks, glancing at Jenner.

"Pretty much since I left you guys. So…last night? Or this morning… I think." Jenner hesitates, scratching dried blood off his chin. "It's a little hard to gauge time when your brain feels like it's melting through your eyeballs." He shrugs as much as his injured body allows, then looks at Ezra, frowning. "I managed to get into The Pit, but they found me just after I made contact with Duke. We barely had time to exchange two words."

The taste of bile floods my mouth. When I was with Ezra, Jenner was here. While I was busy attempting to regain my humanity, Jenner was in agony and alone.

Once again, someone else's pain is my fault. If I hadn't been so caught up in my moment with Ezra, if I had just thought to leave a small space for Jenner available in my head, then I might have seen this coming.

My vision clouds over as I sink to my knees and wrap my arms around my chest, once again holding myself together the only way I know how. I stay this way until something warm prods my cheek, breaking me free from my thoughts of self-loathing.

My eyelashes flutter a few times, my gaze drawn to the finger poking me just below my left cheekbone.

Jenner's hand drops to his side when he whispers, "You're you again…aren't you?"

I choke out a laugh as the tears spill over, the pressure easing off my chest. Sniffing, I wipe the moisture from my face. "How did you know?"

"That." He pokes my cheek again, grinning. "It gives you away. It always gives you away."

Confusion barrels through me just as it did the last time he spoke these words—shortly after we met the first time. Like then, I'm not quite sure what he means. *What* always gives me away?

At one point, I thought maybe he meant my innocence—although, ignorance might be more accurate—but I'm far from innocent now. I'm guilty of the worst crimes imaginable.

When his smile deepens, I decide not to press it.

So long as he's safe, nothing else matters to me.

"I'm glad you're back," he says, taking my hand. "It would've really sucked if I went through hijacking and blowing up a transport helicopter for nothing. Even if it did make me look like a badass."

Snorting, I roll my eyes and wrap my fingers around his, squeezing gently. "I'm sorry it took me so long to come back."

I mutter this same apology, over and over again, as I reposition myself on the floor, huddling between Ezra and Jenner, pressing my back to the damp wall. They don't to interrupt me or minimize my words; they each just take one of my hands in their own and hold me as I let the guilt out.

Eventually, my mumblings fade into silence, and I drift into an uneasy sleep, exhausted by the erratic events of the last few days. Sometimes, my head rests on Ezra's shoulder, and other times, I lean on Jenner's. Their hands remain entwined with mine the whole time.

When I'm conscious again a short while later, I assess the situation. It would be easy enough for me to get the door open; with a little focus, I could rip the damn thing off its hinges. The real problem is the same one that's been plaguing me since I got my memories back.

For as powerful as I am, I lack confidence when it comes to keeping Ezra and Jenner safe from harm. I exist to destroy, not to protect. Anything could happen beyond these walls, and I'm not sure I'm prepared for that. Or for what I could lose in the process of trying to find a way to escape.

I shake my head, biting my lower lip. "Everything is so different now. I don't get it. What happened in the time I was gone?"

I cast a sidelong glance at Ezra, but his eyes are fixed on some distant point at the other side of the room.

When he finally meets my gaze, his brow furrows, his lips pulling down at the corners. "We saw the first changes right after you left. The mission was scrutinized by Nolan, who wanted to understand what went wrong…especially where Rai was concerned. I had no choice but to tell him about Austin. And the truth… Let's just say, it wasn't exactly well-received."

"That was strike one," Jenner mutters. "Although, we didn't know it at the time."

Ezra's expression darkens. "He then pressured us for more details about you. Why you really came to PHOENIX. Why you left. The same sort of questions he began to ask when you were in your coma, except, at that point, he knew we lied the first time around and that we were clued-in on way more than we had initially let on. I could tell he didn't trust me anymore after finding out about Austin, and there was no way he would buy anything I said to him about you, no matter how convincing I made it. Since you had already left, and we were actively trying to figure out a way to get you back, I didn't see the harm in telling him the truth. I thought maybe we could convince him to help."

"Strike two," Jenner croons. "The man hates a liar."

"Ironic," I grumble. "All things considered."

Ezra nods, his frown deepening. "Once Nolan knew the truth about you, everything changed. Especially after he saw the intel Bilken left for us at the magistrates building. Meetings between the Heads became classified, and I was suddenly excluded from information and other resources I had access to previously. Shortly after, the other Heads voted to make Nolan the principal leader of PHOENIX."

"Principal leader?"

"The head honcho." Jenner scoffs, rolling his uninjured eye. "PHOENIX claims to be a democracy, with the Heads serving as the voices of the individual sects. But whatever Nolan said to the others somehow changed all that. Now, we're on the verge of a full-blown dictatorship."

My lips purse, pinching at the corners, as I mull this notion over. As the only living founding member, Nolan probably had some sway with the other Heads that would allow him to take control of the organization. Couple that with his beneficial relationship with Bilken, and I'm not surprised things have turned out the way they have.

The changes I've witnessed are proof of how fragile PHOENIX was…and possibly still is. It only took a little pressure to collapse their way of life, and now, they're resorting to the same brutality and violence they claim to stand against.

Just as I feared, PHOENIX is as corrupt as the State.

"At first, we were on board with the new hierarchy. I mean, anything is better than the State, and he seemed serious about finally making progress with the rebellion. But we were blind. We couldn't see the changes happening right in front of us because we were so preoccupied with getting you back," Jenner explains. "When Nolan asked us to join this sect and help spearhead the next stage of the cause, we agreed without hesitation, thinking it would be our only chance to do just that."

Ezra laughs under his breath, but the sound lacks humor. "Yeah, and we were too absorbed by that idea to realize he was using us."

I glance between them, confused. When Ezra doesn't continue, I look back at Jenner, who carries on where he left off.

"We kept begging Nolan to help, using the file Bilken left us as proof that you were better off with us than with the State. But every time, he made some excuse about why it wasn't the right time to intervene. It took Ezra spilling his guts and professing his love for you for Nolan to budge on the matter. Even then, he made it seem like he was only going ahead with your extraction as a favor to us. On countless occasions, he made it clear we'd be responsible if things went wrong or if you hurt anybody."

"A burden we were willing to bear," Ezra murmurs.

Jenner bobs his head in agreement.

"But he didn't do it for you," I whisper.

He did it for himself, and Bilken helped.

"No," Jenner agrees. "He didn't."

I let out an incredulous huff. I'd wager Bilken used my rescue mission to orchestrate his own exit from the Heart, jumping ship before everything goes to hell. It wouldn't be the first time he used my life as a bargaining chip. After all, two and a half years ago, in a bid to make contact with Nolan, Bilken made a deal with Richter that resulted in my imprisonment. Here he is, once again using me as a means to an end—rescuing me from the State just to save his own ass.

It seems like the only people not using me for their own personal gain these days are Ezra and Jenner. Before, it troubled me to think what they must've offered Nolan in exchange for my freedom, but I realize now they wouldn't have had to give the older man anything. Nolan sold my extraction as a favor to keep them complacent, in turn gaining the key components needed to set his trap for me. And Bilken, always eager to make himself useful, I'm sure—thus, keeping his options open—was all too happy to oblige when his old buddy, Nolan, turned to him for help with the matter.

I can't help wondering what Nolan promised him aside from an escape from the Heart. What part will Bilken play in the new world order when PHOENIX finally takes over?

My heart sinks as my eyes turn back to Ezra. When he meets my gaze, his cheeks burn with shame.

"When you told me about your collar, I began to suspect what was really going on, and what happened just now with Nolan confirmed it. He would've gone through with the extraction regardless of us because he needs you to execute his master plan. We're only here to force you to cooperate. The more I dwell on it, the more I think that's why he kept us close the last few years." His free hand balls into a fist, the knuckles turning white as his fingers curl tighter. "We've been hostages this whole time and didn't even know it."

"Until we busted you out the first time," Jenner says. "After that, he made it pretty damn clear we were getting in his way. And now,"—he runs a hand through his blood-tangled hair and gestures to the concrete walls—"strike three. The warnings about Nolan were there. Like I said, we just didn't see them."

"Or didn't want to," Ezra grumbles.

I contemplate these revelations, lingering on one word Ezra said.

Hostages…

As this concept rolls around in my skull, I think back to my time with Ezra in the farmhouse. If Nolan is as much like Richter as I think, then I bet he had cameras planted up there and was watching our conversation—our *kiss*—eager to see if it would awaken my memories. That's what he wanted, after all.

He wanted me to regain my humanity so he could turn around and use it against me.

Even if we'd had a plan of escape, leaving this place was never an option. Nolan wouldn't have ever allowed me to leave, and there's no way he's going to let us go now. We aren't just prisoners anymore…

We're inmates on death row.

"There's something I still don't understand. Nolan said part of why you waited so long to come get me was because he needed the other Heads to approve my extraction. If he's the leader of PHOENIX, couldn't he have just overruled them?" I ask.

"Even fledgling dictators still need underlings," Jenner jokes.

Ezra heaves a tired sigh. "As the principal leader, yes, Nolan holds the most power, but he's still in a position to be voted out from leadership if the other Heads united to stand against him. Like Jenner said, PHOENIX is first and foremost a democracy. There's only so much he can accomplish without their approval considering they each have authority over dozens of sects that won't answer to anyone else, not even him. I think he's just playing it safe until he can be certain of everyone's loyalty."

"Speaking of loyalty…" Jenner trails off, looking between my face and Ezra's before risking a glance at the camera in the distant corner. Leaning in close to us, he lowers his voice. "Before they threw me in here, I overheard Nolan talking about an attack on the Heart…" He hesitates, peering at me nervously. "He said, after it happens, they won't need you anymore. I'm guessing that applies to us, too."

My heart drops. Ever since my vision of Nolan and Ezra, I knew the older man would eventually make an attempt on my life. I just figured I'd have a solution to this predicament by the time that moment came.

As it stands, I have nothing and our executions are imminent.

"It's all my fault," I breathe, breaking my hold on their hands and pressing the heels of my palms into my eyes. "I should've never come to you for help in the first place."

Every bad thing that's happened since I met Ezra and Jenner all comes back to me.

The people I love always get hurt.

"Hey." Ezra pulls my hand away from my face and draws it close to his chest. "Don't say that. We'll find a way out of this. We always do."

Unable to bear the hopeful gleam in his eyes, I hang my head and yank my hand free again. I don't want him touching me right now—not when all I can think about is how badly I've failed him and Jenner and how I'm about to let them both down yet again by being the reason they die.

I clench my teeth, biting back a growl. For someone who has experienced such terrifying power, it's maddening how limited I am by it now.

Is there nothing I can do to stop this?

I did what Nolan asked me to do, but, by relenting, I've exhausted my usefulness to him. Even if he did still need me alive, he would just keep using Ezra and Jenner as leverage to get me to do his bidding. In place of Richter, he'd become the new puppet master pulling at my strings.

Because of how valuable I am to those who thirst for power, I will forever be trapped in a vicious circle where the only escape is death. There can never be freedom for a weapon of war.

Terror wraps me in a cold shroud as the memory of what Jenner said rings in my ears. If I'm no longer needed, they won't be either.

I can't allow that to happen.

I can't let anyone else I care about die.

Ezra lets out a loud breath through his nose. "So, does anyone have any brilliant ideas?"

Lifting my chin, I fix my gaze on the door, aware that we only have one option if we're going to get out of this alive. "We wait."

And when the time is right, we fight.

TWENTY-ONE

MY EYES DART UP WHEN the door swings open, my body tensing and my senses on high alert in anticipation of whatever—or whoever—waits on the other side, ready to bring us our reckoning. I'm not sure how many hours have passed with us huddled together in this tiny room, but, if I had to guess, I'd say the time has come for me to meet the Heads of PHOENIX.

The screech of the hinges jerks Jenner awake, and grunting, he lifts his head off my shoulder before carefully pushing himself to his feet. Ezra stirs on my other side but doesn't shift much more than that, wincing at the slightest jostle of movement.

Snaking my arm around his back, I use the wall to guide us both up. He groans when my fingers press into his side.

Once we're all standing, I force my gaze in the direction of the doorway. Pitch black eyes bore holes into my skin.

"It's time," Quinn says.

Ezra takes hold of my left hand as Jenner grips my right, and although terror ripples through my veins, it's calmed by a fleeting sense of relief as we inch forward together. Regardless of what happens once we leave this room, at least I won't have to face it alone.

Grimacing at our joined hands, Quinn blocks our path.

"Only her," he growls.

Ezra tenses. "If you think there's any way in hell—"

"It's okay," I interrupt, giving a slight shake of my head when Ezra's eyes dart to mine. He's still recovering from the last time he mouthed off at Quinn. We don't need a re-enactment of that beating right now.

I pull my hands free and plant them firmly against Ezra's chest, putting myself between him and Quinn. He glares at me, lips twisted into a scowl, those hazel eyes alight with fire. Anger and disbelief feed the flames.

"I'll be fine," I murmur.

Beside me, Jenner clenches his hands into fists, and when we exchange a quick look, he nods as if he knows what I'm asking without me needing to say it.

Jenner. Always the dependable one.

Before Ezra can say anything else to escalate the situation, I turn and tail Quinn into the hallway. As much as I don't want to do this alone, I can't keep putting Ezra and Jenner in danger. This mess began because of me, so it's only fitting it ends that way, too.

As the door creaks shut behind us, I examine the burly guard on duty. Although his muscles are intimidating and he could probably crush my skull with his bare hands, I'm more concerned with the rifle slung over his shoulder. It might not do much damage to me, but it could easily be used to kill Ezra or Jenner.

I grit my teeth, my jaw twitching, as I'm once again reminded of what will happen if I refuse to cooperate. I can only hope Ezra and Jenner are smart enough not to do anything stupid while I'm gone.

"Don't try anything," Quinn warns, his voice a low hiss. When our eyes meet, he shoves me hard in the back, forcing me forward.

As we trudge through the corridors, I mimic his steps. I'm unfamiliar with the route he takes, but I know all too well what lies at the end of it.

Are the other Heads of PHOENIX as corrupt as their leader? I try to envision their faces, but all I can picture is an endless sea of masks, not that unlike the Enforcers I always met on my missions, hidden beneath their tactical helmets. In my head, every last one is identical, their true intent concealed from the world.

Just like Dr. Richter.

Pins and needles prickle my skin, and a terrible pain gnaws at my stomach from an uncomfortable combination of anxiety and hunger. The closer we get to our destination, the more unsettled and agitated I become until my nerves are on the verge of a full-scale meltdown. The anticipation is too much to bear.

So look, I tell myself. *See what's coming.*

I consider that option for less than two steps before coming to the disheartening conclusion that looking ahead wouldn't do any good at this point. So long as Ezra and Jenner remain at risk, I'm powerless to change anything I might see. Assuming the future can even be changed. I thought it could, which was why I left in the first place, before I could hurt anyone else or see my vision become reality. And yet, despite my sacrifice, we're back to square one with the threat of the end of the world looming again.

As it stands, my actions haven't changed a damn thing. If anything, they've only brought that future closer.

Plus, there's the added issue of Quinn to contend with. He's made his feelings about what I am perfectly clear, and he may view any attempt to use my power near him as a personal attack on his life. I could deal with him, but—foul attitude aside—at the end of the day, he's just a soldier following orders. We may not like each other, but that doesn't mean I think he deserves to die.

I study his face as we walk, still amazed he's the same person as that frightened young Enforcer I encountered only two months ago. If it wasn't for those eyes, I wouldn't have even made the connection. The change in him is unsettling, and I can't help wondering if he's also hiding behind a mask, just like Nolan and Richter. If so, which is his true persona?

The terrified soldier or the hardened rebel?

"What's your problem with Ezra and Jenner?" I blurt out.

Quinn doesn't look at me when he answers. "They don't respect authority or rules."

"Spoken like a true Enforcer," I scoff.

I ignore the scalding look he gives me.

"So, what made you become an Enforcer?" I continue, pressing him after a few moments of silence.

"I'm not an Enforcer—"

"But you were," I counter.

When he doesn't say anything more, I begin to formulate a plan in my head. It's risky, but we need an ally if we're going to get out of this place alive. As much as I don't like him, Quinn is our best bet to make that happen. Besides, he's already switched sides once, so maybe I can convince him to switch sides again.

"Come on," I plead. "I've never met a defector before, so humor me."

Quinn huffs. "If you must know, I joined because Enforcers are exempt from certain…requirements of our society that I wasn't comfortable with."

"Requirements? Like…getting partnered?"

He clears his throat. "And contributing to population growth. Among other things."

I hold up a hand. "Let me get this straight. You became an Enforcer just to avoid having a family?"

Families are complicated. I would know. And being related to someone by blood doesn't automatically make them trustworthy or incapable of betrayal. But the State is a lonely, isolating place. For some, a family might be the only comfort they have.

How many times have I longed to see my own mother, even after everything she's done?

He shrugs. "I prefer my own company. The thought of being forced into sharing my life with another person doesn't sit right with me. It should be something we choose. Being alone isn't the same thing as lonely."

I arch a dubious brow. "Strange words out of the mouth of a Loyalist."

"Ex-Loyalist," he retorts with an eye roll, and, for a second, I swear the ghost of a smile crosses his lips.

I hesitate for a moment before pushing him further. "Nolan told me you abandoned the State because you don't agree with their methods. Or their rules, apparently," I add under my breath. "Considering the training you would've had to go through to become an Enforcer, I have to say, I find that surprising. And suspicious. All the Enforcers I've met were brainwashed puppets. Not a single rebellious bone in their bodies. So, where did the State go wrong with you?"

A feral noise reverberates in his chest as he whips around and shoves me hard into the wall. Pressing his forearm against my neck, he snarls, "It's *you* I don't agree with. I've seen what you've done. No one deserves to die like that."

"And I deserve what the DSD did to me?" I gasp past the increasing pressure on my throat. "Did it ever occur to you that, maybe, I killed all those people because I didn't have a choice? Because I was under duress?"

Fury pulses through my veins and rips over my skin in a shiver as the edge of the collar digs into my neck, making me dizzy with pain and light-headed from lack of air. My lungs scream out for relief, and gradually, Quinn relaxes his grip on me. He takes a step back as I hunch over, coughing.

Once I've caught my breath, I rasp, "You say I'm the problem. Fine. I don't really care what you think of me. But ask yourself this: why leave the State over one war just to join the side of someone who plans to use my power to start another? By not intervening in the attack on the Heart, Nolan will be directly responsible for the massacre of innocent people, as will anyone who stands by him." I shake my head, looking Quinn up and down with disgust. "Where's your conscience now?" I spit.

Sneering, he bites back, "My conscience is clear."

"Will it still be clear when thousands of your countrymen lie dead in the streets?"

He responds by raising his gun. "Keep walking."

The glassy depths of Quinn's eyes gleam with warning. Holding up my hands in surrender, I continue onward as directed, playing the part of an obedient prisoner.

Throughout the remainder of our journey, our footsteps echo like a ticking clock, counting down to the unavoidable moment ahead. When Quinn slows to a stop, that moment shifts closer.

A steel door stands before us, identical to all the other doors in this place. But unlike the others, I know what's behind it. The moment of our reckoning is finally at hand.

Quinn grabs the top of my arm, pulling me close, then bangs the side of his fist against the metal surface, knocking twice. When the door opens a few seconds later, I don't recognize the tall man who appears in the doorway. I do, however, notice the way Quinn's fingers tense against my bicep when the man glances between us.

"Let them in," a husky voice calls from behind the guard.

Nolan.

The man steps aside as instructed, allowing us access into the dimly lit room. I don't move, instead peering over at Quinn, but he avoids my gaze, dropping my arm and pressing his back to the wall, his stance rigid as if he intends to become a permanent fixture in the hallway. When I still don't move, he jerks his head toward the door, gesturing for me to enter.

Looks like I'm on my own now.

Sweat breaks out across my palms as I take a slow step over the threshold. As I pass Quinn, my eyes search his expressionless face for any sign that what I said before might've swayed his allegiance, even just a little. If it did, he's doing a good job of hiding it.

Upon entering the room, the first thing I notice is the row of armed guards lining three of the walls—at least five for each of the eight Heads sitting along the rounded edge of a large, half-moon shaped table positioned in the middle of the room. The space is empty of any other furniture aside from a single chair facing the crowd of unblinking eyes watching my movements with interest.

I assume that one is meant for me.

A conspiratorial smile curves Nolan's lips when he stands to welcome me from the center seat at the table.

"Ah, Wynter," he says in a pleasant voice. He waves his hand toward the empty chair, only returning to his own seat once I'm settled in mine. "Allow me to introduce the Heads of PHOENIX."

As he rattles off a string of names, I take a good hard look at each of their faces. Six men of varying ages stare at me with uncertainty, accompanied by one severe-looking woman with chestnut skin and curly black hair.

Out of all the Heads, she's the one who frightens me most—not because of the inscrutable way she looks at me but because of the commanding manner she must possess to have been able to infiltrate this select group of men. Men, who may very well turn out to be as corrupt and dangerous as Nolan.

A faint modicum of respect for her swells in my chest despite her support for Nolan's plan.

"I've kept you all in suspense for long enough," Nolan says, his gruff voice pulling me back to the reason for this meeting. "Wynter, why don't you enlighten the other Heads on the details?"

When his shrewd eyes fix on mine, I snort. "I've already told you when it will happen. What more do you want?"

"I want the other Heads to hear it directly from you. So, why don't you start by telling us what sort of attack we should expect," he suggests in a tone that reminds me far too much of Dr. Richter. "What will the fallout be?"

Fallout?

I gape at him, stunned and lost for words. People are going to die because of his plan, and he's brushing it aside behind a technical term that hides what it really is.

Murder.

For the first time in my life, I'm grateful my father is dead. I'm thankful he isn't alive to see this—to witness what PHOENIX is about to become.

This isn't the sort of world he wanted.

Fighting back tears, I force out through clenched teeth, "The attack will be isolated to the Heart, but it will be devastating. Hundreds of thousands will die. Likely more."

"And the State's response?" he presses. "What of the aftermath?"

"Martial law, no doubt," the woman cuts in.

"The attack will result in chaos," says the man sitting at the far left side of the room, his tone skeptical.

I flinch when the elderly man beside Nolan slams his hand down hard on the table, shouting, "That makes it the perfect time to attack!"

The remaining Heads all nod in agreement, though some more begrudgingly than others.

All except Nolan, who considers me with narrowed eyes. "Or a dangerous time," he muses.

I perk up a little at these words, allowing myself a small sliver of hope that he might be coming to his senses and finally realizing how utterly insane his strategy is. The right thing to do would be to warn the State of what's coming and live to fight another day. If he doesn't, there might not be anything left to fight over.

But then, I glimpse that power-hungry gleam in his eyes and that small flicker of hope fades away.

I glare at him. Doesn't Nolan care that his own people—the people he claims to want to lead into the future—will be caught in the crossfire of this attack? He might be safe outside the Heart's walls, but what about the other sects of PHOENIX still residing in the city? Are they disposable to him, too?

"What are your thoughts?" he asks, looking at me.

I scoff. "The entire Heart will be crippled. Isn't that what you want?"

A forbidding smile is the only answer I get.

"It's decided, then." He pushes back his chair, and as he stands, the whispers that arose following my accusation a moment ago fall silent. "We'll move out after the first strike and penetrate the Heart before the State has a chance to respond. We'll utilize the tunnel system to remain clear of the bombings, then reconvene in Zone 1." His pale eyes flash to mine as he claps his hand once. "That concludes this meeting. Everyone, rest now while there's still time to do so. A new dawn approaches and some of us won't live to see beyond the night."

As the other Heads all rise and shuffle toward the exit, the clock counting down over my head reaches zero. Sweat breaks out across my skin, and my pulse thunders in my ears at a speed that tears the air from my lungs.

With the other Heads on board, Nolan now has the manpower he needs to infiltrate the Heart, and thanks to me, he has the know-how to make his ultimate goal a reality. Despite my best efforts, I couldn't change his mind any more than I can prevent the impending attack.

There's nothing anyone can do to deter the next stage of his plan, and unless he's changed his mind about using my powers, Nolan has no reason to keep me alive. Or Ezra. Or Jenner. By trying to shield them both from further harm, I've only put them in more danger than before.

I swallow, biting back tears, as the unnerving realization sinks in. I hear the intent behind Nolan's concluding words as they echo in my ears.

We're out of time.

He's going to kill us.

TWENTY-TWO

ALTHOUGH I ALREADY KNEW IT would come to this, on some level, I had hoped Nolan was bluffing. He went through so much trouble to get me back from the State that I figured he'd find some excuse to keep me chained to his command like a prized pet, just like Dr. Richter. That he'd use me until nothing and nobody else stands in the way of his corrupt aspirations.

Then again, I'm not on his side and he doesn't have the means to keep me controlled if I were to get loose, which makes me a problem. A *big* problem.

A threat.

Considering his intentions with the Heart and my own past experience with unhinged megalomaniacs, I'm not surprised by Nolan's willingness to eliminate any obstacles remaining between him and that goal. What does surprise me is my own inability to stop him and the fact that, at least on one particular matter, I might not want to.

Thanks to Nolan, I'm finally accepting what I've been trying so hard to ignore all these years. He knows it, and I know it, too, even if I didn't want to admit it.

I'm too dangerous to keep alive.

Heavy footsteps approach from behind, drowning me in shadow and setting every hair on my immobile body on end. A chill creeps across my skin as the faint stench of sweat wafts into my nose and travels down my throat, leaving a bitter taste on my tongue. The unbearable heat from the stranger's body is like a hand against my back when they move closer.

"You must be relieved. Your part to play in all this is coming to an end."

Jaw straining, I peer over my shoulder and lock eyes with Wren Bilken, who stares back at me with a smirk on his lips.

"And what about your part?" I ask. "It seems your services are no longer needed here either."

As he considers me, his dark, oval eyes lacking emotion, I revisit the first time we met—when I was sixteen and he interviewed me prior to my work placement exam, back when my life still held some semblance of normality. The fear he struck within me then is a distant memory, a faint tickle I barely feel on my skin. Everything I've seen and been through since that moment has robbed me of the timidness that once made me so afraid of him, and now, I feel nothing toward him except anger.

Now, he's the one who should be afraid.

He steps around my chair, taking deliberate steps, circling me like a ravenous vulture. "I have many talents and qualities that will be indispensable when we build the new world. There's still use for me yet."

"I thought the State was the new world," I counter.

He shrugs one shoulder, his expression disinterested. "Time's change. Those who survive learn to change along with it."

Heat rushes through me, fanning the flames of my animosity, and it takes all the self-restraint I possess to smother the urge to punch him in the face. To calm myself down, I picture Ezra and Jenner locked away in that miserable room and remind myself how their lives depend on my actions. If I act out, what fate am I condemning them to?

Sucking in an unsteady breath, I redirect my unstable emotions into a question, probing him.

Goading him.

"Why abandon what you worked so hard for? It must be exhausting to have to keep starting over."

In my peripheral vision, I glimpse Quinn by the doorway. He watches me with a hand on his pistol.

A brusque laugh draws my gaze back to Bilken.

"War is always inevitable. No matter how successful, the State was always destined to end. I merely refuse to go down with the ship. Those who thrive in this world are the ones who know which side to choose at such crossroads."

My hands clench into fists on my lap. "How can you be so sure PHOENIX will win? You couldn't have anticipated this."

His eyebrows shoot up, reaching for the distant crest of his hairline. "Couldn't I? After all, I've seen this scenario play out before." Ceasing his pacing, he lowers his voice, stooping to whisper in my ear. "You probably aren't aware of this, but the State was once no different than PHOENIX. They began as a small, disillusioned group, and when they saw the opportunity to rise up and make their mark on the world, they took it without hesitation. Unfortunately, not every rebellion has good intentions. PHOENIX included."

Disbelief spreads through my body like poison. While I had noticed similarities between the two, I had assumed the change was recent. A result of desperation. I don't want to believe PHOENIX and the State are the same—two trees born from the same toxic roots. I don't want to believe the cause Ezra, Jenner, and Rai all risked their lives for could be as corrupt at its core as the oppressive government they sacrificed so much to escape.

I don't *want* to believe it…

And yet, I do.

Straightening, Bilken resumes his predatory circling. "Like most failed governments of the past, the State will be destroyed by its own persistent reach for power. It wanted too much too quickly, and as a result, that greed has led to its downfall."

"What next, then?" I press. "PHOENIX seizes control, and ten or twenty years down the line, they end up heading in the same direction. Do you abandon them, too?"

Bilken sneers. "Do not confuse ambition with loyalty, Miss Reeves. Men like me get into positions of power because we do whatever it takes to survive and do not needlessly stand by alliances that only serve us in the immediate moment. Your father chose loyalty over ambition and look where that got him. Perhaps, if he'd been smarter, he'd still be alive."

A swell of power scratches at the underside of my skin, clawing and tearing at every inch of my body in a bid to escape and lash out at Bilken. Red flashes in front of my eyes, and brushing aside all thought of the consequences, I leap out of my seat, springing to strike. The chair tips to the side, clattering onto the floor, and my self-restraint falls along with it—discarded in this burst of madness.

Bilken stumbles backward when I collide with his chest, his feet slipping out from underneath him, bringing us both crashing down to the concrete.

I'm light and quick compared to the middle-aged man, whose muscled frame far outweighs mine, pinning his arms down with my knees before he can rebound and throw me off. As my legs straddle his torso, my fingers reach for his throat.

Rage blinds me. For a split second, I contemplate using my power to snap his neck and be done with it, but killing him that way would be far too easy. Too unsatisfying. No, in this moment, I want him to *feel* me—to feel my hands extinguish the wretched life he betrayed so many others to cling to.

As I tighten my grip, Bilken's eyes glass over and his brown skin darkens, turning a deep shade of purple. My fingers squeeze harder, pressing into his throat.

Suddenly, the air whooshes beside my left ear and then something hard strikes me in the side of the skull, knocking me off Bilken's chest. Pain shoots through my right hip as I topple over, slamming into the concrete.

Vertigo swarms my head as the room spins in dizzying circles, sending the spots dancing in front of my eyes into a frenzy, as if they're celebrating my pain. Fighting through my disorientation, I push to my knees and emit a low growl. An answering click draws my gaze to Quinn's gun, the muzzle nearly skimming the tip of my nose.

"Enough," he barks, his black eyes pleading.

Ragged breaths slither in and out of my lungs, slowing alongside my diminishing fury. Groaning, I slump back onto the cold floor, exhausted.

With his free hand, Quinn grabs me by the neck of my bodysuit and roughly hoists me up onto my feet before pushing me toward the door, pressing his gun into my lower back.

When we're only a few steps away from the hallway, Bilken shouts out in a taunting voice, "If you aren't careful, loyalty will be your downfall as well. Like father, like daughter." He pauses just long enough to unleash a derisive laugh. "At least your mother had the sense to know which side to choose."

I freeze mid-step and glance over my shoulder, choking out a bewildered, "What?" My lips are bone dry as I force out the word.

Question after question stampedes through my brain, but none of them find their way onto my lips. The silence suffocates my voice.

I lock eyes with Bilken, who returns my gaze with a smug grin, but Quinn shoves me through the door before I can even try to get answers.

I stumble forward as shock tears through me. *Bilken knows my mother.* That thought replays in a loop in my brain, opening up a whole new world of possibilities. Bilken and Nolan have been acquainted for years, so it stands to reason Bilken would've known my father, too, given his own past friendship with Nolan.

But my mother? What connection could Bilken possibly have to my mother?

Unless…she knew about my father's activities long before he was arrested. Maybe she never intended to betray him and Bilken was the one who convinced her to.

Maybe Bilken was the person actually responsible for ripping my family apart.

As I trudge along the empty corridor with Quinn's gun digging into the small of my back, urging me forward every few steps, it occurs to me I never truly understood hatred before this moment. Such a feeling wasn't a natural part of my life; like all my other emotions, it had to be repressed or ignored to ensure my survival.

When I met Dr. Richter, I thought I grasped the full extent of what hatred felt like, but I know now I was wrong. Now, I realize I will never despise anyone as much as I despise Wren Bilken.

With one exception, my conscience reminds me.

Myself.

Because loyalty did kill my father. But it wasn't loyalty to his country or PHOENIX, or even to my mother, his wife, that ended his life. It was his loyalty to me.

Because of me, my father is dead, and I will never be able to forgive myself for it.

Quinn nudges me forward again, and with tears in my eyes, I stare down at the floor as he leads me through the compound in silence.

TWENTY-THREE

MY FEET DRAG, SCUFFING THE concrete floor, as I fumble along through the corridors, retracing my steps to my cell where Ezra and Jenner are still imprisoned, Quinn's gun always at my back. The tantrum that took hold of me only moments ago has passed, leaving me feeling deflated and weak.

I recite what Bilken said about my father, repeating his words in my head. *"If you aren't careful, loyalty will be your downfall as well."* I've known since I read my father's journal that his loyalty to me was what led to his death. That guilt is already a burden on my shoulders that I'll never be rid of.

But the second half of what Bilken said… That's the part that bothers me. The part that made it sound like it's a bad thing to die for the people you love. The part that implied family isn't worth protecting.

The part that seemed to empathize with my mother's choice to abandon her husband and daughter to the wolves.

Bilken thinks I'll die the same way my father did, because of loyalty to someone I love. Who knows, maybe I will. Maybe the future I've seen so many times was triggered by my decision to leave Ezra—by my need to find a way to save him and Jenner from the terrible fate we were all unknowingly hurtling toward. I might've had that first vision before our paths even crossed, but I'm beginning to understand that time is a loop and destiny will write itself however it wants, regardless of what steps we take to guide it.

If fate says I'm to die protecting someone I love, then that's the way I'll go. And I'll go happily if it means Ezra and Jenner can live. I can make that sacrifice.

Hell, I've already *tried* to make that sacrifice.

My loyalty to the people I love is what drove me to become Dr. Richter's prized weapon, laying the foundations for the State's current position of power that so many innocent people have paid the price for with their blood.

All I wanted was to protect Ezra and Jenner, but that desire has only pushed us that much closer to death. The fate of our world is intertwined with my choices, and no matter which path I choose, we always seem to end up on the path to that apocalyptic future I've been trying to escape.

Perhaps Bilken is right, after all.

My unwavering loyalty will lead us right into the mouth of destruction.

Quinn grabs my shoulder, stalling me in my mindless advance. Startling out of my daze, I look up, noting that we've arrived back at my cell. I step forward willingly, ready to be reunited with my…friends? That word suddenly seems too weak for what they really are to me.

Family, a voice in my head offers. *They're family.*

I pause, casting a sidelong glance at Quinn when he doesn't move or open the door, but the ex-Enforcer avoids my gaze. His expression is grim, his posture tense, as if he wants to say something but is struggling to find the right words.

My eyes drop to his hands, which now hang by his sides, limp and empty, his pistol returned to its holster.

"Why didn't you use your power on Bilken?" His voice is a rough whisper, scratching against the surface of my sanity. The dark pits of his eyes dart to mine, and in their depths, doubt shines like an old, familiar friend.

I don't blame him for being confused. Everything he knows about me was fed to him either by the State or by Nolan. As far as he's concerned, I'm a monster— all trace of humanity swept under the rug of my power and buried beneath a mounting pile of corpses. But that's not all I am.

That's not all I am.

"I remember who I was before this disease…and before the State started this war. The lost inhuman girl you saw a few months ago didn't have a clue who that person was."

The memory of what I became under Dr. Richter's supervision torments me more than ever now that I remember I wasn't always that way.

Now that I know I became it by choice.

I shake my head. "I don't ever want to lose myself like that again."

I don't bother telling Quinn the other half of the truth. That I wanted to know how it would feel to choke the life out of Bilken with my bare hands. To know I could kill him without using my power.

Shame washes over me. I don't want to be a monster—a *killer*—but it seems that's what I am right down to my core. Evil has been imprinted on every inch of my soul, like tattoos branded into my skin, and soon, there won't a single part of me that's unblemished.

Maybe that's why I no longer care about dying. Every moment, every encounter, is a test against the collar's grip—*my* grip—on control. What will happen when it eventually fails?

When I lose myself, who will be there to stop me?

Quinn averts his gaze and pulls open the door, placing a hand back on his gun as a warning.

I frown. So much for hoping he'd help us.

I step into the room, ignoring the ache in my chest when the door slams shut, locking again behind me. Despite their injuries, Ezra and Jenner leap off the floor and bound across the small space, closing the distance between us in seconds.

Ezra's fingers paw at my face with a heady mix of desperation and relief. I lean into his touch and let out a strained breath.

"What happened?" Jenner asks.

Shaking my head, I push away Ezra's hands and brush between them, nudging their arms with my shoulders. Their eyes burn into my back as I plod to the far wall and slump down to the floor with a whimper.

They're both beside me again almost instantly, crouching close but giving me space to breathe, as if that's what they think I need. I wish they wouldn't. I wish they would hold me and tell me everything is going to be okay, the way my father and Rai would have if they were still here.

The way my mother should have but didn't.

"The other Heads support Nolan's plan." My voice breaks.

A comforting hand slides up my back. "I thought they might," Ezra says, rubbing my shoulder.

I keep my eyes fixed on the floor, but the longer I stare at the concrete, the more it seems to resemble the rubble from my vision.

I blink a few times to chase the image away, but it lingers—a reality I can no longer escape.

"I saw it. The attack on the Heart. There's nothing I can do to stop it now. There's no time. Nolan will keep us alive until it happens, just to ensure I was telling the truth, but after that…" I trail off, unable to finish that thought.

The frustration I've struggled with so many times in the last two months returns to swallow me whole. It spreads through my veins like a surge of adrenaline.

I clamp my eyes shut. "How did things get to this point? Where are your friends? Where are Duke and the others who would've stood by you through this? How are we so alone?" Although I try to keep the accusation out of my voice, it's there, blaringly loud behind every word.

If Ezra and Jenner had cared less about me, if they had made preserving PHOENIX their top priority, then maybe this whole nightmare could've been avoided. If they hadn't cared about me, Nolan wouldn't have known what I can do. If they hadn't cared, no one would have stepped in to extract me. If they hadn't cared, I would've died in that bar in Zone 7 from blood loss like I should have.

If they hadn't cared, everyone would be safe.

I push out a shaking breath through my nose. I know I'm projecting, shifting the blame onto them when, really, the only person at fault here is me. My own inability to change the future is what got us into this mess. My own helplessness is to blame.

Not theirs.

I shiver when Ezra takes his hand off my shoulder. "Nolan chose this place to be a training ground of sorts for the more radicalized members of PHOENIX, the ones willing and able to go to war. Those who didn't fall into that category were redistributed to other sects."

"With the exception of us," Jenner adds, "but we already figured out why Nolan kept us so close. At the time, we just assumed he considered us radical because we were willing to do anything to get you back."

"Yeah, like blow up a transport helicopter," I scoff, rolling my eyes. Skepticism creases my brow. "So, you're telling me Duke wasn't soldier material?"

"Not to Nolan," Ezra answers. "During the redistribution, he said the other sects needed some muscle for protection since many of our members are normal civilians who aren't capable of fighting. I'm guessing the real reason Duke was shunned was because he's our friend and there's a history there that might have made him sympathetic to your plight. That made his loyalty questionable. Nolan prefers his soldiers to be obedient, just like—"

"Enforcers," I breathe.

He nods. "I think we were separated on purpose so we wouldn't have any immediate help available if we did choose to rebel. We thought Nolan was helping us, but, really, he was just securing our isolation. No one even knows where we are."

"Could Duke have traced your call?" I ask, peeking over at Jenner.

His frown is all the answer I need.

Like Dr. Richter, Nolan seems to always be one step ahead of us. He can anticipate what we're going to do even better than I can and *I'm* the one with the power to see the future.

The thought turns my stomach.

Jenner snorts. "You know, for the first time, I almost buy that terrorist label. Nolan is definitely acting like one."

Tears prick at my eyes as I bite back a scream. Things weren't supposed to turn out this way. PHOENIX was meant to save our ruined country.

Not make it worse.

Rai's voice stirs in the back of my head, once again regurgitating the lie that PHOENIX is good. Would she still believe that if she could see what's happening now? Or would she stand against Nolan the way I wish we could?

The people dearest to me have each lost so much and yet found a way to survive with that pain, using it as motivation, as a driving force, to make a difference.

Rai sacrificed love.

Ezra and Jenner lost family.

And my father... He was executed because he dared to dream of a better world. A world with the freedoms he was deprived of.

Freedoms he wanted for his child.

The future we're facing isn't what any of them fought for.

"You know I really do wonder sometimes..." Ezra stares at the door, his warm eyes glazing over, his words barely above a whisper. "I wonder if we are actually any better than the State or if we're just as bad. Maybe we were never good at all."

"Did you see it?"

I look over at Jenner, confused.

"PHOENIX," he clarifies, his gaze piercing, even more so than normal—especially now that his one eye is no longer swollen shut. "Did you ever see anything that suggested it was good?"

Even as a child, I was exposed to the State's warped version of PHOENIX. I heard about the terrorist attacks on the news. I witnessed the fear surrounding our everyday lives. I knew PHOENIX was dangerous, but I never once questioned why.

I know now that those lies were State propaganda, but knowing something isn't true isn't the same as knowing what is. What do I actually know about PHOENIX? How much does anyone really know?

The people I met at the other compound were good and decent, despite their fear of me, but they were never the real members of PHOENIX. If anything, they were victims, just like all the people about to die in the Heart. But where the people in the Heart are being used as collateral damage to prove the State is evil, the people in PHOENIX are a banner of innocence to hide the real horror behind—an instrument to encourage others to join the rebellion and make them believe their new cause is just.

To make them believe PHOENIX is good, the same way Rai made me believe.

Didn't the State once do the very same? Commit atrocities and lie under the guise of creating a better world? If I can trust anything, it's my father's word, and I saw his truth written down in his journal. I saw his truth reflected in the lines in his face and in the sacrifices he made to protect me.

And now, I see that same weariness in Ezra and Jenner. They both stare at me, awaiting my answer.

"No," I mutter in a disheartened breath.

I never once saw anything that suggested PHOENIX was good.

"Everyone who died… It was all for nothing."

The grief in Jenner's voice is heartbreaking, and I know he's thinking of his family who died because of his affiliation with PHOENIX. Meanwhile, I can only think of one person.

Rai.

I don't want to believe her death was in vain. I can't. The guilt is already too much. If I let my thoughts go down that path, I might never resurface from the pain.

"Before, we had a reason to fight," he growls. "But now, we don't even know which side to fight on."

"Neither," Ezra says, defeated. "Neither choice will bring back the people we love."

He's right. How do you pick a side when both options are corrupt and when neither gives a damn about helping the people they're meant to protect?

What do you do when there isn't a third option?

Ezra, Jenner, and I are only three people, and despite my power, I can't fight this war on my own.

But, maybe, this isn't about picking sides.

It's too late to prevent what's coming; if the missiles aren't already on their way here, then they'll be launching soon—within a matter of hours. The attack is less than a day away. But that doesn't mean there isn't still some good we can do or that change—*real* change—is out of reach.

Nolan thinks he can broker peace with our attackers and create a safer world, but he's wrong. Because the only way the world will be safe again is with me completely out of the picture. So long as I live, the death toll will continue to rise as those outside the State strike back—as they retaliate for what our country has done to them first. It's clear this war can only end with my death.

Blood will always demand payment in blood.

Knowing that, the choice isn't really between the State or PHOENIX at all. It's between doing what is right, what needs to be done, or standing by and doing nothing. In this case, doing nothing would mean the end of the world as we know it.

I glance between them. "You still have friends. Those people you defended? The ones you saved from a life of oppression? Who looked to you for guidance? For hope? They deserve a future. You don't need to pick a side, but you *do* need to keep fighting for their sake. They need you, and if we leave them alone in this war, then we're no better than Nolan.

"There's still a chance we can win this. Don't abandon PHOENIX—hold it accountable. Don't let Nolan and the Heads distort what you've all fought and sacrificed so much for."

Jenner bursts out laughing and nudges me playfully with his shoulder. "Nice speech, Wyn. You know, you might have a future in public speaking after this."

A blush warms my cheeks. "My father created PHOENIX, so I feel like I owe it to him to try to preserve it. And we owe it to Rai. Besides, I have to believe there are more people like them and like you in its ranks than there are people like Nolan."

I think of the sole female Head I met earlier and the probing intensity I had glimpsed in her gaze. There was something there and in the overall reluctant air in the room. Something that makes me think the other Heads weren't necessarily corrupt so much as out of viable options. Maybe that means there's a chance we can set them on a new course.

A course for good.

Ezra nods. "Maybe if we get some other members behind us, we can make the Heads listen to reason."

Jenner and I mutter our enthusiastic agreement, although we all agree on one thing.

We need to escape first.

We decide on the best time to make our move, and as Ezra and Jenner discuss which route to take out of the compound, I consider the one part of the plan I intend on keeping to myself.

The world would be safer without me in it. It'll *only* be safe without me in it. And when the time comes, I will do what is right to guarantee a future with peace.

I will surrender myself to the very people trying to destroy us in exchange for them ending this war.

In the meantime, I'll do what I can to hang onto control and to keep the monster subdued until all this is over. Then, I can leave Ezra and Jenner again knowing they'll do what they can to build a better future for everyone.

A future I won't be a part of.

A voice in the back of my head sneers at my resolve, drawing my lingering fear to the surface. As flashes of my vision and the destruction that's haunted me for years cripple my senses, it speaks. I recognize the voice as my own.

If there's still a future to fight for, it says.

TWENTY-FOUR

I ROCK BACK AND FORTH, my arms caging my legs, hugging them close to my chest as my toes tap against the floor, keeping in time with my pulse. The passing seconds tick down to our executions, and I count each one, preparing myself to do whatever is necessary to save us from that fate.

A strangled breath catches in my chest when a blinding flash sears through my head, stabbing my temples and setting my field of vision on fire. I stare into the flames with wide, terrified eyes, glimpsing the impending destruction that will change the world as we know it.

And our futures.

"It's happening."

I snap my head toward Ezra and Jenner a split second before the first impact hits. A tremor rolls through the compound, shaking the room with the vibrating force of an earthquake. Concrete particles knock loose from the ceiling, and the lights flicker, casting us in brief spurts of darkness.

We all glance upward, holding our breath.

I jump to my feet, nodding once at Ezra and Jenner, who nod back, their lips pinching tight into identical determined expressions. We'd already agreed that the distraction of the attack would make for the ideal time to escape, but now that the moment has come to flee, I'm once again overwhelmed by the immense weight of uncertainty. Aside from when Nolan coerced me into providing intel on the attack on the Heart, I haven't been able to find the strength or focus needed to look ahead into the future, too unnerved by the thought of what I might see.

Too frightened that vision might just reveal another death I would be responsible for.

Enough, Wynter, I chide myself. *We don't have time for this.*

Without wasting another second on my fear, I step forward, ready to get the hell out of this prison. Whatever happens from here on out, we'll face it as it comes.

Together.

I shoot a cautionary glance at Ezra and Jenner, who flank me on each side, thrusting my arms out to stop them. "Stand back."

At my warning, they retreat for the backmost wall, standing as far from the doorway as possible. Once they're behind me, I draw in a breath, relishing the electric tingle of power buzzing under my skin.

This time, when I call my power forward, it responds and that familiar pressure builds in my chest, expanding outward like a bubble. Exhaling, I feel the shape of that force in my mind and, with a grunt, push it out toward the door.

As the pressure explodes out of me, the metal caves inward, crumpling at the edges like burning paper. When the hinges snap, what remains of the door falls to the floor with a deafening crash. The concrete shudders beneath our feet, kicking up a cloud of dust.

I widen my stance, shifting into an attack position in anticipation of the barrage of soldiers I expect to find waiting in the hallway, preparing to gun us down. Once the dust settles, the small rectangle of hallway I can see from this side of the doorway is empty. To my surprise, no one comes running to investigate the racket.

All that greets our escape is silence.

Inching forward, I poke my head out of the room and peer down both lengths of the corridor. A coppery odor wafts into my nostrils, drawing my gaze to the steady trickle of crimson seeping out from under the warped slab of steel that once served as the door.

The sight of the blood locks me in place. Although this isn't the first time I've killed, it is the first time since getting my memories back. Accident or not, the guilt immobilizes me, rooting my feet to the floor.

A sickening thought takes hold. *Maybe Richter was right.* Maybe I really am an angel of death. I destroy everything I touch, even without meaning to.

"Like poison," I breathe. I am poison to this world and to everyone near me, even those I want to protect.

Wherever I go, casualties will always follow.

Past visions of Ezra and Jenner resurface in my memory, and I shiver at the flickers I glimpse of their deaths. I shake my head. I can't let that happen. I *will* change that future.

Or I'll die trying.

Warm hands brush my shoulders to console me, but I barely take note of their touch through the shock of yet another pointless death. Ezra pulls me close to his side as Jenner crouches to the floor next to the unconscious guard, checking his neck for a pulse.

Hesitating, he peeks up at me, meeting my gaze.

When he parts his lips to speak, I cut him off. "Please, don't say it. Let's just go."

We take off through the maze-like structure, Jenner in the lead with me and Ezra following at his heels. Each passage is just as empty as the last—as we'd hoped, everyone seems to be above ground, watching the attack in real time, leaving our escape route open. Unfortunately, that route doesn't take us by the Pit, but we ultimately decided the detour wasn't worth the risk of getting caught. Better to get out and not have help than to not get out at all.

As we run, part of me wishes I could be topside as well and actually *see* what I've witnessed so many times in my head. But then the image of mangled corpses and broken buildings assaults me and I quickly push that desire away, forcing myself to concentrate only on the sound of our pounding feet on the floor.

Every few minutes, another tremor ricochets through the compound, even though we're miles away from the Heart.

What kind of weapons are being unleashed if we can feel the shock waves all the way out here?

Dust fills the air, coaxing a cough from my lungs, and I stumble forward as another quake knocks me off balance, pitching me shoulder first into a wall.

Ezra grabs my hand, his palm slick with sweat, and jerks me upright before I hit the floor.

"You okay?"

Before I can answer, the fluorescent lights overhead shudder, threatening darkness with a menacing hum. We cast a wary glance at the long cylindrical bulbs before looking back at each other.

"It's not far now," he promises.

Jenner signals from the far end of the corridor, gesturing for us to hurry. We take off after him again, and after a few more twists and turns, a flight of concrete stairs slinks into view. Upon reaching the base, my eyes are immediately drawn to the round, metal dome-shaped door in the ceiling.

We skip the steps two at a time, sprinting as far up as the shrinking headspace allows. Once we're all huddled at the top of the stairs, Ezra grabs the wheel affixed to the underside of the door, his knuckles turning milk white from the strain of trying to turn it as the metal protests his attempts.

A cool breeze grazes my cheeks when the wheel finally gives way and the door squeaks open inch by deafening inch. I breathe in, gulping down the first fresh air I've been exposed to in days. The wind tastes of dirt and smoke, searing all the way down my throat and burning my lungs.

I suppress another cough as Ezra climbs out of the hole, followed by Jenner, who reaches out a hand to help me up. Grasping his arm, I pull myself over the lip of the doorway, landing on my knees in the dirt.

The open hatch leads us into the overgrown field encircling the farmhouse, which stands a couple hundred yards to our right with minimal cover of plant life to hide us.

I bite my lip, swallowing an anxious whine. I don't like this. We're exposed out here, with nowhere but empty fields and the distant Heart to escape to. All it would take is for one patrol to catch sight of us and we're done for.

My eyes dart from side to side, searching the field, but I don't spot Nolan or any of his guards. They must not be looking for us. Yet.

I breathe in, my senses on high alert, but as far as I can tell, we're alone.

We seem to be safe. At least, for the moment.

"What now?" I hiss, my voice barely above a whisper. "There's nothing out here."

Up until now, we've only had one clear goal: get out of the compound alive. We didn't have enough time or information to expand our plan any further than that. We took advantage of the only opening we'd get, but now that we've accomplished that task, a much more challenging one presents itself.

Where the hell can we go to find the help we so desperately need? Where would we even be safe? The nearest city is the Heart, which is currently under siege by outside forces, and beyond that, the other handful of cities that make up our country are too far away to travel to on foot, assuming we'd even be able to find them. Their locations have never been public knowledge.

Even if we did know where they are, even if they were close, any city still under State control is too dangerous for us to risk approaching without someone in the know who could get us safely inside. Without allies to give us refuge, we'd be as good as dead.

And while that isn't necessarily a bad thing in my case, I can't stomach the thought of anything happening to Ezra and Jenner.

Dread sinks in, settling deep in my bones. There's nowhere else for us to go.

We're trapped. Just like I've always been.

Before either Ezra or Jenner can answer, the skyline around the Heart flashes white, then fades into hues of burnt orange and bright yellow. Explosions dot the distant horizon, the fire from each impact starkly visible even from where we stand, miles away from the devastation.

Goosebumps rise across my skin as the ground shakes, my knees buckling beneath the returning weight of my guilt as the tremors threaten to knock me over. Somehow, I manage to stay on my feet, even as the guilt continues to pummel me into the ground. This destruction and slaughter…

This is all my fault.

The attack on the Heart is retaliation for the role I've played in the State's pointless war. Because of me, because of what I am, more innocent people will die—are *already* dying. The horrors I've inflicted have been piling up for years, and now, the Heart will pay the ultimate price.

Tears carve lines down my cheeks as the attack on the city I once called my home continues. With every strike, I attempt to justify my part in this chaos.

I never had a choice, I chant in my head, but no matter how many times I repeat these words, the burden of my remorse never gets any lighter.

Thick black clouds hang over the Heart, spreading outward like a disease overtaking the world one inch of sky at a time. The irony isn't lost on me. I have done to this planet what Ultraxenopia has done to me, and, unless I act quickly and find a way to prevent further devastation, everything I love will be lost.

The atrocities I committed for the State… I did what I thought was necessary to protect the people I love. And while I'm sure I'm not the only person who would've caved under the pressure of such an impossible decision, I can't be selfish anymore.

I have to set things right.

I have to put an end to this nightmare, once and for all.

Silence falls over the city and stretches across the surrounding fields, descending upon the countryside like a blanket. It's as if the world has been stripped of all sound with only the faint hum of the wind remaining. It whips past, shrouding us in a rain of ash and smoke. Chunky gray flakes settle on the ground like snow.

As I stare at the far-off, burning horizon, I imagine the crumbling remains of the Heart and find myself unwittingly thinking of the people still trapped in the city, wondering if they're dead or alive. Duke and the other innocent members of PHOENIX. My mother. Even—

"Richter," I gasp.

His face fills my head as the vision invades my senses, taking shape before me. My surroundings transform, sharpening to reveal the inside of the DSD, where Richter stands in a familiar exam room, alive and, to my displeasure, unscathed.

When I meet his gaze, he smiles as if he can actually see me.

My heart jumps into my throat as a shudder of fear rolls over my skin. When it comes to my visions, I'm like a ghost, haunting the boundary between two different worlds. But now, it's as if I'm part of what I'm seeing.

Now, it's as if he knows I'm watching.

"Hello, Wynter," he croons in a serpent-like voice.

I take a stumbling step backward and then two to the right, but his eyes don't follow my movements. Relief washes over me. He can't see me. And yet…he's talking as if he can, which is, somehow, so much worse.

Then, it dawns on me. This isn't just a vision but a recorded message he's prepared specifically for this moment.

The moment when I would unknowingly play into his hands.

"I knew it would only be a matter of time before you used your gift to see if I had succumbed to death like so many others in our great city. But, understand that, while I appreciate your concern, I know that's not the real reason you're here."

He smirks, peering at me over the top of his glasses. His expression makes my stomach churn.

"How does it feel to watch your city burn? To see men, women, and children die…all because of what you are."

A sharp, whistling breath seethes through my teeth, my jaw clenching as my pulse thunders under my skin. If I was actually in this room with him right now, I would shove those vile words back down his throat.

"Make no mistake, this attack is as much your fault as it is the State's," he continues. "You bear equal responsibility…which is precisely why you have to come back. Together, we can salvage and protect what's left of our country. We can shelter our beloved Heart and rebuild. Or"—he shrugs—"you can leave me here and do nothing as I and countless others are slaughtered. Perhaps that's exactly what you'll do. It is what you want, after all, isn't it? To see me dead?"

His footsteps resound off the white tiled floor, and as he crosses the room, I shift position, mirroring his every move. I'm like an unwilling shadow. Always connected to this person I loathe.

A malicious grin disfigures his face. "But you wouldn't wish that on an innocent, would you? You're not willing to let *everyone* die, to watch the people you *love* die…are you?"

He pauses beside a white wall-like partition positioned on the right side of the room. I watch his hand with building unease as it swipes across the control panel beside it, the embedded screen jolting to life at the touch of his long, slender fingers.

"You're not willing to let *her* die…"

He presses a button on the computerized panel, and the solid barriers turn transparent, revealing a hospital bed surrounded on three sides by life support machines. An unconscious woman with warm brunette hair and light brown skin lies on top of the blankets like a specimen ready for dissection. Although she doesn't move, the monitor beside her head displays every beat of her heart, each upward tick on the screen coinciding with a shrill beep that I failed to hear before now. Each strike slashes through me like a knife to the chest.

My hands fly to my mouth as her name escapes me.

"Rai..."

It can't be.

"Are you?" Dr. Richter presses.

A blistering pain sets my lungs on fire, and I can't breathe. I can't breathe. I can't breathe.

I can't think.

My vision doubles as the pain shoots upward and grabs me by the throat, strangling me. Black smudges press in at the edges of my eyes, and beyond the growing darkness, all I see is Dr. Richter's smile. It stretches from ear to ear as the vision around me crumbles into ash.

As the last of the image fades away, returning me to myself, the low purr of his voice trickles into my ears, like water trapped behind my eardrums. It goads me with the very same words he used to manipulate me back into his grasp at the magistrates building.

"Think about it, Wynter. You know where to find me."

A sharp gust of wind slaps me hard in the face, and I suck in a breath, wheezing as if I've been trapped underwater and have only just managed to swim my way back to the surface. Each lungful of air burns more than the last.

Gasping, I collapse to my knees, the tiled floor of the DSD replaced by grass and dirt. Ezra's familiar warmth touches my back, but I shy away from his gentle touch. I can't bear it. I can't bear thinking about how much he'll hate me when he finds out what I've seen.

"What it is?" I can hear the apprehension behind his words. "Wynter, what did you see?"

I peek up at him through a blur of tears.

Please, don't hate me, I'm desperate to say. The words nearly tear from my lungs in a scream. "Rai." I swallow, ignoring the way my stomach clenches when my lips shape her name. "She's alive."

Ezra's arms slacken as his face drains of color.

"Wait, what did you just say?" Jenner asks. His eyes whip back and forth between my face and Ezra's.

An invisible hand pushes down on my windpipe. It takes all my remaining strength to choke out the words as I clamber to my feet. "Richter has her."

I don't elaborate. I don't want to. The image of Rai laid out on that bed, her half-naked body unmoving, is branded into the backs of my eyelids so I'm not sure I'll ever be able to unsee it.

Doubt wrinkles Jenner's brow, and he blinks several times, as if he's not sure he heard me correctly.

"How…is that possible?"

All I can do is shake my head.

She died, we all saw it. I saw—

That line of thought cuts off abruptly when it occurs to me that isn't true. Not exactly. I didn't *see* Rai die—not in my vision or otherwise. None of us did. We heard the gunshot and glimpsed her blood on the floor, but none of us were there to witness the actual moment when Dr. Richter shot her. We just assumed he did and then ran like cowards because we all thought she was dead.

I thought she was dead.

My lips peel back into a snarl. "It doesn't matter how it's possible. We have to go help her."

Everything else can wait.

"Are you sure?" Ezra murmurs. His tone is timid. Uncertain. "Did you actually see her there with him?"

Richter's message replays in my thoughts and I see Rai again, unconscious but alive. The memory of it only brings fresh tears to my eyes.

I nod.

"All right." He looks away from me, and my stomach clenches at the sudden distance in his expression. "That's all we need to know. Let's go."

Groaning, Jenner presses a hand to his forehead, then runs his fingers through his mop of black hair. "Let me guess, this means we're going to the DSD."

I catch his gaze out of the corner of my eye but say nothing. What is there to say? If it wasn't for me, Rai wouldn't even be trapped in that hellhole. We owe it to her.

I owe it to her.

I risk a nervous glance at Ezra. He once told me what happened to Rai wasn't my fault, but I was never quite sure if he was telling the truth. I blame me, so, surely, at least part of him must blame me, too.

I part my lips to say something—anything to break the sudden tension between us—but another voice overlaps my own before I can even get a full word out.

"As touching as this is, I'm afraid I can't allow that."

Alarm bells go off in my head, finally breaching the haze of thoughts distracting me from what I should really be focusing on. From what I should've been looking out for.

Too little, too late.

I spin on my heel at the sound of the deep, husky voice, clocking Nolan approaching us from the near side of the farmhouse, flanked by his entourage of guards. Quinn stands among them, staring daggers at me.

My body tenses as I throw myself forward just enough so Ezra and Jenner stand behind me. Nolan won't let us leave here alive, and I don't see anyone stepping in to help us, which means my only choice is to fight. I'm no stranger to murder, and I could easily put down every one of his men before they even lift a finger to stop me. Or, at least, I could have back when I was simply an unfeeling weapon with no recollection of my ties to humanity.

But what about now? I don't want to be a monster, but could I be if the situation called for it?

Once again, I'm racked by the fear that's been plaguing me since I got my memories back. If I use my power that way again, what might happen to Ezra and Jenner? What if, by lashing out, I risk their safety?

What if, by acting out, I accidentally hurt them?

Nolan struts toward us, a frown pouting his lips. "It seems bugging all the exits was a smart move," he comments. "Although, keeping you all alive this long was not." His eyes dance between us as he lets out an exasperated sigh. "You have each been invaluable in getting PHOENIX to this stage, and for that, I give you my sincerest thanks. But this is where that gratitude ends."

The men behind him scatter like ants, encircling us. I count them out of the corner of my eye, tracking their movements.

"Our infiltration and subsequent overthrow of the State are reliant on secrecy and the cooperation of our members, neither of which you are able to provide any longer. And I can't very well leave you to run rampant through the Heart and risk you interfering." Nolan turns his gaze to Ezra, adding, "It's nothing personal."

Pressure explodes in my chest, and I have to bite down hard on my tongue to stop my power from ripping the older man limb from limb. I can't act rashly, not when Ezra and Jenner are standing this close and could get caught in the middle. I need to think.

I need another option.

Nolan offers each of us a lazy salute, then retreats toward the farmhouse, taking all but a handful of his loyal underlings with him. The remaining guards, led by Quinn, keep their guns focused on Ezra and Jenner, guaranteeing I don't do anything foolish.

After a few paces, Nolan stops and looks back at us, his thin lips parting as he holds up a finger, almost like he's forgotten something. When his pale eyes lock on mine, he smiles.

"Wynter…say hello to your father for me."

His next words cut through the air like a gunshot, making my blood run cold.

We're out of time.

"Kill them," he growls.

TWENTY-FIVE

A GRUNT RESONATES IN THE back of my throat as the toe of a boot kicks my legs out from beneath me. Wincing, I drop to my knees in the dirt.

Through a scalding veil of tears, I stare down at the ground. How could I have allowed us to wind up like this? Why did I just sit by and do nothing?

Rough hands pin my arms behind my back, binding my wrists in metal shackles. I don't struggle because I already know from experience there's only one sure-fire way out of this. One way to undo the mistakes—*my* mistakes—that got us into this mess in the first place.

But when that nagging voice of doubt returns, I go still. What if using my power here results in the one outcome I've sacrificed so much to avoid? What if it endangers the very lives I allowed myself to become a weapon to protect?

My eyes dart between Ezra and Jenner as they're both forced down onto their knees beside me. I could do it. I could save them. I could get us all out of here alive. But I also know my plan could go horribly wrong. One wrong move— that's all it would take. One split second of hesitation or miscalculation and they would be dead because of me.

Then again, if I do nothing at all, we all die now, on our knees in this field. When I look at it that way, the decision is easy.

Footsteps plod along the overgrown earth, pacing back and forth behind me. Three sets of tramping boots reverberate in my ears.

One armed guard per hostage, I note.

There were more than that when Nolan left us, but Quinn ordered the others to go on patrol. It shouldn't surprise me that Nolan left the ex-Enforcer in charge of overseeing our executions. Quinn has hated me from the first moment we met. Of course, he would want the honor of slaying the monster.

Considering his motivation for joining PHOENIX, I wonder if his conscience is at all conflicted about gunning down unarmed hostages, or if he sees our deaths as just punishment for the crimes I committed on behalf of the State. He wouldn't be wrong. I've done horrible things for the sake of the people I love and even worse things out of fear of what might happen if I didn't obey. Every step I've taken, every move I've made, was selfish. I can own up to that.

But Ezra and Jenner… They shouldn't die, not like this. They've done absolutely nothing wrong except love a broken girl who doesn't deserve to be loved.

They shouldn't have to pay the price for my sins.

I swallow the rising lump in my throat, asking myself the one looming question I've considered at least a thousand times before.

Can the future be changed?

If I had believed that it couldn't, I wouldn't have left my friends, my *family*, and handed myself over to Richter. If I had thought the future was set in stone, I would've spent what little remaining time I had left with the two people in this world who mean everything to me. I wouldn't have forced myself to forget them. I wouldn't have allowed myself to inflict untold horrors on so many innocent people.

Even now, after everything I've been through, I have to believe I can still make things better.

Otherwise, what am I fighting for?

And if the future can't be changed—if my choices have only led us closer to the fate I've done terrible things to avoid—at least I can take solace in knowing our lives won't end like this, cowering on our knees.

We *will* get out of this, one way or another. Because I've seen it.

I've seen the way we're destined to die.

As the monster stirs inside me, pacing its cage, my trepidation loosens its hand around my throat just a little, just enough to revert me to the detached persona of the weapon the State turned me into. For the first time in days, I remember what it's like to be able to breathe without fear or remorse.

I glance sideways, observing Ezra and Jenner, noting any movement around them, while keeping tabs on the armed guards at all times. My senses all shift into a state of hyperfocus, my power vibrating just under my skin. Straining my ears, I lock onto every muffled word behind us, preparing for the perfect moment to strike.

"Which one do you want?" I don't recognize the gravelly voice of the man who speaks, but the one who answers…

That voice I know all too well.

"I'll take the girl."

Quinn.

The elongated shadow stretched across the ground moves, and I glimpse the darkened shape of a gun a moment before the cold chill of metal presses into the back of my skull. My fingers curl inward and squeeze into fists, my nails biting into my palms. My teeth clench together so tightly my jaw hurts.

"Fine. Then, I'll take this one," the first guard says.

He steps in front of his chosen target, crouching so he's eye level with Ezra. A grin splits his gaunt face, his angular chin lined with a five o'clock shadow several shades darker than his close-cropped brunette hair.

With a gruff laugh, he grabs Ezra by the chin. "Take comfort in knowing that you and your psycho girlfriend will die together," he taunts.

As he speaks, Ezra's hands ball into fists at his sides and lift slightly—a clear indicator he's about to do something stupid. His eyes jump to the guard's gun, then to me, then back again, his fingers flexing.

I clear my throat loudly enough to draw Ezra's gaze, hoping it will be enough to distract him. When his eyes meet mine, I shake my head, mouthing a single word of warning.

Don't.

"Let's get this over with," Quinn grunts.

The other guard glances at me and sneers, then spits on the ground before rising and shifting position until he's standing behind Ezra. Just past him, a third man approaches Jenner, coming to a standstill a few feet from his back.

Time seems to slow as a foreboding hush devours this moment, the silence only broken by three consecutive clicks as the safety is turned off on the guns aimed at our heads.

Breathing in, I close my eyes and concentrate, calling up every ounce of power I have. Doubt and fear twist my gut into knots, but I force them away, determined to fight—determined to feed the monster, *become* a monster, however many times it takes to keep us safe.

I exhale, ready to unleash all hell on our captors, feeling that familiar pressure rise and expand in my chest. My thoughts and attention turn to Quinn, and as he becomes my sole focus, an image forms in my head. The vision rips the air from my lungs.

I hesitate, letting out a stunned breath that's halfway between a laugh and a gasp. Time crawls by—hours seeming to pass in this moment—although, in reality, only a few seconds have elapsed. Long enough for me to miss my window.

A gunshot goes off next to my ear.

My eyes snap open and dart to the left, locking on Ezra before turning to the body now lying prostrate on the ground just behind him. In a panic, I switch my attention to Jenner. The third guard is shouting in my direction, but the ringing in my head is making it impossible to hear what he's saying.

A second gunshot cracks through the buzzing in my ears and skull, and then the guard behind Jenner jerks back and collapses. His top-heavy frame collides hard with the ground.

I glance between the two guards, only looking at each of them long enough to confirm they're dead. Blood pools beneath their unmoving bodies, seeping over the weeds and staining the earth a deep crimson so dark the dirt appears black.

I redirect my gaze over my shoulder, a smile working its way onto my lips. Ezra and Jenner each turn as well, gaping at Quinn in disbelief.

The ex-Enforcer doesn't return our questioning stares or offer any explanation for his actions—he just scowls at us as he always does and fires one final shot in the air.

Three shots. One for each of us…should anyone be counting.

My smile broadens as Quinn squats in front of me and pulls a small, black device from his pocket. As he reaches around to unbind my hands, he rolls his eyes at my expression. The shackles pop open and drop to the ground with a thunk.

"I still don't like you," he says under his breath.

A deranged laugh escapes me. Quinn just saved our lives. Although I had hoped he would come to his senses and help us, I never really believed that he would.

I've never been more glad to be wrong.

Rubbing my wrists, I scramble to my feet and then run over to Ezra, dropping to my knees beside the dead guard behind him. Averting my gaze from the bloody bullet hole in the side of the man's skull, I dig through his pockets, searching for the unlocking device needed to free the others from their restraints. When my fingers finally emerge with the scanner, I graze it over Ezra's wrists just like Quinn did to mine. The shackles pop open and drop to the dirt.

"Are you okay?" I breathe in his ear.

He nods as I help him to his feet, his eyes narrowing at Quinn, who hunches over Jenner now, unlocking his hands.

"Am I missing something here?" Jenner asks. He stands and gingerly rubs his wrists where the shackles chafed against his skin. "I mean, huge thanks for not blowing my brains out and all, but I'm kind of confused why you're helping us."

"You certainly didn't want to help us before. At least, that was the impression

I got when you were kicking me in the stomach. So, what's changed?" Ezra presses. As he reaches for my hand, I can sense his distrust of the situation in his trembling grip.

Quinn contemplates his answer for a moment, then peers over at the burning silhouette of the Heart, the black pools of his gaze reflecting the distant flames. "She was right," he murmurs. "I can't live with it. I didn't sign up to be a killer, and I'd rather help you than be part of the problem."

Ezra and Jenner exchange a quick glance before looking at me, but I don't comment. We might all have our doubts about Quinn's motives, but they don't matter right now—not if having his help means we can get out of this situation alive.

Quinn turns in a slow circle, scanning the area, as he checks the ammunition clip in his gun. "There's a safe place nearby. I could take you all there—"

"No," I cut in. "We have to save Rai. We can't just leave her there with Richter."

"We need to get to the tunnels," Ezra says. "It's the quickest way to Zone 1."

"Are you insane? That's impossible."

I arch an eyebrow at Quinn, pursing my lips. If he's going to reject our ideas, he damn well better offer an alternative option.

He sighs, exhaling through his nose. "Nolan plans to move compliant citizens underground until peace can be established with whoever's attacking us. Every able-bodied person in PHOENIX is being utilized for this task. There won't be a single unmanned route we can use."

Jenner snorts. "If peace even *can* be established. The State has pissed off a lot of people." He quickly meets my gaze. "No offense."

"None taken," I grumble.

Ezra pinches the bridge of his nose between his thumb and forefinger, pushing out a strained breath. "Okay, so how do we get in?"

We all look at Quinn. As an ex-Enforcer, he knows the Heart better than any of us—even better than Ezra and Jenner, who spent so much of their time traversing the tunnels.

Balking under the weight of our stares, he mutters, "Am I going to be able to talk you out of this suicide mission?"

"Someone we care about is in trouble. So, no," I answer.

"Definitely not," Ezra seconds.

"Nope," Jenner adds, popping his lips on the *p*.

Quinn groans, scrubbing a hand over his face. "You're sure your friend is alive?" When I nod, he grumbles something unintelligible under his breath. Then, with a frustrated sigh, he says, "There is one way, but it'll be heavily guarded and will require a bit of"—he looks at me—"force."

I scoff. "*Now* you want me to use my power?"

He shrugs. "I don't like it, but it's the only way in."

No one argues with that. We have to reach Rai, so if Quinn's plan is the only way to get us to her, then that's the path we're going to take.

Ezra raises my hand to his lips, his warm breath tickling over my skin as he kisses my knuckles before pressing my palm to his cheek. Twenty minutes ago, I was certain he'd hate me for abandoning Rai to Dr. Richter's cruelty. For not seeing beyond that splash of blood we mistook to mean death or realizing she's been alive this whole time when I was in such close proximity to her.

But his expression when he looks at me now isn't full of blame, as I expect it to be. If anything, his eyes are pleading. The hazel depths beg me to save our friend.

This is it, I tell myself.

This is my chance to make up for failing Rai.

"We're with you no matter what," Ezra promises.

Nodding, I look back over at Quinn. Although he saved our lives, I'm not sure if I can trust him…or if I should. And yet, if this going to work, I need to.

Holding his gaze, I say, "Show us the way."

The next few moments seem to pass in a daze as we loot the guards' corpses of their ammunition and guns. As Ezra and Jenner arm themselves, Quinn walks us through his plan.

"We'll have to move as quickly as possible since we have no choice but to go on foot. A lot can happen between here and the Heart, so stay close."

We keep low to the ground as we progress through the jungle of weeds that have overtaken the fields. Every so often, a gunshot rings out in the distance, and each time, we drop flat to our stomachs, taking cover out of fear we've been spotted. By the State. By PHOENIX. They're the same to us now.

Both are our enemies.

By the time we reach the outskirts of the Heart, night has fallen and the sky is a blanket of black, the light of the stars extinguished by a thick, suffocating smoke. The border wall marking the edge of Zone 7 greets our arrival, towering over us in a menacing way I never experienced from inside the city. From within, the wall was a guardian. A protector.

But out here, with barbed wire along every edge, it's a threatening sentry denying us entry.

I've never seen the wall this close before. The one and only time I went to Zone 7, it was night and I was too disoriented from blood loss to pay any attention to my surroundings. Prior to that, I never ventured any farther than Zone 2 where the city's boundary was a faint smudge of gray in the distance. Even then, I rarely spared a glance at it. Our society trained us from birth to ignore that we were all prisoners, locked within the State's walls.

Now, those same walls keep us out.

A sealed gate stands a few hundred yards away from our hiding place in the tall, dry grass, hugged by two massive towers topped with turrets. And surrounding it on all sides are Enforcers.

In my head, I tally up how many lives I'll have to take here, how many more lives will bear down on my conscience in order for us to reach the city. The numbers aren't anything I haven't dealt with before, but the thought of further death still twists my insides, as if wringing my body of its remaining humanity.

Quinn waves his hand to get our attention and signals for us to mimic his movements, bolting behind an unoccupied armored convoy truck parked nearby. We shuffle after him one at a time and huddle together, ducking behind the oversized tires to stay out of view of the yellow-toned spotlight, which passes by our position every thirty seconds or so.

After the fifth pass, Quinn hisses at me, "Lookouts are stationed in the towers, and those small dips in the wall are hiding snipers. So, watch out."

"Don't worry about me," I whisper back. "I'll be able to sense them. Just make sure you all stay here and, whatever you do, stay out of sight."

I peer around the edge of the tire and draw in a breath, readying myself for whatever needs to be done to reach Rai.

We're coming, I promise.

As I move to stand, a hand grabs my wrist, holding me back.

"Be careful," Ezra begs when I look over my shoulder.

One corner of my mouth twitches into a smile as I nod, gently squeezing his fingers. Then, without another word, I rise and step out into the open.

TWENTY-SIX

ALTHOUGH I'M AWARE OF YELLING voices, the only sound I hear clearly is my own steady breathing. Each calm inhalation reverberates back in my ears as I stalk forward, deeper into the trap of the spotlight.

Unafraid, I stare up into its glow.

"Freeze!" a voice calls.

I take another step. I'm nearly there now.

The gates are almost within reach.

"Stop!"

I keep walking, my eyes glued to the blinding light, refusing to blink even when the sting of the glare burns my retinas and hot tears begin to stream down my face.

"I said stop!" the hoarse voice shouts again.

A bullet grazes the ground an inch from my right foot, pausing me mid-step. Through the blur of tears, I glance down at the scorched black mark in the dirt, at once reminded of something similar that happened months ago, back when the monster was fully contained and didn't live so close to the surface. Unlike then, the monster now lingers behind every move I make, in the breaths constantly filling my lungs and in each beat of my conflicted heart.

But, for once, I don't see this power inside me as some rotting version of myself that I detest, a harbinger of evil—but as a liberator. An ally. A necessary means to an end. Suddenly, in this moment, I don't fear what I am. I embrace it.

And for the first time since getting my memories back, I become what Dr. Richter warped me into.

I become a weapon.

My feet resume my onward march as my tongue darts out, wetting my lower lip. As the gate draws closer, bullets rain down from above like hailstones, aiming for my body and head.

Aiming to kill.

I exhale, and the pressure in my chest pushes outward, forming a protective bubble around me—an invisible shield that deflects every attempt on my life. Panicked shouts tear through the night as the Enforcers guarding the gate unload clip after clip of ammunition with no success gunning me down.

As I push ahead, many attempt to abandon their posts, but I lash out at them, holding them still, trapping them all in my mental vise grip. Only a brave few hold their ground.

"This is the only way," I murmur.

To reach Rai, anyone who stands in our path must die.

I skirt my gaze over the wall, my eyes wide and unblinking, as the Enforcers guarding the gate drop like flies. As the snapping of each of their necks echoes back in my ears, I try to ignore the scathing voice in my head telling me I'm no better than Nolan—killing my fellow countrymen to achieve my own end. If time wasn't working against us, we might've found another way into the Heart and avoided hurting anyone. But we don't have time.

Rai doesn't have time.

If that makes me like Nolan, so be it. I've already accepted what kind of monster I am.

Silence settles over the field as streams of residual gunfire smoke billow through the warm night air, casting a shallow fog across the dozens of bodies dotting the ground. The gleam of the lingering spotlight confirms the full extent of my monstrosity.

"My own little angel of death," Richter's voice says in my head.

I scrub a hand across my face, wiping away the tears, then avert my gaze, concentrating my strength on the gate. Pressure once again builds in my chest, pressing against my insides as it floods every last inch of my body, filling me to the brim. Gritting my teeth, I focus on my target.

The screech of buckling metal overpowers the hush as the immense twin doors tear free from their hinges and topple backward, crashing to the ground by my feet. Dirt kicks up from the impact, forming a cloud around my head as if determined to choke me.

Once the dust settles, the others approach, and together, we step around the crumpled metal and pass through what remains of the gate. As we step into the Heart, I keep my attention locked on the buildings situated just ahead, ignoring the broken bodies around me. I don't need to look at them to see exactly what I've done. The image of these dead Enforcers is printed onto the backs of my eyelids, just like the vision of Rai in that bed.

Every time I blink, I see them, along with everyone else I've killed.

"What's the fastest way to Zone 1 from here?" I ask, pausing at the first intersection. The insignia for Zone 7 stares back at me from every surrounding building and street corner.

Quinn peers into the shadows, his gun at the ready. "I'm not sure. It's hard to say without knowing how the State is responding to the attack. I imagine all surviving Enforcer units were put on high alert and will be out on patrol. If that's the case, the city will be completely locked down."

"Looks like we may have to use the tunnels, after all," Ezra says.

Quinn rounds on him, his dark eyes flashing with threat. "I told you, it's too risky. Besides, once Nolan realizes I helped you escape, he'll have anyone he can spare out looking for us. Our chances are better topside since the State isn't actively hunting us down at the moment."

Not yet, I muse, but I don't voice that thought.

"What about the trains?" Jenner proposes.

Ezra shakes his head. "They'll all be shut down or in standby mode to keep everyone confined to their zones. Maybe even destroyed depending on which parts of the Heart were hit—"

"You're wrong," I interject, my tone shrill. A vision of the train system manifests in my head, showing me the empty stations. The perfect pathway to Zone 1.

To Rai.

"Even if they aren't operational, we can walk along the tracks and have a straight shot to Zone 1," I explain. "It will take a while, but at least we'd be out of sight."

I glance around the immediate area, peering down empty side streets and around every corner, the pavement drenched in thick pools of shadow. As I turn, my searching gaze falters on Quinn. The hard depths of his eyes stare into mine, his face an expanse of unreadable stone.

"Where's the nearest station?" I ask.

"A few miles north from here, along the eastern perimeter." He points over my left shoulder before breaking into a jog. "Follow me."

Quinn guides us through the abandoned streets, and as we tail his steps through the darkness, it occurs to me that Zone 7 looks just like it did the last time I was here. If smoke and ash weren't blotting the sky overhead, I wouldn't even know there had been an attack. It's as if whoever dropped the bombs on the Heart chose to bypass this zone on purpose.

Either that or the attack isn't over.

The minutes slip by until we've been running for nearly twenty minutes without stopping. The Heart is my home, and yet, this is only the second time I've had to come to terms with its enormity—the first being when I escaped from the DSD and traveled through six zones in a single night on foot. An impressive feat, especially considering the condition I was in at the time. Before that, with few reasons to ever leave my home zone growing up and no other city to compare it to, the Heart's size was inconsequential to me.

But now, with the knowledge of what I learned from my father's journal always present at the front of my thoughts, I'm aware of just how many limitations the State has enforced, not only to discourage contact between zones but between people in general. The cold, detached nature of our society…

The State made us this way on purpose.

The farther we progress through Zone 7, the more I take notice of how empty the streets are. No one's around. The whole zone is deserted. It's possible Nolan already evacuated the residents here, but I struggle to believe PHOENIX could accomplish their goals that quickly, even with all the sects working together. If anything, it's more likely the people are in hiding, waiting for the worst to happen.

The station at the eastern perimeter is just as empty and abandoned as the streets outside. We slink down the steps into the lobby where the fluorescent bulbs overhead spark to life at our arrival, short blinding bursts of brilliant white light interspersed with lengthy seconds trapped in darkness again.

I sidestep the refuse and personal belongings scattered across the gray tiled floor, forgotten amid the chaos before everyone most likely retreated back to their homes. As my gaze absorbs the gloomy scene, I envision the panic that must've ensued here. Fear lingers in the air and presses to the back of my tongue as the ghostlike screams of terror imprinted on the walls seem to scratch at my eardrums. This place is haunted by the recent devastation wrought on our city. Devastation that wouldn't exist if it wasn't for me and what I did for the State.

I'm the one who's brought this ruin to our doorstep.

We cross the lobby to the barricade of turnstiles blocking entry to the platforms beyond. Unlike the others, I hesitate before the glass shield, remembering all the times I waited patiently with my train card in hand behind a gate just like this one.

To my right, Ezra, Jenner, and Quinn each leap over the barricade—Jenner whooping in delight—and as I watch them, I realize my days of being an obedient citizen are long behind me. Breathing in, I follow their lead and catapult my body over the shield.

After two decades of constantly playing by the rules, it's a rush to break them now. Even though I've done far worse in recent years than jump over a turnstile gate without paying, this small act of defiance feels far more significant to me. Symbolic, I suppose, of the complete break from my life before.

We hurry past each platform, searching for the first direct train that will take us to Zone 1. The odds that we'll find the exact train we need—and that it will be operational with the city on lockdown—are slim, but none of us voice this. Negative thoughts breed negative outcomes, and all we can do right now is hope.

When we finally stumble across the right platform, we find the train standing there, the doors hanging open in greeting, as if it's been waiting for us. Breathing a collective sigh of relief, we hurry on board and press ahead in single file to the control cabin at the front of the train.

Red warning lights pulse in each car, casting us in an ominous ruby glow, indicating the train is in standby mode, just like Ezra said it would be. If that's the case, we may very well find ourselves having to follow the tracks like I suggested. Without power to move it, this train is useless to us.

As we make our way through the seemingly endless chain of cars, it occurs to me that anyone attempting to flee from the attack couldn't have used the trains to escape their respective zones, even if they'd wanted to. And considering the gate to the border was shut tight before I tore it down—

A shudder slithers up my spine, and I grimace as an unsettling thought takes shape in my head. Everyone in the city is trapped, just as we've been since the State rose to power. Now, in a bid to hang onto that power, it seems the State is even willing to let its own people die just to keep them locked in its cage.

And here, I thought it couldn't sink any lower.

"Shit."

I stumble to a stop, flicking my gaze toward Quinn, who curses again and kicks at the closed door to the control cabin.

"It's locked," he says.

Holstering his pistol, he reaches for the rifle slung across his back and slams the butt repeatedly into the small glass window embedded in the top of the door. His strikes don't produce even a hairline crack or a chip.

"Move," I growl, pushing him to one side.

In less than ten seconds, I've ripped the door off its hinges, and within another ten seconds, we're all crammed in the tiny cabin. The panel that controls the train stretches before us from wall to wall, but the touchscreen is black.

"Any of you know how to use this thing?" I peer over my shoulder at Ezra, who rubs his hand across the back of his neck.

"Well, the trains are fully automated. Their routes, departure times, even the speed is all pre-programmed. If we can switch it out of standby mode, the computer should just do the rest."

"Yeah, and how do we do that, exactly?" Jenner prods the screen with his pointer finger, but nothing happens.

The panel is locked.

We take turns examining the console, trying to figure out a way to operate the train, while Quinn stands outside the cabin doorway, keeping watch for us. Always the vigilant Enforcer.

After several minutes of repeated failure, Ezra lets out a frustrated sigh. I glance between him and Jenner, and I know, in this moment, we're all once again thinking the same thing.

If only Rai was here.

We stand back and examine the panel in silence, unsure what to do to get the power back on. Every minute we waste here only makes me more anxious. It won't be long before the bombings continue, and if we don't get this train moving soon, we'll have to continue to Zone 1 on foot. Otherwise, we might lose our only chance to reach Rai.

With an exasperated groan, Jenner kicks the side of the console, and the loud *thunk* draws my gaze to the bottom of the plastic casing where the edging seems to wobble a little.

Ezra glares at him. "Try not to break it, will you?"

"Whatever you say, boss." Jenner shrugs. "Pretty sure this thing is indestructible anyway."

As if to prove his point, he kicks the console again. This time, the casing gives way, popping loose from the pristine white frame and clattering to the floor. Behind it, a second, much smaller control panel is just visible, tucked away in the shadows.

"Would you look at that?" Jenner beams, pleased with himself.

Ezra rolls his eyes and bends down to investigate, moving the loose panel out of the way—propping it against the wall to the left side of the cabin—before turning his focus to the hidden control panel, stretching out his hand.

"Wait." I grab his shoulder, and he instantly stills. "Don't touch anything. I have an idea."

My eyes slip closed as I channel my thoughts back to the last time this train was powered down. It's not often the rail system is out of commission, but it has been known to happen on occasion in the outer zones. The State always blames the failures on localized power outages, but now, I wonder if it's just another move to control us.

Perhaps they want to keep certain people confined in their zones, much like they want to keep us all locked in this city.

Ezra and Jenner both fade, dissolving, as the vision unfurls before my eyes, dragging my consciousness into the past. I spin on my heel as the now intact door to the cabin slides open, disappearing into the wall with a whoosh. A man in a clean-pressed navy shirt and gray hat steps into the room and squats down to the floor, popping the false front off the control console to reveal the smaller computer Jenner discovered. With a swipe of his finger, a six-digit keypad ignites across the hidden square panel, the screen burning blue in the darkness.

Upon entering the required code, the train purrs back to life and the larger panel unlocks. I linger in the vision a moment longer, watching as the operator enters a second code into the main console when prompted.

My eyes flutter open.

Ignoring the curious stares of the others, I crouch in front of the hidden panel and tap the screen, holding my breath. Just like in my vision, a six-digit keypad appears, and mimicking the operator, I move my fingers over the keypad. The moment I enter the final digit, a hologram pops up in front of the windshield, casting a green glow onto the long stretch of metal tracks stretched out beyond the glass.

Ezra grips my shoulder when an automated voice booms through the cabin.

"Authorization code required."

Rising, I center myself in front of the main control panel and, when a keypad flashes up on the console, I input the second sequence of numbers I saw the train operator use in my head. Once I've entered all six digits, a musical chime rings through the small cabin and the lights overhead shift from red to white.

"Welcome," the voice says with cheerful acceptance.

With a low hum, the train begins to advance, moving slowly at first as it registers its programmed itinerary, which flashes in front of the windshield in green, displaying the train's intended route. On the other side of the glass, the tracks blur into lines of dim silver as the train picks up speed, racing toward Zone 1.

Grinning, Jenner plants his hands on his hips. "Well, that was easy," he chirps.

Ezra and I both scowl at him.

With nothing else to do now but wait, I trudge into the passenger compartment of the adjacent car. Exhaustion falls over my body as I collapse into the nearest seat.

Closing my eyes, I lean my head back against the window and let out a breath. The minutes pass in a half-conscious daze as the gentle whir of the train lulls me into an uneasy sleep. But even in sleep, I can't escape the tormenting thoughts or the paralyzing image of Rai, unconscious and laid out on that bed beside Richter.

A warm arm grazes my back and drapes around my shoulders, rousing me. As I wrench my heavy lids open, I hear Jenner's voice in my ear.

"Are you all right? You were mumbling in your sleep."

My fingers fidget in my lap, pinching at the suffocating material of my bodysuit. The more I pull, the more the fabric seems to suction to my skin.

"For over *two* years, Rai was right under my nose, and Richter, he..." The words lodge in my throat. Swallowing, I force out, "I should've known."

I let Rai down. I let her down the night we thought she died and again, over and over, every single day I was at the DSD, each time I failed to realize she was alive. How could I have been so blind? Knowing what I know about their past together, how could I have honestly believed she was dead? Richter might be a psychopath, but would he really go so far as to murder the woman he loved?

Then again, it's hard to imagine him being capable of such an emotion. If anything, he's possessive. *Obsessive.*

Neither of those are the same as love.

Jenner wraps his free hand around mine, and tears prick at the corners of my eyes at his touch. A sad smile forms on his lips. "The price of full control," he whispers, nodding.

I choke on a sob, and he pulls me closer, resting his chin on the top of my head.

As he holds me, pangs of remorse stab my heart, cutting into me like small shards of glass. Jenner risked his life to free me from the State, and what have I done since to thank him or prove I'm in any way worthy of his friendship?

You're not, a voice scoffs in the back of my head.

You're right, I answer, resigned. *I'm not.*

Jenner should hate me—if not for the danger I keep putting them in then for the tragedy I've brought upon Rai.

As if reading my mind, he squeezes my hand. "You weren't the only one who thought Rai was dead. None of us had any reason to look for her. You couldn't have known."

He turns to glance out the window, and I do the same, desperate to distract myself from the depressive thoughts beating around in my skull. The tunnel beyond the glass is a solid stretch of unending black, thick and impregnable. I can't see anything except our reflections in the glass.

Jenner catches my eye in the window. "Did I ever tell you the whole story about why I joined PHOENIX?"

I recall him telling me he got into trouble and that his family was executed when he didn't turn himself in to authorities, but he never elaborated on the details and I never thought to press him about it. It felt too personal to ask.

Holding his gaze, I shake my head.

He sighs, letting go of my hand to run his fingers through his disheveled hair. "I was seventeen and stupid. *Really* stupid. I don't know if I was looking for trouble or just bored, but I was always testing what I could get away with, ignoring how I was constantly putting myself and those close to me in danger. I guess I thought all the bad stuff we heard about was just a scare tactic to get us to conform. I didn't think it was actually real.

"One night, I was out past curfew, just wandering the streets looking for something to do, and I saw a girl about the same age as me lying face down on the side of the road. Two Enforcers were kneeling beside her, and I thought maybe she was injured or had fainted or something. She had a bloody gash on her forehead, and it didn't look like they were arresting her. I assumed she fell and hit her head. But then she started kicking and screaming, and I saw one of them cover her mouth as the other..."

He bares his teeth at the memory, and his hand balls into a fist on his knee. A long moment passes before he continues. "Although I couldn't see her face, something about that girl reminded me of my sister. You probably don't know this, but I'm a twin. *Was* a twin," he amends, his frown deepening. "That could've been her. I knew it wasn't at that exact moment, but I couldn't stop thinking... What was preventing those Enforcers from doing what they were doing to that poor girl to someone else? From something like that happening to my sister? If they weren't stopped, there would be a next time and a time after that..." He trails off, loudly clearing his throat.

"Next thing I know, I'm sprinting across the street, screaming at the top of my lungs." He laughs under his breath. "One scrawny seventeen-year-old kid up against two armed Enforcers? I didn't stand a chance. Luckily, Ez and Rai saw what was happening and stepped in to help me before I could get myself killed. They were out searching for new recruits for PHOENIX, and curfew breakers apparently make ideal candidates. You know, because of our willingness to disobey the rules and all that.

"Together, we stopped the Enforcers, but not before one of those bastards shot that girl in the head. In the end, I couldn't save her. Who knows..." He shrugs, shaking his head. "Maybe she would've survived if I had just left well enough alone."

The taste of bile spreads over my tongue. That girl's fate was written the moment she was targeted by Enforcers. If they hadn't killed her then, they would've just dragged her to the DSD and had her executed under the guise of some lie. There was nothing he could've done to prevent her death.

Still, I understand his guilt all too well.

"After we dealt with the Enforcers, I knew there was no way I could go back home. Rai had looped the cameras on the street to eliminate video evidence of our involvement, but the DNA at the scene would've been enough to tie me to their deaths. And the girl's. So, I ran. I joined PHOENIX instead of turning myself in because I was a coward.

"When the news alert about the murders came out the next day, sure enough, I was announced as the culprit. They spun the story like *I* was the bad guy and the Enforcers had died trying to save that girl. It still kills me to wonder if my family believed that.

"At the time, I was so focused on keeping a low profile that I didn't stop to think about how the story might affect my family. Deep down, I knew the DSD would go after them and use them as bait to draw me out. But I didn't take it. I panicked and stayed underground where I knew I was safe. I put myself first and let my family pay for my recklessness. My sister, who I loved more than anyone, who came into this world exactly four minutes and thirty-two seconds before me..." A single tears trails down his cheek. As he wipes it away, his eyes shift to my face. "I'm the reason she's dead."

My heart constricts, not just for his pain but because I recognize myself in his wounded gaze. I see the ghosts that haunt him so clearly now.

After all, the same ghosts haunt me, too.

"Jenner—"

He cuts me off. "I guess what I'm trying to say, in a very roundabout way, is… that's why you mean so much to me."

A trembling breath parts my lips. "Because I remind you of your sister? Or because I remind you of that girl?" I'm not quite sure which option is worse.

"Because," he says, taking my hand again, "you remind me that, until something major changes, there will be nothing I can do to save the people I love. That's my reason. That's why I'll keep fighting until there's nothing left in this world to fight for."

A lump forms in my throat, warning of an incoming onslaught of tears. Jenner's been masking so much grief and pain behind his easy-going demeanor—more than I'd ever imagined. More than I'd ever spared a thought for.

Shame washes over me when I remember how, before I returned to the DSD,

Jenner had asked me to stay, reliving the memory with a new understanding of his personality and how much he had already lost. The ghost of his touch remains on my lips even now, tasting of bittersweet regret.

First, he lost his family. Then, Rai…

No wonder he didn't want me to leave.

"Jenner, about when I left—"

He holds up his free hand. "You don't owe me an explanation. You did what you had to do, I get that. I just needed you to hear my story so you'd understand why I keep fighting and so you'd believe me when I say that all I want is your survival. I just want you to live, Wynter. How you decide to do that really doesn't matter. Besides,"—he sniffs, glancing up at the ceiling—"you and Ez both deserve some peace after the shitstorm of the last few years. I'm happy for you. Really."

His face splits into a grin, and as silent tears trek down my cheeks, it takes all my strength to smile back.

Everyone is silent for the remainder of the journey. Jenner and I sit side by side, our hands intertwined—his touch acting as a barrier between my thoughts and the anxiety threatening to overwhelm me. Ezra sits across from us, staring out into the darkness of the tunnel, while Quinn stands beside the nearest door, possibly questioning his own part in all this.

Just like with the mission to meet Bilken, I can't escape the feeling that we're walking into a trap. Richter is bound to have some tricks up his sleeve, and we need to be prepared for the worst. And yet, each time the future rises before me, I push it away again out of fear.

Whatever we're racing toward, I don't want to see it. I can't bear to see if what we're doing, if our efforts to get to Rai, will be for nothing. For once, I want to just live in the moment and take the future as it comes, no matter what that means.

Even if it all ends in pain.

Drawing in a shaking breath, I glance out the window as the fluorescent lights from the incoming station platform banish the darkness outside. We've reached the end of the line. Whatever happens from here… Success or failure…

The future.

Our future.

It begins now.

TWENTY-SEVEN

THE LIGHTS IN CENTRAL STATION shudder and buzz in time with our steps, but we press on despite their warnings, racing through the abandoned lobby. As we jump over the turnstile barriers, they flicker in quick succession as if saying, *Turn back.*

The overpowering scent of sulfur and smoke burns my nostrils as we approach the flight of concrete stairs leading up to the main street. Ezra pulls me into the dense shadows to one side of the steps just as a spotlight sweeps into the lobby and crawls across a section of the tiled floor, highlighting a thin layer of ash. He hugs me close, one arm across my chest, until the light slinks away.

On the opposite side of the stairway, Quinn and Jenner huddle with their backs to the wall. Meeting my gaze, Quinn jerks a thumb over his shoulder and mouths the words, *How many are up there?*

Sucking in a calming breath, I close my eyes and envision the plaza above us, spreading out the tendril-like fingers of my power, searching for any life forms above us. Exhaling, I open my eyes again and look back at Quinn.

"Two up by the entrance," I whisper, "and three more patrolling the plaza."

Quinn nods and readies his gun, then at the next pass of the spotlight, he sprints up the steps and slams the full weight of his body into the nearest Enforcer. As they tumble to the ground, he strikes the soldier in the head with the butt of his pistol, knocking him unconscious.

At the same moment, Jenner launches himself at the second Enforcer, wrapping an arm around his neck from behind and pulling him into a chokehold. The Enforcer struggles, gasping for air through his helmet, his gloved hands clawing at Jenner's forearms, but every attempt to get free is less desperate than the last, and, after a moment, he stops moving completely.

Ezra helps Quinn and Jenner hide the unconscious Enforcers, tucking them away in a nearby storage closet where no one will stumble across them by accident. While the three of them work, I stand watch at the top of the stairs, taking in the devastation before me.

The last time I was at this station was the morning of my placement exam. I remember that day so clearly, and yet, I barely recognize this plaza—this hub of bustling everyday life—in the aftermath of the attack.

As I breathe in, the dusty air coating my tongue, I glimpse flickers of my vision from earlier reflected in my crumbling surroundings. The darkness of night hides the damage well, but the memory of what I saw is sketched into my brain like a scar on my memory, always haunting me. Even the cover of night can't mask the monumental scale of the destruction.

I jerk my head to rid myself of that image and focus on the distant figures of the three Enforcers patrolling the outer rim of the plaza. Although they're too far away to have overheard our scuffle, they're close enough that I can make out the corpses buried among the rubble in the beams of their flashlights.

A hand skims my shoulder as Quinn and Jenner race past me, darting through the shadows, stooped low to the pavement. Ezra takes off after them but stops in his tracks when I don't follow.

"We can't stay here," he says in a hoarse whisper.

He returns to my side and grabs my hand as I gape at the wreckage laid out before us like a blanket of death. I blink, wishing I could wake up from this nightmare or undo it, but I can't take it back.

All I can do now is try to save Rai.

Nodding, I let Ezra lead me away from the plaza.

We keep to the shadows as we make our way through what remains of Zone 1. The inner zones are rarely cast in such darkness, which suggests the power grid supporting this part of the Heart was targeted by whoever attacked us. That would explain why the surveillance cameras haven't caught sight of our movements and alerted authorities to our location the second we stepped into Zone 1. If they had, the Enforcers would've already found us.

Quinn stops suddenly and holds up his hand, then gestures for us to get back and hide. Ezra yanks my arm, dragging me down behind a partially collapsed wall.

Fear prickles my skin as I lock onto Jenner and Quinn where they crouch behind a smoking abandoned car twenty or so feet away. The stretch of space between us seems to grow over the seconds we wait.

Ezra crushes me close to his chest, his racing heart thumping against my back, matching every frantic beat of my pulse. His grip on me tightens when beams of light flash across the ground just beside our hiding place, shining off a scattered nest of broken glass in which I catch glimpses of my distorted reflection. Although the light shifts away a few seconds later, I hold my breath, recognizing the vibrating sound of tires treading over debris. Each *crack* and *pop* gives me flashbacks to the trucks I was always transported in to my missions.

When the vehicle's engine cuts out, I lick my lips and peek around the edge of the wall. Less than fifty feet away, an armored truck stands vacant in the middle of the road, surrounded by at least ten Enforcers, who descend from the back one at a time, like an assembly line of death. The clomp of their boots against the pavement is deafening.

Their voices echo even more loudly.

"Start over there. Our orders are to have this zone cleared by morning."

Floating dust particles burn in the glow of the truck's headlights as the Enforcers work to move the rubble out of the road, simultaneously clearing the path while searching for survivors. To my dismay, the wounded trapped beneath the collapsed ruins of the surrounding buildings all appear to be dead, their bodies broken beyond recognition.

As they work, clearing the street of all obstacles, the soldiers throw the mangled corpses they find into the back of the truck. They toss body, after body, after body onto the growing pile as if they mean nothing.

"Hey! We have a live one here!" a young Enforcer yells to the others.

The strangled voice of a woman cries out from the other side of the road, and, from my hiding place, I can just make out her face protruding from between several large chunks of concrete. The rest of her body is buried beneath stone and glass.

The senior Enforcer in charge of the patrol joins the others gathered around the woman. "Well, what are you waiting for?" When the soldier who found her doesn't answer, he sighs and gestures to the rubble crushing the woman's body. "She's crippled," he drawls with an indifferent wave of his hand. "That makes her a burden. The State will not support those who cannot contribute. You know our orders."

Reaching for his belt, he unholsters his gun and aims it at the woman's head, squeezing the trigger without even a split second of hesitation. Blood sprays across the concrete behind her as her head flops back with a sickening crack.

Pressure sweeps through my body, hammering under my skin like a second heartbeat. Although I try to contain it, this anger, this rage is unlike anything I've ever experienced. My fingers dig into the dirt, clenching into tight fists, but

I can't hold it back. My hold on my control is slipping, and I can feel my power seeping out through the cracks.

I can feel the monster clawing at the bars of its cage.

Fissures form in the broken wall beside me, starting at the ground by my fists. Grabbing my shoulder, Ezra leans in close and whispers in my ear to calm me. I focus on his voice, letting it ground me, steady me, soothe me, determined to regain myself.

The fracturing ends before it can give us away.

Exhaling, I slump back against Ezra's chest and burrow myself in the safety and warmth of his arms. He holds me as the soldiers continue their search, his body flinching against my back every time a gunshot rings out in the night. Four more shots are fired before the Enforcers finally proceed down the street.

Once the truck is out of earshot, we reconvene with Jenner and Quinn, ready to proceed with our trek through Zone 1. We race through the ruined streets, trying to forget what we just witnessed, but the tragedy of it weighs in the air like a heavy mist, pressing down on our lungs.

Less than fifteen minutes pass before we stumble across another patrol. We group together in the same place this time, ducking into a shadowed side road a safe distance away from the fleet of armored trucks lining the distant end of the street. Wave after wave of armed Enforcers unload from the vehicles and fall into formation.

Beyond the patrol, the road opens up into a wide, pebbled pedestrian footpath that cuts through an expanse of mown grass. At the side of the green, an enormous viewing screen—typically used for news broadcasts and important government-mandated announcements—blinks a few times and then shudders to life, proudly bearing the State's flag.

The other public viewing screens we passed on the way here were all down due to the power outage. If this one is functional, that means the Heart's generators are beginning to come back online, which also means it won't be long until the surveillance cameras turn on again.

If we don't reach Rai soon, we'll be exposed, and if that happens, we'll never make it to her.

We're running out of time.

Suddenly, a booming voice projects from the viewing screen's speakers, startling me out of my thoughts.

"Attention, citizens. Commencing immediately, all zones will be locked down until further notice. You may not leave your homes for any reason during this

period, and failure to comply with these orders will be met with swift and serious consequences. Following this lockdown, restrictions will be lifted incrementally, based on zone and occupation, and curfew will be moved forward from 18:00 hours to 16:00 hours to limit citywide activity. These measures are being put in place for your safety, so we ask that you remain calm in this time of crisis and to obey your local Enforcer units as they work to return our city to normal."

Static disrupts the broadcast, and the screen flickers twice before going black again, hurling the surrounding streets back into darkness.

"The Heads were right," Quinn mutters beside me. "The State is enacting the first phase of martial law."

I glance at him. "What does that mean?"

A grim expression takes shape on his face as he surveys the growing platoon of Enforcers. "It means things are going to get a whole lot worse before they get better. *If* they get better."

"This is exactly what Nolan wanted," Ezra says, shaking his head in dismay. "It won't be long before people begin to catch on to the fact that the State can't protect them from this."

"Then Nolan will swing in with PHOENIX, offering salvation to the masses," Jenner quips. "With a whole army of pissed off civilians behind him, it'll be easy to start a civil war."

"Would that really happen?" I ask, my tone doubtful. "Everyone here has been oppressed and subdued for so long. The people in this city aren't fighters."

Jenner raises a dubious eyebrow before jerking his chin toward Quinn. "It didn't take much to turn him around. Or any of us, really. None of us here were fighters until we were given a reason to fight. And the threat of extinction is a pretty good reason."

He's right. Before joining PHOENIX, Quinn was the perfect example of an indoctrinated citizen. A Loyalist. But, underneath that obedient facade, he questioned what he saw, and now, here he is, sacrificing everything—including his life—because he believes the State's way is wrong.

"A little doubt can go a long way," Ezra muses. "It's a lot easier to flip people than you might think."

As much as I want to believe that, I'm not so sure I do. Maybe Quinn is the exception and everyone else in this city is the rule. Maybe they're all too brainwashed to want to fight back.

Or maybe they won't get the chance to.

The truth tastes bitter on my tongue. "I think the State is far more likely to just kill everyone."

Why else would it keep everyone locked up in a city being bombed? Maybe the State knows it's doomed and wants to take as many people as it can down with it.

Quinn snorts. "If you're all done discussing this, we have to move. We can't stay here any longer or someone will spot us, and then, we're screwed." He jabs a finger toward a narrow street on our right. "The DSD is that way."

We stick to the shadows as he leads us along a zigzagging route that moves us away from the growing contingent of Enforcers nearby. As we follow him through the back alleys and streets, I take in the familiar details of my surroundings—where visible past the destruction—recognizing certain elements from the last time I returned to the DSD.

I remember that moment clearly even now, two and a half years after the fact. How Dr. Richter welcomed me back into his place of torture with open arms and a smile I would've loved to punch off his face.

A weight presses down on my chest, and I can barely breathe past it the closer we get to the facility. My anxiety heightens with every step, but I push it back, keeping my thoughts only on Rai.

Reaching her is all that matters.

When the DSD slinks into sight, my feet trip to a standstill, the shock ripping through me freezing me to the spot. My gaze trails over the crushed exterior of the building, the revolving doors reduced to twisted hunks of metal half-buried beneath smoking mounds of concrete and glass. The entire top half of the building is missing, and I gawk at the remains as a single thought nearly brings me to my knees. This level of devastation…

No one could've survived this.

Shards from the shattered windows crunch beneath my boots when I finally find the will to step forward.

"It's as if they knew where to hit," I muse.

"Maybe they did," Quinn says offhand, kicking aside a hunk of rock.

"What are you implying?" Ezra asks point-blank. "That whoever attacked us chose this exact spot on purpose? How would they even know about the DSD or have its coordinates?" He hesitates, blanching, as a thought seems to strike him. "Unless—"

"They had someone on the inside," Jenner finishes.

The hairs on the back of my neck stand on end. It hadn't occurred to me that there might be someone inside the State responsible for the attack on the Heart, feeding intel to our assailants. The possibility never even crossed my mind, although it should have given the existence of people like Bilken and Quinn, who have each switched sides at least once. We've dealt with double agents enough times now to know what they're capable of.

Then again, what if this wasn't the work of a double agent or someone who changed their allegiance based on their constantly shifting moral compass…but someone who would benefit most from an attack on the Heart? Someone like Nolan, who was around before the State rose to power and has been known to have beneficial connections. Connections to people like Bilken, who not only provided PHOENIX with an untraceable contact channel so he could feed them information from inside the State, but who also helped Jenner pose as an Enforcer.

What other connections does someone like Wren Bilken have? Just how far would he be willing to go to secure his place in Nolan's new world?

"I can't say for sure," Quinn admits, "but anything's possible. I'm helping you, aren't I?"

Jenner leans in, whispering in my ear, "And aren't we just so lucky to have him?"

A grin quickly dies on my lips as I turn my eyes upward, examining what remains of the building. The DSD has always been a looming presence in my life and in the lives of the people inhabiting the Heart. I always assumed it was invincible—that nothing and no one could survive its power or break the hold it has over our city. But now, as I take in this maimed corpse of a building, I realize I was wrong. The DSD was never unbreakable…

My fear was.

And yet, unlike so many others, I *survived* the DSD. I survived its tortuous grasp, not once but twice. And although the fear is still there, itching at the back of my brain every time I draw in a breath, its grasp on me has lessened because I'm not alone. Ezra and Jenner are here with me now and will be with me every step of the way. With them by my side, I'm stronger than I was the last time I stepped back into this nightmare.

Holding that thought close—and with one last appraising glance at the demolished entrance—I jog over to the side of the building, peering into the cramped alley sitting between the DSD and the establishment to its right. The path, which had always been blocked off by a locked gate, is now exposed thanks to the attack, the barrier reduced to smoldering ruins barely resembling what it used to be. Beyond it, lies our only way in.

"There's a back door," I call over my shoulder before submerging myself in the shadows. Ezra, Jenner, and Quinn chase after me, their footsteps light against the cracked pavement.

As I climb over broken concrete and glass, making my way toward the end of the gloomy path, I contemplate what surprises me more—the lack of Enforcers guarding this area or that the back entrance to the DSD, which usually has more security than the rest of the building combined, is deserted.

I take a wary step into the empty courtyard, examining the surrounding wall and the motorized gate that the armored convoy truck would always depart through on the way to the airfield. The gate is still in one piece but closed tight.

To my left, the back entrance to the DSD hangs half off the frame, the hydraulics along the top smashed, as if someone tried to break down the door. Beside it, the keypad affixed to the wall burns red, but other than that, I see nothing.

I sense nothing.

Turning in place, I eye every inch of the darkness for danger, then proceed toward the door. Unease pimples my flesh as the blinking red panel screams a silent warning at me.

I startle at the touch of a hand on my shoulder, and whipping around, I lock eyes with Quinn. His obsidian gaze seems to mimic that warning as he signals for me to get behind him.

He enters the building first, his pistol drawn, and as he clears the entrance, it occurs to me that the fear flooding his eyes when we met is now gone, discarded behind the guise of a soldier. When he gives us the all-clear, I step over the threshold, followed by Ezra and Jenner, who bring up the rear.

The lights in the corridor beyond the abandoned security checkpoint hum to life for a few seconds, then extinguish, shrouding our path in shadow. A few seconds pass before the cycle starts over.

Jenner walks beside me, pausing only to nudge aside a steel tray with his shoe. I shiver when the metal surface scrapes the tile.

"This place is abandoned," he whispers.

Quinn uses the barrel of his gun to push open the nearest door. "Is it?"

I look past his shoulder into the small room, which is pitch-black except for a triangle of floor soaked by the spurts of light flooding in from the hallway. The ceiling has collapsed, and beneath it, a puddle of red is pooling across the visible tiles. An arm peeks out from under the wreckage.

My body goes rigid as the writhing waves of guilt return to swallow me whole. As they work to drown me, Ezra's fingers wrap around the tops of my arms and yank me back to the surface again.

"It's okay," he murmurs, leading me away from the open doorway. "Just keep walking."

As we press on through the facility, checking each room for survivors, the nerves in my stomach twist my insides into knots. The building is empty. No

Rai. No Dr. Richter.

We seem to be alone in this place.

"This doesn't feel right," Ezra says as we enter the large open room at the center of this level. Two of the four walls are caved in, but the way through is clear of any impediments.

I pause. Dr. Richter's assistant would always be waiting for me here after my missions, propped up against the wall opposite where I stand now, staring down at her tablet. I can't help wondering what's happened to her. If she survived or died in the attack, just like so many others.

"Do you think it's a trap?" Jenner breathes, glancing between me and Ezra.

Just like the one we walked into with Bilken. I bristle at the resurfacing thought. "It wouldn't be the first time."

I pause when we turn into a hallway unmarked by the destruction plaguing the rest of the building. Up until now, I've been blindly walking forward with no destination in mind, sometimes following Quinn, other times taking the lead to steer us in a different direction. Now, I realize where I am and where my subconscious has been guiding me.

As I envision what awaits at the end of the corridor, an icy terror spreads over my skin.

"What is it?" Concern swells in Ezra's voice, thick behind every word, but I can't bring myself to look at him.

A distant doorway holds my gaze. The entrance to Exam Room B—the place where Dr. Richter examined me every single day throughout the time I was held here.

Of course, this is where he'd be waiting for us.

"In there." I raise a shaking hand and point a finger at the door. "That's it. That's where I saw him with Rai."

Ezra steps in front of me and cradles my face in his hands, tilting my head back just enough so I can't see the door any longer. As my eyes jump to his, he leans in close and whispers reassuring words against my lips.

"Hey, I'll be with you the whole time, okay?"

Swallowing, I bite down hard on the inside of my lower lip and nod.

Then, together, we continue forward with Jenner and Quinn just behind us. Ezra never lets go of my hand, and his touch is the only thing keeping me afloat in the treacherous tide as we swim farther into the depths of my fear.

But even his touch can't save me from drowning, and as we walk, I struggle to breathe, choked by the thought of what horrors await us on the other side of that door.

TWENTY-EIGHT

MY HEART POUNDS IN MY ears as I enter the code Dr. Richter's assistant always used to gain access to this particular room into the keypad on the wall, holding my breath as the door to Exam Room B slides open, as if welcoming me home. As I inch over the threshold, the shadows swarming the room seem to swallow me. Emergency fixtures line the base of the walls, emitting a faint blue light, but the dim glow barely puts a dent in the encompassing darkness. Still, it's enough to see by.

Enough to see him.

My pulse spikes when a smile forms on my tormentor's lips, and as he meets my gaze, all I'm aware of in this moment is fear. I can't move. I can't breathe. I can't think. Suddenly, I'm that damaged ghost of myself again—the one who cowered so many times before the will of her captor. Perhaps I never stopped being that girl.

Maybe I always will be.

"I knew you'd come," Dr. Richter purrs. "I was so confident, in fact, that I even left the back door wide open for you."

The Enforcers, I realize, my stomach dipping. He sent them away so nothing would stand in the way of our reunion.

Quinn and Jenner storm into the room with their guns raised, flanking me on both sides. Ezra falters behind me, his breath hot on my neck, but when I pull on his hand, he doesn't move.

I remember the day I came back to this place. I remember hesitating not far from the entrance, thinking of all the things I was giving up—the people I was protecting in exchange for my freedom. I remember how frightened I was.

And I remember conquering that fear.

For Ezra, this is that moment. Once he steps inside this room, there's no turning back. We can't run from the person responsible for so much of our heartache and pain any longer.

The time has come to end this twisted game of cat and mouse for good.

A fraught silence permeates the air as Dr. Richter cocks his head, his cold gray eyes tapering behind his thin-rimmed glasses. His gaze never falters from mine, and the longer he stares at me, the more I can feel my strength slipping, the unease of being this close to him again eating away at my composure.

My fingers grip Ezra's, clenching them for support, and to my relief, he squeezes back, letting me know he's still there. A stilted breath spills from my lungs when he steps forward, standing tall beside me.

"Where is she?" Ezra spits the words.

The smile on Richter's face deepens, spreading wide and peeling back his lips to reveal two rows of perfect white teeth. Knitting his hands behind his back, he shifts a single step to our left, and with that one movement, it's as if the spell he has over me has broken, at once freeing my body from my paralysis.

I blink, peering hard through the subdued light in the room, finally noting the set-up behind him. The opaque partitions from my vision stare back at me—the final hurdle separating us from what we came all this way for.

Richter looks at me, then swipes his forefinger across the control panel embedded into a freestanding podium situated beside him. The screen illuminates beneath his touch as the milky surface of the partitions fades, revealing the bed on the other side of the barrier.

Although I already knew what to expect, a tear still slides down my cheek at the sight of Rai stretched out on the mattress, her whole body exposed except for her torso and pelvis, which are covered by a rectangle of white surgical paper. Tubes protrude from her arms, each one connected to a different machine that either tracks her vitals or keeps her alive. A heart monitor beeps with calm repetition less than two feet away from her head.

My trembling fingers clamp over my mouth, holding back the rising wave of nausea pushing at the brink of my lips. Beside me, Ezra staggers forward, his hazel eyes wide and glassy.

Dr. Richter clicks his tongue. "I wouldn't do that if I were you."

Ezra freezes. "Is she alive?" His voice breaks on these words, and he swallows loudly.

Dr. Richter laughs, and I flinch, that demented cackle grating my senses. For as long as I've known him, he's been a vicious man, but I always suspected I was never witnessing the full extent of his cruelty, although I'm sure I came close.

But, now, as he laughs at Ezra's pain, I glimpse every dark and maniacal side of him. Now, I see just how dangerous and deranged he really is.

"Of course." He scoffs. "Did you really think I would kill her?"

"What did you do to her, then?" Ezra presses. "If she's alive, why the hell isn't she conscious?"

Richter slinks backward, stepping around the now invisible partitions, and emerges around the opposite side of the bed, pausing just beside Rai's head. Quinn and Jenner keep their weapons aimed at his chest at all times, repositioning where they stand in the exam room to align with his movements.

"I did what I had to do. Sound familiar?" He gives me a knowing look as his mouth hitches up at the corners, then looks down at Rai. He touches a hand to her cheek before trailing his fingers upward, tracing circles around a dark pitted scar on her forehead. "But I was careful. I made sure she survived."

An involuntary gasp escapes me.

When that vision of Richter revealed that Rai might still be alive, I only believed it because of the daunting realization that we never saw her die. The only proof of her demise was that soul-destroying gunshot and the splash of blood on the floor that still burdens my every waking thought.

As I gape at the small, round scar on her forehead, I grasp what really happened that night.

"You did shoot her," I breathe, aghast.

In his sick, twisted way, Dr. Richter was telling the truth. Rai isn't dead, but I'm not sure the state she's currently in could be classed as being alive. Can someone survive getting shot in the head? The heart monitor beeping beside her seems intent to prove so, but what of her mind and the person living *inside* her unmoving body? Is Rai even in there anymore?

Or is that part of her gone for good?

Grinning to himself, Richter moves the back of his hand along the exposed curves of Rai's torso and hip. The violating way he touches her, like he's entitled to put his hands on her body—like he has ownership of her—fills me with disgust, and I grimace, shivering as my powers scratch at the underside of my skin, searching for a release. Eager to hurt him. Although he's put me through hell time and again, what he's doing to her is so much worse than anything he ever did to me. What I experienced here at the DSD was inhuman, but this...

This is just *wrong*.

"I'm sure you're all familiar with our story by now. Raina..." He pauses to chuckle at some unspoken memory. "She was always stubborn. She never would've come back to me willingly. This was the only way."

My eyes prick with tears. "So, you're keeping her like this? Like some living doll you can just preserve behind glass?"

"She is *mine*," he snarls, each word a separate threat. "She always has been, ever since we were children. I will do whatever it takes to keep her close, even if that means I can only have her like this."

Like so many times before, I'm shaken by the thought that, if I had only been in control of my power, maybe I could've prevented what happened that terrible night. Maybe then, Rai wouldn't be here, laid out like some prize on display, doomed to spend the rest of her life as a prisoner in her own comatose body.

"I wonder,"—Richter paces behind the bed, fixing his hawk-like gaze on his brother—"how long it took you to realize that Wynter is the one Mother used to speak of?"

Ezra's face turns white, his eyes darting to mine, and in his gaze, I glimpse the memory of our conversation in the tunnels that night we went to Zone 1. What he said about his mother… What he said about me…

In this moment, I remember it all.

"You were always her favorite." Richter sneers, his tone mocking. "After the visions started, Mother couldn't even bear to look at me, but you? She always looked for you."

"She probably saw what you'd become," I cut in. "What you would do to people like her."

Like me.

He brushes off my comment with a shrug, unfazed. "Perhaps. Or maybe I only became this person *because* my mother cast me aside. Remember, Wynter, cause and effect. I'm sure you understand that notion better than anyone. If she had never shut me out in the first place, maybe I wouldn't have become someone she hated."

"Or feared."

His eyes sharpen as if I've just uttered the most offensive words possible.

"My mother had nothing to fear from me. Even my father, who had her institutionalized and who I blamed every single day for her death… Even he had nothing to be afraid of. But you?" Richter growls, turning his wild gaze back to his brother. "If you had just listened to her, she wouldn't have become so agitated and Father wouldn't have locked her away. We could've had more time. *I* could've had more time to find a way to help her."

He shakes his head, his lips curling back with disgust. "But you didn't believe her, and he locked her away, and she died in that godforsaken place. If it wasn't for you, if it wasn't for those damned visions, Mother might've survived. And if she'd survived, you never would've left home to join PHOENIX, and Raina—" He pauses, heaving a manic breath. "Raina wouldn't have been poisoned against me!"

I jump at the thunderous roar of Richter's voice, the crazed look in his eyes making me take a step back in response out of self-preservation.

I know exactly what visions he's referring to—*"One green, one blue. Look for Wynter."* That's what their mother used to say to Ezra. At first, he depicted those words as a warning, but when we met, he took it upon himself to protect me instead, believing that was what she intended.

The truth is, we don't know what she wanted as neither of us know exactly what she saw that warranted her asking him to seek me out in the first place. Whatever she saw... It was clearly important enough for her to want Ezra to find me.

Unfortunately, her other son found me first.

I wonder, did their mother's repeated ramblings about me become ingrained in Richter's brain? Was that what led to his career selection—this need to decipher his mother's cryptic words and find a cure for her condition? To discover not only the meaning behind her rantings but the reason for the visions that plagued her? The visions that likely were the cause of her death?

I remember what he said to Rai just before he shot her—how his mother's illness was why he initially showed an interest in this line of science, although he then went on to claim his past holds little bearing now. Still, I can't help wondering...

From the beginning, have I been at fault?

Was it his mother's visions about me—the riddle of my existence—that made him this way?

A short, barking laugh parts Ezra's lips. "How much of what you're doing here is out of loyalty to the State and how much out of some misconstrued sense of revenge? Your work here won't bring Mother back and it won't undo the fact that Rai chose to leave you."

Richter's eyes flash, his expression vindictive. "The State has provided me with a home for my research and financial backing, a necessity in my line of work. But, make no mistake, it is only a tool. Without the DSD, I wouldn't have had access to the resources needed to find someone like you, Wynter. Someone who would help me bring Raina home."

I balk at his words, unable to comprehend why he would carry on pulling my strings, playing the part of puppet master, if he already had what he wanted.

"I-I don't understand," I stammer. "You got Rai back over two years ago. She was in your grasp this whole time, so why keep using me? Why keep *torturing* me?"

His answering smile sends a chill racing through me.

"Because I wasn't done with you."

Ezra tightens his grip on my hand and shoves me behind him, putting himself between me and his brother. In my peripheral vision, Jenner takes a step forward, his finger hovering over the trigger of his raised pistol.

Dr. Richter merely huffs at the threat. "Call it pride or whatever you will, but when you dedicate so much of your life to one thing, it's only natural to wish to see it through to the end. To witness it used in the manner for which it was intended. For which it was born.

"Once, I may have concerned myself with petty politics, but I have only worked so hard to further the State's agenda because its interests aligned with my own. Our fearless government wished to take over the world, and by doing so, it gave me the opportunity to observe my creation in action."

"Project W. A. R.," I whisper. I can practically feel the color drain from my cheeks.

His sinister smile stretches from ear to ear, goading me. "I'll admit, I have conflicting feelings toward you, Wynter. On the one hand, you were the focus of the visions that killed my mother and, in turn, led to the chaos that uprooted my life. I should *despise* you, and yet...I find myself drawn to you. I've never experienced such attachment to anyone, not even to Raina, who is the love of my life. She is my heart, but you, Wynter... You are my greatest achievement. You are my soul."

I let out a nauseated breath at the same moment Ezra expels a low, throaty growl, his shoulders rigid as he tenses in front of me. The same revulsion tearing through me seems to emanate from his body like heat.

Dr. Richter snorts at my disgusted expression. "Don't misunderstand me. You are nothing more than the physical embodiment of my life's work. But that work is important to me and has become as necessary to my existence as breathing. I couldn't pass up the chance to witness your glorious rebirth." His focus shifts to Ezra. "And knowing you will be forced to watch it all happen makes it that much more satisfying."

My eyebrows pull together. "Wh—"

But before I can get the full word out, an ear-splitting ringing explodes from inside my head, making my teeth chatter together as pain vibrates through my skull, bringing me to my knees. As I scratch at the sides of my face, a scream forms on my lips, but I can't hear it past the noise in my ears.

Ezra whips around, mouthing my name, but only silence emits from him as a volley of power projects from my body against my will, throwing him backward several feet. As he collides hard with the floor, Jenner rushes toward me from the side of the room, fear and panic etched across his face, exposing his confusion. The pressure in my chest turns on him next, tossing him aside as if he weighs nothing.

Tears stream down my cheeks as pain stabs through my temples, pinning me down on all fours, my breathing shaky as my fingernails claw at the tiles, trying to find the purchase needed to push me back up again. An invisible force holds me down.

What's happening? I try to cry out, but my voice doesn't work. I can't speak. I can't breathe. I can't hear. A vibration in the air draws my gaze, but I can't pinpoint which direction it's coming from.

Tears burn my eyes as the pressure in my chest continues to build, crushing my lungs from the inside. Why is my power lashing out? I don't understand. I'm in control. I—

Understanding dawns suddenly. Raising my head, I lock eyes with Dr. Richter, who struts across the exam room, holding a sleek black gun in one hand and a small remote control in the other.

My eyes widen, searching for Ezra and Jenner, but they're both eerily still on opposite sides of the room, unconscious at best, dead at worst. Behind Richter, Quinn lies on the floor a few feet from Rai's bed, a puddle of blood forming beneath him.

My gaze flicks back to Dr. Richter, terror curdling like spoiled milk in my stomach. Since he put this collar on me, I've wondered if he could really control me like he often claimed—if his constant warnings held any real weight or were just empty threats intended to frighten me into submission. Now, I know he was telling the truth.

All this time, he's only been holding my strings, and now, he's finally decided to pull them.

"I've never been one for idle threats." Squatting in front of me, he tilts his head to one side and pockets the remote control and gun before wiping the tears from my cheek with his thumb. I'm not sure if it's his proximity that's letting me hear him or his control on my collar. Regardless, every word out of his mouth makes me tremble.

"If you had just been a good girl as I'd asked, I wouldn't have had to resort to such methods. But, just like Raina…" He pushes out a disappointed sigh through his nose before muttering, "You've left me no choice."

I choke on a gasp as he pulls back his hand and slaps me hard across the face. Tears spring from my eyes as my head snaps to the side, the metallic tang of blood flooding my mouth, tasting strongly of copper.

"Please," I whimper, my words slurring, "don't do this. We can stop what's happening. We can fix things, just like you said. No one else has to die."

He laughs under his breath before brushing his hand in a tender caress across my sore cheek. He clicks his tongue, shaking his head. "My precious angel of death… Do you really believe that I *wish* to fix this?"

A cold rush of fear tears through my body, freezing me under him. I want to get up and run away from this room, but I can't move.

I can't move.

"For years, my mother spoke of you, and from the moment I looked into those mismatched eyes, I knew you would alter the course of my life. The question as to what my mother saw… The source of the repetitive visions that killed her… It was as if fate had hand-delivered you to me so I could discover those answers."

I force out the words past the weight on my chest. "I thought your work had nothing to do with your mother?"

A smug grin warps the edges of his lips. "Like Raina, you confuse my ambition with sentiment. My mother's condition might've been the stepping stone for my career, but it was an entirely different motivation that kept me on this path. The truth is, I desire justice for her as little as I desire an end to this conflict."

"But—"

He cuts me off, scoffing at my startled expression. "Why, I wonder, would I cling to the love for a mother who was so quick to cast off her child? You should understand where I'm coming from more than anyone, Wynter. After all, look at how quickly your own mother abandoned you."

I swallow, my mouth painfully dry. "But Rai… She abandoned you, too."

"She was misled!" he shouts, grabbing my arms, his fingernails scratching my skin through my bodysuit. "She wouldn't have left me if Ezra hadn't encouraged her to. He has that effect on people, my brother. Always seems to know just what to say to get others to follow. To get them on his side." He snorts. "A trait you two seem to share."

Peering at me over the top of his glasses, Richter rises to his feet, dragging me up alongside him. I try to find my footing, but I can't feel my legs. I can't move at all, paralyzed by whatever hold he has on my collar.

Or maybe my fear is what's keeping me still.

"In the early days of your stay here, when Ezra appeared in your first successfully triggered vision, I recognized something in the way he looked at you. And I saw it again that night at the magistrates building, when we were all blissfully reunited.

"Whether or not he knew it then, it was clear to me what he stood to lose. Only by tempting you away could I hurt him in the same way losing Raina had hurt me. You see, it had to be your choice. *You* had to leave him willingly. That was the only way to make him feel the same pain I had suffered for so many years.

"After you returned to the DSD, it was a matter of waiting and keeping your unstable powers contained until the right moment. I had planted the seeds for my greatest triumph, unbeknownst to any aside from our mutual friend, Wren Bilken, who it seems had as much to gain from sharing that report with PHOENIX as I did."

"So, you knew?" I blink, my disbelief crippling. "You knew Bilken was working undercover for PHOENIX? You knew they were going to steal me back?"

"You. PHOENIX. Bilken… You're all pawns in a game I've created and I'm the one moving the pieces. I see much more than you know." He brushes a finger across his bottom lip and gives me a devious grin. "Ambition is a curious thing, Wynter. Ripping you away from my brother would never be enough to satisfy my need for retribution, and you… I knew you couldn't reach your full potential so long as you remain trapped by control. Our time apart was necessary to bring us to this next stage of your evolution. PHOENIX was vital for that." A scathing laugh cuts through the small space between us. "I must say, you've all played your parts beautifully. Especially you."

His hands move up to the back of my head and glide through my hair, pulling me close to him. A shudder rockets up my spine at his touch.

"You know," he whispers in my ear, "I spent the last two years trying to create more of you at the urging of my superiors, but every single time, the experiment failed. No matter what I tried, none of the others could come close to matching your genetic perfection. You are one of a kind, just like the beautiful poison blood that runs through your veins, and it was always meant to be you and me. We were meant to come together and see this through to the end. And now that you're with me again, we can. We can finish this, just as my mother predicted."

That terrible smile—the one that always contorted his face when he tortured me—spreads over his face again now, and he laughs a truly mad laugh, clutching me tightly by the back of my head and pulling me close until our noses are touching.

"What you fail to understand is that I don't wish to save this world. I wish to see it *burn*. Now that I have Raina again, my greatest desire is to witness the denouement of your vision. To see how this planet will come to its end." When I whimper, he lets out another low laugh. "Have you worked out the reason she saw you yet?" Determined to torment me, he doesn't elaborate, instead saying,

"The best part is…Ezra will only be able to watch as everything that every mattered to him is destroyed."

Bile burns my throat. This was all planned. Every single part. Yet again, I've fallen into one of Richter's traps, just like he knew I would from the very beginning.

"You knew where I was the entire time, didn't you?"

Richter knew I would come back because he was watching me. But how? Was it the surveillance drones Ezra and I saw outside the farmhouse? Or did he have some other method to keep tabs on where I was? To ensure that I would come back when he called?

He cups his hand around the back of my neck and trails his thumb along the edge of my hairline, tapping twice with the tip of his pointer finger just behind my collar. "I've been with you all along. Right. Here."

Vomit burns my throat at the thought of a hidden tracker embedded at the top of my spine. "No. No way. PHOENIX checked me over. They disabled the chip in my collar. They didn't find—"

"A useful feature of this particular piece of technology is the built-in countermeasure. The second your friends shut off the tracker in the collar, it sent out a jamming signal, blocking their scanners from picking up any trace of the chip in your spinal cord. The collar has never been just a device to control you, Wynter. It's a shield." His fingers press against the back of my collar until the metal bites into my skin. I squirm, swallowing a cry as he pulls back enough to look me in the eye. "And now that we're together again, you don't need it anymore."

"If the world dies, so does Rai—"

"We will be together until the end, just like we were meant to be." He leans in again to whisper in my ear, and my body convulses at the feel of his hot breath on my skin. "Now, show it to me. Show me the destruction you spoke of. Show me the destruction you and my mother both saw."

His fingers graze my collarbone, and time seems to slow as I stand immobile, trapped in his grasp, helpless and alone. *Click.* The tightness around my throat disappears as the collar drops to the floor by my feet.

A hollow humming sound fills my head, and my hand trembles over the exposed skin of my neck as a stabbing pain shoots through my temples, lancing me with unthinkable pain. My lips part to scream, but my voice is lost behind the realization crashing to the front of my thoughts. It taunts me, telling me my worst fear has come true.

My control is gone.

And now, the monster inside me is free.

END OF BOOK TWO

BOOK THREE
SUBJECT ZERO

AT THE PINNACLE OF WAR,
ONLY SACRIFICE STANDS BETWEEN
DESTRUCTION AND SURVIVAL.

ONE

PAIN, VIOLENT AND MADDENING, TEARS through my body like a rush of heat, boiling my organs and burning every inch of my limbs on its rise to my skin from the inside out. The agony pounding through my head is only interrupted by the clang of metal against tile, the sound of the impact a sharp, grating scratch that draws my blurring gaze to the floor. My breaths reverberate in my ears, and blinking a hazy film of tears from my eyes, I glimpse the outline of my discarded collar.

The one tool keeping my power in check now a hunk of useless metal, destroyed, at my feet.

For the last few years, I wanted nothing more than to be free of this tether to Dr. Richter and to the constant trauma I endured at his hands. But, as the understanding of what losing this link will mean sinks in past the expanding surface of pain, I find myself mourning its loss almost more than I grieved over my father or Rai. Perhaps because, without it, I know there's nothing I can do to save anyone from the monster living and thriving within me—the monster its removal has unleashed on this world.

Without the collar, the few people I have left are dead.

A convulsion barrels through my weakening body, and as the seizure intensifies, my legs buckle, no longer able to support the burden of my weight. What little strength I've been clinging to slips away like heat escaping my skin in the cold.

My lungs constrict as small gasps of air leach from my lungs. I can't breathe. I can't breathe. I can't think. A black mist unfurls across my eyes, and through the expanding fog, I glimpse the exam room floor rushing upward like the jaws of hell opening to swallow me whole.

My kneecaps slam hard into the gleaming white tiles, coaxing a strangled cry from my lips. Although unpleasant, the jarring jolt to my bones is insignificant compared to the fire of pain raging through me. I can feel it—the returning threat of death as it infiltrates my veins like a fast-acting poison, spreading quickly. Burning my insides. The monster has been patient, awaiting this moment, while I've been living on borrowed time, foolishly hoping and, at times, even allowing myself to believe, this day wouldn't come.

Time this disease will now strive to steal back.

Without the collar, the only thing in this world capable of ensuring my survival is gone. There's nothing else in existence that can slow or cure the parasitic plague of my condition. Without the collar to pause the advance of my illness—to keep me in much-needed control—my symptoms will just resume their assault from before the respite of Richter's so-called cure and lead me into the smothering tides of what is sure to be an agonizing death. Now, when all hope is lost, the monster will win. And soon, Wynter Reeves, as I am at this moment…

This side of me will cease to exist.

The unrelenting full extent of Ultraxenopia—finally free of its cage and running rampant inside me—seems to take on a physical form with its assault, sinking its claws into my flesh without mercy and reclaiming the hold it lost the day Dr. Richter ensnared me in this collar. It grabs me, squeezes me tight in its suffocating embrace, whispers familiar taunts in my ears.

Goosebumps pimple my flesh as it hisses those three weighted words, which have followed me since I was a child.

"I'm sorry, Wynter," the monster says. It speaks in a strange muddled voice, half my father but also half Ezra—a hybrid of the two people I love most in the world, created from my most painful memories and torn straight from the one moment I want to avoid.

The one moment that haunts me now more than ever.

As the mental image of it manifests in my thoughts, the exam room melts away to reveal a warped twin version of myself, the deep pools of her soulless eyes staring back into mine, black, empty, and unblinking. Around us, ash and dirt hang heavy in the air like smog, the taste of death and decay thick on my tongue.

The silence between us is unnerving, but when I part my lips to break it, the ground quakes, signaling the impending end of all life, as if that one unspoken word is the catalyst for the future I've been trying to run from. A moan rips through the desolate landscape, vibrating through the musty air and under my feet, and on all sides, the buildings of the Heart tremble for a moment before caving inward. Surrendering to their fate, they collapse, crumbling into jagged mountains of rock and glass.

"I'm afraid!" the other me shrieks, her voice clear despite the thunderous rumbling all around us. My gaze darts back to hers, my heart racing. But, to my bemusement, her lips don't move and her face is composed—a mask of stone. Unmoving. Unfeeling.

Resigned.

I furrow my brow, staring into her eyes where I see myself reflected in their inky depths. Like her, I've lost what little semblance of humanity I had retained in my appearance. Now, I look inhuman.

Like the angel of death Richter and the State shaped me into.

As my black-eyed twin continues airing her woes, her lips eerily still despite her cries, it registers that the ranting I'm hearing isn't coming from her—from this manifestation of the monster I'm becoming. It's coming from me. *My* fears. *My* emotions, long bottled up.

All of it, every word…

I'm the one saying it.

Tears slip down my cheeks at this realization and gather on my lower lip, filling my mouth with the tang of salt when I speak.

"I don't want to kill anyone else. I don't want to do this. I don't want to die!"

Nodding, the monster extends her hand and touches her fingertips to my right cheek, as if to ease my fear with her touch. But the relief I anticipate doesn't come.

Instead, I feel only terror when her skin grazes mine, my stomach turning as the contact between us triggers the world to tilt on its axis, throwing my center of gravity off balance. Darkness seeps in at the edges of my vision, smudging her face and the surrounding apocalyptic wasteland, both fading into black as I tip to the side, falling…falling…

Falling.

A searing pain spreads through my left shoulder and arm as I collide with the floor, the chill of the ceramic sinking into my bodysuit like a rush of ice water. I'm cold, so cold, and my lids are heavy, but I fight against the temptation of sleep, forcing my eyes to stay open.

Slowly, as I cling to waking, the features of the exam room slide back into focus, and I concentrate on each detail before me in turn, a shaky breath parting my lips. The dim blue light. Rai's body stretched out on the bed. Ezra, Jenner, and Quinn…all motionless on the floor. And *him*.

The man behind this chaos.

Dr. Richter leans over me with a smug smile, squatting down to the floor, his elbows perched on his knees. "Shh…" he croons, brushing the sweat-matted hair from my eyes. "Everything is going to be all right. Soon, this will all be over."

Holding my gaze, he reaches inside his coat, his hand emerging a few seconds later from the interior chest pocket, fingers clamped around a syringe. With a quiet laugh, he flattens his palm, presenting the capped needle like a trophy. I suppose, to him, it is. A symbol of his power and control over me.

Dread turns my stomach. There's nothing I can do. He'll inject me with the syringe's contents and I won't be able to fight back or stop him, every inch of me held down by debilitating pain. I'm helpless. No…worse than that.

I'm powerless.

More tears track down the sides of my face. This is like the collar all over again—another way for him to show he owns me and can do whatever he wants with my body, my own desires and wishes be damned. Just as he's proven time and again throughout the years we've known each other, I can never outsmart him.

Dr. Richter will always win.

I glance down at the shimmery silver liquid inside the transparent barrel, which glistens in the minimal light illuminating the room. It would be beautiful if the threat of it wasn't so obvious.

Pinching the syringe between his fingers, Dr. Richter removes the plastic cap with his teeth, spitting the clear shell back out on the floor. With his other hand, he grabs me by the back of my neck, raising my rigid body upright.

I whimper, my pulse throbbing deep in my ears. "What…is…that?" I wheeze, glaring down at his hand.

"Shh…" he says again, his grip on me tightening.

His nails dig into my neck, and I wince as the needle punctures the skin at my throat. The liquid is bitterly cold when it enters my body, and I shiver as it passes through me, spreading along the underside of my skin. The sensation—a freezing prickle followed by fire—sends all my nerve endings into a frenzy, igniting the pain receptors in my brain until I feel the frigid burn everywhere.

A rising sense of panic swells deep in my chest, but when I try to scream, the hoarse cry that rips from my throat is a broken sob barely louder than a breath. Every second is drawn out by the agony swelling inside me. I can't take it.

I just want it to stop.

Another seizure strikes without warning, the tremors tearing through me more violent this time. Discarding the syringe, Dr. Richter smooths a hand over my forehead, considering me with a spine-chilling fondness. As his fingers move down the side of my face, caressing my wet cheek, my limbs jerk uncontrollably and bile surges up from my stomach.

It's only now, as the pain sinks deeper and death creeps closer, that I realize my plan has failed. I can't turn myself over to the people attacking the Heart and end this war I'm responsible for…because I'm going to die before I can even attempt to. I'm going to die before I can change a damn thing, and Richter will watch, smiling, as the world dies, too.

My teeth chatter, threatening to bite off the tip of my tongue, when the convulsions intensify, each spasm—along with Dr. Richter's hands—pinning my hips and legs to the floor. My tormentor cocks his head to one side, his eyes tapering behind his silver glasses, appraising my twisted expression with glee.

"Even when you fight against me, you're still the perfect obedient pet, always doing precisely what I expect. And now, thanks to the accelerant taking root in your veins, it won't be long until you fulfill your purpose on this planet." Shifting, he eases my shoulders and head onto the floor, then straightens, his smiling face cast in shadow. Although I try to move, the spasms rocking my limbs and the stabs cutting into my brain hold me down.

As Dr. Richter looms over me, drinking in the spectacle of my pain, the gentle glow from the emergency lights reflects across the lenses of his glasses, obscuring his eyes behind a blue flash. His grin widens, revealing his teeth, and with that one gesture, he looks less like a human and more like something out of the fairy tales my father would read to me when I was young. Like something not of this world, but like something else entirely.

Something truly, unspeakably evil.

Grimacing, I force my gaze to the side, glancing at the three immobile figures spread out across the floor at different points in the exam room—on Ezra, Jenner, and Quinn, who have all been caught in the middle of this warped game between me and Richter. I never wanted this. I never wanted to involve any of them with this part of my life. I only wanted to keep Ezra and Jenner safe. I only wanted to protect them from certain death and destruction.

I only ever wanted to protect them from me.

Guilt constricts my chest, but my nagging thoughts of self-reproach are fleeting, my brain unable to focus for long on anything beyond the crippling pain in my head. Another turbulent fit rocks my body as my eyes shudder open and closed, then wrench open again, my pulse skyrocketing at the sight of the wicked smirk twisting Richter's lips.

He claps his hands together with a low, mocking chuckle. "Everything has fallen into place just as I envisioned. All that's left to do is wake Ezra so he can witness the finale to this grand production. He did, after all, help us get to this point. We wouldn't want him to miss a second of it, now would we?"

"There's only one problem with that—"

My eyes jerk wide, and the same surprise overwhelming my senses flickers across Richter's face as he spins around, putting his back to me. I follow his startled movements as much as my increasingly sluggish vision allows, my heart racing a mile a minute with recognition, anticipation, and fear.

That voice—

My heart constricts when I see him, my brain only managing one coherent thought.

I didn't kill him.

Ezra's name springs free of my throat in a gasp, but he doesn't spare me a glance. Blood is matted in his unkempt hair—dripping down his already bruised cheek from a wound on his scalp I can't see—but instead of worry, all I'm aware of is the relief coursing through me just knowing he's okay. And alive.

I choke out a breath, desperate to coax those hazel eyes in my direction, but I lack the strength to speak. I silently beg him to look at me, but if he's aware of me here on the floor, he doesn't show it, his attention fixed on his brother.

A smirk hooks up one edge of his lips. "I'm already awake."

Ezra thrusts his arms upward, slamming a large, flat object into the side of Richter's skull with such force that, for a moment, I allow myself the gleeful belief that my tormentor might be dead. The collision makes a tinny, metallic sound that results in a wobbling echo.

On impact, Richter's head snaps to the left, his glasses knocked to the floor, the frames bent and broken, the lenses cracked. For a few seconds, he teeters on his feet before crumpling, his gray eyes rolling back in their sockets.

Exhaling, Ezra drops his weapon, the medical tray clanging loudly against the white tiles. His chest heaves as he lets out a breath, and after checking with a nudge of his foot that Richter is unconscious, he finally looks in my direction.

"Wynter?" he rasps. Even in my disoriented state, I'm aware of his panic as he races forward, sliding to his knees at my side. His hands are cold as they press to my face. "Wynter, can you hear me?"

Although I try to stay awake, my eyelids droop, and the exam room melts into an indistinct smear of shades as the finer details fade.

"I'm sorry," I breathe as darkness rises to claim me. "I didn't...mean to..."

"Hey. Hey! Wake up. Stay with me." Ezra grabs me by the shoulders and shakes me gently until I pry my eyes wide. "I got you," he murmurs, wrapping his arms around my torso and pulling me close to his chest. His fingers graze my aching skin through my bodysuit. "Everything is going to be okay."

I manage a weak nod, feigning belief, even though his words are a lie. I know all too well what's coming for us.

Everything is far from okay.

Tears carve lines down his cheeks but he wipes them away, setting me back down on the floor. Ripping off his jacket, he bundles the fabric and places it under my head like a pillow. If I have another seizure, the material should at least protect my skull from any direct impact with the tiles. Not that it really matters.

Seizure or not, I'm already dead.

Jaw straining, Ezra wipes a rogue tear from his chin. "We never should've come back. We should've left—" He falters, and the column of his throat shifts when he swallows, the sound audible in the hush of the room. Clenching his teeth, he mutters, "We should've left when we had the chance."

Mere hours ago, after saving our lives, Quinn offered us the chance to escape, saying he'd take us to a safe place outside the Heart. But we didn't go, we didn't flee, because I encouraged Ezra and Jenner to fight—to hold PHOENIX accountable—and because we were all adamant about saving Rai, even though I think part of me always knew she couldn't be saved. But also, because I knew running wasn't an option.

And, deep down, I had already accepted this war would only end with my death.

Tremors ripple over my arms as I reach for Ezra's hand, my movements lethargic and clumsy. He meets my near lifeless grip and squeezes, his brows tugging together when I guide his fingers to the naked skin at my throat.

His eyes drift down to my neck, then to my discarded collar on the floor, understanding forming in his gaze. Realizing what I'm trying to tell him, he scowls. "We're going to get out of here," he promises, "and we're going to figure something out. I refuse to lose you, too. I won't."

A traitorous tear dashes from my left eye. Blinking it away, I turn my gaze from Ezra and take in the scene of ruin I've wrought upon the people who were only trying to help—to protect me, even though I don't deserve it. Two bodies lie on opposite sides of the room, one on his back in the far left corner and the other prostrate in a pool of blood not far from the right side of Rai's bed.

Quinn.

"Alive…?" I wheeze, my voice breaking.

Ezra blinks, his face pale with shock, but at the sound of my voice, he snaps out of his stupor and jumps to his feet, stumbling across the exam room. He shakes Jenner by the shoulder, who rouses with a groan and sits up, disoriented but unharmed. Ezra then scrambles over to Quinn, carefully flipping him onto his back.

As Ezra examines him, my vision fades in and out, the clarity of the room changing every few seconds like the ebb and flow of a tide. I squint, watching as he checks for Quinn's pulse before rifling through the ex-Enforcer's pockets, retrieving the very same shackles our former enemy removed from my wrists after saving us from execution. That moment seems like it happened in another lifetime rather than only a handful of hours ago.

So much has changed so quickly. That thought turns my stomach, and as the blood collects beneath Quinn's body, it occurs to me that I never thanked him.

I make a mental note to do just that if he survives.

Exhaling, I press my cheek to the cold floor when another wave of pain slams into the walls of my skull. Through the darkness swelling over my vision, I can just make out Ezra's expression as he jumps to his feet and stalks toward his motionless brother. Rage burns in his eyes as he hoists Richter upright and props him into a sitting position against the metal table on the left side of the room—the same table I was examined on every single day for over two years in this hell.

Nostrils flaring, Ezra binds Richter's wrists in the shackles, his attention flicking between his brother's limp hands and his white DSD-issue coat. Once the restraints are secure, he crouches, removing two objects from the deep pockets—the remote control for my now defunct collar and the pistol Richter used to shoot Quinn.

And possibly Rai, I consider, shuddering.

For a moment, Ezra stares at the remote, understanding darkening his gaze as his eyes drift from the black device in his hand to me. He must know I would never attack him or Jenner. Not willingly.

Not unless I was forced to.

"I didn't mean…to," I whisper again, pushing the words out with effort.

Ezra's face loses the last of its color as his eyes blow wide, returning to his hand. As the realization forms in his gaze, his lower lip quivers, peeling back in disgust.

Raising his hand, he growls, just loudly enough for me to hear, "That piece of shit."

With a shout of frustration, Ezra smashes the remote control against the floor, his chest heaving as the device explodes into several pieces, scattering across the white tile. Rising, he shoves Richter's gun in his belt—replacing the pistol he stole from one of Nolan's lackeys, which seems to have gotten lost in the chaos—before fixing me with the full force of his gaze.

"He will *never* control you again," Ezra vows, voice hard and hazel eyes silvered with tears.

Then, in the time it takes for me to blink, he's on the move again, dropping to his knees beside Quinn and clamping his hands firmly against the right side of his torso. Blood seeps up through his fingers, gushing over his hands.

"Jenner, a little help?" he pleads.

Jenner, whose face is awash with confusion, turns slowly, locking eyes with Ezra. "What the hell happened?" he asks, sounding dazed.

Ezra sneers. "My asshole brother happened."

A loud cough punctures the silence, followed by a few breathy grunts as Quinn jerks into waking, his obsidian eyes bulging in confusion and terror. When he tries to sit up, Jenner jumps into action, scooping his gun off the floor—which was torn from his grasp when Richter forced me to attack him—returning it to his belt before racing across the room to help Ezra by forcing Quinn back down again. As he restrains the ex-Enforcer against the floor with his forearm, Jenner grabs a spare sheet from under Rai's bed with his other hand, pressing it down on his wound.

"Hey, man, don't move! You're really hurt."

Quinn's only response is a croak as his head lolls to the side, his tongue darting out to wet his dry lips. Although ashen from blood loss, he's awake and alert and makes repeated attempts to move despite Ezra and Jenner insisting he needs to keep still. Ignoring them, he fans his arm out to the side, his hand curling into a fist, except for one finger…which points directly at me.

All three sets of eyes fix on my face as my body contorts, my limbs locking and back arching unnaturally, foam spitting from the sides of my mouth. Ezra calls out to me, but his voice seems so far away, like time and space are separating us, placing us on different fields of existence. Still, he reaches out, crossing that distance, although it feels so impossibly far.

His arms wrap around my back, holding me tight, as a strong, metallic stench fills my nose and a warm, sticky wetness seeps from between my lips, tasting of copper and something acidic. Ezra wipes his hand over my mouth, and although he tries to hide it from me, I glimpse the smudge of red staining his fingers.

Blood, I realize, aghast.

My blood.

Just like I feared, now that the clock on my disease has resumed, the time I have left is being siphoned away as payment for the extra years I survived. Thanks to Dr. Richter, how long do I have?

When is my time going to finally run out?

Ezra shifts position and draws my head into his lap, gently stroking my face. As the seizure subsides, I search for his eyes through the expansive fog of pain weighing on my senses, making me groggy. The hazel depths gazing at me will me to speak.

Despite my exhaustion, I muster the only words I can think of—those at the core of our connection to each other.

Words that always make my past and future collide.

"I'm...sorry..."

His mouth fights a grimace as his face contorts with resurfacing rage. Taking care not to jostle me too much, he props my head on his jacket again, then returns to his feet, yanking Richter's gun free from his belt. The fire in his gaze continues to burn as his finger folds around the trigger.

I force myself to stay awake, focusing on Ezra's retreating back as he storms toward where Richter is slumped, shackled to the table. Leaning down, Ezra slaps him hard, then grabs him by the neck of the shirt, shaking him.

"Wake up!" he shouts, venom lacing his tone.

As Richter comes to, his gray eyes flicker from his younger brother's face to mine.

Ezra releases his grip on his shirt and shoves him hard into the table leg. "Help her." He glances at me, his hand shaking as he repositions his grasp on the gun.

A wry, gloating smile shapes Richter's lips. "I'm sorry to disappoint you," he says, slurring the words, "but I can't do that."

"What do you mean you *can't*?" Ezra barks. He backtracks, reappearing at my side just long enough to pluck the collar off the floor before rounding on Richter again, tossing the thick metal ring in his lap. "You're the one who did this to her, so fix it!"

A nefarious laugh reverberates through the room and ricochets through every inch of my body. As the horrible, calculating echo of it beats in my ears, a rising terror swallows my sanity whole.

"Surely, you're aware by now that collar was the only thing keeping her alive?" Richter asks. "Without it, she's doomed. There is no other cure for her condition."

Ezra cocks the gun, reaffirming the threat in his hand. "Put the collar back on, then," he snarls.

Richter glances between us, his expression triumphant despite the fact that he's the one handcuffed on the floor. Squaring his shoulders, he rests the back of his head against the leg of the table.

"That collar is a sophisticated piece of technology, the sole of its kind created with the singular focus of protecting and preserving the security of the State. It was designed to cease all functionality should it ever be removed or tampered with. So, you see, Little Brother…" His grin widens, his face splitting into a demented smile. "It cannot be fixed."

During the two and a half years I served as, first, the DSD's guinea pig, and then, the State's weapon, there wasn't a day that went by when Dr. Richter didn't assess the collar for faults. To ensure it was doing its job. He never took it off. He never spoke of upgrading it or altering the model. He only made certain the leash that kept me chained to him and in control was working.

I knew the collar was valuable—possibly even more so than I was—but I always assumed that was because we went hand in hand. Without one, the other was useless.

Except, now, I realize it was more than that. The collar was valuable because it was unique, the sole of its kind…just like me. And since Dr. Richter had no other patients to subjugate, no other victims to turn into weapons since his other attempts to create more had failed, the State had no reason to produce other collars. That technology my control is reliant upon…

It can't be fixed or replaced.

"So, make a new one," Ezra demands, losing patience. "I'm sure you know how."

Richter scoffs. "That one collar took years of development to create and an entire team of qualified engineers to manufacture. Somehow, I doubt all the needed components survived the explosion…"

I lie still, a silent witness to this conversation, picking up what words I can in my lethargic state. At the mention of the bombing, my eyes drift to Quinn. I recall our conversation outside the DSD, before our confrontation with Richter. At the time, I didn't think much of it—of Quinn's suggestion that someone was working with the enemy from within the State, giving them the intel to target this place. Now that I allow the thought to sink in, I can't help wondering if maybe he was right. Perhaps the enemy isn't really an enemy at all and just wanted to erase what the State had created before it could be used to hurt anyone else.

Before *I* could be used to hurt anyone else.

What little hope had stirred within me at Ezra's words—at the notion of the possibility of a new collar—promptly dies at the amusement in Richter's voice. "Even if, by some miracle, the required parts were all intact, it would still take months to construct a new one. Something tells me she doesn't have that much time."

Lunging forward, Ezra jams the muzzle of the pistol against his brother's forehead. Richter doesn't even flinch.

Instead, a derisive snort pierces the silence between them.

"Are you going to kill me?" Richter asks.

"Tempting," Ezra considers, drawing back the barrel, "but no. As much as I want to pull this trigger, Wynter should be the one to kill you, not me."

Richter chuckles. "She's had the opportunity to end my life countless times, and yet, here I am. Alive. Why do you think that is?"

A lump swells in my throat at his confession. In all the time Dr. Richter held me captive, I had several chances to kill him; there were so many moments when we were alone and I could've ended his miserable life without lifting a finger. But I never attempted to out of fear. Fear of what would happen to me if he wasn't around to guarantee my control. Fear of why I was allowing myself to do his bidding.

Fear of what I was forcing myself to forget.

But now, I remember everything and, unlike before, Richter no longer has the threat of my collar to use against me. He's severed those strings from my body, ending my unwilling stint as his puppet. The control I've been clinging to is gone, along with any reason to keep him alive.

No reason other than Rai, I remember.

Drawing in a tremulous breath, I cut my eyes to the bed in the corner. As much as it breaks me to admit it, she's dead, broken beyond any hope of repair. Her heart might be pumping blood through her veins, but the hard truth—the truth I now have to face—is we lost her that night at the magistrates building.

And for that, Richter doesn't deserve to live.

In my peripheral vision, I glimpse Ezra shrug. "I really couldn't say, but I have a feeling you might've just changed her mind."

Richter responds with a sharp, biting cackle. "You think you know her so well, but the only person who truly understands her is me. She is death incarnate. *Mors vincit omnia.* 'Death conquers all,'" he translates. "Have you seen her kill before, Brother? You think I'm a monster and yet you defend someone who has decimated entire armies—"

"Stop talking," Ezra warns.

"Or what?" Richter goads. "You don't have the stomach to kill me."

Ezra tilts his head to one side and taps the barrel of the pistol to his lips, as if contemplating the idea. "Yeah," he agrees with a tentative nod, "but I never promised not to shoot you."

An ear-splitting bang rattles the remains of the building, which threatens to cave in and crush us to death, entombing our bodies in a grave of sterile surfaces and glowing blue emergency lights. Black spots emerge in front of my eyes, and my ears ring from the gunshot, making the pounding in my head unbearable.

My eyes slam shut, as if doing so will help fight the pain. I'm so tired. I just want to sleep—to slip away from this madness and escape into dreaming, even if where I end up is a nightmare.

A memory jerks me awake, and with fear, I remember something from before I returned to the DSD two years ago. The days spent before the mission to Zone 1. Days I spent in a comatose state.

If I go to sleep now, who knows when I'll wake up? I can't afford to lose any more time.

Not when the clock is already ticking.

Blinking away the shadows from my eyes, I peer at Ezra and at the gun at his side before turning my drowsy gaze to his brother. Richter clutches his leg, his face draining of color as his teeth grit together, biting back what I hope is a scream. As he grunts, blood oozes from a hole in his pant leg situated just above his left knee. His restrained fingers claw at the wound to no avail, only making the blood bubble faster.

As if sensing my joy at his suffering, his wild eyes dart to mine—the hue of his irises nearly identical now to his complexion, his skin growing whiter by the second. Sweat beads along his hairline as he bares his teeth and lets loose an animalistic snarl, spit flying from between his chalky lips.

As the pool of blood building beneath Richter's leg expands across the tiled floor, the room begins to spin, making me nauseous. Dizzy, I close my eyes to settle my stomach only to be assaulted by images I'd rather not see. The one nightmare I can never escape projects onto the backs of my eyelids and in every thought until I see it all over again, just as I did the first time.

Darkness.

Destruction.

Death.

Every aspect of my vision is exactly the same. No matter what I do, no matter which path I take or who dies along the way, the future never veers from its intended destination. It always ends with me…

And with the desolation of our world.

A scream cranks open my lips, ripping free of my throat, as the images fade and yet another wave of convulsions rise to take their place. Leaping up from where he kneels at Quinn's side, Jenner crosses the distance to my thrashing body, tugging my back against his chest and holding me upright and still through my seizure. But he can't protect me from the wrath of this disease.

No one can anymore.

Ezra's eyes find mine as Jenner shouts out his name, but I can't tell if they belong to the Ezra of the present or the Ezra I always see in my vision—the one who's sorry and who I'll have to watch die because I failed to find a way to save him and Jenner from that terrible future. From me.

Whichever version it is, I hang onto his voice as the world around me is engulfed by darkness, his every word the only anchor between me and unconsciousness.

"If she dies, so do you!"

"Don't you understand yet?" Although weak from his wound, Richter laughs again—a cruel, malicious sound that cuts through me like a knife to my chest.

His voice is the last thing I hear before the darkness finally pulls me under.

"We're already dead."

TWO

OVER THE YEARS, I'VE LOST track of how many times I've been forced to return to this moment. Regardless of what I do in the real world, regardless of the choices I make, the future awaiting me is always the same. The same destruction. The same outcome.

The same deaths…over and over again.

I turn in place, my eyes trailing across the rubble and skeletal buildings, emaciated frames of steel and broken glass, that are soon to be all that remain of my home. Maybe the world was always doomed to end this way. Maybe every step I've taken since the day this disease first awoke only took us closer to our pre-destined demise. Whether through the assault on our city or through my own increasingly unstable powers, maybe the violent eradication of mankind was always inevitable.

I let out a tear-soaked breath and wait for Ezra, fearing his appearance more than ever now that I know this vision's eventual re-enactment in reality is certain. At any moment, he'll manifest, muttering the same three words that have plagued me for years. He'll apologize, although I still don't know what for.

Now that I no longer have my collar, I suppose it won't be long until I find out.

My eyes dart side to side, scanning my surroundings for movement. Aside from the occasional flicker warping the dusty air like static distorting a picture, everything looks the same as it has since unconsciousness dragged me back to this hellscape only moments ago.

An uneasy confusion sends my already erratic pulse racing. The last time this vision took an unforeseen turn, I had to watch Ezra and Jenner both die, a helpless spectator to their gruesome deaths. I don't want to relive that again. My fragile sanity can't take it.

My breath hitches at the soft crunch of footsteps in dirt, and I throw a panicked glance over my shoulder, expecting, dreading, *hoping* it's him. Hoping the vision hasn't changed for the worse.

If anything can be worse than death.

Ezra's name hangs on the tip of my tongue, but I swallow it, stopping short, my chest tightening at the sight of the familiar brown eyes staring at me.

I blink, choking out a single word.

"Rai?"

She fixes me with that maternal gaze that was once so warm and full of life but is now dull and empty by comparison. She takes a step toward me, dragging her feet, while I stumble back, bringing a hand to my mouth.

She's wearing the same clothes she was the last time we saw her—the night we thought she died in Zone 1. Blood has saturated the top half of her long-sleeved gray shirt and pools around her pronounced collar bone, an endless flow of red streaming down the side of her face from the small circular wound in her temple.

"Wynter…" Her voice penetrates the shell of shock freezing me, once again opening the door to my grief. A door I've been trying so hard to close. Great, heaving cries rack my lungs as tears leave thick scalding lines down my cheeks.

"I'm sorry," I gasp, fighting for breath. "I tried. I-I tried to save you—"

She extends a hand toward me, a gentle smile curving her lips. As her fingers cup my face, I close my eyes, trying to remember her touch, her warmth…but no matter how hard I try to recall even the smallest detail, I feel nothing. As much as I want to believe this is real, as much as I wish she was here with me, the truth is I'm alone and Rai is still comatose in the bed Richter fettered her to, forever trapped somewhere between life and death. And this, our bittersweet reunion… It isn't a vision at all but a dream.

A nightmare born of my guilt to torment me.

Steadying myself, I open my eyes and force myself to look at her. The bullet hole at the right side of her forehead has healed, leaving a pockmarked scar in its place, and the clothes she was wearing have been substituted for the minuscule rectangle of surgical paper covering her sleeping body in the real world.

Now, instead of the Rai we remember, she looks like the lifeless doll belonging to Richter.

Her smile transforms, dipping into a frown. "You were never going to be able to save me, you know that." She lowers her hand from my cheek, then drops her voice to a whisper. "But there's still time."

I shake my head, blinking the tears from my eyes. "Time for what?"

As if precipitated by my words, an alarm blares in the distance, the whooping scream of it faint but shrill. I take stock of my surroundings, trying to locate the source, but the air is a thickening whirlwind of dirt and ash, obstructing my sense of direction.

Two voices swirl around me in a vortex, carried by the raging wind. They echo in time with the screeching alarm.

"What is that?"

"Sounds like our not-so-friendly reminder to get the hell out of here."

"Ezra. Jenner." As their names leave my lips, a shudder turns my skin ice-cold and I remember where they still are at this moment. When I remember the danger I've led them both into.

My heart hammers against my ribcage when I look back at Rai.

"Time for what?" I ask again, my voice breaking.

A sheet of dust blows between us, blurring her face. Through the debris, I can just make out her eyes—two deep glistening pools of burnt umber that, despite their warmth, chill me down to the bone.

She stares at me, her gaze pleading. "To save them."

As these words permeate the air between us, the ground caves in beneath my feet and I fall, plunging into the depths of the earth, as a blanket of black blots out the world. Above me, Rai watches, her expression unmoved, looking down at me as I fall...fall...

Fall.

Her voice is all I cling to in the deepening shadows as the echoes of her warning-like plea flood my ears. I hear it, over and over again, telling me what I have to do. But how? How can I possibly hope to change anything or save anyone now that I've been stripped of control?

A few moments pass before I realize I'm no longer free-falling and the darkness around me is lifting, pulling me back into the cruelty of consciousness. The soft blue haze of the emergency lights seeps in at the edges of my sharpening vision, revealing the details of Exam Room B.

My own personal purgatory.

The repetitive wail of an alarm attacks my eardrums, but the sound is muted by the thick gray walls, as if it's been confined to the hallway. Although distant, the racket is more than enough to awaken the throbbing pain in my head, thrusting me the rest of the way into waking.

The arms wrapped around my torso flinch when I rouse, and I glance up to find Jenner leaning over me, his face upside down, those bright blue eyes teeming with worry.

Wrinkling my nose, I part my lips on a moan. "What's that awful sound?"

His warm breath tickles my cheeks when he laughs, his chest spasming against my back with a tearful sigh. He shakes his head at me, his cheeks twitching in an aborted smile. "You had us all worried there for a minute."

"I'm fine," I assure him.

Testing the strength in my limbs, I cautiously push myself into a sitting position. Jenner rises beside me and helps me up onto my feet, keeping one hand on my arm and the other on my back to steady me, should I need it. Every inch of my body screams in protest, but it's far easier to stand than I thought it would be given whatever Richter injected me with.

An accelerant, he called it. I frown at the thought. My brief paralysis might've elapsed but I'm sure such reactions will only become more frequent as the episodes continue and my condition worsens, chipping away at what little still remains of me, Wynter Reeves, before revealing the monster beneath. Before the collar, a single episode could cripple me for days, sometimes longer. How long before I return to that point, especially with Richter's unknown drug in my veins to push me closer to that edge?

How long before this disease destroys everything?

"Just had a minor relapse, that's all." I try to give Jenner a reassuring smile but fail, only managing a grimace.

"Minor?" a voice behind me shouts.

My stomach clenches as I turn and find myself face to face with a furious Ezra. A scowl pinches his brow, his arms stiff at his sides. The anger in his eyes smolders in the hazel depths like embers threatening to spark into full flames.

"You call that *minor?*" he asks, his voice raised over the persistent howl of the alarm. He holds my gaze for a moment before letting out a breath. Then, stepping toward me, he grips my upper arms, dropping his forehead down onto my shoulder. "I…" He trails off, shaking his head, brushing my neck and collarbone with his hair. "I thought that was it."

His voice is barely audible, but I hear it, pressed up close to my ear. I hear it as clearly as I sense his fear.

My arms tremble as they snake around his back. "You don't have to worry." I speak loudly enough so he can hear me but low enough so no one else will. "I've seen it. That's not how I'm going to die."

I'll die surrounded by ash and dirt—the remnants of a world I've destroyed.

Ezra snaps his head up and pulls away just enough to look me in the eye. Placing his hands on either side of my face, he says, "We're going to make our own future, you hear me? Don't let my brother get in your head." His gruff words are a tender kiss on my lips, but as comforting as they are in this moment, they're powerless to change my fate.

Or the future.

Beside us, Jenner clears his throat. "As much as I hate to break up this lovefest, we really need to get out of here. Whatever that alarm is, it can't be anything good."

Ezra lowers his hands from my cheeks, and I follow his forlorn gaze to Rai, the sorrow on his face beyond any comprehensible words. Quinn sits propped upright against the plastic and metal frame of her bed, eyes closed and dusky brunette hair askew, with the bed sheet Jenner was using to staunch his bleeding now tied around his midsection like a tourniquet. The pallid hue of his complexion is worrying. The only indicators that he's even alive are the gentle rise and fall of his chest and the wheezing breaths occasionally seeping through his lips.

"What about…" But Ezra doesn't finish the sentence.

I reach out, taking his hand, and behind me, Jenner touches my shoulder, forming a chain of support. In our mutual silence, I know we're all thinking the same thing.

The sole point of returning to the DSD was to rescue Rai from Dr. Richter, and now, that decision might have cost us the one ally—although begrudging—who was willing to help us. While I had suspected from my vision that something was wrong, I didn't grasp the full extent of Rai's injuries until I saw her with the clarity of reality and realized exactly what Richter had done.

When it became evident that she wasn't going to ever wake up, I knew then that our mission had failed. Rai wasn't leaving the DSD. She can't, not when the array of necessary machines connected to her body make any notion of escaping impossible.

As for Quinn, who knows how long he has? I never saw him in any of my visions. For all I know, he'll die here, right next to Rai.

I take in her face, perfectly still in eternal sleep. Comatose.

Vegetative.

"You were never going to be able to save me, you know that."

Tears prick my eyes at the memory of what she said in my dream. Real or not, she was right. I wrote her off as dead over two years ago, and our quest to save her from Dr. Richter was nothing more than a misguided attempt to assuage the guilt I was struggling to rid myself of. Part of me always knew she was already gone.

"But there's still time," her voice says again in my head.

Is there? I desperately wish I could ask her. How do I know that for sure when it wasn't even really her I was talking to? Machines might be keeping her body alive, but Rai—the Rai we knew—is lost and has been for a while now. I know that. Ezra and Jenner know that, even if some of us aren't ready to admit it.

Just as we all know you can't talk to the dead.

I'm about to tell Ezra that Jenner is right, that staying won't do anyone here any good, when he pulls his hand from mine and storms across the room to the bed in the corner. Even in the shadows, the denial is as clear on his face as the shimmer of tears coating his eyes.

"We just need more time! If we can figure out a way to transport her, maybe we can find someone else to help. To bring her back. And Quinn"—he gestures to the unconscious ex-Enforcer—"he might be an ass, but he saved our lives. He doesn't deserve to die like this, and neither does she."

"Like who?" Jenner asks, exasperation bleeding into his tone. "Do you know any doctors? Because the closest thing we had in our sect was Rai, and even she only knew enough to get us all by." He tightens his hand around my shoulder, his fingertips trembling against my skin. "No one is going to help us, Ez. Not your brother. Not the State. Not even PHOENIX." He pauses, drawing in a shaking breath before letting it out through his nose. "This is a lost cause, you know that."

Laughter rings out beside us, drowning out the alarm.

"Raina isn't going anywhere. None of you are," Richter crows.

Ezra peers back at his brother and scoffs. "And who's going to stop us? You?"

Richter's lips curl into a smile. "I don't need to. The second that alarm began to go off, every door on this floor locked from the outside. We're all stuck in this room until someone comes to investigate, and I have a feeling whoever that is will be on my side, not yours."

Ezra, Jenner, and I all exchange panicked looks before throwing nervous glances back at the closed door, the apprehension hanging in the air so thick and pervasive I can practically taste it.

Steeling myself, I limp across the room until my hand is within reach of the door, shivering when the cool metal grazes my fingertips. I pause for a moment, holding my breath, silently praying that Richter is lying...but knowing in the darkest depths of my own corrupted black soul that he isn't.

I reach for the keypad and enter the unlocking code branded into my memory.

As expected, the door doesn't budge.

"It's locked," I try to say, but my mouth is a desert and the words come out garbled.

I take a step back, assessing our options. I could break the door down like I did to the one in my cell in the PHOENIX bunker outside the Heart, but when I try to summon the energy to do so, I don't even manage a dent. My body is spent, and my head feels like a cracked egg, the pain lingering far too close to the surface.

I glance back at Ezra, and whatever he sees on my face must tell him everything he needs to know about what I'm capable of at this moment…and what I'm not. He holds my gaze for only a moment before pulling the gun free of his belt and aiming it at Richter, his finger hovering over the trigger.

"Shut it down!" he shouts, spitting the words, crossing the exam room until the end of the pistol is less than an inch away from his brother's forehead. "Get that door open or, I swear, I'll shoot you again."

Dr. Richter huffs, his face deathly pale. "And how would you like me to do that?" He jerks his chin toward his restrained wrists. "In case you failed to notice, I wasn't the one who set it off."

"I was."

My heartbeat drums in my ears as my focus shifts to where Quinn sits hunched on the floor, his black eyes locked intently on mine. In answer to my silent question, he lifts one hand, his fingers wrapped around a black device not that dissimilar to the remote Richter used to overpower me through my collar.

"This"—he grimaces, his other hand pressed flat to his side, holding the bloody sheet in place as he pushes off the tile and up onto his feet—"was given to me in the event you ended up back here again."

Dropping the mechanism next to Rai's foot, he grabs onto the side of her bed for support, wincing at the effort of holding himself upright. Beads of perspiration dot his upper lip, glistening in the low light of the room.

"What the hell is that?" Jenner asks, his voice trembling.

"RF transmitter," Ezra answers, his back stiffening like hackles on a growling dog. "They shoot radio frequencies between two points and can be used to remotely trigger alarms. We used them once or twice when I first joined PHOENIX, but they're unreliable since…" He trails off, a wary look crossing his face.

A shudder creeps up my spine. "Since what?"

His eyes narrow on Quinn. "Since most alarms these days are protected against outside interference. For it to work, the security system would have to be either extremely vulnerable or pre-programmed to accept that specific frequency. Which means…" He hesitates, his mouth a thin line. "Whoever gave you that transmitter has access to this facility."

I bristle, gaping at the ex-Enforcer. Why would Quinn have a transmitter capable of prompting the DSD's alarms? And what did he mean it was given to him in the event I ended up back here?

Given to him by who?

Dr. Richter bursts out laughing, cackling like a madman, his expression deranged. Euphoric, even. "Once an Enforcer, always an Enforcer." With a contented sigh, he leans forward until his skull nudges the muzzle of the gun in Ezra's hand. A malevolent smile contorts his lips. "Betrayal stings...doesn't it, Brother?"

"I knew it," Ezra breathes, staggering back a few steps, his arm dropping but his grip on the gun never easing. "I knew you couldn't be trusted—"

"You're a real bastard, you know that?" Jenner seethes, his hands balling into tight fists at his sides, his knuckles turning white from the pressure. "So much for helping us. I should've let you bleed out on the fu—"

He advances on Quinn, but I pitch forward and grab his arm, pushing myself between them. Jenner gapes at me, stunned by my intervention.

Ignoring him, I round on Quinn, my body aching as what little strength I've managed to conjure up seems to leave me in the space of a heartbeat. Quinn doesn't look to be in a much better state. Sweat lines the curve of his hairline and the sides of his neck, drenching the collar of his black shirt, and the white sheet around his torso is stained red, sodden with blood.

Wound aside, he seems so exhausted, so weary. Like someone who's tired of running. Of hiding. The question is...what is it Quinn's running from? Has he always had this hunted look in his eyes and I just never noticed it?

Or am I to blame for that, too?

I shuffle closer. "I don't understand. You saved our lives. Why do that just to turn on us here?"

His jaw strains and he groans, catching himself on the edge of Rai's mattress when his knees buckle, weakened from blood loss. Nostrils flaring, he shoots me a knowing look, hissing, "You don't get it. This *is* me saving your life—"

As suddenly as it appeared, the alarm cuts off, and that's when we hear it— the rumble of booted footsteps outside in the hallway. I recognize that sound, remembering it all too clearly from that night in Zone 1 and from all the months I spent fighting in the State's pointless war. Those tromping, heavy footsteps, a telltale sign of approaching death...

They belong to Enforcers.

Ezra and Jenner both whip around to face the incoming threat while my own gaze turns toward Dr. Richter, who smiles at the apprehension rolling through me. I know he can sense it, just as I can practically hear his snide voice in my ear whispering, *"I'd like to see how well you perform without your precious control to help you."*

The imagined taunt is quickly drowned out by the memory of what he said in those final few seconds before removing my collar. *"Show it to me,"* he had murmured, his breath hot on my skin. *"Show me the destruction you and my mother both saw."*

I swallow as a tingle like static electricity passes over my skin, raising the hairs on my arms. Maybe what I'm feeling is my unrestrained power creeping back to the surface, preparing to finally force me to yield. Or maybe my dread and fear have taken on a tangible form, wrapping around my lungs and choking my airway like a hand gripping my throat.

Whichever it is, I try to breathe past the sensation, hoping my panic won't show as Ezra and Jenner stand side by side, forming a shield between me and the door, even though we all know they'll do little against a team of Enforcers. Our only real hope in this dire situation is me, except…I don't have my collar and I'm too weak and tired to fight.

But I have to. Like I told Ezra before, I don't die here. Neither does he. And Jenner won't either. I won't let him.

I shake my head, shoving all doubt aside. I was in control of this disease for two years. Collar or not, I know how to summon my power. I can do this.

I can find the strength to protect us.

The footsteps cease just outside the door, and everyone in the room goes quiet and still. Ezra peers over his shoulder, meeting my gaze, and I nod, consoled by the thought that this—getting gunned down here in my tormentor's lair—isn't what I saw in either of our futures. Whatever happens here, whatever comes in the next few moments, we'll survive it. I have to believe that.

Otherwise, my terror might actually crush me.

A dull sequence of beeps hums through the closed door, singing out from the keypad outside in the corridor. The metal panel separating us from yet another danger then slides open with an ominous *whish*, and I suck in a sharp breath, tamping down my nerves. Closing my eyes, I beckon my power, just as I have a thousand other times before. Just as I used to when I had my collar.

That familiar pressure begins to build in my chest but far more slowly than I would like, my hold on it shaky. I inhale again, pushing myself, but a hand grabs my shoulder, warning me to stop.

I recoil, glancing back at Quinn, ready to kill him myself for putting us in this position…then pause, taken aback by the look on his face. He retracts his hand, his fingers sticky with blood, and stares at me the same way Rai did in my dream—like they both know something I don't. He opens his mouth, soundlessly muttering a single word, confusing me even further.

Wait.

Before I can ask him why, the click-clack of high heels draws my attention back to the door, my senses alert. A tall woman stands at the threshold to the exam room, wearing a white blouse and dark gray knee-length skirt, framed by a long DSD-issue coat identical to Dr. Richter's. Her light blonde hair is pinned back in a bun and bright, intelligent cobalt eyes sweep across the scene before her, vaguely amused.

"Well, well, well," she croons. "What do we have here?" She signals with a crook of her pointer finger to the group of Enforcers in the hallway behind her. Brushing past her into the room, the soldiers take position around us.

Ezra steps back and pulls me close to his side as Dr. Richter lets out a devious, albeit weak, laugh.

"Fancy meeting you here, Dr. Adler. Your timing is impeccable, as always."

"Adler?" Jenner's tone straddles the line between afraid and incredulous, his cheeks draining of color, as if he's just seen a ghost.

I watch him for a moment, unnerved by his reaction to the woman standing in the doorway. A reaction he only had once he heard her name.

Just who is this Dr. Adler?

Reading my mind, Ezra whispers in my ear, "Evelyn Adler. She's in charge of Termination."

I want to ask him how he knows that, but the words fail to form as I take a closer look at the newcomer—at this woman Jenner seems so afraid of. As the features of her face sharpen before my drug and fatigue addled gaze, I realize that I've seen her before. But not here. Not at the DSD where I spent nearly three years of my life being tortured and experimented on.

No, I know her from somewhere else. It just took me a minute to recognize her and to see past the disguise of her blonde hair and clothes. She looks so different—not at all like the woman I remember from what might as well be a different life. A life where she was someone else.

Someone I once thought I could trust.

It can't be.

I step out of Ezra's arms as my memories of her slide to the front of my brain, unbidden. As the name I used to call her unfurls on my tongue, moisture drips down my cheeks and gathers in a pool on my lips, the taste of each bitter tear triggering the recollection of one of her lies. Of what I now recognize as deceit.

And betrayal.

"Mother?"

THREE

"HELLO, WYNTER," MY MOTHER SAYS from the doorway, her voice steady and placid, as if we're discussing the weather. A reluctant, forced smile hooks up the corners of her lips. "I'm sorry we had to meet again like this."

I jerk my head in disbelief, my mouth opening and closing several times, trying and failing to form the words, *any* words, that will help me make sense of what I'm seeing—of this impossible reality where my mother is not only standing before me after not seeing her for nearly three years but that she's... wearing a DSD-issue coat?

The irony is almost enough to make me laugh. Didn't Ezra once falsely claim my mother worked here as an alibi to cover up my escape from this place? The recollection of his calculated lie flits through my mind, and I wonder if he's remembering that moment now, too. If I could move, if I could just break through the shock of this moment and look at him, I'm sure I would find him wearing the same disturbed expression slapped across my own face.

Never in a million years did either of us ever think he would be right.

I swallow, and the sound is gratingly loud in the silence. No matter which angle I look at it from, the woman looming at the threshold to the room—the woman I once called my mother—is unrecognizable to me. And, in this moment, I realize she's just another lie I've been force-fed my whole life by the State.

No, this woman isn't my mother at all. She's a stranger, just like any other I would pass on the street. Evandra Reeves, if she ever existed at all, is a ghost.

Dead to this world, just like my father.

I eye her carefully, tasting the name Ezra referred to her by just moments ago on my tongue. Evelyn Adler. *Dr. Adler, Richter called her.*

Sneering, I push that thought away. If this is all true—if this isn't just another twisted nightmare intent on unhinging me—then that means the woman who raised me is a torturer.

A murderer.

This time, I can't help the choked-off laugh that escapes. *Like mother, like daughter,* a voice says in my head.

I might be personally responsible for the genocide of thousands of people, maybe more, but I always acted under duress. Can my mother say the same? How many lives has she taken? How many people has she killed all for the sake of keeping our country shackled with fear? After all, that's what Termination does.

They're exterminators and the people living in the Heart are the bugs.

I shake my head again, the threat of madness teasing the edge of every thought. How did I not know? How did my father not know?

A sudden queasiness clenches my stomach, and I let out a stilted breath when an epiphany floods my head. Maybe my father *did* know. They were married for years before he was executed, years during which he was still active with PHOENIX. Years where she must've known, or at least suspected, what he was up to before something made her decide to turn him in to the authorities. Upon learning of my father's involvement with PHOENIX, I had assumed she only reported his crimes because he exposed me—their child—to the danger of his affiliations. But what if I was wrong? What if she turned on him for a different reason altogether?

What if she killed him because he found out the truth?

Pain tears across my forehead again, and my legs wobble as a wave of vertigo disorients my senses, leaving me unsteady on my feet. My lungs constrict with the effort of trying to breathe, as if something is blocking my airway, suffocating my every inhalation.

Confusion and denial both crawl up my throat.

"How?" I gasp. It's the only word I manage to force out.

My mother takes a step into the room, and as the glow of the faint emergency lights reflects off her face, I notice the skin beside her eyes is creased and the corners of her mouth are downturned now. It's the same expression she used to wear whenever she'd scold me for not abiding by one of her rules. Rules she always claimed were for my survival and safety. I never quite understood that look, the way the fear invaded her otherwise severe gaze. But now, I realize what it was she was afraid of—what she didn't want me to know and always tried to hide behind a cold, aloof mask. Now, I realize why she was so desperate for me to remain invisible, unseen from the very government I've fallen victim to. Because if I didn't, I would've found out about her…

And she would have had to deal with me the same way she dealt with my father.

Is that why she's here? I wipe the tears streaming down my cheeks away with the heel of my hand.

Did my mother come here to kill us?

"Wynter—" she begins, her voice careful and low.

Behind me, a scratchy laugh cuts her off.

"It isn't possible."

I pivot, glancing back at Dr. Richter where he sits propped up against the leg of the examination table, his complexion pasty and putrid. The left corner of his mouth twitches every few seconds into a warped expression that's somewhere between a laugh and a grimace.

My brow furrows at the doubt in his voice. Surely, he had to have known who she was, unlike me, who lived her entire life with a liar, her deception beyond comprehensible limits.

Richter swallows, the lump in his throat bobbing, and his lips part, but no other words come out. Like me, this revelation seems to have rendered him silent.

Realization grips me like claws sinking into my skin. Is it possible he really didn't know who she was—of our connection to each other?

Just how many people has my mother fooled?

I peer back at her, bemused, and the lines beside her eyes ease, smoothing out, as she turns her attention to Richter. With that blank expression, she's suddenly that poised stranger again—the one I barely recognize.

The evil monster in charge of Termination rather than the woman I once called my mother.

Keeping her unblinking gaze locked on his, she proceeds deeper into the room with a calm assuredness to her steps that twists my stomach in knots and prods at the barely restrained anger inside me. I push back against it, suppressing that anger, afraid that—if I cave to it for even a second—I'll snap and kill every single person in this room. It doesn't matter how tired I am, how weak. The threat of my power thrums under my skin as if in direct response to my rage.

When my mother struts toward me, Ezra places a hand on my arm to pull me back out of the way, but I shrug him off and step forward to meet her, hardened by my growing outrage. I'm done with being subjugated by people who think they can control me, with being a tool and always cowering out of fear of what monstrous people like Richter might do to me or to someone I love if I refuse to obey. After all, there's nothing anyone can do to me now that's worse than what

Dr. Richter has already done.

Not even my mother has that kind of power.

As the distance between us diminishes and her emotionless gaze shifts from Richter to me—the depths the same blue as my own right eye—I ready myself to unleash everything I've wanted to say to her since she abandoned me the day of my placement exam. My mouth opens once more, my lower lip quivering with the weight of every word.

Words that falter on my tongue when she brushes past me as if I don't even exist.

"I assure you it is," she says, her tone biting.

It takes me a few seconds to collect myself—to grasp that she isn't speaking to me but to Richter. She stands beside him now, her back tall and arms crossed.

Although I can't see her face, I can easily envision the expression she's wearing. I picture it all too clearly in my mind from the day my father was taken away and, again, when she surrendered my life to the State. When she handed me over to be tortured as if I meant absolutely nothing to her. That cold, detached look like he is beneath her, like he is a nuisance...

Like my father and I must've been.

Dr. Richter gapes at her, his skin dewy with sweat. "We've been working together for over ten years. How could I not have known about this?" His eyes flit around the room, agitated in their movements, but they settle on nothing, almost like he's watching the frantic nature of his thoughts unfolding before him.

For the first time, I really glimpse the madness lurking in the monochromatic pools of his gaze. I suppose it was always there; I just failed to see it through his near constant insistence that someone else was always to blame for all the terrible things he's done.

The mother who saw what he would become.

The brother who stole the one person he loved.

Even me, the broken girl who would become his obsession.

"No," he breathes, shaking his head. "The girl's mother relinquished her custodial rights *in person* here nearly three years ago. The woman I met then wasn't you. And Hastings—he was there at her house. He saw her mother's face."

Hastings?

Understanding dawns, and I realize Richter is referring to the DSD attendant who was present when I was apprehended following my placement exam. The one who jammed a needle into my neck and drugged me.

Begrudgingly, I accept that Richter has a point. That man saw my mother's face—

"Hastings works for me." My mother's tone is callous, and she waves a dismissive hand. "You're a clever man, Austin. But you're young, and I've been playing this game a lot longer."

I can sense Ezra's eyes burning into my face, but I avoid his gaze and keep watching my mother, mesmerized by every word out of her mouth…and unsure what to make of any of this.

The heels of her shoes click against the white floor—the once gleaming tiles spoiled by Richter's blood, leaving a trail of red smears in her wake—as she turns around and backtracks toward me. This time, her hooded eyes take me in as if I'm the only other person in the room.

She reaches out a hand to touch my left cheek, but her fingers freeze when I flinch away. Her eyes brim with hurt as they sweep over my face, but behind that surface sheen of pain, there's something else there in the way she looks at me. Understanding, perhaps.

Or regret.

Dropping her arm, she directs her gaze over my shoulder and nods, smiling slightly. "Thank you for bringing Wynter to me. You've upheld your end of the deal and I will see to it that I uphold mine."

Deal?

Acid sloshes against the walls of my stomach and my heart drops into my feet when I turn, following her line of sight to the unapologetic sable eyes watching me.

A breath catches in my throat. Was this what Quinn meant when he said he was saving my life? By making a deal to return me to my mother? But how would they even know one another?

He says nothing as I stare at him, his face increasingly pale, his breathing ragged. Any sympathy I felt for being the reason he got shot has evaporated like water in dry heat. Of course, he never really wanted to help us. He never cared about us finding Rai or preventing the war against the Heart that he helped to ignite by being Nolan's lackey and keeping me out of the State's hands. By keeping me captive. The whole time he's been playing both sides. The whole time he's been playing *me*, moving me around like a chess piece across a board I wasn't even aware I was on.

Positioning the pawn everyone sees me as exactly where my mother wants me. But why?

I glare at him, silently demanding answers, but his expression is blank despite the probing heat of his gaze. I wanted to trust him. I wanted to believe he really did oppose this war and had turned to our side, but it was idiotic of me to hope that anyone who once worked for the State might have some sort of conscience.

I bite down hard on the inside of my cheek, suppressing a scream of frustration. A million questions make a home in my skull. How did they meet? How long have they been working together? How did Quinn manage to get in so tight with Nolan so soon after leaving the State? Obviously, that had to have been part of the plan. Otherwise, he couldn't have intervened the way he did when we were about to be executed.

Some rescue, I think to myself, laughing under my breath.

As if sensing my unraveling sanity, Ezra grabs my hand, his palm sweaty and hot as his fingers weave around mine, clenching tightly. I stagger toward him, pressing my back to his chest—the only safe place I know as the lies once again build up around me, threatening to bury me alive.

"Can someone explain what the hell is going on?" he barks, his voice loud in my ear.

"All in good time," my mother answers, barely taking the time to spare Ezra a glance. Instead, her blue eyes lock on mine. "We will discuss everything once we're out of here. But first…there's something you should see."

Jenner, who has been silent throughout this exchange, seems to break out of whatever trance had ensnared him upon my mother's arrival and rushes forward, shoving himself between us.

"We aren't going anywhere with *you.*" He yanks his gun free of his belt and trains it on her face, his shoulders shaking with a fury I've never seen from him before—not even when he thought Ezra and Rai had been lying to him.

Around us, the Enforcers react to the threat, weapons raised and aimed on Jenner—my terror forming a rancid taste in my mouth as his life flashes before my eyes. Observing me out of the corner of her eye, my mother raises a hand, signaling for the soldiers to stand down.

My heart races a mile a minute, and my pulse only settles when the Enforcers all lower their guns—some holding pistols, others rifles—and return to their at ease positions. I reach out to Jenner, tugging on his shirt to yank him back toward me. But he doesn't budge, and when he finally looks back at me, his eyes are almost feral in their intensity.

Startled by his reaction, I replay the moment of my mother's unexpected appearance in my head, trying to figure out what about her triggered this hostility in him. When Dr. Richter greeted my mother, Jenner had whispered her name with an unnerving familiarity—a familiarity that was explained when Ezra revealed her full alias.

No, not her alias, I realize. *Her identity.*

Her *true* identity.

I wish I could scrub the revelation from my mind. At the time, I didn't have a chance to examine Jenner's shock any deeper, assuming it merely aligned with my own—born from the sheer horror of realizing my mother's position here at the DSD. But now, as I glance between his face and hers, I recall what he told me on the train earlier about the events that led him to join PHOENIX.

About his family.

My stomach sours. If Jenner recognized her name, that must mean my mother was the acting Head of Termination when his parents and sister were killed. If that's the case, then Jenner has good reason to believe she was not only involved with the death of his family…but directly responsible for it.

Vomit rises in my throat, and I glare at her. "Why?" I rasp through tears. "Why should we trust you after everything you've done?" My voice breaks on that last word, and I can see in the way her eyes widen that she knows what I'm asking. How can I possibly trust her after what she did to my father?

After what she did to me.

She huffs out a breath through her nose, as if this conversation is beginning to bore her. "I understand there's some distrust and hurt feelings between us—" Jenner scoffs, earning him a cutting glare from her as she raises her voice, continuing over him. "But I am your one chance to get out of this city alive."

As she says this, she peers at the bed, and the uncertain look I find on her face makes my body go rigid.

"Who says we *want* to leave?" Ezra counters.

Lifting her chin, my mother averts her eyes from Rai, meeting my gaze again. "Then, you will die. Staying in the Heart is suicide at this point." She allows a moment for her words to sink in before speaking again. "I'm offering you and your friends help, Wynter. Are you going to accept it or not?" When I don't say anything, she gestures toward the Enforcers. "If I was interested in harming any of you, I would've given them the order to start shooting already."

Everyone in the room seems to watch me, waiting, as I consider her offer. I know I won't be leaving the Heart alive—if my vision comes true, none of us will—but I don't want to close that door or the potential for a fresh start elsewhere on Ezra and Jenner, especially if there's no hope of ending this attack or preventing the downfall of our home. I might have told them to stand up to PHOENIX, but we've been back in the city for only a few hours and we're already in way over our heads. Even if we try to intervene, it won't matter if PHOENIX doesn't win this war.

And that's assuming I can find a way to prevent the future I saw. Otherwise, anything we do now is futile.

"There's still time," Rai reminds me, her voice a soothing croon in my ear. Maybe this is how I protect the people I love moving forward. By ensuring there's an exit in place for them, even if there isn't one for me.

I glance at each of the Enforcers around us and then at Quinn, who looks down at the floor, his hand clamped to his still bleeding side, his upper lip curled back, exposing his teeth. With a groan, he eases himself back down to the floor, propping his head against the side of Rai's bed. Although his face is crumpled in pain, he looks almost relieved, his eyes sliding shut—as if he's done what he came here to do and now, can finally rest.

Frowning, I take in the Enforcers again. Quinn might not be much of a threat at the moment, but the soldiers surrounding us are a whole other story. Would they let us leave if we refused to go with them?

Where would we even go if we do?

Jenner's fingers tighten around the grip of his pistol—the barrel still aimed at my mother's face—making me swallow the bitter taste of my fear and come to a decision, as much as I don't like it. Although she's a liar, I can sense that she's telling the truth when she says they're not here to harm us. And while I detest the thought of spending even a second longer with the imposter wearing the face of my mother, given the revelations the last few minutes have exposed, I know accepting her offer will give Ezra and Jenner the best chance of survival— especially if she's telling the truth about having an escape route out of the city. If we don't go with her, we're on our own, surrounded on all sides by enemies who would kill us without hesitation.

My life might be forfeit to this disease, but that doesn't mean theirs have to be.

Plus, in the event I'm wrong and the future is more malleable than I've been led to believe, I don't want my stubbornness to be the reason we all die in this place or by the hand of the Enforcers guaranteed to swarm the building if we turn down her offer.

With a deflated sigh, I release Ezra's hand and step forward until I'm shoulder to shoulder with Jenner, my fingers carefully folding around his wrist as I push down his arm, forcing his gun away from my mother. His face burns red as he shoots an accusatory glare at me, his bright eyes wordlessly asking how I could possibly side with her over him. I'm not—far from it—but I doubt anything I say at this moment could ever make him believe that.

Straining my jaw, I stare down my mother. "I have questions and you have answers. *Both* of you." My gaze slides to Quinn, who pries one eye open, sensing the weight of my attention. When he peeks up at me, I grind out through clenched teeth, "That's the only reason I'm agreeing to this."

My mother purses her lips and nods. Quinn looks like he's about to be sick but does the same, wincing with the effort, before letting his eye slip closed once again. Behind me, Ezra and Jenner say nothing.

My mother tugs back her coat sleeve, peering between her silver watch and the door. "Well, if there's nothing anyone else has to say on the matter—"

"We're not leaving. Not without Rai," Ezra protests.

Confusion flashes across my mother's cold face, followed quickly by comprehension as she once again glances past us toward the bed in the corner. "There's not much that can be done about *that*," she says tersely.

"The only reason we're even here at all is because of Rai," I interject.

For a moment, my mother just looks at me, her face pinched, the wheels of deliberation turning behind those familiar eyes. Finally, with a sigh, she relents. "It's unlikely I'll be able to help her, but I'll try. *After* you come with me."

"What about him?" Jenner asks, jerking his chin toward Richter, who is still staring up at my mother with a baffled look on his face, his eyes glazed over and wide with derangement.

If the blood loss doesn't kill him, the shock might, I note.

She shrugs one delicate shoulder, as if the thought of his fate hadn't even occurred to her. "Oh, he's coming with us. We have unfinished business." The menacing edge to her voice makes me shiver.

I stiffen. "Coming with us?"

Coming with us where?

My mother rolls her eyes. "Don't worry. He won't leave this building alive."

Snapping her fingers, she signals to the two nearest Enforcers, who step forward and grab Richter by the neck of his coat, hoisting him up off the floor. As he's pulled upright, the broken collar falls from his lap and strikes the tiles with an ominous *thunk*.

A strangled cry escapes Richter's lips and he reaches for his injured leg as much as his restrained hands allow.

"We were partners!" he shrieks, finding his voice again through the pain, his expression crazed as his eyes find my mother's. "We were on the same side!"

"Stop." At her clipped command, the Enforcers wrestling Richter toward the door cease mid-step.

Clearing her throat, she stalks toward my captor, her steps balanced and steady despite the tiles underfoot being slick with his blood. Once beside him, she grabs his chin with one hand, tugging until their faces are only inches apart. With the other, as she holds his gaze, she sticks a manicured finger in the bullet hole above his left knee.

When he screams, she forcibly closes his mouth, gripping his jaw so tightly her nails dig into the skin, drawing blood. She then leans in even closer to him, her voice a low and guttural whisper.

"I stopped being on your side the second you took my daughter."

She spits in his face before releasing his chin, and as she steps back, her eyes flick to the floor where my collar sits undisturbed on the tile behind him. She waves at the Enforcers restraining Richter's arms, gesturing for them to take him into the hallway, then brushes past as they make for the door, plucking the device up in her nimble fingers and immediately shoving it in her pocket. Part of me wants to ask why she's grabbed the collar, while another part would rather not know. Whatever the reason, it's useless now.

As my mother turns to exit the room, she beckons to the remaining Enforcers, who instantly abandon their posts at her command.

"What about Quinn?" Ezra calls after her. "You aren't just going to leave him here, are you?"

His words draw my attention back to the ex-Enforcer, and I feel the tiniest twinge of guilt at the wan, near colorless hue of his skin. Surely, dying from a gunshot wound wasn't the outcome he was meant to see from the deal he made with my mother.

"You don't get it. This is me saving your life—" he had said. Whatever his motivations were, Quinn also thought he was helping me, someone he openly considered a monster. Regardless of why he did all this, he still saved our lives.

And for that, he doesn't deserve to die.

My mother pauses in the doorway, throwing an impatient look over her shoulder. The Enforcers tailing her mimic her movements, coming to an abrupt halt behind her.

"How bad is it?" she asks, peering at the bloody sheet wrapped around Quinn's mid-section, one imperious brow raised.

"The bullet went clean through," he mutters. "A few stitches and I'll be fine."

Nodding, she cuts her stern gaze to Ezra. "There you have it. We'll come back for him and your friend once we've dealt with the more pressing matter at hand." She raises her chin, side-eying the door where Richter waits just outside in the hallway.

Deal with it how? I wonder before deciding it's probably best not to ask.

Steeling myself, I step forward to follow when my mother and the Enforcers leave the room, but a hand grabs my upper arm before I can get far, roughly yanking me back.

"Are we really doing this? Are we really *trusting* her?" Jenner asks.

As I turn, my eyes drift between him and Ezra, who lets out a strained breath through his nose.

"Even if she is your mother, she still works for the DSD," he says. "She can't be trusted, you know that."

I hesitate, forcing myself to pause and consider the situation from their perspective. They only know Evelyn Adler as the enemy whereas I've always known her on a different, more intimate level—as the woman who tried to protect me and shield me from danger the first eighteen years of my life. As much as I hate her for her duplicity, I have to believe she won't actually hurt me. And, regardless of the risks, I need answers.

Answers I don't think she'll give me unless we cooperate.

In the silence, Ezra and Jenner mimic my stillness like shadows made of flesh and bone.

Uncomfortable, I clear my throat. "I'm not sure we really have much of a choice. It's not like we have any other options."

Jenner blanches. "She murdered my family," he counters.

"Do you know that for sure?" For some reason, I feel defensive, like I'm somehow an extension of my mother's crimes. Maybe I'm in denial. Maybe I just don't want to believe the woman I relied on for so many years is capable of something so heartless.

At his wounded expression, shame punches the air from my lungs.

"I mean…was it actually her who did it?" I amend.

Jenner runs a shaking hand through his hair, pushing the thick black strands off his forehead. "After my family was taken to the DSD, I begged Rai to hack into the citizen registry database and see if she could find out what happened to them. I had hoped, if we could determine where exactly they were being held, then maybe we could get them out. But we acted too late; all Rai found was their death certificates, signed by none other than a Dr. Evelyn Adler, complete with her smiling mugshot, like the bitch was gloating about what she had done." Nostrils flaring, he glares at the doorway where my mother stands just outside in the corridor. "It took me a second to make the connection, but it's her. I'd know that face anywhere."

Anguish swells in my chest, and I wipe at the tears streaking my cheeks, the residue leaving my skin sticky and raw. I can envision that picture too easily—I can see the subtle smirk shaping her lips just like the one always worn by Dr. Richter. Who knows, maybe being a psychopath is a job requirement to work in this place.

"I understand why you don't trust her—" When he snorts, I lower my voice to a fierce whisper, growling, "Remember, the same woman who murdered your family also sentenced *my* father to death. We've both lost something because of her." Jenner averts his eyes, and I swallow, pushing out my next words with effort. "But, right now, that's secondary to me, to *knowing* I was held captive in this place for nearly three years and she was here the whole time, just watching it happen. She was *here* and never once did she try to help me." I pause, my throat thick, only daring to speak again once I'm sure my voice won't betray me. "I need to know what she wants from me and why she waited until now to come get it."

Jenner might not understand, but, for my sanity, I have to at least try to get answers.

Extending my arm, I touch his hand, tentatively interlacing our fingers. "Plus, we need help, and I think we all know that no one else is going to offer us that."

We came back into the Heart on a whim, without a plan as to what we would do once we got here or an exit in place to ensure we'd actually get out again if we had to. We didn't have the time or information to formulate a strategy, emotions were running high, and we were all only thinking about one thing: saving Rai. But now, things are different. Now, there's a clock ticking over our heads, with every second hurtling us all toward certain doom.

"There's still time," Rai says yet again.

Maybe, I muse, hoping she's right.

And maybe trusting my mother is how I get it.

A pained expression darkens Jenner's gaze, but he doesn't protest my reasoning.

"Fine," he grumbles, yanking his hand free of mine and shoving his gun back in his belt. "But don't expect me to be happy about it."

As Jenner trudges away, Ezra touches my shoulder. "He won't stay mad forever."

Forever.

A lump rises in my throat.

The problem is, I don't have forever.

"Are you sure about that? At what point will I be unredeemable to the two of you?" My chest tightens. "Maybe this crossed the line for him."

A curt laugh fills the space between us. "He blew up a transport helicopter while he was still on it just to save your life. He'd go to the ends of the earth for you. We both would." Planting a swift kiss on my forehead, he whispers, "We're with you. We're always with you, even if we don't like it."

My mother clears her throat from the doorway, and when I look in her direction, she taps her foot impatiently against the floor, beckoning us to hurry. With a sigh, I glance up at Ezra again, but his gaze has shifted, his attention on Rai.

"We'll come back for her," I whisper, but I don't dare utter the other thoughts in my head. The ones that force me to acknowledge that I know she won't be leaving this place.

Unable to bring myself to look at her sleeping face for a moment longer, I peer at Quinn, tugging on Ezra's sleeve. "Do you think he'll really be okay?"

"I can hear you, you know." Quinn groans, lifting one lid to look at me. "And like I said before, I'll be fine. It's really little more than a flesh wound."

The blood still seeping through your fingers says otherwise.

"I meant it when I said I want answers," I say, my tone clipped. "So, try not to die while we're gone."

He lets out a low chuckle, which turns into a wracking cough, his face scrunching as he cringes at the pain. "Don't worry. You'll get them. Just not here. Not now."

"Soon then?" I press.

He exhales through his nose as his eye falls closed again. "Soon," he promises.

FOUR

WHEN EZRA AND I JOIN the others in the hallway, my gaze catches on my mother's face, her lips pursed and eyes lowered, locked on our entwined fingers. I straighten, standing tall under her scrutiny, her disapproval only encouraging me to grip Ezra's hand even harder.

With a *humph*, she falls into step beside me, and without saying a word, we progress down the darkened corridor—the lights still flickering at random intervals, exacerbating the apprehension writhing in my gut. Jenner walks a few paces in front of us, hands thrust in his pockets and shoulders slumped slightly, but the way he keeps looking back tells me he's listening, hanging onto every impending word in the silence.

"What are you going to do to him?" I finally ask, glancing between my mother and Richter, who is sandwiched between two Enforcers at the front of our group. They drag him, ignoring his pained whimpers, just like the orderlies used to do to me when I was a patient here, leaving a staggered line of blood behind them. It streams steadily from Richter's pant leg, marking the tiled floor like a trail of breadcrumbs. "What unfinished business were you talking about?"

"Why?" She crosses her arms, frowning at me. Her irises flash like a cat's in the shadows. "Do you want him to live? After everything he's done to you, do you think he deserves to?"

I gape at her, the sharp edges of a retort poking at the inside of my lips. Even if she wasn't directly involved with the torment I experienced the last few years, even if she didn't have a hand in what Dr. Richter put me through in this place, she still allowed it to happen. She didn't fight for me the day of my exam—the day the Enforcers came to take me away—when, as Head of Termination, she had power. Power that might have changed everything.

Instead, she hid behind her false life and simply let the chips fall where they may, abandoning me to my fate as if I was nothing to her. As if I *meant* nothing. She let me go…the same way she let go of my father.

And because of that, I will never forgive her.

"And whose fault is that?" I bite back. "Remind me who it was who abandoned me to suffer through that tortur—"

She stops walking, and the white coat representing who she really is swishes around her knees as she rounds on me, clutching my left arm hard enough to make me hiss.

"This is neither the time nor the place for this discussion. He needs to be dealt with. *Now*." She gives me a quick once-over, and her eyes narrow, as if she doesn't recognize this person, this *thing*, I've become. Clicking her tongue, she adds, "I wouldn't have thought you'd be foolish enough to extend mercy to such a monster."

A cruel laugh escapes, springing up from my throat. "Haven't you heard? The real monster here is me." I tug my arm back, throwing her off, challenging her judgmental gaze with my own. My upper lip curls back in a sneer. "And I never said I don't want him to die."

If anything, I don't want you to steal that from me.

Ezra stands close to me on my other side, his grasp on my hand tightening. Out of the corner of my eye, I notice Jenner has stopped walking as well, his body turned sideways, his fingers hovering over the gun at his belt as if it's the only thing he can trust.

My heart clenches at the sight of them, always ready to intervene on my behalf and protect me, even when I don't need it. I feel weary, exhausted right down to my bones, from all the fighting and all the lying and pain that's consumed my life in recent years. But, in so many ways, they've had it worse, and I can only imagine how they must be feeling—what they must be thinking—given what they've both been through.

Ezra, whose brother has embraced his madness and who now sits on the brink of death, too dangerous to keep alive. And Jenner…whose family was executed by mine.

I'm overcome by the urge to reach out to him, to console him, but it doesn't feel right. Not here. Not in this place, surrounded by the ghosts of his family. Not when I'd only be seeking to comfort him as a way of easing my own pangs of conscience.

My chest tightens, and I wonder how we cross the canyon of guilt that seems to keep growing between us. How do I release them from the unending shadow my existence always casts over their lives when they're too far lost in the darkness to even remember the light?

I swallow, fighting back resurfacing tears…because I already know the answer.

Soon, I vow, keeping my eyes on my mother so as not to expose the heartache in my gaze to them. *Soon you'll be free of me and this will be over.*

My mother's brows dip into a vee, and her lips press into a tight, thin line, her hawkish eyes assessing me closely. Whatever suspicion I glimpse in her gaze is fleeting as she lifts her chin, seemingly content with my reaction.

"Hm." She pivots and carries on walking, stroking a contemplative finger along the line of her jaw. "If you feel that way now, I can only imagine what you'll have to say once you see what I have to show you."

My stomach dips at her cryptic words, but I can't bring myself to press her on the matter or ask her where she's taking us.

Because—

"Where are we going?" Even wrapped up in the warmth of Ezra's voice, this question is a sledgehammer to my skull, smashing a hole in my composure.

"One of the sublevels." My mother's face darkens. "There's a…warehouse, of sorts, down there."

"That's only slightly ominous," Jenner grumbles.

She shoots a scathing look at his back. "Yes, well, you'll want to prepare yourselves. I promise you, what's down there isn't pleasant."

Because I know—

"So, then, why are we going at all?" Ezra presses. "Let's just grab Rai and Quinn and get out of here. You said—"

"Not until I've destroyed it!" she snaps. Her scathing response echoes down the length of the hallway, and when her gaze cuts to mine, my blood seems to freeze in my veins. "I can't allow that research to survive. The attack should have—" Her mouth snaps shut, as if she didn't intend to say those words. As if they forced their way out on their own.

As I gape at her, I'm reminded of what Quinn said just before we came back to the DSD. When we were standing outside the ruined entrance, remarking on the damage the building took from the bombing.

"It's as if they knew where to hit," I had said.

And then Quinn answered, with words that resurface as the realization sinks in, *"Maybe they did."*

"It was you," I breathe. My feet drift to a stop, and the others all stop walking as well, as if our movements are linked by some invisible force. I drag in a shaking breath, then more forcefully add, "You were feeding intel to the people who bombed us."

"Someone on the inside," Jenner mutters, echoing his own earlier words.

"Why the hell would you do that?" Ezra steps toward her, releasing my hand. "Why the *hell* would you attack your own people?"

"I did no such thing," my mother counters. "Not directly, at least. There was an agreement made, and we…" She hesitates, her expression pensive, as if she's looking for the right way to phrase it. "We supplied them with the coordinates to destroy this place, that's all. But the damn bombs didn't hit deep enough."

"We?" Jenner presses, but she ignores him, brushing a hand over her face, which suddenly appears a decade older than it did only seconds ago. Does she mean her and Quinn?

Or is there someone else my mother has been working with?

With a sigh, she sweeps back a loose strand of hair. "Yet another spectacular failure. Maybe this is karmic justice at work."

Slowly, the disjointed pieces before me connect until the picture forming begins to make sense. My mother's appearance here. Her unfinished business with Dr. Richter. Her desire to eradicate his research…

She wants to destroy this place for the same reason I'm terrified of seeing what she has to show me.

Because I know what's waiting, I realize.

Bending forward, I plant my hands on my knees as the rancid taste of bile floods my mouth. My legs tremble as the revelations tally up, building one on top of another until I can barely keep hold of my rising emotions as each betrayal, each discovery, stacks up before me. Pressure grows in my chest, but I beat it back. If I'm not careful, my power will slip through the cracks in my mind and unleash who-knows-what kind of devastation.

Except, I do know because I've seen it before. And now that my control is gone, there is nothing to hold back what I'm truly capable of.

Sweat trickles down the sides of my neck, and a wave of vertigo swirls through my head as a black fog encroaches, disorienting my senses. I gasp, fighting to keep myself conscious.

My vision blurs as I think of Rai in that bed, her body still, her serene face frozen in sleep. A metallic stench fills my nose as she once again whispers those warning words from my dream.

"There's still time," I whisper under my breath, wiping the back of my hand across my nostrils. When I pull it away, blood stains my pale skin.

Just stay on your feet, I chide myself, shaking my head to clear the haze and hopefully stop the hallway from spinning. My gaze drops to the floor, but the red streaks of blood across the tiles swirl into a nauseating pattern that makes my light-headedness worse.

I squeeze my eyes shut to escape the vertigo, to escape the images haunting me, but the memory of the blood and future destruction is already there, branded into the backs of my eyelids, always ready to greet me. To tell me there's nowhere to hide. That it's coming.

To remind me of the monster I am.

"Wynter?" A warm hand wraps around my shoulder and presses gently, steadying me. I know without having to look that it's Ezra. "What is it?" he asks, bringing his mouth close to my ear.

I gulp, trying to force out the words, quickly wiping my bloody hand on my bodysuit. I open my eyes to find Ezra staring at me, visibly concerned, but I avoid his questioning gaze, instead glaring at my mother.

"They're still here…aren't they?" I ask.

My pulse quickens when I glimpse the answer reflected in the piercing storm of her eyes.

"So, you know."

I nod, turning my head to observe the Enforcers holding Richter's sagging body upright between them. Although his eyes are closed, I suspect he's awake. That he knows exactly where we're going and what we'll find once we get there.

"Know what?" There's a wariness to Jenner's tone that I don't want to fuel, but I can't control my lips. They move of their own accord, even as the lump in my throat threatens to choke me.

As I speak, I'm brought back to that tiny cell under the farmhouse where Nolan kept me confined after PHOENIX extracted me from the State. Even now, I can envision him sitting in front of me. I can hear his gruff voice in my ears.

"Nolan…told me what Richter was attempting to do with my blood," I say, breathless. Although my mouth is dry, the words keep coming. "How he was injecting it into other people with Ultraxenopia, trying…to create an army of soldiers."

Once again, my focus settles on Richter, and before I can talk myself out of it, I'm stumbling toward the heartless man who abused me for years. Ezra and my mother both call after me, while Jenner tries to grab my arm, but I don't stop, evading his grasp.

"That's what you meant, right?" I shriek, the accusation like a hot brand on my tongue. "Before, when you said you spent the last two years trying to create more of me. You were making—" Soldiers.

Weapons.

I grimace, suppressing the overwhelming urge to scream. "And they're here, aren't they?"

They're still here.

Dr. Richter's eyes glide open, the skin around them mottled with shades of brown and purple, the sockets darker than normal, concave from the pain of his wound and blood loss. A bruise forming across the left side of his jaw tells me one of the Enforcers must've struck him at some point—probably to stop him from struggling when they dragged him out of the exam room.

He grins at me, revealing teeth stained with red. He deserves far worse than he's already gotten.

You deserve to die.

The sly smile contorting his lips stretches wide. "Would you like to meet your brothers and sisters? Would you like to see why your blood is so special?"

I blanch at his words, unable to speak, as the guilt I've tried so hard to press back washes over me in a devastating wave with a singular purpose—to crush me. My chest constricts, and I can't breathe. I can't breathe. *I can't breathe.* I don't want to see them. I don't.

Not when, at the heart of it all, I know I'm the one who's at fault for their deaths.

"Shut him up."

My mother's heels snick against the tiled floor as she approaches from behind my right shoulder, the harsh growl of her voice a hammer against the walls of my paralyzing panic. I glance at her when she stops beside me and rests a hand on my upper back, breaking me free of its hold.

At her pointed look, one of the Enforcers shoves a gag into Richter's mouth before swinging his arm back and bringing it forward again without restraint, punching my tormentor hard in the stomach. A muffled groan leaches out around the gag, sending an odd surge of satisfaction racing through me.

My mother shifts her hands onto my shoulders and carefully spins me around to face her. "I wouldn't speak to him anymore if I were you," she warns. "He's smart, but he's desperate. He knows he's been cornered, and he'll be looking for a way out at every turn. He'll use that against you if he can." Although she lowers her hands, there's a moment where I sense real motherly concern coming from her, but as soon as it appears, it's gone. The blue eyes staring down at me— so much like my own right eye—are reproachful now, holding all the warmth of ice. "He'll only try to get inside your head."

I let out a deflated breath, a wry smile pulling at my lips.

Too late.

I lift a hand to the back of my neck, my fingernail grazing the knobbly flesh where the tracking chip Richter implanted in me remains, lodged in the top of my spine. A cackle of laughter swells in my chest, expanding in my lungs, the sound unhinged, the madness finally leaking through.

"He's already there," I mutter, certain that, as I speak, I'm donning the soulless black eyes of the monster I always wear in my visions. "He has been since you let the DSD have me."

My mother's gaze holds me in place for a moment, her face an unreadable mask. Distant. Perhaps that's how she shields herself.

How she keeps her own guilt at bay.

Sidestepping me, she grinds out, "Let's go," before resuming her onward march. The Enforcers follow her lead as if they have no will of their own, the two at the front towing a barely conscious Richter toward the one place in the entire world I don't want to see. The one place I know I *have* to see if my mother is going to give us her help—whatever that entails.

The one place where what remains of my sanity will surely shatter into a million, irreparable pieces.

We continue the rest of the way in silence, my mother trudging several paces ahead with the Enforcers while Ezra and Jenner bring up the rear, lingering close to me at all times. I'm not sure how long it's been since we left the exam room—five minutes? Ten minutes? Fifteen? It all feels the same.

"How much farther?" Ezra asks, echoing my own silent thoughts.

My mother doesn't respond. It's possible she doesn't hear him but it's far more likely she can't be bothered to answer, which wouldn't be at all surprising considering her intolerance for questions during my childhood.

I frown at the memory of the naive little girl I used to be…and clearly still am, even now, after everything I've endured. How did I not know or ever suspect who my mother really was? Was she simply that good at hiding the truth? Or did she have me so well-trained to just accept what I saw, to never question anything around me, that I wouldn't think to question her?

Bitterness prickles my skin, and I shudder against it, once again swathed in the understanding that everything I once thought I knew was a lie. And here I am, about to face the worst one of all: the lie I keep telling myself. That I'm a good person at heart. That I never wanted to be a monster.

Even though the blood coursing through my veins and the horror awaiting us say otherwise.

My mother leads us around several corners, then down a flight of stairs to a dead-end passage, bringing our procession to a grinding halt in front of an elevator I've never seen before. A small scanner on the wall positioned at eye level blinks to life when the sensor registers movement.

"Open it."

The Enforcers restraining Richter shove him forward at my mother's command, one pinning his arms behind his waist while the other tugs his head back by his hair, the fingers of the soldier's black gloves intertwining around the auburn brown strands and squeezing. Shifting Richter in front of the sensor, the Enforcers hold him still while the device scans his face, the blue glow emanating from the panel making his skin look sallow in the minimal light.

"Facial recognition scan complete," an automated voice intones from the device. *"Commencing retinal confirmation."*

Richter doesn't fight the scan, his back heaving, no doubt laughing around the gag—thrilled by the notion of me finally coming face to face with what a monster I am. With what he and the DSD turned me into.

"My own little angel of death."

I press a hand to my mouth at the recollection of his voice in my ear, holding back a scream or a sob. Honestly, I'm not sure which. Maybe both.

I don't want to see this.

I have to see this.

I don't want to know.

I have to know.

My thoughts vacillate back and forth until—

"Retinal scan complete. Welcome back, Dr. Richter," the scanner bleats in greeting.

The steel doors slide apart with a hiss, granting us access and beckoning us on board, ready to take us down into the bowels of what will surely be hell.

A crippling fear overwhelms me, and my body goes rigid, my boot soles glued to the floor. I wish the ground would open up and swallow me—anything to stop me from having to step foot on that elevator.

I don't want to see this, I think again, trembling.

I could leave right now and never turn back. I could walk out of this place, pretending what Dr. Richter said is a lie, just like his promise of a cure.

You could, my conscience says, *but you won't.*

"No," I say in a near inaudible breath. "I won't."

Because to do that—to run—would mean rejecting my own culpability.

Bristling, I push forward one step at a time, inching into the cramped metal box, the air inside somehow both hot and cold and smelling strongly of sterilizer. It's claustrophobic, and with the others gathered around me, the walls seem to shrink, pressing in on all sides, the matte metal surface warping our reflections.

"Do you really think an elevator is the safest place to be after the building's *just* been bombed?" Jenner asks. His tone is snide, his skepticism thick behind every word.

Annoyance creases my mother's brow, and she glares at him, her upper lip curling slightly. "It's the only way down. Don't like it? Get off. Otherwise, kindly do us all a favor and shut up."

I try to focus my thoughts elsewhere. To shut them out. To shut *everything* out. But I can't. All I can see in my head is the very real horror I'm responsible for. Not just the deaths I'm destined to cause when this world comes to a violent and catastrophic end, but the countless fatalities that already stain my conscience.

The doors sweep shut, and the air leaves my lungs, my panic an intense living thing that gnaws at my insides, trying to rip me apart from within.

"Hey," Ezra says, his voice soft in my ear, his soothing tenor instantly calming me. "I'll be with you the whole time, okay? You aren't alone."

I shudder as his arms wrap around me from behind, and although I don't deserve his kindness or his sympathy, I lean into it. Because I want it. I crave it.

I *need* it to not lose my flimsy hold on what little sanity I still manage to cling to.

"No matter what?" I breathe, my voice breaking.

No matter what we find?

Even if I'm the cause of it?

As the elevator begins its descent, Ezra's hold on me tightens, his fingers a comforting cage around mine. His nose brushes the back of my neck when he nods.

"No matter what."

FIVE

JENNER SULKS IN THE CORNER closest to me, on my left, chewing on his bottom lip, the entire ride down to Sublevel B—our destination according to the automated voice projecting around us in the overcrowded elevator. The monotone words are distorted by the occasional crinkle of static, likely a result of the damage to the building caused by the bombings on the city.

Bombings my mother helped orchestrate.

The voice announces our arrival at the same moment the doors ping open, letting in a rush of cold air. At first, all I can see is a gloom so thick and foreboding my first instinct is to cower and hide. A chill rolls over my skin as I stare into the darkness—my feet rooted to the spot and legs stiff—unable to bring myself to move forward even as everyone else steps off the platform into the shadows.

Nausea hits me like a brick wall as I drag in a breath, the sour undertone of a noxious odor in the stale underground air potent enough to make me retch. Cupping a hand over my mouth, I recoil, shrinking deeper into the elevator until my back collides with the hard metal.

Crinkling his nose, Ezra stops at the threshold and sniffs, but the revulsion contorting his face dissipates, replaced by a familiar concern when he looks back and sees me flattened against the far wall.

"Hey," he says, closing the distance between us again. "Just say the word and we'll go."

No. I have to see this. I have to know.

"I'm fine," I lie, dropping my arm and finally forcing myself to take a step forward. "Let's just get this over with."

I exit the elevator, pushing ahead into the dim glow of the emergency lights, which burn red on this level. As my eyes adjust to the darkness, I note that the floor is an uninterrupted slab of gray concrete, plain and unassuming compared to the sterile tiles that are so prominent throughout the rest of the building. The smooth surface stretches forward in a broad, half-moon shape, and along the curved edge, the floor collides with a wide pane of glass that stretches the full breadth of the space. The glass slants upward at a forty-five degree angle until it connects with the ceiling, forming an observation deck overlooking another much larger room.

My mother stands in front of the window, looking down at the space below, while the Enforcers accompanying us have separated into three pairs. One duad lingers near the elevator with another waiting beside a door off to the left, which I can only assume leads through to whatever nightmare awaits on the other side of the glass. The remaining pair stands at attention on the right side of the observation deck with Richter wedged upright between them.

Ignoring them all, I press on toward the glass, holding my breath as that stale odor grazes my nostrils, my lips, my tongue, my throat. Trepidation grabs at my skin, trying to find purchase and pull me back away from the window, but I brush the sensation off and tell myself to just keep moving. Even if I don't want to see what's beyond those glass panes.

Even if I know seeing it will be what breaks me.

The cavernous space just past the window is massive, at least fifty times greater in scale than any other room at the DSD—at least, of the ones I've been in or seen. The warehouse spans the height of two levels, and above, industrial fans pattern the ceiling, their constant whirring thunderous, even through the barrier of thick glass.

I watch the blades spin, focusing on the droning hum of each lethal rotation as the fans circulate oxygen, picturing myself standing under their currents. When I imagine the brush of that cool air on my skin, an involuntary shudder rips through me and my mind conjures images of what it is the fans are being used for.

What it is they need to keep cold.

Sinking my teeth into the inside of my lower lip, I press a hand to the glass and lower my gaze to the room below, wholly unprepared for what I know I'll find but unable to delay facing it any longer. If I don't look now, I never will. And by refusing to look, I'd only be denying the cruelty that went on in this place.

Cruelty that I unknowingly contributed to.

Hundreds of metal tables are laid out on the floor, lined up in perfect rows, the mid-section of each covered in a single white sheet—clinical and frigid, just like the rest of this place. At a glance, they remind me of the table I was tortured on in Dr. Richter's laboratory or of the table in Exam Room B, where I endured countless inspections during my time as his unwilling pet. It's only when I look closer that I notice the difference.

It's only when I look closer that I notice the faces.

"What the hell…" Ezra breathes beside me.

Although I already knew what I'd find here—knew in my bones what my blood is responsible for—my eyes still widen in abject horror, locked on this barbaric disregard for human life displayed in the room below like some kind of spectacle.

The acid in my stomach roils as I wonder how many others have stood in this exact same spot, watching as Richter committed his crimes. Why else have this window here? Why else make it so people could see what's occurring downstairs if Richter didn't expect spectators to his torture?

Bile burns my throat. *I'm going to be sick.* But I can't look away no matter how hard I try to. I can't bring myself to tear my eyes from the bodies.

Like Rai, each of Richter's victims is naked, their dignity only protected by the thin, white sheets draped over their torsos, pelvises, and the top half of their legs, offering far more modesty than my friend has been afforded. And yet, unlike Rai, the pallid hue of their unmoving faces tells me they lack the one thing she still possesses, even if she's otherwise dead to the world.

A pulse.

My quickening breaths leave patches of fog on the glass as my fingers tighten into a fist, my knuckles trembling against the broad pane. The power inside me rears to life, vibrating along the underside of my skin, a hum in my blood that threatens to shatter this window.

Gulping down the lump in my throat, I sweep my blurring vision across the organized grid of bodies. These people… They're just like me. Or they were before Dr. Richter got hold of them.

Before my blood was forced into their veins.

A tear cuts a line down my face, and as I wipe it away with the back of my hand, I pivot, shooting an accusatory glare at my mother. She stands a few feet to my left in funereal silence, staring down her nose at the grotesque sight below. A flicker of disgust burns in her eyes.

"You knew about this," I hiss. "You knew what he was doing here."

The biting edge to my voice makes her flinch, as if she had somehow forgotten I was here in the few seconds she's spent looking upon Richter's den of death. Her lips part—probably to excuse her role in this massacre—but Jenner cuts in

before she can speak.

"*Of course*, she knew." His face is hard as he sidles up beside me, crossing his arms. "Killing people is what she does."

"Were you in on it?" My whispered words feel pointless because I already know what she's going to say. After all the senseless killing I did on behalf of the State, and then seeing what's happening now in the Heart, I know all too well what sort of evil can be born from ambition.

Richter, Bilken, and Nolan—all three have gone to extreme lengths for their twisted aspirations or to gain or maintain a position of power, so I can only imagine what my mother had to do, what crimes she had to commit, to get to where she is.

To become the Head of Termination, feared and revered by all in the Heart.

Fresh tears flood my eyes. Although the logical part of my brain has already accepted the truth, there's another part—the ignorant child buried deep inside me, screaming out—that still clings to the pipe dream that my mother is good. That my own flesh and blood isn't capable of such monstrosities. That my evil wasn't inherent but made. Because if she really did help Richter do this, then that means half of me—the half of me I got from her—was always a monster, even before he set that side of me loose. And if that's the case, then Richter was right.

I really am an angel of death, born to be a scourge on this planet.

"Not so much recently but yes," she admits and, exhaling through her nose, shifts her body to face me. "Richter and I met ten years ago, at which time I helped him procure his test subjects. He was just a junior researcher then, and he lacked the authorization needed to carry out his experiments. Had he tried, there would have been consequences. So,"—she lifts her chin, shrugging one shoulder—"I helped him be…discreet…and offered my support and backing for his eventual promotion with the proviso I get partial credit for his findings."

Jenner snorts. "And the benefits that came with it, no doubt."

Her eyes dart to his, then back to mine, her lips pursed in annoyance, but she doesn't deny it.

"I stepped back two years ago," she says defensively. "When he moved all his research down here and built *this*." She gestures to the room beyond the glass, her upper lip peeling back into a revolted sneer.

"What about before then?" I manage, my voice a rough whisper.

Were you involved when I was here the first time?

She shakes her head. "I haven't had a direct hand in the experiments themselves for some time, not since Richter was elevated to department Head nearly seven years ago. Once he had the State's full support and internal obstruction was no longer an issue, my active participation became unnecessary. Frankly, there were other people more suited to the type of hands-on assistance he required in the lab, and my specialty was always more…behind the scenes. Like I said, I worked in procurement. Besides, I had my own department to run. So, I observed, I offered my input when he asked it of me, and I continued to provide test subjects for his experiments as and when he needed them.

"The first time you were here, I kept a close eye on you. I knew the only way to avoid suspicion of our familial connection and to stay fully apprised of your situation was to monitor everything, as Richter had come to expect of me. I knew about every experiment, down to the smallest detail…and I knew of their outcomes. The second time, when you came back and Richter's relentless experimentation resumed, I knew I couldn't carry on watching you day in and day out and pretend not to know you any longer. And this…" She casts a sad glance through the glass. "It got so far out of hand."

Her eyes drift to mine, her gaze pleading, as if this confession is somehow supposed to make me feel better. As if she didn't just admit to handing innocent people over to be tested on and killed, all in the name of Richter's research. As if she didn't just come out and say it's because of her support that he reached a position of power that allowed him to commit these atrocities.

My arms shake at my sides, but my building outrage and resentment don't seem to discourage her. She continues, even though I wish she would stop.

"At this point, thanks to his success with both you and that collar, Richter had limitless resources at his disposal and entire teams dedicated to subject retrieval, so it wasn't as if he needed my help. In truth, there was little I could do that wasn't already being done by somebody else. So, I stepped back in all regards except one."

"Which was?" Ezra presses.

My mother flashes a wicked grin. "Despite the endless array of tools at his disposal, there was still one thing I could give Richter that no one else could. You see, over the last decade, I have proven myself to be an indispensable confidant. A valuable ally he could trust. And now, I'm using that trust to destroy him."

My mouth and throat are a desert, arid to the point of pain, as I drag my gaze back toward the window and, once again, peer down at the bodies below. Forgotten. Discarded. Useless.

"How did you do it? Where did you…" My jaw clenches.

Where did you get his test subjects?

Her smile fades. "Termination," she murmurs, and when my head snaps up in response, she makes it a point to avoid my gaze.

I can practically feel the blood drain from my face. I always knew criminals and anyone determined to be unredeemable in the eyes of the State—those sent to Termination for the ultimate punishment of death—were often tested on first, used as guinea pigs in human experimentation, like I was, or tortured for information they likely never had. The goings-on at the DSD have always been common knowledge, and yet, knowing my mother was the one who handed these people over to suffer the kind of horrors I experienced at the hand of Dr. Richter—

Vomit rises in my throat, and it takes everything in me to swallow it down.

"Why?" I blink hot tears from my eyes. "Why would you do this? Why would you help him?"

She raises a skeptical eyebrow but still refuses to look at me. "The only true security in this country is power. Believe it or not, everything I've ever done was for you. To keep *you* safe. I just never imagined—"

"What?" I scoff. "That I would become a weapon?"

I glower at her when she doesn't answer, clicking my tongue in disgust.

"I want to see them," I say after a moment, and when she still doesn't speak, I grab her hard by the wrist. "Isn't that why you brought me here? So I could see this for myself? To show me what a monster he is?" Releasing her, I thrust a finger at Richter.

To show me I don't really know you at all?

Rather than answer, she looks past me at Richter, who now sits slumped on the floor, his face ashen and head nodding forward as if he's falling asleep. When she struts toward him, he jerks awake at the ominous clicking of her heels on the concrete.

She extends her hand, palm up. "Hand it over. I know you have it on you."

He lets out a wheezy laugh, his eyes shuttering closed again.

Crouching to the floor, my mother grabs a handful of his sweat-matted hair and yanks his head back. "We can do this the easy way, or I can have one of my friends here blow out your other kneecap. Which will it be?"

Dr. Richter hesitates for only a second before reaching inside his coat's interior chest pocket and pulling out a plastic keycard clenched between his bloodstained fingers. As he holds it out for my mother to take, his eyes slide to mine and his lips curve into a venomous smile.

That smug expression—that damned, gloating grin I've seen more times than I care to recount—triggers something inside me, a surge of anger I can't contain. In this moment, I want nothing more than to wipe that smile clean off his face and make him regret ever messing with me.

As the rage consumes me, I seem to become an invader in my own body, trapped inside it but helpless to act, watching the scene unfold as a spectator. In my place, the monster uses its newfound freedom to slink to the surface and seize control, just like it did before I had my collar to act as a needed leash on my power—like that night in Bilken's office when I butchered those Enforcers, who, despite working for Dr. Richter, didn't deserve to die. Like then, the monster uses the far-reaching grasp of my mind, ripping the plastic from my tormentor's fingers like it turned those Enforcers' guns back on their owners.

The card whips past my mother's hand before she can touch it. She follows its trajectory with startled eyes as it zips across the observation deck toward my outstretched arm, which the monster raises, pulling my strings like I'm a marionette. An abrupt shock passes through me like a jolt to the heart when the flat side of the plastic collides with my palm.

Disoriented, I peer down at the keycard, confused, the last few moments lost in fog. One second, it was in Dr. Richter's hand; the next, it was in mine. I didn't even actively try to use my power to obtain it. It just happened.

Completely beyond my control.

Oxygen evades me as I draw in a steadying breath, my head dizzy as that familiar metallic odor fills my nostrils and sits on the back of my tongue, tasting strongly of copper pennies. Pain stabs behind my eyes, my surroundings going dark at the edges of my vision, and for a moment, I think I might pass out. The vertigo is too powerful, the stench of my blood too overwhelming. But then my fingertips tighten around the card in my hand, reminding me what I have to do, and that resolution gives me all the strength I need to find my balance again. To cling to consciousness until this is over.

Ignoring the heat of everyone's bewildered—and frightened—stares on my face, I turn on my heel and make for the door at the left side of the platform, glaring at the two Enforcers positioned in front of it, who step aside without a word at my approach. As they shift out of the way, I lift my hand to swipe the keycard through the black sensor box on the wall beside the door, then freeze, my fingers an inch from the wall, suddenly uncertain if I want anyone else to witness what awaits beyond this point any closer.

That same terror and shame that shook me at the magistrates building when Ezra saw my file and witnessed the depth of the treatment I received under his brother's care grips me again now, the trauma of what I've been through like a hand around my throat, squeezing tightly until I can't breathe. I didn't want him to see that then, and I don't want him or Jenner to see this now. I don't want them to look at me like I'm broken. Or worse.

Like I'm the monster everyone else thinks I am.

"On second thought, maybe I should do this alone," I announce.

Ezra comes up behind me and touches my shoulders, turning me around to face him, before leaning in close until the tip of his nose brushes mine. "I've gone through hell to get you back," he says, his voice low, his breath hot on my lips. "I'm not leaving you now. Besides, remember what I told you?" He cups one hand around the back of my neck and trails the other along my right cheek. "We're always with you, no matter what."

I glance behind me at the closed door, wondering who it really is I'm trying to protect by choosing to face this nightmare alone. Is it Ezra and Jenner? Or is it me? Am I just running away like I promised I wouldn't?

"Promise me, you won't run away this time."

The promise I made to Ezra... It seems like I said it so long ago now—like it happened in another lifetime to an entirely different person rather than only two days ago. But it didn't. It happened to me, and if I push him away here when he's offering much-needed support, I would be doing exactly what I promised I wouldn't. Running away. And despite everything I've done, despite my guilt, I'm so tired of running and trying to face my problems on my own, even if, in the end, I have to. For now, I want him and Jenner to stay by my side, to ground me, to soothe me, for just a bit longer. For them to keep fighting for me until the time comes when fighting is no longer an option.

Until we need to say goodbye.

As Ezra's hand skims down the length of my arm, I find myself nodding absentmindedly at his touch. "Okay," I concede with a sigh, meeting his gaze again.

But as these words leave my lips, something doesn't feel right. As much as I want him to stick with me until the bitter end, there's a part of me festering in the darkest depths of my soul that hopes this will be the moment his love for me dies. Maybe, by seeing the crimes I've contributed to with his own two eyes, he'll finally decide I'm not worth fighting for and let me go...the way he should have when we were last at these crossroads two and a half years ago.

"Ready?" he asks, nodding toward the closed door behind me, and I nod back despite my growing apprehension, clutching his hand even tighter.

I peer past Ezra's shoulder at Jenner, who stands nearby with his hands thrust in his pockets, his gaze purposely avoiding the glass. The warmth I'm so accustomed to seeing in his expression is missing, and my fingers ache with the urge to reach out and grasp at the essence of what makes him *him* and somehow draw it back out again. The coldness I find instead makes me shiver.

At my questioning gaze, he shakes his head. "I'm going to stay up here.

Someone trustworthy needs to keep an eye on this asshole." He jerks a thumb over his shoulder toward Richter.

Unease swells in my gut as my eyes shift from my mother to Jenner, and then to each of the Enforcers standing like sentinels on the outskirts of the deck. I don't know how I feel about leaving Jenner up here alone with them. While my mother hasn't made any move to harm us, I can't be sure that amity will extend to Jenner if I'm not in the immediate vicinity to ensure his well-being and safety. Especially since he's not exactly looking to play nice with the woman he blames for the death of his family.

The mental image of her touching even one single hair on his head is almost enough to make me lash out.

"If any of you so much as look at him the wrong way, I'll kill you," I warn, speaking loudly enough so each of the Enforcers can hear the threat in my voice. My gaze hardens on my mother. "That goes for you, too."

She rolls her eyes, waving a flippant hand in disregard. "I'm coming with you. So, rest assured, your friend will be safe from my judgmental glaring. For now, at least."

I arch a brow. "Why? Looking to repent?"

She blinks slowly, unfazed by my withering tone. "I've learned to live with the weight of my sins long ago. I'm not looking for forgiveness."

Not even for what you did to Father?

"Good," I retort, letting the acid eating away at my insides bleed out in that single word. "Because you won't get it from me."

Scowling, I turn back toward the locked door behind me with Dr. Richter's keycard clenched between my fingers. Beside me, Ezra clasps my hand, and I nod.

"Let's go." I swipe the rectangle of plastic through the dip in the black pad on the wall, skimming the strip where Richter's security clearance has been embedded across the sensors. It only takes a moment, the light at the top of the panel switching from red to green almost instantly.

When the door slides open, my body goes rigid as the fans waft the warehouse smells onto the observation platform, the putrid stench of death even stronger without the airtight barrier to block it.

I bristle, glancing at Ezra, who squeezes my hand for reassurance.

"Just breathe through your mouth," he murmurs.

I part my lips, ignoring the foul taste that assaults my taste buds, and breathing in, I urge myself to move forward. To take just one single step over the threshold.

"Wynter, wait."

The panic in Jenner's voice halts me dead in my tracks, and pulse quickening,

I glance over my shoulder as he crosses the deck, his blue eyes round, their depths gleaming with fear.

Stopping directly in front of me, he says, almost breathlessly, "I get it. I get why you need to see this and why you're doing what you're doing, just—" He brings himself closer until our noses are nearly touching, lowering his voice. "Don't let this mess with your head, okay? The real monster here isn't you, no matter what you keep telling yourself."

I resist the urge to scream—to shake some needed sense into him, and into everyone else who keeps trying to help me. His words don't bring me comfort; if anything, they only make me realize how difficult it will be to get him and Ezra to stop fighting for me. To finally see me as I am. After all, how can they still believe I'm worth saving when the proof of my monstrosity is right here on the other side of that glass?

I can't bring myself to agree with him. I can't even manage a half-hearted nod because doing so would make me a liar, just like my mother. Jenner, seeming to sense my internal struggle, offers me the barest glimpse of that lopsided smile I love—that light, that forgiveness I desperately crave, emerging from behind the more prominent dreariness in his expression, making him seem like himself again, even if only for just a moment.

With as much of an answering smile as I can manage, I turn my back to him and proceed through the doorway, my eyes locking on the steep metal staircase on the other side, which will take me down into Richter's lair of torment.

Ezra and my mother follow me through the door, which slides shut, locking again behind us once we're clear of the threshold. Together, our hands glued palm to palm, Ezra and I take the unlit stairs one grated metal step at a time, proceeding with caution, my mother trailing behind us and mimicking our every move like a shadow. The rancid odor I first noticed on the elevator only gets stronger as we descend. The frigid temperature might be slowing the corpses' decomposition, but not enough to avoid the inevitable smells that accompany death.

Breathing through my mouth like Ezra suggested, I set my gaze on the vast space, which only seems to grow larger as we near the bottom. I shiver, the air touching my skin getting gradually colder, escaping my lips in small puffs resembling smoke. When we step off the stairs into the hangar-like warehouse, I notice the bodies we viewed from the observation deck are even more disturbing to look upon than they had seemed from above. Up close, I can see their skin—grayish blue and chalky—is riddled with boils and scabbed-over sores, and their mouths—all slightly parted, as if caught in a scream—are stained at the edges with dried, flaking blood.

My lower lip wobbles as I release Ezra's hand and inch toward the table closest to me, risking a terrified glance at the disfigured body obscured by the white sheet. It looks so small, and upon further inspection, I discover the face belongs to a boy, probably no older than nine or ten years old. Even stretched out at full length, he doesn't come close to covering the surface. The cold steel seems to swallow him, as if to demonstrate how tiny and fragile he is.

Was. Unfettered rage boils my blood at the thought. *The bastard killed a child.*

Was this what my mother meant by the experiments getting out of hand?

Was murdering children where she drew her moral line in the sand?

Pressing a hand over my mouth to stifle a sob, I shift my gaze away from the boy's face, unable to bear the sight of the pain and fear frozen permanently in his youthful features for even a second longer. As I take a step back, my eyes catch on his arm, the slender limb hanging lifelessly off the table, peeking out from under that crisp white sheet. To my revulsion, the crook of his elbow is riddled with needle marks identical to mine.

Vomit rises in my throat as I stumble back, my eyes flitting around the warehouse. *No, not a warehouse,* I correct myself. *A morgue.*

This place is a morgue.

Tablets are placed at the end of each table, positioned between the subjects' feet, the screens black aside from a subtle, pulsing blue light situated in the corner of each—so faint it was indiscernible from up on the deck.

Needing to see the full scale of the experiments that occurred here for myself, I skirt around the table beside me and tap my fingertip against the screen placed by the boy. As his medical records illuminate the dark space, I'm instantly brought back to that night in Zone 1. The night we thought we lost Rai.

The night I discovered exactly what the State was planning for me.

My heart races, drumming in my ears, as I flip through the file, skimming every note and detail regarding the boy's brief imprisonment, comparing it to my own time here. If what Nolan said about Richter using my blood is true, then everything I went through was just a precursor to what this poor boy had to suffer. His death, along with the deaths of the others around us... Every last one is on me.

Regardless of what Ezra thinks, or of what Jenner says to try to convince me otherwise, this... What happened here...

This genocide...

This is my fault.

My finger stills as two lines of text flash across the screen, and a tear slips down my cheek as I read them.

Cause of Death: Cardiac Arrest Following Transfusion
Days Completed in the Type X Trial: <1

"Type X," I breathe. A strangled laugh erupts from my chest, and despite the cold, despite the fog of mist that forms whenever I exhale, sweat coats my upper lip.

Nolan was telling the truth, after all.

Dr. Richter really was attempting to weaponize my blood.

One day, I digest, reading that second line again, the words fuzzy and nearly indistinct through my tears. This boy lasted less than one day with my blood in his veins.

Looking up from the screen, I swing my eyes to the other tables around me, from body to body. Corpse to corpse. And as I take in each one, my hysteria grows. If this boy only survived one day after being exposed to my blood, how long did the others last? Was their misery drawn out for days? Weeks? It couldn't have been that long if Richter never pushed for production of other collars.

But that thought brings me zero comfort when I think of what they still had to go through. When the end finally came, were they in agony? Or did their deaths come quickly?

Were they at least granted that one small mercy?

Tears curve over my cheekbones as I divert my gaze back to the boy's stony face. Reading about what happened to him here isn't enough; I need to see it for myself. I need to witness what Richter put him through.

I need to witness what *I* put him through.

Tremors roll over my hand as I reach out and brush my fingertips against his limp leg, and as I graze his chilled skin, I draw in a breath through my nose despite the terrible smell. My stomach turns, but I push all thought of my own discomfort away and focus only on calling on my power—on triggering a vision, just like I've done so many times in the past. Control or no control, I remember how to do this.

As easy as breathing, I once told myself.

My lungs deflate, a wavering breath breaching my lips, as my thoughts encompass the bodies around me. Other victims to this dreadful disease. When I was first brought to the DSD, Dr. Richter told me the condition was rare. But if that's true, where did he manage to find so many people with Ultraxenopia to serve as his test subjects? Were all these people in the Heart this whole time, all of us unaware of each other?

Or is something far more sinister at play?

A light sparks in the corners of my eyes, bleary at first, then sharpening as it spreads in front of me, filling my full range of vision. Unlike the other times I've done this, what I experience now is a jumbled mess of distorted images rather than the clarity I grew accustomed to with my collar. Sweat beads across my forehead, suctioning my bangs to my skin, as I fight to control the racing images, which fly through my thoughts in a blur.

As I feel my hold on the images strengthen, the vision finally steadies, revealing itself. Time seems to slow as I'm taken back through the battles I participated in on behalf of the State, but I'm not glimpsing my role in the destruction nor an impending retaliatory attack. Now, I'm seeing the aftermath.

Of what my involvement in the State's sieges allowed.

Enforcers roam the war-torn streets, pulling civilians from their homes and shining small flashlights into their eyes, searching for—

Heterochromia, I realize with a start, remembering what Richter said when we first met.

"Like the people in these documents, you have a rare genetic defect known as Heterochromia. To put it in simple terms, your eyes are two different colors. Although the disorder itself is harmless, we are beginning to link it to a more serious condition. A phrenoextratic disease called Ultraxenopia."

My blood curdles as the truth sinks in and I grasp what it is I helped Richter achieve. I helped him pillage countless cities, and the Enforcers... They were never there to support me but to ravage what remained afterward. To search for any survivors with even the slightest sign of having heterochromia, all on the DSD's orders.

In country after country, the men, women, and children who survived the attacks were all herded into transporters like sheep; I see it happen all over again in my head. And I recognize with increasing dismay that I was not only directly involved with their eventual deaths but personally responsible for their enslavement.

I did this to them.

No wonder the State always sent me in first to neutralize the threat. Minimal damage meant fewer casualties and more potential candidates for Richter's research.

The picture in my head warps, transforming, until a room almost identical to the Research laboratory manifests around me. Fear and anticipation prickle my skin, but instead of reliving my own torture, each of Dr. Richter's other victims flash through my head. I watch as they're strapped down to a metal table identical to the one from my own nightmares and then injected with my blood, their screams shredding what remains of my sanity. By the fifth one, I can no longer bear to watch.

I let out a gasp when the images fade, darkness swathing my eyes and taking the shape of the graveyard that is Sublevel B. Dazed, I step back, my fingers slipping away from the boy's leg, and as the contact between us ends, my knees buckle.

Ezra rushes to my side when I collapse, catching me just before I hit the floor, his arms acting as a safety net, drawing me close. The familiar wetness of blood drips from my nose to my lips, and my head throbs, slices of agonizing pain cutting into my temples, making it difficult to focus on anything other than the burden of my guilt. It's crushing me, but I don't fight it. I can't.

I can't…

"My blood did this," I breathe, my voice cracking. "I did this."

Ezra sweeps my sweaty hair back from my forehead and wipes the blood off my quivering lips with the sleeve of his shirt.

"No, you didn't," he says fervently. "You were just…"

The pawn. The murder weapon.

Fresh tears slide down my cheeks, singeing my skin with their heat, as Ezra pulls me against his chest, hooking his chin over the top of my head. "I know it's hard to see otherwise, to *believe* otherwise, but none of this is your fault," he whispers.

I want to believe that, but how can I?

After everything he's seen me do, how can he?

My gaze drifts up to the observation deck window where I envision Dr. Richter just on the other side of that glass. I never wanted this. I never chose to become this tool, this weapon.

I never wanted to hurt anyone.

Every single thing I've done since finding out I have this disease has been forced upon me. I might not be blameless in what happened here, but I didn't choose for it to happen either.

Whether or not my blood was the underlying cause of these deaths, I never consented for it to be used this way, and I certainly never had a say in what I became or in how my powers were used by the State. I didn't want this—I would *never* want this—but like these people, I wasn't given a choice. My path was dictated for me from the start.

Like them, Dr. Richter also made me a victim.

"You're right," I agree, pushing myself upright, swaying at first but finding my feet.

My jaw clenches as the guilt in my chest relents, surrendering to a much stronger emotion.

I glare up at the glass. "It isn't."

SIX

THE PAIN IN MY BODY is secondary—an afterthought—as I push away from Ezra and stumble back toward the stairs, my fingers gripping the handrail so hard the metal squeals and bends beneath my touch, distorted by the pressure and rage pouring out of my body in an invisible wave. In my peripheral vision, I glimpse my mother, her expression resigned, perhaps even contrite, almost as if she knew this would happen.

Hell, maybe she intended it to.

"Wynter, where are you going?" Ezra asks, his tone panicked.

He races after me, hot on my heels, as I bolt up the shadowed stairs, retracing my steps toward the observation deck up above. For so long, I've been blaming myself for so many things that were beyond my control. But this disease didn't turn me into a killer—my fear of the State and the DSD did. I didn't *want* to go to war. I didn't *want* to murder countless innocent people.

Just as I wasn't the one who pumped my blood into the bodies around me.

No, Dr. Richter did that. All the suffering I've witnessed the last three years, and the pain and the guilt that have nearly consumed me—it's all been because of one person. Him. And Rai, whose death has haunted me for years…

Jenner was right. I repeat this sentiment in my head several times until I believe it. *The real monster here isn't me.*

It's Richter.

"Wynter?" Ezra grabs my wrist, and I stop halfway up the stairs to the deck.

Slowly, I turn, looking over my shoulder. "If my blood did this to people like me," I muse, my voice devoid of emotion as my eyes skim over the bodies below, "I wonder what it will do to someone who isn't."

Without meeting his gaze, I rip my arm from his grasp and continue up the stairs, too hell-bent on revenge to care about his reaction to the implication behind my words or the way his steps falter behind me. If this is what ultimately flips the switch and makes me the monster in Ezra's eyes, then so be it.

One way or another, Dr. Richter will pay.

As I near the top of the stairs, I slide the door open with a single look, forgetting the keycard and crumpling the metal before me as if it were paper. The lock panel protests my forced entry, the automated voice dropping an octave, its tone wavering in pitch as it moans its refusal before shorting out, going silent.

A searing pain threatens to melt my brain as the pressure building inside me expands, spreading along every inch of my skin in an uncomfortable, electrifying tingle that radiates through me right down to my bones. Fighting through it, I step over the threshold.

The Enforcers stationed on the outskirts of the observation deck all jump back in alarm, raising their guns as I tear through the door. Their fear and uncertainty as they regard me is as potent as the stink of death in the air, but they aren't my targets. They aren't who I'm here for. Still, they hesitate, peering past me at my mother, who emerges from the warped doorway behind me.

"Stand down," she commands.

The Enforcers exchange unsettled glances, their confusion apparent, even as they lower their weapons. Jenner seems to share in their bafflement, his black brows furrowed and pupils dilated in fear, but I ignore him, focusing on Dr. Richter, who smiles up at me from his place on the floor.

"Do you believe me now?" he coos. "About how remarkable you are?" He raises an arm, gesturing toward the glass, then drops it back to his side in exhaustion. "Just look at what we've achieved together."

Together.

My loathing ignites a fire inside me, the flames burning in my chest savage and hungry, driving me berserk. They guide my movements, and as I storm forward, blind in my rage, I recall all those times on the battlefield when I surrendered myself willingly to my power. Unlike then, the power coursing through me now is unstable, and every second of use is paired with the worst kind of pain imaginable. But I can't help it, the pressure needs a release.

And I need to make my tormentor pay.

Blood streams from my nose, coating my lips, as I thrust out an arm and lift Richter off the floor without even touching him. The Enforcers standing nearby duck out of the way as I throw him to the side, slamming his back flat to the window. As I pin him to the slanted surface, a spiderweb of cracks branch out across the glass beneath him.

"There is *nothing* remarkable about what I just saw." I clench my fingers as if squeezing his windpipe. His eyes bulge, and he paws at his neck, trying and failing to pull away the invisible touch of my hand on his throat.

Gritting his teeth, he chokes out, "You are…Subject Zero. You lived…while they died…because…you are special. It's a pity…you can't…appreciate…what evolution has…gifted you."

"Gifted?" I scoff, sneering at the notion. "This disease is a *curse*. Seeing this"—I wave a frantic hand at the glass—"has only opened my eyes to just how dangerous you are."

I tighten my hold on his throat, and his washed-out complexion blooms with color, turning red first before darkening into shades of purple, then blue. When his eyes roll back into his head, it occurs to me that letting him die this way would be easy. Too easy. And unsatisfying.

No. I can't allow that. He deserves to suffer the same way all those innocent people downstairs had to suffer at his hands. He deserves to suffer the same way *I* had to suffer. And like hell do I plan on making it quick. Death by asphyxiation would be too merciful an end for someone like him.

My fingers slacken, relaxing my death grip, before I release my mental hold fully, dropping Richter back to the floor. A mewling sound escapes him on impact, and he curls into a ball on his side as he greedily drinks in gulps of fetid air until the normal color returns to his face. Tears shimmer across his pasty cheeks.

The second I release him, that build-up of pressure flows out of my body and my strength slips away just enough that I momentarily lose my balance. From behind me and to my right, I sense Ezra and Jenner stepping forward to help me, but I hold out a hand, shooing them back.

"What do you say we do one more experiment?" My voice is an ominous drawl as I fix my blurring gaze on Richter's face. "We've seen what my blood can do to someone like me. Now, why don't we see what it can do to you."

He blanches at the threat, his deranged mask cracking. For the first time in the few years I've known him, the man responsible for the downward spiral of my life actually looks afraid. The thought gives me a twisted sense of pleasure I didn't know I was capable of feeling.

I look back at my mother to find a complacent grin on her lips.

"This is what you wanted, isn't it?" I ask. "Why you brought me here? You want to destroy him."

"Not just him," she amends, her stare hard and calculating. "All of it."

All of it. His research. The bodies of his victims.

Destroy it all so it can't happen again.

"Good." My eyes flash to the two nearest Enforcers before snapping to Dr. Richter's trembling body. "Take him downstairs."

When they don't move, my mother says, "You heard her. Escort him downstairs immediately."

"W-Wait!" Richter protests when the Enforcers return to his side and yank him up off the floor. "You can't do this! You *need* me! No one else understands your disease! No one else can help you control it!"

As he kicks and fights against the two Enforcers, I hold out an arm, blocking their path.

"You're wrong," I growl, clenching my hands into fists. "I don't need you. I've *never* needed you."

And you already stole that control from me, just like you stole everything else.

Baring his teeth, he lets out a low chuckle. "Without me, you will die. You know this."

I fight back a laugh. Richter doesn't care if I die. Hell, I don't even think he cares if *he* dies. His only concerns are his own sadistic ambitions and living long enough to see them to fruition.

"I don't wish to save this world. I wish to see it burn."

That was what he said to me in the moment right before removing my collar. Blinded by his obsession with this disease, he wants to witness the destruction I've seen in my vision, to see the full extent of the power I'm capable of with his own two eyes, even if that means decimating an entire planet and killing billions of people in the process.

As I challenge his gaze, I can feel the fire of disdain burning inside me, although I hide it behind a detached facade. The mask sliding into place is one I've worn so many times. The mask of the unfeeling weapon *he* created.

"I'd rather die and deprive you of the one thing you want than let you live for a second longer. It's what you deserve."

My mother places a firm hand on my shoulder, and at her touch, I lower my arm. She nods at the Enforcers restraining Richter, who shoots me one final terrified glance as he's hauled across the observation deck toward the door.

Dr. Richter shouts obscenities at me, but his cries become dulled as he's led down the darkened stairway into the warehouse below. My mother's hand disappears from my shoulder as she follows behind the Enforcers, her heels ticking on the metal steps, beckoning me to join her. But I can't seem to bring myself to move.

My eyes shift to the glass, and I stare blankly up at the fans, entranced by their rotations. I don't know why I'm hesitating. It's not as if I haven't killed before. I've taken innumerable lives in cold blood. But then, those deaths were meaningless to me whereas *this*, what I'm about to do, is different. Killing Dr. Richter will sever a toxic, abusive bond that has kept me captive for years.

Killing Dr. Richter will set me free.

"Wynter."

At the sound of Jenner's voice, I avert my eyes from the window to find him and Ezra standing beside me.

"You don't have to do this," he says, his tone pleading. "I know what he is, but you don't have to sink to his level."

"We should just shoot him and be done with it." Ezra looks down at the floor as he speaks, refusing to look me in the eye.

My heart trips at the possibility that what I'm planning will hurt him, even if any love or affection he once held for his brother is gone. As I consider this, I decide that whatever happens in the moments to follow can't just be about me. I'm not the only one Richter has hurt. Ezra deserves a say in his sentence. This decision can't be mine alone.

And yet, I can't bear the thought of leaving this place with Richter's heart still beating.

"I..." Raw emotion strangles my voice. "I know I'm a monster. I've accepted that." I hold up a hand before Jenner can protest, giving him a look that tells him I'm not finished. "But *he* was the one who made me this way. And Rai..." I shake my head, unable to say it. To put what Richter did to her into words. "Someone who would do that doesn't deserve to live. Not if he's only going to do more of this."

I wave toward the window, gesturing weakly to the mortuary reeking of death just below. Ezra's gaze follows my hand, his expression unreadable, while Jenner's hard stare remains locked on my face.

"This isn't the same," he insists. "This is the first time you would be killing another person by *choice*. Your mother has been back in your life for five seconds and she's already manipulating you into doing her dirty work. Don't let her turn you into something you're not."

Compassion soothes the jagged edges of my heart. I understand why Jenner has reservations—why he's worried what influence my mother might have on me when I'm already so close to the edge. But this isn't about her. Or even about me.

This is about making Richter pay for his crimes.

Before I can argue and tell him he's being short-sighted, Ezra breaks the silence. Every word that escapes resonates with the same vitriolic hatred I feel.

"Austin signed his own death sentence the moment he *chose* to shoot Rai."

Jenner glances between us in shock. "I can't believe what I'm hearing. Murdering an unarmed hostage isn't right, regardless of if they deserve it. You know that," he says, his eyes cutting to Ezra. "That mercy is part of why I agreed to join PHOENIX."

"And look what PHOENIX has become," Ezra scoffs. "The world will be a safer place once he's gone."

"This isn't the only option—"

"What else do you suggest, then?" Ezra asks, his tone bitter. "Who, exactly, will punish him if we let him go free? Nolan, when he creates the new State?"

Jenner doesn't argue further; he must know there's no logical argument to counter the brutal, honest facts before us. Besides, he wants Richter dead as much as we do—I can see that written all over his face. He's just worried for me, as he always is. About what price I'll pay for taking this life.

About what cost it will have on my sanity and what little flicker of humanity I'm still holding onto.

"I feel trapped," I whisper, glancing at Jenner, whose eyes soften at the hardship behind those three words. "And, so long as he's alive, I will be tethered to him and he will always find a way to drag me back. You must know that or else you wouldn't have killed all those Enforcers to get me away from him. So, please," I beg, "don't think less of me for needing this. For needing to finally set myself free."

I watch the shift in his throat when he swallows, his eyes gleaming with tears as he steps forward and tugs me into a suffocating embrace. His voice is rough in my ear.

"I'll always stand with you, no matter what. Hell, I'll pull the trigger myself if that's what you need. Just…make sure it's your choice, not hers."

My choice…

As he pulls away, putting space between us again, I realize everything he said just now was a test—a chance for me to back out if I needed it. He doesn't want the burden of guilt that comes with taking a life to crush me, despite the fact that I've already taken so many and the guilt is a tidal wave I will never escape. An inescapable ocean in which I am drowning.

Luckily for us both, this is one death I'll never regret.

"It is my choice," I promise.

Jenner exhales, then rolls his shoulder in a slow circle, cracking the joint. "Okay. If you're sure, then let's go kill this prick."

"No. Go back to Rai and check on Quinn. The code to the room is 84912. I'll meet you there as soon as I'm done here."

Ezra cocks a brow at my words, and even Jenner looks at me as if he doesn't understand what I'm saying. "We're going with you," he argues.

I shake my head. "No. Not this time."

My chest aches at the nonplussed look in their eyes. Even when they don't agree with my choices, they would still walk to the ends of the earth by my side rather than let me face any kind of danger or pain alone, even the kind I inflict on myself.

But I can't let them do that this time.

Meeting Ezra's wounded gaze, I whisper, "You don't need to see this."

Just because he deserved a say in what befalls his brother doesn't mean he needs to witness the outcome.

Before either of them can change my mind or object, I brush past them, crossing the deck to the stairs, unbending the squashed remains of the door to block the path behind me, even though the effort is exhausting.

Ezra's eyes follow me through the observation deck window, and I can only hope that he'll realize what I'm trying to do—that I'm trying to protect him from the images and regret that will torment him should he have a hand in his own brother's death. I'm protecting him the same way he and Jenner have always gone out of their way to shelter me, even when we were little more than strangers.

And with that protective instinct at the front of my mind, I descend into the chilly darkness of the warehouse.

When my feet touch down on the sublevel floor, I scan the empty, cold space for my mother. At the far end of the vast room, past the rows of my dead brethren, I glimpse a faint light outlining a doorway I didn't notice the last time I was down here.

As I near it, weaving through the maze of tables—ignoring that several I pass display children—I notice the door is slightly ajar, and through the crack, I see Dr. Richter propped up in a chair. Shackles bind his wrists and ankles to the metal arms and legs, and he's surrounded by machines and instruments that eerily resemble the laboratory upstairs I was tortured in.

I push the door open the rest of the way but waver at the threshold as recognition pummels my senses. Images of the barbarity I glimpsed when I touched that poor boy's leg flash through my head again.

This is where he tested on them, I realize.

"Are you ready?"

My mother appears before me, and nodding, I shuffle into the laboratory after her, my decision to do this now fully cemented. The echo of her heels clicking against the concrete is bitingly loud in the silence as she leads me over to a silver cart where a syringe is already prepared.

"This won't be pretty," she warns me.

My jaw tenses. "It can't be any worse than what he's done to me."

To encourage her, I push up the left sleeve of my bodysuit and hold out my arm, exposing my vein, which seems to pulse in anticipation, giving her permission to draw my blood. Her mouth purses when she spots the dozens of track marks littered across the crook of my elbow.

Fingers trailing over my wrist, she sweeps an antibacterial wipe across my clammy skin, her touch surprisingly gentle. She doesn't warn me in advance of the pinch that follows from the needle pushing into my vein. She doesn't need to. I already know what to expect.

Silence swells like heat between us, the seconds ticking by at a near stagnate pace, as we both watch my blood—blood that's to blame for so much needless tragedy—fill the attached plastic vial. When my mother finally frees the needle from my skin, she offers me a small square of gauze to staunch the bleeding, which I refuse with a terse shake of my head. Pulling down my sleeve, I turn to face Dr. Richter.

His gray eyes—eyes that once filled me with fear—now stare at me with the same trepidation. "You don't know what you're doing," he says, the words hurried. "If you go through with this, your life and the lives of everyone you care about are over. But, if you stop this, I *will* fix your collar. I'll give you your control back, I promise!"

A laugh churns deep in my chest. "We both know that's a lie. Besides, what was it you once said to me?"

Stepping forward, I jerk his head back, cranking open his mouth with one hand while grabbing fistfuls of his auburn brown hair with the other. Sweat bubbles up on my skin as I focus my thoughts on the pile of gauze layered on the silver cart behind me. Square after square floats through the air toward us and straight into Dr. Richter's mouth, gagging him.

A smile hitches up the corners of my lips. "Sacrifices must always be made for the advancement of science."

The scent of his terror is palpable and almost cloying in my nostrils, strong enough to overwhelm the stink of death emanating from the adjacent room. His eyes widen, flicking between me and my mother, who appears beside me, holding the syringe in her hand.

Offering it to me, she points to a vein on his neck. "Inject it here. The results will be more immediate." I shift the needle toward Richter's neck as instructed, but before I can pierce his skin, my mother grabs my hand, stopping me. "You need to be sure you'll be able to live with this. What we're about to do will haunt you for the rest of your life."

Precisely what I wanted to spare Ezra from.

The smile fades from my lips. "Good thing I won't be around that much longer, then, isn't it?"

Dr. Richter mutters something, his words unintelligible past the wad of gauze in his mouth. I meet his gaze—his eyes gleaming with fear—and to my surprise, I feel strangely calm.

The smile returns as I prick the needle into his neck.

"Don't worry," I murmur. "You'll only feel a minor discomfort at most."

SEVEN

I STARE DOWN AT DR. Richter's slumped form in the chair, his posture slack, his heart and lungs still. His face is shriveled like a grape that's been left out in the sun, and his complexion is stained with varying unsettling shades of brown and black, the skin riddled with multi-colored contusions. Although he's only been dead for a matter of minutes, it's as if the flesh on his bones is already rotting.

Beside me, my mother whispers, "Are you all right?"

My lips pinch into a disgruntled frown. I'm not sure what to say. Am I all right? I thought watching Richter die—I thought being the one to kill him after everything he's done—would somehow make what I went through here worth it. But now, as I graze my eyes over what remains of the person who made me what I am, I don't know what I should be feeling. There's no sense of relief or anger or any of the emotions I anticipated.

Instead, I feel nothing, as if what just happened was meaningless.

My eyes shutter closed, and I watch the vivid memory of his death replay in my mind. I see myself plunging the needle into the side of his neck, injecting him with the same blood he used to kill so many others like me.

As it entered his body, I observed the outcome without remorse, my pulse a steady, satisfied tempo. I didn't startle when his breaths became labored or when his eyes flashed up to mine, terror-stricken. If anything, his pain was a drug and I was an addict fixing for more.

Within seconds of my blood penetrating his body, Richter's skin jaundiced, his ivory complexion turning yellow. Sweat bubbled along the sides of his face, which was breaking out in purple bruises that extended down past the neck of his shirt. As his chest heaved, his lungs constricting—fighting for breath—blood dripped from his nose and the vessels in his eyes all popped, turning the whites a bleak red. His irises rolled back into his skull, then his jaw unlocked and a scream unlike anything I'd ever heard before unleashed from his throat as if his soul was being torn from his body.

When the room fell silent again, he was dead.

The echo of his agony lingers in my ears, the shrill, grating resonance worse than what I remember of my own screams in this place. Worse even than the screams of the young boy, which linger still in my memory.

Why don't I feel better? The man responsible for the suffering of so many—of *my* torment and pain—is dead. He's finished. His experiments are finally over.

Except…they aren't. Not really. Not while there are plenty of others just like him out in the world, ready to rise up and take his place and start this cycle all over again so long as they have access to the right subject. Nolan was just the tip of the iceberg and I have no doubt in my mind that others impacted by the State's war have considered how I could be used to their own advantage, like Nolan stole me away from Richter for his. For all I know that's what the bombings on the Heart are about and the attack on the DSD was a smokescreen. I can't be sure of anything anymore.

Not when I've seen how quickly power corrupts.

And even if I don't live long enough for that to happen—to become someone else's unwilling stooge—Dr. Richter still wins in the end. The destruction and death he wants to inflict on the world will come to pass, no matter what I do.

No, the horror isn't over at all.

So long as I'm alive, it will never be over.

As I open my eyes, it takes all the willpower I possess not to fall to my knees and weep. Not out of regret for what I've done—my hatred for Richter like a red-hot poker burning into my skin, branding me permanently—but because the reality of my situation is closing around my neck like a new collar. One I can't remove.

I've understood for a while now how dangerous my existence is to the well-being of this world, but this is the first time I truly grasp just how much of a threat I really am. Apocalyptic visions aside, the greed of mankind is an enemy I will never be able to defeat. Because even if I found a way to overcome this disease and prevent the decimation awaiting us…

Someone, somewhere, will always attempt to leash me, just as Richter did.

I startle at the touch of my mother's hand on my forearm, and jerking away, I put a few steps between us. When I meet her gaze after a moment, her brow is drawn and she's staring at me with an odd look in her eyes, as if she somehow knows what I'm thinking.

"Let's go," I mutter, cutting her off before she can comment.

I don't look back as I storm out of the laboratory and back into the large open warehouse where the sharp, tangy smell of disinfectant gives way to the stomach-churning stink of decaying flesh. The fans spinning overhead waft cold air over me, chilling me down to my bones, and goosebumps raise all over my body, as if the death in the room is a tangible presence caressing my skin. Around me, the corpses of Richter's victims tempt my gaze, but I keep my eyes on the floor. I can't face them again, not after witnessing what they went through here.

Not when I know it could have all been avoided if I'd never gone back to the DSD in the first place.

If you hadn't, they would still be dead, my conscience reminds me. *And so would you. So would everyone.*

I grit my teeth. Would they? Is it certain the destruction I saw would have occurred any sooner had I never left PHOENIX? And even if it is, why are the only options before me always death or more death?

As I near the stairs, I pause, glancing back at my mother, who follows a few steps behind, keeping her distance. She meets my gaze with those inquisitive blue eyes that are so familiar and yet, make her seem like a stranger.

"This…" I trail off, my tongue suddenly too big for my mouth. Tears disfigure what I can see of her face in the restricted light as I bite out the only words I can manage. "How will you destroy it?"

She considers me for a moment, her expression wary. Does she think, because my eyes are wet with tears, I want to preserve this place? Does she think I want any evidence of what Richter has done here?

Of what my blood can do?

Finally, she says, "By finishing what the bombs started."

Holding her gaze, I swallow around the lump in my throat and nod before resuming my march up the stairs, trudging one leaden step at a time. My movements only seem to get heavier and more sluggish as I climb, as if the darkness below is trying to pull me back into its depths and keep me here amid the death and decay where I belong. I can almost hear the screams of the dead— of my brothers and sisters in this disease. Of my blood in their veins calling out to me, begging me not to abandon them here. Their cries of blame are like nails digging into my skin, regardless of how many times I tell myself I'm not the one who did this.

The heels of my mother's shoes clang on the steps behind me like the unchanging beat of a metronome, the rhythm only fluctuating in the moment it takes for me to peel back the door at the top of the stairs. As the rumpled metal yields before me, the pain I've been staving off fills the remaining space in my head like water seeping through cracks, flooding my pounding skull like a bowl.

A silent scream forms on my tongue as a warm, sticky wetness drips from my nose onto my lips, but I clench my jaw and power through, wiping the blood—both fresh and old—from my face. Stumbling onto the observation deck, I search for Ezra and Jenner, but they're nowhere to be seen. I can only hope their absence means they went upstairs to wait with Rai and Quinn like I asked.

My mother's entourage of Enforcers remain, standing by to accompany us back up to the ground level. I ignore them, crossing the platform toward the elevator, the steel doors hanging wide like open arms eager to embrace me. Out of the corner of my eye, I glimpse the streak of blood staining the floor where Dr. Richter sat, awaiting my judgment, only minutes ago, and I falter mid-step, wondering if he suffered enough—if I shouldn't have drawn his death out longer as punishment for everything he inflicted upon this world.

Upon me.

Shivering, I wrap my arms around my torso and shrink into the back corner of the elevator, trying to escape the thoughts stirring inside me. Thoughts that threaten to plunge me into a dangerous state of mind I might not be able to escape. My fingers rake through my hair, clutching my aching head, as I sink into a crouch on the floor.

Outside, on the observation deck, my mother pauses before the broad window, staring down at the horrific scene below in quiet contemplation. Without looking up, she simply says, "Burn it."

There's an edge to her tone that speaks to something inside me. That makes me wonder if destroying this place is as much about revenge for her as it is about closure and justice for me.

I consider that idea of vengeance as the Enforcers all reach for their belts at my mother's command, each retrieving one of several transparent tubes of carmine-colored powder I only now notice affixed to their uniforms. Without needing any further instruction, they proceed in a single-file line down the stairs, pouring the contents on the floor in a trail starting from the deck and continuing all the way down into the warehouse.

My mother lingers in front of the glass, hands clasped behind her back, watching them work. They return to our level a few minutes later, and as the last Enforcer steps onto the platform, he wavers by the crushed remains of the door, pulling a silver cylinder from his pocket. Twisting the top, he tosses the device down the stairs and quickly steps away from the threshold.

At the clink of the triggering device striking concrete, flames ignite throughout the mortuary, casting everything in a fiery haze. The glow of the fire sends orange and yellow flickers of light through the slanted glass, which dance across the walls in celebration of the impending destruction.

The soldiers don't hang around to witness the blaze, quickly crowding around me in the elevator. When black puffs of smoke cloud the windows—the flames reaching up from below, licking the glass—my mother joins us, swiftly pressing the button to ascend, leaving the warehouse behind to burn. She doesn't look at me once, not even as the doors close.

I can feel the heat of the fast-spreading flames beneath our feet as the cramped metal box carries us in silence back up to the ground floor, but still, my mother doesn't spare me a glance. She doesn't even speak until the doors open.

"The sublevel will keep the fire contained, but another attack could be imminent. I'll see to your friend, as promised, but we need to be quick."

Despite her warning, my steps are lethargic as we make our way back to Exam Room B where Ezra and Jenner are waiting for us. The Enforcers shadow my every move—so much like my personal bodyguards when I was a ward here— while my mother walks a few feet to my left, her steps hurried and clipped, more quiet than she was before.

When I can no longer bear the discomfort of her silence, I murmur, "Did you know?"

"Know what?" she asks, tone tentative.

"That I would be exactly what Richter was looking for." My eyes cut to her face as she lifts her chin, but still, she doesn't look at me. "You said it yourself, you were the one who got him his subjects. You had to have known I would fit the criteria."

She finally meets my gaze, her face a pitiless mask, wearing the same expression she always reserved in my childhood for the rare moments when I was being a nuisance. The ice in her gaze reminds me far too much of the man she just helped me murder.

"For eighteen years, Richter was ignorant of you, and I made sure he stayed that way. He didn't search for subjects himself; he relied on me to find them for him. If I hadn't gotten involved, if it had been someone else doing his dirty work—" The muscle in her jaw clicks when she snaps her mouth shut, as if physically restraining herself from even entertaining that thought. After a moment—and a steadying breath—she continues. "Like I said, everything I did was for *you*. To keep *you* safe. Even when they took you..." She shakes her head. "I wouldn't have let them if I didn't know that I would be able to watch over you after."

A dubious laugh more like a gasp parts my lips, and I slow to a stop, glaring at her. "Watch over me? You call what you've been doing *watching over me*? Where were you when I was trapped in a cell for days on end? Or when I was trying to kill myself by throwing up everything I ate? Where were you when Dr. Richter started torturing me? Do you even know what he made me do?"

"Of *course*, I know." Her tone is sharp, but when she opens her mouth to say something else, she hesitates, seeming to think better of it. Pinching the bridge of her nose between her thumb and forefinger, she lets out a long, weary breath. This time, when she speaks, her tone is more gentle. "Why else do you think I intervened?"

Intervened?

"What, you mean earlier with Richter? *After* he removed my collar and shot Quinn?" I snort. "You were a bit late helping anyone there, don't you think?"

"I'm not talking about today," she says vaguely.

My brow furrows, and I blink at her, confused. "What—"

She holds up a hand. "I promise to tell you everything as soon as we get somewhere safe. But not here. Not right now. It's far too long a story and we don't have that kind of time." Her eyes flash back in the direction we came from, reminding me of our current predicament.

We walk the rest of the way to Exam Room B without another word between us. When we arrive, I pause at the threshold, my eyes sweeping over Ezra where he sits at the edge of Rai's bed, his back hunched and hands splayed through his hair, his fingers mussing the strands in his frustration. Jenner, who had been pacing the room, goes still the instant he sees me in the doorway. Ezra looks up a few seconds later, his eyes finding mine like two magnets drawn together.

I glance between their unnerved faces and shove my hands behind my back. Although clean, they feel dirty with Richter's death, as if his blood is a permanent stain on my skin. If they see my hands, they'll see what I've done, and then, they'll finally see me for the monster I am. And while they should, while part of me wishes they would, my heart can't bear the thought of either of them looking at me the way I looked at Richter.

The lump returns to my throat as I force myself to acknowledge Ezra's questioning gaze. He stares at me, those hazel eyes swimming with tears, asking the one thing his lips seem unable to voice.

As the answer pushes at the boundary of my lips, the sharp, stabbing pain of anguish cuts through my heart, and it dawns on me there's one death I've been ignoring. The only death I will never come back from—that I caused when I *chose* to kill Dr. Richter. Regardless of all the lives I've taken, *that* was the defining moment when I truly decided to become the monster instead of fighting it. Because, for the first time, I didn't just have to kill.

I wanted to.

"It's done," I gasp, pressing a hand to my chest, balking under the sudden hollow feeling inside me.

For so long, I viewed my humanity as the switch to my emotions; that I could abandon them if I just shut it off. But now, I realize it's something else—the only thing standing between who I was before this disease and the monster hovering at the edge of every thought, waiting for me to relinquish myself to its whims. Without that wall separating the two, there's nothing to stop me from losing myself, and nothing to help me come back again should that happen.

Without that small thread, however small, tying me to who I used to be, who will I become in the time I have left?

As this question nags at me, gnawing at the last of my composure, I surrender myself to the barrage of emotions building up in my chest. And in this moment, despite everything I've done, despite all the lives that have been lost and that I've personally ripped from this world…

Despite knowing that I don't deserve to be saved…

The death of my humanity hits me the hardest.

EIGHT

THE TENSION IS PALPABLE, LIKE a thick morning fog, as we stand congregated around the narrow bed, waiting for my mother to deliver a verdict on Rai's condition. Her prognosis. I hold Rai's right hand clenched between both of mine while Ezra clings to her left, as if his own life depends on it, his knuckles white as his fingers squeeze tightly. Jenner sits perched on the foot of the mattress, staring over at her sleeping face in silence.

Our escort of Enforcers all wait in the hallway with the exception of Quinn, who has been moved to the examination table that marked so many of my days here. Propped upright against the wall with his legs stretched out across the full length of the metal surface, he's bloody still but bandaged properly now, the bed sheet replaced with a large patch taped to his side that I glimpse through the ragged remains of his shirt, which my mother cut through to get to the wound. She also gave him some pills, I assume for the pain, and got his bleeding staunched enough that his face is steadily regaining color, stealing away any threat of death.

As for my mother, she stands behind us, tapping and swiping at the screen of Richter's tablet, scrolling through the notes he left behind about Rai and whatever it is he did to her, her face pinched in concentration.

She sighs, her eyes glowing in the light of the screen. "I'm surprised he managed to keep her here without anyone finding out about it. I can only assume he had your friend somewhere else in the building and then relocated her to this exam room after the attack." Frowning, she places the tablet down on the mattress, meeting my gaze across the bed. "The man was always good at hiding his secrets."

"He wasn't the only one," I comment.

My mother refuses to wilt under the heat of my glare, staring back at me for a long moment. She only looks away when Ezra clears his throat.

"Can anything be done to help her?" he asks.

We hold a collective breath in anticipation of her answer, although the dread pooling in my stomach tells me I already know what she's going to say. Rai told me herself.

"You were never going to be able to save me, you know that."

I've known since the moment I saw her in this bed. There's nothing we can do for her. She's gone.

She's *been* gone since Richter shot her.

"No." My mother's voice is flat. "The damage to her cerebrum is too significant. Although her vital functions are still in working order, there's no evidence here to suggest she will ever wake up. Going off this data, I'm afraid her vegetative state isn't reversible. Whether or not Richter intended that, I can't say. But if there is a way to rouse her, I'm afraid I don't know it."

"So, that's it?" Jenner whispers, his eyes haunted. "All this was for nothing."

His face twists with outrage and anguish, which I can't help feeling responsible for. Even though Richter was really to blame for what happened to Rai, I can't ignore the facts. Both times we fell into Richter's traps because of me—because of my decisions—and both times, we lost her as a result. If it wasn't for me, none of this would've happened.

If it wasn't for me, Rai might still be alive.

I recall the soothing words she spoke in my dream, once again hearing the lie she so easily spun that there was nothing I could have done to prevent this. The lie I know was really just my own brain trying to ease the burden of responsibility crushing me. But it can't be true that we were helpless in this. I can't believe that. I *won't*. Because if I did—if I were to allow myself to follow that line of thought for even a second—that would mean there really is nothing I can do to prevent the future I saw in my vision.

From losing everyone else I love the same way I lost Rai.

My mother's frown deepens, and she offers me a pitying look. "I'm sorry, but we can't take her with us. Now is the time to say your goodbyes."

Panic flashes across Ezra's face followed by a stricken acceptance that dulls his warm eyes, cutting me deep. Swallowing, he squats beside the bed and touches his forehead to the back of Rai's hand.

"Where is it we're even going?" Jenner asks, his voice rough with a suspicion I find myself sharing.

"And why are you taking us there?" I add, my own tone edged with doubt.

Despite what I said earlier about going with her, the truth is, I don't trust my mother. I'm not sure I ever can after all the betrayals that have tarnished our family with tragedy. She might have helped me put an end to Dr. Richter's reign of terror, but that doesn't make us allies.

And it certainly doesn't make her good.

"A safe house," she answers, frustratingly vague again. "Everything else will be explained once we're there."

"Whose side are you on?"

My eyes bolt to Ezra, who glares at my mother, skepticism creasing his face, as if he's not sure what to think of her. As if he's not sure he should believe what she says.

With a forceful breath through her nose, she mutters, "I'm on no one's side. As far as I'm concerned, the State and PHOENIX can battle this out on their own." Her expression hardens, and she crosses her arms. "All I care about is keeping my daughter alive and, from what I've heard, that's what you both want, too."

She's not wrong. All Ezra and Jenner have done since we met is try to keep me safe—to protect me, even when I didn't need protecting. But how does she know that?

What else has Quinn told her?

I examine the details of her prim face, trying to see past the mask of cold detachment she keeps in place like armor. Her tightly pursed lips give nothing away.

"Ma'am." One of the Enforcers appears in the doorway, saluting my mother, who gestures for him to speak. "Rogers has reported an increase in blockades across the zones. If we're to have any hope of reaching the rendezvous point, we need to leave soon."

Nodding, she swings her eyes back to mine. "Whatever you're going to do, decide now."

With one final glance at Rai, she turns on her heel and makes her way to the door. To my surprise, she pauses beside the examination table mid-route, extending her hand to help Quinn up instead of calling for an Enforcer to do it. He scoots forward at her beckoning, grunting as he slides off the metal, landing unsteadily on his feet, and I watch as she snakes an arm around his back when he stumbles, taking the brunt of his weight. It's the first time I've ever seen her do anything at the expense of herself, and I stare, mesmerized, as she leads him out into the dim light of the hallway.

As the door glides shut behind them, I peer down at Rai's limp hand still clutched in my own. Her skin is soft and cold against mine.

"She's right. Rai is gone. I might not have known her well, but I don't…" My throat constricts around the words. "I don't think she would want us to stay here. She'd want us to go."

Ezra raises his head, and he and Jenner both look at me, the same unspoken question burning in each of their eyes. When I say nothing, comprehension darkens their gazes. They know I've seen something, but I can't find the strength to explain it to them. Not now.

Maybe not ever.

"If there was a way, I wouldn't leave," is the only explanation I can offer, my voice a barely-there whisper.

"You were never going to be able to save me."

These words seem to live in my ears, in my skin, in the very essence of who I am—an unpleasant reminder of a truth I will never escape. But they also remind me of something else.

Something that gives me hope.

Although I failed Rai, I have to believe what she said in my dream is possible. That, even though she's beyond helping, there is at least still time to save Ezra and Jenner. To change their fates the way I couldn't change hers.

Releasing her hand, I trail my fingertips across the pitted scar on her forehead, then through her hair, brushing the strands over the skin to hide the evidence of the gunshot that stole her from us. With it covered, she looks perfect—like she could be sleeping. Reality buries its claws deep in my heart.

Leaning forward, I press my lips to her right cheek, no longer able to hold back the tears. They pour out of me, collecting on her skin like dew drops, before dripping down her neck and pooling in the dip at the apex of her collarbone.

As my gaze follows their downward descent, I glimpse a thin silver chain I never noticed her wearing before. Curious, I lift it away from her throat, noting the subtle weight tugging down on it.

Careful not to yank it too hard, I spin the chain around until a small silver locket emerges from the sleek mane of her hair. It's round and thin, easily mistaken for a simple pendant if not for the hinges, and etched into its surface are beautiful ornate swirls that come together to form some sort of pointed flower or star.

A trickle of unease creeps over my skin, and I shiver at the realization that Dr. Richter must've been the one to give her this necklace. Otherwise, I'm sure he would've discarded it.

Exhaling a shaky breath, I touch my fingertips to the engraved metal, and upon contact, an image explodes inside my head, nearly knocking me back off my feet. A bright, white flash fills my range of vision as a stabbing pain cuts into my temples, threatening to rip a scream from my throat. When the light finally fades and the details of my surroundings return, it dawns on me that I'm not in Exam Room B anymore, nor anywhere at the DSD.

This, I realize with growing horror, staring aghast at the long hallway forming before me.

This is the magistrates building.

The corridor is dark, almost pitch-black, and empty, just like that night two and a half years ago. I turn in place, my eyes swinging left and right, unsure what I'm meant to be seeing, when the echo of a female voice slips through the crack of a door standing open to my left. Her muffled words beckon me forward.

My heart races as I follow the sound, my feet stumbling forward as if my body is being pulled by some invisible force I have no control over. When I approach the room, the door swings wide, revealing an office identical to Bilken's. Rai sits at the glass desk within, staring blankly out the large window—forming a mirror image of Dr. Richter and how he looked in the vision I saw of them meeting. In her extended hand, the silver locket lies open against her flattened palm. A blue light shines up from its depths, reminding me of the glow of a hologram.

"If you're watching this," she begins, her voice low. Hesitating, she seems to reconsider her words, and shaking her head, she lets out a sigh. "Okay, let's be honest. If you're watching this, I'm dead. I'd be lying if I said I didn't expect it. I only wish I had enough time and words to tell you just how sorry I am."

I hold my breath as I cross the room toward her, hypnotized by her words—by how real she feels to me in this moment. If I reach out my hand, I can touch her again; I can feel the warmth of her skin. I can remember what she was like when she was alive instead of the shell Richter turned her into.

But then I remember that she isn't real—not like this, not anymore—and my chest hitches with a sob when I comprehend what this vision is trying to tell me. When it hits me what event this moment is preceding. She knew what would happen.

She knew by approaching Richter, she would die.

"I know you're going to blame yourself, but this isn't your fault, Ezra," she says. "No matter what he thinks, no matter what I'm sure you've wondered yourself countless times, you didn't make me leave. It was *my* choice to join PHOENIX, no one else's. Just as this…facing him again… It's my choice. I didn't tell you what I was planning because I knew you would try to stop me, and I love you for that—for caring about me in this messed-up world where love is so fragile and fleeting. But, the truth is, I'm tired of running from everything we left behind. The past haunts me, and I owe it to myself and to Austin to finally put all this to rest. Put *us* to rest. I need you both to let me go."

A smile spreads across her lips as she spins in the chair, her dark eyes flicking upward to look at the ceiling. I'm amazed by how calm she seems despite her impending death looming over her head.

Not calm, it occurs to me the longer I watch her. *At peace.*

"You and I have been through so much together, and every step of the way, you've always trusted my advice and guidance. Okay, maybe not *always*, but most of the time. So, let me impart some final words of wisdom, all right?" She kicks out a leg, halting the chair's rotations, and, once still, peers down at the locket with the stern expression of an older sister. "Look after Wynter. I know you wouldn't hear it before, but she's important. I can *feel* it. And not just because of what she's capable of…but because of what I know she could be to you."

My feet freeze beneath me as I suck in a breath, and triggered by her words, my memory drifts back to this same night, focusing on our trek through the tunnels as we made our way into Zone 1. I recall, verbatim, my conversation with Ezra and how he said he felt compelled to protect me. On some level, I've always wondered if his feelings for me boiled down to obligation because of his mother. But now, hearing this, I feel reassured that I didn't imagine it when I sensed something between us from the very beginning, even when I wasn't sure what that was. Knowing that Rai could see it—what we were destined to become to each other—fills me with the best kind of joy and the worst sort of fear. Because Ezra has to let me go.

And now, more than ever, I'm terrified that he won't.

"You've shut yourself off for so long that you probably don't even realize it yet," she muses. "I guess it's my own experience that allows me to see what you're trying so hard to fight. You're curious about her. And maybe that doesn't seem like much now, but I can see what it could turn into." She leans back in the chair, a slight smile forming on her lips. "Take it from someone who's made this mistake and doesn't want to see you make it, too. Embrace it. Take a chance. Allow yourself to experience something *real* for once. Something other than the fear and hatred we've all blindly surrendered ourselves to. This life is far too short, and the seclusion we suffer prevents us from having what you've been fortunate enough to have dropped in your lap. So, look after her. Find a way to help her survive. Oh, and Ez?" She cocks a disgruntled brow. "Try not to be too stubborn about it, okay? If you wait too long, Jenner might beat you to it!"

Rai throws a quick, alarmed glance toward the door before looking down into the blue light again. It's only now, as she crouches over the desk and the glow of the hologram recording illuminates her face, that I notice the tears in her eyes.

"It's time for me to go now," she whispers. "I know the odds of you ever seeing this message are slim, but I couldn't allow myself to die without saying this. I'm only sorry I didn't say any of it to your face when I still had the chance. If I get lucky and you *do* see this, just know that you have the power to create great change. So, go out there and do it. Don't spend your life searching for vengeance. Regardless of what Austin does to me, stay focused on what really matters. And remember…"

The room around me darkens, and, all too quickly, Rai's features fade into the shadow of memory. Panic gives me the strength to lunge forward, and as I scream for her not to go—not to leave us again—I reach out a hand. But she slips from my grasp, now nothing more than a ghost.

In the thickening gloom, as the darkness envelops me, I can just make out the bright warmth of her smile.

"I love you and I will always believe in you."

Stabs cut through my skull in quick succession, and my lungs burn with a scream that seems to set my soul on fire. My legs give out beneath the weight of my pain, my knees slamming hard into the floor. Through my blurring vision, blue smudges at the edge of my eyes tell me the vision is over.

I'm back at the DSD.

Ezra and Jenner both yell out my name, but their voices are dull behind a shrill ringing beating against my left eardrum. The familiar taste of blood fills my mouth and nose—the one commonality I've come to expect from these episodes— and yet, something is different about the effects this time, as if I can sense myself moving one step closer to death. It hangs over me like a constant shadow.

"Wynter—"

Ezra and Jenner come at me from both sides, arms outstretched to offer their help and support, but I brush them off with a strained "Don't," clutching at the side of the bed. Ignoring the agony slicing my brain to ribbons, I carefully pull myself upright until I'm on my feet again.

Fingers shaking, I reach out and grab the locket, which now rests against the top of Rai's chest. My heart pounds in my throat as I pry the latch open with my thumbnail, and inside, I find a small picture—the same photograph Ezra was staring at the night we lost Rai at the magistrates building. The picture of them as children with Richter.

Gritting my teeth, I peel the picture away, searching for the recording device hidden underneath. Rai must've planted it there before we left for Zone 1 with the intent of leaving Ezra a message, even knowing he might never see it.

A sob grips me at the thought, and I bite my lower lip hard to hold back the pain in my chest as I unclip the chain from her neck and extend my trembling hand toward Ezra. Cautiously, he takes the locket from my grasp, confusion alight in his eyes.

Two words break free of the cage of my throat before the tears and grief consume me.

"From Rai."

NINE

I PRESS MY BACK AGAINST the cold wall and tilt my head toward the door, listening for any trace of sound inside the silent exam room. It's been several minutes since I handed Rai's locket to Ezra and left him to listen to her message alone. Everyone else had the decency to follow my lead and give him the privacy needed to process our friend's final words, even though every moment we spend here only increases our chances of being discovered by Enforcers not on the DSD's payroll—assuming that's who the soldiers accompanying us work for—or, worse, falling victim to another attack. Even my mother, who has the authority to talk us out of trouble with any passing patrols, should it come to that, is visibly perturbed by how long we've spent here.

I peek at her out of the corner of my eye where she leans against the wall on the other side of the doorway, standing opposite me. Although her expression is drawn, she keeps checking her watch. It's strange to see her fidget when she used to scold me for that same habit when I was a child, but I don't blame her for being antsy or feeling on edge. My own nerves are shot, and the hush that's engulfed the building since I stepped out of the exam room has been stifling. Even Jenner is unnervingly quiet.

My mother huffs, peering at her watch for at least the twentieth time in half as many minutes. "We can't afford to waste any more time. If we don't leave now, we'll miss our window."

"Window?" Jenner asks from where he stands on the other side of the corridor, his voice strained with unshed tears.

She tugs on the crisp lapels of her coat, her severe eyes cutting to mine. "The patrols in this area aren't the only ones we have to worry about."

It takes me only a moment to grasp her meaning.

"The safe house," I breathe.

Her brows draw into a vee as she nods. "We only have a brief stretch of time in which we can get to it unnoticed, assuming a blockade isn't already obstructing our path. That window gets smaller the longer we linger. We've already been here"—she glances at her watch again, that solemn frown deepening—"nearly an hour. We can't afford to dally much longer."

Pushing off from the wall, I let out a breath and drag a hand across my face, brushing the hair from my eyes, which burn uncomfortably, aching with exhaustion.

When was the last time I slept?

"I know." I hesitate, casting a remorseful glance at the door. "I'll tell him. Just...give us a minute, okay?"

The dread that keeps biting at my insides resurfaces, and my stomach turns at the thought of walking back into this room...and what it will mean when I come out. Even though I've already been through this loss and suffered this pain once before, the thought of never seeing Rai again is somehow so much worse this time. Maybe because it's real now and we actually have to say goodbye to her—a chance we were robbed of when Richter shot her.

Now, any hope we had of reuniting is lost.

And that's largely because of me, because I didn't see her fate soon enough to prevent it. So, how can I face her again, even in death?

How can I face Ezra when so much of this is my fault?

"Wait." My mother grabs my hand and, turning it over, presses something hard against my palm. My eyes dart downward, narrowing on a syringe not that unlike the one we used to kill Dr. Richter.

"What—" I begin, but she cuts me off.

"I've been holding onto this just in case anyone ever caught on to what I was up to. I figured a quick death was preferable to torture, and I didn't want—" She breaks off mid-sentence, as if the words are too painful to say, then clears her throat, straightening. "Well, it doesn't matter now. Use it on your friend. You'll need it to end her life humanely."

"She's already dead," I whisper, my voice breaking.

"Her brain might be, but her heart isn't," my mother murmurs in a strangely consoling tone. "Leave her in peace. Better you do it than abandon her as she is for someone else to find. At least, this way, she can go surrounded by people who love her."

Abandon. That word cuts through me like glass. Isn't that exactly what we did the night Richter shot her? If we hadn't fled the magistrates building—if we had stayed and fought to bring Rai home or, at least, gotten her back to the tunnels—then she could've died peacefully among her friends, her found family, the way she should have. The way she would have wanted. Then, she wouldn't have been turned into a living representation of Dr. Richter's twisted obsessions. Then, we wouldn't be faced with the terrible decision placed before us now.

A decision which isn't really a decision at all.

My fingers close around the syringe.

I won't make the same mistake twice.

Resolved, I turn to face the door, my fingers trembling as I enter the unlocking code into the keypad. As the barrier yields, sliding open to welcome me, a hand brushes my upper back and I startle.

I glance up at the sudden warmth at my side, meeting Jenner's gaze, the blue depths the same icy shade of water or the hottest burning fire—a combination of cold and heat. My heart swells when a gentle smile forms along the edges of his lips. There's no joy in it, only sadness.

But it's a sadness we share.

"I'll go with you," he says, taking my hand. "This isn't something you should do alone, and I—" He grimaces, closing his eyes for a moment. "I want to say goodbye, too."

Alone… I don't know any other way to survive. Ever since Ezra and Jenner came into my life, I have always tried to shoulder the burden, always tried to prepare myself for the inevitability that I would lose them or that they would be taken from me. Because that's what my life has always been—a never-ending cycle of solitude and loss. Our final impending moments with Rai only confirm that.

Inside the exam room, we find Ezra in the same place where we left him, except now, he's kneeling beside Rai's bed, his forehead on his hands, gripping hers. There's a vulnerability to this pose I haven't seen from him before—not even when he was weeping over the photograph of him and Rai as children the night we first thought she died. The night that also marked the first time we ever kissed.

My heart breaks at the sight of his pain.

"Ezra."

He lifts his head at the sound of my voice, and his eyes—the whites red and raw from crying—shift to meet mine, his expression dazed. Drawing in a shaking breath through his nose, he clambers to his feet.

"It's time to go…isn't it."

A lump blocks my throat, and the syringe in my hand suddenly seems to weigh several tons, threatening to drag me down to the floor along with the regret and remorse of what I know is the right thing to do. It takes all the strength I possess—that I've *ever* possessed—to force myself to nod.

Jenner and I make our way to the other side of the bed, giving Ezra some space. As one, we all look down at Rai.

This is it.

It's time to say goodbye.

And yet, none of us seem able to do it, the silence consuming every word and breath before we're even able to make them. I never thought I'd mourn someone as much as I've grieved for my father, but as my eyes dance over Rai's comatose face, it strikes me just how much I miss her. I barely even knew her and my heart still aches for the hole in our lives created by her loss, the pain of that emptiness crippling. I didn't even know it was possible to feel anguish this deep and unrelenting.

Jenner squeezes my hand, drawing my watery gaze, and once again offers me that same timid smile he gave me only a few moments ago. The smile that tells me I will never be alone in my pain…even though I know he's wrong.

When what I saw in my vision finally transpires, I will be alone in the darkness I've cocooned around myself—darkness born out of guilt for the part I've played in the deaths and tragedy I only wanted to prevent. Even if everyone in the world dies alongside me, in the end—in the moments before I destroy the world, when everyone realizes what's about to befall them—*I* will be the person they blame. Because Richter didn't give me this disease. I was born with it. Fate dictated I would be the real villain in this tale. And if Richter's death has taught me anything…

It's that villains deserve to die alone.

Jenner's whispered voice shakes me out of my thoughts, and I blink, staring at him as he looks down at Rai.

"I never thanked you." Tears streak his cheeks. "Not just for saving me that day but for convincing me to live. To hold on. I promise you, I'll keep living… and I'll keep fighting. Until there's nothing left to fight for."

As he speaks, I'm reminded of something he said long ago. In the tunnels under the Heart, Jenner told me what PHOENIX stood for and why those joined under its banner would fight for the cause until their dying breaths. A message that corruption warped over the years.

Now, those words are a promise to Rai, a vow to keep fighting for the better world she wanted. A world she'll never see.

A world I'm destined to raze.

Jenner swallows, the sound audible in the hush, then gives me a small, encouraging nod, and I realize it's my turn to impart whatever farewell I want to leave her with. I wish I knew the perfect thing to say—something that would close the door on this pain. But what *is* there to say?

What *can* I say that could possibly ever erase these feelings of self-condemnation?

I draw in a breath, letting it out with a whimper, before muttering the only words I can think of. The one truth I can manage in my grief. "I wish I'd had more time to know you."

Leaning forward, I brush my lips across her soft cheek again, and as I pull away, I lament the inevitable goodbye that I'll have to say to Ezra and Jenner. My throat thickens with tears, the thought taking hold like barbs in my skin, piercing my lungs. My heart.

I wish I'd had more time to know them all.

Biting back a sob, I watch as Ezra bends down and plants a careful kiss on Rai's forehead, avoiding the spot where Richter shot her. His lips linger for a moment, his breath a kiss of its own as he whispers, so softly I barely hear it, "Message received."

Our tear-filled gazes meet across the bed, and I lift my hand to show him the syringe. It sits unmoving against my palm.

"For Rai," I breathe, and my voice breaks on her name.

I turn toward the metal infusion stand, which remains situated, undisturbed, near Rai's head, and carefully collect the transparent tubing trailing down into her right arm between my fingers. A tremor rolls through me as I try and fail to insert the needle into the injection port beneath the IV bag.

I hear footsteps behind me, then a familiar hand touches my shoulder before moving to my wrist, steadying my grip.

"Together," Ezra murmurs.

Guiding the needle, he presses my shaking thumb down on the plunger, then takes me into his arms as we watch the silver liquid travel through the length of the tube.

It takes less than ten seconds for the poison to enter Rai's body. When it reaches her heart, the monitor tracking her vitals beeps erratically, screaming in protest like the alarm we heard earlier. Unlike the alarm, it dies quickly, settling into one continuous tone.

As the tears roll fat and hot down my cheeks, the flatline rings around us like a death knell.

TEN

A CHILL HANGS HEAVY IN the air, pressing down on my lungs and constricting my breaths a bit more with each step I take away from Exam Room B and the nightmare of the time I spent trapped in this hell. Even now, the imprint of my trauma remains like a brand only I can see and feel, its presence a constant weight on my shoulders. I had thought, with Richter gone, that weight would lift, but it lingers, like a new sort of tether attempting to keep me tied to this place. Even in death, Richter haunts my every waking moment.

Even in death, I can't fully escape him.

No one utters a word as we file out of the back entrance of the building into the smoke and ash polluted air, stepping past the broken door and emerging into the empty courtyard—the night silent aside from the occasional thump in the distance or resounding shot of gunfire. The resulting echo of triggers pulled without remorse sends a jarring shiver over my skin. I can only imagine how much innocent blood has been shed in the wake of the attack of the Heart, not only from the bombs but from the Enforcers, who now gun down their own people without mercy.

"The State will not support those who cannot contribute. You know our orders."

I shiver again at the memory of that callous voice and the murder of the poor woman that followed, the thought of which tugs my attention to Quinn. He stands propped up between two of the soldiers in my mother's employ, his skin still on the paler side but less clammy than it was twenty minutes ago. Whatever medication my mother gave him to fend off infection and pain seems to be working quickly.

Sensing my gaze, he looks over at me, and as our eyes meet, I wonder if he would be out in the streets tonight, murdering the blameless victims of the attack on our city had he remained an Enforcer and not defected to PHOENIX. Or to work for my mother, or whatever the hell he is now. Doubt about his intentions troubles me, and yet, behind that uncertainty, I can't help remembering what he said after saving our lives.

"I can't live with it. I didn't sign up to be a killer, and I'd rather help you than be part of the problem."

Did he mean that? Or were those impassioned words a lie—a ploy to gain my trust and sell his role in my mother's scheme to have me returned to her, like lost property?

"This way." My mother's sharp tone draws my focus.

I glance in the direction she struts in, her gait purposeful and determined, if not a little too fast to seem completely natural. She walks like someone who can't get away fast enough, her discomfort apparent in her quickening pace and the way her hands clench and unclench at her sides.

The rest of us follow her lead without protest, but as she makes for the motorized gate at the far side of the courtyard, skittering toward it like a bug fleeing death, I find a small measure of peace in knowing that even the Head of Termination isn't immune to fear.

Especially now, when I'm so close to drowning in it.

With every step, I sense the towering presence of the DSD behind me like a living, breathing thing—a malevolent entity that will reach out and claim me again if I don't get away quickly. Matching my mother's stride, I push ahead without looking back, eager to get beyond the extensive reach of its shadow.

The large gate buzzes open as we approach—although I can't see who opened it—and as the steel rack glides along the wheels, I squint into the darkness, unnerved by the thought of what might be waiting on the other side.

It takes my eyes a moment to spot it, the black metal blending into the unlit surroundings. Where the property line of the DSD intersects the street, I can just make out an armored truck facing us, the rumble of its engine a deep purr in the night, its headlights shut off. Behind it, a short distance away, I glimpse a second identical truck.

The sight of the two vehicles gives me pause. How many of these very same trucks were I transported in over the last year, always surrounded by soldiers and treated like a dangerous convict who needed constant surveillance?

How many times did these same trucks carry me to a war I never asked to be part of?

My mother continues, undeterred, and as I pass through the open gate behind her, I can't shake the growing apprehension that I've made a mistake in deciding to go with her—that we've escaped one trap just to fall in another. At my sides, Ezra and Jenner inch closer to me, seeming to share my concern.

My mother looks back at us briefly before nodding to the Enforcer walking beside her, who—on her unspoken command—trots ahead and circles around to the rear of the truck nearest us. The squeal of metal hinges is thunderous in the night as he pries open the doors.

As for my mother, she stops beside the cab.

"All aboard," she says, sweeping her gaze to the back of the vehicle before pivoting to face us. The Enforcer there mimics her instruction with a silent gesture for us to get in.

Ezra, Jenner, and I all waver, our eyes straying from the propped open back doors to the driver seat where yet another Enforcer sits as still as a statue, awaiting his orders. Although his head is turned in our direction, his face is hidden beneath the opaque shield of his helmet.

At our hesitation, my mother crosses her arms. "You can trust him. He's under my employ."

I peer over my shoulder, noting the other soldiers spread out around the courtyard. Including the driver, that makes seven Enforcers working for my mother. Eight if I count Quinn. Nine if there's a driver in the second truck.

How? I wonder, flummoxed by their involvement.

How did she buy their loyalty?

Jenner snorts. "Like that means anything."

She glares at him, her stern brow creasing, and lifts her chin with a disparaging sniff.

The dignified air she swathes herself in as she scoffs at our reluctance is familiar. How many times did she look at me with this same exasperation when I was a child? How many times did I brush it off as normal?

But normal people—the average inhabitants of the State not in positions of power and authority—don't behave this way in our society. They don't command respect. Or demand it, as my mother always has. Like the day my father was charged with treason when she boldly told an Enforcer to remove me from the room. I always assumed she said it to try to shield me from that trauma—from the distress of seeing my father get beaten—but now, as her words from that day stir in my memory, I realize it wasn't a request at all.

It was an order.

I grew up believing my mother worked in the Financial sector, that she was a law-abiding, run-of-the-mill citizen, so why did I never question it when she dared to order around an Enforcer? And why did her past behavior never stand out to me until now? I suppose I didn't want to see the truth, even though it was right there in front of me from the time I was young.

The truth that she was always a traitor.

My breathing stutters at the thought of my father, but the pain in my chest reminds me why I agreed to do this. Why I'm going with her.

Answers, I say to myself, finding my courage again. *Go along with this until you get answers.*

"Come on." I grab Ezra's hand and step forward, then look over at Jenner, his cheeks smeared with streaks of gray from the ash. Glancing between them, I incline my head toward the truck.

Ezra follows me without question, his face drawn with the distraction of his grief over Rai, but Jenner hangs back, gaping at us as if we've both lost our minds.

"Wait," he hisses, his bright eyes flashing to my mother. "This doesn't strike you as a *really* bad idea? Going with them is one thing. Being trapped in the back of a locked, armored truck is another. Who knows where she could be taking us."

Although I'm sympathetic and understanding of Jenner's distrust, I've reached the limit of what I can take in terms of pushback and second-guessing. I know he's only concerned about me and doing his part to point out any potential pitfalls—to be the voice of reason and sense while Ezra and I both spiral, barely hanging on by a thread—but we're running out of time. *I'm* running out of time. And every second we stall only brings the terrible future I've seen that much closer.

If we're going to do this, we need to go now.

While there's still time to save you, like Rai said.

A tired sigh parts my lips, but Ezra breaks his silence before I can speak. "We'll just have to trust she meant it when she said she wanted to help us."

"*And*," I add in a harsh whisper when Jenner begins to protest, "if, at any point, we suspect she's leading us into a trap, I'll kill her myself. Sound good?"

As these words escape me, I realize I mean them. To protect Ezra and Jenner, I would slaughter anyone who even *thinks* about harming them. Even if that person is my own mother, the woman who brought me into this cruel, unforgiving world.

Jenner stares at me for a moment, then snaps his mouth shut with an audible click. Grumbling under his breath, he storms past us and makes for the rear of the vehicle, purposely knocking into my mother's shoulder in passing. Sneering, she clears her throat and straightens her jacket, shifting her focus to me.

Ezra shoots me a questioning look, and I nod, urging him to give us a minute.

Words need to be said, and I'd rather tackle the subject without an audience.

With a warning glance at my mother, he releases my hand and follows after Jenner, casting one final look over his shoulder before climbing into the back of the truck.

Once we're alone—or alone as we can be with her nearby team of Enforcers—my mother arches a judgmental eyebrow. "Interesting friends you've made."

Baring my teeth, I lunge forward and grab her by the coat, shoving her into the side of the cab. "They aren't just my friends, they're my *family*," I spit, relishing her reaction to my choice of words. She flinches, as if every last one has cut her.

"Wynter," she starts to say, but I interrupt her.

"I love these people, and I swear on my life—on *your* life—that if you hurt them, if this is a trap—"

She huffs, attempting to push me off, but I don't relinquish my hold. If anything, her resistance makes my fingers grip tighter.

Nostrils flaring, she rolls her eyes. "I wouldn't waste time herding you into a vehicle if my intention was to kill you. I could've done that job three times over already."

Although she's right—although I've told myself this very same thing at least twice in the last hour—I scowl, unconvinced.

My fingers clench, the knuckles bone white, and I pull her closer until we're nose to nose. "Just don't delude yourself into thinking the fact that you're my mother will stop me from ending your life."

As I watch her process the threat, her lips trembling slightly, I relax my hand. I then take a step back, putting much-needed distance between us.

It's only when I turn my back to her that I acknowledge how fast my heart races or the burning in my eyes that can only be tears. I draw in one deep breath, then another, until the danger of my emotions fades, refusing to give her any reason to doubt me.

If I'm going to protect Ezra and Jenner from her—the way I wish I could've protected my father—then I need her to believe that I would kill her if the choice came down to them or her. If I'm going to ensure they survive, that they have a future without me after I'm gone, then I need her to *want* to honor my wishes. And not just because I'm her daughter…

But because she's afraid of what I'll do if she doesn't.

I don't spare her a second glance as I skirt around the side of the truck to the open back, mentally preparing myself for whatever unknown danger awaits us from here. Ezra and Jenner stare out from the hold, looking equally nervous as I climb in and settle on the empty bench seat beside them.

Even with the doors hanging open, exposing us to the night air, the interior of the truck is a claustrophobic box. Like in the elevator to the sublevel, the metal walls press in on all sides until each breath is a struggle and the persistent ache behind my eyes makes me dizzy. Part of me can't help wondering if my reaction is all in my head—if the heat burning across my skin is real or imagined, born from the reminder of the many times I was forced into a vehicle just like this one.

Muffled voices outside draw my attention, and I listen, trying to hear what my mother is saying. If she really expects to take us to a safe house where we won't be discovered, I doubt she'd risk detection by bringing her small hoard of Enforcers with us. Despite that, I'm relieved when two masked figures appear at the doors and help Quinn up into the truck. As angry as I am with him for his deceit, he promised me answers and I intend to get them. And, as loath as I am to admit it, I still feel an inkling of gratitude toward him for saving our lives, even if he only acted because my mother ordered him to.

"I'm glad to see you haven't died on us," I say flatly as the two Enforcers plop him down onto the bench seat across from me.

To my surprise, he chuckles. "Not yet. But I suppose there's still time."

"There's still time."

Stiffening at his mimicry of Rai's warning, I part my lips to shoot back a scathing remark, but the words die on my tongue when the Enforcers disembark and my mother appears between the open doors in their place, her eyes sharp and intent. She looks at me but says nothing before exchanging a meaningful glance with Quinn. As if in answer to some unspoken question, he nods, and then, my mother slams the doors shut, drenching the hold in impenetrable darkness.

An hour seems to pass in the space of mere seconds as the front door to the cab opens and shuts and the engine roars as the truck is thrust into drive, sending a rumbling vibration through the interior that causes the metal floor plates to quake under my feet. The shadows are too thick for my vision to adjust, and despite the seat under me, I feel like I'm floating, the pressure building in my chest like a balloon.

I reach for Ezra's hand, needing his presence to ground me, and as I interlace our fingers, he squeezes, although he's in far more need of consoling at the moment than I am. Whispering just loudly enough for me to hear, he croons, "It'll be all right. I'm here."

The crunching of tires over broken glass and debris agitates every last one of my nerves as the truck rears forward, leaving the DSD far behind. I don't hear the rumble of the second truck trailing us—which I assume was for the Enforcers—and it's hard to tell how much time passes in the darkness. While

I attempt to keep track of the direction the vehicle moves in to have some idea where we're going, I give up after the fifth or so turn. The sensory overload of being temporarily blind makes it too hard to focus on anything other than the reassuring sensation of Ezra's hand in mine. Wherever we're going, we'll be together.

At least, until my time runs out.

The thought sobers me, and I close my eyes, trying to steady my breathing, which grows more uneven with every bump we cross in the road. My mind drifts back to our journey to the DSD only a handful of hours ago and what we witnessed the Enforcers doing to the injured people they found in the streets— the brutality of cold-blooded murder for the sake of maintaining a society built on our usefulness.

My stomach churns at the vivid recollection of what we might be driving over.

A bright light abruptly fills the sweltering hold, and I wince, glaring across the small space at Quinn, who stares down at the communicator clutched in his hand. Frowning, he looks up at me after a moment, his obsidian eyes hooded in the shadows. "We're coming up on a checkpoint. Don't make a sound."

My own eyes flash to Ezra and Jenner—desperate for a momentary glimpse of their faces when, any second now, the situation could take a turn for the worse and we may be separated for good. But Quinn shuts off the communicator, extinguishing the light before I can see them, throwing us all back into the stifling gloom.

Beneath us, the large tires roll to a stop. As the engine cuts off—engulfing us in silence—each thud of my pounding heart is so loud I'm certain the others can hear it.

I strain my ears, noting raised voices coming from outside near the cab, and as the growing tension crushes my lungs, I can feel Quinn's eyes on my face even though I can't see him, his steely features washed in shadow. Part of me wonders if, with our dooms so close at hand, he once again resembles that frightened young Enforcer I encountered a few months ago. It's still so hard for me to reconcile the two—the terrified soldier charging into his first battle and the hardened double agent, whose real motivations remain a mystery to me.

In the darkness, with no one to see him—when he can be his real self—which one is he?

A sharp knock against glass snaps me out of my thoughts, and I listen intently, catching the motorized hum of a window being lowered.

"ID," a gruff voice demands. Even obscured by the thick walls around us, the hostility in his tone is clear.

I hold my breath. There's a shuffling sound and then, for a torturous moment, nothing.

"Evelyn Adler," the Enforcer managing the checkpoint drawls in a bored monotone. "Where are you coming from, Doc?" A sudden pounding on the side of the truck sends my heart jumping up into my throat. "What's in the back?"

"Medical equipment," my mother responds coolly. Her alibi is convincing, even to me, as she adds, "The DSD was hit during the strike and I thought it best to salvage as much of the equipment as possible—"

"Who gave you clearance to do that?"

Goosebumps rise on my flesh at the suspicion behind the soldier's question, and that bubble of pressure in my chest grows larger, my power expanding under my skin like heat. I swallow, trying to tamp it down. If I don't keep my emotions, my terror, contained, then an outburst isn't only likely. It's unavoidable.

And without my collar, everyone in this truck and outside of it will die.

"I am the Head of Termination," my mother snaps, her authoritative tone bordering on malicious. "I don't need clearance to protect my work." There's another pause, and in the momentary hush, I envision her face. The irritation I imagine printed into her features is present in every word she growls. "Don't you have better things to do than hold us up over ridiculous formalities? Like searching for survivors, perhaps? Or evacuating the areas affected by the attack?"

The Enforcer mutters something I can't quite make out and is answered after a few seconds by a garbled voice projecting from a communicator. I can only understand one or two words past the frequent bursts of static.

"Roger," he huffs before clearing his throat. Then, he reluctantly says, "You can go."

Sweat breaks out across my forehead and hairline when the truck finally jerks forward again. Beside me, I can feel the others keeping perfectly still, as if waiting to see if we'll be followed or if the Enforcer guarding the checkpoint will change his mind and stop us again out of spite.

The unease permeating the air is like a perfume I can taste on my tongue, and I hold my breath, counting the seconds as we drive away. But no matter how many pass, I still don't feel safe. No length of time or distance is enough.

I stifle a breath of surprise as a light floods the interior again, illuminating Quinn's face. His brow is puckered as he stares down at the communicator clutched in his hand.

"We're all-clear," he breathes.

No one dares speak another word for the remainder of our journey. As we pass through the city, heading who knows where, I focus on the noises beyond the truck, searching for anything to distract myself from the recollection of the past few hours and the untold horrors which may still come to pass. A faint siren rings in the distance, but other than that, the Heart is eerily silent, as if the bombings have somehow robbed the world of all sound. It's a sobering reminder of the fate awaiting us all if I don't succeed in preventing my vision.

The tires slow their rotations, rolling to a gradual stop, and the engine cuts off, eliminating the constant reverberations beneath my feet. I bristle in anticipation, but when no questioning voices greet us and the doors to the cab creak open and slam shut again, I let out a sigh of relief.

It seems we've reached our destination.

Bracing myself, I stare hard at the back of the truck as the repetitive clicking of high heels on concrete signals my mother's approach. Her face is just visible, her body a black silhouette, as she pulls the doors open, letting in a rush of night air.

"We're here. You can get out now," she says. Her eyes sweep from side to side as she steps away from the truck, searching the shadows for movement.

Quinn descends first, wincing as he eases himself onto the pavement, followed closely by me, then Ezra, then Jenner. Once we're all free of the stuffy hold, I turn in place, taking stock of our new surroundings. We're alone inside an empty parking structure, encased on all sides by broad concrete walls with only small slips of open stretches that let me see out into the city beyond. Smoke from the explosions seeps in through the gaps like rays of sunlight determined to burn, stinging my nostrils and throat, and although it's summer and the air is warm, there's an undeniable chill to the night. Almost as if the world itself is shivering in fear of what's coming.

Despite the fluorescent strip bulbs overhead, the lights in the structure are off, drenching the vast space in darkness. But I'm not sure if that's to mask our presence or because of the power outages across the Heart.

Completing my rotation, I note that the second truck is nowhere to be seen. Curious, I meet my mother's probing gaze, her eyes reflecting the minimal light.

"Where are your other lap dogs?" I ask, jerking my chin toward the sole Enforcer beside her—the driver—who stands at silent attention.

Her lips twitch. "Scouting the area and keeping a watchful eye on our route out of the city."

"So, you really *do* know how to get out of the Heart?" Ezra asks, surprised.

I've been wondering the same thing. After what we saw on our way to the DSD, it's hard to imagine escape of any kind being possible.

Jenner scoffs. "I hope you aren't planning on using the tunnels. Your little pet

Enforcer here already told us they're a no go."

Quinn's upper lip curls back into a sneer, but my mother holds up her hand, cutting him off with a pointed look before he can get a word out.

Scowling at us each in turn, she says, "Being in a position of power has its perks. So does being universally feared. It affords me the connections to make the impossible possible. So, no," she adds, glaring at Jenner, "We will *not* be using the tunnels. But this is not the place for this discussion. We need to get inside. Then I will answer your questions."

My eyes drift along the concrete walls, noting there isn't a single entry in sight. *Get inside where?*

At my confused look, she turns, waving for us to follow.

We trail after her without further question, Ezra and Jenner sticking close to my sides, while Quinn limps along behind us with the help of the other Enforcer. His grunts of pain stoke the embers of my guilt again, fanning the sparks into an inferno. He didn't betray us, not really. If anything, he saved our lives not once but twice by working with my mother. Who knows what might have happened at the DSD if she hadn't shown up. If he hadn't been there to lead her to us.

Knowing that, I struggle to cling to my anger. Haven't I done questionable things to protect Ezra and Jenner? Besides omitting the truth, what has Quinn done that can remotely measure up to my own countless crimes?

Haven't we all done things we're not proud of to survive?

My attention shifts back to my mother, and I stare at her back, deliberating over what possible motives inspired her actions over the years. Did she become what she is to protect someone else?

Or to protect herself?

She doesn't lead us very far, guiding our group into a narrow corridor less than twenty yards from the truck that I failed to notice from where we stood before, the entrance obscured by one of many flat protrusions of concrete that I had mistaken for a design feature rather than what it actually is. A nook for masking a secret passage. At first glance, the space beyond appears to be a dead end—a short hallway of concrete and pipework that, under any other circumstances, I would disregard as little more than a utility closet.

"This way." My mother signals to a minuscule gap in the pipes to our left barely wide enough for one person to slip through.

The passage we enter is cramped. The gloom thickens as we progress down a flight of slippery stairs, then down another, our trek continuing until the air grows damp and cool, just like every other time I've found myself in the underbelly of the city. My hand skims the wall in the blackness, the glow of my mother's communicator the only light guiding us forward.

Underground again, I note, shivering at the thought.

"This isn't creepy at all," Jenner mutters behind me, echoing what I'm thinking. Directly in front of me, Ezra says nothing, but I can sense his apprehension in the uncertain grip of his fingers.

"What zone are we in?" I ask with a sidelong glance at the walls, which seem to draw closer together the deeper we descend.

"Three," my mother answers.

Three? I stare at the back of her faint silhouette. That seems like an odd choice of location for a safe house, but then, I suppose that's the point. No one would think to look for us here.

At the base of the stairs, my mother turns right into what looks like another utility area, except, unlike the dead end upstairs, this corridor contains a single door. Proceeding toward it, she presses the palm of her hand to the small black screen above the handle.

"Access granted," an automated voice bellows before the door swings inward, flooding the chilly hallway with light.

I shield my eyes as my mother puts her hand on my shoulder, pulling me over the threshold into a large open-planned living area, which reminds me in some ways of my home in Zone 2. The design—white walls and sparse gray furniture—is almost identical to that of the quarters I shared with her for the better part of ten years.

"Please, make yourselves comfortable," she urges.

Ezra, Jenner, and I all stand frozen, gawking at our surroundings, while the Enforcer plods past us, helping Quinn over to the large L-shaped sofa, which is positioned to border a white marble table that seems to serve as the centerpiece of the space. The back of the longer side of the couch is facing out into the room, toward the door we came in by, while the shorter side is pressed up flat against the wall to my right. The only other furnishings are two glass tables at each end of the sofa and a television screen mounted on the wall opposite the seating. Aside from that, the room is bare.

I spin slowly, taking in the clean decor. "Where are we, exactly?"

We all turn to face my mother as she closes the door behind us, her expression carefully blank.

"A safe house, like I promised."

Beside me, Ezra stiffens. "I've been wondering, what would the Head of Termination need a safe house for?"

The unease and doubt in his voice set me on edge, and I glare at my mother as all the many reasons I had not to trust her pop into my head again.

Her lips curl almost imperceptibly at the corners. "It's not mine," she clarifies.

My blood runs cold at the scuffle of footsteps behind me, and wheeling around, I choke back the murderous instincts of my power as I come face to face with our true host.

Wren Bilken meets my gaze with a glower. "Hello again, Miss Reeves."

ELEVEN

THE LAST TIME I WAS in the same room as Wren Bilken, my hands were wrapped around his throat, my thumbs gouging into his windpipe with a single pressing intent: to kill. Was it really only yesterday we had that altercation? It feels like it happened so much longer ago. Then again, the chaotic events of the last twenty-four hours have completely skewed my perception of time, making it seem like the past few days have spanned weeks. I don't even remember when I last properly slept. If the heaviness in my bones is any indication, it's been a while. Too long, maybe. And just like this disease—or perhaps even because of it—my exhaustion seems to be taking its toll.

Legs suddenly weak, I stumble forward, reaching toward the back of the sofa to steady myself, the room spinning around me. The resurfacing pain in my temples coaxes a fresh dew of sweat to bead along my forehead, the heat flushing along the underside of my skin making me nauseous. Ezra rushes forward to support me, his hands firm on my waist, but I wave him off, assuring him I'm okay. When he steps back, I clench my jaw and snap my eyes between my mother and Bilken as a dozen different emotions go to war in my chest, my heart the battlefield where they collide. I don't know what I should be thinking or feeling, or what game these two think they're playing with us. Hell, I don't even know which side they're on.

"At least your mother had the sense to know which side to choose." That was what Bilken said right after I nearly killed him for insulting my father. Was this what he meant? This…collaboration between them, or whatever this is I'm witnessing. At the time, I thought he had been referring to my mother's decision to surrender my father to the State for being a traitor in the unforgiving eyes of

the law. But now, I can't help wondering if he meant something else entirely.

Bilken's callous expression relaxes into a smirk that makes me want to choke him all over again. "I'm glad to see you've all arrived in one piece."

Ezra scoffs, the sound abrasive, like the unsharpened edge of a knife against metal. "Why am I not surprised you're the one behind this? You always were a two-faced snake. What, tired of working for Nolan already?"

"Nolan is a power-hungry fool," Bilken growls, his momentary amusement gone.

"What happened to playing for the winning side?" The words are grainy as they roll off my dry tongue.

Bilken's responding look is scathing. "There is no winning side if everyone's dead. Surely, you've seen enough to know that by now."

His gaze is shrewd, and I wonder just how much he knows about what I've seen, both while as a weapon for the State—witnessing the resulting carnage of war with my own two eyes—and in my visions. Nolan might've used me for information to make his move when the Heart was defenseless—information Bilken was privy to—but Richter was the only one aside from Jenner who knew the full breadth of what I've seen. Who knew about the havoc I'm destined to wreak. I never even worked up the nerve to tell Ezra the truth, though I'm sure he's well aware of it by now. That's a secret I doubt Jenner would've kept to himself once he and Ezra realized I'd fallen for Richter's lie about a cure and gone back to the DSD.

I can only assume Bilken doesn't know the truth about what the future holds for the world, otherwise why is he helping us—helping *me*, the monster destined to inflict it? What's his angle here?

My eyes snap to Jenner's, and the suspicion I glimpse in their blazing blue depths gives me the impression he's wondering the same thing I am.

"So, you had a falling out with Nolan and since you can't exactly go back to the State after jumping *that* sinking ship, you're helping us. Why, out of the goodness of your heart?" He snorts. "Funny how you didn't care about our well-being when Nolan had this asshole put a gun to our heads."

Jenner shoots a scornful look at Quinn, which the ex-Enforcer returns from where he sits, reclined, on the sofa.

"Who do you think it was who told me to get close to Nolan?" Quinn asks. "If it wasn't for me, you would all be dead."

My eyes widen as that word fills every available space in my head.

Dead.

A lash of pain cracks through my skull like a lightning bolt, and I clamp a hand over my mouth, suppressing the violent urge to throw up. I can't make sense of any of this. Quinn was working for Bilken? I thought he was working for my mother?

How does one tie into the other?

"At least your mother had the sense to know which side to choose," I hear Bilken say again in my head.

Sides… Maybe I'm focusing on the wrong thing, too busy scrutinizing Quinn's part in all this and not looking closely enough at my mother's. Who Quinn is working for is irrelevant, but he *is* the common denominator. The link connecting the two pieces I have yet to put together, forming a picture I can't comprehend.

As it stands, only one thing is clear. My mother and Bilken are working together and possibly have been for a while, if what Quinn said about getting close to Nolan is true. But why? To what end?

What am I missing?

I recount everything that's transpired since the day Jenner blew up the transport helicopter. What he had said after, about an inside man helping them to accomplish the job…

Well, now that my initial shock and anger have both worn off from when Nolan revealed their informant was Bilken, I'm not surprised by the latter's decision to leave the State to join PHOENIX. Such betrayal is in line with his character, abandoning one side to join another if he has reason to believe it will keep him alive and, more importantly, in a position of influence. He told me as much himself, and by helping Nolan secure the State's precious weapon, he would've had the new life he desired at his fingertips. A just reward for a worthy prize.

But this? This I don't understand. Why throw it all away? What could he possibly hope to gain by having Quinn intervene in our executions? By turning on Nolan?

And what does any of this have to do with my mother?

Someone says something, but I can't pinpoint who, their voice dull behind the high-pitched ringing now filling my ears, penetrating deep. I can feel the reverberations in the roots of my teeth, as if I've just bitten an exposed wire. My fingers weakly reach for my ears to claw the sound out, but it only gets louder and more shrill, as if reacting to the protesting voices assaulting me from all sides.

My eyes search for Ezra, my vision blurring as his mouth forms words I have no way to hear, a plea for help lost in the cage of my own throat, impeded by the pain. It's unbearable, growing worse with each passing second, and I need it to stop. I need it to—

"Stop," I beg in a thready whisper. The clanging in my head is deafening, igniting another, stronger wave of pain, which drags an inhuman scream from my lips. "Stop!" I shriek.

The voices buzzing around me go silent at the same moment the world seems to tilt on its axis. My hands flail, reaching for the sofa, but miss as my eyes roll upward, my gaze skimming across the smooth ceiling. The rows of circular embedded lights burn fuzzy dark spots across my failing vision.

"Wynter!"

Muscular arms catch my body when I collapse, supporting my limp neck and head, and the shadows swathing the room clear just enough for me to make out Jenner's face, those kind eyes shining with concern. Ezra rushes to his side, leaning over me, but falters as he begins to say my name, his worried gaze catching on my mouth. Frowning, he presses a hand to my face, his thumb gently grazing my upper lip. I know without having to ask what he's seeing. I *feel* the warmth of it on my skin as clearly as I can smell its metallic stench, like rusty coins shoved up my nostrils.

A fearful look passes between him and Jenner, and Ezra's skin pales as he pulls back his hand. At the sight of the blood on his fingertips, another agonizing pain rips through my skull, stabbing behind my eyes, blinding me.

"My head," I gasp, writhing in Jenner's firm grip. Tears cut hot lines down my cheeks. "It's…killing me."

"Move." My mother's face appears in front of me now, her expression distant and detached like always, filling my field of vision like a storm cloud overtaking the sky. Cold fingertips brush my wrist. "Her pulse is weak. She needs to rest and recover her strength—"

"Recover her strength?" Ezra spits through gritted teeth before letting out a harsh, barking laugh. "She's *dying* because of what you assholes have done!"

Dying…

From the beginning, ever since our paths crossed, Ezra has known that's what this disease would amount to—that its parasitic hold on my life would always inevitably result in my death. He never shied away from that knowledge, and sometimes, I think it's that outcome—knowing that our time together is limited—that's coaxed him to fight as hard for me as he has. In a world where so much has been beyond his control, he wants to challenge fate.

And finally overcome it.

But now, hearing that word—"*dying*"—escape his lips so easily makes my fate all the more real…and that much more terrifying. I had accepted my impending death. On some level, I've even welcomed it. And yet, the strain in Ezra's voice as he mutters that single tragic word threatens to undo me.

My mother's sharp riposte jerks me out of my thoughts despite the darkness creeping in at the edges of my eyes. "*I* didn't do this to her. Your bastard brother did. And *you* did. She's in this condition because of *you*."

Because of Ezra?

I blink slowly, clinging to consciousness, searching for Ezra's dimming face through the haze. He recoils at her words, his confusion apparent in the vee of his brow.

"*Me?*" There's a defensive edge to his tone.

"Oh, yes, I know exactly who you are, Mr. Laramie." My mother glances down at me, and for the first time in my life, I notice what looks like a hint of regret in her gaze. When she next speaks, I'm not sure who she's talking to. Ezra…or me? Maybe both. "The question is," she mutters, "do you?"

What are you talking about? I try to push these words through my lips, but any remaining strength I had slips away and the darkness takes hold before I can speak. Pain, all-consuming and unrelenting, returns to wrap me in the cocoon of unconsciousness.

As my eyelids slide closed, Ezra's face is the last thing I see, the sorrow in his expression reminding me so clearly of another moment in time. A moment we haven't lived yet.

A moment I know is unavoidable.

And when that end comes—with me and him alone at the end of the world, my power raging out of control and a gun gripped in his hand—I can't help wondering if he really will pull that trigger. Or if he'll fail me as badly as I've failed him…

And let that gun fall, unused, to the ground.

TWELVE

THE WORLD IS FROZEN. ASH and dust hang in the air like suspended snowflakes, and I push them aside with my hands as I progress through the wasteland that's become as familiar to me now as the reality I live in. Perhaps this vision—this unavoidable outcome—is even more real to me by this point. More real than Ezra or Jenner. More real even than the trauma I've endured at the hands of the one person who was a bigger monster than I am.

Because this destruction, this chaos, is certain. Whereas everything else—Ezra and Jenner and the lives of all those residing on this doomed planet…

Those fates still hang in the balance, dependent on what I do moving forward.

The gravel and debris crunch beneath my steps as I traipse this desolate landscape alone. The wreckage stretches as far as the eye can see, but for once, I'm not afraid of it or of the knowledge that I am the one who will bring this hell upon us.

Finally, acceptance has sunk in, settling over my skin like drops of water I can't brush away. And as that rain pummels into my flesh, spreading over me, I know I would do anything to avoid the horrific consequence of my disease destined to follow this destruction. Anything to avoid creating further casualties to my unwanted power.

No one else should have to suffer because of me. Because of what I've become.

This is one burden I should bear alone.

Quiet laughter tugs my gaze over my shoulder, and turning, I glimpse the distant shape of three young children chasing each other. Two boys—one taller than the other—and a girl with a shining curtain of glossy brown hair that hangs down to her waist. Their giggles, although stifled behind tiny hands clamped over their mouths, are genuine and infectious, and I find myself stumbling toward them, needing to see their faces more clearly, even though I know in my heart who they are.

As I draw closer to where the children play, the ruination of the Heart ripples like a mirage, the details around me changing. Now, instead of standing among the craterous remains of the city, I'm in a small, confined courtyard surrounded by blocks of lower-income apartments from a time long before the attack. Smog puffs in a thick, black cloud overhead, dragging my gaze toward the looming crematorium—just visible through a gap in the buildings.

This is Zone 4, I realize as I pivot in a slow circle, observing the scene before finally looking back at the children, my eyes settling on one in particular.

The beautiful boy with golden hair and a smile that breaks my aching heart.

This must be where Ezra grew up.

I watch the children play their game, taking in each of their faces in turn. Ezra, so carefree, his smile so bright. So unlike the man I know, the weight of the world always pressing down on his shoulders. Rai, youthful and full of vigor. Unlike now…our lives robbed of her light. Then there's Richter, the oldest of the three, and serious even at such a young age. He's no older than ten or so in this memory, but there's a glint to his eyes as he assesses his brother and Rai, as if he's mirroring their actions, wearing the mask that's expected of him in this moment. As if he's only *pretending* to enjoy himself to appease the other two children.

And yet, I can see a hint of fondness slipping past his carefully poised expression each time he looks at them. He cared for them. He *loved* them.

Until he thought they betrayed him.

Rai trips and falls hard in the dirt, and I gasp, rushing forward to help but stopping dead in my tracks when Richter sprints toward her at the sound of her cry, which she dampens by biting down on her lip. As he tends to her scraped knee, she wipes the tears from her eyes and nods to something he says to her, the words beyond my range of hearing. Grinning, he pats her on the head.

Once he's finished, he helps her back onto her feet, but as he resumes their game, she pauses, glancing down at her leg, head cocked to one side like a curious puppy. The expression on her face strikes me as familiar, and I find myself thinking back on my feverish recollection of how she cared for me when I first sought out PHOENIX after escaping the DSD. How she kept me on this side of death in the days after I cut out my tracking chip. Now, as I stare at the childlike incarnation of her, the irony hits me. The medical training Rai had, however minimal…did she learn it from Richter?

Was the heartless man responsible for so much suffering—*my* suffering—the one who taught Rai what she needed to know to save me?

A sob catches in my throat, and I turn, averting my gaze, no longer wanting to see this. To see how many lives have been torn apart and changed for the worse. By our country's oppressive ways. By rebellion.

By me.

If I had never existed, Ezra's mother wouldn't have told him to find me and maybe Richter wouldn't have grown to become obsessed with my disease. Maybe then, he would've turned out differently, *become* a different person than the madman I knew. And maybe, if I had never existed, these three children would've been able to share a happy life together, free from the moral differences that tore them apart.

Or, at least, as happy as anyone can be in the State.

If I had never existed, Ezra would be safe. And Rai… Sweet, kind Rai…

She would still be alive.

The sound of nearby footsteps has me looking to the right side of the courtyard, and I gape, wide-eyed, at the beautiful but tired-looking woman standing there, dressed in a tattered white hospital gown. At first, I think she's part of the vision—out of place, but part of it. Until, I realize her gaze isn't following the playing children but locked intently on me.

Her skin crinkles beside her pale eyes when she smiles. "Hello, Wynter."

I startle at the sound of my name on her lips, spoken so easily, as if we're acquaintances. I blink, unsure if I heard her correctly, but there's no mistaking what she said. She said my name. She *knows* me. She's *speaking* to me.

But how?

Before I can ask, she holds up a hand. "Don't be afraid. I just want to talk. You have no idea how happy I am that I'm finally able to reach you."

"Who—" The word comes out broken and raspy, and I clear my throat, ignoring the shiver of fear sweeping over my skin. "Who are you?"

The woman clasps her hands loosely in front of her waist. "My name is Alivia Laramie. I'm like you."

Laramie…

My eyes widen. "You—" The words stick to my tongue in protest, as if they can't believe what I'm seeing or hearing. "You're Ezra's mother," I finally mutter after a moment.

She pushes out a relieved breath through her nose and dips her chin, bowing her head in acknowledgment. When she looks up again, her eyes—an usual combination of honey and pewter—are sad. "I'm so glad he managed to find you. And so terribly sorry for everything you've had to endure."

I shake my head, stumbling backward a step. "How is this possible? How are we communicating right now? You—"

You're dead.

I stare at her, my thoughts jumbled. Death aside, Ezra's mother was institutionalized, her mind fractured in the months, or maybe even years, leading up to her death. But this woman, she seems sane, for lack of a better word, her words and eyes focused and clear.

I think back over what Ezra told me—how his mother would say the same thing to him whenever she saw him, repeating it like a chant. *"One green, one blue. Look for Wynter."*

Did she only say these words so he would pay attention…or was that all she was able to say? If so, does that mean I'm seeing Ezra's mother before her inevitable breakdown? Or is this just another frustrating outcome of this disease?

Will I eventually lose the ability to communicate, too, except for with the visions I see in my head?

At the confusion on my face, Alivia smiles. "You and me…" She looks away, gazing fondly at the children running back and forth between us, their laughter now a distant hum despite them being so close, as if the volume on the memory has been turned down so as not to overwhelm this conversation. "We are the epitome of what shouldn't be possible, and yet, here we both are. I'm looking ahead at you. You're looking back at my children and their darling friend, Raina." Her expression darkens. "That poor, poor girl."

She closes her eyes for a moment and draws in a steadying breath, the silence between us morose. When she meets my gaze again, she shrugs.

"I'm no expert, but I suppose we could say it's like our wires are crossing."

My heart jumps up into my throat at her words. She knows about Rai? But then… How much has she seen?

How much does she know?

"This is a dream," I whisper, shaking my head again. "This isn't real. It can't be—"

"And so what if it is?" Alivia asks me. "Dream or not, who's to say what's real and what isn't? You and I have both seen enough to know what we can do shouldn't be possible. If this is a dream, it's a dream. Let's not lose ourselves to semantics and what ifs."

"But…" I trail off, unsure what to say. I don't know what to think. I don't even know why I'm seeing this.

I don't know what she wants with me.

As if reading my mind, she cocks a thin, auburn brow—her wavy hair so much like Richter's in color. "You're running out of time. You know that, right? The moment you've been dreading is fast approaching." She lets out a long-suffering sigh and gestures around us with a wave of one hand. While the children remain, our surroundings have reverted to what they were before.

Once again, we're encompassed by the destruction and death I will inflict on this world.

"It's inescapable…as it has always been," she says.

I lurch forward a step, my jaw clenched, my hands drawn into tight fists. "How much have you seen?"

I narrow my eyes, glaring at her drawn face, her skin pallid and aged beyond her years from the disease wreaking undeniable chaos on her body. If she really has witnessed as much as I fear, then how long did she live with Ultraxenopia before it finally took its toll? The visions she saw and her descent into madness… Is that what I would have experienced if Richter hadn't intervened and escalated my own condition?

My evolution. A spiteful laugh catches in my throat at the thought.

"How much have you seen?" I ask again when she doesn't answer, my tone bordering on hysterical.

As these words leave my lips, I remember what Richter said before removing my collar. *"Have you worked out the reason she saw you yet?"*

A shiver of terror crosses my skin, and the sadness in her eyes tells me everything I need to know.

"Enough," Alivia whispers before glancing at the children again. I follow her gaze only to find they have ceased their playing and now lie dead on the ground at my feet.

A hand flies to my mouth and I scramble backward, nearly tripping as I flinch away from the small, eerily still bodies in the dirt. A strained cry escapes me.

"So, that's it?" I shout, tears streaming down my cheeks. "There's no way to avoid it?"

Her eyes snap to mine. "There is one way."

I shake my head. "I know what you're thinking and I can't," I protest. "Not until I know Ezra and Jenner are safe from what's happening in the Heart."

Alivia's expression changes and she gives me a look I recognize all too well. I've seen that disappointment enough times on my mother.

"They will never be safe so long as you are alive. You know this—"

Anger, hot and fierce, rips through me, exploding like a burst of fire off my tongue. "Of course, I know that! You think I don't? I—" The rage leaves me suddenly, and I deflate, beaten down by the memories of everything that's occurred since the fateful day of my placement exam. "I've tried to change it," I breathe, my voice shaky. "But every time, I only end up making things worse."

No matter what I do, I always put the people I care about in danger. I want to protect them, not just from this world but from me. And to do that, I know, better than anyone else...

There's only one option left.

"Why did you tell Ezra to find me? He would've been safer if we'd never met."

Alivia turns in place, taking in our surroundings. Holding out one hand, she collects the ash and dust hanging stagnant in the air on her fingertips. "Would he? His fate has always been tied to yours. As has Austin's." She inhales deeply, then looks up at the sky and says, as if reciting a poem, "Two brothers—one, the creator of a terrible weapon. The other...destined to destroy it."

I balk, my skin going cold. "Destroy..." I go still, the realization gripping my chest. I swallow, my voice breaking. "You mean kill."

Ever since I had that first vision of Ezra, his solemn words have haunted me. Gun in hand, tears streaming down his cheeks, he said, *"I'm sorry, Wynter."* Always those same three words. I never knew what he meant or what he would do that would warrant such a distressed apology. But now...

Now, I think I do.

"Have you worked out the reason she saw you yet?"

Richter knew. Or he deduced enough from what I told him and from that initial vision at the DSD—the first time I saw Ezra—to come to his own conclusion. Which means my mother, his trusted confidant, who admitted to knowing the details and outcome of every experiment he put me through...

She figured out Ezra's role in my vision, too.

"I'm sorry, Wynter."

I shake my head again. No. He dropped his gun. He wouldn't—

Alivia frowns, as if reading my thoughts. "That has always been Ezra's purpose—"

"No," I say, out loud this time. "If that's true, then fate is cruel for letting me—letting *us*—" I snap my mouth shut, unable to bring myself to say anymore. Instead, I close my eyes, tears slipping through, as I imagine every moment I've ever shared with Ezra. His anger. His distrust. His affection.

His love.

I remember it all. I *feel* it all.

And for the first time, I realize how unfair this world is.

Alivia gives me a pitying look. "Fate may lead us to a destination, but the path we take to get there is entirely up to us. We each carve our own path."

"Do we?" I ask, wiping away the sticky residue of tears on my skin. "Because nothing I've been through has felt like my choice."

She nods, then steps forward, crouching down beside the innocent child version of Richter lying on the ground between us. Trying and failing to brush the hair from his face, she says, "I understand that frustration, more than anyone possibly can." Her eyes—such a peculiar combination of the person I love most and the man I hate with every fiber of my being, even now, after his death—lock onto me, hawkish and demanding. "But you need to be strong, Wynter. I—" Her voice breaks. "I don't want to lose another son."

"But—" I bite my tongue, hesitating. She's so worried about what *I* need to do, but does she know what fate awaits *her*? Given what she's seen, surely, she knows this, too. Finally, I force myself to say, "But you're already dead."

She offers me another doleful smile. "But Ezra isn't."

A sudden unbearable shame washes over me. By only mentioning Ezra, it dawns on me that she must also know that Richter is dead. And more so, that I'm the one who killed him.

And yet, there's no trace of blame in her words. Just a matter-of-fact undertone I can't ignore.

"There's still time to change the course of your path," she continues. "To ensure he lives."

As she says this, I hear the echo of Rai's words from my dream. Like Alivia, she had said there's still time, and when I had pressed her for what, she had answered with three simple words that even now torment me. Three words that shape my every moment.

"To save them."

How? I want to scream. *How can I change it?*

What if I only end up making things worse?

But I don't give voice to these thoughts because I know they're only excuses for the terror that threatens to cripple me. If I do nothing, Ezra and Jenner will die. Saving them is simple. All it would take is one sacrifice.

One sacrifice I know I'm capable of, and yet, according to Ezra's mother, I'm not the one meant to enforce it.

He is.

I bite down hard on my lip. "He won't do it. Not after everything he went through to get me back."

"He will," Alivia counters, "because it's what needs to be done. No one else can do it but him."

"Why?" I press. "Why does it *have* to be him?"

Why is fate so set on hurting us? And if it does have to be this way, why can't I just do it myself or hand myself over to someone actually willing? There are plenty of people out there who would happily kill me.

Why does Ezra have to do it?

Rising, she closes the distance between us and presses a clammy hand to my cheek. I startle at her touch, but she smiles...the way I always imagined a mother would.

"Because you will ask him to," she murmurs, "and because, at the end of all this, he is the only one you won't try to stop from pulling the trigger. This disease likes to protect itself. It's like a parasite and we are the unwilling hosts, used until our bodies are depleted. You heard what Austin said. He called it the next stage of human evolution." She scoffs. "Who knows for sure what it is. But, I can tell you, it won't let you do what you're thinking while it still has a use for you. And anyone else who tries will be killed. You know I'm right...even if you don't want to admit it."

Images of the many battles I was forced to take part in on behalf of the State rush into my mind all at once, assaulting me with the guilt of the lives I've taken and of all the times I gave myself over to the monster living inside me, even though I knew all along it was gaining control. Even now, with the monster unleashed, I'm still here—still present—but it's gradually taking over, consuming me slowly as if to taunt my weakness.

And, in the end, it will win.

"And if he doesn't do it?" Or worse, if I lose all sense of myself and murder him for trying?

"You will still die," Alivia says, her tone sober. "But so will he. And so will everyone else on this planet."

Her eyes glisten with unshed tears, and in that sadness, I hear the words she left unspoken. The words we both know to be true.

No matter the outcome, you will die.

She wraps her arms around her torso, shivering against the bite of the wind, even though it's a barely-there caress against my own skin. "You and Ezra... Neither of you deserve what's coming, but it doesn't change the fact that it is still your future. We both know it can only end one way." She nods then, as if she senses what I'm feeling. As if she knows those emotions all too well herself. "It's okay to be afraid. Just don't let it stop you from doing what's right."

Suddenly, the ground rumbles beneath our feet, and Alivia falters, thrown off balance, shock and dismay etched into her features. Her face blurs and turns slightly translucent, like a radio frequency losing signal.

I stare at her, alarmed. "What's happening?"

With a watery smile, she meets my gaze one final time. "It seems fate has finally caught up with me."

She doesn't seem afraid so much as resigned. Still, I'm overcome by the urge to help her, even though we both know I can't. Her destiny is already written. She will die. Richter will become a monster. And Ezra will set out on a journey during which he'll unknowingly honor his deceased mother's wishes.

As Ezra's face fills my thoughts, Alivia grips my hand. "Wynter?" Her tone is pleading and as she vanishes into the landscape, her words sink into my skin alongside those raindrops of acceptance, branding themselves into my flesh.

Every last one burns me with a pain I deserve.

"Tell my son I love him."

I collapse to my knees as her hand fades from my grasp until, once again, I'm alone with only the destruction I will cause as my sole companion. I stare at the emptiness around me, and, in this moment, as wracking sobs reverberate deep in my chest...

I know my fate is the one thing in this world I can't run from.

THIRTEEN

I WAKE UP IN A dimly lit room, curled in a ball under a thick blanket, fully naked with a thin layer of drying sweat on my skin. My surroundings are sparsely furnished and bleed together, blurring into a continuous gray and white streak, and the air is cold, as if the room is conditioned. Or as if—

I'm underground.

My head spins as I slowly force myself into a sitting position, trying to figure out where I am. Everything is hazy, and my gaze snaps to my bodysuit where it's crumpled in a heap on the floor—my armor of the last year discarded, leaving me vulnerable and exposed. Fleetingly, I wonder who undressed me but the thought is cast away when I take a closer look at the bodysuit. Even from across the room on the bed, I can spot the dark patch soaked into the collar.

I wipe a trembling hand across my nostrils and mouth, and when I glance down at my fingers, I grimace at the flakes of old blood spotting my skin like freckles.

Bilken's safe house, I remember abruptly, my eyes narrowing on the door as the broken recollections of the events that led me here begin to slowly piece back together. The DSD. Richter. Rai. My mother. Our trek to this hidden, clandestine apartment. I remember it all.

Even my dream.

Alivia Laramie's face is a stain on my mind, as clear to me in waking as it was in my vision. As much as it scares me to think that I spoke to Ezra's dead mother, I can't ignore the twisting sensation in my gut that keeps telling me she was real. Everything she said was a reflection of the hard truths I've been struggling to accept, and maybe, it was for that reason I was able to connect with her now when it sounded like she'd been trying for some time to reach me. Maybe I needed someone to give me a push, to put into words what I already know. Or maybe none of what I saw was real after all and my subconscious was merely manifesting my fears in a form that would finally force me to listen to reason.

As if to remind me what I stand to lose if I fail—what will happen should I bow to cowardice—another face bursts into shape in my head, pushing all trace of Alivia out. A searing pain stabs my eye sockets like ice picks, and as tears obscure my surroundings, I hear a familiar timbre in my ear. I look behind me, following the trail of the voice, sliding off the bed onto my unsteady feet as the small, frigid room melts away.

Shadows wrap around my eyes like a blindfold, but gradually, the darkness lifts, unveiling a cramped space I've been in before. This place… It's the room where I found Ezra tucked away the night of our mission to Zone 1. The night we thought Rai died. The room where he was mourning her loss and I dared to kiss him for the first time.

Just like that night, he sits hunched on the floor like a neglected child, his back to the wall and gaze hooded, cast down on the concrete. The only visible light floods in from the hallway, forming a line of yellowish white, which begins at the door and ends just past his feet, only kissing a few inches of his body and face.

The soft echo of steps draws my gaze to the doorway, and I glance at the silhouette standing at the threshold, his tall frame snuffing out the faint pool of light.

Jenner.

Once again, his soothing voice fills my ears, repeating the faint words that pulled me into this vision.

"Wynter's leaving. You have to stop her."

Ezra's eyes crawl upward, his face expressionless. "What do you expect me to do?" he asks.

Jenner steps forward, throwing his hands up in frustration. "Go after her!"

Shoulders slumping, Ezra looks back down at the floor. "What's the point? If she wants to go, then let her."

"You…" Jenner blanches, his voice faltering, as he gapes at the downcast, broken shell of his friend. His hands curl into trembling fists at his sides. "You can't be serious right now."

Ezra's answering silence is deafening.

Sneering, Jenner tilts his chin up, defiant. "Fine. Sit here in the dark and mope"—he all but spits that last word—"but I'm not willing to just let her go—"

"She's dying, Jenner," Ezra says bluntly. Tears flood his eyes when he finally looks up again. "Wynter is *dying*."

Understanding dawns as Jenner's pupils blow wide. "And you think, if she leaves, your brother might actually cure her?" A humorless laugh cuts through the minuscule space. "I'm calling bullshit. You're deflecting, Ez. Why are you so goddamn stubborn and unwilling to actually face the truth?"

Ezra scoffs. "And what truth is that?"

Jenner swallows, and the wounded look on his face nearly brings me to my knees.

"I'm not blind," he mutters, his voice walking the tightrope of a whisper. "You put on a good show, but anyone can see you're half in love with her already. Even when you acted like she was a threat, I saw the way you looked at her. You were constantly watching her, and when she fell into that coma..." He shakes his head. "You barely left her side for *six* days. Hell, since she woke up, this is the first time you've let her out of your sight."

When Ezra doesn't respond, doesn't so much as blink an eye, Jenner sighs.

"I know what you're thinking," he continues. "You're thinking, if she stays, there's nothing to prevent you from losing her just like we lost Rai." His voice catches on her name, and he clears his throat. "It's a risk, sure, but if you don't go after her now, you'll regret it for the rest of your life. You'll always wonder."

Ezra leans forward and, propping his elbows on his knees, runs a shaking hand through his hair. The dirty blond strands stand on end where he touched them. Grimacing, he bites out, "If she's so set on leaving, what makes you think I can change her mind? Clearly, you couldn't convince her."

He smothers his face in his hands, but despite his obvious misery, I find myself looking at Jenner, lured by the sad smile curving along his lips as he squats to the floor beside his friend.

Pain grips my heart as he murmurs gently, "Because I'm not the one she wants to ask her to stay."

As Ezra looks up, realization alight in his gaze, the shadows return, swathing his face in blackness and ripping me out of the vision. When the blindfold lifts for a second time, I open my eyes to the colorless room I woke up in, naked and alone.

An all too familiar coppery scent fills my nose, and I brush away a dribble of blood from my nostrils as the pain in my head fizzles to a dull ache. I swallow the rising bile in my throat, scrubbing a hand quickly over my face as a knock drags my sluggish gaze to the door.

"Wynter?"

Ezra pokes his head into the room as I tug the thick blanket off the bed and wrap it around my shoulders, his watchful eyes like flames licking over my exposed skin. The goosebumps pimpling my flesh soften within moments of the warm fleece cocooning my body, and with one last shiver, I let out a breath, plopping back down onto the edge of the mattress.

Without saying a word, he crosses the room and sits down on the bed beside me. I can feel the concern practically vibrating off him like tremors felt after an earthquake, but thankfully, he doesn't ask me if I'm all right.

After all, we're both smart enough to know that I'm not.

I peer at him out of the corner of my eye. It's strange to look at him now, knowing what I know. That we were always destined to meet for a single purpose. For him to kill me. I think I've always known as much, I just didn't have the strength to admit it.

The elements in our lives have always been too closely aligned to brush off as coincidence. And yet, accepting it now doesn't change how I feel. If anything, it only makes my heart hurt—makes this love feel cruel and unjust, like something beautiful that's been poisoned against me.

A broken laugh forces it way up my throat.

I guess I do know how Richter felt.

A frown pulls at the edges of my lips. There's so much I want to say to Ezra and there's the matter of the message his mother asked me to relay, but how do I even begin to tell him something like that? How do I navigate his emotions when I can barely handle my own?

Tears line my throat, distorting my voice when I speak. "I feel like everything I've ever been told is a lie. I'm not even sure what's real anymore."

Quinn. My mother. Bilken. Ezra. Nothing makes sense to me anymore.

Hell, maybe it never did.

Calloused fingers wrap around mine and squeeze. "I'm real," Ezra says. "*We're* real. And I love you. That isn't a lie. It never was."

I turn into his shoulder, nestling my head under his chin so he won't see the heartbreak on my face.

So, what if you do? I'm tempted to ask. *That won't change what needs to be done. That won't change why fate brought us together.*

A whimper escapes me, and I stifle a sob.

"Hey," he breathes, brushing his knuckles against my cheek and tilting my head back until I'm forced to look up at him. "There's still time. We'll figure this out."

There's still time. Those words seem determined to haunt me—to define my remaining moments on this planet. The trouble is, they aren't true.

What time I do have left is nearly expired.

"You know just as well as I do there isn't." My tongue darts out over my lower lip, tasting the tears now running freely. I shake my head. "I don't want to waste what little time we have left together pretending otherwise."

I stroke Ezra's bruised cheek with my fingers, but he moves away, pushing up to his feet.

"So, you're just going to give up? After everything we've been through?"

"No," I counter. No, this isn't giving up. Because my death won't be the end. "I'll keep fighting until this is all over. For Rai." *For Jenner,* I add silently. *And for you.*

A flicker of hope crosses his face, and he kneels on the floor, taking my hands in his once again. Bringing my fingers to his lips—the skin still battered from the beating he took at the PHOENIX compound outside the Heart but now finally beginning to heal—he says against my skin, "Okay, then let's figure out what to do."

"I already know the answer to that," I assure him with a careful, forced smile, "but, for it to work, I need you to promise me something."

He nods, and all the love he has for me seems to pour out in the single word he exhales. "Anything."

Leaning forward, I slant my mouth over his, and as his lips part to let me in, eager to reciprocate my touch, I remember his mother's words from my vision. With a heavy heart, I whisper, "Promise you'll kill me."

He jerks away as if I've burned him, his eyelids fluttering like a moth's wings. "What?"

Tugging my hands free of his tightening grasp, I cup his face, holding him trapped to my gaze. He knows the truth. He said it himself when he lashed out at my mother.

"She's dying because of what you assholes have done!"

Now, he needs to be reminded of it.

He needs to know there's no happy ending where he and I end up together.

"I'm dying, Ezra. And when this sickness finally reaches its pinnacle, I won't be able to stop what I've seen. I don't want that. I don't want to kill the people I love."

"And you think I do?" he growls. "No. *No,*" he says again, more firmly this time. "We'll find a way. We always do. I'm not going to *kill* you when there's still a chance I can save you."

"And if you can't?" I ask. "What then? When we're out of options, what else will you do?"

His cheeks flush red, but he says nothing. Because there's nothing to say. There's no magical solution to our problem.

A stray tear darts from his left eye.

As I brush it away, I kiss him again. This time, his mouth is still against mine.

"There's no other way," I mutter against his lips. "Please. If you really love me...you'll do this." I pull away just enough to look at him, all gentleness gone from my voice. "Please."

Ezra climbs to his feet and leans over me, placing his hands on my upper arms and pushing me back onto the bed, the blanket falling away from my shoulders as he joins me on the mattress. As he hovers over me on all fours, his head bows and tears splash onto my chest, sliding in hot streaks across the curves of my torso.

Lacing my fingers through his disheveled hair, I snake my other arm around him and tug him down until our bodies are flush. As I hold him to me, stroking his back and head, he shakes with silent sobs.

"Please," I whisper again, pleading.

He swallows loudly. Then, nodding against my shoulder, he gives me the only thing I'm asking him for.

"I promise," he says, his voice husky.

My lips find his in the pained hush that follows, but as our fingers interlace, our bodies joining, a flicker of doubt seeps into the cracks in my thoughts. And as that doubt festers, I can't help wondering if, like so many other aspects of my life...

If those words are just another lie.

FOURTEEN

I HAVE NO IDEA WHAT time it is when we finally emerge from the bedroom, out of our little pocket of darkness into a sterile light that seems blinding by comparison. The artificial white glare reminds me too much of the DSD, of Richter and the flashes of memories always sitting too close to the surface, ready to tear my already fragile composure to shreds.

A shudder rolls over my skin, tempting me to slink back into the refuge of that bedroom, where the seconds—which now rush by as if to taunt us—seemed to at least stand still for a moment. Now, out here in the open space of the safe house, reality is something I can no longer avoid or put off.

The future is coming, whether I like it or not.

Ezra squeezes my hand, offering the only physical comfort I have aside from the fresh clothes brushing my skin—the first clean ones I've had the privilege of wearing since PHOENIX extracted me from the State. The black pants, short-sleeved shirt, and jacket are soft and less restrictive than my bodysuit was, allowing me to breathe for what seems like the first time in years. Although, I imagine that has less to do with the fabric and more to do with what my previous attire represented. Now, instead of a weapon of mass destruction and war, I'm just me. Just Wynter. Now, the physical representation of Richter's hold over me is gone, discarded like trash.

I glance at the others, who sit perched on the sofa, their postures awkward and tense, drawing attention to the intentional gaps between them, as if they're all afraid to exist too close to each other. The only ones who sit side by side are my mother and Bilken, who—for reasons I have yet to discern—seem to have no issue sharing the same space.

A grimace twists my lips as I narrow my eyes at them, wondering what the nature of their relationship is. Are they just colleagues in their master plan, or are they something more?

Where does her betrayal to my father end?

They stare back at me, although neither one says a word, instead waiting for me to break the silence. My mother cocks a delicate eyebrow, urging me to speak.

I exhale through my nose before crossing the room and plopping down with a grunt onto the empty cushion beside Jenner. He grabs my hand as Ezra looms behind us, standing over me like a protective bodyguard. His fingertips touch my shoulder for reassurance.

As I sit, my gaze never strays from my mother. "You promised me answers. So, talk."

Her face is a stone mask, irritatingly blank and unreadable. A skill no doubt mastered at the DSD.

"Where would you like me to begin?" she asks.

"My father," I bite back.

She begins to recoil but catches herself, as if determined not to show any weakness. Straightening, she clears her throat. "You might not believe it, but I loved your father—"

I scoff. "Handing him over to be executed is an interesting way of showing it."

A scowl mars her lips. "You don't know the whole story."

"Then tell us," Jenner urges.

I glance at him. Although his tone is calm, there's a hardness behind his words that I can't ignore and a hatred in his gaze I understand far too well. I don't blame him for loathing my mother for the tragedy she inflicted on his life.

For the same reasons, I despise her, too.

My mother lets out an indulgent sigh. "Before the State became what it is now, it was an underground political movement, a group of like-minded individuals who were unhappy with how the previous government ran things and were confident—or, I suppose, arrogant—enough to believe they could do better. Not unlike PHOENIX," she adds, her tone frigid.

"I know this already," I snap, glaring at Bilken, whose expression remains frustratingly impassive. "He told me. What's your point?"

She leans back and studies me, crossing her arms. "Did he also tell you I was part of that group?"

Shock strips the heat from my skin. "What?"

Exchanging a brief look with Bilken, she nods. "I didn't grow up in this city, like you. Neither of us did," she says, gesturing to our still silent host. "Together,

Wren and I were sent into the Heart in the early stages of the State's rise to power, before it had actually seized control and word of a new government was still merely rumor, to work undercover and weed out any possible rebellion before it could grow. We were each given aliases and false lives, then told to make connections and report back on any treasonous activity we encountered." At my stunned expression, she adds, "It's much easier to smother an ember than it is a flame," as if that justifies what she did.

"So, my father…" I trail off as acid sloshes in my stomach, making me nauseous. She can say what she wants about loving my father; in the grand scheme of things, only one fact matters.

He was a target to her.

"At first, Wren and I had different marks we were each told to watch and report on. We were young, barely adults ourselves, so we could easily move in social circles and public spheres where those most likely to be involved with an insurgency would be present. Several years passed before I actually crossed paths with your father. I met Freston in a bar in Zone 7 that we had heard was frequented by a growing rebel group, which Wren had been cozying up to for years, since shortly after we first came to the Heart."

"The Vega," Ezra mutters at the same time Jenner says, "PHOENIX."

She nods again, looking me square in the eye. "Wren had already secured connections there, which led to our discovery of the group when it was still a fledgling idea more than an actual rebellion. But once it became more established, there were too many marks for him to cover alone. So, I stepped in to help. That was six years before you were born."

"Six *years*?" Disbelief stains my words as I try to line up the events of my past in my brain. I was just shy of turning seven when my father was beaten and dragged out of my house by Enforcers, taken away to the DSD to be executed. What could've possibly made my mother wait over a decade to turn him in to authorities?

My frown deepens as a more pressing question nags at me. How did she hold off the State for that long? Given my own experience with the DSD and Dr. Richter, I find it hard to believe whoever my mother reported to would've been that patient. Thirteen years is a long time to not deliver results.

"Then why—" I begin, but my mother cuts me off, as if she knows what I'm going to say.

"Do you really think I would've waited so long if I actually had any intention of turning him in?" she barks. "I told you," she mutters, her tone softer now. "I loved your father. I protected him for as long as I could."

Leaning forward, I rub my hands over my face. "I don't understand. Why didn't you just turn him in the second you learned he was with PHOENIX? You know he was the one who founded it, right?"

Why marry him only to betray him?

Her expression darkens. "Why else do you think I made it a point to get close to him? Wren worked out fairly early, through sheer proximity, who the ringleaders were in the group, and once I got involved, we agreed I would focus on Freston while Wren would foster his growing association with Nolan, that way we had two shots at infiltrating the insurgents. Sure, we could've named names from the get-go, but we didn't want to be too hasty in case either of us was being fed false information. The State was playing the long game, so the accuracy of our intel was more important than how quickly we got it. And believe me when I say, accuracy was paramount. The State has never been tolerant of misinformation, so with our futures and positions at risk, it was imperative we didn't make presumptions or do anything that might expose our identities, in turn jeopardizing our mission. With that in mind, we agreed to wait, to dig deeper, and only report back to our superiors with information that would prove we were assets and not liabilities. We wanted to make ourselves indispensable."

Jenner snorts. "Even undercover operatives weren't safe from the State, then, I take it."

My mother unleashes a cold laugh. "Far from it. We were promised esteemed positions in the new bureaucracy should we deliver the head of the snake, but were we to fail..." She laughs again. "Well, as you all are aware, the State doesn't take kindly to failure."

"But you didn't fail. You did eventually turn in my father. You got your *esteemed* positions," I spit. My gaze locks on Bilken again, and as I glare at him, picturing him gloating in his tall, glass tower, I remember what he said to me back at the bunker.

"Men like me get into positions of power because we do whatever it takes to survive..."

"There was more to it than that," he rumbles, finally breaking his silence, his voice a low, threatening boom. "You think it was easy for your mother to do what she did? We both had people we cared for. People we didn't want to see suffer."

"But my father did suffer!" I shout. "He died! He died because of *you*." I cut my eyes to my mother, who winces at the accusation in my words. Shaking, I suck in a trembling breath. "Tell me, were you partnered because you actually loved him, or was that just another part of your cover? Of the fake life you used to trick him into trusting you?"

Her lips purse, and she snaps back, her tone defensive, "I had every intention of just going in and doing the job I'd been assigned. But intentions change when you're in love." She scoots forward a few inches, as if to bring herself closer to me. "I didn't partner with him because I had to. I partnered with him because I *chose* to. I couldn't bring myself to betray him."

"So, why did you?" Ezra asks. "Obviously, something changed."

Her face falls. "Just because I didn't want to betray him doesn't mean I had another option. You don't say no to the State." She chews on her bottom lip for a moment, then shrugs. "Wren and I stalled for as long as we could, giving the people we reported to obscure leads and lesser names whenever pressed for information, making excuses about needing more time to build up the required trust to uncover who was really in charge. I'm not proud of it"—she glances at me then looks down at the floor—"but I sacrificed others in your father's place to buy myself time." Her voice drops to a whisper. "To buy *him* time."

Sitting back, she brings a hand to her mouth and bites down on the tip of her thumbnail. For a moment, she's silent, her eyes averted and glassy, as if lost is some distant recollection.

"Eventually," she continues, her voice melancholy, "his views became too outspoken, and I knew it was only a matter of time until his role in PHOENIX would become known to the wrong people. I couldn't think of any other way to protect him than to make myself a threat."

A threat…

The words I read in my father's journal take shape before me, rewriting themselves across my thoughts. I recall the entry he penned, expressing the divide that had formed between him and my mother and how he feared her allegiance to the State. In that same entry, he swore to put PHOENIX aside for the sake of his unborn child.

For me.

But despite stepping back from the organization, he never really put it aside. The siren of rebellion always called to him, and when I was a child, he exposed me to its song, even though doing so would have put me at risk.

It's only now, with my mother sitting before me, that I can see the situation from a different angle. If she hadn't done what she did—if she hadn't positioned herself as a threat to my father—would he have allowed that siren to pull me into the water?

Would he have allowed me to drown alongside him?

Exhaling, my mother shakes her head. "It killed me to put that distance between us, but I could accept his distrust if creating that rift meant he'd live. I had hoped, by making him afraid of me, he'd choose to give up the rebellion—

that he'd pass on the torch out of self-preservation. And he did…but only once I told him I was pregnant with you."

Once again, I recall my father's words from his journal. *"I must abandon everything and all that I stand for, and, for the sake of my unborn child, I must stay and wear the mask of a man who conforms."*

My mother scoffs, as if reading my mind, and when she next speaks, her tone is surprisingly bitter. "I thought we were free. That we'd be able to rebuild our love. But my pregnancy only subdued him. It didn't extinguish the fire he had burning within him, and when I discovered he was exposing you to that danger, that *world*, I knew he hadn't let PHOENIX go. He was simply biding his time, and what was worse, he had every intention of bringing you into the fold." Her voice breaks, and the desperation in her eyes as she meets my gaze is completely alien to me. "He left me no choice, Wynter. If I had let things carry on, I would've ended up losing you both. You were only a child. You were guiltless. I needed to protect you before he drew you in, too. Before there could be no saving you, either."

I hate the feeling expanding in my chest—this fear that my father was so blinded by his love for the past that he failed to see the danger that love put me in. A danger I'm now beginning to realize my mother tried to shield me from, even if, to do that, it meant making me hate her.

"So," she says, wringing her hands in her lap, "I did the only thing I could. I reported him. By this point, the State was no longer interested in eradicating PHOENIX. Instead, it saw the benefit of using the insurgency as a common enemy to unite the people against, amassing further power with the threat of domestic terrorism, which the State itself was actually responsible for. PHOENIX's mission and ideals were warped to create a smokescreen that would align the public under the government's rule."

Beside her, Bilken hooks one leg over the other and laces his fingers around his knees. "All the precautions the rebellion has taken to stay hidden over the decades have been fruitless. Even with the limited intel we provided, the Enforcers could've easily tracked PHOENIX under the city and eliminated the entire movement at any time. Especially once Freston was taken into custody. But the State opted not to do that, instead using PHOENIX to oppress the people and your father's execution as an opportunity to remind everyone of what happens when you act against the State, further cementing the fear it utilizes so expertly to manipulate public perception."

My brow furrows under the weight of my confusion, and although I'm wary of the answer, I ask, "What are you saying?"

Bilken gives me a sympathetic look then says, with a clarity that makes my lungs deflate, "Your father's execution was broadcast."

Vomit rises in my throat, and it takes all the willpower I possess not to spew across the sterile white rug. My father's execution was broadcast? I never knew that, and I certainly didn't see it, which means my mother must've gone to great lengths to ensure I wouldn't have to—an incredible feat considering everyone in the State is required to tune in to public executions.

I don't have to ask how she kept the truth from me. Growing up, no one ever said anything to me about my father being a rebel leader or about his involvement with PHOENIX, and why would they? Fear of suspected association would've tied even the bravest person's tongue. Besides, my mother was the one who reported him. She cemented our devotion to the State with that action. If anything, she made it clear to all those around us just how far she was willing to go for that loyalty.

Beside me, Jenner raises his hand. "Wait a minute. So, when you turned in Wynter's father, no one found it odd you had somehow failed to notice your own husband's involvement in the rebellion?"

"I said what I had to," my mother retorts. "That he covered his tracks. That he would've made a great operative for the State had he not been a traitor." She rehearses the words so convincingly that it's easy to envision her saying them.

"And they bought that? The people you reported to?" Ezra asks. Even without looking at him, I can picture the dubious expression he must be wearing just based on the tone of his voice.

My mother snorts. "What other choice did they have? They had no proof I knew anything of his connection to PHOENIX. The only other person who knew the truth was Wren, and we were careful with what we documented so as not to incriminate ourselves. But…" She falters, her gaze once more distant. "Just because they didn't have proof doesn't mean they were accepting of my ignorance." Her eyes flick from Ezra, settling back on me. "I was punished for falling victim to what they believed to be your father's duplicity, but I accepted that punishment because it meant that I could stay with you. That you would be protected. *Safe.*"

My pulse picks up speed, thrumming under my skin.

"What punishment?" I whisper, breathless.

"Aside from losing my husband, the man I loved, the father of my child?" She huffs, peering up at the ceiling, as if to hide the sheen of tears in her eyes. Sneering, she sniffs and looks down at her hands. "I was given my current job at the DSD."

Behind me, Ezra squeezes my shoulder. "How was being given a position of power at the most feared establishment in the State retribution?" His voice is unnervingly calm, the opposite of how I feel at this moment. Because I already know what she's going to say—I *fear* it—the weight of her unspoken confession hanging heavy in the air between us.

My mother considers Ezra for a moment, and I can sense the way she measures every word before she dares to speak. "The job wasn't the punishment," she finally says. "Killing Freston was."

Ezra's fingers tighten their grip, and next to me, Jenner stiffens, the hand wrapped around mine suddenly sweaty. I can feel the heat of his gaze on my face, as if he expects me to leap off this sofa and strangle my mother for this revelation. But I can't bring myself to move. I'm held still by the resurfacing pain in my chest and by the words that keep spilling from her lips, intent on torturing me with the truth.

"The State is often backhanded with its rewards. Everything must be a lesson—a reminder of where that reward came from and what happens when you bite the hand that feeds you," she says, as if I need further explanation for why she chose to turn on my father.

Her level tone sparks a writhing fury within me that tears at the underside of my skin, but still, I don't move, trapped in place by the small part of my mind that's led by reason and determined to listen to her side of the story. That needs to fully understand what she did.

"I was awarded an elevated position at the DSD for my devotion to the State and for making the ultimate sacrifice by reporting my husband's activities. But of all the jobs they could've assigned me—" Her breath catches, and she swallows, the sound audible in the encompassing hush. "It wasn't enough that I handed him in. The State wanted me to prove my loyalty by ending his life."

Tears scald my eyes, and I bite hard on my tongue to keep my rising sobs at bay. For so long, I've blamed my mother for what happened to my father. First, for not intervening when the Enforcers came to take him away, even though I've always known no one can intervene with the State. Then, once I learned of the full extent of her betrayal, I blamed her for turning him in. For being the one to steal my father from me. I blamed her in every sense of the word for his death, but never once did I think she was the one who killed him, that she was the one who snuffed out his existence like water on a flame.

In my mind, she was responsible for his death but not his murder, and that disparity mattered. The separation between the two was what allowed me to keep seeing her as a mother—that let me live under the same roof and still love her all those years before my placement exam. Before she inevitably betrayed me, too.

My mother blinks when tears slip down my cheeks, burning raw lines into my skin. She inches forward on the sofa again, the temptation to console me etched plainly across her face, even though she has never been one to show outward affection. But I don't want her comfort.

I don't need it.

Wiping the anger and grief from my face, I growl, "You could've said no. You could've turned the job down."

At my words, the mask of the woman who pulled me away from my father in our final moments together and who handed me over to the DSD to be tortured slides back into place. Any hurt I thought I glimpsed in her gaze dissipates, vanishing behind a wall of ice.

"Do you honestly believe that?" She arches an eyebrow. "Wynter, the job was a test. There was no saying no, or I would've ended up just like your father."

"Okay, so why not just hand you a gun?" Ezra presses. "That doesn't explain why they would give you a job at the DSD. The staff there is all doctors and scientists—"

"As am I," she interrupts, her voice hard. "I had already begun my training in healthcare when I volunteered to infiltrate the rebellion, and it was agreed I would receive a prominent position if I delivered information that would strengthen the State's foothold. As part of my cover, I began working in a small local health center, but when the DSD was established, I was sent there as a way of protecting my cover and alias, albeit in a junior position. One that wouldn't draw needless attention. At work, I was known by my birth name, Evelyn Adler. But everywhere else, I was Evandra Wright—then later on, Reeves— an insurance broker from Zone 2. Any intersection between my two lives was minimal, if altogether non-existent. And I insisted they stay that way, even when I turned in my husband and they offered me Head of Termination as my reward. A reward that came with a hefty condition."

"That you murder my father," I finish flatly.

She nods. "Don't you see? I never really had a choice in the matter. I was forced to accept the job. If I hadn't, my allegiance would've come under question and I was already being scrutinized at every angle. My options were accept or die." She sighs. "I know what you're thinking, but turning the position down wouldn't have saved your father. Besides, if I hadn't agreed to their terms, if I *had* resisted, what would've happened to you?"

My mouth opens to snipe back a scathing retort, but then closes as understanding sinks in. Everything my mother did back then…she did to protect me. I know all too well how powerless the individual is against the State, and as much as I hate her for betraying my father and for handing me over to be experimented on by Richter, I can empathize with being forced into a position where, no matter which option you chose, you lose. How many times have I been torn between two terrible choices and acted out of a desperate desire to protect someone I love?

How can I condemn her when I'm guilty of the same crimes?

She might not have been an affectionate mother, but she loved me enough to do what she did and to live with the burden of that choice. I'll never forgive her for it, but knowing her loyalty wasn't to the State, as my father had thought, but to her daughter. To *me…*

Well, that has to at least count for something, even if that loyalty has caused us both pain.

"And you?" I ask, shifting my gaze to Bilken. "What was your reward for your role in all this?"

He regards me for a moment, appraising me with those knowing dark eyes, one hand scratching along the scruff of his facial hair.

"Just before your father's untimely death, your mother warned me what she was going to do. So, I gave Rodrick a heads-up. I told him he needed to stay underground and out of the limelight until I gave him the all-clear. He had gone to ground several years earlier, more out of fear of getting caught by Enforcers than out of any real desire to help those who had fled the State's reign, but we were still in contact—"

"Wait," I interrupt, and the air punches from my lungs as I choke out two words. "He knew?"

Nolan knew my father was going to be executed and he did nothing to help him.

"I was sorry to hear about what happened to him." Nolan said that to me. He looked me in the eye and acted as if his own inaction didn't play a part in my father's death.

"You *both* knew," I seethe, fighting back my re-emerging tears. "You both knew and you did nothing."

"And what would you have liked us to do?" Bilken asks. "I wasn't going to act against your mother's wishes, and had Nolan offered your father refuge with PHOENIX, what would have become of you?"

Me?

Had my father survived, had he gone underground as he always intended, what *would* have become of me? I might've gone with him, I might've grown up with a different life than the one I was forced into. Or…

I glance at Jenner, his hand eerily still around mine, that *or* in my thoughts like a tangible presence in the silence between us. When he joined PHOENIX, his family suffered—not because he had become a rebel but because the State needed someone to blame for the two Enforcer deaths that resulted from his actions that night. And it would have been no different for us. My mother would've been punished for not turning my father in—as an operative working for the State, it was her job to be on the lookout for potential insurgents—and I, as her child, would've ended up caught in the crossfire.

Swallowing, I blink the fresh mist from my vision. As much as I want to believe my father would've protected me, the reality is—

"They would've killed us," I whisper.

"Or worse, in your mother's case," Bilken says cryptically, although I know all too well what he means.

Torture, at the hands of the very institution she works for.

Pushing the image of that place from my mind, I press, "What was the plan, then? Other than letting my father die."

I don't look away from Bilken, although, in my peripheral vision, I see my mother flinch at my words. Good. The barb hit its intended mark.

Leaning back, Bilken crosses his arms. "Well, I knew Rodrick would be insulated well enough from the fallout of your father's execution. The trouble was, your mother and I wouldn't be. Nor, by extension, you. Not unless I came up with a damn good excuse to explain why we had been blind to Freston's involvement with PHOENIX. Something big to soften the blow."

"You needed a scapegoat," I realize.

He nods. "And Rodrick was the perfect fall guy. But I couldn't exactly tell him that he was in danger and to keep out of sight for the foreseeable future without telling him how I came by that information. So, I told him the truth about me— that I was an operative working for the State but that my loyalties had shifted and I wanted to help him. That I believed in his cause."

"And did you?" Jenner asks, his tone snide.

Bilken hesitates, as if considering his next words, then says, "As much as a double agent could, I suppose, although nowhere near to the same extent Rodrick did. He genuinely believed it was his mission—his divine purpose, even—to lead our country into a new age. I, on the other hand, saw PHOENIX for what it was: a back door, should the State eventually fail. Not that Rodrick ever knew I held that mindset. As far as he was concerned, I was a changed man, brought into the light of reason by this grand thing he had helped build.

"Years earlier, prior to Freston leaving PHOENIX and before Rodrick—who had fallen victim to his own paranoia and growing extremism—moved underground to fully devote himself to the cause, they both extended personal invitations for me to join PHOENIX. Up until that point, I toed the line between supporter and friend, always making the same excuse as to why I couldn't properly join the movement. That I had someone I didn't want to leave behind, who I couldn't bring with me had I agreed, a reasoning Freston deeply empathized with."

I blink at him in surprise, wondering if there's any truth to that statement or if it was just a lie to fend off my father and Nolan. It's hard to believe Bilken could care about anyone more than he cares about himself. Considering he's not from the Heart, I doubt he has any family here. Hell, I don't even think he's partnered. I can only assume his *esteemed* position got him out of that requirement.

Unaware of my internal musings, he continues. "But, at that moment, I leaned into that foundation of trust built between us, letting Rodrick believe I was ready and willing to not only turn against the State but to help dismantle it from the inside. I told him what I stood to gain in my career and how that aid could, in turn, eventually bolster the rebellion and elevate it to new heights with the information that would be at my disposal. That he would need that information if he ever wanted to knock the State off its pedestal and install PHOENIX as the new ruling power. All he had to do was lie low for a while and wait for me to contact him."

"And you're saying he happily waited for over *twenty* years?" I ask, incredulous.

My father was executed in the year 2050. That was fourteen years ago, when I was just shy of turning seven years old. From what I read in my father's journal, Nolan had already gone to ground before my mother found out she was pregnant with me. That means he sat by and waited for Bilken to contact him for twenty-two years. *Twenty-two years* spent underground, obsessing over a message that may not ever come.

"That's a hell of a lot longer than a *while*," Jenner mutters under his breath, echoing my own thoughts.

Bilken glares at him. "Rodrick valued the cause more than he cherished his freedom. Or, should I say, he valued the notion of what the cause could become. He was skeptical, of course, when I relayed my intentions to him, but considering I hadn't turned him in to authorities in all the years we'd known one another… Well, he was inclined to believe me."

"So, Nolan made himself scarce and you, what?" I ask. "Gave the State his name?"

"Along with an in-depth report outlining how he had founded PHOENIX alongside Freston Reeves. I gave detailed descriptions of their movements and how they had been clever with who they allowed into their circle, explaining why it had taken so long to get usable intel and uncover the true roots of the organization. I manufactured false leads and presented them as fact, selling the idea that we'd been led astray. *Both* of us," he emphasizes, gesturing to my mother. "But I did it in such a way as to balance our shortcomings against the value of the information we were providing to make our overall mission seem like a success. Remember, the State valued accuracy and we were risking much by admitting fault. That was why I needed to give our superiors something that would overshadow our failures and, in turn, guarantee our safety and preserve the futures we'd been promised. We told whatever lies we had to in order to make the story work, and there wasn't any tangible evidence to refute our claims. Like your mother said, they couldn't question our guilt if there was never any proof that we knew."

My brow hooks upward as I peer between my mother and Bilken. He could've left her to fend off the wolves on her own, to suffer the consequences of her actions, regardless of what they might've been, but he didn't. He secured alibis for them both, even though doing so would have put his own life at risk. If he hadn't acted, if he had stayed silent, what might have happened to her? And why did he care? Why did he emphasize that his report was meant to protect both of them, unless—

"I toed the line between supporter and friend, always making the same excuse as to why I couldn't properly join the movement. That I had someone I didn't want to leave behind, who I couldn't bring with me had I agreed, a reasoning Freston deeply empathized with."

Shock passes through me, rattling me to my core. Was my mother that someone he mentioned? When he said they both had people they cared for, people they didn't want to see suffer…

Was he actually talking about her?

Is she the person he wants to protect above all—like Ezra and Jenner are for me, and I apparently was and maybe still am for my mother?

Bilken's rough tenor steers me away from that thought. "Despite my best efforts to allay their suspicions, your mother's loyalty was called into question. For whatever reason, our superiors didn't feel the same need to test me. I suppose because I wasn't sharing a home with the enemy. And as we were careful not to make it known that our collaboration as field operatives had transcended into friendship, they didn't suspect I would know anything of real consequence about her partnership with Freston. If I had, surely I would've reported her... or so I'm sure they assumed." He casts a sidelong glance at my mother before fixing his perceptive eyes back on mine. "My reward for my dutiful service was my position at W. P. Headquarters."

"Which you would later use to make yourself an asset to PHOENIX, just as you told Nolan you would." Ezra lets out a low, deliberating hum. "Did he know why you wanted him to lie low? That you were planning on selling him out?"

Bilken waves a dismissive hand. "He was already on the Enforcers' watch list as a rebel instigator, much in the same way you are. And as the State had just been given a public face for the rebellion, divulging the true extent of Rodrick's involvement barely put him in any additional danger. He was already in hiding, and he was smart. He knew not to stay put in one place for too long. Besides," he adds, "he wouldn't have left the door open for me to join PHOENIX if he didn't believe I could deliver what I promised."

"Which was to smash the hierarchy!" Jenner says in a jubilant voice, slapping his left fist against the palm of his opposite hand. "Seems strange, though," he comments, tone suddenly languid, "that you'd willingly destroy a system that worked so well to your benefit."

Bilken shrugs. "You forget, I made that promise to help the rebellion before I had any real power, so, at that moment, I was living under the State's thumb just like everyone else, my life governed by constant fear. But even if I had been in a different position at the time, the fact remains. You can only oppress a people for so long before they choose to retaliate. It was always inevitable the State would fail and a new regime would rise to overtake it. I merely saw the warning signs early and wanted an exit strategy in place for when that time came."

"Okay, so if PHOENIX was your exit strategy, your 'back door' as you called it, then why are you here now instead of out there with Nolan?" Jenner points a finger towards the white concrete ceiling. "If he's your friend, why help us when he wants us dead? Surely, by now, he's worked out you betrayed him."

Bilken exhales an indignant laugh. "Rodrick and I are *not* friends. We were once, but we haven't been for a long time now, not since I told him the truth about who I was. That is, if you can really call yourselves 'friends' when the other person doesn't know the real you." He sighs. "I believe he could have killed me that day. He might have tried had he not seen the value in keeping me on this side of the living." He laughs again, the sound more callous this time. "What we have had since is a mutually beneficial relationship, one that I consider over now that I've gotten what I need from him."

Apprehension settles deep in my bones when his eyes narrow on mine.

"You mean me," I breathe.

Bilken turns his head, looking again at my mother, but this time with a fondness I didn't think the stern man capable of. When she returns his gaze, it dawns on me that it isn't just friendship I glimpse in his face when he looks at her, but something else. Something more. Something that would make him go to the ends of the earth to protect her, like Ezra and Jenner keep doing for me.

He loves her, I realize.

"I have only ever had one real friend, Miss Reeves," Bilken says, his eyes never straying from my mother, "and, long ago, I promised I would do anything to ensure the survival of her daughter."

FIFTEEN

MY HEARTBEAT HAMMERS IN MY ears, and every jagged breath I exhale is deafening in the hush that follows Bilken's admission. Like always, I feel like I'm dangling at the cliff edge of understanding, so close to losing my grip.

"You're confused," Bilken says, cocking a wiry eyebrow.

Jenner blows out a frustrated breath through his nose. "Who isn't?"

Prickles of pain speckle my forehead, and I wince, rubbing my fingertips across my right temple. The influx of information being laid out before me is proving difficult to keep track of, and my head spins as I try to make sense of the tangled web of words my mother and Bilken are weaving.

Her story is too elaborate to be fabricated, and I want to believe her just to put the pain of my past to bed. Besides, what reason would she have to lie at this point?

That's what I keep asking myself, and yet, there's a niggling voice of doubt in the back of my head, ever present and jeering, that keeps drowning out whatever reason I still cling to.

Bilken has been trying to protect me? it repeats on a loop.

I suppress the overwhelming urge to laugh.

Noting the skepticism creasing my brow, Bilken frowns. "Everything your mother has said is true. We were sent into the Heart to infiltrate the rebels as a pair, although we were told to target its members separately, so that should one of us be compromised, the other's cover would remain intact. We were strangers isolated in a unique situation together, and, believe me, leading a double life takes a toll—"

"You would know," Jenner grumbles.

Bilken ignores the interruption. "It was a lonely job that spanned many long years, and throughout that time, Evelyn needed someone to lay her burdens on, just as I, in turn, laid mine on her. Our friendship was one built on secrecy and trust."

A shudder of revulsion creeps up my spine, my shoulders raising like hackles on a hissing cat, and I grimace as something inside me snaps.

The loyalty these two found in their deceit was stronger than anything my mother could have had with my father. Bilken said it himself—can you really be friends, or more in my parents' case, if the other person doesn't truly know who you are? Bilken always knew the truth of who my mother was, whereas my father died thinking she was someone else. If our paths hadn't crossed again at the DSD when she intervened with Richter, I suppose I would have died thinking that, too.

It doesn't seem fair that my mother could create victims of her own family while Bilken got off clean. He never intentionally hurt the people he loved. After all, the only person he clearly loves is my mother. If he did have anyone else he cared for, he wouldn't be here, helping us. Helping *her*.

A sour taste floods my mouth at the thought that he is the only person who really knows her.

I breathe out, grazing my palm against the sofa cushion, concentrating on the brush of the soft fabric against my skin—focusing on anything other than the resurfacing urge to jump up from my seat and strangle Bilken. I don't want to hear about this. I don't want to hear about the bond he shares with my mother.

I don't want to hear him say how he helped me when, because of him, Rai is dead.

Sensing my distress, Ezra presses his fingertips into the skin just above my collarbone, his hand a comforting weight on my shoulder, grounding me when I need it most. His touch calms the building pressure in my chest.

"That explains your relationship, but what does any of this have to do with Wynter?" he asks.

"It has everything to do with her," Bilken counters. The deep mahogany pools of his eyes lock on mine. "When the DSD apprehended you following your placement exam, your mother came to me. She begged me to find a way to help you, to get you both out of the State. To make you disappear so no one would be able to find you. And because of that friendship between us, I agreed—"

"At the risk of your own life?" I interrupt. "I find that hard to believe." Even knowing that he did so once before—in the events leading up to my father's execution—I struggle to associate that notion of a selfless Bilken with the man I know.

He sneers. "Because you know me so well, Miss Reeves?"

I lurch forward on my seat, but Ezra and Jenner both grab me, restraining me as I shout, "You were the one who told me not to confuse ambition with loyalty! *You* told me you don't stand by alliances that only serve you in the immediate moment!"

"I was baiting you!" he fires back. "Everything you know about me is a carefully constructed facade, a role I tailor to whomever it is I need to manipulate. And, in that moment, I needed to fool you. To *make* you believe I was your enemy."

"Why?" I gasp, sinking back onto the sofa.

He scrubs a hand across his face, his collected composure finally slipping. "To understand, we need to start from the beginning." He draws in a deep breath through his nose. "During your first stay at the DSD, your mother kept tabs on you from within while I worked on a plan to get you both out of the State in one piece. But increasing security over the years has made it difficult to expatriate anyone from the Heart, especially an individual under such heavy surveillance as you were under Richter's guardianship. My options were limited, and I knew the only way I could help my friend, help *you*, was to seek assistance from somewhere else."

"Assistance?" Ezra repeats.

Bilken nods. "After Freston's execution, I kept in contact with Rodrick, mainly to ensure the offer to join PHOENIX still stood, even if I wasn't sure I ever intended to take it. But, over time, it was a risk maintaining that contact. Not in the way you're likely imagining—not out of fear of getting caught, although that's the way I pitched it to him. I told him contact channels were being monitored and that, if we weren't careful, his location would be discovered, once again reiterating how vital it was he remain out of sight, feeding his growing paranoia. In reality, I needed to keep a healthy distance between us so I wouldn't inadvertently encourage him to do anything that might jeopardize my position in the event I ultimately decided against joining PHOENIX. Deniability, Miss Reeves. It is how one stays above the law.

"Still, when your mother came to me, I almost reopened that contact for her sake. The only reason I didn't was because I knew, even as Freston Reeves' daughter, PHOENIX would never willingly involve itself with the DSD. Rescuing you from that fortress would've been a suicide mission for all involved. But then, you escaped and sought PHOENIX out all on your own, solving that little logistics problem for us. All I had to do to guarantee your safe return was make good on the promise I had once made to Rodrick. To remind him of why I was a good friend to have."

"The transmission to Nolan," I breathe. "It really was bait to get me, but not for Richter—"

"No, not for Richter," Bilken echoes, "although, luckily for us, he didn't know that. As far as he was concerned, I had offered my help to retrieve you for *him*. For the State. And it worked. Unfortunately, the rest of our plan didn't go as intended."

A mocking laugh punctures the air beside me. "Which part would you be referring to?" Jenner asks. "The part where you didn't bother to turn up? Or the part where we were ambushed by Enforcers? Oh"—he holds up a finger—"I know. You mean the part where our friend got shot and was turned into a human trophy by that sadistic dick." Clicking his tongue, he rakes a hand through his mop of black hair. "And while you're answering that, I'd love to know why the *hell* Richter would trust you."

Bilken shrugs, unfazed by Jenner's outburst. Like before, he directs his next words at me. "The same reason he trusted your mother. We have a history, a rapport that we were both careful to cultivate. To build trust, you need to sometimes give someone what they want without expecting anything in return. Then, when the time is right, you can turn that trust to your advantage. That's one lesson I learned long ago, thanks to the State—that power on its own is never enough. To be truly safe in this world, you need to have other powerful people in your pocket."

"What do you mean?" Ezra presses. There's an edge to his voice that closely mimics the unease unraveling my insides.

Bilken picks at a loose thread on his shirt cuff. "I gave Richter what he needed to expand his research when the pool from Termination was no longer fruitful, ultimately paving the way for him to claim his position as Head of the Research department. *Access*," he clarifies when none of us utter a word. "Once he knew what prerequisites needed to be met, it was easy to find him new subjects among the general populace of the Heart."

Stunned, I turn the full brunt of my gaze on my mother. Back at the DSD, when we were in Richter's underground morgue, she told me she procured test subjects for him before he became Head of Research. Before the State gave him free rein to inflict his madness on his victims unhindered. And now, I know she didn't do it alone. She and Bilken both fueled my tormentor's ambitions, enabling his research like it was an addiction.

I glance back at Bilken as the apprehension pooling in my stomach turns sour.

"The key to true security—not power, *security*," he emphasizes when I try to interrupt him again, "is to make yourself an asset to those you wish to use. Let them believe they have the upper hand, that they're the ones calling the shots.

That way, when you steal from them or depose them, they'll never see your treachery coming. Richter saw me as such an asset, and because of that trust, it took very little convincing on my part to involve myself with your retrieval. I presented the idea to coax PHOENIX with the offer of inside intel and used that transmission as my one opportunity to reach out to Rodrick directly.

"As for your other questions," he drawls with a sharp glance at Jenner, "I was never meant to be there that night, nor was Richter. The plan was to send in a group of Enforcers, who were under orders to detain Wynter and bring her to a secure location, where Richter was told to meet them and aid with transporting her back to the DSD. The part of the plan Richter wasn't aware of was that we planned to intercept his Enforcers with our own team en route to that secure location." His eyes shift back to mine, and the corners of his lips twitch, offering me a frown which borders on sympathetic. "You needn't feel bad about killing them, by the way. The plan was always for those Enforcers to die."

I remember the outcome of that moment so clearly, the way the Enforcers' blood soaked into the white carpet underfoot in Bilken's office. The way the bullets perforated so many priceless artifacts of a time long lost to us.

My stomach churns at the memory, and I grimace at Bilken's brazen disregard for human life.

He snorts. "You judge me, Miss Reeves, but everything that transpired that night was done in an effort to help you—"

"Help me?" A disdainful breath slips through my lips. "Rai *died* because of that mission." I became a weapon because of that mission. If I hadn't gone that night, I wouldn't have encountered Richter again and he wouldn't have swayed me back into his clutches. If I hadn't gone, I would've escaped years of torment and torture and succumbed to my disease surrounded by people I love.

No, you wouldn't have, a small voice lurking in the back of my head has the indecency to remind me. *You would've ended the world and taken everyone with you.*

The unavoidable fate which now awaits us despite everything I've done to alter my path.

"Let me see if I have this right," Jenner says. "Your strategy was to intercept the Enforcers before they could drag Wynter kicking and screaming back to the DSD, but then Richter turned up where he shouldn't have, derailing that plan."

Bilken grunts in confirmation. "I was ignorant of his connection to Mr. Laramie and Miss Dorne, so had no reason to suspect he'd intervene. In hindsight, I should have anticipated that he would do something so...inconvenient."

"Inconvenient?" Ezra parrots, his words dripping with anger.

"The man was a complete narcissist," Bilken drawls. "He needed to believe he was the smartest person in the room. That every move made was by his design."

My teeth roll over my lower lip as I drop my gaze to the floor, staring blankly at the carpet as my mind revisits the tragic events of that night. If I didn't already blame myself for what happened to Rai, I do now that I know the real purpose of the mission that put her back in Richter's path.

Sniffing, I wipe my nose with the back of my hand and glance up again, glaring at Bilken. "Was the transmission a genuine offer? Or was it just another lie to get what you wanted?"

Cocking his head to one side, he says, "It was genuine in as much as I was willing to give Rodrick what he wanted to see you returned."

"Which was what, exactly?" Ezra presses. "You gave him reason to come after Wynter the moment you handed over her file. If the intent was to get her off everyone's radar, you failed."

"It's called a back-up plan," Bilken retorts. "By the time Rodrick saw the file, Wynter would've been far away from the Heart and out of his and Richter's reach for good. The information would've been useless to him…unless things didn't go as planned, which we are all well aware that they didn't."

Jenner leans forward, exhaling a startled laugh. "You devious bastard. You *intended* to give him a reason to want Wynter for himself, didn't you?"

Bilken squares his shoulders. "Hence why it's called a back-up plan. I needed a reason to get PHOENIX involved in the event our mission to retrieve Wynter failed."

I stare at him in amazement, begrudgingly impressed. And here I thought Richter was a maniacal genius. He never stood a chance against my mother and Bilken.

"And the connection mentioned in the transmission?" I ask. "The person who was supposedly equipped to handle my illness?" Before tonight, I always thought it was Richter—that Bilken's aid was just a ruse to force me back into my tormentor's shackles. But now… Understanding dawns and I glance at my mother. "It wasn't Richter, it was you."

She straightens slightly under my scrutiny. "I'm no expert on your disease, but I did know of the collar Richter had been designing and that it could potentially curtail your symptoms and prolong your life. Maybe even allow you a shot at a normal one."

My brow furrows. "And what, you were going to steal it?"

Once, it would've been impossible for me to imagine my mother stealing from the State—from the very government I was always so convinced she was loyal to.

Now, I'm beginning to see just how shallow that loyalty really is.

"If I had to," she says without hesitation. "But then the mission failed and you went back to the DSD and Richter fitted you with that collar himself. At that point, all we could do was wait and hope Nolan would take the bait Wren had dangled in front of him."

"Which he did," Bilken mutters, grinning smugly. "As expected, your file exposed just how valuable you could be to him. After that, Rodrick merely came to conclusions I had already predisposed him to see."

"How?" Jenner asks.

Bilken's grin widens, unsettling me. "By stoking the flames of his megalomania and forcing him into the background of his own creation. And by making him believe he would need my help if he ever *truly* wanted to take on the State.

"Between the two founders of PHOENIX, Freston was always the realist and Rodrick the fantasist. He was willing to do whatever it took for the pipe dream of power, even if that meant receding into the shadows and waiting for a signal that may not ever come. As I hoped, he saw the transmission as that signal and the file as just the beginning of the goldmine of information I had promised all those years ago. Having bided his time for so long, he was ready to finally take control of PHOENIX and emerge to fight the war he felt destined to lead. And, as I knew he would, he viewed Wynter as the prime tool needed to do that.

"When he contacted me for my help with extracting you,"—Bilken meets my gaze—"I made it a point to only agree to offer my continuing aid under the condition that I could join PHOENIX, like he once asked me to. I wasn't going to make the same mistake I made with the mission to the magistrates building. This time, I would be present to see to your safety myself. And between my ability to pass your friend here"—he nods to Jenner—"off as an Enforcer and the drugs needed to restrain you, which PHOENIX wouldn't have otherwise had access to, he couldn't very well refuse my demands."

The drugs…

I remember the paralyzing effects of whatever I was injected with when I woke up at that bunker. At the time, I didn't remember Rai or what she once told me about PHOENIX's lack of access to medical supplies. Otherwise, I might have suspected a bigger player's involvement.

A swell of laughter fills my throat. "See to my safety…by allowing Nolan to execute me?"

Jenner stiffens at the same moment Ezra's fingers tighten around my shoulder, and I know they're thinking of the same thing I am, the memory of our almost executions vivid in my thoughts even now. It could have gone so much differently. And it would have, if—

"Whose idea do you think that was?" Bilken snaps. He glares between the three of us, staring at each of our faces in turn. "Are any of you dead now? Why do you think that is?"

Because Quinn saved us, that voice in my head whispers.

My attention jumps to the ex-Enforcer, who has been silent this whole conversation, a spectator to the revelations assaulting me. His cheeks are flush with color—a sign the medication my mother gave him must be working—and there's a clarity to his obsidian eyes that wasn't there the last time I looked at him. His drug-addled haze seems to be wearing off.

"You were working for Bilken the whole time," I murmur. "You were planted there to get close to Nolan."

His eyes flick briefly to my mother and Bilken, as if seeking permission before he answers. "I was planted there to get you out…by any means necessary."

I shake my head. Why would Quinn—or any Enforcer, for that matter—abandon the State when the consequences of that betrayal were significant? What was he getting out of such an arrangement?

And how the hell did he cross paths with my mother?

"Why?" I ask, confused. "Who are you, really?"

"An Enforcer, who could no longer fight for a country that was so quick and willing to commit genocide." Anger burns in his gaze, the black depths like chips of hard onyx. His chest puffs out as he draws in a steadying breath, and pushing it out through his nose, he speaks slowly, as if every word is an effort. "I was drafted into the State's war a year before it began—I wasn't old enough to become an Enforcer yet otherwise—but I joined willingly because of certain privileges the position afforded."

Like getting out of the partnership requirement, I muse, recalling our conversation back at the bunker when he escorted me to meet the Heads of PHOENIX.

"My first time in the field," he continues, "I saw what they had you do, what you were capable of, and what you would *continue* to do until there was no one left to conquer or destroy. After that battle, I knew I couldn't be part of it, and upon returning to the Heart, I abandoned my post, thinking 'to hell with the privileges.' I didn't really have a plan, and I had no desire to join PHOENIX, unlike some other recruits who had fled—"

Nolan's lackeys, I note, remembering the Enforcer-like guards the PHOENIX Head seemed to constantly surround himself with.

"—and, of course, I had no clue how to get out of the city, so it wasn't long before I was caught. They didn't even ask why I ran away. They just branded me a traitor and sent me straight to Termination."

"It's always bad publicity when an Enforcer goes rogue," my mother chimes in. "It sends the wrong message about their authority. Because of that, their executions are never broadcast."

Her focus drifts to the closed safe house door, and as I follow her gaze, I allow the tentacles of my power to unfurl, reaching beyond the thick slab of reinforced steel. Beyond it, I sense a presence—the steady rhythm of a heartbeat belonging to the Enforcer who brought us to this place, ever silent and obedient. Even now, he stands watch, loyal to my mother, although I don't understand why.

My mother's eyes swing back to mine, as if sensing my unspoken question. "I have Enforcers loyal to me because I saw the opportunity they presented. The few I keep close were all spared from execution and, thanks to Wren's extensive reach and connections, given forged identities that allow them to roam the Heart freely and aid me whenever the situation calls for it. For all intents and purposes, each of them died when they were meant to. Including Quinn here." She nods toward the ex-Enforcer slouched on the sofa, who dips his chin in acknowledgment, then repositions himself on the plush cushion, wincing as he pushes himself fully upright.

"In exchange for sparing my life, we made a deal," he explains, picking up where my mother left off, as if the silence is pressing him for his side of the story. "Per our agreement, Bilken would help me seek asylum with PHOENIX, and he coached me on what to do to gain Nolan's trust. It wasn't particularly hard. AWOL Enforcers make good little soldiers the Heads can shape to be cannon fodder for the cause. Once they're sure we hold no loyalty to the State anymore, that is."

Although his words should surprise me, they don't. My most recent encounter with PHOENIX had all too clearly demonstrated how its priorities have shifted over the last few years. Instead of helpless, terrified refugees, the only members in that bunker were armed muscle for Nolan.

"I was with Nolan for nearly two months prior to your extraction, and in that time, I did everything I could to make myself invaluable to him," Quinn says. "I ran his errands like a good little minion and force-fed him a story about how much I hated and feared you." When I cock an eyebrow, he adds, "I needed to give him a good reason to let me be on the firing squad."

"Oh, so, *that's* why you were such an asshole to us," Jenner scoffs.

Quinn's responding glare is icy. "I couldn't do anything that would make Nolan suspect my allegiance or put my mission at risk. I'm sorry if I hurt your *feelings*," he spits, "but your opinion of me meant absolute shit."

Snorting, Jenner stretches his arms out along the back of the sofa.

"What did you get out of this bargain, other than your life?" Ezra asks. "Surely, there was something more in it for you since you had to have known you couldn't stay with PHOENIX."

The ex-Enforcer crinkles his nose. "Nor did I want to. The plan was to 'execute' Wynter and then reconvene with Dr. Adler and Bilken at a safe place a mile southeast of the bunker's location where we would all then escape the State together. You two"—he wags a finger, pointing between Ezra and Jenner—"were just excess baggage."

"Excess baggage?" Jenner squawks at the same time I say, "Escape?"

Quinn ignores Jenner, locking eyes with me. "That's what I was promised. The chance to begin again somewhere else. Somewhere far away from the State's ideologies."

"And this fresh start included you two?" I ask, once again peering at my mother and Bilken, who traces the shape of his well-manicured, close-cropped beard with his fingers.

"This country has gone to hell, and we were tired of playing both sides," he admits. "Sometimes, power isn't worth the struggle it takes to hold onto."

His words take me aback, and a long moment passes as I once again try to align this version of Bilken—the man behind the mask—with the cold-hearted coward I assumed him to be.

He and my mother sit silent, waiting for me to speak. In the seconds that follow, I note the traces of exhaustion lining each of their faces. Faint purple smudges ring my mother's eyes, and Bilken's salt and pepper hair is beginning to look more gray than black. All that scheming must be catching up with them.

With a strangled breath, I sink back into the cushion. "Let's say everything you've told us is true, and that everything you've done really has been to help me. Why goad me into attacking you? Why not just tell me the truth?"

Why make me hate you?

"Just another part of the plan, Miss Reeves. You and I were never going to be able to speak freely with Rodrick always watching you. There were cameras everywhere in that bunker. He and his soldiers were aware of every move you made, even when you thought they weren't." He cocks an eyebrow at Ezra and Jenner, and I know he means when they broke me out of my cell. "There was no opening to expose my plan to you, and frankly, the less you were aware of, the better. The way it played out was far more believable than if you or your friends had been in the know." He pauses for a moment, and his lips part again on a sigh. "As for why I provoked you? Simple. It gave me the opportunity to plant a tracker on your person. That way, had you refused Mr. Stohler's offer of refuge, which you did," he grumbles, his eyes swinging to Quinn before returning to me, "your mother and I could have traced your location. Which ended up being a necessity given your...detour."

Inside me, sparks of outrage threaten to burst into flame, and I glower at Bilken, once again repressing the urge to strangle him. He's just like Richter, treating me like some possession that needs keeping track of.

I wince as a sharp pain stabs behind my eyes, the agony chipping away at my brain. This is all too much. I'm drained just trying to unweave this complicated web of endless lies and deception.

Shaking off my growing fatigue, I cut my gaze back to Quinn. "And the RF transmitter? If they were already tracking me, and if you had the means to contact them,"—I nod toward the communicator on his belt—"then what was the point of having that?"

"Because the DSD is the one place the trackers and communicators don't work," my mother says, answering for him. "That place is...*was*," she corrects herself, "a fortress. It was constructed with materials designed to prevent anyone on the outside from accessing the sensitive intel and equipment stored inside, or from anyone already inside from transmitting to an exterior location. That included access to personnel movements." Frustration leaches into her tone as she glances between Ezra and Jenner. "Why do you think PHOENIX never managed to hack the DSD's systems? Because it can only be done from *within* the building. Sure, we were able to track you to the DSD's doors, but beyond that, we were blind to your location. The RF transmitter Quinn used had a short range and only targeted alarms—and, in turn, the locking mechanisms— in the immediate area." Her gaze flicks back to mine, and her expression softens. "That's how I was able to find you so quickly. I was already there, I just needed to know where to look."

I blink, stupefied into silence. They really did think of everything—covered every possible angle and outcome.

And yet, there's still one thing I don't understand.

"If the plan was to escape the State, then why help us get back into the Heart?" I ask Quinn.

He cocks a dark brow at me and snorts. "That ticket out was entirely dependent on delivering you to Dr. Adler. You insisted on going back into the Heart. Would I have been able to stop you?"

He's right. We would've just gone on without him if he hadn't agreed to come with us, and he couldn't exactly tell us the truth. I had just tried to kill Bilken with my bare hands and I never would've believed my mother was working for the DSD, let alone serving as the acting Head of Termination. Not that it would have mattered if he had. Rai was still our priority.

To uphold his end of the bargain he made with my mother, Quinn had no choice but to return to the one place he was so desperate to leave, to accompany me for as long as it took to fulfill his mission, all in the vain hope that the path to escape would still be there at the end of it.

"What's done is done," my mother says brusquely. "The decision was made and now, we have to work with the hand we've been dealt if we are to get out of this city alive."

"And your plan is…what?" Jenner prompts. "Because I'm assuming you have one."

Sitting forward, Bilken props his elbows on his knees and steeples his hands, touching his fingertips to his lips in contemplation. "You forget, Evelyn and I are not from here, and my position has allowed me a certain degree of, shall we say, freedom and accessibility not afforded to others? All that to say, I have made valuable friends and connections abroad over the years. Connections, who would be willing to harbor fugitives and aid their escape from"—he shrugs, gesturing vaguely with one hand—"an oppressive regime that's currently under attack?"

Surprise ripples through me. "You have a way to contact people outside the Heart?"

He might've provided PHOENIX with the instructions to set up a secure contact channel between them that night at the magistrates building—even if it wasn't entirely necessary, based on what he's since revealed about stoking the flames of Nolan's delusions—but that communication line was still within the boundaries of the State. Whereas, what he's talking about now… He's implying that he's had access to the outside world this whole time—that he's always had the option of freedom, while those of us trapped inside the Heart's borders didn't.

Just how far can one man's reach extend?

"My dear, when you work at the center of something, you familiarize yourself with its loopholes and flaws. You learn to play those weaknesses to your advantage. Take the DSD, for example. These connections of mine wanted to eliminate the threat before it came to them, so I gave them what they wanted— the beating heart at the foundation of the State's war."

As Bilken's eyes hold mine, it sinks in what he's saying. He doesn't just mean the DSD. He means Richter's research and the weapon it created that allowed the State to pursue such ruthless endeavors. And now, with this attack, his *connections* think they've destroyed the threat.

They think they've destroyed me.

Fear is a hand tightening around my windpipe. What will happen when they realize they didn't?

"And my reward for orchestrating an end to the State was a one-way ticket for us out of the Heart," Bilken says, but I barely hear his words past the terror soaking into my thoughts.

"The inside man… It wasn't Adler, it was you," Jenner accuses, sitting upright, his arms slipping down onto the cushions beside him. His tone holds neither question nor surprise. He's simply voicing what I think we all suspected from the moment we arrived at this safe house.

I glance at Quinn, who—given his part in this conspiracy—must have been aware of Bilken's role in the attack despite claiming otherwise. Our conversation outside the DSD replays in my thoughts and, again, I hear Ezra and Jenner theorizing that someone might be working with the enemy from within the State as a double agent. At the time, although he was the one who brought it up, Quinn had shrugged the notion off as a mere possibility rather than a fact.

Can't say for sure, huh?

Bilken lets loose a rough laugh. "Did you not wonder how I would continue to make myself useful to PHOENIX after fleeing the State? I know *you* did," he adds, nodding at me. "I'm not a fool. I know Rodrick would have disposed of me the moment I was no longer working for him from the inside. That was the only worth I held for him. So, I gave him his tool to take on the State and then outlaid what he had to do to use it. It wasn't enough having the DSD's weapon at his disposal. He knew as well as I did you weren't going to attack your own home—"

"But that didn't mean someone else wouldn't," Ezra mutters behind me.

Bilken nods. "The plan, at least as far as Rodrick was concerned, was for me to tip off the 'enemy.' To give them a reason to strike the Heart, offering a potential end to our global conflict by means of an attack, which would provide PHOENIX with the opportunity to broker peace and establish themselves as the new governing power. Once peace was publicly made, military support from outside would sweep through the Heart, allowing the rebellion to supplant the State. I simply made the introduction between him and these friends, at which point, they stated their terms and Rodrick agreed."

"PHOENIX planned this?" Disgust roils in my gut. Now, I know why Nolan was so willing to let millions of people in the Heart suffer. He isn't just some power-hungry opportunist seizing an opening. He *created* the opening with Bilken's help.

He brought this chaos to our doorstep.

Bilken frowns. "Believe it or not, this conflict was inevitable. Had you remained Richter's puppet and continued forging a path of death across the globe, someone would've retaliated—"

"They wouldn't have succeeded," I cut in, but Bilken is already shaking his head.

"They would have found a way," he insists, "just like I found a way to take down your transport helicopter. As for PHOENIX... Well, like Rodrick, many were tired of withering away in the shadows. They would've come to a head with the State at some point."

"Not like this," Jenner whispers, his head jerking side to side in disbelief like the sway of a pendulum.

The weight of Ezra's hand disappears from my shoulder, and he steps around the sofa until he's standing beside me. "All this, a war with millions of lives sacrificed, just to get Wynter back for her mother?" Shock distorts his voice, and his face is unnervingly white, painted pale with the same revulsion I feel ripping a hole in my chest.

As he meets my gaze, I know I made the right choice in acting on his mother's words and asking him to kill me. Ezra would never risk so many lives to save mine. He would choose right. He *will* choose right.

And the right choice isn't me.

"And to secure our escape from the State, although that wasn't the only reason," my mother protests. "You saw for yourselves what Richter was hiding in the DSD. He was attempting to create an army, and I think we all know he would have succeeded eventually. Then, it wouldn't have mattered where we went. We wouldn't have been safe anywhere. That was all the incentive we needed to intervene, casualties be damned."

The mention of the bodies in the sublevel of the DSD churns the minimal contents of my stomach. I wish I could bleach my eyes and scrub the memory of that room from my brain.

The memory of what I am indirectly responsible for.

The memory of what Richter was trying to create with my blood.

A dour laugh presses at the wall of my lips, breaking through. "Let me guess, that was the price for their help. That all the weapons of the State be destroyed."

"The price," my mother clarifies, "was that PHOENIX provide the coordinates to the source of the weapons, where they were being created and stored. But when the blast didn't wipe out the full scope of the DSD as intended, I knew I had to finish the job myself or else risk them reneging on their side of the arrangement where our escape was concerned. And..." She hesitates, wringing her hands in her lap again. "So no one else would ever have to go through what you have. So no one else could continue what Richter had started."

I brush off her forced attempt at reconciliation as a blanket of calm settles over my senses, extinguishing my simmering rage. I've heard enough. I understand why my mother and Bilken did what they did, but their actions change nothing. They offer no way to put an end to this war—only the offer to run away from it like a coward.

But there can be no running away, not for me. Not for any of us.

Not if the future plays out as I know all too well it will.

Slowly, I rise from the sofa, taking a few calculated steps back toward the bedroom before pausing, glancing over my shoulder.

"Everything you did was in vain. The collar is broken—there's no way to control this disease. And you do realize these 'friends' will never let me go once they realize what I am, right? They'll want me dead, just like everyone else with Ultraxenopia."

"We won't let that happen," my mother assures me. "Wren already drafted a new identity for you just in case they learned your name. No one needs to know who you really are or that you're sick. We have options." As if to prove her point, she pulls the remains of my busted collar from her coat pocket, setting it on the marble table before her. Hand shaking, she gestures to it and says, "Once we're out, I'll find a way to fix it. To cure you myself. We have time—"

Even if I believed her—which I don't since there can be no hiding the severity of my illness or fixing a device none of us knows the first thing about, not in the time I actually have—it doesn't change the fact that she would willingly leave everyone else in this city to a fate they don't deserve. What's to stop her from doing the same to Ezra or Jenner if it came down to protecting them or me?

I won't risk it.

"Except, we don't. Because I'm not leaving the Heart. My time is almost up. I'll die in this city." Turning fully, I fix a cold glare on my mother. "And if you keep trying to 'help' me, you'll die, too."

You all will.

SIXTEEN

COLD WATER STRIKES MY FACE, an icy deluge that brings relief for all of five seconds before the nausea rolls through me again. My tongue darts out across my chapped lower lip, and I swallow, pushing down the bile burning the inside of my throat as I raise my gaze to the mirror. Gripping the sides of the polished stone basin, I grimace at the gaunt face staring back at me. Whatever healthy color I had to my skin has faded, resulting in my chalky complexion, and shadows mark the edges of my now protruding cheekbones, the skin around my eye sockets mottled with blistering shades of purple and black. Even my eyes seem to have lost some of their vigor and hue, the irises dull, taking on tones of gray.

I splash water on my face again before peering down into the sink.

"It really is trying to make up for lost time," I mutter, biting back an unhinged chuckle, which quickly fades into a sob. I clamp a hand over my mouth to keep quiet.

This disease really is determined to kill me.

Pain slashes through my skull as if in response to that thought, and I cry out as a searing flash of light explodes behind my eyes, blinding me. The room spins, my surroundings blurring, and my knees buckle, dragging me down to the floor.

As my fingertips graze the tile, searching for a way through the sudden fog obscuring my vision, a voice calls out from the distance, calm and collected.

And, above all, familiar.

I glance in the direction it's coming from, unsurprised when the light fades and I find I'm no longer on the floor in the washroom in Bilken's safe house but in the magistrates building in Zone 1. Standing, as if this disease isn't killing me.

I recognize the office I'm in, and my chest tightens as I peer down at the carpet, the fibers bleached white, erasing the evidence that it was once soaked with the blood of at least a dozen Enforcers. Erasing that Rai was shot in this room.

Resurfacing bile burns my insides like acid as my focus drifts to the broad wall of windows and the looming figure standing before them, looking down at the city below.

Even from behind, I know him.

As if sensing my presence, Nolan turns on his heel, but his pale eyes look past me because I'm not really here. I follow his gaze to the line of still people behind me, awaiting his next words in silence.

"It's time," he says to the other Heads of PHOENIX. Then, clearing his throat, he takes a seat at what was once Bilken's desk.

Folding his hands on top of the glass surface, he straightens as three floating black balls take position a few feet in front of him, buzzing softly in the hush. Spotlights project from the recording drones, illuminating Nolan's face.

"Citizens of the State," he announces, enunciating every word. "I come to you in this dire time to offer you much-needed hope for the future."

Behind him, flames cast an orange and gray smoky haze across the city. I stumble forward, approaching the window, my hands flattening against the panes as I stare out at my home, so much of the immediate area now reduced to rubble and ash.

Tears thicken in my throat as a list of people I blame for this shuffle through my head on a loop. Richter did this. My mother and Bilken did this. Nolan did this.

I did this.

"For so long," Nolan continues, and I pivot to face him again, staring into the cameras, invisible in my grief, "you have all been led to believe that PHOENIX is the enemy. That *we* are the threat. But now,"—he gestures to the ruin beyond the windows—"our borders have been breached by those the State has goaded into a war. So, I ask you…who is the real enemy here?"

"You are," I whisper. "Because you did this." Once again, I rehearse that list of names.

Richter.

My mother.

Bilken.

Nolan.

Me.

"The State does not care about you," Nolan says. "You are cattle with one purpose: to produce. To be productive members of society or perish under the umbrella of uselessness. Now, when outsiders come here to slaughter you, who are the ones offering you shelter and safety? Is it the State? No, it's us—the terrorists the State has conditioned you to fear."

He shakes his head, clicking his tongue in disdain, and as I skirt around the desk again to look at his face, it dawns on me that he isn't acting. The rage and fear in his gaze are both real.

And, despite his scheming and planning, he's afraid.

For all Nolan's faults, he's right—the State doesn't care about us. It never has. We're all just cogs in a machine, oiled just enough to keep us working and discarded without thought the moment we break. But the problem is, regardless of what he says to try to calm the peoples' terror, he isn't any different. And the disheartening truth I'm beginning to realize is…I'm not sure any government can be. We are all part of the machine, and those who are smart enough to be the ones turning the wheels are aware that, if the machine stops working, they lose their hold on power. So, it's inevitable. Once PHOENIX takes control, it will only be a matter of time before the people become victims again, used to serve someone else's greed until someone new steps up who wants to be different.

But Nolan isn't different—he's more of the same. Any words he utters to suggest otherwise are just lies wrapped up in a pretty bow of denial.

"But PHOENIX is not a terrorist organization—"

I grimace. That might have been true once, but he made it one with this attack.

"We are like you," Nolan continues, insistent. "We are also afraid, but we want to cure you of that fear. We desire peace and the freedom to live, just as we desire that freedom for you. The State has kept you all in a prison, which we will liberate you from in return for your trust. Let us lead you down this road, back to the haven of freedom."

What even is freedom? I wonder. Has anyone living ever truly experienced it? Or is it just a dream? More pretty words to use as a weapon of oppression?

"This attack…" He averts his gaze from the cameras. Perhaps to hide the truth from the people watching who are bound to see the guilt in his eyes. "The State has brought this upon itself with its unnatural experimentation and greed. Its greatest interest has always been expanding the cage instead of protecting its lifeblood. Its *people*. I promise you," he persists, shaking his head, "the State will not protect you from this. Even now, it executes you in the streets like sick dogs instead of offering aid when another attack could be imminent." He pauses for a moment before looking back at the drones, and goosebumps pimple my skin, reacting to the sudden change in the air. There's a peculiar weight to this silence.

An expectation.

"And so," he finally says, "I come to you with a proposition. *Join* us. Turn away from the State, let us help you, and together, we can create a new future of peace and prosperity where war is a thing of the past—a distant, terrible memory we tell our children about to warn them away from making the same mistakes we have. Rise up!" He slams his fist on the desk. "Rise up against the Enforcers who seek to enslave us! Help me prove to our attackers that we are not the enemy. We are *not* the State."

I stumble back a step. "No," I breathe, then more forcefully repeat it. So much for wanting to save the people—Nolan wants to turn them into his own personal army. Doesn't he see how that will backfire? Isn't he aware of the Enforcer patrols lined up throughout the Heart? They won't hesitate to shoot; by encouraging a revolt, he's only going to get everyone killed. And if everyone's dead, who then will he lead?

My hands curl into fists, my nails biting half-moons into my palms. I don't know what arrangement Nolan and Bilken made with the people attacking us, but I'm assuming this is all part of their plan—this unspoken assumption that the attacks will stop and they'll swoop in to help him seize control. That's the only explanation that makes any sense. The only reason I can see as to why even he would suggest this madness.

But someone coming to PHOENIX's aid at the eleventh hour isn't what's going to happen—I see that now as Bilken's old office disintegrates and I find myself outside the magistrates building, watching helplessly as Enforcers gun down unarmed citizens as they, in turn, are bombed from above. Corpses litter the ground, while before me, the massive structure—where Nolan and the other Heads wait out the attack—burns like a sacrificial pyre.

My surroundings change again until, once more, I'm back inside Bilken's office where Nolan screeches into a communicator. He coughs into his fist as a cloying gray smoke billows under the door and wafts into the room.

"That wasn't the deal," he rasps between coughs. "You never said you needed physical proof, just that she needed to die!"

My brows draw together as I take a step closer, straining my ears to hear the other side of the call past the mayhem and noise just outside.

"No. *No*, that's not what you said. You *said* to take her out of the picture, which we've done. Not to mention we handed you the DSD on a goddamn silver platter. You have the coordinates and the girl is dead, I swear it. I saw to it myself after I used her to convince the others of the attack—" His eyes widen. "W-What? That's not—"

The hum of an angry voice on the other end of the line interrupts him.

Indignation paints Nolan's cheeks bright red. "I'm not hiding the girl! She was a stain on this world. I wanted her gone as much as you did." He jerks his head in vehement denial, although there's no one here except me to see it. "Call off the attack as you agreed," he pleads. "Do that and I'll produce her body. I just need a little time to get out of the city to fi—"

He blanches, pulling the communicator away from his ear. He then stares at it for a long moment, his face draining of color when a message lights up the small screen. Inching toward him, I squint at the words which appear in bold letters, reading them over his shoulder.

PROOF OR NO PEACE

A short video clip replaces the words, showing a high-resolution image of my face close-up before panning out, giving me a better idea of when this footage was shot. Between my clothing and the length of my hair, it's clear this video—likely filmed from an enemy drone—was taken several months before when I was still under Dr. Richter's control and engaging in battle on behalf of the State.

My stomach sinks as Nolan throws the device to the floor. I was right. These people do know what I look like.

And just as I feared, Nolan's plan—his hope to establish peace between them—will fail.

"Damn it!" Nolan sinks to his knees, and as he combs his fingers through his ashy hair, he looks as helpless as I feel. But I have no sympathy for him, and a large part of me hopes he burns inside this building.

Like the State, he brought this upon himself.

Around me, the office goes black, my vision blurring as it always does when I'm dragged through time and thrust back into the present—into the grim reality where I belong. The walls of Bilken's washroom rebuild around me brick by brick, stone by stone, the concrete repainting itself snow white as I slump to the ground.

Heaving, I scan my bleary surroundings, and with my target in sight, I fling myself forward, spewing into the toilet as I clench my eyes shut. Pain is a sledgehammer against the inside of my skull, and when I finally pry my eyes open, it takes a few seconds for my horror to penetrate the agonizing pressure in my temples. Blood. There's so much blood. And not just dripping from my nose, but on the ground…and in the toilet bowl, the white porcelain stained with smears of crimson and black. I didn't so much as vomit as hurl my actual insides out of my body, and the sight of it triggers a terror stronger than any fear I've ever known in my life.

I collapse back against the nearest wall, sobbing. And not just because of how close I am now to death—its presence touching my skin like a phantom caress—but because of how pointless this destruction has been. Nolan was never going to get his peace. Even if he did have proof of my death, I'm sure our attackers would still change the terms at the last minute, citing some new stipulation for them to cease their attack on our home.

And I'm certain Bilken knew this would happen. His only concern has been getting us out of the State because that's what my mother asked of him. He's never cared about the damage left in our wake or what casualties would rack up as payment for our survival. He made that clear enough when he sentenced those Enforcers to death at the magistrates building two years ago.

I always thought Richter and Nolan were clever, but Bilken has played us all like fools. He is the real mastermind behind everything, dictating our movements while we carry on, none the wiser. And Nolan...

Nolan was just his latest victim, and behind the scenes, Bilken was whispering in his ear, using decades of desperation and lust for power to his own advantage.

Where does it end? I wonder weakly.

When do we stop manipulating each other?

I cough, and blood speckles the palm I press to my mouth, but I'm too tired to care or move. I can barely even find the strength to lift my eyes when a knock on the door pulls me out of my stupor.

"Wynter?"

Jenner opens the door before I can protest, stepping into the small, single-person washroom. He stops when he spots me in a near lifeless heap on the floor, the confusion creasing his brow immediately giving way to alarm.

"Shit!"

Rushing forward, he drops to his knees beside me, dirtying his pant legs on the blood-smeared tile. Without hesitation, he lifts his arms and bends as if to scoop me up, but then pauses, as if he's not sure he should touch me. I don't blame him. I don't think I've ever looked quite this sick before.

"I—" he begins to say, but I shake my head and he goes silent.

"Nolan," I manage.

He blinks. "What about him?" Then, understanding registers on his face and he says in a softer voice, "What did you see?"

"A broadcast. He..." The dryness in my throat is unbearable, making it too hard to speak. I try to swallow, but every effort is wasted and I only end up gagging, my tongue like sandpaper.

Realizing what I need, Jenner jumps to the sink and cups cool water in his hands. Then, lowering himself beside me again, he brings his fingertips to my lips. As he feeds it to me, the water dribbles from the sides of my mouth, but it satiates me enough to speak.

"He's going to try to stop the attack," I wheeze. "But...but it..."

"Stop it how?" Jenner asks.

"A public call for a ceasefire." I nod to myself, rewatching Nolan's one-sided conversation in my memory. "I think... I think that was...the plan. The way they intended to...establish peace, like Bilken said." I wince as another jagged cough escapes me. "But...it won't work."

Jenner is quiet for a moment as he considers the severity of my words. When he finally speaks, his tone is somber. "So, Bilken's connections go back on their deal?"

I shake my head as much as I'm able to.

"I'm not sure...they ever intended to honor it. At least, not the part of the deal...made with Nolan. They don't trust him. They know he was holding me outside the city, and now, they want proof of my death." *Proof or no peace*, the message to Nolan said. I shiver. "Without it, they won't honor the ceasefire... and they'll continue to bomb us until there's nothing left."

Until the Heart is nothing but ruins, like the desolate future I've seen so many times in my visions.

Jenner's mouth pulls down at the corners, and the misery in his gaze mirrors what I feel so acutely that I can't help wondering if I'm somehow sharing my pain with him.

"So," he mutters, "decimating the DSD was never going to be enough."

I wish it was. I wish this could have all ended with Richter's death.

But, like always, fate has other ideas.

I let out a pained laugh. "They know what I look like. If my mother were to try to smuggle me out, they'd recognize me. A new identity isn't enough. I'd need...a new face." I smile, laughing again under my breath, as if that notion is the funniest thing in the world.

Jenner's frown deepens, causing my smile to slip.

"They think Nolan is hiding me, keeping me in his back pocket. They want proof...or—"

"Let me guess, we all die?"

My silence is answer enough.

With a weary sigh, he runs a hand through his hair, pushing the strands back off his forehead. "What do we do?"

"Regardless of the role the State and Richter had in this war, I can't help... feeling responsible, too. I...want to find a way to stop it." *And to save you and Ezra.*

He shoots me a cautious glance. "Okay," he hedges, "but how do we do that?"

The only way we can.

"I think we need to pay PHOENIX a visit," I murmur.

Jenner's ebony brows shoot upward, making a reach for his hairline. "What? Why?" He holds up a hand as if to stop me. "You *do* realize they'll kill us—"

"They already tried that, remember?" My chest heaves, my lungs aching with the effort of each strenuous breath. Exhaling, I whisper, "They want a ceasefire… and thanks to Bilken, Nolan has a direct line to the enemy…even if they don't trust him. The Heads will hear me out, especially when I tell them about his hand in all this."

Jenner scoffs. "That's assuming they weren't in on it, too."

I offer a barely perceptible shrug, too exhausted to raise my shoulders any higher than the half-inch I manage. "It doesn't matter. The only way to end this attack is to make peace, and I…can offer that to them. I'll give them their proof."

Jenner's pupils blow wide at my words, and he lurches forward, placing his hands on my arms. His nails dig into my skin through my shirt. "If you think for one minute that Ezra or I will let you—"

"It isn't your decision, Jenner."

As this sentiment leaves my lips, a convulsion tears through me, and I gasp for breath as my lungs cough up fresh blood onto the floor. Jenner reaches for me, this time not hesitating to wrap an arm around my back to keep me upright.

"Shit, this is bad. I'm going to get your moth—"

He props me into the corner and moves to stand, but as he rises, I grab his shirt in my fist.

"Don't," I gasp. "Not yet. Please…just stay."

His lower lip wobbles as he crouches beside me. "You're not well. You need medical attention, which I can't give you."

My eyes flutter closed, and I huff out a laugh. "What good will that do at this point? I'm a…lost cause. The sooner you accept that, the better."

His warm fingers cup my cheek, and I lean into his touch, forcing my eyes open again. The swirling blue depths of his gaze in this moment remind me of the sky on the verge of a storm.

When he speaks, his voice is gentle but stern. "That won't stop Ezra or me from trying to find a way to save you. You're our family." Leaning in, he presses his forehead to mine. "We both love you. You know that, right?"

Family.

My heart clenches as tears burn the corners of my eyes. "I know." My fingers tighten in his shirt, and I peer up at him, pleading. "You won't leave, will you?"

He glances at the ajar washroom door for a moment before settling on the floor beside me, wrapping me in a towel and wiping away the crusting blood from my face. As he snakes an arm around my shoulders, pulling me close, I rest my cheek on his chest, listening to the soothing *thump thump* of his heart.

The consistent sound guides me away from the pain, and as my eyes drift closed, Jenner whispers, "Never."

SEVENTEEN

A **COMFORTING WARMTH ENVELOPS MY** body, and I wake to find myself back in bed, blanketed under the heat of the duvet. Blinking the sleep from my eyes, I raise a hand to my face and wipe at the skin just under my nose, expecting the dried blood—evidence of my worsening symptoms—to flake off at my touch. But, to my surprise, nothing comes away on my fingers. I'm clean, as if someone washed me while I was sleeping.

The memory of my last waking moments rush back.

Jenner.

I press a hand to my forehead, a dull pain lingering behind my temples. He must've brought me here after I passed out.

Groaning, I push into a sitting position, pausing mid-movement when my gaze snags on the dozing figure in the chair beside the bed. My chest tightens and I instantly relax.

As if attuned to my movements, Ezra snaps his eyes open, and he looks at me for a long moment, trapped in that disoriented stage between sleep and awake. When I offer him a smile, he draws in a breath and leans forward.

"Hi," he murmurs, his deep voice husky.

"Hi," I mutter back, my own croaky.

Rising from the chair, he shifts himself onto the mattress beside me. "How are you feeling?"

I shrug. "Okay, I guess. Did Jenner bring me here?"

A frown tugs at his lips as he nods. "I thought—" The words catch in his throat, and he swallows. "There was a moment there where I thought…"

I press a hand to his cheek when he looks away, turning his face back toward mine. "I'm fine," I whisper. For the moment. "Trust me, you'll know when it's time to worry."

Because you'll be there, holding the gun that will kill me.

But this seems to be the wrong thing to say because he jerks away from me, his lips pulled taut. Swinging his legs over the side of the bed, he stands to leave.

"Ezra—" I begin.

"No." He glares over his shoulder at me for a second, then looks away again. "You keep talking like it's inevitable. Like I'm supposed to just accept that you'll die."

Because it is. Because I will. But I can't bring myself to utter these words.

Exhaling, he lets his arms fall to his sides before slumping down onto the bed beside me again, this time with his back facing me. "I won't let you go. I've already lost too much."

The sorrow in his voice is like a blade edge against my skin, cutting so deeply I'm not sure the wounds will ever close. Biting back tears, I plant my cheek on his shoulder and wrap my arms around his torso, hugging him tightly from behind. His heartbeat drums under my fingers.

"I'm sorry," I gasp, but the apology sounds hollow, even to my own ears.

I wince at the dry ache in my windpipe. There's so much more I want to say, but the words get stuck in my throat and stay there, never reaching the liberation of my lips.

The time we had together might've been brief but at least it was ours.

The tears break through now, soaking the back of his shirt, but still, I don't speak. I can't bring myself to.

Not when there's nothing I can say to undo what we both know is coming.

My breath catches when Ezra pivots in my embrace, turning around to scoop me into his arms. His fingers weave through my hair, pulling my head into the space between his chin and chest.

"I won't give up," he says low in my ear, "even if you already have."

The door swings open and we startle apart, our eyes locking on Jenner, who stands at the threshold. "It's happening," he breathes, his eyes wide.

There's only one "it" he can be talking about. Straightening, I fist my hands in my lap to hide that every inch of my body is trembling. "The broadcast?"

He nods, then gestures for us to follow before turning and vanishing from the doorway.

Ezra and I don't exchange another word as he helps me up from the bed, and he keeps one arm latched around my waist as we exit my temporary quarters, stepping back into the open living space of the safe house. Everyone else is gathered already…or maybe they never left the room? It's growing increasingly difficult to keep track of time, and I can't say for certain how long we've been down here. One day? Two?

Too long, a snide voice says in the back of my head.

A dull ache spreads through my skull, each throb like the tick of a clock, reminding me that every second spent here is draining what little time I have left in this world. At this rate, my disease will kill me long before I get to Nolan. And if that happens…

Well, at that point, any hope of salvation for anyone is lost.

Sliding out of the loop of Ezra's arm, I pause beside the sofa and sink down onto the armrest, training my gaze on the illuminated screen on the wall, watching—as transfixed as the others—as Nolan makes his futile plea for peace. It's always strange to witness an event that's previously played out in one of my visions, like I'm being forced to watch a broadcast I've already seen. Even if I turned it off, the memory of his words would remain. As would the knowledge of their outcome.

"Eerie," Jenner mutters under his breath, shooting me an unsettled look. "You told me it would happen, but it's still weird as all hell actually hearing it."

An amused grins tempts the corners of my lips. "Now, you know what it's like for me."

Knowing the future is a curse disguised as a blessing, an unending nightmare that fuels me with the constant false hope that I can change what I've seen when time has proven, over and over again, that I can't. Even after everything I've been through, even after all the pain and loss I've suffered, part of me still clings to that hope.

Now, so close to the end, it's all I have left.

As Nolan rambles on, I watch without really listening, calm and content in my decision. I'll do whatever needs to be done to put an end to this war, so if that means surrendering myself to PHOENIX so they have their proof, then that's what I'll do. It's no different than what I was initially planning, and at this point, it's all I *can* do.

Before returning to the DSD to save Rai, I had already begun to realize this conflict would only end one way. There's no turning back, no altering the path or decisions that led us to this outcome. But that doesn't mean I'll go down without a fight or let Nolan use my death for his own personal gain. My end might be written in stone, but there's still time to change the future for everyone else.

Or die trying.

"There's still time," Rai whispers in my head in agreement.

When the broadcast concludes a few minutes later, the picture cuts out with a burst of static, then goes black before transitioning to a gray screen with the words PLEASE STAND BY stamped in the middle. In the bottom right corner, the State's insignia looms under the text—a clenched fist bursting out of tree roots; the general populace being the roots the State draws power from—as if to remind us who is really in charge. But the damage of PHOENIX's interference is done. They've exposed a chink in the State's armor by hacking its television servers and making this very public declaration of war, and now, doubt will begin to fester and spread through the Heart. Between the attack and Nolan's announcement, the people's eyes will be opened and they will see how tenuous the State's hold on them really is. They will switch sides, led by the belief they now have the freedom to alter the course of their lives.

Quinn is the first to break the silence, blowing out a loud breath through his nose. "Nolan was convincing, I'll give him that."

"Not to everyone, it would seem." Bilken's baritone draws my attention, and when our eyes meet, he cocks a questioning eyebrow, his stern gaze lingering on my face. I stiffen, challenging his stare for a moment, before it registers that he's talking about me.

Relaxing a little, I shrug. "Because I know it won't work."

"Of course, it will." He shoots me a patronizing look that seems to say I'm too naive to understand such matters. "A ceasefire was always the arrangement—"

"I don't *care* about your damn arrangements, or scheming, or plans," I snap. "Once your connections find out I'm alive, they won't honor any deals you made. Or, at least, not any made with Nolan."

Assuming they ever planned on honoring them at all.

My eyes spring wide at the thought. "You know, I'm starting to think maybe that was intentional. I mean, the only deal you really care about is the one that ensures you two"—I wag a finger back and forth between my mother and Bilken—"survive this whole mess, am I right?"

"And you," my mother protests, but I talk over her, keeping my eyes locked on Bilken.

"Or"—I shrug again—"maybe I'm wrong and you aren't as clever as you think. I mean, if you are, then I'm surprised you weren't prepared for this. That you weren't aware, despite your *extensive connections*, that our attackers would know what I look like." As a weighted silence descends on the room, I click my tongue. "Seems you didn't account for every possibility after all."

My hands curl into fists as I remember the harrowing scene that followed my vision of the broadcast. What I saw while the magistrates building burned.

Although I only witnessed one side of the exchange between Nolan and the people attacking our city, it was clear what our assailants were demanding.

My death.

Furious words spill from my lips in a rush. "Did you really think they'd just take Nolan at his word? Or that they wouldn't change their demands at the last minute?" Bilken is smart enough to know what people are like once they believe they have the upper hand. That notion of power makes us brazen. I saw it enough with Richter to know. "What was the deal you made, anyway?" I press.

Before he can answer, my mother throws her arms in the air with a frustrated huff. "This is ridiculous. Why wouldn't they honor the ceasefire? As far as they're concerned, you're *dead*. We did our part. We gave them the DSD—"

Jenner snorts. "Well, clearly, that wasn't enough. It seems your *friends*"—he hooks his fingers into air quotes—"knew, or at least suspected, that Wynter was being held outside the Heart, and now, they want proof of her rotting corpse. Those are the new terms."

"Proof or no peace," I murmur, repeating the words I saw blazing across Nolan's communicator screen.

My mother flinches, and her eyes are daggers cutting into my soul as her gaze jumps to mine. "You know this?" she asks, and I can hear in her tone how desperately she's hoping I'll say no. When I nod, her frown deepens and she looks down at the floor. "Well, all the more reason for us to leave immediately, then. We need to get out before leaving is no longer an option."

"I'm sorry, did you not hear the part where they'll know who she is?" Jenner leans forward, his expression mutinous. "They're willing to let this entire city burn on a hunch that Wynter is alive, so what makes you think we have a chance in *hell* of getting out of the Heart unnoticed? Or that we'd even want to leave? This is our home. Someone has to fight for it—"

I shake my head. "No, Jenner, she's right." Before he can protest, I shift my tired gaze to my mother's. "You're right. You *should* go. In fact, you should *all* go...as far away from this place and from me as possible."

Except Ezra, a voice that sounds eerily like Alivia Laramie breathes in my ear. A somber reminder of the role he has yet to play.

Echoing that thought, Ezra says, "That isn't happening." He touches my left cheek, pressing slightly, forcing me to look up at him where he stands resolute on my right. When our eyes meet, he murmurs, "Where you go, I go. Remember?"

Jenner tsks, knocking my shoulder with his. "Seriously, how many times do we have to say it?" When I glance at him, he rolls his eyes. "You know we aren't leaving you alone in all this."

My chest tightens at their words, and I bite the inside of my cheek to hold back the resurfacing threat of tears. I wish they would stop fighting for me. I wish they would just let me go.

After all, we're nearing the point when they'll have to.

Bilken lets out a chastising laugh. "After everything we've done to get you away from the State, you now want to stay behind and burn along with it? Or are you misguided enough to think you can stop this war, Miss Reeves? You are the one who created it."

White hot anger floods my body like heat, and scowling, I push forward onto my feet. "Which is precisely why I'm the only one who can stop it. These people attacking us are only here because of what *I* have done."

And because he gave them incentive to strike.

I step forward, and Bilken recoils a little, like prey caught in the gaze of a predator. His hand flies to his throat on reflex—a trauma response from when I choked him at the bunker—and the apprehension radiating off him as I approach is so palpable I can almost taste it, like a dank odor permeating the room.

I look down at him where he sits next to my mother. "I don't care how valuable you think you are, they wouldn't have made that deal with you unless they viewed me as a threat. And it doesn't matter if Richter and the State were behind all this, I'm still the one who did the killing. I'm still the one who decimated entire armies. This began with me—"

"Wait a minute," Ezra interrupts, his tone wary. "What exactly are you proposing?"

I hesitate for a moment, worrying my lower lip between my teeth before forcing myself to peer over my shoulder at him. Those hazel eyes I've looked into so many times stare me down, their warm honey depths rife with a fear I know all too well from my vision.

Keeping my expression neutral, I glance at Jenner, who slumps back into the sofa cushions, making it a point to evade my gaze. His avoidance is all the confirmation I need.

It seems he didn't tell Ezra about our little bathroom conversation, and I'm not sure how to feel about that. On the one hand, if he already knew what I'm planning, that would take the sting out of what I'm about to say. On the other, it's only fair if he hears it from me.

Breathing in, I force my eyes back to Ezra, and when I speak, my voice is a jagged-edged whisper. "That I give them the proof they want."

Understanding drains the color from his complexion. "No." He stumbles forward, and fury instantly hardens his face. "*No.* I won't let you die for this—"

"What other choice is there?" I ask, and he stops dead in his tracks. Looking around the room at each of the others' silent, staring faces, I growl, "Whether or not any of you want to admit it, I'm running on borrowed time. You might not want to hear it, but I'm going to die. Soon." *And leaving this city won't escape what's coming. This war isn't the ticking time bomb, counting down to impending explosion.*

I am.

But ending this conflict is the right thing to do, and if handing myself over for execution kills two birds with one stone, then I'll do it. I'd do anything to guarantee Ezra and Jenner survive and to preserve the future for them. Even if I'm not part of it.

"Go or don't go," I mutter, "but I'm staying."

And nothing any of you say will change my mind.

I can't let it.

Rising from the sofa, my mother steps toward me. "Wynter, I didn't do all this for you to stay behind and try to be a hero—"

She raises a hand, but I step back before she can touch me.

"I'm no hero," I counter, "and I didn't ask you to intervene. Every choice you've ever made was done on your own and without my input or consent."

A crazed laugh escapes me at the realization of how much I've changed since the day of my placement exam. Before this disease, I would've never spoken this way to anyone, least of all my mother. But I'm not that frightened little girl anymore. I'm different. Stronger. And I've found my voice.

That thought encourages me to be brave.

"I've had very little say in the events of my life. So, this?" *The last thing I ever do...* "This will be my choice, understand?"

I turn again, locking eyes with Ezra, who grimaces, arms tense and shaking at his sides.

"Do you really expect me to just stand by and watch as you hand yourself over to be *killed*?" His words are a furious growl, and the pain in his heart is reflected on his face, swarming those warm eyes in shadow.

Closing the distance between us, I flatten my hands against his cheeks and rise onto the tips of my toes, gently pressing my lips to his. "No," I whisper, so softly only he can hear. "I expect you to remember your promise."

"Promise you'll kill me."

When I release him, he takes a step back, his gaze distant as his anger fades and he wilts under the weight of my words. Jenner glances between us, his confusion evident in his downturned brow. He looks at me, his intense gaze relaying his unspoken question, but I shake my head.

Silence swallows the room like a black hole sucking all sound from the world, and I stand still, feeling the hot touch of everyone's watchful gazes as exhaustion creeps through me. I can't delay any longer. If I'm going to go, it needs to be now.

"I'll go with you."

With a grunt, Quinn pushes off the sofa and stands, keeping one hand on his injured side. Holding my gaze, he extends the other toward me.

A peace offering.

I blink at him, stunned. "What? You're injured, and last I checked, this arrangement was your ticket out of this city."

"True," he agrees. "But I left the Enforcers because of moral differences. How can I stand here and say I'm any different than the State if I leave this city to burn?" When I still don't take his proffered hand, his lips pinch into an offended glower. "Look, do you want my help or not?"

I consider him for a moment, wondering how much I can trust him before reminding myself of the only fact that matters. Quinn saved our lives. Twice.

And in this world, you can't get much more loyal than that.

"Okay," I breathe, taking his hand. And we shake.

"Although..." Quinn says, trailing off.

"Although what?" I ask, unable to mask the uneasy edge to my tone.

As I retract my hand, he frowns. "Well, it won't be easy getting to Nolan. He's holed up in the magistrates building, and since we can't exactly use the route PHOENIX planned to get there, we'll have to travel topside again, like before. Trouble is, there are at least a dozen checkpoints between where we are right now and there. We'll need transport...and cover."

His eyes swing to the left and mine follow, landing on my mother. Quinn's right. We got lucky before, getting, first, to the DSD and then to the safe house undetected, and now that Nolan has challenged the State's rule, it's all but guaranteed it will respond in force, deploying Enforcers to stop anyone who tries to freely move throughout the city. Hell, we already had a few close calls.

Although I don't want to rely on her any more than I have to, I face my mother, my decision made. "Everything you've done has only gotten people I love killed. I don't *want* your help...but I need it. So, help us. Get me there."

Her cobalt eyes are piercing. "If I do this, I'd be leaving you in this city to die. After everything I've done to get you back, how can you ask me to do that?"

"I'm already dying," I remind her. "Besides, you did it once before." A rueful smile twists my lips, and I shrug. "How hard can it be?"

A pained expression flits across her face, and she lets out a near silent laugh.

"You'll never forgive me, will you?" she rasps.

Drawing in a calming breath, I take a tentative step toward her and hold out a hand like Quinn just did to me. Then, looking her square in the eye, I nod.

"I will if you help me end this war."

EIGHTEEN

 depart Bilken's safe house. While, under normal circumstances, the cover of darkness would have masked our movements, there are too many blockades erected throughout the city now to reach the magistrates building unnoticed. Going at night would've only aroused unwanted suspicion, leaving us with no other option but to proceed during the day and hope no one questions what we're doing or looks too closely at the vehicle we'll be hiding in. If they do, I'll have to act—to create a path for us—which I don't want to do unless I absolutely have to. I'm so tired of killing, and using my power will only push me that much closer to death.

A risk I can't afford until this is over.

We emerge from the obscured path into the empty parking structure above the safe house, the only sound in the morning the cacophony of our footsteps as we approach the truck. The smoke and dust clouding the air have both settled a bit since I was last outside, the ash a thin layer of gray on the pavement, resembling a fresh dusting of snow that shouldn't be possible considering the structure is under cover and any exposure to the elements from here is limited.

My eyes shift to the nearest open stretch in the wall before me, scanning what I can see of the silent city beyond. Despite the returning clarity to the air, my nose wrinkles at the sulphuric stink that seems to cling to every surface around us. I breathe through my mouth to escape the scent, but the taste it leaves on my tongue isn't much better.

Grimacing, I hang to one side of the truck as my mother and Bilken prepare for our departure, conversing in hushed voices with the Enforcer who served as our driver before—then our watchdog while we were all hunkered down in the

"""

safe house—and with Quinn and Ezra, who are actively involving themselves with the plan. Although I should be listening, I find myself tuning their voices out on reflex, too mentally drained after the endless chatter of the last two or however many days it's been since we got here to take in any new information.

So, instead, I observe. I observe and I try to force myself to stay calm despite knowing how close I am now to my death.

And to the deaths of everyone if my plan doesn't work.

Shaking the thought from my head, I watch, bemused, as the Enforcer gestures for Quinn to join him in the truck, extending a hand to help him up onto the bed before advising him to strip off his clothes.

As I turn away to give them privacy for whatever it is they're doing, my eyes land on the only member of our party keeping his distance from this congregation. Jenner leans against the wall just beside the concealed entrance leading down to Bilken's safe house, arms crossed and eyes downcast on the floor.

My fingers fidget with the hem of my jacket, my teeth sinking into my bottom lip as I cross the large, empty space, closing the canyon of distance between us. So much has happened in only a few days, with Jenner focusing solely on me and my problems while suffering in silence, shoving his own heartache aside. My chest tightens at the thought of what unspoken emotions he must be bottling up even now, and I fear the resentment that might be growing inside him.

Resentment towards me for forcing him into such close proximity with the woman responsible for his pain.

I gulp, pushing down the rising lump in my throat. I see him, I see his grief, and the last thing I want is for him to think that I don't.

His eyes find mine as I draw closer, his sullen expression easing a little. In typical Jenner fashion, he offers me a lopsided smile.

"I see I'm not the only one who's grown tired of the planning brigade over there."

He arches a brow, peering past me, and with a quiet laugh, I follow his sardonic gaze, looking over my shoulder at the rest of the group. He's not wrong. All they've done since last night is discuss routes, potential pitfalls, and just about anything else we might encounter today.

Sighing, I step forward and turn on my heel, leaning against the smooth concrete wall beside him.

"I'm sorry if I've made you feel like you have to go through with this or tolerate my mother for my sake. I know you don't like accepting her help. Believe me, I don't either," I mutter. Shifting so my back is facing the others, I look him square in the eye, lowering my voice to a whisper. "But we need it. If something goes wrong…" I shake my head. "I can't take out that many Enforcers. Not without the collar." Not unless I want to risk decimating an entire city block and everyone near it. Or triggering the vision I'm in a race to outrun. "We need to at least *try* to get there without bloodshed."

Raising his hand in a fist, Jenner gives me a gentle, playful knock on the chin. "You haven't forced me into anything, Wynter. I am and will always be there for you, no matter what. And no matter who else might be, too. But…" Frowning, he glances over my shoulder, and the silence between us stretches on for a moment too long.

Reaching out, I touch his hand. "But what?"

His frown deepens. "Will you really forgive her after everything she's done? After what she did to your father? Some people don't deserve forgiveness…or to live in peace."

I nod, repositioning my back to the wall. "Maybe not. But if telling her I'll forgive her means keeping you and Ezra alive, then it's worth it to me. They're just words," I mutter, shaking my head again. "If they mean that much to her, she can have them."

The clomp of boots on tarmac draws my attention, and I look to my left, spotting Quinn, who walks toward us dressed in an Enforcer's uniform, tugging at the collar with one hand while the other holds the matching helmet tucked under his arm. His face is set in a scowl and he looks uncomfortable, reminding me of the first time I saw him.

Once we're within earshot, he stops and jerks his head toward the truck. "It's time to go," he says.

"Ready?" I ask with a backward glance at Jenner.

He shrugs, the barest grin touching his lips. "As I'll ever be."

We make our way toward the others without exchanging another word, Quinn proceeding at a clipped pace a few strides ahead. Once we reach the truck, he indicates for us to get in, and upon approaching the open back doors, the first thing I notice is the unfamiliar man standing at attention nearby. He's dressed in black clothes I know I've seen before, the fabric soiled with blood on the side of the torso.

Quinn's clothes, I realize on closer inspection.

Although a fresh outfit was waiting for me—spare garments my mother prepared to replace the DSD-issue clothes I was wearing—Bilken didn't have anything on hand for the others, not even Quinn, who was an active part of their plot. Our pit stop at the safe house was never included in their plan to flee the State and it's possible, even if it had been, he didn't anticipate having so many extra bodies to account for.

Still, given what I know about him, I found this lack of preparation odd, further fueling my assumption that he never intended to ensure the safe escape of anyone other than himself, my mother, and, begrudgingly, me. When I pointed out his poor planning on the matter, he merely scoffed and said arrangements had been made to accommodate us once we fled the city, although who that "us" was referring to, he didn't say. The bitterness in his voice when speaking of these arrangements—arrangements I was purposely rejecting—was enough to dissuade me from asking.

We didn't talk about clothes or leaving the city again after that.

For Ezra and Jenner, the lack of new attire wasn't a pressing issue. They weren't wearing anything branded with insignia or visibly recognizable that might put our identities or mission in jeopardy, unlike me with my military grade bodysuit. But for Quinn, not having that option to change meant remaining in garments stained with his own blood.

My gaze jumps back and forth between him and the Enforcer in my mother's employ, and as I once again observe the regulation uniform on Quinn, I find myself wondering why, exactly, they swapped.

"Planning on rejoining?" I joke, cocking a brow at him.

He doesn't even crack a smile, his tone husky as he says, "It'll be easier to get through this unchallenged if they think I'm one of them. Call it a fail-safe."

"And him?" I press, nodding at the Enforcer, who looks strangely naked without his uniform and helmet. "I take it he's not coming with us?" If I had to guess, the deal my mother made with Quinn wasn't extended to everyone in her employ.

Quinn responding snort is dismissive. "Don't know. Don't care. Ask your mother or Bilken if you want to know so badly."

Wincing, he climbs into the back of the truck, then kneels, releasing a circular spring-loaded plate in the floor with his thumb. The button—no larger than a watch face—pops up with a click, exposing a catch, which Quinn grabs and yanks back to reveal a hidden compartment under the metal sheeting.

Leaning forward, I peer into the dark, empty space, confusion spreading through me like a chill.

"You need to hide," Quinn clarifies when I look up at him.

Hide? My brow furrows as I assess the cramped space. *In there?*

"Another fail-safe?" I ask.

Beside me, Jenner balks. "I know you don't expect me to climb into *that*. Small spaces aren't really my thing." He shudders.

Quinn clambers to his feet and looks over us like a disappointed parent. "Need I remind you, we got lucky last time. There's no way we'll make it through a dozen checkpoints without at least one Enforcer checking back here. They won't suspect me if I'm dressed like one of them. But you?" He scoffs at the thought. "We need to get *there*"—he points in what I assume is the general direction of the magistrates building—"with as little fuss as possible. Unless you'd prefer to just kill everyone in our path?" He narrows his eyes at me.

Jenner and I both shake our heads before silently doing as we've been instructed, climbing up into the truck and exchanging one last dubious look before taking turns to lower ourselves into the hidden compartment, lying flat until we're squished under the floor like a pair of sardines.

A moment later, Ezra appears overhead and climbs in beside us without saying a word. Grunting, we shift as much as we can to make room for all three of us to fit, but it's snug and the space is overwhelmingly warm, already making me sweat.

"This will be cozy," Jenner grumbles under his breath.

On my other side, Ezra's fingers wrap around mine. "You can still change your mind," he whispers. "We can go out the way we came in and all leave this city together."

The strangled hope in his voice draws my gaze.

"And then what?" I counter. "Regardless of where we go, I still…" *Die*, I finish in my head. *Regardless of where we go, I still die.*

Drawing in a shaking breath, I dare to imagine a life outside this city's walls. A life where I am healthy and free. A life where Ezra and Jenner are safe and *stay* safe from the threat of war.

But only one of those things can happen, and I know, without a doubt, which life I choose.

When I swallow, the shifting of my throat is deafening in the confined space.

"I've seen what's coming, and if we abandon the Heart now, the people we leave behind will be slaughtered. If that happens, especially when we had the means to prevent it, then Quinn was right. We are no better than the State. Or PHOENIX. Or the people attacking us. All sides are guilty in this." *Even me.* A tear escapes, sliding down the side of my face. "It needs to end."

"Okay," Jenner says, jumping in before Ezra can speak. He grabs my other hand, and when I look at him in the darkness, he smiles. "Then, let's end it together."

NINETEEN

THE CRAMPED COMPARTMENT IS UNCOMFORTABLE as the truck bounces along the empty streets, the tarmac littered with glass and debris. Even without seeing it, I can envision how badly Zone 1 has been hit by the bombings, the impact devastating, even in the areas beyond our attackers' targets. I can feel every rock, every pop of the broken shards beneath the tires, and the vibrations marking our forward progression flood the metal coffin-like space, whirring in my ears like white noise.

Beyond the low hum of the truck, I can just make out the occasional sprinkle of gunfire, but trapped in the darkness, I'm blind to what's happening outside— what mayhem is raining down over the city. My imagination doesn't help, filling the empty seconds that follow with screams.

I clamp my eyes shut and draw in one deep breath after another to steady my heart, which only grows more frantic in my confinement. My pulse skitters under my skin until I feel the racing tempo everywhere. In my throat. Behind my eyes. I can even hear it in my ears, a low *ba-dum ba-dum* that only escalates my increasing anxiety.

A sheen of sweat coats my skin, and drops of perspiration slide from my forehead down the sides of my face. The space under the floorboards is a hot box cooking me alive.

Hysteria grips me as I squirm against the two bodies pressed close on each side of my own, the proximity making it hard to breathe. Swallowing despite the grating dryness in my throat, I focus on satiating the burning need in my lungs, but no matter how many times I draw in a breath, each inhalation feels like my last. The pressure building in my chest is a crushing weight pinning me down to the floor.

Whatever self-control I had learned with my collar is lost as I succumb to my panic, leaving my fragile mind unguarded to the vision that suddenly strikes in the blackness. Gunfire. Bodies. Flames. One after another, these images enter my thoughts, showing me what I can't see with my eyes.

Just as I knew it would, the Heart has devolved into a state of complete anarchy. Everyone has turned on each other. The Enforcers against the people. The people against each other. Around me, all I see is death. So much loss.

So much needless destruction.

The gunshots I hear beyond the reinforced walls of the truck echo in my head, projecting from the images like I'm in two places at once, the vision mimicking reality. My eyes burn, and I tremble against the hard floor, weeping and wishing for this assault on my senses to stop. But it doesn't. If anything, the vision only strengthens its hold, digging deeper into my consciousness.

Forcing me to see what my existence has led to.

A sticky wetness pools under my nose as pain slashes through my temples, pulling a scream from my throat, which is quickly muffled by a hand over my mouth. A gasp slips through my covered lips, and I startle at the touch of hot breath on my ear. "It will end. You'll get through it, but you need to be quiet. Breathe, Wynter. Just *breathe.*"

The tension in my body eases at the soothing sound of Ezra's voice, the violent tide of the visions instantly ebbing. On my other side, warm fingers wrap around mine.

"It's okay," Jenner whispers. "We're right here with you."

Above us, a booted foot stomps down hard on the floor, rattling the metal plating. "We're coming up on the first checkpoint," Quinn warns.

My insides turn liquid, and tears squeeze from my eyes as I bite my lower lip to tamp down my whimpers. As we come up on the checkpoint, Ezra keeps his hand clamped over my mouth.

We make it through the first two checkpoints unscathed. At the first, the Enforcers guarding the blockade granted us passage almost immediately upon learning my mother's identity, satisfied with her story about transporting medical equipment to a safe location. They didn't even consider checking the truck. But at the second, the Enforcers only relented once Bilken intervened, although not before questioning why he and my mother were together—their positions in our society unrelated, rousing suspicion as to why their paths would cross if they weren't partnered. He didn't dignify them with a response, instead—rather haughtily—taking a moment to remind the soldiers who he is. Bilken holds one of the highest positions in the State, and while he isn't personally in charge of our country's military force, he *is* partly responsible for its recruitment. To join the Enforcers, the CEO of W. P. Headquarters must personally approve and sign off on every transfer request. Without him, the State wouldn't even have a military to speak of.

Once the truck is far enough away from the second checkpoint, Quinn stomps his foot on the floor again. "How are you three doing down there?"

Jenner laughs under his breath, then shouts back, "We're having a grand old time, aren't we, guys? Couldn't be more comfortable!"

On my other side, Ezra snorts.

By the time we reach the third checkpoint, the seconds feel more like hours and the minutes more like days until it seems like I'll never get out of this truck. My whimpers have ceased, the pain in my head fading to a dull ache, and Ezra has long since removed his hand from my mouth, although his hand never strays far, his fingers gently stroking my cheek. I turn into his touch, matching my breathing to his, as the tires beneath us roll to a stop.

Like at the last two checkpoints, I can just make out the muted conversation.

"Identification?" a gruff male voice asks. There's something peculiar, something I can't quite pinpoint, about the way he says this word.

There's a brief pause, and I can all too clearly envision my mother presenting her wrist to their scanner along with the look of sheer disdain on her face. If she's nervous or afraid, I highly doubt the soldier would know it.

"Dr. Evelyn Adler..." The Enforcer trails off, but there's a deliberating edge to the way he says her name that triggers goosebumps all over my body, even in the suffocating heat of the underfloor box. I strain my ears, waiting for him to continue, and in the lull, I'm certain I could hear a pin drop. "You work for the DSD?"

My mother's answering tone is bored. "That's what it says, doesn't it?"

The Enforcer whistles, as if signaling to someone out of earshot, then shouts, "Everyone out of the truck!"

"For what reason?" my mother questions, but the usual authority behind her words wavers a little. "You are interfering with sanctioned—"

I suck in a breath at the sharp click of a gun being cocked.

"Shut your mouth, lady, or I'll shut it for you. Now,"—there's the tinny sound of the driver's side door wrenching open—"get out of the truck." After a short pause, he adds, "You two, check the back."

I note the heavy tromp of boots approaching, the sound all too familiar after all the time I spent accompanied by Enforcers. It grows louder as the weight at the front of the vehicle shifts. My mother and Bilken must've climbed down from their seats and disembarked the truck as instructed.

"I think this is all a misunderstand—" Bilken begins, but his protest is silenced by a blood-curdling *thwack* that sends a ripple of dread racing through every inch of my body. A heavy thud follows, and even with the thick, metal carcass around us, I can hear my mother gasping.

My panic burrows deeper, making the cramped compartment feel even smaller, but I barely have time to process what's befallen my mother and Bilken before the back doors of the truck are forced open.

On each side of me, Ezra and Jenner go still, holding their breath, and I do the same, listening. Above us, Quinn is perfectly quiet.

"Hey, you," a new voice grumbles. "Why are you alone back here? Where's the rest of your unit?"

Like the first Enforcer who spoke, his accent is slightly clipped. Strange. Did the State call in reinforcements from the other eight cities that, along with the Heart, form our country—assuming they haven't also been caught up in the assault? I've never met anyone from outside the capital to know if we all sound the same.

Quinn clears his throat. "I've been reassigned as a temporary escort for Dr. Adler until the crisis is over. I was instructed to stay with her and Mr. Bilken until they're at a safe location."

There's a tremor in Quinn's voice, but I doubt it's from fear—I've seen him in worse situations and he's a far cry from the spooked soldier I met months ago. If anything, it sounds like he's in pain, and I wonder if the medication my mother has been giving him to stave off the discomfort of his injury is wearing off. He was only recently shot, and I'm still amazed he wanted to come with us considering how close to death's door he had seemed that first day, in the hours after it happened. I suppose it says something about his stubborn need to maintain his moral high ground on the issue of our country that he's on this mission at all.

"Get out of the vehicle," the Enforcer barks.

Quinn does as he's told, his boots bearing down on the metal plating in slow, careful steps as he inches toward the open doors and the awaiting Enforcer below on the pavement. The truck shifts again from the displacement of weight when he jumps down into the road.

There's a second of agonizing silence, then the harsh slap of palms against the floor right above us.

"It isn't customary to search one of our own," Quinn grunts. He bites back a groan. The Enforcer must've grazed his wound.

"I'll do a lot worse if you don't shut up."

I frown, staring hard at the ceiling—even though I can't see anything in the darkness of the box—imagining Quinn's hands on the other side. He's right. Why would an Enforcer target another Enforcer? I've never seen that happen, not even in the year I worked closely alongside the State's military.

My frown deepens. Something about this whole thing feels off. There's the faint rustle of clothing as Quinn is patted down and his weapons are confiscated, his muttered cursing just audible through the floor.

My breaths grow increasingly ragged in the enclosed space, my heartbeat thunderous in my ears. But past the building cacophony of my hysteria, I note a near imperceptible click in the panel above my face—my ears acutely aware of every sound in an effort to balance my deprived senses.

"You find it?" the first voice calls out from the front of the truck.

"No," the soldier nearest us answers, yelling back, "She isn't here."

She?

Comprehension is a hand tightening around my lungs. Enforcers are searching the city for me—what other "she" could they possibly mean? But why? Richter is dead and no one in the State has seen me since I boarded the transport helicopter Jenner blew up to extract me. For all I know, everyone I was in contact with during my time at the DSD assumed I perished in the explosion that claimed so many others. Even if they *had* thought I survived, I didn't think anyone other than Richter and Bilken knew I was back in the Heart. I killed all the soldiers guarding the East Gate, and anyone in power still living after the attack would have no reason to believe I'd be in this city, let alone alive.

So, who could've sent them? Are they being directed by someone I'm unaware of? Someone hoping to use me to control the outcome of this war?

What am I missing?

"Where is she?" the first Enforcer shouts, drawing my split attention to the front of the truck.

"Who?" my mother coos with mock innocence.

When the soldier next speaks, his voice is a threatening growl. "Your little monster. You work for the DSD, so you should know. *Where is she?*" he asks again, enunciating each syllable slowly.

"I don't know what you're talking about—"

A sharp slap cuts her off. "Don't lie, bitch!"

My body is a tightening coil springing to snap. I resent my mother. On some level, I hate her. But that doesn't mean I want her to die or to be executed like some helpless animal in the street.

I have to do something.

I have to stop this before anyone else gets killed because of me.

Ezra, sensing the change in me, moves his hand from my mouth to my wrist, his grip tight, bordering on painful. "Don't," he warns, his voice a fierce whisper, but I barely hear him, too preoccupied with the scuffle of footsteps outside the truck.

"Get them down on the ground. And shoot that one. See if it jogs her memory."

Panic writhes within me, and my insides feel slippery, like I'm going to be sick. Who was the Enforcer talking about? Shoot who? Bilken?

Quinn?

The thought of the ex-Enforcer taking another bullet after everything he's done to help not only me but Ezra and Jenner is one step over a line I'm not willing to cross. Driven by my protective instincts, I shoot my hand out, clawing at the panel above me.

"Wynter—"

I ignore Ezra's protest, shaking off his and Jenner's combined attempts to hold me back. The false floor gives way with ease when I push, and as I climb out of the shadows of our hiding place, it occurs to me what that click I heard before was.

Quinn unlocked the compartment, I realize. When he was being searched against the truck bed, he popped the latch in the hidden door, setting us free.

No, not free, I correct myself. Because he didn't intend for us to run.

What he wanted was to set me loose.

The back doors of the truck hang wide on their hinges, offering me a perfect view of Quinn, who faces me on his knees in the road, hands clasped in surrender behind his head. The Enforcer who searched him is standing to his left, aiming a pistol at his right temple—his back turned toward me as he barks orders at another soldier beyond my line of sight.

I step forward, drawing in a steadying breath, and as my feet reach the edge of the truck bed, Quinn's gaze shoots up from the cracked pavement, locking on mine. Inhaling again, I close my eyes.

The power in my mind is like tentacles reaching out, searching for the soldiers' heartbeats and using the draw of each *thump* to pinpoint their positions around us. I sense six in total.

This time, instead of expanding outward, the bubble of pressure in my chest is like a black hole, ready to suck everything in.

To destroy.

I call that destructive force to the surface before the soldiers are even aware of my presence, envisioning the bone structure of their spinal columns as I jerk my own head to the side. The sole Enforcer in my range of vision drops to the ground. To the side of the truck, I note the identical thud of a limp body hitting dirt.

Two down, I muse, stumbling backward. I try to reach out again to the Enforcers at the front of the vehicle—to make sure I got them, too—but the flash of pain cutting into my temples makes it too hard to zero in on them a second time.

I thrust out a hand toward the side of the truck to catch myself when my legs buckle. Chest heaving, I look down at Quinn, who lowers his hands, a harrowed frown on his face. He glances around, his complexion ashen, before calling up to me, but whatever he says is drowned out by the hum in my skull.

Exhaustion drains the strength from my legs, and my knees bend on reflex, giving out and pitching my body forward over the lip of the truck bed. Strong arms catch me mid-fall, tugging me back, and I instantly recognize the warmth and smell that encases me despite the added odor of sweat.

Eyes glassy, I peer over my shoulder at Ezra. "I'm fine," I mutter, finding my feet. "I'm okay."

Holding onto his arms for support, I push myself upright then glance down at Quinn, who is crouched over the body of the Enforcer who held a gun to his head, a puzzled look crossing his face.

"What is it?" I ask as Ezra helps me down from the truck. Jenner follows closely on my other side, brushing the sweat-dampened hair off his forehead.

Quinn glares at us. "These aren't Enforcers. Look."

He rolls the dead man onto his side, propping him up with one hand on his shoulder while pointing with the other to the embroidered crest on the left sleeve of his uniform. The symbol is barely visible against the black fabric.

As if they intended for it not to be seen.

Quinn lets go of the dead soldier, letting his lifeless body flop back to the ground. "The uniform isn't exactly the same but it's close, especially with the helmets. If I had to guess, they took those off the Enforcers who were originally stationed here."

"And who are probably dead now," Jenner mutters.

Quinn nods. "What better way to ambush someone than to pose as one of their own?"

My eyes widen when the answer clicks in my brain. The unusual accents. The strange, black insignia.

"It's them," I whisper. "The people Nolan made his deal with."

In my memory, I glimpse flashes of the magistrate's building burning and of innocent people gunned down in the streets. This invader Bilken brought into our lives—no, that *I* brought into our lives—is only here because of me. Only killing our people because of me. Because of what I have done to countries like theirs, my actions on behalf of the State merciless. And now, because of the fear I've instilled within them, they're inflicting the same kind of slaughter on us, killing without remorse, carving a path through the city while looking for me.

Just as I knew they would.

Ezra snorts. "So much for waiting until peace was established."

I glance at him, suppressing a grimace. He's right. Bilken said the enemy would offer military support to PHOENIX—that they would sweep through the Heart, offering the needed numbers to supplant the State. To remove it from power. But this feels much more covert. Like these soldiers were here on a specific mission.

Not to help establish peace in the city.

A shout drags my attention back toward the front of the truck, and glancing at the others, it dawns on me that our party is short two members. My voice is hoarse, my mouth bone dry, as I force out the words, "Where's my mother?"

Quinn retrieves his weapons from the body of the enemy soldier. Then, nodding to Ezra and Jenner, he skirts around the right side of the truck while they both go around the left, guns drawn and at the ready. I follow closely at Quinn's heels despite the exhaustion pushing at the underside of my skin.

As we come around to the front of the vehicle, sticking close to the cab for cover, I glimpse my mother on the ground less than ten feet away, kneeling beside Bilken, who is on the ground, unconscious. Maybe even dead. Her hands are pressed to his head, blood seeping between her interlaced fingers. Around them lie the prone bodies of three soldiers, their necks bent at unnatural angles. The fake Enforcers I killed only moments before.

That only makes five, I note with unease, and then I see him—the sixth soldier I sensed. The one my power failed to reach.

He's cowering behind the barricade erected across the road, but, unlike the others, he's not wearing an Enforcer's helmet, his pasty, stricken face on full display. Shouting again, he aims his rifle at my mother.

"You're not her! I've seen her face… You're not her!" His cries are incoherent, and his eyes bulge with terror as they dance across the crumpled bodies of the soldiers between them. "What did you do to them?" he screams.

Quinn crouches, aiming his gun, but before he can shoot, I brush past him and walk out into the open street, exposing myself to the soldier. Recognition flashes across his face.

"She didn't do this. I did."

As these words leave my lips, I jerk my head to the side, using my power again despite the excruciating pain that follows. Pressure squeezes my skull, and the tang of blood coats my nostrils and the back of my tongue, but I barely notice either beyond the war occurring in my thoughts. All I can focus on is that soldier.

When he falls, I find myself torn between succumbing to the guilt of all the deaths I keep causing or slinking back into the safety of numbness, far away from where I don't have to feel anything, just like I did when I was the State's weapon. The numbness is tempting, and yet, I know feeling nothing would be giving the monster exactly what it wants.

And I don't want to exit this life as the monster everyone thinks I am.

Clenching my teeth, I choose to embrace the guilt but push it aside for the moment, my blurring gaze tripping on my mother and Bilken, whose face is slack, his eyes closed. His head wound is still bleeding profusely despite my mother's best attempts to stop it.

Stumbling forward, I wipe away the fresh blood from my nose. "Are you okay?" I ask, standing over her. Although I can sense them behind us, Ezra, Jenner, and Quinn all keep their distance, giving us space.

My mother doesn't look up at me. "Yes, but Wren's injured."

"What happened?" I press, although I'm certain I already know the answer.

She shakes her head. "That asshole struck him with the butt of his rifle. I think he might have even cracked his skull. I need to clean the wound and stitch it up before he loses too much blood." Lifting her gaze, she glances past me toward the others. "There's a first aid kit in the truck. Will one of you grab it?"

Ezra yanks open the vehicle's passenger door and climbs inside, emerging a few seconds later with the first aid kit clasped in his hand. When he presents the metal box to my mother, she nods for him to put his hands on Bilken's skull in place of hers, offering the needed pressure to staunch the bleeding while she prepares the supplies to disinfect and close the wound. To my surprise, Ezra does so without question, planting his hands on Bilken's head. He only moves them once my mother is ready to work, handing her gauze and whatever else she needs when she asks for it.

As my mother sets to stitching the broken skin together, I kneel beside her. "You should go," I say point-blank. "Call your Enforcers, take the truck, and go back."

Her fingers pause their movements, and she blinks at me, confused. "What? No, I'm taking you—"

"You don't get it. These soldiers?" I wave a hand toward the broken bodies around us. "They *weren't* Enforcers. Those people Bilken and Nolan made their deals with are here and they're looking for me. Helping me will only get you both killed, especially if they find out you work for the DSD. They'll blame you. For Richter's research. For me. For everything." I add that last part in a soft breath, hoping my words carry the weight to make her understand.

"So, they aren't just attacking while waiting for proof of your death, they're actively looking for it?" Jenner asks.

I roll my lower lip between my teeth, thinking. "It's…more than that. This is retaliation. Even if they had proof of my death, I'm not sure it would be enough to stop the attack."

"Then what's the point?" Ezra snaps, his eyes shooting daggers at me over Bilken's unconscious body. "Why hand yourself over if it won't put an end to all this?"

Annoyance grips my chest, and a fury unlike anything I've ever known washes through me. Ezra's upset—he wants to find justification in agreeing to what I've asked of him—but I'm tired of trying to make them understand.

Of trying to make them see what will come to pass if they don't let me go.

"What do you think will happen when this disease kills me?" My eyes flash to Jenner over my shoulder. "Or have you forgotten?" Although I spit the words, they come out more cruel than I intend, and I find myself averting my gaze, not wanting to see the hurt look on his face.

With a tired sigh, I look back at Ezra. "This war will only end one way. Because I *make* it end. And if the way to do that is to hold the entire world hostage unless they agree to my demands, then so be it. I will gladly let them burn if they refuse."

"Even if it means burning us, too?" Ezra breathes.

The dejected notes in his voice extinguish my rage, and I immediately deflate. We stare at each other for a long moment before I can finally bring myself to answer.

A regretful smile pulls at my lips. "If it comes to that…nothing I do will save you anyway."

Glowering at me, Ezra jumps to his feet and storms away from us back toward the rear of the truck, raking a bloody hand through his hair. Jenner and I exchange a look, and with a quick nod, he follows after him.

Beside me, my mother is unnaturally still.

"Wynter, I—"

"I forgive you," I say suddenly, and as the words rush out, I realize there's a part of me that means them.

My mother gapes at me, as surprised as I am.

"I understand why you did what you did," I continue before she can utter a word, "and I'm grateful you came back for me and helped us get this far, but…" I hesitate, shaking my head. "But you need to let me go. *I* need to see this through, but you don't." I glance between her and Bilken and at the delicate way her hands cup his head. Before, their closeness infuriated me, but now…

Now, I'm just glad she won't be alone at the end should the future I'm trying to avoid come to pass.

My throat thickens. "You two can still get out. Use Bilken's connections or sneak out some other way if you have to. Just get as far away from here as you can."

My mother's gaze hardens, and she clenches her jaw. "Even if I agreed, how do you expect to get the rest of the way without transport? We're still miles from the magistrates building."

"You got us this far, but going through the remaining checkpoints isn't an option. Not anymore." My eyes drift across the dead soldiers around us. "We'll be better off on foot from here. A truck will draw too much attention."

Leaning toward me, my mother reaches out a tentative hand, using her thumb to wipe away the bead of sweat building on my forehead. Then, she carefully touches my nose, and when she pulls away, I glimpse the blood on her fingers.

"I didn't want to accept it before, but I see it now. I recognize it from—" Clearing her throat, she drops her hand, as if she can't bring herself to touch me and mention her crimes at the DSD at the same time. Still, although the heat of her hand is gone, her eyes burn me when she says, "Your body is failing, Wynter. At this rate, you'll be dead before you even get there."

A strange calm settles over me, and I nod.

"Then I better make every second count."

TWENTY

MY MOTHER FINISHES BANDAGING UP Bilken's wound, then rouses him with a capsule of smelling salts from the first aid kit, which I catch an unpleasant whiff of from where I kneel beside her. His eyelids snap open, his dark eyes unfocused, and nostrils flaring, he lurches away from the stink of ammonia with an agonized groan.

"Don't," she warns, grabbing his wrist in a pincer-like grip when he lifts a shaking hand to his head.

Bilken's gaze is bleary as she forces his arm down, pinning it to his side with her knee. "Wh—" he begins, his confusion evident in the crease of his brow, but she hushes him.

"*Don't,*" she says again, more forceful this time. "Just be quiet for a minute. I need to examine you before you can move."

Pulling a small flashlight from the box, my mother clicks on the white beam and shines it in Bilken's eyes, watching in silence as his pupils respond to the light. After a moment, a hum of consideration breaches her lips.

"Your pupillary response is slower than I would like. Do you feel nauseous at all?" she asks.

"No," he mutters, then, with a heaving sigh, adds, "I'm sure I'll live, Evelyn. Can I sit up now?"

With a disgruntled huff through her nose, she glances over at Quinn, who waits by the truck, gun in hand, standing lookout. Frowning, she looks at me. "Do you think you can help me get him up? I'm not sure Quinn is in the best condition for this."

Nodding, I follow her lead, wedging one hand under Bilken's back and placing the other on his shoulder while my mother carefully cradles his neck, slowly easing him into a sitting position.

"Are you dizzy?" my mother presses him. There's an undercurrent of worry in her voice I've never heard before.

"A little," Bilken admits, waving her off. "But, like I said before, I'll be fine."

I snort. "Of course, you will be. You're a human cockroach," I mutter, but my words hold no malice. If anything, I'm beginning to revere Bilken's stubbornness when it comes to his survival, and not just in political situations where he exploits the playing field to his advantage but now from an actual assault that could have easily killed him. Either fate is watching over him or he's incredibly lucky. If it's the latter, then I wish that fortune was contagious, so I could force him to pass it on to Ezra and Jenner.

My mother arches a surprised brow at me, her shock at my caustic tone clear on her face. As I glance at her, I'm certain I know what she's thinking. What does she glimpse when she looks at me? Does she see a stranger much like I do when I look at her? After all, I'm nothing like I was before my placement exam. What happened that day changed me—not just physically but mentally—and although there's so much that's transpired along the way since then that I wish I could have done differently, I'm free in a way I never was when entangled in the restrictive rules of the State. Even with a timer counting down over my head, at least I can approach the end of my life knowing I had the chance to find the real me. The person I lived as for eighteen years, the person my mother must think I still am…

She died that day I escaped the DSD, cut out of me alongside my tracking chip.

Bilken exhales a strangled laugh, drawing my gaze. "Well, I'd rather be a cockroach than dead. So, I'll take it."

Once she's convinced his injury isn't life-threatening, my mother gestures for me to help her lift Bilken and, together, we ease him up onto his feet. Reluctantly, he slings an arm over my shoulders, and although the dead weight of his arm is heavy, it's light in comparison to the invisible burden I already carry.

Soft breaths part my lips as I trudge forward one step and then another, stumbling along beside Bilken as we lead him over to the truck. Quinn, unable to do any heavy lifting in his condition, holds open the passenger door, keeping one hawk-like eye on our surroundings at all times, ever the watchful soldier even when injured.

"Quinn, a word?" my mother says once Bilken is settled in his seat.

The ex-Enforcer's obsidian eyes flash to mine, then he turns, heeding my mother's summons, tailing her away from the truck. I watch their retreating backs for a moment before peering at Bilken, his skin slightly sallow. His breathing is hitched, like every inhale is a struggle.

"How's the head?" I ask, turning my back to the propped-open door.

He groans, sliding his eyes shut for a moment before wrenching them open again with a sigh. "Like a cracked egg. I suppose I should take this as a sign that I'm getting too old to be mixed up in this business."

I press my trembling fingertips into my tired eyes. "I know the feeling." *Well.* "Time for retirement, I guess."

Bilken lets out a low rumbling hum of agreement. "Looks like it." Averting his gaze, he stares out through the windshield at my mother. "For both of us," he adds under his breath.

The fatigue I've been fighting back hits me tenfold at these words, and I slump against the door, my knees wobbling uncertainly beneath me. Silence, as thick as the tears in my throat, hangs between us for an uncomfortable moment, and I follow his distracted line of sight to my mother, watching as she hands something small and indiscernible to Quinn. Even from here, I can see the dazed stupefaction on the ex-Enforcer's face.

There's something about the way she looks back at him that I struggle to put into words. Something so final, like what I envision a goodbye looks like without the spoken sentiment.

Heart clenching at the thought of my own impending goodbyes, I return my focus to Bilken. "You'll take care of my mother?" I murmur, my voice soft.

He begins to nod but stops mid-movement, wincing. "I've been doing my best by her for the last thirty-one years," he mutters on a broken exhale. "I'm not about to abandon her now."

"Good," I whisper. Then I say nothing else, content to let the quiet return.

The scrape and crunch of approaching footsteps draw my sluggish gaze to my mother and Quinn, who walk back toward us now—my mother with a somber frown on her face and Quinn still wearing that same shell-shocked expression from a few moments ago. Ignoring me, he presses on past the cab and continues onward to the back of the truck, while my mother makes a beeline for me, jerking her head once she catches my gaze.

My stomach twists at her unspoken command—at this gesture of beckoning for me to go to her—and as I push away from the door, closing it behind me, I feel strangely nervous. Like waking believing everything was a dream and instead learning the nightmare is actually real.

She lingers several feet away from the truck, pacing and chewing on the tip of her thumbnail. Her agitation surprises me. I don't think I've ever seen my mother look overwrought.

"What's wro—" I begin to say, but before I can finish, she grabs my hand, flipping it over.

"Take this." She places a gun on my outstretched palm, then curls her fingers around mine as if she just gave me the solution to my problems rather than a weapon that will be useless to me.

I blink, staring at the pistol where it touches my skin—the sleek black metal cool against my overheated flesh.

"I don't—"

"Please," she begs, her plea drawing my gaze to hers. Anguish dulls her eyes as she tightens her grip. "I know, just…please. Let me leave here feeling like I've at least done something to protect you."

Her hands relax, and with a stilted breath, she pulls away, quickly retracting her fingers. Her eyes slip from mine, dipping to the ground.

As an awkward hush rises between us, I find myself staring at the spot where she touched me. She's touched me before but never like this. Never with this desperation.

Never like my life has depended on it.

For all the attention I received from my father, I think that might have been the first time my mother has outwardly shown me she cares.

The first—and last—physical affection she will *ever* show me.

"Are you sure I can't get you to change your mind?" she asks, her voice just a step above silent.

Shaking my head, I tuck the gun in my waistband, shivering when the metal brushes up against the small of my back. "Even if that was an option…no. This is the right thing to do."

The *only* thing to do.

She nods. "For what it's worth, I think…" She hesitates, clearing her throat, her eyes shiny, then gifts me with an unexpected smile. It's despondent and screams of regret, but there's also something else behind it. Something almost like pride. "I think this is what your father would've done, too."

With a shuddering breath, she caresses the side of my head, her fingers lingering for just a moment, brushing over my hair. Then, her hand is gone, her touch nothing more than a memory, almost as if I imagined it.

Flicking a tear off her cheek, she turns and struts toward the truck without looking back.

My mother and I don't speak again. She returns to the driver's seat of the cab and, after checking on Bilken, turns over the engine. We don't even make eye contact as she reverses the vehicle, heading back in the direction we came from.

As I watch her drive away, I don't know what to feel. Anger? Sadness? Regret? Relief?

All of the above?

Or, maybe, nothing at all.

"Are you okay?"

I jump at the sound of a gruff voice in my ear, and I look back to find Ezra standing behind my left shoulder, a concern I'm all too familiar with swirling in the warm hazel depths of his eyes. My gaze darts from his, scouring our razed surroundings, searching for Jenner amid the rubble, who I spot across the street, talking to Quinn. I wasn't even aware they were all back yet from wherever it was they stormed off to.

With one final glance down the road, I turn, squaring my shoulders to face Ezra head-on. If he's still upset with me, the drawn expression pinching his lips into an emotionless line doesn't show it. Regardless, I feel the need to say something. To clear the air. To preserve whatever time, however little, we have left together.

Even if it's tainted by the understanding of the roles we both have yet to play.

I draw in a breath, preparing myself, but before I can get a single word out, he closes the distance between us, scooping me into a firm embrace that punches the air from my lungs. My body freezes in his arms as he whispers, "It's okay, you know. To *not* be okay."

I pull away slightly, unsure what he means. He mimics the movement, looking me in the eye in that cryptic way he does, the silence saying so much more than words ever can. Brushing my hair behind my ears, he leans in again, cupping my face in his hands.

"Putting aside what she's done, who she's hurt… At the end of the day, she's still your mother. It's okay for you to be upset by how things have turned out or pissed off or whatever you want to feel. And if that means talking about it or crying or, hell, screaming as loud as you possibly can, then just do it. You have my ear and my shoulder. Whichever one you need is yours."

As he lowers his hands, I push out a slow breath through my nose and bow my head until my cheek rests on the top of his chest. "How do you do it?" I mumble.

His heartbeat is strong and steady, and his voice is a throaty purr as he asks, "Do what?"

Console me when your pain outweighs mine.

Console me when all I've done is hurt you.

I burrow my face against his neck. "You're angry at me, and I don't blame you for that—"

"Stop." Grasping the tops of my arms, he pushes me back a step, forcing space between us again. When I look up at him, confused, he growls, "I know what you're going to say, and you don't need to say it. You don't *ever* need to say it. Because you and I both know I'll always be here for you, Wynter. Even—" He grimaces, choking on some unspoken thought, as if he can't bring himself to vocalize what we both need to hear. Tears shine in his eyes, and he swallows loudly. "Even at the end," he breathes.

I hear the pain in those four words as clearly as I sense the acceptance behind them. Ezra finally understands. Jenner *made* him understand. Or maybe he got there on his own and has merely been wearing his denial as armor.

Whichever it is, I can't help feeling a certain sense of loss, like the embers in a hearth burning out. Those embers were what remained of Ezra's lingering belief that I might actually survive this.

And now, that hope is gone. Extinguished.

As he pulls me in again, holding me close, I'm reminded of the dream-like conversation I had with his mother a few days ago.

"He won't do it. Not after everything he went through to get me back," I had said to her, adamant Ezra would never agree to what I backhandedly made him promise to do.

"He will," she had countered, *"because it's what needs to be done."*

I nod against his shirt, pressing my nose into his collarbone, as tears—fiery and unrelenting—slip down my cheeks.

He will, I think, repeating those words.

He has to.

Behind me, someone clears their throat, and I lift my head, breaking away from Ezra, even though every atom in my body screams for me not to. He keeps a hand on my back as I turn to face Jenner and Quinn, who flings a rifle he must've retrieved from one of the soldier's corpses over his shoulder. Beside him, Jenner flashes me a small doleful smile.

"We'll have to go quite far on foot from here, and the road ahead will be dangerous. I hope you're all prepared," Quinn says, his dark eyes scanning our surroundings.

Ezra's responding breath tickles my ear. "Sure you're okay with this? Your ticket to freedom is driving away as we speak. I'm sure you could still flag them down if you wanted."

We all turn, watching the shrinking form of the truck as it turns a corner at the far end of the road, disappearing from sight. As Quinn stares off into the distance, as silent and stoic as ever, I observe his drawn face, wondering if he regrets his decision to stay. When we reach the end of our current path, will he wish he'd run when he had the chance? Or has he realized what no one else seems to understand, no matter how loudly I shout it?

That if we fail to end this war, we're all as good as dead.

Scowling, Quinn jerks his gaze to mine, as if he somehow heard my thoughts. "Do you want me to help you get to Nolan or not?"

When I nod, Ezra grabs my hand and interlaces our fingers.

Before leaving the relative safety of the now unmanned blockade, we spend a few minutes discussing our revised plan of action, pouring over a map of the Heart that Bilken gave Quinn just before we departed the safe house—in the event we needed to resort to Plan B—trying to work out which roads we should take from here to avoid any further obstructions. Although the map doesn't reveal the locations of the roadblocks standing in our way, Quinn's past experience as an Enforcer, however brief, lends us knowledge of how the State would enact martial law, including what areas they would prioritize in cutting off access to when locking down the city.

"We're currently in Zone 2, and the magistrates building is on the opposite side of Zone 1 from where we're approaching it from, so we have a bit of a trek ahead of us. We'll likely have to adapt our route as we go, and it won't be the most direct path, but we'll get there," he mutters, tracing a finger along the hologram.

My eyes dip, honing in on the side of Quinn's torso, his wound masked by the thick armor plating of his borrowed uniform. "Think you can manage the journey?" I ask, unable to hide the concern in my voice.

His eyes lock on mine, probing in their intensity. "I could ask you the same question," he murmurs.

"I'm fine," I insist. But as I say this, I catch a glimpse of my reflection in a window to the left of the roadblock, the broken pane visible over Quinn's shoulder. Eyes, mostly black, stare out from the web of cracks in the glass, calling me a liar.

"Well, you have us," Jenner says with a swift glance at Ezra. "We'll make sure you get there in one piece."

No one says another word as we pass the blockade and proceed down the road, the streets in the immediate vicinity silent, as if everyone still alive in the area is holding a collective breath. As we advance, Ezra scouts just ahead while Jenner takes up the rear, leaving Quinn and me in the middle, our steps slow with exhaustion and the aches of wounds both visible and unseen.

I peer at him out of the corner of my eye, watching as he fidgets with something small in his hand before stuffing whatever it is in his pocket.

"Is that what my mother gave you?" I ask, unable to keep the curiosity at bay any longer. Inching closer to him, I press further. "What is it?"

He cocks an inky brow, and I shrug.

"I know it's none of my business," I mutter.

"And yet, you asked anyway," he grumbles.

My face flushes at the admonishment in his tone. "You don't have to tell me—"

"Her gratitude."

At my confused expression, he fishes the object free of his pocket and extends his hand toward me.

"What is this?" Plucking the silver disc up with my fingers, I turn it over on my palm. It's a thin piece of steel carved with an ID number, but, beyond that, I'm not sure what I'm looking at.

As I hand him back the disc, he scoffs. "I 'died' when I quit the Enforcers, remember? As far as the State is concerned, I was executed the day of my arrest. This"—he pinches the minuscule piece of metal between his thumb and forefinger, holding it up to eye level—"is how the government records our deaths. At the end of our lives, this data chip is all that remains, containing every morsel of information the State deems important about us. *That* way our sins can follow us even beyond the grave."

"Our sins?" I echo, my stomach souring.

Quinn snorts. "What the State sees as sins, anyway. I prefer to call it having a conscience."

I give a weak nod. The list of my own sins is extensive, something my conscience often reminds me of. But with so many of my crimes committed on behalf of the State, I can't help wondering… What would my data chip say? Likely something about dying in service of my country, the thought of which makes my skin crawl. Especially when, by comparison, someone like Quinn, who abandoned the Enforcers in protest of mindless killing, would be seen as a criminal.

"Okay, but why keep these records?" I press. "Once a person is dead, their crimes die along with them."

He shrugs. "Not always. Not if there are indications others may have been involved. The records help pinpoint where the State should be watching for any potential…subversion."

"You mean *who* it should be watching," I correct him.

Like Jenner's family, who paid for his crimes. Or my mother and me, who were probably under surveillance because of my father. Just how long did the

State watch us after his death before we were no longer considered a threat?

Shaking away that thought, I ask, "Why would my mother give that to you?"

Quinn shifts his hand so the disc is laid out flat on his palm. "Because of this." He pulls a compact device free of his belt—an ID chip scanner identical to the ones I've seen Enforcers carrying a hundred times before—then runs the red light it projects over the ID number engraved in the metal.

"*Record deleted,*" the scanner intones. "*The information stored on this data disc is no longer accessible.*"

My brow furrows. "I don't understand."

Quinn curls his fingers around the data disc, then stuffs it back inside his pocket. "Your mother… She wiped my entire identity, taking it back to a clean slate, so regardless of what happens or who ends up in power here, it'll be as if I never existed. There's no information for anyone to access about me. No pictures to cross-reference, no record of my past. *Nothing.*" As he fixes the scanner back on his belt, a rare smile tugs at his lips. "By doing that, she didn't just make me a ghost. She gave me my life back. I can start over, like I would've done outside the State if I had gone with her and Bilken as planned."

I balk at his words—at this notion that all evidence of his life and deeds are somehow gone, erased from public knowledge like an ocean tide washing away footsteps in sand.

Envy scratches at the underside of my skin.

What he's describing almost sounds like freedom.

"Is that even possible? What about your ID chip? Wouldn't it still—"

He shakes his head. "The servers linked to our mandated chips were all fried by a localized EMP in the initial attack. The State isn't tracking anyone now, not that they even could in my case. PHOENIX disabled mine as soon as I joined."

My feet stumble to an abrupt standstill. "Wait…what? The chips don't work?"

I gape at the ex-Enforcer, my body rigid with shock. This is news to me, and I wonder why my mother and Bilken didn't feel the need to tell us about this— especially when Bilken admitted to putting a tracker on me back at the bunker. Then again, that tracker was discarded when I tossed out my bodysuit, and Ezra, Jenner, and I—and now Quinn—don't have functioning ID chips anymore. The State wasn't tracking us for such news to matter.

The skin at the base of my skull tingles, and I suddenly remember the chip Richter planted there. Well, one person was tracking me, but, thankfully, he's no longer a problem.

"Nope," Quinn answers. "According to your mother, it was part of the plan to cause as much mayhem as possible during the attack and to make it harder for the State to rebuild, should it *actually* win this war."

"You say that like you don't think it will," I note. Although part of me doesn't believe it will either, another part is well aware of just how far the State is willing to go. At this point, it has nothing to lose, which only makes it more dangerous.

I wouldn't count it out of this battle just yet.

A harsh laugh breaches his lips. "Of course, it won't. And when it falls and PHOENIX or whoever the hell takes over, I can rest easy knowing they'll have nothing to link me to the State."

I consider that for a moment, turning the knowledge of everything Quinn has done since abandoning the Enforcers over in my head. Finally, I say, "Won't it be worse for you if they link you to me?"

I'm being hunted down on all sides by every enemy in our path. The State wants to use me. PHOENIX and our attackers both want me dead. If Quinn is found aiding me, surely that will put him in a far worse position than he ever was as a double agent.

A thoughtful expression darkens his face, and he nods, as if coming to some internal decision. "Not if I help you put an end to all this."

I consider him, a frown tugging down on my lips. It didn't occur to me how Ezra, Jenner, and even Quinn might be impacted by their connection to me even after I'm dead. The last thing I want is for them to survive this only to then be punished for my crimes.

One more thing to negotiate with PHOENIX, I muse.

We continue for a few minutes in silence, but with every step, what Quinn said before about my mother eats away at me until I can't stand the question burning through my thoughts any longer. I can't make sense of it—why she would honor her agreement with him if she didn't get what she wanted.

"So, my mother upheld her end of the deal…even though she walked away empty-handed?"

The ex-Enforcer might have delivered me to her as they agreed, but the rest of the plan went to shit, making everything she did over the last few years meaningless. And while none of that is Quinn's fault, my mother has never exactly struck me as the generous type.

Once again, that contemplative expression crosses his face. "Maybe she didn't," he says, then shrugs. "Maybe she got something else she wanted instead."

Something else?

My eyes widen as the realization hits me, and a soft laugh escapes as I resume my forward march, fixing my gaze on the far-stretching road ahead. My mother's actions were never defined by her need to save me from my illness or even from the State but by her desire to ease the burden of guilt on her shoulders—a weight I'm far too familiar with. And all she needed to lighten that load was one thing. The *only* thing I still had in me, even after everything, to give her.

My forgiveness.

TWENTY-ONE

THE TEMPORARY SILENCE THAT ENVELOPED us back where we parted ways with my mother is shattered completely as we progress toward the border to Zone 1. Sprinkles of gunfire pierce the musty air, seeming to come from every direction at once, and explosions light up the horizon with smoke, the black smudges visible as they rise in the sky against the rapidly dwindling daylight.

The stink of sulfur I noticed back in Zone 3 touches my nostrils again, but there's something else behind that smell—something rancid that makes my stomach roil. Although I wish I didn't know that stench, I recognize it from the battles I fought in and from the carnage I helped the State inflict on our unwilling victims.

Grimacing, I flinch away from the smell of burning flesh as if it has physically struck me.

Exhaustion weighs down my movements until every step is a struggle, but I push ahead despite the increasing pain in my skull, determination coursing through my veins like blood. Overhead, the sky shifts as we press forward, the evening light dimming until the city is swallowed by night.

Zone 2—a place I called my home for many long years—is unfamiliar as we navigate the empty streets. Quarters, not unlike the terraced house I lived in with my mother, are now more like empty husks, quiet and dark within, aside from the ones we pass that are burning. The flames, almost white in their fiery rage, eat through them as if they're made of paper.

At the sight of one house in particular—so close in appearance and color to the home I once shared with my father—I stumble, jolting to a standstill. Could it be the same quarters? I was so young when we were relocated that I can't help believing it's possible.

I inch toward the front door, led by a strange, trance-like sensation washing over me. I almost make it when a hand grabs my shoulder, stopping me dead in my tracks.

"Wynter?" Ezra asks.

Disoriented, I blink once, then again, before finally turning and meeting his gaze.

"Are you—" he begins, but he cuts off mid-sentence. His hazel eyes spring wide in horror.

My stomach seems to fold on itself as I stagger backward an unsteady step. "I...don't feel very well," I manage, resisting the sudden urge to throw up.

A trickle of wet heat slides from my eyes down my cheeks, and swaying, I shift my gaze back to the house only to find it ablaze, shining white like a beacon of light.

My brow creases in confusion. The house wasn't burning a moment ago.

"Wh—" But before I can get the full word out, a reel of images explodes inside my head like a single fatal gunshot. My legs shudder and I fall, my knees slamming hard into the asphalt, as a deranged, inhuman scream escapes me.

Around me, the windows of the quarters lining the street implode one after another with a resounding *pop-pop-pop*, the glass cascading down onto the pavement like a rain of knives. A shadowed figure shields me from the torrent, but I can't make out their face through the terrifying crimson haze in my eyes. All I'm aware of is the scream clawing at the inside of my throat, and as my shrill outcry persists, the ground quakes underfoot, fissures sprouting under my hands and knees, as if the planet is reacting to my pain.

Rough fingers clamp over my mouth, dulling my scream, as familiar voices coo my name, but I'm only half-aware of them calling to me through the violence carving a path through my brain.

Like the vision I had at the safe house, I see chaos devouring the Heart, eating through the streets like a ravenous worm, leaving only destruction and death in its wake. Soldiers gun down innocent civilians running for their lives, but the images move too quickly for me to know if the murderers are Enforcers or this new enemy merely posing as them, like the ones we encountered at the barricade earlier. The images flicker, shifting from past to future to present and back again until I'm not sure what's already happened and what atrocities are still yet to come.

"Wynter!" someone calls to me, and I latch onto that voice, using it as a tether to guide me home. The images flashing behind my lids slow in response, instead merging to create a new picture.

My heart drops when a familiar wasteland rises before me, my surroundings barren and still except for the ash and dust stirring in the breeze and the far-off figure standing with their back toward me.

I know, even at a distance, it's Ezra.

As I cross the space between us—momentarily unbound by the crippling confines of reality—he turns, meeting my gaze, his own silvered with tears. When I stop a few feet away from him, there's a split second where I swear I see the ghost of his mother standing just behind his left shoulder. But as suddenly as I thought I saw her, she's gone, and as the two of us face-off, he raises his gun—

"Wynter!" Ezra says again in my ear.

I snap my eyes open to find him leaning over me, holding me in his arms close to his chest, his features and what I can make out of our surroundings dyed red. Before us, the terraced quarters I mistook as my childhood home is no longer burning.

Maybe it never was in the first place.

My back arches against him as I let out a soft whimper. I can feel it—this disease eating away at my brain. I'm beginning to see things that aren't actually there, and it feels like I'm one vision away from exploding and taking an entire city block with me.

Strange, I note.

How I can feel so weak and so capable of total obliteration at the same time.

"I got you," Ezra murmurs, holding me close, his hand sliding away from my mouth. "You're okay—"

"I can feel it," I rasp, my voice hoarse.

"F-Feel what?" he stammers.

I touch a hand to my damp, sticky cheeks, wiping at the skin under my eyes. My fingertips pull away coated in blood.

Biting back a sob, I force out the words, "I'm running out of time. Remember—" I gasp when a sudden pressure squeezes my skull, and a moan rumbles in my chest as sweat beads along my forehead and upper lip. "Remember what you promised."

He shakes his head, his voice taking on a panicked edge. "What if I can't do it? What if I don't?"

A wheeze rattles my lungs and the taste of copper floods my mouth when I cough. "Then we all die," I breathe once the fit passes. "And I don't—" The lump in my throat distorts the words, and I let out a shaky breath before trying again. "I don't want that, Ezra. Please."

A tear dashes from his left eye as he tugs me closer, gripping my body so tightly it hurts. "There's still time," he whispers in my ear.

I swallow, biting back a laugh. Of course, he would utter the very words that keep haunting me. *Is* there still time? I'm starting to think maybe there isn't and the belief that's pushed me this far is wrong.

There's still time, Rai echoes in my head, as if to tell me not to lose hope.

I grit my teeth. *You've made it this far, Wynter.* If I give up now, then everything we've done, all the sacrifices we've endured to get to this point, would be meaningless. I can't give up. Not now.

Not ever.

"Help me up," I beg, gripping Ezra's hand.

He considers me for a few seconds then nods, looping his arm behind my back, and as he climbs to his feet, he brings me up with him, using his weight to support my own. It's only once I'm upright again that I finally notice Jenner and Quinn. Jenner stands close on my other side, ready to step in if needed, while Quinn keeps his distance, fear and uncertainty teeming in the charcoal pits of his eyes.

"I'm okay," I assure them as I wipe my face clean on my sleeve, clearing my gaze. "Let's keep moving."

It takes longer to reach Zone 1 than any of us would like, our advance proceeding at a much slower rate and getting slower by the minute as my symptoms worsen. Ezra and Jenner take turns acting as my crutch and bearing the brunt of my weight, even going so far as to carry me in the moments when I can't carry myself, my vision sporadically clouded by incomprehensible hallucinations of past and future overlaid on our present surroundings, blinding me to our current path.

We stop sparingly and only when needed, although the chaos in Zone 1 makes those pit stops frequent. The anarchy I witnessed playing out in my head is a real stain on the Heart now, painting every street we walk in red. We often find ourselves having to hide from passing patrols to avoid detection—to avoid us ending up just as dead.

The acrid stench of smoke and death is a cloying, almost tangible presence in the air, choking my throat and lungs the closer we get to the center of the city. The devastation seems so final, so irreversible, that part of me worries there isn't anything we can do to change it.

There's still time, Rai reminds me, her voice inescapable, like a beating pulse in my ear.

It takes all the lingering strength I possess to believe that.

The nearer we get to the magistrates building, the harder it is to steer clear of the mayhem, and with every breath, I fear I won't have the strength in me to act—to protect us if it comes to that. Ezra, sensing my exhaustion, corrals our group into an abandoned health center, the glass front doors broken by large chunks of shrapnel, offering us uninhibited entry.

"Let's rest here for a minute," he says, depositing me carefully on the gray waiting room sofa. When I wince on impact, he drops to his knees before me, taking my face in his hands. "Just a bit longer. We're almost there," he says before brushing a chaste kiss across my lips.

Jenner searches the office and adjacent exam room, running back into the lounge after a moment with a few bottles of water, the first of which he extends to me before sinking down onto the sofa. I drink the liquid down greedily as Quinn props the map of the Heart—specifically Zone 1—on the low table between us.

When the hologram manifests, glowing blue in the shadowed room, he points to an intersection of roads not far from our location.

"We're close. Less than two miles, barring any unforeseen obstacles." A pensive scowl warps his face, and his eyes dart to mine. "Once we get there, that's it. You know that, right? No more dodging patrols. No more hiding in side streets. The second they spot us, we'll be seen as the enemy. What's to say they won't think you're there to attack them?"

I shrug, even though the movement makes my skull ache. "That's a chance I'll have to take."

"So, what's the plan?" Jenner asks. "We stroll up to the magistrates building and surrender? Remind me again why we don't just contact Nolan on his communicator and handle this from a safe distance? Also, how do we even know all the Heads will be together? Seems kind of risky for PHOENIX to have all their leaders convened in the middle of a war zone."

"It's not a risk if they think they'll win," I mutter.

Ezra rubs a hand across his chin, blowing out a slow breath through his nose. "This is the first time PHOENIX has initiated an all-out offensive, and to get everyone on board with the plan, the Heads would've needed to display a united front, which would've meant throwing themselves into the fray. If they don't win here, they won't win at all. It was everyone and everything or nothing. As for why we can't just call Nolan, contacting him takes away the element of surprise, and we need the other Heads there when we talk to him so we can expose the part he played in this attack. The easiest way to get in front of both and kill two birds with one stone is to turn up unannounced, even if that means surrendering."

Quinn snorts. "If we surrender, they'll take our guns, and I guarantee someone will put a bullet in our heads before we even get to Nolan."

The thought of that happening ignites an unexpected fire of adrenaline within me. "I won't let that happen," I growl.

My heart races like a hummingbird trapped in my ribcage. Maybe I do still have the strength in me for this, after all.

Ezra's hand grips my shoulder, and I instantly go still, as if his touch has smothered the flames of my rage. "Wynter, you can't fight everyone," he chides. "You can barely even stand."

My eyes snap up to his, determined. "I won't hesitate to protect you. All of you," I add, looking at Jenner and Quinn.

Jenner leans forward, planting his elbows on his knees. "Let's hope it doesn't come to that and that the Heads will hear us out."

We don't drag out our stay at the health center any longer than we need to, only remaining long enough to hydrate, catch our breath, and plot the final part of our path. When we leave, we go out the back entrance of the building and stick to the alleys and side roads, staying as far away from the sounds of gunfire and screaming as we're able to.

It's well into the early morning hours by the time we reach the magistrates building, its silhouette a towering, visible presence even against the black clouds behind it. Unlike the last time we were here when the plaza was empty, this time, the open stretch of cobbled ground is swarmed with people waiting to get into the building.

Citizens seeking shelter from the attack, I realize.

For a while, we loiter out of sight in a narrow backstreet offering an unobscured view of the plaza. Jenner and Quinn hang to one side of the alley while Ezra and I keep close on the other, his arm around my waist at all times to steady me.

"Do we just join the crowd and try to pass ourselves off as refugees?" Jenner whispers.

Quinn sighs, then retorts, "That's unlikely to work and it wouldn't get us anywhere close to the Heads. Besides, it doesn't look like that line is moving quickly, if at all."

I trail my eyes over the maelstrom of bodies, flinching when the pandemonium from the vision I had at the safe house flickers on top of the scene, fading in and out like a mirage. Flames lick across the massive structure before vanishing, as if nothing more than a temporary figment of my imagination.

Shaking my head to clear it, I say, "The fastest way to reach Nolan will be through one of his lackeys. Or by making a big enough scene."

"Option A," Ezra deadpans. "Making a scene might draw attention we don't want."

Slumping back against his chest, I nod, acknowledging that he's right. If the enemy discovers my location and comes for me, then whatever hope I had of using the Heads to barter an end to this war will be forfeit. We need to get in front of Nolan with as little fanfare and fuss as possible.

And soon.

Quinn wipes a dew of sweat from his brow before pointing to the far end of the plaza, just past the densest part of the crowd. "The soldiers not blocking the entrance to stop these people from overrunning the building will be on rotation, doing patrols around the immediate area." He draws a large circle in the air with his finger, indicating where he means. "We just need to find one of those sentries and hope they don't shoot us."

Ezra lets out a soft laugh that wafts the hair against the back of my neck. "I know just the guy."

Before I'm even aware of what's happening, Ezra is retracting his arm from around me and, after propping me against the wall to ensure I won't fall over, runs off into the night toward a tall figure skirting the edge of the large mob. All I can see clearly about the vague man in the distance is the rifle he carries.

My heart jumps into my throat, pushing a terrified cry from my lips.

"Ezra!" I shout before slapping a hand over my mouth. Fear is a writhing entity inside me as I silently scream for him to come back.

"Where the *hell* is he going?" Quinn snarls from the other side of the alley, looking as conflicted as I feel.

Beside him, Jenner just cocks his head, his bright blue eyes narrowing. "Wait… is that?"

"Duke!" Ezra calls out.

The hulking man pivots at the sound of his name, and when he turns, his face becomes a degree or two clearer in the minimal light smeared across the plaza. At the sight of the figure running toward him, he raises his gun, but recognition stills his hand.

"Ezra?" Duke lowers his weapon and races forward, meeting Ezra halfway, slowing to a stop less than twenty feet from where I remain in the shadows, exhaustion gluing my weak body to the wall.

To my right, Jenner seems to explode out of the alleyway, and when Duke's gaze tracks the movement, he gasps.

"Holy shit, Jenner." His eyes, almost black in the darkness, dance back and forth between his two friends. "When the transmission cut off, I didn't know what to think," he says, pulling them each in for a hug. "Gotta admit, I panicked. Thought maybe you guys were dead."

"Came close a couple of times," I hear Jenner say, "but we're still kickin'."

"More like lucky, you son of a bitch," Duke retorts with a gruff laugh.

"Who is that?" Quinn hisses at me across the small side road.

I only met Duke once and we didn't exchange a single word at the time, but he was there the night we lost Rai. *Here*, I correct myself with a sullen glance past him at the magistrates building. He shared in the grief we all felt in the tunnels; he *knows* what we went through that night. And he was the one Jenner tried to contact for help from the bunker when we were cornered by Nolan.

He's older than I remember him seeming in the darkness of the tunnels under the city—his mid-thirties, maybe older, weathered by the hardships of underground survival—and while I don't know much else about the man besides his name, there's a kind sincerity radiating from him as he speaks with Ezra and Jenner that lets me believe, lets me *hope*, we can trust him.

"A friend," is all I say in response.

Quinn grunts, either in disapproval or acknowledgment. I'm not quite sure which.

"Listen," Duke mutters to Ezra and Jenner, "it's good to see you both and I'm relieved as shit you're okay, but everyone's on high alert...and we have our orders. Specifically about what we're meant to do if we see you. If they find you here—"

Duke stops short when his gaze catches mine, and he gawks at me, his mouth hanging wide, as if he can't believe what he's seeing.

Clapping him on the shoulder, Jenner steers Duke toward the shadowed recess of the alley. The large man lumbers along obediently, never once tearing his eyes from mine.

"What have you heard about us, exactly?" Jenner asks once we're all crowded in the narrow side road, out of sight of everyone in the plaza and—more importantly—any passing patrols.

Duke doesn't respond at first, too shell-shocked by my presence to speak. Or maybe it's my appearance that has him lost for words, just like he was that night in the tunnels under Zone 1 when he looked at me in a similar manner. If that's what's troubling him, I wouldn't blame him for feeling unnerved. I can only imagine what I must look like right now.

Finally, he shakes his head and grumbles under his breath, "I've heard a lot of shit, man."

"Give us the abridged version," Ezra presses.

Duke white-knuckles his rifle as he peers over his shoulder, probably checking for any sign of the next patrol amid the nearby crowd. After scanning our surroundings for a moment, he turns back to face us. "All right, so word around the rumor mill is *this one*"—he jerks his chin toward me—"went insane and tried to murder Nolan…and that you two then helped her escape." Duke glances between Ezra and Jenner.

"Well, they got it half right," Ezra mutters.

"Everyone's callin' you traitors, sayin' you've been brainwashed by the State or some shit. It's *serious*," Duke growls when Jenner scoffs. "Our instructions are shoot to kill upon sightin'."

Jenner snorts. "Shoot to kill? What are you, Enforcers now?"

"Wait," Ezra says, confusion creasing his brow. "Why has Nolan issued shoot to kill orders if he thinks we're already dead?"

Jenner considers this question, then shrugs. "Maybe he knows we're alive?" Tilting his head in Quinn's direction, he adds, "Which means Nolan's also gonna know you betrayed him."

The ex-Enforcer rolls his eyes. "If he doesn't, I think he'll figure that out the moment we reveal ourselves to him."

Recalling the vision I had of Nolan back at the safe house, I shake my head, interjecting, "He doesn't know we're alive."

Jenner cocks an ebony eyebrow at me. "How do you know?"

"I saw it," I answer simply. "Believe me, he doesn't know." I glance past Duke toward the magistrates building, remembering the flames that consumed it in my vision—or *will* consume it…at some point. Considering the structure isn't currently burning, I can only assume what I witnessed within hasn't happened. "Not yet, anyway," I mutter.

Dread is an icy trickle down my spine. That vision could play out at any moment. The attack I saw could happen the second we step foot in the building with us all trapped inside. I could be leading the only two people I love straight to their deaths if we proceed, and yet…what other choice do I have?

All I can hope now is that we reach Nolan first and finally prove the future can be changed.

Once again, I picture the words I saw light up across Nolan's communicator after he spoke to our attackers, feeling their presence like a weight on my skin.

Proof or no peace.

This is the only way, I remind myself.

"Why would Nolan think you're dead?" Duke asks, peering at each of us, his expression perplexed. His deep voice drags me out of my thoughts.

"Because he ordered our executions," Ezra says bluntly.

"Maybe that's precisely why everyone in PHOENIX still thinks you're alive,"

Quinn suggests, glancing between us.

I frown at him. "What do you mean?"

The ex-Enforcer gives me a condescending look. "Think about it. Nolan has used this situation to establish himself as some sort of benevolent leader—"

"A savior," I whisper breathlessly, reciting Nolan's words from the broadcast in my head. Once again, I hear how he appealed to the masses with promises of security and peace, offering a better world where the State no longer exists.

"He has always liked to keep his hands clean," Ezra muses. "Better to let someone else do the dirty work so he always seems like the good guy."

Jenner crosses one arm over his chest and drums the fingertips of his other hand against his chin. "Looking at it that way, he must think our executions would somehow tarnish his image."

"And deter people from siding with him," I murmur.

Quinn nods. "Which is exactly what would happen. I mean, would *you* seek shelter with a man who ordered the executions of two of his own and an unarmed hostage?"

Ezra huffs out an incredulous breath. "I'd hardly call Wynter unarmed."

Quinn raises one shoulder, then lets it fall again in a dismissive gesture. "Me neither, but almost no one at that bunker saw her use her power. Come to think of it, few have outside the Enforcer units. And she knew people in PHOENIX before, right? People who saw how sick she was?" An *I'm just saying* look crosses his face. "Remember, it only takes one person to sow a seed of doubt. Besides,"—he lowers his voice—"if word got out he was playing judge and jury, the DSD comparisons would be unavoidable."

"So, he lied and turned us into the bad guys, and now, everyone thinks we're just running amok." Clenching his jaw, Jenner slams the side of his fist against the brick wall to my left. "This is *bullshit*. We aren't brainwashed traitors. Hell, the real traitor here is Nolan. Did you know he planned all this?" Peering at Duke, he waves an arm, gesturing vaguely all around us.

Duke blinks in confusion, attempting to follow Jenner's erratic movements. "What?"

"It's true," Quinn asserts, his tone grave, still not bothering to introduce himself to Duke. "This attack is only happening because of a deal he made to push the State out of power. A deal he used to coerce the other Heads into giving him full control of PHOENIX."

The broad, muscled man slings his rifle over his shoulder before raising his hands, palms out. "Whoa, whoa, wait a minute. Everyone is sayin' this happened because of *you*."

Once again, his wide eyes shift to mine.

"Also true," I admit, drawing everyone's gaze.

With a slow, calming breath, I push away from the wall, and Ezra's hand shoots out, his fingertips pressing against my waist to steady me. Wrapping my hand around his forearm, I look over at the magistrates building and at this chaos I helped to cause.

"This attack is retaliation for everything I was forced to do for the DSD, but that's only half of it," I explain. "The other half is down to the deal Nolan made with these people—"

"Whoever the hell they are," Jenner grumbles under his breath.

I pause only long enough to lick my dried lips. "In return for helping him overthrow the State, Nolan agreed to a set of demands, which included destroying the DSD's weapon. But he trusted the wrong person to do the job, and now, the ceasefire is at jeopardy without proof of my death."

My eyes flash to Quinn, then quickly look away. I don't bother explaining to Duke that the "wrong person" in question is currently standing here with us.

"Okay." Duke runs a hand back and forth over his head, the blond hair there so closely cropped to his skull that, from some angles, he almost looks bald. "Okay," he says again, looking at Ezra now. "Tell me everythin'. Start at the beginnin'."

TWENTY-TWO

"SHIT," IS ALL DUKE CAN manage once Ezra finishes relaying the events that led us here, beginning with my extraction. At that part, he had gaped at Jenner in awe, as if he couldn't quite believe his friend had not only infiltrated a State airfield but that he had managed to bring down one of its helicopters and live to tell the tale.

But his focus on Jenner is fleeting, and as Ezra continues, I often catch Duke's eyes on my face, their depths brimming with an apprehension that makes me wonder if he'll actually help us.

"You know how crazy this all sounds, right?" he asks a minute or two after Ezra falls silent.

My pulse trips at his skeptical tone, but I find myself unsurprised by it. Of course, it sounds crazy. Unfortunately, that doesn't make our story any less true. Or our situation any less dire.

"It's all true," Jenner counters, as if voicing my thoughts, his tone barely above a growl.

"Oh, I don't doubt it," Duke says. "Hell, it actually explains a lot."

Quinn cocks a dubious brow. "Like what?"

Duke scoffs. "Like the fact that all our transmissions have gone completely ignored."

My fingers tighten around Ezra's forearm. "Transmissions?"

Glancing at me again, the burly man nods. "Since the Heads established themselves in the magistrates buildin', they've been puttin' out transmissions every hour to every possible frequency, tryin' to initiate a ceasefire. Between those and Nolan's very public declaration of war on the State, there's no way these assholes attackin' the Heart haven't heard us by now."

"Are we sure the State isn't jamming the signal?" Jenner asks.

Across from me, Quinn shakes his head. "Unlikely." Pulling the palm-sized device from his belt, he turns on the hologram map we used to get here, his hooded eyes following the glowing lines hovering over his hand for a moment before shutting it off again. "If they were, then GPS would be affected as well. It wouldn't be just communicators." He looks at Duke. "I'm assuming PHOENIX hasn't had any issues with theirs?"

Duke, who stands at least half a foot taller than Quinn, meets the ex-Enforcer's questioning gaze. "Nope. Everythin's been working fine. It's more like the bastards just aren't listenin'."

"And they won't," I mutter under my breath. "Not until they know I'm dead."

A fraught silence fills the backstreet at my words—only broken by the ominous murmuring of the crowd—and for a while, no one says anything else, the tension permeating the air speaking for us. I loosen my grip on Ezra's arm, but as I pull away, he grabs my hand, interlacing our fingers. Refusing to let go.

Duke stares at our conjoined hands for all of five seconds before glancing upward, narrowing his muddy brown eyes on my face. "So, your plan is to do what, exactly?" he asks, the slight waver in his voice giving away his unease.

My lips press into a determined scowl, and I say, shoulders tensing, "To make them listen."

Once again, that uncomfortable hush floods the alley, and a long moment passes before anyone dares to break it. Nodding, Duke lets out a loud breath, the husky sound caught somewhere between a sigh and a groan.

"Okay," he murmurs, peering between me and Ezra. "You've convinced me. What can I do to help?"

"We need to speak with the Heads," Jenner answers.

"And with Nolan," I add reluctantly.

While I want to expose his crimes—to tear him apart and make him pay for being willing to sacrifice an entire city—I'm not foolish enough to deny we still need him. Among the Heads, he's the only one who can make direct contact with our attackers and negotiate terms with them that will actually end this merciless assault on the Heart. No number of blind transmissions will sway them, but if Nolan reaches out and says he has me in custody…

That he's willing to trade my life for peace—

Duke exhales again, scratching his chin. "I can take you to Nolan, but after that…" He hesitates, his eyes flitting from my face to Ezra's, then to Jenner's, and finally, to Quinn's. "There won't be anythin' more I can do, especially if the other Heads take his side."

Ezra's palm is sweaty as his fingers clench a little tighter around mine. "We understand. Just get us in front of them."

Unloading the rifle from his shoulder, Duke grips his weapon in both hands and turns his back toward us, facing the plaza and the sea of bodies congregated before the magistrates building. Then, taking a step out of the shadowed alley, he says in a gruff voice, "Follow me."

We all tail Duke's hulking frame without question, my stomach dipping when we walk out into the open despite the increasing cover of night. I've never felt so exposed, and with every step we take across the plaza, I know there can be no turning back.

The faint buzz of frantic voices and weeping grows louder as we approach the dense throng ahead, the sinister din forcing me to cast off any lingering trace of doubt and fear still clinging to me like sweat on skin. There's no room for either anymore, only courage.

And yet, although I've stood against entire armies alone, I feel anything *but* brave as we carve a path through the crowd, balking under the brush of curious eyes observing my every move.

Despite the early hour, no one is asleep, the noise in the city impossible to tune out. Faces dirty with the residue of ash and smoke surround me on every side, like a sea of judgment ready to rise up and drown me. A shudder crawls up my spine, and I'm struck by the overwhelming urge to shy away from those piercing gazes—to bury my face in Ezra's chest and squeeze my eyes shut to hide from their scrutiny. But I don't let myself. Their suffering is my fault. *I* caused this.

And I deserve the weight of every glare focused on me, even if I'm only imagining them.

"All these people..." A lump sits heavy in my throat. Clearing it with a quiet cough, I force out, "Did they come here seeking shelter from the attack?"

Ezra must hear the tremor in my voice because he releases my hand and slides his arm around my hip, pulling me close to his side. "Why haven't they been moved underground yet?" he asks, his words equally soft. "If this building is hit, they'll—"

Duke flashes a warning look over his shoulder, as if to tell Ezra to watch what he says, before slowing his pace until he's barely keeping two steps ahead of us.

"It's madness out there," he murmurs. "Enforcers are prowlin' the streets, people are dying..." He tsks, shaking his head. "We've been evacuatin' as many areas as we can, but honestly, I don't think any of us anticipated it being this bad. We're movin' them underground, it's just been slow-goin'. Every time we relocate a group, another ten times the size shows up on our doorstep. We can't keep up." He gestures to the surrounding horde, proving his point.

"It isn't safe for them here," Ezra breathes.

"No," Duke agrees, "it isn't. But if we tried to tell them that, considerin' what the rest of the Heart is like right now, would they believe it? Are they in any more danger here than they would be elsewhere in the city?" He shrugs. "Are any of the zones even safe anymore?"

My teeth sink into my bottom lip, biting hard enough to draw blood.

Probably not.

Nowhere in the State—or in this world—will be safe until I'm dead.

Snorting, Duke rubs a hand across his shaved head. "It's actually too bad the outer cities aren't real. Then we'd have someplace to escape to."

My chest constricts, and the air rips from my lungs as my eyes flash to the back of his head. "What?"

Disbelief threatens to suffocate me. What does he mean the outer cities aren't real? That can't be true…

Can it?

All my life, I've been raised to believe there are eight other massive cities just like the Heart—nine total that make up our country, demonstrating the extensive reach of the State. The Heart was always the grandest, the capital, but it was never alone in its power.

Yet, if what Duke is suggesting is true, that means the State is so much smaller than I ever imagined, isolated to just this one city—this walled-in metropolis everyone is forbidden from leaving.

Throughout our years of education, we were always taught that certain high-ranking officials and, sometimes, Enforcers could travel to the other cities with special permission, for purposes we were unaware of. But…have I actually seen that happen?

Before my own involvement in this conflict, did I ever even see a helicopter leave this city?

No, I realize, and my stomach turns as it registers just how much I've been lied to. And not just about the limits of the State's borders but the actual reasoning behind this whole war.

A war the State only started once they had me to use as a weapon.

Because its army isn't as big as it wants people to think.

My alarmed gaze swings upward, locking on Ezra, whose face is unnervingly composed.

"You knew?" I hiss, my tone accusatory. It takes a moment to collect my thoughts enough to frame the rest of my question. "You knew the outer cities aren't real and you never thought to mention it?"

A sheepish look crosses his face, his cheeks pinking a little as his hazel eyes snap to mine. "I didn't mention it because it changed absolutely nothing about our situation. The outer cities were never going to help us, so it wasn't relevant. But yeah," he admits. "We've known for a while now. For over two years, actually," he adds, his words weighted.

Two years?

I gape at Ezra, stunned, trying to discern his meaning when the answer strikes me.

"Bilken," I mutter.

This time, when Ezra speaks, his expression is sullen. "Why else do you think Nolan got it in his head that he can actually overthrow the State?"

I blanch, a staggering nausea hitting me. "Because Bilken told him it's only one city."

Why did my mother fail to mention this when she was disclosing the details of her past to us? Because it wasn't relevant, like Ezra said? Or maybe she didn't see the point since, as members of PHOENIX, he, Jenner, and Quinn were already well aware of the truth. Maybe, she assumed I was, too.

I roll this concept around in my head, going back through everything my mother told us about her life in the early days of the State. When she said she and Bilken weren't from the Heart, she didn't mean they were from one of the other cities in the State… They were from a whole different part of the world. Which also means the people who founded our so-called country weren't merely part of an underground political movement that rose to power…

They were conquerors, and they sealed us in this city as if it was a cage.

Ezra nods. "Whatever this country was before, the State infiltrated it piece by piece and tore it apart from within until only the Heart was left standing."

My eyes widen as I recall the content of my father's journal entries. The rumors he heard. The reason no one around him seemed to blink an eye when the State seized power…

"The State didn't begin with the Heart," Ezra continues. "It just ended here."

In front of us, Duke lets out a harsh laugh. "Well, that certainly seems to be the case now."

Duke leads us around to the side of the building, and there's a rumble somewhere in the distance behind us as we make our way through the rest of the densely packed crowd. Thunder, maybe. An incoming storm.

Or a sign of what's to come.

I shake off that thought as we pass several heavily guarded doors before approaching what I instantly recognize to be the same entrance we used to gain access to the premises the last time we were here. The night of our mission to meet Bilken, before we knew of his role in all this. The mob is thinner around here—most of the refugees have gathered back by the front of the building—and there's only one guard stationed at the door, with no other wandering patrols in sight.

Not yet, at least, I muse.

As Duke escorts us to the door, his agitation is almost palpable, like a rancid odor in the air. His unease does nothing to ease my own dread, and I find myself leaning in closer to Ezra, whose arm instinctively tightens around me.

"It's okay," he whispers in my ear. "Just a little bit farther."

At our approach, the PHOENIX member stationed at the entrance—a young man, who doesn't look to be much older than me—straightens and repositions his grip on the rifle he's holding. Alarm burns behind his warm ocher eyes, which narrow, locking on Duke in confusion.

Face scrunching in surprise, he calls out, "Aren't you supposed to be on perimeter patrol, Masterson?"

Before my eyes, Duke seems to grow in size—his chest puffing out, as if to block our presence behind him—as he closes the distance to the younger man, his own weapon in hand. "I need to see the Heads," he barks back. "It's urgent."

The guard scoffs, then averts his gaze from Duke, observing the rest of us one at a time, blatantly searching for a threat in our group. "They're in a meeting. Besides, kinda late for a house call, don't you thin—" he says, but then cuts off abruptly, his attention fixed on my face. "Holy shit." He takes an uncertain step back. "Is that…?"

"Like I said…" Duke peers over his shoulder at me, then looks back at the guard and repeats, "It's urgent."

The color drains from the man's face as he fumbles his rifle, nearly dropping the gun to the ground. Catching it, he raises the barrel, taking aim at his intended target. At me. "S-Stay back. Stay right where you are."

Shifting the full breadth of his muscled body in front of me, Duke reaches out and grabs the barrel of the man's gun. "Lower your weapon," he snarls.

I blink at Duke's large back in surprise. He might be friends with Ezra and Jenner, but he doesn't know me. He owes me no loyalty, and I certainly never expected for him to put himself between me and a bullet.

"Don't—" I start to say, but the guard's frantic voice overshadows my own.

"Our orders are shoot to kill!"

"You *really* don't want to do that," Jenner insists, stepping forward until he's nearly shoulder to shoulder with Duke.

No, you don't, I add in my head. *Please, just let us pass.*

Duke shoves the guard's rifle downward until the muzzle is safely pointed toward the ground. "I know what our orders are, but they have information the Heads *need* to hear." Then, in a low voice, he says, "She'll kill you before you can even pull that trigger. Do you want to die for this?"

The man falters back another step, and in the minimal space between Duke and Jenner where they stand side by side, I glimpse him shaking his head.

"W-Weapons," he chokes out after a moment. "You can't go in with your weapons."

Heaving a resigned sigh, Duke surrenders his rifle, handing it to the guard. "Fine." He then gestures for us to do the same. "You'll have to leave them here," he instructs, staring pointedly at Ezra's hand where it hovers over the gun on his belt.

Ezra and I exchange a quick look, and I can see my own worries reflected clearly in his conflicted gaze. Going up against the Heads defenseless is a risk. And if something goes wrong and I can't protect them—

Ezra's sharp retort interrupts my thoughts. "I really hope you know what you're doing," he grumbles, turning over his pistol.

The muscles in my stomach constrict as I watch the gun slip from his fingers before begrudgingly following suit, tugging the farewell present my mother gave me free of my waistband and handing it to the soldier. Although useless in so many ways, that gun was her small sentiment of love and protection when nothing in this world can save me. And now, it's gone, like everything else will be if I don't get to Nolan.

That makes two of us.

Once everyone has relinquished their weapons, the guard steps to the side of the doorway, hesitantly granting us entry into the building. Duke goes in first, leading the way, and although the man doesn't attempt to deter us again when Ezra and I move to follow, his eyes burn their distrust into my face and then my back as I walk past.

Whatever momentary concern I have that the guard will try to shoot me once my back is turned is forgotten as soon as I step over the threshold. I had assumed all the refugees were being kept outside in the plaza for some inane reason, like to keep them separate from the Heads—who, if they're anything like Nolan, likely prioritize their own safety over that of the citizens seeking their help. What I hadn't expected was the grim reality before me.

On both sides of the hallway, survivors line the walls as far as the eye can see, some injured but conscious and others half-dead, if not already all the way there. One woman sits slumped under the sill of a bay window, her dark head of hair flopped forward, the strands hanging limp, obscuring my view of her face. Beside the woman, a young child shakes her by the shoulder, crying for her to wake up.

"Mother," the girl whimpers, tears streaking her filthy cheeks, and in her terrified gaze, I see myself.

"They…" My voice breaks, and I swallow a sob.

"Just keep walking," Ezra breathes against my neck, one hand against my lower back, gently nudging me forward.

"This is…" Jenner whispers behind us, but he doesn't finish the thought, as lost for words as I am.

"We brought in as many of the injured as we could," Duke says, keeping his eyes turned ahead. "But like I said, they just keep comin'."

Just keep coming…

Tears filter in from the edges of my vision, then expand, blurring the path ahead. There are too many people to help and not enough people to help them. Or enough time.

Time. The thought is like a weed taking root in my brain. It grows regardless of what I do, even if I try to starve it.

There isn't enough time.

Sweat breaks out across my skin, and a long moment passes before I realize I've stopped walking. Somewhere, a distant voice calls to me, but I can't see who it belongs to. All I'm aware of is the crowded hallway, which seems to grow longer, extending before me indefinitely, with no visible end in sight.

Static distorts my surroundings as it has so many times before, but in the uninterrupted stretches of stillness, I see the weary faces congesting the corridor. Every last one glares at me—even the ones that were dead, alive again in their hatred—their unblinking eyes declaring that I am to blame for this.

I stagger forward a step as an overwhelming heat flushes through me, perspiration trickling down the sides of my face, neck, and back. The warmth seems to blister my flesh, my body consumed by invisible flames.

Static again. The hallway warps, and in the flickers, I glimpse the future awaiting us. It blankets itself on top of the present, warning of its outcome. Devastating, unavoidable…

And immediate.

A harrowing cry wrenches open my mouth, but the sound breaching my lips is swallowed by the volatile fire now raging around me.

"Wynter?" that faint voice calls again.

Hands grip my shoulders and shake me roughly, yanking me out of the vision like a lifeline pulling me from under a wave. When I blink, my face is turned toward the ceiling, my jaw hanging wide, frozen mid-scream.

A terrified breath escapes me as I lower my head, finally noticing Ezra, who stands before me, his hands on my arms, his fingernails digging into my skin through my jacket. Tears burn lines down the sides of my face, and the metallic taste of blood coats my lips, which I lick to ease the dryness there.

"Wynter?" Ezra says once more, and the uncertainty in his voice mirrors the unrelenting panic racing through me.

Just as I feared…

Trembling, I inch backward out of his grasp, my misted gaze sliding to the nearest window. Although the panes are coated with ash, hiding the city beyond from view, I can sense the incoming danger behind the glass.

My heart sinks. I glance back at Ezra, who stares at me, expectant, a confused fear in his eyes. And as one thought plays through my head in a tortuous loop, my lips hurry to shape another.

We're too late.

"Run."

TWENTY-THREE

SMOKE BURNS MY NOSTRILS AND throat, and I cough on reflex, spitting blood onto the hard wooden floorboards. Jagged glass shards cut into my palms as I push myself upright, my arms shaking under the weight of my aching body, which lies prostrate in the middle of the sweltering corridor. Every inch of me hurts, and the building pressure in my head only adds to my disorientation.

A shrill ringing reverberates deep in my ears, and my vision is cloudy as I lift my head, squinting through the rippling waves of heat and potent smog filling the hallway. I cough again. All I can make out around me are indistinct silhouettes.

The injured refugees, I realize. Some are screaming. Some are attempting to flee. Others no longer move at all.

Panic digs its talons into my fracturing sanity, and I scramble to my feet, my head spinning as I scour my surroundings for Ezra. I barely had time to tell him to run before the explosion hit behind us. The blast projected me several feet forward from where I was standing before, but he was directly in front of me when that happened. He should be here.

Why isn't he here?

I brush the sweaty hair away from my forehead, wincing when my fingertips graze a deep gash near my temple. As I check the extent of the damage, something sharp pokes my thumb. Clenching my teeth, I pull a small piece of glass free of my skin. I glance at the bloodied fragment then drop it to the ground, my eyes shifting to what remains of the windows lining the wall to my left. The panes in every last one are shattered, giving me an unobscured view of the madness outside.

Like in the vision I had at the safe house, Enforcers storm the plaza, gunning down the unarmed civilians whose only crime was seeking shelter with PHOENIX, while gunfire and small-target bombs rain down from above, turning this part of Zone 1 into a battlefield. Enemy aircraft whirr overhead, but I can't see them through the black smoke shrouding the air.

I inch backward, a ragged breath parting my lips as I clamp a shaking hand over my mouth. The attack came out of nowhere, even though I knew it would inevitably come. Death and destruction follow me wherever I go. I was foolish to think we could outrun fate.

And now, everyone here is paying the price.

Once again, I search the hallway for Ezra, desperation igniting a fire in my bloodstream that sets my whole body ablaze.

"Ezra!" I shout, turning in circles.

The hazy corridor blurs, and my stomach lurches as the ringing and pressure in my skull intensify in tandem. Somewhere in the distance, I hear the distinct sound of gunfire, but I don't know if it's coming from outside or approaching from the far end of the hallway.

I stumble forward in the direction we were heading before, staggering a few steps to the left. I squint again. More screaming. Then gunfire again—closer this time.

My pulse skitters under my skin, and I swallow, sneering at the acrid taste of smoke on my tongue.

"Ezra! Duke!"

No response. I look over my shoulder, searching the path behind me for the others, but the smoke is so thick, it's like a tangible wall.

"Jenner! Quinn!" I cry out, my voice breaking as another hacking cough racks my lungs.

Sweat drips down my face as I look forward again, the hallway painted with orange patches of fire. Everywhere I turn, smoke or flame blocks my path.

I sway, light-headed, and my shoulder collides with the wall, my elbow brushing against the protruding remains of a window, the serrated edge tearing a hole in the arm of my jacket. Wheezing, I grip the broken frame for support, ignoring the searing cut of glass in my palms.

We're all going to die here and it's my fault.

"Jenner," I whimper. "Ezra..."

"Wynter!" a frantic voice shouts from somewhere behind me.

Blinking slowly, I veer my gaze to the left, toward the growing wall of smoke, when the voice shouts again.

"Wynter! Ezra!"

My heart trips as recognition sharpens my senses. "Quinn?"

Pushing away from the window, I trudge through the hallway, going back in the direction we came from, even though every logical part of my brain is telling me to run away from the smoke and flames instead of into them. Pressing my mouth and nose into the crook of my elbow, I push on toward the blaze, my eyes watering from the heat and fumes.

"Quinn!" My voice is hoarse from the tainted air and my sleeve muffles his name. I try again. "Quinn! Where are you?"

"Wynter! Over here!"

A burst of adrenaline surges through my body, and without sparing a second thought for the danger, I charge ahead, sidestepping the flames.

It takes less than ten seconds to find them, the tears clearing from my eyes just enough for me to spot Quinn kneeling in front of a broken ceiling beam, trying to lift its weight off the man pinned to the floor underneath it.

"Where's Jenner?" I ask as I race forward, squatting and planting my hands on the beam, my nails digging into the wood. My stomach clenches when I spare a glance at the injured man on the floor below us, taking in his inky sable hair, his bruised jaw and cheeks blackened with soot, and his wide blue eyes, which lock on me, freezing the blood in my veins.

"Pre...sent," Jenner says, his voice strained.

His name is a petrified breath on my lips.

"Help me!" Quinn pleads as he shifts position, propping his back against the debris. Blood trickles from a cut near his hairline and seeps through the side of his uniform, where he's probably burst his stitches trying to lift the beam on his own. Despite still suffering from his own wound, he puts all his strength into the task, but even with our combined efforts, the wood doesn't budge.

The beam snaps at one end, bringing its full weight down on Jenner's chest, stirring a panic within me that makes me want to rip the flesh from my bones. If I don't do something, he'll die.

"Get out... Go... Leave me...here..." Each word is a struggle as Jenner gasps to breathe.

He's running out of time.

"Move," I command when Quinn lets out a howl of frustration. If he keeps this up, he'll die here, too. "Move!" I bark again, grabbing him by the shoulder and pulling him away from the beam.

He shoots me a wary look but doesn't fight me, slinking to the side of the hallway and looking more frightened than I've ever seen him.

Fear and anger are my driving forces, and I look to them in place of the control

I had become so reliant on, using them as fuel to feed my power. I'm weak, and so close to the brink of death, but I know I can do this.

"There's still time," Rai says in my head, as if to say she believes I can, too.

A shiver rolls over my skin despite the broiling heat, and my right eye twitches as I focus every ounce of strength left within me—both mental and physical—on the length of wood. Pain, agonizing and all-consuming, cuts through my head like the shards of glass on the floor and window frame that bit into my hands.

If I had my collar, this would be easy, like lifting a twig, but I'm exhausted. No, not just exhausted, depleted, like an empty tank running only on fumes.

My eyes narrow on the beam, but the harder I push with my mind, the more my grip on the wood seems to slacken. Sensing my struggle, the monster drags its claws along the underside of my skin, reminding me of its inescapable presence now that it's unleashed. I could do it—I could surrender and let it take over if doing so would let me save Jenner. But I'm afraid...*so* afraid...that if I tap into that monster—if I yield to it again for even a moment—that will be it. There will be no coming back from that precipice and any hope I have of changing the future will be lost.

"Move, damn you!" Blood drips from my nose, pooling on my bottom lip, as an inhuman shriek tears from my lungs. My hands thrust out in front of me, as if to strengthen my mental hold on the beam, and when the sound of my scream fills the corridor, I finally feel the power I need rushing through me.

The monster nods its approval as the force of my mind slams into the hunk of debris, blowing it backward off Jenner where it then splinters, crashing into a wall several feet away.

My chest heaves as I watch the pieces land, my concentration wavering. Others could be trapped here, too. Others might need my help, even though I'm not sure I have it in me to help them. Still, I reach out with my senses, searching for anyone who might be alive among the wreckage.

Aside from Quinn's, the only heartbeat I sense in the immediate vicinity is Jenner's.

Staggering forward, I drop to my knees beside him. "Jenner—"

I look him over, searching for broken bones or any other visible damage while trying not to fear the worst—the damage inside his body I won't be able to see. His shirt is torn where the beam struck his chest, and I can already see the black and purple bruises forming on his torso through the slashes in the fabric.

His eyes shutter open and closed a few times. "I'm...okay..." he says between gulps of air.

Curling my hand around the back of his neck, I help him into a sitting position, taking care not to move him too quickly. Before he's even fully upright, he recoils from my touch, his face scrunching in pain.

"Shit." He grimaces, his hand darting to his side. "I think...I might have broken a rib."

Worry envelops me, its grasp suffocating. If his rib *is* broken and it punctures a lung—

"We need to find help," I breathe.

Remembering Quinn, I look over my shoulder, locking eyes with the ex-Enforcer where he sits on the floor, propped up against the wall. My gaze falls to the hand clamped tight to his side.

"Quinn?" I ask. I can't help wondering if he can hear the tremor in my voice.

A shaky breath parts his lips as he nods. "I'm good," he says, even though I know he isn't. Based on the blood seeping through his fingers, he definitely reopened his wound.

Grunting, Quinn rolls over onto his knees, then pushes up to his feet before straightening, only pausing in his movements to cough. He jerks his head, fighting to stay conscious in the encompassing heat, then wobbles toward us, his balance precarious.

As he squats on Jenner's other side, the fire roars—lashing out around us with hungry intent—and more debris falls from the ceiling, the remaining wooden beams overhead cracking, threatening to come down on us at any moment.

"Help me get him up," Quinn barks.

Panting, I fling Jenner's right arm over my shoulder while Quinn does the same with his left. Then, together, we lift him up off the floor, displacing the majority of his weight between us.

"Stay awake," I murmur, and he nods, although the movement is weak.

Jenner is conscious, but his breathing is unstable, and his eyelids keep fluttering, making me fear sleep—or something much more final—is beckoning him. If only I could tell just how badly he's hurt.

"Where are Ezra and Duke?" Quinn shouts to me over the crack and hiss of the spreading flames.

Shaking my head, I peer at him from under Jenner's arm. "I don't know. I haven't seen them since—"

The crash of falling timber behind us drowns out my voice, and we trip forward when a rush of heat strikes our backs, nearly knocking us all to the floor.

"Damn it," Quinn hisses, regaining his balance as I struggle to do the same. "We need to get out of here."

His obsidian eyes glow orange in the light of the flames as he looks around for an escape route. The way we came from is blocked, desecrated by one of many ongoing explosions if the rumbling quakes intermittently rocking the building are any indication of the hell raining down on us from above.

"This way," Quinn says in a rush, guiding us forward toward the nearest broken window.

When we reach the sill, I stop dead in my tracks. "We can't leave. We need to find Ezra and Duke."

Quinn pauses with one hand on the frame, gaping at me in disbelief. "You hear that?" he asks.

I follow his leery gaze down the hallway—in the direction we were heading in before the attack—noting the sprinkle of gunfire and screaming. So much screaming. Both closer and louder…

So much louder than they were when I last listened for them.

Sneering, Quinn meets my gaze. "They're probably already dead."

"No!" Ezra's face fills my head, and my heart seems to cave in at the thought of never seeing him again, even though our time together was already close to being over. "He isn't!" I protest, my scream edging on hysterical. "Ezra isn't…"

I sink my teeth into the inside of my cheek. Ezra *has* to be alive. He has a part to play still. I *need* him. He can't be gone, because if he is…

Then there's no one left to stop me.

"He isn't," I say again, softer this time.

"Wynter's right," Jenner murmurs, drawing both our stunned gazes. Lifting his head, he lets out a low, crackling exhalation, and once again, I worry about the state of his lungs. "We can't…leave them behind."

"Damn it," Quinn mutters under his breath. But, to his credit, he doesn't fight us on the matter, instead leading us away from the escape of the window and down the seemingly unending hallway.

Others seem to have had the same idea as Quinn, and as we push ahead, the three of us hobbling as one unit, I watch as refugees climb out through the windows, while others die on the floor, succumbing to the choking smoke and flames.

I cough into my elbow, feeling the smoke's grasp on me growing, my head increasingly dizzy with each step and with every breath drawn into my lungs. Still, I push on, consoled only by knowing that I won't die here in this burning building—that there *is* still time, like Rai keeps saying.

My eyes scan our murky surroundings, searching for any sign of Ezra or Duke's hulking frame among the wave of civilians racing toward us, away from the gunfire, which is so close now I can smell the sulfur in the air.

Panic. Havoc. Both consume the overheated corridor as the bodies pile up.

"Do you see them?" I bellow, grunting when an elderly man limping past knocks into my shoulder.

The source of the gunfire is visible now, the soldiers forming a black mass in the distance that moves toward us like an unstoppable plague. Even if the guard at the entrance hadn't taken our guns, the reality is, we're vastly outnumbered.

If we keep going, they'll gun us down.

"No!" Quinn answers, quickly followed by, "Wait! Over there!"

He steers us through the frenzied throng, pointing his free hand in the direction of a junction up ahead where the corridors intersect. The pack of Enforcers approaching have cut off the opposite side of the hallway we're in, leaving only three paths open—the way we came from, which is blocked by fire and debris, to the left, which will only lead to certain death at the hands of the chaos outside, or to the right, the only viable option if anyone hopes to get out of this alive.

My heart pounds in my ears as I follow Quinn's outstretched finger, spotting Ezra and Duke, who take cover from the gunfire at each side of the crossing, facing us with their backs to the wall of the passage cutting horizontally through the main hallway. Although faint, given the mayhem around us, I can hear them both shouting—directing the innocent civilians who have been caught in the middle of this war to take that right-hand path and flee.

"Ezra!" I cry out, unable to contain my relief.

His gaze snaps toward us at the sound of my voice, and when our eyes lock through a gap in the crowd, the entire world seems to stand still for a moment.

"Wynter!" he calls back, bolting away from the safety of the wall and sprinting toward us.

He pushes through the mob, closing the distance between us in seconds. "Are you okay?" he asks, roughly taking my face in his hands before glancing at Jenner and Quinn. "You guys hurt?"

"We're coping," Jenner mutters with a wheezy laugh.

Ezra nods, and when his eyes turn back to mine, I notice the dirt and ash on his cheeks, hiding the bruises underneath. The filth on his clothes. His disheveled hair...

Just like he always looks in my vision.

"I couldn't find you," he says, his voice thready. "The blast knocked me out cold, and when I woke up, it was chaos. People trampling each other. I—"

"It's okay," I interrupt, pressing my palm to his cheek, wiping away a rogue tear with my thumb.

He looks over his shoulder when the gunfire draws uncomfortably close, grabbing hold of my hand. "Come on. Follow me."

"No." I dig my heels into the floorboards when he yanks me forward. "We still need to find Nolan."

Quinn scoffs. "If the Heads aren't dead, they will be soon. Just like us, if we don't get out of here."

He's right. I *know* he's right, but we came all this way and the plan is falling apart right in front of my eyes at an alarming rate. I don't know what to do.

I don't know how to fix this.

"Ezra! We have to go! Now!" Duke shouts from the intersection, manically waving us forward.

Ezra's hazel eyes swing to mine, imploring. "We'll come up with another plan."

Another plan.

I frown, my tongue darting out and licking across the blood drying on my lower lip.

We don't have time for another plan.

"Behind you!" Jenner rasps suddenly, throwing the full weight of his body on mine and whirling us around until we've swapped positions.

At the same moment, a deep voice yells out, "Target sighted!"

I barely have time to process the soldier aiming at me through the shattered window when a gunshot cuts through the surrounding commotion like a knife through butter. Jenner shudders against me, and my heart goes still.

"Jenner?"

In my peripheral vision, I'm aware of Ezra launching himself at the enemy soldier, wrenching the pistol free of his grip before turning it on him and pulling the trigger. The man's head snaps back, and he falls away from the window, crumpling to the ground out of sight.

Jenner's arms go slack around my torso, and with a stilted breath, he stumbles backward a step, his face pale under a thick sheen of sweat. "Ou…ch…"

I can barely breathe, time and space slowing around me as Jenner tilts his head, looking down. His eyes are glassy, and terror strangles my throat as I force myself to follow his gaze.

"Jenner?" I whisper again, tears streaking my vision as red expands across the front of his shirt.

The blood is like a blooming flower, unfurling across his chest until almost every inch of the pale fabric is drenched. I can't move. I can't think. I can't breathe. This is just like that vision I had after we met when it dawned on me that I would be responsible for not only the end of the world…but for the deaths of the people I love.

People like Jenner.

"Today…is not…my day," he stammers before collapsing to the floor.

"Jenner!" Ezra and Quinn both rush to his side, but I stand rooted to the spot, the shock racing through me like ice in my veins, freezing me.

I can't move.

I can't think.

I can't breathe.

Inside my head, the monster seethes. *They did this,* it says, and I lift my gaze, my eyes locking on the black mass of approaching Enforcers. Or maybe they aren't Enforcers at all, but this new nameless enemy.

It doesn't matter who they are, I tell myself, and the monster agrees. *They're all the same.*

And every last one of them deserves to die.

"Wynter?" Ezra's voice is distant, like he's speaking to me from behind a glass wall. The ear splitting ringing returns to my head, and my right eye twitches as my hands clench into fists at my sides.

The soldiers have breached the intersection now. The civilians who haven't escaped are shot, and in the back of my mind, I'm aware of Duke running toward us to escape the spray of bullets, even though the path this way is a dead end.

Kill them, the monster croons in my ear as the surfacing pressure in my chest seeks an escape. *Let me help you kill them all.*

Whatever lingering hold I had on my sanity is lost as I cede control to the monster. Power stretches under my skin, and Ezra screams my name as I break free of the shock binding me, storming ahead with only one goal in mind: to destroy anything that stands in the way of my anger.

I use my rage as both a shield and a weapon, projecting it at everything in my path. The civilians who screamed in terror of the soldiers now run the other way in fear of me, trapped between the two like a mouse caught by two grappling vipers.

"They did this," I mutter to myself, stalking forward, and for a moment, I can't stop the flood of grief washing through me as I'm reminded of all the people I've lost because of the State's obsessive need for power. My father's face fills my thoughts followed by Rai's. Then, I see Jenner.

His face lingers the longest.

"The State did this," I growl, possessed by my fury. It's a fire curling under my skin, stoked by the monster, who wants to see the chaos I can bring to this world.

Just like Dr. Richter, I realize.

"I hate you!" I scream as a wave of energy explodes out of me, shattering the few remaining windows and rendering anyone unfortunate enough to be near me to mere piles of ash. "I hate you all!"

The State did this.

Richter did this.

The soldiers, so close now and aware of the danger I pose, aim their weapons at me, pulling the triggers. The bullets don't get far before I turn them back on their owners, like I did the last time I was here in this building when I murdered the group of Enforcers sent by Richter. Just like then, I watch as they drop, one by one, to the floor like dead flies. And as the light leaves their eyes, I realize I am Death, just like Richter said. But more than that, I am chaos incarnate.

And this is what I was created for.

"Wynter, stop!" someone shouts, grabbing my arm, but I throw them off, refusing to let them stand in my way. They crash to the floor with a grunt, and as I turn to face them, I take in the result of my wrath. Bodies everywhere—some soldiers, most not. Few, if any, are left standing.

I turn, concentrating on the figure bold enough to attack me, ready to eviscerate him like I did the others, when I glimpse the pitiful gun in his hand and the hazel eyes staring at me, pleading for the monster to stop. The pistol shakes in the man's grip, but he doesn't lower the barrel or point it away. His finger hovers over the trigger.

A tear cuts down his cheek. "Please," he begs, and I can see in the furrowed lines of his brow that he doesn't want to do this. He doesn't *want* to shoot me.

But he will.

He'll kill me to put an end to my rampage.

He'll kill me even though he loves me.

That thought is what finally snaps me out of my frenzy, and I gape at Ezra, mortified at how close I came just now to ending his life.

"Ezra—" His name is garbled in my mouth as a spurt of blood breaches my lips, and I gasp, gripping my skull in both hands, as the pain in my head brings me to my knees.

Darkness is a snake slithering over my vision, sheathing my surroundings in black. And like so many times before, I sense the taut leash of unconsciousness, pulling me back into its grasp against my will.

As it rises to take me, I have just enough time to meet Ezra's gaze—to let him know I'm me again. That I don't want to hurt him or anyone else…

But that I'm glad he'll do what needs to be done to stop me when I do.

"I'm sorry," is all I manage to say as the world turns sideways and my head hits the ground.

TWENTY-FOUR

I WAKE WITH A START, a jagged groan splitting my lips as the minimal contents of my stomach threaten to remove themselves from my body. My head feels like it's been cracked in half, the pain like a hammer behind my eyes and temples, each swing chipping away at my skull in time with every beat of my pulse.

When my eyelids wrench open a few seconds later, I flinch away from the gentle light on my face, my retinas oversensitive, even though the room around me is dark. Tears distort my vision, blurring the blue light stretching before me into streaks.

What is that? I wonder.

With another groan, I shift myself upright, feeling the rough fabric of an armchair grazing my fingers. My entire body hurts, like my bones have all been broken and reset wrong.

Wiping the moisture from my eyes, I blink several times, forcing the details of my surroundings into focus. At first, I think I'm back in Bilken's office—back in the setting of so many of my worst nightmares and of one of my most guilt-ridden memories—but the more I take in the encompassing space, the more I notice the differences. Instead of white carpet, the bare floorboards underneath are exposed, and in place of a glass desk, a steel conference room table stands before a windowless wall. Most striking of all, unlike in Bilken's office, there are no extra spaces or adjacent nooks in this room to display possessions paid for with the people's blood.

Breathing in, I squint at the source of the light—a vast depiction of the building projecting from a small device in the middle of the table—and just behind it, I glimpse Duke, Ezra, and Quinn, assessing the schematics while in heated discussion, their faces drenched pale blue in the glow.

As if sensing me watching him, Ezra turns his head, meeting my gaze through the flickering hologram.

"Wynter." He quickly skirts the table, crossing the room to my position in seconds.

Relief and guilt go to war in my chest as he kneels before me, those hazel eyes brimming with a concern I don't deserve. Does he feel the same way? After coming so close to pulling that trigger—although I asked him to do it—can things ever be the same between us?

Or is this almost tangible sadness I feel in the shared air we breathe as permanent and inescapable as our fates?

My mouth is dry, and I can taste the bitterness of regret on my tongue as I force out the words, "How long have I...? Where..." Trailing off, I press the heels of my hands into my aching eyes. "Where are we?"

"Not long," Ezra murmurs. "Only a few minutes. We're in one of the western annex offices, as far from the fires as we could get for the moment."

Trepidation prickles along my skin as I lower my arms. "The exits?" I ask.

I draw in a breath through my nose, noting the stench of smoke isn't quite as potent as it was before when we were caught in the thick of it. Still, the smell of it clings to my nostrils, and I know it's only a matter of time before the flames reach us and force us out of our hiding place.

He averts his gaze, his lips set in a serious line. "All blocked. There's no way out, at least not from this level. The doors are either all inaccessible because of the explosions or pinned down by soldiers shooting anyone who tries to leave the building. I think the fire is what's keeping them at bay, but who knows how long it will be before they send in the next wave."

"Are we sure they were Enforcers?"

When we were ambushed at that roadblock in Zone 3, the soldiers looked just like Enforcers. It wasn't until Quinn pointed out the blacked-out crests on their sleeves that we realized they were this new enemy in disguise. At a glance, it was virtually impossible to tell them apart.

Ezra nods. "We checked a few of the bodies, and the ones you took out in the hallway definitely were. I think, between the number of patrols in the city and Nolan's call for citizens to side with PHOENIX, it's probably safe to assume the soldiers outside all belong to the State."

Not all of them, I muse, but I can't bring myself to utter those words.

"Regardless of the attack, the State was never going to tolerate such outright betrayal and treason," Ezra continues. "Besides, with PHOENIX out in the open and their whereabouts on full display, it makes sense the Enforcers would choose now to strike. Eradicate PHOENIX and you eliminate half the current problem."

Images of the massacre occurring just outside this building's walls stain my mind yet again. "That isn't..."

A tear cuts down my cheek.

"What is it?" Ezra whispers, leaning in.

I shake my head. "It isn't only Enforcers. That soldier you killed..." I swallow, and my throat is unbearably thick. "He wasn't with the State!" I cry out. "He was going to—" Pressure squeezes my chest, and an inconsolable sob breaks free of my lungs. "But Je—" A spasm restricts my diaphragm as my fingers frantically tear at my eyes, trying to rip out the memory branded to the backs of my lids.

That crimson flower of blood blooming across Jenner's chest is a nightmarish image I will never escape.

He shielded me. He put himself in my place and took the bullet intended to end my life, even though all I've wanted to do since the day we met is keep him alive. I didn't ever want him to protect me.

I only wanted to protect him.

Why did you do that? I wish I could ask him. *Why did you sacrifice yourself for me when my life is already over?*

"Jenner," I gasp, weeping into my hands.

A warm hand brushes the hair away from my face. "Hey, it's okay."

No. No, it isn't.

How can Ezra say that when his best friend not only died...but died because of *me*?

My grief is a bottomless ocean, and once again, I find myself drowning in it. This time, I fear I'll never find my way back to the surface.

Maybe I don't want to.

"Wynter, listen to me!" Ezra pleads, grabbing me by the shoulders and shaking me. "It's okay! Jenner's alive!"

Jenner's...alive...?

Those words are a wrecking ball against the walls of my heart as I finally meet Ezra's gaze. His pupils are blown, his own chest heaving.

"Wh-What?" A soft hiccup breaches my lips, and the shock of this revelation calms me enough that I manage to say, "Jenner's...okay?"

He nods, wiping the tears from my cheeks with his thumbs. "I'm so sorry. If I had known that's what you thought—"

I grip the backs of his hands, pulling them away from my face. "That's why..." But I can't find the will to finish the rest of that sentence. To admit what I did to all the refugees trapped out there in the hallway alongside us, whose only crime was trying to escape the terror inflicted on their lives by me.

By being in the same proximity as the people I wanted to blame for my pain.

Fresh tears well in my eyes, but I push them back. "Where is he?"

Understanding and pity both flit across Ezra's face as he helps me up from the chair. When he points out where Jenner is—propped up by cushions on the floor in the corner of the room to keep him upright and take the weight off his lungs—it requires all the self-control I possess not to throw myself at him and hug whatever life he still has out of his body.

As I stumble toward him, his eyes flutter open.

"Hey," he croaks, gifting me with that lopsided smile that always warms my chest. When he looks at me like that, it feels like home.

"How?" I breathe, dropping to my knees beside him, noting the belt tied across his chest right under his armpits. "You… You were shot."

He chuckles, then goes still, his face contorting in pain. "Yeah, I remember. Son of a bitch really hurts, too. But I guess now we know why Quinn was being such a baby," he says between strained breaths.

"I heard that," the ex-Enforcer grumbles from the other side of the room.

I scowl at Jenner. This is no time to be joking. This is serious. He could have *died*.

"But you…" I shake my head. "I saw—"

Jenner taps the belt, then tugs down the neck of his bloodstained shirt, revealing a wad of fabric against his bare chest. It looks like the torn remnants of a shirt, the original gray of the cloth only visible at the edges. The rest is soaked almost entirely red.

I risk a quick glance at the others. Considering no one in this room is short on attire, I'm not sure I want to know where they got it from.

You mean who, my brain corrects me.

Shuddering, I stare at Jenner, wide-eyed, as he says, "The bastard caught me in the shoulder. So, thanks to his shitty aim, I'll live."

I blink, looking closer at the makeshift dressing and tourniquet. He was shot in the shoulder. Not the chest. Not the heart.

His *shoulder*.

"I-I thought…" I stammer, fresh tears spilling over as I raise a trembling hand to my mouth.

"I know," Jenner whispers, playfully poking me in the left cheek. "And I'm touched you'd go on a murderous rampage to avenge my death."

These words aren't said with any humor but with a morose understanding of just how much he means to me…and of how far gone I am. Of how willing I am to let the world burn for daring to harm one hair on his head.

It would be easy to blame the monster. To plead innocence and shift the guilt of my actions onto this parasitic illness and claim some invisible entity taking over my body made me do it. But the truth is, there is no monster. Only me.

Me grappling with my own inner demons as I lose myself to the madness of this disease.

"I…" The lump in my throat is thick enough now to choke me. When I swallow, it hurts. "What I—" Tears curve over my fingers and lips, tasting strongly of salt and cinders.

Of ash, like all that remains of some of my victims.

"Those people—"

Ezra wraps his arms around me, kneeling directly behind me and pulling me back against his chest before I give into the guilt. Pressing his face into the crook where my neck meets my shoulder, he murmurs, "It doesn't matter now, Wynter. They all would've ended up dead anyway."

There's a pain in his voice that makes me realize he's right. He said it himself— the soldiers outside are shooting anyone who tries to leave the building. That would mean any of the people I didn't kill in my frenzy would've been met with the same end once they fled outside. Just like all the refugees he and Duke tried to help, their act of selfless bravery reduced to nothing.

Ezra's arms squeeze me tighter, and I can sense his anguish in the hot breaths on my neck and the way his fingers dig into my skin. I don't want him to hurt anymore.

I just want this nightmare to end.

Sinking into a chair to my right, Quinn scoffs. "And now, we're all going to die here, too."

Ezra's arms retract from around me, and as he stands, he grinds out through gritted teeth, "Don't be a dick. It isn't helping anyone."

Quinn flops his head against the back of the chair, as if he's lost the will to argue. "I'm only speaking the truth. I stayed behind to help end this conflict. To *fix* things. Not to die like some scared sewer rat in hiding while innocent people are slaughtered." With a disgruntled sigh, he scrubs a hand across his face. "The whole plan's gone to shit."

"No," I breathe, clambering to my feet. "Not yet it hasn't. We can still find Nolan."

I turn into the heat of Ezra's eyes on my face. He stares at me, his expression dejected, and in this moment, it occurs to me that Quinn isn't the only one among us who's lost hope. "Wynter, he might be dead—"

"He's not," I blurt out, my voice jumping an octave. "He's not," I say again, softer this time, the words barely above a breath. "He's alive. I've seen it." I look down at Jenner. "That vision I told you about? Proof or no peace? When I saw him get that message, he was *here*, in this building, in a room that was filling with smoke."

"So, you're saying you think that vision only just happened? Or maybe hasn't even occurred yet at all?"

Meeting Ezra's gaze again, I nod. "They think Nolan's lying about me being dead—that he's hiding me to use against them later. But they've offered him an olive branch. The chance to prove I'm dead and to end this."

"Bombing us doesn't seem like much of an olive branch," Quinn points out, grimacing as he raises his head.

I shrug, conceding his point. "No, but something tells me that's the idea. They want Nolan to know they're serious about not letting up until he gives them what they want. This attack…" The whiplike snaps of crackling flame and the echoes of gunshots resound in my head, and I wince at the memory of the horrors we left beyond this room. "I think it was only a warning."

With a long, low whistle, Duke leans against the side of Quinn's chair. "One hell of a warnin'."

Quinn's black eyes narrow on my face. "Even if he *is* alive, we don't have time to search every damn room in this place hoping to find him—"

"We don't have to," I interrupt, ignoring when he cocks a dubious brow at me. "We can contact him on his communicator, like Jenner suggested earlier."

Ezra, Jenner, Quinn, and Duke all exchange pensive glances, as if considering the validity of my idea.

I look between them, annoyed by their silence. "Is it not possible or something? Surely, one of you knows what frequency band he's on?"

"What happened to the element of surprise?" Jenner asks, repeating Ezra's earlier words. "If we call him, won't that run the risk of the other Heads never finding out what he did?"

I falter, worrying my lower lip between my teeth, unsure what to say to that. He's right. Calling Nolan directly removes what leverage we have over him from the equation. As much as I need him to make a deal with this enemy and help me put a stop to this war, I can't agree to anything until I'm certain my friends, my *family*, will be safe from threat. That includes not only Ezra and Jenner but Duke—who had no real reason to get involved and help me but did anyway— and Quinn, who for all his grumbling isn't quite as surly as he wants us to think. The ex-Enforcer might have a real chip on his shoulder, but we wouldn't have gotten this far without him. I owe him the fresh start my mother promised.

But how can I protect any of them when there's no one left alive I can trust? No one I can be certain will see that my wishes are honored long after I'm dead?

"I can try Jaed," Duke suggests.

My eyes flick to his. "Jaed?" The name sounds familiar, but I can't place where I've heard it before.

"Jaedyn Vance," Duke clarifies. "She's Head of the sect I was transferred to after…" He hesitates, looking first at Ezra, then Jenner, and in that shared glance between them, I know what he isn't saying—what moment he's referring to with his silence.

After I went back to the DSD where, for all they knew, Richter would've tortured me for information about PHOENIX's whereabouts.

I stare at Duke for a long moment, processing Jaedyn's name and searching for her face in my recent recollections—in particular, from when I was forced to recount my vision of the attack on the Heart before the Heads several days earlier at Nolan's request. I remember her now, just as I remember the fear that had swelled in my chest, alongside a begrudging respect. As the only female in a group of ambitious men, she deserved that much from me, even if, at the time, I thought she supported Nolan's plan for the Heart. A thought, which I'm hoping was misguided, if Duke really believes she's someone we can turn to.

Clearing his throat, Duke folds his arms across his broad chest. "The Heads were meetin' when I was bringin' you to see them, so, if she's alive, there's a good chance she's with Nolan right now. She can tell us where they are or, at least, give us a clue where Nolan might be if they aren't together. Then, we can still go directly to them as planned. Or, if we can't, we use her as the go-between, so someone else knows what's goin' on."

Ezra is the one to ask the all-important question. "Can we trust her?"

My heart catches in my throat, and my palms are sweaty as I curl my hands into fists.

More importantly, I add in my head. *Will she help us?*

Duke offers a noncommittal shrug. "I'd like to think so given what I know of her. If any of the Heads are goin' to have a lick of sense, it's Jaed. Plus, she's against this whole operation."

"Against it how?" I press.

She didn't seem against it when all the Heads were nodding their approval regarding the attack. Then again, some did seem more reluctant in their agreement than others.

Duke gives me a look that says the answer is obvious. "Against lettin' thousands of innocent bystanders die. She thinks we should have tried to prevent the attack rather than use it to benefit PHOENIX. Unfortunately, she was in the minority, and, as we all know, majority rules."

A frown tugs at the corners of my lips. "And you know she thinks this…how?" I stifle an exasperated sigh, sincerely hoping this isn't another case of half-truths running wild and becoming rumor. We can't risk the only opportunity left to us on second-hand information.

Duke lowers his eyes to the floor. "She told me."

Quinn snorts. "You're saying the Head of your sect just so happened to confide this very timely and relevant information to you?"

The stocky man flushes to the tips of his ears and swallows so loudly I'm certain everyone in the room can hear it. "Uh… Yes," he says, looking uncomfortable.

"Why?" Quinn asks. I cock my head to one side, appraising Duke and wondering the same thing.

Jenner barks out a laugh that quickly turns into a yelp of pain. Glancing between me and Quinn, he deadpans, "Wow, if you two were any denser, you'd be robots. For clarity, I blame the State for that, not either of you." Then, with a mischievous grin at Duke, he purrs, "Bedding a Head. You sly dog, you."

I didn't think it was possible for Duke to turn any redder, but his skin burns deep crimson at Jenner's teasing words. It takes a second for their meaning to click in my brain. When they do, "Oh," is all I can think to say.

Coming up behind me again, Ezra loops an arm around my waist. "So, there's already a precedent there for her to hear us out. And maybe the other Heads, too, now that the plan hasn't gone the way they hoped."

I peer up at him, nodding my agreement, before turning to Duke once more, steadfast in my commitment to seeing this through. To get to Nolan and end this the way I always intended to.

"Do it," I say, my voice a determined growl. "Make the call."

TWENTY-FIVE

WE EMERGE FROM THE OFFICE ten minutes later, after Duke has made contact with Jaedyn. I could only hear his side of their conversation, which lasted maybe two minutes but seemed to span hours as the rest of us waited with bated breath, hoping whatever information he gleaned from the Head would help us track down Nolan.

The memory of their one-sided exchange plays again in my head as we weave a path through the smoggy, smoke-stained hallways.

"Don't worry about me," Duke said when Jaedyn answered the call. "I'm fine. Where are you?"

A pause.

"Is Nolan with you? What about the other Heads?"

A longer pause.

"Tell me how to get to you. We need to talk to Nolan immediately."

Duke hesitated then, his mossy brown eyes finding mine in the darkness of the office.

"The State's weapon," he muttered, staring at me. "She's here. Along with some others who just want to help."

Silence again.

"I know what we've been told, but it isn't true. Nolan's lied to us," Duke growled after a moment. Then, softer, he said, "Jaed… You'll just need to trust me on this. Please."

The call ended shortly after that plea, at which point, Duke had returned to the schematics of the building's layout hovering over the table. Inserting a location marker into the hologram map, he grabbed the projector and crossed the room, tossing the device to Quinn before squatting to help Jenner up from the floor.

"Seein' as you're hurt, I'll give Jenner a hand and you can lead the way," he had grunted, nodding at the ex-Enforcer in passing as he made his way to the door. "I think *your* hands are already full," he then added with a knowing glance at Ezra.

He wasn't wrong. Since my outburst, I can barely stand on my own, let alone walk anywhere unaided. As we progress through the first floor of the building, avoiding the fire-ravaged paths, Ezra keeps close beside me, never letting me stray too far in my disorientation.

When I do, his fingers draw me back.

"So, where is it we're going, exactly?" he asks, tightening a hand around my waist.

"Jaed said the Heads are hunkered down in a safe room in the basement while they figure out what to do next," Duke answers.

"This place has a safe room?" Jenner slurs, stumbling along beside Duke, his uninjured arm draped across the older man's shoulders.

"Most of the government buildings do," Quinn asserts, calling back to us from where he keeps pace a short distance ahead. "Considering the State's most influential members have offices here, it makes sense they'd have a secure location to evacuate to in the event of an attack."

A humorless laugh parts my lips. "Ironic."

"What is?" Ezra murmurs.

I lift my shoulders in a half-hearted shrug. "That PHOENIX emerges for the first time in decades, and now, it's right back underground where it started."

No one says another word as we traverse the long hallways, searching for the entrance to the basement Jaedyn mentioned to Duke. We find it—an unassuming door hidden in plain sight, surrounded by others just like it, with the only difference being a keypad where the handle should be—back in the eastern side of the building, which seemed to take the brunt of the damage from the explosions. Access to entire passages are blocked off from caved-in ceilings and other varying forms of burning debris, and the fire is still raging, though spreading far more slowly than I would expect.

It's possible the stunted growth of the inferno is a result of the chemical compounds used in the bombs, the slow spread intentional to drive home the warning message behind the attack—to threaten PHOENIX, to maim it, but not to destroy it. Though, it's just as likely due to the lack of flammable objects, or any objects at all, in the corridors. Either way, the flames still find prey to devour, the blackened corpses lining the floor adding the stink of burning charcoal to the air, turning it putrid.

The resurgence of smoke in my lungs is debilitating, and the temperature of the flames scoring the walls nearby is unwelcome against my already overheated skin. Sweat trickles down the sides of my face and the back of my neck as I watch Quinn enter the code Duke recites to him into the keypad. When the last digit is entered, the door unlocks and swings inward on sturdy hydraulic hinges into an unlit passage beyond, blasting us with a rush of unpolluted air.

With a hacking cough into the crook of his elbow, Quinn removes the flashlight from his belt and staggers forward into the darkness. The brilliant beam of light cuts into the shadows, revealing a set of stairs leading down.

"How did the Heads know the code to get down here?" I ask. But as we descend, I note the similarities between this space and the pathway beneath the parking structure in Zone 3 that my mother took us down to get to the safe house.

The words have barely left my lips when I make the connection.

Coming to the same conclusion, Ezra grumbles, "If I had to guess? Bilken."

That would explain why the Heads chose the magistrates building as their base of operations and acting headquarters during the siege. Aside from being in a central location, insider intel about the layout made it an ideal place to go to ground and wait out the attack.

Unless there's no way out, I muse.

In that case, the safe room might as well be a tomb.

At the bottom of the stairs, I glimpse a faint light on our right, then movement, a face taking shape in the murky shadows of the passage.

"Duke?" a hesitant voice calls out.

"It's us," the brawny man says in response.

There's a moment of hesitation, and then Jaedyn Vance steps forward, her features sharpening in the beam of Quinn's flashlight. Her chestnut skin is flushed, her expression caught somewhere between relieved and nervous.

"Are you okay?" she asks Duke. Her eyes find mine, and she stills, making no move to come any closer.

Duke answers with an affirmative grunt. "You?"

Jaedyn heaves a shuddering sigh. "I will be once this is over." Her eyes hang on mine, and I can sense her silent deliberation. Finally, she nods and says, "Right. Follow me."

Jaedyn leads us along a winding passage, the gloom thick enough to swallow us whole even though glass sconces line the walls, offering—but failing to provide—the solace of light. Come to think of it, the only place I've seen fully operational power since the attack began was at Bilken's safe house. Even the DSD, which has a back-up generator, was limited to the use of emergency energy; the only functional lights on in the entire building were mere strips of ominous blue lining the floors. Is the State's infrastructure really that fragile and crumbling that quickly as a result of the bombings?

Or is it purposely keeping the city in darkness to demonstrate how much control it has over us?

"It's so empty down here," I whisper, a shiver crawling up my spine.

How many of the terrified refugees outside in the plaza could have been saved in this most recent assault if the Heads had diverted the civilians who looked to them for help down here in the interim? Why didn't they take advantage of this sprawling space if they knew it was here?

I can only assume it was because Nolan didn't want to sacrifice the Heads' only access to shelter to the very people he believed expendable in this war.

Jaedyn stiffens, her shoulders raising defensively. "The attack happened so quickly," she says, her voice curt. "There wasn't time…" She shakes her head, then mutters something unintelligible, sweeping a black curl behind her ear before repeating, "There wasn't time. We only just made it down here ourselves and we barely managed that much with our lives." This time, her tone is regretful, and I can't help imagining that she *did* want to save those lives, but something—or someone—stood in her way.

Her reaction to my unspoken accusation is telling, and I realize, maybe Duke was right, after all. Maybe there is one Head of PHOENIX left we can trust.

One who still has a firm grip on their conscience.

"Does Nolan know we're comin'?" Duke asks, falling into step behind Jaedyn as Jenner grunts, working to keep up.

Her large, round eyes cut to his over her shoulder, her lips pursed in a deliberate scowl. "No. Given what *little* you told me, I figured it would be better this way."

"I'm sorry about that," Duke mumbles, and Jaedyn shifts her attention back ahead with a *humph*. "There wasn't time to fill you in on the details."

She falters then, only pausing long enough to look back at me where I linger at the back of our procession. Molten brown eyes gleaming black in the darkness, she says, "Well, I assume we'll all find out the truth soon enough."

We continue the rest of the way to the safe room in silence, the trek taking less than five minutes in total, even with our listless pace, although, mentally, the journey seems never-ending.

While the path we take is similar in style and layout to the one we took to Bilken's safe house, in so many ways, this underground passage reminds me of the tunnels we traveled that night two and a half years ago. The night we first lost Rai and the course of my life was altered, turning me into this monster.

In many ways, this moment mirrors what we went through back then. The difference is that I won't make the same mistakes. I won't be tricked or fooled by the cunning of someone else and their immoral motivations.

This time, the outcome will be decided by me.

The glow of Jaedyn's flashlight illuminates a reinforced bulkhead door at the end of the corridor, which is once again devoured by shadow when she turns to face us.

"Before I open that door…" She hesitates again for the breadth of a heartbeat, then raises her chin, forceful and resilient, unflinching as her glare pins me down. "I don't know what's going on, but I sincerely hope you came here with a solution. Not to create more problems for us."

I can feel the weight of the others' stares on my face. This is it—the do or die moment. Once these words leave my lips, there can be no going back, no changing my mind or running away from my fate or searching for another way out of this mess. The moment I walk through that door, my life is over—surrendered as payment to guarantee the survival of others.

Ezra squeezes my waist, and I lay my hand on top of his, squeezing back. Like always, his touch grounds me and serves as a stark reminder of what I'm fighting for.

Of what I'd gladly pay any price in the world to protect.

Leveling my gaze at the Head, I retort, "I came to you with a way to end this war."

Once again, Jaedyn's eyes hold mine for a moment. "Good." She lets out another shuddering sigh. "That's what I was hoping you'd say."

Like the door upstairs on the ground level, the door to the safe room is controlled solely by keypad entry. Deadbolted shut, the entrance is impassable without the code. Or a strong enough explosive.

Or someone who can tear through metal with their mind.

Fortunately, we don't need to resort to the two latter options—I'm too drained for anything more taxing than walking, and an explosive would be more likely to cave in the passage than to actually break into the room, not that we have any on hand to find out.

But we do have the code, which Jaedyn inputs after casting one final apprehensive glance in my direction, that single look exposing her indecision as to whether she should trust me. In that split-second when our eyes were locked, I could see the doubt so clearly in her gaze, the swirling depths of her eyes alight with the question of if I really am here to help them end this war like I claimed.

Regardless, she enters the code, and when the keypad registers the final digit, the buzzing of a motor fills the passage, the sound vibrating through the floor into my feet. Beyond the hum, I hear the click of tumblers shifting and the whirring crunch of gears turning as the deadbolts sealing the entrance slide free.

Gripping the handle, Jaedyn pulls the door open, then steps over the lip into the darkness beyond. We follow behind her one at a time—Duke first, then Jenner, who he helps over the threshold, trailed by Quinn, Ezra, and finally me. We proceed single file into a narrow corridor, which continues for a few steps before feeding into a larger, more spacious compartment lit by the familiar glow of blue emergency lights.

As we shuffle into the safe room, I realize it's less of a room and more of a fully equipped bunker with hallways branching off from the main area, likely leading to sleeping quarters and other living spaces built to help wait out whatever event would usher its eventual occupants down here.

Occupants like Nolan, who rises from a chair as we enter, eyes pitched wide in disbelief.

He looks different than when I last saw him, as if he's aged ten years over the span of only a handful of days. His ashy blond hair is sweat-slicked back off his forehead, his beard longer, like overgrown weeds on his face. Scorch marks riddle his clothes—his fingers and cheeks smeared black with ash—but, physically, he otherwise appears uninjured. Mentally, I can't say the same, noting the alarming disconnect behind those pale, unblinking eyes.

A few other figures turn as we enter the room, and I immediately recognize them as the other Heads of PHOENIX. Of the eight I stood before less than a week ago, only five are here, including Nolan. One of them, a man with red hair—whose left arm and the left side of his face are covered in superficial burns—gapes at me from where he sits slumped in a chair.

"Is that—" he chokes out, while the elderly Head looks around at the others in dismay.

The last Head—a man not much younger than Nolan—inches as far back into the room as he can get, gawking at me but saying nothing.

"Rodrick—" Jaedyn begins, but an explosion of unhinged laughter drowns her out.

"So, they were right," Nolan rasps, staring at me. "You really are back from the dead."

He takes a step closer, those almost colorless eyes narrowing, assessing first my face then the way my chest heaves as I lean into Ezra for much-needed support. Without him, I'm not sure I'd be able to stay upright, my body worn out, stripped of any lingering energy.

Nolan's attention lifts back to my face, and he flashes an unnerving smile. "Though, from the looks of it, you might not be far off."

Behind him, the other Heads look confused, and their bewildered expressions remind me of the rumors Duke told us about earlier. About how Nolan claimed I attacked him and escaped from the bunker where I was being held as PHOENIX's prisoner. Although Nolan had said he'd rescued me from the State because of my father, that was a lie—an excuse to get me back in his grasp. The truth was, all he desired was my power. To use me and then discard me once I'd given him what he wanted.

Clearly, the Heads had believed these lies, too.

Running a hand through his bedraggled hair, Nolan scans our group, sneering at Ezra and Jenner on my right—undoubtedly irked to see them still alive—before his gaze passes me by, catching on Quinn. Understanding pulls the edges of his lips taut.

"I suppose I have you to thank for sparing their lives?" He clicks his tongue. "How disappointing. Although, I suppose there's a lesson to be learned in all this as to who we allow into our ranks moving forward. After all, how much loyalty can we really expect from someone who used to be the State's dog?"

Quinn bristles beside me, his expression mutinous, his shoulders trembling under the force of his rage.

It's only now, with us positioned side by side before Nolan, that I realize how much we have in common. Unlike Ezra and Jenner, who escaped the toxic clutches of the State sooner than either of us, we weren't just victims of oppression and fear like so many others in the Heart.

We were tools used to inflict them.

But we both broke free of the shackles that bound us, and like me, Quinn isn't anyone's pawn anymore. Or dog.

Least of all the State's.

The hair stands up on the back of my neck, my fury rising at Nolan's insult. A snarl rips from my throat as I jerk free of Ezra's hold, my fingers curling, reaching for my power—the monster inside me hungry for blood.

"Wynter, don't," Quinn says as I put myself between him and Nolan, his panicked breath shaking me free of my rage.

Nolan's brow furrows as he peers back and forth between us. "Last I saw you two together, he was about to kill you. And you as well," he adds with a dismissive wave at Ezra and Jenner. His eyes flick to Quinn, curiosity written in the grooves of his weathered face. "You were always so adamant that she's a monster. I'm interested to know what changed your mind."

Low mutterings erupt now among the other Heads, but Nolan either doesn't care or is too lost in the moment to notice.

My pulse flutters under my skin. Does this mean Nolan hasn't figured out that Quinn was a double agent placed in PHOENIX by Bilken? That the man who helped him orchestrate this attack—who he once considered a friend—was actually the one behind our escape?

Would it even matter at this point if he did?

I consider the repercussions that might arise if Nolan determined the true scope of how—and why—I survived that day. Would Bilken's perceived betrayal affect his willingness to make a new deal with our attackers? Surely, Nolan still wants an end to this war. Even if I plan on making damn sure he never gets the power he lusts for, he must still value his life. He must want to live.

At least, enough to make the call.

"What *changed*," Quinn seethes through clenched teeth, and my already erratic heart rate ratchets higher as I anticipate his answer, "was knowing I was working for another version of the State." He spits each word, feeding Nolan a story in the same vein as the one he gave me when he saved our lives in the field outside the farmhouse.

While it's not a lie by any stretch, it's not the whole truth. Quinn might be guided by his morals, but I doubt he would've ever helped me to begin with if there wasn't something worthwhile awaiting him at the end of that aid.

Still, half-truth or not, Quinn's outrage is explosive as he continues. "I wasn't going to sit by and help you murder thousands of innocent people—"

"Murder?" Nolan balks, his cheeks ruddy as his own anger flares. "I'm trying to *save* this country!"

"You can cut the act," Ezra growls. "We know all about the deal you made with the people attacking us."

"Deal?" The elderly Head reels back, squinting at Nolan. "What deal?"

For the first time, the cowering Head at the back of the room finally speaks up. "Rodrick, what is he talking about?"

"Yes, Rodrick," Jaedyn croons, crossing her arms. "Tell us. What *is* he talking about?"

"I don't—" Nolan begins, but I cut him off.

"Don't try to deny it. I *saw* it," I say, pausing to let the meaning of my words penetrate. "You betrayed us all, admit it. Tell them how you arranged this attack so you could seize power."

Nolan's lips peel back, exposing his teeth. "I used a terrible, *unavoidable* situation to our advantage. But that's not exactly a secret. Don't you remember,

Wynter? You were there. You were the one who told us the details of the attack." There's a note of accusation to his tone that suggests I am to blame for how things have turned out. While there's truth to that—while I might be guilty of igniting this war—that doesn't negate the fact that he is responsible for letting it escalate this far.

Hell, as much as he influenced the situation, I can't even blame Bilken for this. He might have handed Nolan the gun by introducing him to our attackers, but Nolan was the one who pulled the trigger. He, and he alone, shoulders that blame.

"Cut the shit," Jenner barks, his voice surprisingly strong given his weakened condition. "That's not what she's talking about and you know it." Taking a limping step forward, he looks around at the other Heads now, meeting each of their startled gazes in turn. "Nolan already knew the attack was coming because he's the one who arranged it. He then used Wynter's vision—a vision that was only triggered at all because of his actions—to coerce you into agreeing to this coup."

"But it hasn't exactly gone to plan, has it?" Quinn asks, his tone derisive.

Nolan's upper lip quivers with contempt, his nostrils flaring. "Everything I have done has been for the betterment of our society—"

"If you really believe that, you're delusional," Ezra scoffs.

Sweat beads the Head's upper lip, and his right eye twitches as he glances around the room, as if searching for a target to lock onto. Silence falls among the remaining Heads, who all stare at Nolan like he's lost his mind.

"What does it matter how we got to this point?" Saliva flies from his lips as he turns in place, a greasy tendril of hair falling into his face. "All that matters is that the State is crumbling before our eyes—"

"People are *dyin'*, damn it!" Duke shouts, making me jump. His muscles pulse as he glares down at Nolan, his large frame towering over the older man, even with the space between them.

Nolan scoffs. "Sometimes, sacrifices must be made to pave the way for a better tomorrow."

A stunned breath escapes me. "You really are just like him," I whisper.

All eyes swing in my direction.

"Like who?" Nolan asks, his tone mocking.

"Richter," I bite back through clenched teeth.

I remember thinking it once before—when Nolan said I would be doing the people of our country a great service by helping him. The Head had tried so hard to make his plan seem noble, like he really was acting on behalf of the people. But now, with failure on his doorstep, I see just how little they mean to him. He'd sacrifice an entire city of innocents if it helped him take the power he believes he deserves.

I blow out a furious breath through my nose. From the stunned looks on the other Heads' faces, I can only assume Nolan never voiced these particular viewpoints before to anyone other than me. If he had, they would realize what I already know—what I can see them all now beginning to realize.

Nolan doesn't deserve to lead. Not PHOENIX. Not whatever the State becomes after this war. Given his actions, he's lucky I'm not ending his life the same way I ended Dr. Richter's.

"Richter's dead, by the way," I say, my tone blunt but the words sharp enough to cut. "In case you were wondering."

Nolan's expression hardens. "Is that a threat?"

A fresh surge of fatigue creeps through my body. I shake my head, more than ready to be done with this conversation. "I don't need to threaten you because, without me, you're all already dead."

The red-haired Head visibly stiffens. "What are you saying?"

I swallow, my mouth and throat painfully dry.

No turning back.

"As we speak, there are an unknown number of soldiers in the city posing as Enforcers, and soon, the bombings will continue, regardless of your calls for a ceasefire. Once that happens, they won't stop. Not until..." I trail off, the rising lump in my throat blocking the words.

"Not until what?" Jaedyn asks, trepidation rife in her voice.

I glance at her, then at each of the Heads, before turning the full force of my gaze back on Nolan. "Not until they know I'm dead. You see, that was the deal Nolan made with these people. Power in exchange for the DSD...and my life."

The silence that follows this revelation is strained, and the Heads wear matching scandalized expressions that reassure me as to how little they actually knew about Nolan's plans. While their confusion before when Ezra mentioned the deal Nolan made would've been enough to convince me of this, their shock at this moment confirms it. It tells me PHOENIX hasn't been completely corrupted, like I feared it had. That my father's legacy wasn't destroyed, just tainted.

Tainted but redeemable.

Jenner snorts, his disgust apparent, even though every word that breaches his lips is labored. "Why are you all acting so shocked? Like you didn't agree to just sit by and watch as the Heart was attacked?"

"We believed the attack was futile," Jaedyn murmurs, her eyes downcast on the floor, "not that—"

"It was a power play by the very person you all chose to be your leader?" Quinn mocks.

Nolan's complexion is gray now, and I glimpse a level of panic in his wandering eyes as he tries to figure out how he can retake control of the situation. His manic mannerisms remind me of Richter when we returned to the DSD to find Rai, that mask of brilliance slipping, revealing the madness under the surface. Like Richter, Nolan's mask has slipped and I can see the real man underneath, exposed now in his desperation.

"Proof or no peace," I mutter, just loudly enough for everyone to hear. "That was what they said to you."

Nolan's gaze snaps to mine, his remaining composure unraveling at these words. As he crosses the room, storming toward me with murderous intent, Quinn roughly shoves me behind him. At the same moment, Ezra steps forward, pulling me protectively back against his chest.

Duke lunges forward, shoving Nolan, who thrusts a finger toward me, spitting, "Stop acting like this isn't your fault! This war is happening because of *you*. Because of what you've done!"

My chest squeezes. "I know." More than anyone, I know what I'm responsible for. What my existence has caused. I live with the guilt of it every day. "And that's why I'm here trying to fix it. To give them an alternative to this destruction. To *end* this."

Nolan stills, and a momentary hope flickers behind his blue eyes. "End this, how? They want proof of your *death*. Are you willing to die to put an end to this conflict?"

I always thought, once I reached this moment, I'd hesitate to answer this question. That part of me would be so overcome with fear, I would need some final push to make me say it. To agree to do what needs to be done, even though there was never a doubt in my mind that I would make this sacrifice willingly.

But now, as Nolan's words hang in the air between us, I feel only a calm acceptance. An eagerness, even, to finally shift the weight of this burden off my shoulders.

"If I'm given certain assurances, yes."

The four lesser Heads exchange furtive glances, while Nolan just laughs, the sound biting and callous.

"*Foolish* girl." He grimaces, and whatever hope I thought I saw in his hooded gaze is swallowed by the bleak darkness of defeat. "There is no end to this. Even if we give them what they want, it won't be enough. It's over. We aren't safe.

Not down here. Not anywhere." The color drains from his face as he stumbles backward, his eyes glazing over as his fingers reach for the edge of the nearest chair. "We're all going to die."

Ezra's arms tense around me. "Why do you say that?" His breath beats hot and fast against the back of my neck, his heart pounding so violently I can feel it through my jacket.

Nolan just shakes his head. "Because it wouldn't be enough for me, and it sure as shit isn't enough for them. They had already agreed to decimate the State, to help install PHOENIX as the new ruling power. But now…" He clamps his teeth onto his lower lip before crying out, "They don't trust me! Don't you see? To these people…everyone in this city is a threat. And the only way to ensure a threat is eradicated is through total annihilation. Extermination," he adds, muttering that last word under his breath.

Tears spring into my eyes. After all this, after everything we've been through, that can't be the only outcome. Death can't be the only option.

Otherwise, what am I fighting for?

"They aren't you," I breathe.

Nolan raises his head, fixing me with lifeless eyes. "Are you so sure about that? Would you bet *their* lives on it?" He gestures to Ezra, then to Jenner and Quinn, his expression smug.

"No," I counter, and I step free of Ezra's arms once again, finding strength in my resolve. "But I'm willing to bet mine."

A low hiss escapes through Nolan's clenched teeth, and there's a deranged glint in his eyes that unnerves me. "Have you not listened to a word I just told you? It won't be enough—"

"It will." *It has to be.* "I can see the future, remember? I'll know." *And if they go back on their deal, I'll kill them.* "I just need you to contact whoever you made your deal with and make a new agreement. My death in exchange for peace."

For a long moment, Nolan just gapes at me, and though no one else in the room dares to speak, I can sense the gravity of their unspoken thoughts in the encompassing silence. Finally, Nolan clears his throat.

"Why would you do that?" he asks, his voice hoarse.

Two faces flash through my head—not just reminders of why I *should* do this but the reasons why I will without doubt or regret. Why would I sacrifice myself, Nolan wonders?

For friendship, I muse, glancing over my shoulder at Jenner, who gifts me with that lopsided smile. The smile that made me know what it felt like to be unconditionally accepted.

For love. My eyes drift to Ezra's and linger there, taking in every detail of his face and imprinting them on my mind alongside the memories we've made together. Memories which are so few but more precious than anything else I possess in this world.

When I look back at Nolan, a third face fills my thoughts. As it manifests, a smile tugs at my mouth, calming the waves of fear, doubt, and unease rising up and beating against the walls of my heart.

"Because I have something I want to protect," I assert, "and because…I want to follow my father's example."

I've been called many things over the last year. Monster. The State's weapon. Richter's angel of death. But if I am anything, I am my father's daughter. My father, who tried so hard to defend what he cherished. Who only wanted to preserve a piece of the world—a kinder world—he once knew for his child.

Just like I want to guarantee a life after all this for Ezra and Jenner.

Nolan blinks at me, as if he can't fathom a scenario where someone else's life is worth the surrender of his own. And, for a brief moment, I pity him until I remind myself that monsters like Richter and Nolan—people who would intentionally cause such carnage—are undeserving of pity. Like Richter, Nolan deserves what's coming to him. But unlike the man who tormented me for years, I want Nolan to live.

To watch as the world moves on and becomes better without his influence.

Jaedyn steps toward me, drawing my focus from Nolan, her gaze skeptical despite her confident tone. "You said you wanted certain assurances," she says, and the other three Heads watch us closely, hanging onto every word. "What are they?"

I lick my lips, weighing my thoughts before I voice them. The Heart can never go back to what it was before. Even if the State did manage to stay in power after this conflict, the death toll would only rise once they catch and punish all those who ran to PHOENIX for aid. The battle beyond these walls might end but the war would continue for those who remain in the Heart. The oppression and terror that afflicts their everyday lives would only worsen.

That leaves two alternatives: seeing our city razed to the ground…

Or PHOENIX.

While the rebellion alone isn't a threat to the State—as proven by the swarm of Enforcers outside—the people assaulting the Heart have the means and the will to ensure the State is removed. Without me, the State is at a huge disadvantage. Even with every Enforcer at its disposal, it can't wage a war against the whole world. Its days are numbered.

But so are PHOENIX'S without peace and support.

At one point, despite what's occurring right now, our attackers were in favor of PHOENIX seizing power. Even if they don't trust Nolan, there's time to make them support PHOENIX again. To work together to put a stop to this madness.

Only days ago, I saw PHOENIX as the lesser of two evils, but it doesn't have to be that way. Without Nolan, it can once again be what my father created.

It just needs someone else at its helm.

Nolan once said to me that power can always be taken away. Time to put that theory into action.

"We can't have peace as long as the State is in power," I say carefully, "and I know our attackers feel that way, too. But"—I observe the faces around me— "we can't have peace with Nolan leading either."

"What are you suggesting?" the Head standing at the back of the room asks.

A pang in my forehead makes me wince, but I shake it off, ignoring the way the room seems to spin under the glow of the emergency lights overhead.

I swallow, trying to steady my voice. "Rodrick Nolan is to be stripped of his title—"

When Nolan begins to protest, Ezra steps forward, pulling out the pistol he wrenched away from the now dead enemy soldier upstairs. "Shut up and listen," he snaps, aiming the barrel at the older man.

My eyes shift to Ezra's face, then to his finger, which hovers over the trigger. He's more calm and steady than I've ever seen him, but there's a resignation in his gaze that breaks my weary heart.

That makes me realize he's finally accepted how this situation will end.

Swallowing again, I glance at Jaedyn, who nods for me to continue.

Drawing in a deep breath, I repeat, "Nolan is to be stripped of his title and is to have no involvement in what you choose to build in the State's place once this is over. I don't care who takes charge, but it needs to be someone who actually has the people's best interests at heart, not their own." I spit that last part, scowling at Nolan.

Jaedyn considers me for a moment. "Anything else?"

"My friends—" My voice catches, obscured by the tears in my throat when Rai's face appears in my thoughts, followed by Alivia Laramie's.

Say it, my conscience chides me. *This is your last chance to save them.*

Glancing first at Ezra, then at Jenner and Duke, I whisper, "They've only ever tried to do what they thought was right, to protect those who couldn't protect themselves." I lock eyes with Quinn next, who nods, his obsidian eyes aglow with an emotion I never thought I'd see from him.

Respect.

"I won't let them be punished for my actions," I declare, facing the Heads once more, "and they deserve a say in what the Heart becomes next. I won't agree to anything or do anything until I know for sure they'll be safe."

The elderly Head huffs out a breath. "Any other demands?" he drawls.

I narrow my eyes at him. "Be better. Be better than what came before us."

Scowling at the old man, Jaedyn steps toward me, extending her hand. "Your requests are perfectly within reason. If you help us, I will *personally* see to it that it's done."

Behind her, the red-haired Head pushes up from his chair. "I think we can all agree it's time for a clean slate." He looks to the last Head, who nods in agreement.

As I reach out to take Jaedyn's hand, Nolan lets loose a demented, bone-chilling cackle. "Jaedyn, you don't need to make concessions for this traitorous child." He spits the word *traitorous* like it's left a sour taste in his mouth. "She's the reason this war is happening. If she's so convinced her plan will work, let's just hand her over and be done with it."

Ezra moves so quickly I barely register the movement, his lips peeling back in a snarl as he pushes the muzzle of the gun between Nolan's eyes. "You will *not* touch her," he growls. "This is *her* choice, not yours." He laughs once, the sound bitter. "You should be thanking her for saving your worthless life, you arrogant shit."

Flop sweat glistens across Nolan's brow, but I don't tell Ezra to lower his weapon. Instead, I say in a bored monotone, "Need I remind you, I have slaughtered entire armies. If you think you can make me go without giving me what I'm asking for first, then try." Nolan's eyes flash to mine, and I shrug. "But don't for a second think I won't let you die to get what I want. All of you," I add, peering at the other Heads.

As much as I desire a peaceful end to this war—a world in which Ezra and Jenner can thrive—I am more than ready to let everyone and everything burn if there's a chance they won't be safe once I'm gone.

My time is running out. I can feel it. But I won't hand myself over without these assurances, and without the deal, we're all dead anyway.

All I can hope for now is that the Heads don't call my bluff.

Jaedyn blanches at the unfeeling threat in my voice, and the column of her throat shifts when she audibly swallows.

Good, I think. *Now, they know I'm serious.*

Jerking her head, Jaedyn says in a rush, "That won't be necessary. We agree to your terms." Then, glaring at Nolan, she barks, "You got us into this mess, Rodrick. Now, you're going to get us out." Closing the distance between them, she thrusts a communicator into his hand. "Call them. Broker the deal."

Nolan's expression turns stony. "And if they don't agree?" he asks. "What then?"

With the mask of the monster firmly in place, I smile.

"If they don't, tell them I'll kill them all."

TWENTY-SIX

I LEAN OVER THE METAL basin in the washroom, choking back the urge to throw up. It's been twenty minutes since Nolan vanished into one of the sleeping quarters to make his call—accompanied by Duke and Jaedyn, who were intent on keeping a close eye on him to ensure he wouldn't betray us. Every second since then has been like a knife slowly sinking between my ribs, the blade tip piercing through muscle and tissue until the lung it punctures fills with blood, suffocating my breaths from within.

The pressure I've sensed building over the last few days is everywhere now, clawing at the underside of my skin, and the vibration of my power as it slips further beyond my control is a constant taunting hum in my ear. I feel the current like an ever-present itch at the roots of my hair, and my fingers tingle with the urge to rip the strands from my scalp if it will make the sensation stop.

I retch, but nothing comes up, my stomach empty in a painful way, as if something is eating me from within. My inability to ease the gnawing ache only drives me that much closer to the brink of madness.

Assuming I'm not already there.

Cupping some cold water into my mouth, I lift my gaze to my reflection, recoiling from what I find staring back at me in the small square mirror above the sink. My skin has a mottled, grayish hue, and the whites of my eyes are bloodshot, the harsh red veins converging at the edge of my irises, which bleed black, blotting out the green and blue.

"There's still time," I whisper, repeating Rai's words, willing them to be true. Since that dream, I've been heeding what she said, even though, deep down, I know it wasn't really her speaking to me but a figment of my imagination created in my grief to console me. To give me a shred of hope to hang onto.

All this time, I've been chasing a ghost, and now, so close to the end, that manufactured hope feels so far away, like it might slip through my fingers if I'm not careful.

Still, real or not, I cling to those words, repeating them again and again. I repeat them until my voice is hoarse and tears streak from my eyes, burning my cheeks.

I repeat them until I believe them.

A sudden knock makes me jump, and I startle, choking on the half-spoken word in my mouth. Wiping my face dry with my hands, I turn from my reflection and fling the door open to find Ezra waiting at the threshold.

His expression is solemn. "Nolan's made the call," he says. He doesn't elaborate more than that.

Like me, Ezra couldn't bring himself to be present when Nolan contacted the people attacking the Heart. Perhaps he feared he wouldn't be able to restrain himself and didn't want to jeopardize the outcome of the call. Or maybe listening in on that conversation would've made what's coming far too real. Too immediate.

Too inescapable.

Swiping my wet palms on my jacket, I exit the washroom behind Ezra, following him back into the main area of the bunker where the Heads all look nervously at each other, as if fearing this moment will spell out our doom. They all remain seated except Jaedyn, who stands with Duke off to one side of the arrangement of chairs, shooting him the odd worried glance. On the other side of the room, I spot Jenner and Quinn, who linger at the periphery of the space, using the wall behind them for support.

Concern swells in my gut as I observe them, my fear like spoiled milk, turning my stomach. They're both pale, *too* pale, and while Jenner's arm is now tied up in a makeshift sling—his chest bandaged and the belt tourniquet gone—his shirt is soaked through with an alarming amount of blood. Who knows how much he's lost by this point.

My chest tightens as I take in their faces again. All this standing and waiting around can't be good for either of them. They need help. *Real* help.

Help they won't get down here in this bunker.

Help they'll only get if I succeed.

Nolan clears his throat, and after a split second of hesitation, I meet his gaze, acknowledging him for the first time since re-entering the room. He looms, frowning, at the front of the space, like an instructor about to deliver a lesson— the communicator clenched tightly in his right hand. Behind him, I can just make out the outline of the locked bulkhead door in the shadows of the hallway we came in by.

My thoughts drift, wondering if the flames have penetrated the passage by now and if we'll still be safe in here once they reach the safe room entrance.

Shaking that fear from my head, I focus on Nolan's lined face, the skin wizened beyond its years, making him look at least a decade older than he actually is.

"Well?" I ask, breathless.

With a disparaging sniff, Nolan raises his chin just enough to glare down his nose at me. "They've agreed to the ceasefire, providing our evidence is legitimate."

I cock an eyebrow. Whether those words are his or the enemy's, one thing is clear.

He doesn't think I'll go through with this.

"They said to deliver the proof to Central Station—"

"The proof?" Ezra's voice is a threatening growl, and I grab his forearm when he takes a step forward. "She's a *person!*"

Nolan scoffs but doesn't spare Ezra a glance, trapping only me in the heat of his stare. His pale eyes burn with indignation. "If they saw her that way, we wouldn't be in this situation—"

"When?" I interrupt, tightening my grasp on Ezra's arm. He trembles, rigid beneath my touch.

One corner of Nolan's lips—the skin dried and flaking—hooks upward, part smile and part sneer, raising goosebumps all over my body. There's something about the detached way he looks at me, like he no longer cares how this conflict plays out.

Like he doesn't want this plan to succeed.

Maybe he doesn't, I consider. With everything he's been working toward for years ripped away and no prospect of power to look forward to, what does he stand to gain from a peaceful resolution?

His life, my conscience retorts, but I'm beginning to think maybe that alone isn't enough.

But if it isn't, then why make the call?

Nolan's quivering upper lip catches my eye, and it occurs to me that I might have it all wrong. He isn't looking at me with such fervent hatred because he *doesn't* want this to work; he's looking at me that way because he *does*. He's just convinced himself that failure is inevitable and our impending demise is futile. And for that—for the dire outcome, the *only* outcome, he sees before us—he blames me.

The weapon whose mere existence foiled his plans.

"Two hours," he grinds out, pulling me out of my thoughts.

"So soon?" Jenner asks, his tone panicked.

I meet his gaze across the room, then quickly avert my eyes to the floor. It was already hard enough to look at him knowing he's hurt because of me, but the dejection on his face now makes it unbearable. I'd rather never look at him again than see him stare at me that way.

As if determined to test the limits of my heartache, Ezra mutters under his breath, "That doesn't give us much time."

I'm not sure whether he's referring to how long it will take to get to the agreed location or if he means for us to savor these final moments together. Knowing just how soon we'll have to say goodbye to each other makes me not want to ask.

I draw in a deep breath, then let it out, repeating the process twice to steady the tremor I sense at the edge of my voice. Once I'm certain I won't break, I look back at Nolan. "Did they make any new conditions?"

Arching a wiry brow, he chokes out a low, scornful laugh. "Well, the fact you're alive after I told them you were dead has made them…reasonably wary. They don't understand why you would—"

Why I would surrender myself to die…

"They don't need to understand," I snap, cutting him off. *No one does.* "They just need to agree to our terms."

"And they have," Nolan counters. "Or rather, they will," he amends.

I stiffen at the vague threat in his words.

"What do you mean, 'they will'?" Ezra asks. The suspicion in his tone mirrors the dread and uncertainty twisting my thoughts into every worst case scenario I can imagine.

"They *will*," Nolan repeats after a moment, that eerie half-sneer half-smile returning, "so long as when you arrive, you're still breathing."

This revelation takes me aback, and I gape at him, confused. "I thought they wanted me dead."

"They do." His fatalistic expression hardens into the cold, calculating leader of PHOENIX I met in the bunker outside the Heart. The man I recognize now, not as a savior as he professed to be, but as a monster.

Like me.

In this moment, with our facades shed, I see the man behind the mask more clearly than ever.

"But they want to be the ones to do it," he explains. "To be sure the danger you pose is eradicated for good."

The danger. It takes everything in me not to laugh. If only they knew what I was protecting them from by choosing to hand myself over like this. By *choosing* to die instead of waiting for this disease to end everything the way fate intends.

I don't bother enlightening Nolan to the truth—to the real danger he's oblivious to. In his eyes, and in the eyes of everyone else here, except for Ezra and Jenner, and possibly Quinn now, I would still be a monster. The harbinger of their deaths or, at the very least, a life-threatening hazard. Nothing I say at this point will change that. Not after everything I've done. Not after all the suffering I've caused.

So, instead, I just say, "If those are their conditions, so be it."

Regardless of the road I take to get there, all paths lead me to the same end.

Shaking his head, Nolan rubs a hand over his mouth, his nails scratching at his scraggly facial hair. "This is all going to blow up in your face," he warns. "You're going to die for nothing."

There's a cruel undertone to this premonition that makes my body go rigid, like he's said these words, or some variation of them, to someone before. The frustration and disdain in his gaze when he looks at me strikes a familiar chord, and it makes me wonder if the person in question, the one who received this warning, was my father.

I can envision it—Nolan reprimanding him, telling him his eventual death would be meaningless if he abandoned their cause. That if he wasn't part of PHOENIX then he was against it.

That his betrayal made them no different than enemies.

My teeth clamp down on the tip of my tongue as I recall how Nolan knew my father would be executed and did nothing to stop it. And as a fresh wave of hate rushes through me, I realize I don't just want him to be stripped of his title and role in whatever new world PHOENIX makes. What I want is for him to feel just as helpless as my father must've felt that day, bloody and beaten on the floor of our home.

I want him to feel just as powerless.

My lips harden into a scowl. "Then I guess it's a good thing you won't be there to watch it."

Terror ignites behind Nolan's eyes, and he takes an involuntary step back, the fear wafting off him so potent I can practically smell it. The sudden tension permeating the silence is thick, and I can feel the others watching me closely, anticipating what I'll do next. Wondering if I'll act on the obvious threat behind my words.

I stare at Nolan without blinking, letting him stew a while longer in the uncertainty of this moment. Letting him debate if I'd actually kill him.

I would, it occurs to me as I scan his face, noting the droplets of sweat beading along his hairline. But I won't. Not because he doesn't deserve it, but because enough people have already died because of me and my soul can't take anymore. I'm done.

I don't want to be the reason anyone else has to die.

When I turn from Nolan, he lets out a small gasp, as if I was forcibly holding his gaze in mine and that connection is broken now that I've looked away. Quiet, distressed breaths escape him, but I ignore them, focusing on Jaedyn.

"Does this bunker have a secure room that can be locked from the outside?" I ask.

I can sense an unspoken question on the tip of her tongue as she glances between me and Nolan. Her furrowed brow smooths out a moment later as understanding dawns in her gaze.

"There's a storage room filled with nonperishables just down that hallway"— she points over my shoulder to the corridor leading past the washroom. "I only had a quick look inside a few minutes ago, but it should be fit for purpose. Duke?"

She casts an expectant glance at the brooding hulk of a man standing close beside her, who snaps to attention with a jerk of his head.

"On it," he barks before crossing to Nolan. "Come on, old man," he growls, grabbing his arm. "Let's put you someplace where you won't go around causin' any more trouble for anyone."

Nolan curses under his breath, his eyes flashing to mine as he fights against the larger man's grip. "You need me!" he shouts. "Without me, *everything* will fall apart!"

This time, I don't bother suppressing my laugh. "Richter said the same thing to me just before I killed him."

I take a slow step forward, relishing the way Nolan flinches back when the space between us shrinks. Duke's grasp on his arm holds him steady, and on his other side, Ezra appears, wielding his gun like a whip. There's nowhere for Nolan to go. Nowhere for him to escape to this time.

You're helpless now. Just like you deserve.

"Move," Ezra growls, pressing the pistol's muzzle into the older man's side.

Grimacing, Nolan does as commanded.

"Wait," I breathe when they've only taken two steps.

Ezra and Duke both pause, the latter holding Nolan in place by the nape of the neck. Ezra's eyes cut to mine, and I nod toward their captive's trembling fist.

"You won't be needing this," I murmur, reaching forward and tugging the communicator free of his fingers.

Now, you're not just helpless. You're also alone.

As Duke and Ezra lead Nolan out of the room, I hand the communicator to Jaedyn, who comes to stand beside me, her expression sullen.

"I'm ashamed I didn't challenge him sooner," she laments with a sigh.

I shake my head. "The past doesn't matter." Although it haunts me, it can't be changed. Only one thing can. "Only the future," I whisper.

"And what is it you see when you look at ours?" Jaedyn asks.

For so long, I've wondered if it was even possible to change the future—to alter course on our preordained paths. Has anything I've done to prevent the terrible fate I've seen awaiting us made any difference? Or was every act of perceived rebellion on my part already planned by some greater power? In trying to change the future, did I inadvertently cause it?

These are the questions I've been running from since I first found out about my disease.

Questions I now need the answers to.

Drawing in a calming breath, I slide my eyes shut and slip into that state of deep focus I've been to many times before. It's harder to reach now without my collar, and my head pounds with the effort, but I push through my discomfort.

My hands shake at my sides as I search inside myself, reaching for that mental thread that will draw a line between me and the future I'm now desperate to see. When I find that thread, I latch onto it without hesitation.

A shiver of apprehension runs through me as the image takes shape behind my closed eyes. My heart sinks when the destruction that plagues my every waking thought rises in front of me like a wave, although the vision isn't as clear this time, the scene almost translucent.

That ember of hope I've been holding onto so tightly bursts into a flame as another image appears behind the first, sharpening as the desolation I've grown so accustomed to gradually fades. The image isn't fully opaque, the picture quivering, like this possible future might vanish if I so much as breathe wrong, but the details are clear enough for me to make out a different version of the Heart—not untouched by war, the scars still visible in the details around us, but *healed* from it.

The people walking the streets smile and nod to each other, no longer afraid of untoward attention or proximity, and children run and laugh freely among them, a sight I don't think I've ever witnessed except for that one glimpse of Ezra's childhood. Bright colors bring life to the cold grays of the buildings in the form of expressive clothing and flowers, and a beautiful melody floods the air instead of the strict, enforced silence I've always known.

A piano, I realize, and a tear slides down my cheek at the unbidden memory of my father.

I scan my changed surroundings with interest, faltering when I suddenly find myself before the East Gate, the wall enclosing the Heart looming over me. As I look up, I notice the wall is intact, but the gate stands open without an Enforcer in sight. No guards. No closed metal doors.

The gate is just open, granting passage to anyone who wants to leave.

Clamping a hand over my mouth, I stifle a cry, an intense relief filling me until it feels like my body might explode. This vision… It means there's still a chance. A chance for the Heart to thrive. A chance for a new world where the city is no longer a cage and fear is no longer a prison. A future where, after so long, the sacrifices of the people I love will be realized. A world where we will finally have—

"Peace," I gasp, my eyes wrenching open. A thick line of blood trickles from my nose to my lips, and a headache beats against the inside of my skull, but despite the nagging pain, I smile.

Because after everything we've endured, if that future I saw just now is what awaits at the end of this war…

It will all have been worth it.

I meet Jaedyn's stunned gaze, and she exhales sharply, as if releasing a breath she was holding. "That's reassuring. It means your plan will work."

I nod, reaching for something to hold myself upright when the room starts spinning. My fingers find the back of an unoccupied chair.

"Any idea how I can get there?" I rasp, wiping the blood from my nose on the sleeve of my jacket. "I don't think going back the way we came is an option."

"Probably not," she agrees. "Even if the fire wasn't an issue, there are still the Enforcers outside to contend with."

I nod again, swallowing the acidic burn of bile as it sweeps up my throat. At this point, I'm not sure I could overpower even one soldier let alone the dozens, possibly hundreds, waiting in the plaza above us.

"*But,*" Jaedyn adds, and I shoot her an expectant glance, "there's a passage that leads from the back of this bunker and feeds out into the tunnels, which you can take to get there. I haven't seen it myself, but Rodrick told us about it when he was leading us down here. We were planning on getting out that way."

I snort. "So much for them being unusable."

"Unusable?" she echoes.

I shrug, brushing the sweaty hair back off my face. "It's just something Ezra told me Bilken said." When she raises a brow for me to elaborate, I sigh. "According to Bilken, the State believes the tunnels were filled with toxic gas and that's why they never thought to monitor the system for PHOENIX. But clearly that was a lie, otherwise why build an escape route leading into them that would be used by the State's leading officials? People they wouldn't want to die."

The Head scoffs. "Because, sometimes, lies are easier than the truth. Especially when you can benefit from them."

Like how the State benefited from PHOENIX's reputation as a danger to our society.

If what Jaedyn is insinuating is true, then the State didn't just know the tunnels were perfectly usable… It *wanted* to keep people away from them. But why? So, citizens wouldn't seek out PHOENIX for themselves?

Or so they wouldn't start asking questions, like why the State hadn't eliminated the threat?

"If there's one thing governments thrive on, it's bullshit. Those at the top of the hierarchy will always spout lies to their underlings to keep them from asking questions or poking their noses where they don't belong." Jaedyn crosses her arms with a huff. "The State has always loved its rules, but if there's one thing I've learned over the years, it's that rules are created for everyone *except* the people in power."

I nod. Bilken's office and his collection of hypocrisy were proof enough of that—of the laws disregarded by the very people who helped to create them.

Mulling over that thought for a moment, I glance at the other Heads seated behind us, the three men huddled together in quiet discussion.

"I hope you'll do things differently." Although the words are soft so only Jaedyn can hear them, there's an edge to my voice—an unspoken warning that, if they don't, any peace I saw will be forfeit.

Jaedyn cocks her head slightly, drawing my gaze. "Everyone thinks you're a monster, that you brought this hell into our lives,"—she peers at me as if she's trying to see behind the guise this war has forced me to don—"and while that may be true, do you know what I see when I look at you?"

Silence. I go still, all nausea and light-headedness forgotten.

I don't want to know, I try to say, but I can't find the words.

When I don't answer, she says, "A scared little girl." There's a note of uncertainty in her tone, and the pitch when she speaks is uneven, like someone fighting back a strong surge of emotion.

Like someone who thinks what's happening to me is wrong…even when it's the only option.

She steps closer now, lowering her voice to a whisper. "Can you really follow through with this knowing the cost?"

The cost?

What is one life worth when weighed against millions?

What is *my* life worth when weighed against the people I love?

"It's overdue," I breathe, then clear my throat, eager to change the subject. "What will you do about Nolan?"

Her eyes shift in the direction of the storage room. "For now, we'll keep him confined." Then, nodding to herself, she says with more force, "But once things have calmed down, he'll need to answer for his crimes. A trial, I think. Like the way things used to be done."

A smile lifts the edges of my lips, and for a second, I hear my father in Jaedyn's words. The way he used to talk about the old world and what life was like before the State. The way his recollections held a glimmer of hope.

Like we could someday return to that place.

She is exactly what PHOENIX needs.

For the first time, that peace I saw really feels possible.

There's only one thing left to do.

"I should be going."

Jaedyn's gaze snaps back to mine, and she frowns. "I could accompany you—"

"No. We have no idea what they'll have planned for me. Besides…" I swallow, the words thick in my throat. "I need to do this alone, and *you* need to survive. I'm counting on you to honor our agreement."

Her frown deepens, but she acquiesces, nodding. Then, looking me up and down once, she offers me her hand again. "Goodbye, Wynter."

Pressing my palm against hers, I grip tightly. "Good luck."

As our hands slide apart, my vision goes bleary. It's time to go talk to the others—the one thing in this world I'm not ready to do. My chest tightens when I think of Jenner, as I picture his face when I utter that final, tearful farewell.

By comparison, surrendering myself to be executed sounds easy.

Still, it needs to be done, and so I draw in a breath—mentally ready but emotionally unprepared to go say my goodbyes—only to turn and find Jenner and Quinn standing behind me. I didn't even hear them approach, and a surprised squeak escapes me as I glance between them.

Although physically they look like a strong wind might blow them both over, their eyes are bright and determined, their faces set in matching glowers.

"Jenner—" I begin, but Quinn cuts me off.

"We were eavesdropping," he says in a blunt monotone.

Jenner shoots the ex-Enforcer an appalled look. "No, we weren't."

"We *were*," Quinn says again, rolling his eyes.

Misery softens the hard edges of Jenner's frown, and for a moment, he just stares at me, a sense of pleading behind those blue eyes. Finally, he admits, "We heard you say you were leaving."

The ex-Enforcer scoffs, and before I can respond, he adds, "What he *means* to say is we're coming with you."

"What?" I blurt out. Panic rockets through me as I envision the two of them topside again, caught in the chaos outside in their current conditions. "You can't. It's too dangerous—"

"And everything else we've done hasn't been?" Quinn retorts.

My lips press into a line. "This is different," I hiss.

"No," Jenner mutters gently. "It's not."

"I..." My heart hammers against the inside of my throat. I need to say something. *Anything* to convince them I should do this without them. Ignoring the danger, I don't want them to see it.

I don't want Jenner to watch as I die.

"Don't try to talk us out of it, Wyn." Jenner's expression is pained, as if the concept of me leaving without him is a betrayal he can't bear to put into words. "We've come with you this far, haven't we?"

"He's right."

I whip around at the growl of a third voice behind me, a voice I would know anywhere. Jaedyn is gone—I glimpse her walking away to meet Duke, who lingers at the edge of the room—and in her place, Ezra stands a few feet away, staring at me, as if he can see into my battered soul.

When I meet his gaze, a tear slips down my cheek, but I can't find the strength to lift my arm and brush this tangible evidence of my fear and heartache from my skin. Closing the distance between us, Ezra takes my face in his hands, like he has so many times, and wipes the wetness away with his fingers.

"We go together...remember?" he breathes.

Once again, I glimpse that bleak resignation behind the familiar warmth of his eyes. I wanted to part with Jenner and Quinn here—to spare them from what comes next in my journey—but Ezra never had that option. Like his mother warned me, he has a role to play yet. A role only *he* can step into.

"No one else can do it but him."

Her words haunt me, and more than ever before, I feel the truth to them in my bones. Regardless of my intentions to hand myself over, to let the enemy handle the threat as they see fit, I fear we won't make it that far. And even if we do—

"This disease likes to protect itself."

A shudder rips through my body. What's stopping me from losing the last of my flimsy control and massacring everyone who lifts a finger to harm me, even if I agreed to it? What if Alivia was right, and surrendering alone won't be sufficient to prevent the destruction I'm destined to cause? I might've seen a different path in the Heart's future, but that's all that image was: a possibility. A glimmer of light at the end of the tunnel.

It wouldn't take much for the darkness of death to extinguish that glimmer and swallow us whole.

That's why Ezra needs to come with me—so he can do what he's destined to do before that prospect of peace I witnessed is jeopardized. If the plan goes to hell and no one else can kill me, he needs to do it himself, like he promised. Even if it means killing me before I surrender to avoid further bloodshed... So long as they *see* it...

So long as the enemy *knows* that I'm dead...

That might be enough.

I had hoped it wouldn't come to this, but I realize now that as much as I wish I could spare Ezra from this task, I can't. Even I don't have that power. Still, my chest aches at the thought of what this might do to him. Of the trauma I'm thrusting upon him by asking him to pull that trigger.

"His fate has always been tied to yours."

Ezra might've made me a promise, but I made a promise, too, even if I never said the words out loud. A promise to myself. A promise to his mother, her dying words a painful blemish on my memory. If I'm going to save his life and put an end to this war for good...

This is the only way.

A sob catches in my throat, and I exhale a soft whimper. Then, looking him in the eye, I whisper, "Together."

TWENTY-SEVEN

THE PASSAGE AT THE BACK of the bunker feeds into the tunnels, just like Jaedyn said, and after a quick goodbye to Duke—who opts to stay behind with the Heads and help them once it's safe to resurface—we set off, ready to meet my fate.

Water soaks into my boots as I trudge through the murky run-off flooding the tunnel floor, our forward progression lagging, slowed by injury and illness. Still, I push ahead through my exhaustion, and as we follow the curve of the path in the general direction of Central Station, I'm struck by a dizzying sense of déjà vu, just like I was in the weeks before I got my memories back.

This moment… This is just like when I returned to the DSD, except, there's no promise of a cure awaiting me at the end.

Still, there is one glaring difference to that night that brings me comfort now, even if all I see at the end of this road is darkness.

Unlike then, I'm not alone this time.

My pulse trips as I glance ahead at Jenner and Quinn, then over at Ezra, who stays close beside me, crushing my hand in his grip, a weighted silence saturating the damp air between us. No one has spoken since we left the bunker over an hour ago, even though there's still so much to say.

"Tell my son I love him."

Alivia's words trouble my thoughts, stirring all too familiar feelings of guilt.

Feelings I never seem to escape.

I urge myself to relay her message to Ezra, but how? How exactly do you tell someone you spoke with their dead mother? I can't imagine there is an easy or right way to do it. All that matters is that I do. He deserves to know—to hear her final words.

To be given the chance to finally put his unresolved feelings about her illness and death to rest.

"Ezra," I force out, slowing my steps.

My fingers tighten around his, and he pauses mid-stride, looking back at me, his expression worried.

"I…" A growl of frustration rumbles deep in my chest, leaching into my voice. "This is going to sound insane."

Ezra offers me a small consoling smile. "More insane than seeing the future?"

A melancholy laugh parts my lips. "Probably."

Although his tone and gaze are teasing, there's a heart-wrenching sadness behind both that grab me by the throat and squeeze. I try to swallow, to free myself of the suffocating sensation, but my mouth and tongue are dry and every breath feels like broken glass in my airway.

When I don't say anything more, the corners of Ezra's mouth twitch, dragging down into a telltale frown that betrays the panic undoubtedly rising to the front of his thoughts. I see it flashing behind his hazel eyes when he steps closer to me.

"Wynter, what is it?"

Say it, my conscience chides.

"A few days ago," I blurt out, wincing at the harsh croak of my words. Clearing my throat, I start again. "A few days ago, back at the safe house, I had a vision of you as a child. Your brother and Rai were there, too. And…" I hesitate, steeling myself. "Your mother."

His brow, which was furrowed, now raises in question. "What were we doing?"

"Playing, but—"

"That's strange." His eyes drift away from mine, narrowing. "I don't remember my mother ever watching us play."

For a moment, he stares blankly over my shoulder, as if searching for the memory. Unable to find it, he looks back at me, intently now, and I can hear each beat of my heart in my ears. I know what he's thinking—that it wasn't safe to play out in the open the way he, his brother, and Rai did as children. That they wouldn't have done it with parental or *any* watchful eyes in sight—not considering the way we were all raised to understand the potential consequences of drawing unnecessary attention to ourselves.

Thinking back on that vision, I recall their stifled laughter and the way Rai tried to hold in her cries, like they were aware that what they were doing was dangerous. Even as young children, they knew—just as I learned early on—it was better to be neither seen nor heard.

"Wynter," Ezra presses, and goosebumps wash over my skin at the gentle prodding way he says my name.

I let out a choked breath. "That's because she wasn't there," I confess, shuddering under the weight of each word. "Not the way you were."

His expression contorts, vacillating between shock and trepidation. "What are you saying?"

My palm is slick against his, my grasp faltering. I curl my fingers tighter.

"She was there the same way I was. We spoke."

Ezra blanches, and a surprised sound escapes him that makes me feel sick to my stomach.

"That's…not possible," he stammers.

"We are the epitome of what shouldn't be possible, and yet, here we both are."

As his mother's voice stirs in my memory, I recall the sharpness of her face in my vision. How alive she had seemed to me. How real.

And, more than ever, I'm certain it wasn't a dream.

"We were both looking at the same moment," I murmur, repeating Alivia's explanation. "Me, from the future, and your mother—"

"From the past," Ezra finishes, the realization stretching across his pale face. Then something else occurs to him and he gasps, the words that follow almost inaudible. "She was still alive."

He averts his gaze for a moment again, digesting this information, before abruptly snapping his eyes back to mine. There's something different about the way he looks at me now, with suspicion burning behind his stare.

And when he next speaks, his tone is harder than it was a moment before.

"What else did she say, Wynter?"

This time, there's a coldness to the way he utters my name—spoken not without love but like that love is encased in a thin layer of frost, the warmth underneath barely perceptible.

"She…" Sweat prickles the back of my neck as the nerves writhing in my stomach twist my insides in knots. *Damn it, Wynter, just speak.* "She explained why she told you to find me."

Ezra's eyes narrow again, his gaze now accusatory. "That's why, isn't it? Why you made me promise that I'd—" Voice catching, he wrenches his hand free of mine, and running it over his face, he takes a step back. His expression under his palm is aghast.

My heart breaks at the sudden distance between us, and without thinking, I reach out to take his hand again, needing his touch to ground me like I need air to breathe.

"It's the only way," I manage through tears, clutching his fingers, pulling them away from his face. "No one else will be able to do it—"

"Why?" he growls, shaking me off. "If you're so eager to die, I'm sure there's a firing squad waiting for you at Central Station."

I resist the inclination to flinch, hearing the quiet venom in his tone for what it is. Pain. His words might be cruel but so is what I'm asking of him. He's the one who will live with the repercussions of our words and actions, not me. I have an escape from that heartache.

Even if it's an escape I don't want.

"I don't *want* to die," I whisper, fighting to keep my voice steady. "But I don't want you and Jenner to either."

His jaw trembles, and a tear breaks through the hard exterior he's pushed into place until the stone facade cracks completely. He grimaces, trying to force the tears back, but they just keep coming.

Rising onto my toes, I press my forehead to his. "If I have to choose…every time, I will choose you."

As I erase the remaining distance between us, I taste the salt of his grief on my tongue. At first, he doesn't kiss me back, his body stiff and unyielding to mine. But, gradually, his lips part as I knew they would, giving into me the same way I always find myself giving into him. His free hand curls around my waist, his fingertips slipping under the hem of my jacket, grazing the skin at my lower back. I shiver at his caress, which is both reluctant and desperate—his hand pulling me closer but not close enough.

When we break apart, he cups my face in his hands and leans back just enough to look me in the eye. "I won't talk you out of this…will I."

It isn't a question but a statement of cold realization, which robs me of the warmth his touch stirred within me only seconds before.

"'Two brothers,'" I breathe, holding his tear-soaked gaze. "'One, the creator of a terrible weapon. The other…destined to destroy it.' That's what your mother said." My fingers circle his wrists as I let my own tears fall. "The truth is…this disease won't let anyone else pull that trigger. It *has* to be you."

"Because my mother *said* so?" He spits the words, vehemently shaking his head. "Just because that's how she interpreted what she saw doesn't make her word law—"

"Because I love you!" I cry.

As these words leave my lips, I realize this is the first time I've said them, *really* said them, out loud to the one person who deserves to hear them most. The proclamation is long overdue, and I hate myself for saying it like this—for throwing such beautiful words around as nothing more than an angry riposte.

Chest heaving, I force myself to continue. To *make* him see why there's no other way. My tone holds a pleading edge. "Every time I come close to hurting you, I *always* snap out of it."

Bilken's office when I became consumed by the flashback of my father and us playing the piano together.

Earlier today when I lost control and snapped, killing however many Enforcers.

Both times, I came close to hurting Ezra. Or worse.

And both times, I got my senses back before I could.

The only two times I *did* hurt Ezra—first, when I choked him shortly after PHOENIX extracted me and then, when Richter pulled at my strings and made me lash out via the remote for my collar—I was in a subdued state of manipulated control. My powers weren't awake and wild, in need of taming. Not like they are now.

With the collar, the monster was asleep, but now, it's awake, and the only person it will answer to isn't me.

It's him.

"My power… It won't stop you," I whisper, more certain than ever as the hum of pressure building under my skin seems to calm for a moment, reinforcing this line of thought. Maybe this disease doesn't actually want the release it's been leading me toward all this time. Maybe what it actually wants is an end.

Maybe what the monster really desires is peace.

"You were right," Ezra mutters, lowering his hands from my face. "This does sound insane."

A joyless smile finds its way onto my lips. "Maybe. But since you made me that promise, I've seen the possibility of a different future. A world where the Heart can have peace. The image was weak, almost like fate hadn't decided its course yet. But I saw it, Ezra. It can happen."

"You aren't making this any easier," he grits through clenched teeth, his arms shaking under the lingering touch of my fingers.

"It's not meant to be easy." I lift a hand to wipe away his tears, trailing my thumb across his wet lower lip. "But that doesn't change the fact that you still need to do it."

I drop my hand, and for a long moment, we just stare at each other, neither one daring to speak a word. When I can't bear the silence any longer—or the uncertainty of whether or not he'll fulfill his promise—I clear my throat, ready to play the only card I have left.

"Your mother," I begin, and Ezra's eyes blow wide, the hazel depths terror-stricken. "I was with her in her final moments, and do you know what she asked me to do?"

I note his small intake of breath and the way his chest ceases movement in anticipation and dread of what I might say. He gapes at me, but I don't waver under the intensity of his gaze.

"She begged me to save you. To die to ensure you would live." A sacrifice I was ready to make before she even asked it of me. "So, if you can't do this for me, because *I* asked you to do it, then do it for her. Do it because it was her dying wish to see her remaining son live."

"Wynter," Jenner calls suddenly, and I turn my head toward the uneasy sound of his voice, peering down the length of the tunnel to where he and Quinn watch us from a respectful distance away. Even in the thick cover of shadow, I can see the discomfort on each of their faces—can see the way their eyes flick from me to Ezra, as if the tension between us is a tangible thing they can see.

Maybe it is, I consider, pursing my lips.

Maybe they can see it as clearly as I can feel it pushing me and Ezra apart.

When I meet Jenner's gaze, he nods toward the left side of the tunnel where a ladder stands a foot away from the curved wall, leading up into a circular opening in the ceiling.

"We're here," he says, and those two words are like lead in my gut.

I risk a glance at Ezra, but he doesn't return it, his eyes downcast on the floor, ringed with tears. Gulping down the lump in my throat, I brush past him and continue through the shallow covering of turbid water to where Jenner and Quinn wait up ahead, pausing beside the ladder. I'm not sure if they overheard our conversation or if I care one way or the other. What I can't stand is the pitying looks on their faces.

"Is the station far from wherever this leads out?" I ask, eager to direct their focus elsewhere.

"Not exactly," Quinn mutters. When I arch a questioning brow at him, he points at the ceiling. "It's directly above us."

My eyes dart to the unlit hole above as the air expels from my lungs in a nearly silent "Oh."

Everything that's transpired since my placement exam—both the good and the bad—has been leading me to this, to the culmination of my existence. It's strange to finally be here after so long, and at the same time, it feels like this moment has come too quickly, like my death—however prepared I am for it—has snuck up behind me without warning. I haven't had enough time, not only with Ezra and Jenner but with myself. With the *real* me, freed from the constraints of our society.

I haven't had enough time to live.

Shaking my head of those thoughts, I breathe out through my nose to steady my nerves and place a hand on the closest ladder rung, the metal rusty and flaking beneath my grip. My fingers tremble, but I tighten my hold. Then, placing one hand over the other, I climb.

I don't look back, but I hear the clink of each step as the others follow, trailing me into the claustrophobic darkness of the maw-like opening. My panting breaths reverberate around me, and I can't help imagining they belong not to me but to some great beast, like the ones from the stories my father used to read to me when I was young. I feel the heat of every exhalation reflected back on my face as if I'm trapped in its mouth, about to be swallowed whole.

Desperate for fresh air, I hasten my movements, but the ladder doesn't go as high as I expect and my head soon collides with the underside of a manhole cover at the end of the vertical tunnel. Profanities unfurl on my tongue, but I swallow them and direct that anger at the metal, pushing against it with all my strength. Thankfully, it lifts without much hassle. My fingers curl around the lip of the cover, finding leverage, and I shove it out of the way, reveling in the brush of cooler air on my face.

I scramble out of the tunnel onto one of the station's platforms but remain on my hands and knees as I work a little too hard to catch my breath. My lungs feel like they're on fire and my head is swimming with a disorienting vertigo that blurs my surroundings. Or what I can see of them in the minimal glow of Quinn's flashlight.

"Wynter?"

I glance up at the sound of my name, but it takes me longer than I would like to register Jenner standing over me. He plants a tentative hand on my back.

"Are you okay?" he breathes.

With a grunt, I nod and push up to my feet, then look over my shoulder, scanning the shadows for the others. I spot Quinn first—also struggling to climb to his feet—then Ezra shortly after, his light hair drawing my gaze as he emerges from the hole in the floor.

Once all four of us are upright on the platform, I ask, "How long do we have?"

When Quinn checks his communicator, a frown immediately forms on his lips. "Fifteen minutes, give or take."

This revelation sombers us, and we head for the lobby without another word.

Just like when we were last in Central Station, there isn't another soul in sight. The fluorescent bulbs overhead, which had worked intermittently when we passed through here before, don't even buzz this time, trapping us in a shroud of darkness broken only by the beam of Quinn's flashlight. He guides the way, shining the light in a straight path, and the trash and abandoned possessions littering the floor get caught up in its glow, all coated now in a fine dusting of ash. There's a permanence to seeing them like this that unsettles me. Perhaps because I know, if my plan goes wrong, life will never return to this place.

When we reach the turnstiles, I fumble over the barrier without the rush of excitement I experienced only days ago at the train terminal in Zone 7. The others seem to share my lack of enthusiasm, their movements hurried but reluctant, as if they're the ones walking to their deaths and not me. I try not to dwell too much on that thought—on what awaits me outside this station—but I can sense the clock ticking down over my head like a physical presence I can't shake. Each passing second weighs me down.

Our steps are gunshot loud in the silence as we proceed toward the stairs leading back aboveground, and with every inch of the lobby we cross, my heart beats faster, pummeling into my ribs. When we finally ascend, emerging into the gentle light of the breaking dawn, I go still, pausing beside Quinn, who clicks off his flashlight.

The immediate area outside the station is still dark, but the pink light creeping across the sky has drastically softened the shadows, revealing enough of the plaza for us to make out the contingent on the other side. A clear path stands between us and them, as if some greater power has shifted the rubble and buried corpses aside.

Once again, I'm struck by an overwhelming sense of déjà vu. I suppose, like my many returns to the DSD and our repeated trek through Central Station tonight, this is just another example of fate guiding my steps and turning the wheel that is my life full circle. After inflicting so much pain on this world, it's fitting my final moments would look like this. That my death would be witnessed and initiated by an army just like the ones I helped to slaughter.

It really is a firing squad, like Ezra said. I suppress a bitter laugh at the thought.

A delegation of at least one hundred soldiers lines the opposite edge of the city square, their commanding officer—possibly even the same person Nolan spoke to earlier—standing at the front of the congregation, his face a pale smear in the distance. I'm not surprised by the show of force. If anything, I expected it.

"That must be the welcoming party," Quinn grumbles.

Jenner snorts from somewhere on Quinn's other side, but the sound, while derisive, lacks humor. When he speaks, I can hear his voice waver. "They don't look very welcoming to me."

Sucking in a breath, I turn to the left, aware of Ezra standing a few steps behind me on my right. As much as I want to, I can't bring myself to look at him. Not yet.

Instead, I focus on Jenner and Quinn. "Before I go, I'd like a moment to speak with each of you alone…if that's okay."

Jenner's eyes drop to the ground at my words, the vibrant blue depths glistening with unshed tears. Quinn, on the other hand, looks unfazed—his expression pinched into a disgruntled frown that I've come to learn is his normal face.

And yet, I spot an unexpected tenderness from the ex-Enforcer when, after a glance back at Jenner, he sighs and gestures with a leading tilt of his head that he'll speak with me first. It might not seem like much of a sacrifice, but he's bought Jenner the delay of a few precious moments. Moments before he'll have to finally acknowledge the reality of the situation…

And say goodbye.

Quinn and I move away from the others until we're out of earshot, pausing beside a message board several feet away, on the left side of the station entrance. His obsidian eyes watch me closely, but he doesn't force the conversation, instead giving me time to find the right words.

"Once it's done, call Jaedyn," I say, keeping my voice as low as possible. "Let her and the other Heads know it's finished and put them in contact with their commanding officer over there, if you're able to." Quinn listens intently as I repeat the frequency band Jaedyn told me just before we departed the bunker, then he follows my gaze when I jerk my chin in the direction of the distant figure standing front and center at the opposite edge of the plaza. "Whatever you do, don't let *them*"—I nod again toward the enemy army—"see you or Jenner as a threat. Especially Jenner."

Terror floods my chest at the thought of how he might respond once this is over. I've seen it—seen how he reacts when emotion gets in the way of sense. But I've also seen him show remarkable strength when everyone around him is falling apart. I have no way of knowing which way the scale will tip—if the pain of loss will outweigh his resilience. So, the only option is to make sure someone is watching his back once I'm gone. Someone objective to my death who won't let him try anything stupid.

Never one to waste words, Quinn nods, his expression as sullen as ever. "I can do that."

"Quinn—" I grab his arm, and for the first time, genuine surprise fills his eyes. When he looks at my hand, I loosen my grip and instead wipe my sweaty palm on my pant leg. "I-I don't really know how to thank you. I know you don't like me and I understand why, but I'm still grateful you helped us get this far. Without you, we wouldn't even be here at all. And…" A broken breath jumps from my throat, and I stifle a sob. "You saved Jenner's life. If I could repay you for that, I would—"

"Don't worry about it," he interrupts, and this time, I'm the one gaping at him, lost for words. Frown deepening, he shakes his head. "Besides, after this, I think we're the ones who will owe *you* a debt. You're doing the right thing, by the way."

A startled laugh rips from my throat. "Are you just saying that so you can finally be rid of me?"

His eyes, always hard like chips of onyx, do something I didn't think them capable of. They soften. To my ongoing surprise, the ex-Enforcer, who once hit me over the head with a rifle, cracks a smile.

"Maybe."

The disdain I was always so certain Quinn feels for me seems to dissolve with this single word, leaving us with a mutual respect and something almost resembling friendship. As that realization sinks in, I suddenly find that everything that's happened between us, the lies and deceit… They no longer matter.

All that matters is this moment.

"Hey," Quinn says, placing a steady hand on my shoulder. "I'll keep an eye on them for you. I'll make sure they come out of this okay."

"Thank you," I breathe, and wiping away a tear, I peer over my shoulder at Jenner, who watches me with bloodshot eyes.

With one final appreciative nod at Quinn, I inch back toward the stairs, ignoring the way my heart seems to cave in on itself. Although Jenner's only a short distance away—in the very spot I stood in nearly three years ago, the day of my placement exam—the effort it takes to cross over to him is immense, every step more draining than the last. I'm exhausted in both my body and my soul, and with each passing moment, I feel more ready than ever to do what I came here to do if only to find the freedom of relief at the end of it.

"Why does it seem like I'm always begging you not to leave?" he asks when I reach him, the words strangled and raw in his throat.

"I wish I didn't have to," I whisper.

He gnaws on his lower lip for a moment, avoiding my gaze. "First, Rai. Now, you," he rasps as a tear curves over his cheekbone. "I won't be able to bear it."

Reaching out, I grab his hands and tug on them, urging him to look at me. "You underestimate yourself. You're the strongest person I know, Jenner. If anyone can make it through this, it's you."

His face scrunches into a grimace as more tears follow the first, their trails colliding at the point of his chin.

"Listen to me," I plead, and releasing his hands, I grab him by the sides of his face. "They're going to need someone like you, so I need you to keep fighting, okay? To make this place better than how I left it." My arms snake around his shoulders, pulling him in for a hug that I wish could last forever. "You're the only person I'd trust with the job."

When my hand combs through his thick hair, he nods, pressing his face into my shoulder.

"I wish—" he begins, but I cut him off, hugging him tighter.

"I know."

There's a lot I wish. There's a lot I would've done differently in my life, but not this. Never this. If given the chance to go back and do everything over, I would make this sacrifice time and again without hesitation. There isn't a timeline or world that could exist where I wouldn't put his life or Ezra's above my own.

Where I wouldn't gladly die if it meant they could live.

When we pull apart, Jenner offers me a barely-there smile, even though all I see in his eyes is pain. I cup his cheek in the palm of my hand, hoping to leave him with some sense of lasting comfort, just as he's always comforted me. My lips turn upward, mirroring his, but it feels wrong to look at him this way and say the words that still need to be said.

By the time they breach the silence between us, my smile is long gone. As is his.

"Goodbye, Jenner," I murmur.

He leans into my touch, never once breaking my gaze. Not even when I pull away.

"Goodbye, Wynter."

My tears stream freely and without effort as I turn my back toward him and cross the pavement to the only person remaining in our group who I haven't spoken to yet. Ezra stares me down with furious eyes and is already shaking his head before I can even open my mouth.

"I won't say goodbye," he growls. "Maybe, if we make them *see* that you're not a threat, we can—"

"Your mother told me to tell you she loves you." At his startled expression, I step closer, lingering beside him just long enough to say one more thing. "Remember your promise," I whisper.

Before he can respond, I continue into the plaza, my gaze fixed on the blurring line of soldiers ahead. As I walk, the surrounding shadows lighten, the sky overhead filling with the soft glow of morning. Unlike earlier, the city is silent now, as if the entire Heart—or at least Zone 1—was abandoned in the time we spent underground getting here. I glance left and right, assessing the buildings on each side of the square, and just like in my vision, there isn't a single light to be seen or any signs of even the slightest movement or life.

If I don't look straight ahead or back, it's easy to imagine I'm the only one left. That I really am the sole survivor at the end of a world I am responsible for destroying.

A strange sensation takes root at that thought, and I stumble, falling carelessly to one knee. My torn palms slam into the asphalt, but I barely notice the ache in my hands, the terror and resurfacing pain spreading through me seizing my undivided attention.

I've experienced this kind of pain before, but there's something different about this time—something truly terrifying about how fast that violent, familiar heat rushes through me, like liquid fire in my veins.

Blood drips from my nose onto the backs of my hands and spatters the ash-covered ground, and time seems to slow as the crimson collides with the stone, each splash echoing back in my ears. Behind me, I hear someone calling my name, but the dull ringing in my head is drowning them out.

My arms shake beneath me as I push myself upright, but I manage only a single step before staggering again. Around me, the buildings stretch into disfigured streaks, and the rippling waves of static distorting my vision wash the world in tones of sepia until all I see are varying shades of muted brown.

It takes me a moment to realize the brown I'm seeing is actually dirt, the wind whipping the small particles up around me in a frenzy.

No, not the wind, I correct myself, lurching forward one more graceless step. Me. I'm the one doing this.

The impairing fog is just like what I always saw in my vision, the city and destruction just discernible through the thick haze. But that's where the similarities end. The fear, the hysteria bubbling under my skin—those are stronger than they ever were when I was just a spectator to this moment.

Considering how many times I've seen this, I thought I would be more prepared. Less afraid. But I'm not. Any and all bravado I felt before slips away.

Muffled shouts reach me, and the pressure building in my chest reacts through the pain, my powers locking onto the soldiers at the far edge of the plaza, who are indistinct smudges of black in the distance. By now, they've all realized something is wrong. And, like so many before them, they're going to make the same mistake that left thousands of others dead.

Stop, I try to say when they reach for their guns, and as that word fills my thoughts, it occurs to me this might be the escalating moment—the trigger that sends my unstable powers into meltdown.

I never saw what caused my world-ending outburst, and I never stopped to consider what the vision wasn't showing me, too focused on the details it always repeated. On the elements I hoped I *could* control.

Now, I just want to laugh at my idiocy. Every aspect of my visions really have been self-fulfilling, like I feared. After all, I was the one who pushed for the deal that led us here into the arms of aggressors, just as it was the bullet meant for me that injured Jenner and left him bloody, like he was in my nightmare. Everything I've done to change the future and steer us from this course has only cemented our path.

When the world ends, it will be entirely my fault.

And yet, through the suffocating weight of my guilt, doubt grabs at me, pulling me back up for air. If these visions are self-fulfilling, then what about that glimpse of peace I saw?

How can I make that our new future?

The answer comes to me so quickly, it knocks the breath from my lungs. The options I saw were destruction or peace, there was no middle ground. Destruction is simple—my natural tendency. But peace?

For that, I need to die.

"Ezra." His name is a whimper on my lips, and slowing, I turn back toward the station, searching for him through the growing storm of debris. The ground rumbles beneath my feet, and my fingers tremble at my sides as the howling wind grows more wrathful. I don't see him, but I know he'll come. I've seen this moment enough times to be sure of that.

Still, despite that certainty, something breaks inside me when I catch sight of his face, his features the picture of clarity against the obscured backdrop of the city. I see him more clearly than I've ever seen him, and a tear slides down my cheek as he races forward, closing what feels like an insurmountable distance between us.

For so long, I've seen Ezra as two different people—the Ezra I know and the Ezra from my vision. But now, as he shouts out my name, a terrified distress in his voice, they are one and the same. And in his hand, he holds the gun from my vision.

Ready to end this just as fate intended.

A wet heat seeps from my ears, and as the pain in my head intensifies, I know this is it. For good, this time. No collar could fix me now, even if I had one.

The end is finally here.

"I'm afraid!" I admit without thought, my rising panic pushing me over the edge into madness. It's a cliff I've been stranded on for a while, and now, there's nowhere to go but down.

Down into the tides below where I will surely drown.

Ezra falters, and as his pupils blow wide, I can imagine all too easily what he's seeing. The blood streaming from my nose and ears. The black, soulless eyes of a monster. I have completed my transformation just like he has become the stranger from my vision. Now, we will step into the roles we were destined to play, offering two different paths for the future.

And I know which path I want to win.

"I don't want to kill anyone else," I cry, even as the ground quakes beneath my feet. Straining my jaw, I try to push back the power pouring out of my body, but I can't grab onto it, feeling it slip through my fingers like wisps of smoke. "I don't want to do this," I scream, hoping to goad Ezra into action or that fate will hear me and spare me from this terrible burden. Then, a choked sob escapes, and a truth I don't mean to utter spills out. "I don't want to die!"

Ezra gapes at me, horror spreading across his face like spilled ink, and I instantly wish I could unsay those words—that I could withdraw them from his memory just like I would erase all recollections of me if I could. Anything to make this easier on him, which is the opposite of what this confession will do. If anything, it'll only make this harder. Even if I meant those words with every fiber of my being as much as when I told him I love him, even if they're the truth, I would still take them back in a heartbeat. Because he needs to see this through. He *needs* to secure a future for this world. For him and for Jenner and Quinn.

And for that to happen, he needs to pull that trigger.

A bullet whizzes above my head, stirring the monster's impulsive rage, and I know if I don't end this quickly, that vengeful, savage power inside me will destroy everything, including the peace we've been fighting so hard for.

Focusing the pressure seeking a release from my body into the dirt whirlwind around me, I build it up to act as a shield between us, hoping to buy a few additional moments. Then, finding a thread of sanity to hold onto, I push back my retaliatory reflexes and shout, "You have to do it now before it's too late!" But Ezra doesn't move a muscle, not even when I scream *"Kill me!"* at the top of my lungs.

Running out of time and strength, I stumble forward, desperation guiding my steps, and drop to my knees in the dirt before Ezra. His lower lip quivers when I grab the hand holding the pistol destined to end my life, and raising it, I press the cold metal of the barrel against the middle of my forehead.

"Please," I breathe, and when I close my eyes, tears slide through, scalding the cuts and scrapes on my cheeks. "Please," I repeat, wrapping my fingers around his. "I don't want anyone else to die."

"But it's okay if you do?" Ezra asks. His voice is strained but the words are as loud as if he had shouted them to my overstimulated senses.

My lips part on a shaky breath, and I peer up at him through tear-soaked lashes. "If it means you live…then yes."

"That's the thing…" Shaking his head, he takes a step back. As the distance between us grows, the chilled metal of his gun slides away from my forehead. "I don't want to live without you. I won't."

The pain in those words is a noose around my neck, tightening around my windpipe and ripping the very air from my lungs. I stare at him, eyes burning but unable to blink. Unable to move.

Unable to breathe.

"I'm sorry, Wynter."

When he finally says it—the three words that have haunted me almost my entire life—the realization that comes with it is devastating. A tear cuts a line in the ash on his cheek, and shaking his head again, he slackens his fingers. The pistol falls from his grip to the ground.

Just as I always knew it would.

For a while, I've wondered what this part of the vision was trying to tell me—if Ezra really wouldn't carry out his promise or if these words would only come after he had. Once I saw the possibility of a future with peace, I hoped the outcome would be the latter, but now, disbelief stings me as it occurs to me just how wrong I was. Ezra might not want to lose me, but I also know he isn't that selfish. He can't really be willing to sacrifice the whole world just to avoid doing this…can he?

Doesn't he grasp that, even if he refuses to kill me, I'm still going to die?

"What are you—" I gasp, but he's speaking again before I can get the words fully out.

"I can't do it," he confesses, the tears coming fast now. "I know I promised, but I can't. I *won't*. Screw what my mother said!" he shouts into the howling wind. "Screw *fate*! I'd rather die with you than pull that trigger."

As this admission leaves his lips, I'm assaulted by that image I saw of him years ago—of that nightmare where I watched as he was reduced to ash, his remains blown away by the wind as if he never existed at all. If that's what awaits, then what was the point of every atrocity I committed and every choice I

I'M SORRY, WYNTER

made to protect him? He'd be depriving those sacrifices of meaning…

And robbing the world of a chance to exist and thrive long after I'm dead.

"You have to," I beg. "If you don't—"

"No one else has to die." He looks half-crazed, the words tumbling out of his mouth in a rush. "There's another way. You just need to believe it."

Believe it?

I can taste the swarming dirt on my tongue, and the throbbing in my head only grows more brutal, distorting his face as he moves closer, sinking to the ground before me.

"You're capable of control. I've seen it," he says.

"With my collar!" I protest, letting out a deranged cry of pain as the agony in my head threatens to gouge my eyes out of their sockets.

His hands shoot out to steady me, gripping my shoulders. "You saved us from those soldiers," he counters. "And you did it without my brother's leash."

I blink at him through the tears obscuring my vision. He said soldiers, not Enforcers, and I realize he isn't talking about the moments after the explosion when I lost control and murdered almost everyone in the magistrates building. He's talking about the blockade with my mother, when I saved our group from certain execution by the task force sent to track me down.

He's right. I did control it then. Just as I called on my power to look into the future when prompted by Jaedyn. It was difficult, harder than any other time I used my power, but I did it using my own strength, without the borrowed control of the collar.

I did it without Dr. Richter.

"So, if you can't stop it…" Ezra looks up, his eyes trailing the swirling vortex around us. "Redirect it," he urges. "Contain that power."

"Where?" I press, my tone frantic and shredded. "There's nowhere to contain it to—"

"Here," he murmurs, taking my hand and pressing it over his racing heart. He then knocks me gently under the chin, forcing me to meet his gaze, before placing his other palm against my chest in the same place mine rests against his. My pulse beats like moth wings under his touch. "Contain it *here*. Find your control and think of us. Only us."

Think of us.

My eyes widen. "If I do that—" Everyone will live except for him. No…except for *us*. But then, my death was always inevitable. It was his that wasn't, and I never wanted a scenario where everyone else would survive this except the one person I wanted to save.

"I know."

His left hand never moves from on top of mine, his palm hot against my skin, his fingers squeezing, offering reassurance…and making it clear what he's chosen.

For over two years, every decision I made was with Ezra and Jenner in mind. I only wanted to shield them—to spare them from the monster inside me and a terrible future no one, not even Richter, deserved. But, the thing is, they never asked me to protect them, and I never once stopped to consider what they wanted. If they even *wanted* to be saved or if I was just too afraid to let them go. To see history repeat itself, the way it did with my father and Rai.

Ezra's eyes scan my face, pausing to take in every detail. I can see it now, the acceptance in his gaze. He's made his choice just as I've made mine. I won't be able to talk him out of it.

Even if I wish I could.

"But…I only wanted to save you."

A sympathetic smile tugs at his cheeks, and when he speaks, I hear the heartache in his words…as well as the haunting truth behind them. "That makes two of us."

"Ezra, please—"

The full extent of my power slams against the invisible wall of my resistance, and I feel a crack form in that barrier—in the last remaining defense between life and all-consuming death. Any moment now, it could break.

I reach for the discarded gun on the ground, but he grabs my hand before I can touch it.

"No," he says firmly, and this time, it's his tone that holds the pleading edge. Shaking his head again, he pulls me close until I can feel his breaths against my cheeks.

"All I've wanted the last two years and five months," he begins, his voice thready, "was for us to be together again. This way…we can."

He looks down at our hands, nudging my chest with his palm, and as he pulls me close, my mind reels back over every time he uttered that word.

"Together…" I echo. How many times have we said this? How many times have we sworn it to each other—sworn not to leave the other behind?

A vow that outweighs the promise he's broken.

His hand combs through my hair, brushing the sweaty strands away from my face, and as I stare at him, taking in his features for the last time, I realize his tears have stopped. His expression is resolved, the love in his hazel eyes undeterred.

"Always," he swears.

Time seems to slow as a memory drifts to the forefront of my thoughts, and suddenly, I'm back at the blockade in Zone 3, just after parting ways with my mother. The words Ezra spoke then come rushing back, setting every hair on my body on end.

"*...you and I both know I'll always be here for you, Wynter. Even—*"

"Even at the end," I breathe.

"Forever," Ezra says.

His lips brush mine for a moment that's far too short, draining me of the last of my resistance. Both against him and against this disease.

And as the pressure rises inside me, I do as he asked.

I focus on us.

For years, I've wondered if the future could be changed, and I've carried the burden of that task, but maybe it was never only up to me.

The promise of a future was only possible once Ezra made his decision. Not to kill me as I asked but to *join* me.

As the dust thickens and the world fades to black, I consider that maybe Ezra's real role in our star-crossed paths wasn't to subdue the monster. It was to love it.

Maybe, all along, that was the real cure.

EPILOGUE

JENNER

THE AIR BURNS MY NOSTRILS, reeking of smoke and a musky, sweet odor that turns my stomach. Even now, weeks after the conflict has ended, the scent of burning flesh still lingers. It's a smell I don't think I'll ever get used to. A smell I can only hope will fade as the memory of what happened here fades along with it.

The dirt crunches in protest beneath my feet, the earth outside the city's walls a tangle of dehydrated weeds and other struggling plant life born from many long years of neglect. Perhaps, one day soon, with the gates of the Heart now open, life will thrive out here again. After everything we've been through, I have to believe it will.

Otherwise, what was the point of all this?

I carry on, taking the same path I've walked every day the last two months. The sun is setting, beginning its steady decline toward the distant horizon behind the darkening silhouette of the city. As it sinks, the rays stretch across the dried grass, and the glowing orange light against the yellowing vegetation makes the world around me look as if it's on fire.

My feet falter as I'm reminded of a night not that long ago when we tore through these very same fields to save Rai. I recall the pounding of my heart against my ribcage and the painful hitching of my breaths, which only grew worse with each frantic step we took toward the Heart. Our progression was hurried and desperate but determined despite the potential threat before us. We knew what we were running into, and we embraced the unknown outcome regardless.

In that moment, nothing else mattered except saving our friend.

A lump rises in my throat as a gravelly, humorless chuckle escapes through the seam of my lips. I never thought I would miss those days—the days where I looked death straight in the eye and laughed without hesitation or fear. But I do. They held pain and true, immeasurable grief, and yet...

I miss them more than anything.

A spasm shoots through my right arm and I wince, trying to clench my hand to ease my discomfort, but my fingers don't move beyond a twitch. To my frustration, my arm sways limp at my side, the nerve damage in my shoulder rendering the entire limb useless—just as it's been since the day I was shot. The wound might've healed, but the lack of mobility and the ever-present ache I'm left with are inescapable reminders that nothing I did was ever going to matter. I could have jumped in front of a thousand bullets and, at the end...it still wouldn't have made any damn difference.

My feet slow to an unsteady halt, the dirt kicking up in a small hazy cloud around the toe of my boots. Although I'm no stranger to this place, every trip here feels like the first one all over again, my grief now just as ardent as it was in the beginning, the pain in my heart never easing. I keep hoping this is all only a dream and that, any second now, I'll wake up to a different reality where that day—the day that changed everything for this city, for the world, for *me*—ended differently. Where we managed to find an alternative to the decision that gave us this tenuous peace.

I remember those final moments as if they only happened yesterday. The violent dome of swirling dust that formed over the center of Zone 1. What we all saw once that dust finally settled.

The uncertainty that hung in the murky air while I waited to see if the war was over.

In the hours that followed, a covenant was made between the remaining Heads of PHOENIX and our attackers. The discussions didn't last long; they all agreed, with the threat at the source of the conflict eliminated, there was no further need for bloodshed.

In the end, our reformed enemy got what they came for.

And so, the people who were once our assailants became our allies, honoring the initial arrangement made with Nolan. An arrangement he had no hand in this time. There was only one unresolved matter to settle: the residual presence of the State in the Heart, which both sides wanted to see abolished.

Over the next few days, our attackers turned allies worked with PHOENIX to liberate the city before withdrawing their troops and parting with the promise of amity between us. With the proviso, of course, that we nourish this peace and do nothing to jeopardize it. That we be better.

Just like Wynter wanted.

But although the Heart is now at peace, there were sacrifices that came with our newfound freedom that I struggle to reconcile. Our world feels so different now. *My* world feels different.

And each morning, I wake up wishing this wasn't real.

Lowering my tear-streaked eyes to the ground, I sink into a squat and flatten the palm of my good arm against the sun-warmed surface of the erect stone slab jutting out of the earth. I'm at least a mile away from the Heart, and yet, the acrid smell that still plagues the city seems to have tagged along with me today, trailing my steps like an unwanted companion. The odor shrouds my body like a suffocating blanket, accosting every one of my senses. But the worst part isn't the odor—it's the memories that smell triggers within me.

Memories I fear I'll one day forget.

Scrubbing my hand over my face, I close my eyes and drag in a slow, calming breath. With my eyes squeezed shut, I can see her so clearly. How long will that last? How long before I can't remember the details of her face any longer?

How long before she's nothing more than a distant memory I can't recollect?

Swallowing my rising nausea, I force my attention to the heat of the rays on my face and the orange-tinged darkness beneath my lids. The solitary silence is peaceful, and as the seconds tick by, I try to forget where I am, as I often do when I come out here. Instead, I pretend I'm someplace else. In another time. Another life.

In a world where the people I love are still here.

But, eventually, my eyes have to open again, and when they do, I'm reminded, as I always am, that the past will always be out of reach. It can't be changed, no matter how many times I dream otherwise. The events that led to this moment are written, etched into the timeline of history.

Just like her name in the graffitied tombstone before me.

Anger rocks me, and my lips peel back into a grimace at the sight of the untidy word scrawled into the smooth gray surface above her name. Because of the State's greed, many knew who she was, her notoriety like a phantom presence. At first, knowledge of her was limited to those directly involved in this war, but over time, especially since the conflict ended, normal civilians living here who knew little of the State's outside actions heard of her, too. And, in turn, began to shift their blame. They grew to view her as the State had wanted her to be seen—as a weapon of their war. She became the villain, the one they viewed as culpable for the losses we suffered and the destruction we're still working to rebuild, all the while ignoring what else she was responsible for.

The reality that it was because of her they survived.

Scowling, I pluck a sharp rock from the ground and scratch the slur out with the jagged edge until the letters are illegible. Then, I scratch new words beside it. Ones that speak the truth of her actions that day regardless of what she did all the days before it.

Wynter knew what people thought of her, and she wore that label despite the burden it carried because she believed it as much as they did, maybe more. But she was never a monster—not the way Richter was—even if she was forced to do monstrous things. In the end, she proved that.

Dropping the rock, I admire my handiwork through tears, brushing away the resulting sandy residue with my fingertips. Even if no one else agrees with these words, even if I'm the only one who knows the truth of what almost happened that day, *I'll* always know.

And I'll carry that truth with me like a promise carved into my heart.

Wiping my palm on my pant leg, I push to my feet and direct my gaze to the grave marker standing to the right of Wynter's. Whenever I think of Rai, my mind instinctively pictures her on that bed in Richter's lab, a living doll he kept for his own sick amusement. I can barely stomach the thought of what that asshole did to her—what he *took* from her, not only in life but in death. Every day, I'm grateful he suffered. That he got exactly what he deserved.

But the satisfaction of his death is never enough to ease the festering sickness of regret inside me, and I often find myself dwelling on all the missed opportunities—the moments I could have told Rai how much she meant to me. That she didn't just draw me out of my own self-destruction after my family died, but that she *was* my family. The one I went to for advice.

Advice I could desperately use right now.

The thud of boots on dead earth resounds in my ears, and out of habit, I reach for the gun at my waist. Whipping around, I brandish it with my good arm, although my grip falters a little, the weapon awkward in my left hand.

"Calm down," Quinn grunts, raising his arms in mock surrender. "It's only me."

Exhaling a ragged breath, I holster my pistol. I'm not sure why I'm so on edge. We finally have the peace we fought for, and since the war ended, I haven't had to use my gun once. I shouldn't feel the need to even carry it anymore, let alone direct it at every sound.

Then again, maybe the fact that I do is proof the paranoia and fear instilled by the State will never go away. For some of us, we'll carry these scars forever.

As I rub my hand across my face to erase the evidence of my mourning, I clear my throat, forcing my voice to be steady. "What is it?" I ask. "Everything okay?"

"Jaedyn's looking for you," he says, but I can tell by the look on his face there's something else he wants to say.

"What?" I press.

He hesitates for a moment before taking a cautious step toward me, his dark eyes flicking between my face and the graves. "Was it worth it?"

I stare at him blankly, slightly raising my brow.

Discomfort stretches across his face. "Losing the people closest to you," he clarifies. "Was it a justifiable cost for this?"

I follow his gaze to the Heart, envisioning the ways our society has changed since Jaedyn and the other Heads took over. Several high-ranking officials were captured when the allied forces swept through the city, and the Enforcers who didn't surrender were killed. Those who did yield were put in Detention alongside Nolan to undergo a trial and determine if they can be safely reintegrated into society since many were only following orders. But that process will take time, and there's always the risk the State's brainwashing may be irreversible.

As for the city itself, PHOENIX has been slowly shifting the rubble outside the walls and rebuilding the areas the bombs hit the hardest. There are plans to restructure the wealth system and citizens have been told they'll have a say in what jobs they do moving forward, although nothing has been reorganized as of yet. Like everything else, it will require time for the roots of change to take hold, but once they do and the ripples of that change are felt, this city should function the way it did before the State seized control thirty years ago. Instead of creating something new, we're returning the Heart to what it was always supposed to be.

To what it was before tyranny crushed it.

With the mental picture of that potential future taking shape, I ask myself the same question Quinn posed only a moment ago.

Was it worth it?

"Losing them won't be for nothing," I vow.

Quinn scoffs. "Are you sure about that? The city is in shambles. We're divided, no one trusts each other. This peace you lost everything for is so fragile the smallest mistake might break it. I know you're an eternal optimist but, surely, even *you* can see we're in over our heads."

There's an unreserved fury in his voice that fails to mask his fear. I don't blame him for feeling this way.

Those are two emotions I know all too well.

Quinn and I, along with a few others like Duke, have been providing support to the Heads through this uncertain period of change, which has meant that a lot of burdens have straddled our shoulders. Oftentimes, that weight is unbearable, but we struggle through it because we have to. Because we're *choosing* to survive, and survival means finding the strength to continue.

"It's okay to be afraid," I murmur, and Quinn bristles at my words as if I've admonished him. "What we have right now might be broken, but change doesn't happen overnight. It will take time, but we have that time now, thanks to them. What they did…"

I look over my shoulder at Wynter's tombstone, then at the one on its left. For so long, I've avoided looking at that grave—at reading the name inscribed on the stone surface. I suppose part of me hoped that if I never read it, I could pretend this wasn't real.

That I could somehow convince myself that my best friend, my *brother*, is still here.

But now, as I finally face Ezra's grave, I don't feel the pain or sorrow I expect. Only comfort in knowing that, at the end, they were together…as they were meant to be.

My thoughts drift back to that day, and I relive the apprehension of staggering forward through the settling dust and clumsily sliding down the side of the crater that formed where the plaza in front of Central Station once stood. I relive the agony of finding my two friends on the ground, hand in hand—their bodies embraced, limbs tangled, like two halves of a whole rejoined. Grief had consumed me as the realization of what I was looking at sunk in, but past the pain tearing my heart to shreds, I noticed the matching looks on their faces.

The gentle smiles that made me hope they both finally found some small measure of peace.

A fresh tear slips down my cheek, and as I wipe it away, I whisper, "We wouldn't have a future at all if it wasn't for them."

Quinn is silent for a moment, and when he next speaks, the anger and disdain are both gone from his voice. "So, what's the plan?"

The plan…

I glance up at the darkening sky—at the stars peeking through the fading light—and for the first time in what seems like forever, my loneliness stings just a tiny bit less. I feel the ghost-like presence of my friends beside me, and when I imagine their encouragement, the answer comes easily, as if I've known it all along. As if we were always meant to end here, like this.

"We take it one day at a time and do whatever we can to create a world they would be proud of."

Quinn cocks a dubious eyebrow, crossing his arms. "Just like that, huh?" he asks skeptically.

Drawing in a trembling breath, I turn my gaze to the Heart, which, although fractured, will heal with time. The last of the diminishing daylight glows around it like a halo, giving me hope.

And before it all, in the distance, I swear I see Wynter. She looks at me with that shy smile I loved from the first time I saw it and has one hand outstretched, urging me forward.

As I take a step, lured by her beckoning, I recite the words I carved into her tombstone, and through my pain, they give me courage. The courage to keep fighting for the future she gave herself to protect.

SHE SAVED US ALL

"Yup." A smile tugs at one corner of my lips. "Just like that."

FOR A BONUS CHAPTER FROM EZRA'S POV,
SCAN THE QR CODE BELOW

THE END

DEAR READER,

THANK YOU FOR READING the *Project W. A. R.* trilogy! This series has been a huge part of my life, so I hope you enjoyed Wynter's story as much as I loved writing it. For more from this world, check out *The Richter Files*, a companion narrative in the form of journal entries from Dr. Richter's perspective.

To keep up with the latest news about my work, sign up for my newsletter at **WWW.BOOKISHDEN.COM**.

For more information about the *Project W. A. R.* series and for an interactive version of the map found at the beginning of this book, please visit **WWW.MAPHIPPS.COM/PROJECTWAR**.

I love to chat with readers, so feel free to get in touch! You can contact me through my websites or through any of my social media accounts. Or you can join my fan group on Facebook—just search for **THE BOOKISH DEN**. We'd love to have you!

Lastly, if you enjoyed this book, please consider leaving a review on your retailer of choice, BookBub, and/or Goodreads. Reviews help authors, like myself, gain exposure, so we can keep sharing our stories with the world.

Thanks again for reading the *Project W. A. R.* trilogy. I hope you'll continue to enjoy my work!

ABOUT M.A. PHIPPS

M.A. PHIPPS is an American-born British author, who resides near the ocean in picturesque Cornwall with her husband, daughter, and their Jack Russell, Milo. A lover of the written word, it has always been her dream to become a published author, and it is her hope to expand into multiple genres of fiction.

Project W. A. R. is her debut series.

Visit her online at:
WWW.MAPHIPPS.COM or **WWW.BOOKISHDEN.COM**